THE GOLD BUG
VARIATIONS

BY
RICHARD POWERS

THE GOLD BUG VARIATIONS

PRISONER'S DILEMMA

THREE FARMERS ON THEIR WAY TO A DANCE

THE GOLD BUG
VARIATIONS

RICHARD POWERS

WILLIAM MORROW AND COMPANY, INC.

NEW YORK

It is the policy of William Morrow and Company, Inc., and its imprints and affiliates, recognizing the importance of preserving what has been written, to print the books we publish on acid-free paper, and we exert our best efforts to that end.

Library of Congress Cataloging-in-Publication Data

Powers, Richard, 1957-
    The gold bug variations / Richard Powers.
       p.   cm.
    ISBN 0-688-09891-6
    I. Title.
PS3566.092G65   1991
813'.54—dc20
                                                                                          90-20267
                                                                                          CIP

Printed in the United States of America

First Edition

1   2   3   4   5   6   7   8   9   10

BOOK DESIGN BY BRIAN MOLLOY/CIRCA 86, INC.

RLS CMW DJP RFP J?O CEP JJN PRG
ZTS MCJ JEH BLM CRR PLC JCM MEP
JNH JDM RBS J?H BJP PJP SCB TLC
KES REP RCP DTH I?H CRB JSB SDG

ARIA

The Perpetual Calendar

I.

What could be simpler? Four
scale-steps descend from Do.
Four such measures carry over
the course of four phrases, then home.

At first mere four-ale, the theme swells
to four seasons, four compass points, four winds,
forcing forth the four corners of a world
perfect for getting lost in

or for filling, by divide and multiply.
Four secret letters, tetragrammaton,
start to speak themselves, the tune
doubling down a net of no return.

What could be simpler? Not even music
yet, but only counting: Do, ti, la, sol.
Believing their own pulse, four tones
break into combinations, uncountable.

II.

From language to life is just four letters.
How can that awful fecundity come
from four semaphores, shorthand and dumb,
nothing in themselves but everything?

Gene-raining cascade, proliferating green
tints, varieties senseless except for their own
runaway joy in the explosion. Fresh phloem-
pipes, palisades, leaves ripe for insect-aping.

All patterns patented: gyro, chute, receiver,
fish that track ocean back to first stream
or steer pitch black by trapped bacterial beams.
Can egg-chaos really be all the blueprint needed

to father out this garden-riot from just seed?
No end to the program except a breaking out
in species-mad experiment, sense-shattered shout,
instruction-torrent: live, solve, copy This, repeat.

III.

Two men, two women, their requisite friends,
acquaintances, strangers and impediments,
two couples at arm's length of thirty years bend
in ascending spiral dance around each other.

All four have traveled far from home
and, in the hour when they need it most,
the grace of reference works won't come
to cure the persistent call of tonic.

"Picture those pay telescopes," he said,
"that sprout up at scenic views. Ten cents,
a minute's panorama, then it snaps dead.
Clicks shut. Cut off. And you with no more change."

All four must make a full tour of the curse,
and deep in variation, for a moment, lose
the four-note theme, sight of each other, worse.
Drowned by the pump and swell, the flood of dates.

IV.

The calendar's fresh beauty is how it runs
through perpetual days, calling us on
to the urgencies of life science, old names,
genus, species: May Thirds, March Twenty-ones.

Everything that ever summered forth starts
in identical springs, or four-note variations on that repeated theme: four seasons,
four winds, four corners, four-chambered heart

in four desire-trapped bodies in the thick
of a species-swarmed world where green thrills
to countless change while the calendar holds still.
Winter works again, through autumn's politics,

its call to action, critical count of votes:
Look, speak, add to the variants (what could
be simpler?) now beyond control. How can we help
but hitch our all to these mere four notes?

I

The Care and Feeding of Foreigners

Word came today: four lines squeezed on a three-by-five. After months of bracing for the worst, I am to read it casually, jot down the closing date. The trial run is over, Dr. Ressler dead, his molecule broken up for parts, leaving no copies. I can neither destroy the note nor keep from rereading it. The news is a few days cold. I've had a year's advance warning. But I haven't time enough left in my own cells ever to figure it. The mechanical music box, his body, has had its last crack at the staff. Those four notes, four winds, four corners of a world perfect for getting lost in are lost in a sample mean.

Once, when he talked, I could almost follow in him the interior melody from the day of creation. For a few months, I'd had that tune by ear. Now nothing. Noise. I read the note all evening, waiting for the clause that will make sense of it. The only volunteer words are his: Dr. Ressler, leading the way through winter violence, the snowstorm that trapped the three of us in a vanished cabin, laying out all natural history with an ironic shrug: "What could be simpler?"

I had a hunch it would come now. For a week, unseasonably cool—brisk, blustery, more like summer's end than its beginning. Last night the cold peaked. I slept under a parfait of wool, the weight required to keep me under. Giving in to an irrational fear of *courants d'air* brought on by too much literature as a girl, I sealed the apartment. No one around any longer to object. Excited by night chill, the signal hidden in temperature, I fell asleep only by degrees. I lay in the metal-cold sheets aware of every pore, unable to keep from remembering. Something was about to hap-

11

pen. Hurried lingering, hope, as always, a function of weather.

I passed through that hybrid state just short of dream, back to that iridescent weekend in the woods. The familiar world overhauled, encased in silver sealant. We three waded again across the glacial surface: spectral trees glazed with lapidary. Bird and squirrel fossils marked the drifts. Snow obliterated paths, spun power lines into flax, confected hedgerows, dressed our cabin in gothic buttresses and finials. I walked through the transmuted place beside my two males, one in herringbone, the other in navy pea. Dr. Ressler walked between Franklin and me, pointing out astonishments in the altered world, his features as angular as the shepherd's wonder from my childhood crèche. The seashell loops of his ears, his fleshless nose, reddened in the acute cold, while his lashes doilied with flakes that beaded across his mat of hair.

We pressed deeper into the snowscape, the bronchi-passages of a walk-in lung. Franklin and I placed our hands under each other's coats, pleading conservation of heat. In bed, my skin still recorded the year-ago cold of that boy's fingers against my ribs. Ressler saw everything: the bark swells of insect galls, the den entrance punched through hardened powder. He certainly saw how Franklin and I kept warm, and treated it as easily the most explicable of winter mysteries. At his finger-points, the arcade of frosted branches became vault ribbing. His each wave populated the landscape, pulling Chinese lanterns out of flat sheets. He crumpled to his knees in the snow, shook his head in incomprehension, and like the crystal world, seemed about to splinter. He must have solved again, with fierce looking, the ladder of inheritance, because his face turned and he swung his eyes on us expectantly.

Piled in blankets, I slowed the dream, kept him from speaking, prolonged the endangered moment that would shatter at the least formula. His throat tensed; his lips moved soundlessly like a remedial reader. He became that pump organ we had played six-hands, about to produce the one phrase sufficient to hymn this mass of brute specifics. The traces of creatures, all the elaborating trills and mordants of winter seemed a single score, one breathing instrument whose sole purpose was to beat the melodic line of its own instructions—four phrases, four seasons, every gene the theory of its own exposition. He was about to hum, in a few notes, the encoded thread of everything happening to us and everything that would fail to happen. But his lips—thin, boyish, blue, wasted in middle age—could not shake loose the first pitch.

As before, Franklin challenged him. "You're the life scientist. Tell us what's afoot here." Every detail of Ressler's face grew magnified: the interstate lines of folded neck, his frozen-brittle lobes, the spot on his chin thawed by breath. His viscera, the process even then growing more variegated, already knew the tumor. This time Dr. Ressler gave no reply. He had gone, slipped out from under the weight of white.

Then, this morning, just waiting for me to commit wrongly, summer chose its moment to break. The pressure system stalled above the city passed over, at last bringing the weather the calendar called for. Overbundled in the airless room, I woke up soaked in flannel. I sponged clean, washed my hair, ate an insignificant breakfast, and brushed my teeth without conviction. I sat in the dining nook, in the first, full heat of summer, trying to retrieve that snowscape. Awake, I let the man ask the question I'd earlier forestalled: *what could be simpler?* He remained a geneticist despite everything, partial to the purposive pattern, the generative thread. But his four-phrased, simple explanation was as unrecoverable from my breakfast table as that New Hampshire weekend, the whole aborted year.

Fragment, endorphin-induced, absolutely commonplace: easier to count the nights when I don't dream of those two than when I do. Still, this one torched my morning. I filled with the urge to make the call, but had no number. I came within a dot of dashing off the telegram composed since last spring, but knew no sending address. The way back, the suggestion forced open again overnight was sheer perversity. I sat at the breakfast table until the moment passed. Then I made my way to the archives.

I was first at work, always easiest. I unlocked the library and headed by rote to the Reference Desk, my half-dream still an embryo in me. The day would have been long in any event. The longest day of the year, even had I gotten eight good hours. By ten, I found myself seriously questioning the charter of a big-city branch library. Our catalogued, ecumenical clearinghouse of knowledge was running at about double average gate. Kitty-corner to me, a pack of pubescents prowled the genre racks, eyes on the signaling flesh at adjoining tables. A few bruised retirees, two years from terminal Medicare, pored over magazines, persisting in forcing the weekly news into a parody of sense. In the adjoining children's room, a pride of early readers, spirits not yet broken by summer camps, disguised the fact from their unwitting parents

13

that books mystified them more than the real world. Behind the Reference Desk, on the peak day of our peak season, I fielded questions from this community of needs. First day of summer: briefly, everyone wanted to know something about nothing. I shook off Dr. Ressler's rhetorical question, agitating out of all proportion to the intervening silence, and busied myself with questions that were at least answerable.

This morning, I was glad for the diversion. By noon, I had solved a burning problem concerning obscure wording on W-4 forms, pointed out the Bridge and Dog Grooming books, and located, for an earnest navigator of sixteen, a side-by-side comparison of Mercator's, Mollweide's, and Goode's projections. I went home at noon. I've taken to it lately, despite losing most of the hour in the trip. I felt the urge to buy a car, not to drive, impossible in the city, but as prep for the increasingly likely evacuation. Home, I swept the mailbox by limp reflex. Franklin's note cowered in protective coloration amid bank statements and time-limited offers. I took it with the numbness of months. I can't remember the flight up or breaking through the deadbolts. I set Todd's calligraphic scrawl on the kitchen table and began pulling vegetables systematically from the bin. Hysterical affectation of indifference: make myself a bite to eat before settling down to death. The snowstorm came back, the hunch that sent me home for lunch, and I tried on the idea: I'd *known*. Then I remembered Ressler's definition of chance: the die is random, but we keep rolling until we hit necessity. Hunch long enough, and premonition will one afternoon be waiting for you at home. I left the vegetables salad-bar-style across the cutting board and sat down, worried open the seal. Stiff, white invitation card:

Our Dearest O'Deigh,
    It's all over with our mutual friend. I've just this instant heard. The attendant at the testing center assures me that all the instruments agree: Dr. Ressler went down admirably. No message, or, I should say, no new message. I wanted to inform you right away, naturally.

Naturally. Also naturally, no signature. He printed "FTODD" at the end, as if authorizing a change of date on a bank draft. But he could not help adding an afterthought at bottom: "Oh, Jan! I miss you right now. More than I would miss air."

14

I spread my hands on the table and divorced them. Through a tick in my eyelid, I pointlessly read the note again. All over with our friend, his four-letter tune. I knew the man for a year, one year ago. Before everything fell apart, he became one of the few who mattered to me in the world. Once, when he was young, he stood on the code's threshold, came as close as any human to cracking through to those four shorthand semaphores. Then, for years, he went under. Slowly, astonishingly, as Franklin and I watched, he awakened. Now, stripped of content, he was gone.

What did it mean, "went down admirably": resisting or acquiescing? And what possible difference could it make to me now? Dr. Ressler was dead. No shock, not technically. Given his disease, he wasted and died per timetable. But, backwater organism, I'm no good at abstraction. A lifetime of practice unmade in a minute. And I learn again, in my nerve endings, that information is never the same as knowledge.

Today in History

I met him in ignorance, a day into autumn of 1982. Another half year passed before I learned his name. I pinpoint the date through the Event Calendar, one of those well-meaning services I supervise daily for an indifferent audience. Research, edit, type, and list for the consumption of the dabbling public what, if anything, happened today in the past, ignoring the contradiction in terms. For five years I've posted the day's event, finding exactly the right bite-sized fact to feed the public library patron. Five years times fifty weeks times five days is 1,250 daily facts. The public librarian's knocking out of the weekly cantata. Something to do. Until today.

The race is constantly sneaking up to something: space shots, cathedrals, mill strikes, expeditions, inventions, air disasters, revolutions, epochally indecisive battles, world-shaking books, commercial upheavals, pogroms, putsches, treaties. A few sources provide enough grist for every day of the solar mill for years to come. If I'd ever run out, the human activity since I began hunting would have carried me through at least another year. I never fell back on birthdates of famous people, cheating in my book. I still have on file every Event I ever posted. After five years, my selections blend into a reference work in their own right. Years after

15

my first run-in with the ex-scientist, putting together the stray pieces, I can look up the particular notice that caused the Franciscan of 4th Street to break down and—against character—address a perfect stranger. I arrived at the library early enough one September in '82 to pick, type, and post the item within fifteen minutes of the branch opening for business:

Today in History
September 26
In 1918, after four years of total war, the Allies launch an offensive along the Western Front that will break the Hindenburg Line. Two weeks later, World War I formally ends on the eleventh hour of the eleventh day of the eleventh month. The following year, touring the U.S. to drum up support for the new League of Nations, Woodrow Wilson collapses with his first incapacitating stroke. With him collapses any hope for the League.

I have the provoking entry here in front of me. As I pinned it to the board, a hand chopped me on the clavicle. I fell back at the capacitance, thinking that someone had stuck me with a knife. I now know that the man had gone so long without touching that his muscles had simply forgotten how light a tap need be to attract attention. I turned to see a figure shorter than average, small-framed, with a beautiful, skeletal face and skin resisting the sag of age. His forehead arced down into thin nose cartilage, and his lower lip shaded indistinctly into a long chin. Had he not been anemic, his crew cut might have made him an astronaut. His extraordinary moist eyes monitored me with the soft hurt of animals, encouraging me to say the worst. He seemed not to blink, like a camp refugee or feebleminded ward of state.

He wore a forgettable light suit, a narrow maroon tie not seen since the fifties, and an immaculate oxford button-down, carefully ironed but pilled to exhaustion around the collar. He emitted the aura—accurate, it turned out—that he found buying clothes too embarrassing. He was over the median age by twenty years. As I stared, wondering if this was an assault, the figure said, in a voice rattling like a cracked distributor, "Excuse me, Miss. There's been a mistake." I hadn't a clue what he was talking about. Worse—the ultimate terror for my profession—I had no source to appeal to. Just his being here disturbed me; at that hour, in autumn, the library was the tacit domain of retirees and transients. A male of employable age, able-bodied albeit as emaciated as a Cranach

Christ, upset the statistics. "There's been a mistake. I'm afraid the date is off."

Influenced by earlier having identified the relative strengths of shipmast flags and Aldis lamps, I thought I'd been singled out to receive a cryptogram canceling some covert operation. *All-points bulletin: Date off.* His fastidiously soft-toned grammar, in best academic fashion, removed all trace of personal involvement: *There's been..., The date is....* I gawked at him, mutely rolling my head to either side, Galileo's pendulum experiments with my brain the deadweight. "I apologize for being so unnecessarily elliptical," he added. A frail finger directed my attention to the Today in History. "This account, which I don't for a minute doubt to be accurate in particulars, is, unfortunately, irrelevant." He gave me an apologetic smile, an attempt to be amenable despite having just run over my pet dog. I still produced nothing but an uncomprehending stare. "I'm afraid those things did not take place today. In history."

My response surprised even me and jeopardized my standing in the ALA. I blurted out violently, giving in to that contempt the specialist stores up for the lay passerby, "And how would *you* know?"

He paled and pulled his mouth into a grimace. "I don't. That is, I wouldn't be able to tell you when, if ever, that particular item took place." He trailed off, considering it unnecessary to explain. Noticing my look change to clinical concern, he added, "To resort to an allusion that won't be lost upon a person in your line: 'You can look it up.'"

I brayed out loud, astonished at the combination of scenic-route syntax and citation. I didn't stoop to ask how he could possibly correct my events while admitting ignorance of when they'd happened. Instead, I adopted professional patience and hissed, "Let's just do that." I set off to the Reserves without looking to see if he followed. In seconds I was furiously buzzing over the historical almanacs, amazed at myself for losing equanimity. As the pristine derelict appeared at my side, I hit upon September 26 with a vengeance, confirming both Wilson and the Allied offensive. He passed a cupped hand across that stretch of forehead—God; his quintessential gesture!—and nodded. "I'm convinced, beyond question. Your skill with an index is impressive. Nevertheless...." He pointed politely to the massive wall calendar that, even from where we stood, broadcast today for all to see. I broke out for a

17

branch-record second laugh in one morning. September 24.

Just what empirical precision prevented him from asserting the obvious more obviously? His radical skepticism had required me to run the full, clumsy experiment of heading to the stacks in the outside event that the offensive *had* begun on the 24th and I'd committed the less likely error of date substitution. I sank into the nearest Breuer chair and exhaled. Thinking I was put out by the effort required to find a replacement, he said, "Might I make up for some of my incurred guilt in this matter by suggesting a substitute? Say, Eisenhower's heart attack; 1955." Making matters worse, he mumbled, "Should that be too obvious, you could take alternative refuge in 1789. Congress passes the Federal Judiciary Act. I'd rate that as fairly crucial, wouldn't you? But perhaps you've used it?"

I couldn't decide if this was burlesque or the fellow's genuine attempt to repair unmeant damage. I tried for knowing reserve. "Ike's heart attack will do just fine."

He straightened like a teen coming clean from the confessional. "Terrific. We're even, then." He shifted weight from one leg to the other and tucked a stitch back into his coat seam. I reestimated his height: five-nine, with a full moon. He coughed and took a nervous step backwards. "I like Ike. How about yourself?"

My introduction to Stuart Ressler's sense of humor. I could think of no answer in the world to give such a thing, so I returned to the almanac. Through the miracle of cross-referencing, I reverse-engineered Ike's coronary and the Federal Judiciary Act. He must have arranged the stunt in advance. But I'd only posted the fact the instant before he jabbed my shoulder. He watched my bewilderment for a few seconds, hunched his back, waved apologetically, and walked away. He was almost gone when I called after him. "I give up," I said, offering a respectful truce. "How'd you do that?"

"Never complain, never explain." He looked furtively around as if it could not have been *him,* violating this place of public research by talking in full voice.

My propriety vanished. For the first time in years, I stood face to face with another who wanted to force his way into the indifference of data. I slid from hostility to good-natured self-effacement in under a second. "Piece of cake," I baited him back. "Disraeli. I was *born* knowing that one."

"I'll have to take your word for that. I'm afraid I'm worse than aphasic with quotes." And he abandoned me. Too soon to be leaving. Never would have been too soon.

The rest of that day was dense with its own transactions, but erased from the retrievable record. I half expected him to return a week later, drop in for another chat about retrieval. He didn't. The whole encounter had been an elaborate setup. With no other way to explain it, I unprofessionally let the incident drop until this evening. Friend, why aren't you here now? The date's off again. I too have grown worse than aphasic with quotes. What was it you said to me once? What was it I said back? What had been so urgent for a while, so in need of saying?

But What Do You Do for a Living?

From that clueless beginning dug up from corkboard clippings, to Today in History, 6/23/85: Stuart Ressler—who once put his hands cleanly through the molecular pane, subsequent second-shift recluse, late-in-the-day returnee to the world—dead. I met the man by fluke, the universal architect. I will not meet him ever again. The meeting place he opened for us imploded with him.

Knowing the course of the disease, I thought I was prepared for Todd's mercifully curt devastation. I saw it in the envelope before opening. But when I sat and read, the veins of my neck thickened with chemical fight or flight, as if death dated from the minute I heard of it. Two billion years, and my body is still stupidly literal. My neck-gorge refused to shrink, however hard I rubbed. No RSVP required; just return to work, an afternoon dispensing citations. But I couldn't move from the chair. Something specific was required, some word I had to identify before I lost the few lucid moments grief ever allotted.

I reached for the envelope, my first indication in a year where Franklin was. The name in the cancellation circle pushed me over the edge. My throat hemorrhaged; violent self-control broke into hatcheted crying. Franklin, Dr. Ressler's only student, had posted the note from that Illinois university and farming town where the old man had wandered off the path of human sympathy. Of all the towns packed with all the impotent intensive-care facilities in the world, Ressler chose that one to return his metastasized cells to at the end, as they ran him back into randomness.

I believed, until that minute, that business as usual was the only consolation life allowed. But now the idea of going back to work right away—ever—appalled me. I returned to the vegetables on the kitchen counter and heaped them into a semblance of salad. But eating anything was beyond me. I put the food on the sill for whatever not-yet-extinct birds still braved the Brooklyn biome. A sympathetic mass took over my chest. The block spread into my legs, threatened to stiffen them if I didn't keep moving. So I did what I always do in the face of unnameable grief. I began straightening things. I picked up the books dispersed over my study. I threw away the accumulated advertising fliers. Dusting the record collection, I suddenly knew what I had been delaying, the act I needed to send him off.

There, in my front room, trembling the record from its dust jacket, I set on my ancient turntable the piece of music the newly cadenced man most loved. I sat limp and listened all the way through, the way he had listened once, motionless except to flip the record. Four notes, four measures, four phrases, pouring forth everything. The sound of my grief, my listening ritual, will be the closest the professor gets to a memorial service. Franklin, wherever he now is, must have resorted to the same. Two listeners to that simple G scale and all the impossible complexity spun from it. I heard, in that steady call to tonic, how Dr. Ressler had amortized bits of himself for decades. Now he was paid off. Back at Do.

The music—I can't say what the music sounded like. Whole now, with none of its many endings the last word. That emotional anthology is so continuous that I could not tell whether my discovery dated from a year ago, under the dead man's guidance, or this afternoon, at his private wake. Only Dr. Ressler's perpetual running commentary was missing: the amateur's gloss that always made the piece so difficult to listen to when he was in the same room now left it unbearable in his silence. "Here it comes. *There.* What a chord. Hear? The left hand, the interior dissonance . . . ?" Every embedded line became painfully apparent with no one there to point it out.

Only when the reprise, the last da capo bars resolved their suspension and fell back into generating inertness did I leave, lock the place, and climb the blocks back to the branch. Two hours late in returning. My colleagues, old maid Marians to a man, seeing me drag in late, stared as if I had just sprouted a full-fledged, handlebar-mustached mania. One of the eternally punctual, I had committed blatant inconsistency. Settling behind the Reference Desk as casually as possible, I resumed answering the public's questions as if nothing had happened.

But everything had. I worked like the worst of bush-leaguers. It took me twenty minutes to identify, for a polite woman not a day less than ninety, the river that had a funny name beginning with a vowel and probably lying in Africa or India. She and my atlas at last compromised on the Irrawaddy. I did almost as poorly naming the one-armed pro baseball player from the forties who puts in an appearance every five years and should have been child's play. By four, badly in need of a break despite less than an hour's work, already suspecting the break I needed, I attended to the Quote Board.

Old institution, child of the fresh days of my M.L.S., when I still believed in the potential of democratically available facts: the Quote Board began as my experiment in free expression. An open corkboard with blank cards broadcast a standing invitation to "Add your favorite passage here." We did well for a while, if not producing any transcendental insights. But the inevitable appearance of the limerick Ladies from Lunt and the Lonely Master Painters soon forced the notice "All quotes subject to final approval by Staff." After-the-fact justification of censorship, first fatal realization that the body of literature had its obscene parts in need of covering.

By the early eighties—just before I fell in with Todd and, through him, Ressler—the Quote Board was clearly fighting a losing cause against creeping nihilism. It filled with the work of junior Dadaists: random passages from sports magazines or cereal boxes, meaningless but too inoffensive to suppress in good faith. Disenfranchised blind mouths, wanting nothing better than to deface any suggestion of need. One morning the whole wall sprouted Day-Glo, spray-painted genitalia. After that, the project shrank from its first, ambitious conception to a square of plate glass around a single, daily quote selected by a librarian. As a sop to the old belief in public speech, I attached a locked submissions box with the condescending invitation, "If you have any suggestions for quote of the day...." The project kept its old name through force of habit.

Not that the public abandoned the Quote Board entirely. Over the years, it's had the periodic inspired submission. Much of my original intention felt paid by one doubtlessly quarantined high school girl who, from an astonishingly broad reading, conscientiously culled the best of everything she came across. Last year she sent me an aerogramme from Eritrea reading:

> Even a proverb is no proverb to you till your life has illustrated it.
> Keats

I let that one run two days. This girl and a few others have kept up a steady submissions trickle. A few hundred other contributors give once or twice, usually that private byword they've taken to heart: the St. Francis prayer or the Desiderata. Otherwise, the box bulges with teenage death or torch lyrics, proper names artlessly altered. Of tens of thousands who finance the branch, only a fraction of card-carriers make a point of reading the quote of the day, and fewer still ever go out on a limb and contribute. Still, the Quote Board provides its service. Recognition, learning a thing by heart: life will be nothing after these go.

This afternoon the box was empty. Cupboard bare, I fingered my skirt pocket where Franklin's note had somehow accompanied me back to the library, a coconut floating to populate a virgin, volcanic island. Franker once promised to keep me in permanent quotes: "You'll never have to stuff the ballot box again." For a long time he did. But today, as so often before he began to frequent me, I again had to come up with a fresh saying, never before used. One that might mean something, anything, to that fractional percent of my clients who hang on the choice of words.

I felt an urge to use "Two loves have I, of comfort and despair. . . ." But remembering the public in public library and feeling little better than the prolific submitters of plaintive lyrics, I didn't. Despite my small stockpile of emergency reserves, I could find no quote that satisfied. I couldn't shake the features of the dead man's face, the constriction of my gut. I took my neck by the hand and my fingers went all the way in. I tried to lose myself in the search, to turn up the quote that had absolutely nothing to do with grief. I stood in front of the Quote Board for some time before admitting that what I required in today's quote was a private, particular eulogy.

As I pretended to think, the passage I was after presented itself. I went straight to the stacks and found the source, a posthumous work by Dr. Arendt on the dangerously detachable, oddly convincing life of the mind. I remembered the words practically verbatim. I knocked out the excerpt on one of the antique staff manuals and posted it. Stuart Ressler had probably never come across the passage in his life. But it stood for him, summed up his permutation as well or better than any other:

> The God of the scientists, one is tempted to suggest, created man in his own image and put him into the world with only one commandment: Now try to figure out by yourself how all this was done and how it works.

Tacking up this charm, locking the glass cover that would keep it safe from an uncomprehending audience until I replaced it, I headed back to the Reference Desk. But on the upbeat of my return footstep, I felt the first of Dr. Ressler's astonishing variations visit. Music. Unasked-for, self-generating attacca singing. Unable to help myself, forcing my heels into professional clicks, I succumbed to syncopated desire, the skip hidden in the sound of sole against tile. The most powerful intellect, the most remarkable temperament I ever met was dead of a slow horror. And all I could feel was this urge to dance. Grotesquely inappropriate—*what could be simpler?*—I felt the need to move in as many directions as possible, to assume all the virtue of virtuosity. I knew what measures I would be forced to take.

The mood annihilated the incapacitating silence of lunch hour. In the time it took me to walk the hundred meters back, the syncopation clamping itself deeper into my walk, I caught sight of the scientist, the god of the scientist. Frozen like a deer in car headlights, the thing he'd figured out: how all this works. Dr. Ressler, hearing the world burst its reservoir. The empty separation of the last year dissolved in one upbeat; the first hint of a two-step, and everything changed. The constant anticipation of a handful of months before came flooding back. I saw the three of us, the small circle drawn into our orbit, as we all had been. I heard the words we wasted late into the night, stabbing at something beyond saying. I felt, with a mix of hot shame and pleasure, what a talker I'd overnight become. Months of verbal drunkenness, when once or twice I'd even known what I was talking about. I saw the sharp lines of the design that obsessed him as if I'd drawn them myself.

In that instant my afternoon's routine, my surviving professional life, wholly unconnected to that other run, sounded the subtlest

23

exercise in multifoliate counterpoint: a short-short-long in the right hand completing a simultaneous long-short-short in the left. Those two out-of-step tunes, in their off-beat separateness, not only seemed deliberately thrown together, they also harbored, hidden and distant, other voices peeling off in parallel structure, coming apart at the seams. No other way to describe what came over me: I began to hear music. Literal music, music flying along under the fingers, the same music I had listened to earlier this afternoon, only radically changed. I was at last *hearing*, picking out pattern with my ears, knowing what sound meant, without translation: that tune—four notes by four—Dr. Ressler's life theme, the pattern-matching analog he had always been after.

That syncopated dance back to the Reference Desk—elaborate, contrary motion—called on me to make a deliberate, irrevocable sashay. Music, his music, melodic balls tossed freely back and forth between the hands, begged me to discover how wide an arpeggio might emerge from single notes. He led me to the center of the ballroom with those thin, cancerous hands, took my body in his timid, skinless arms and commanded, "Ready? On one."

But the meter of that music was too rich and ambiguous to stick. By the time I reached the Reference Desk, the inappropriate euphoria over Dr. Ressler's life—its triumphant grammar, however brief and bungled—was gone. Anticipation fell off into fatigue. I wanted only to go away from here for a moment, a lifetime, stay away as he did until I'd forgotten the layout of this place. Lose the old fixtures, erase what had happened, then wander back in at the beginning, take it from the top, enough time having passed to reclaim the sense of place, the time of year we had once lived through.

I spent this afternoon in my usual capacity, doling out facts. The ten most frequent letters in English. The weight of protein in a pound of peanuts. Each answer bitterly dedicated to my distant colleague in the information sciences, whom I once met over the Event of the Day. The events he set in motion were now the stuff of archives. But then it struck me, what I'd known and forgotten any number of times: the calendar is not a fixed record, an almanac of everything that ever happened indexed by a few hundred slots. Every calendar page also contains the anniversaries of everything that has not yet happened. Slowly, the ambushing tune came back—that exercise in stretching an unassuming dance beyond the counterbreakingpoint. Quieter, richer in independent voices, now a confident and compelling tempo, certain I'd take the required response. And this afternoon, just before closing shop, I gave, to the astonishment of my coworkers, my two weeks' notice.

I am not sure, as I write this, too late at night, what I meant by quitting. I don't know what I hope to do, what, if anything, I still *can* do to put things right. I only know that I am inextricably involved in what happened to the man. His story has become my story, and no one is left to tell his but me. Our showdown—our fight with the anniversaries that haven't yet happpened—lasted just a little under a calendar year. But those few months were the only ones of my life that I experienced firsthand. I've wasted a year since, convinced that my continuing the quarrel alone was out of the question. Funny, the idea hitting me only now, so late in the day, so long after the fact. Tonight, for the first time in I can't remember how long: the hint of possibility that always arrives with death. With news.

I sit typing in the dark. He's really dead, then. Nothing works against it. I tick away, sick in the chest at all that never happened. Outside my window, on the river, the shortest night of the year already lifts. This absurd hour: I'd call Todd in a second, just to speak to the one other person who knows Dr. Ressler's tune by ear. His note, brutal announcement of the end, provides me with entrée. Impossible; no idea how to reach him. I half expect my force of concentration to tip him off. Make my phone ring from sheer telepathy. But air is always the worst of carriers.

I must break for an hour's sleep. The urge for something less ambiguous than more silence is unbearable. What do I have left to work with? What have I ever had but four seasons, four corners, four nucleotides? How can I name the man's changes with only that? Only, once, touring the snowdrifted world, pointing out the spore, he asked, "What could be simpler? We all derive from the same four notes."

II

Who's Who in the American Midsection

For all that we finally discovered about him, Dr. Ressler still came from and returned to nowhere. His life was a cipher, his needs one of those latent anthologies, safe deposit boxes filled with tickets to urgent, forgotten banquets. Our sustained misreading of the man was my fault. Todd put me on his trail, and I went after him as an abstraction, a chemistry unknown that, mixed with the right reagent, reveals itself by going rose or precipitating. I looked for a postulate, completely missing the empiricist's point. Now, when it no longer helps, I see the person he stood for is the one who is gone.

Our search for the reagent began two years ago. The branch again swelled to summer capacity with bored children and adults too ashamed for bathing suits. The alien figure from the previous autumn who'd known all about Ike's coronary but hadn't a sufficiently straightforward command of syntax to tell me I'd flubbed the day's date had not returned, and my recollection of the run-in followed the standard extinction path. Months on, after a numbing bean curve of requests, I looked up from the Reference Desk at a face so untroubled and trusting as to instantly trigger any thinking woman's suspicion. A man in mid-twenties lingering patiently like a parasitic vine for me to finish. His nose tilted friendlily when he at last got my attention. His eyebrows flashed greeting, sure I'd be as happy to see him as he was to see me. I returned the survivalist's stare I'd learned on hitting the city: stand where you like—here, there, under the traffic in Columbus Circle. His grin persisted as we slid onto business footing. If anything, he got a kick at my failing to respond as effusively as invited. Without a trace of agitation, he said, "I want to know someone."

I squelched the facetious comeback. Cutting cleverness, the chief weapon of my social life, was worthless at the branch. I kept mum until the clear-faced questioner corrected himself. He did so without the diffidence I expected from such ingenuous features. "I mean I'd like to identify someone. Find out who he is." I waited, but he was in no hurry. Apparently he felt that anyone who couldn't sift the evidence before it was spelled out would be unable to handle it after. "I'd like some information. Whatever you can find. I need an ID on this fellow." He slipped me a scrap torn from a drawing notebook. Florid acanthus letters formed a man's name. Aware that his writing was more cryptic than Linear A, he read out: "Stuart Ressler. Mean anything?"

I set the scrap down with exaggerated care. "Could you please be a little more vague?" I pride myself on working impartially, even for those whose sole purpose on earth is to propagate ravaging inanity. But this man was clearly too bright to be forgiven such a time waster. Bright enough to register facetiousness, in any case.

"Perhaps I ought to narrow the scale a mite. It's just that you're such a mind reader over the phone."

"Sir, we have several librarians on staff, and any one of them . . ." I tried to catch the eye of the security guard, just coming around the periodicals.

"Oh, no. We've spoken a couple times. The text of Luther's 95. Fast Fourier transforms. How much IBM to buy. Names of the flying reindeer."

I cleared my throat; we were not yet amused. But he had proved himself at least marginally safe, unlikely to tote handguns down into the subway. "All right. I'll help you, so long as you pay your taxes. This name: animal, vegetable . . . ?"

"Funny you should ask." He turned his face away, hiding. When he looked back, his boyish clarity had changed barometrically. "I'm *certain* he did important work once."

The catch in his voice revealed that this wasn't a simple round of Botticelli. "All right. You believe he's in the records. I'll trust you. What was the man's line of work?"

My client grinned. "Don't know for sure." Sheepish, tickled. "Something hard. Something objective, I mean."

His odd adjective reminded me of a quote I'd once identified: *Who seeks hard things, to him is the way hard.* That one had

27

fallen trivially at the push of a concordance. But this: qualitatively different. Why associate difficulty with objective disciplines? Certainly the subjective morass is harder. "We can eliminate professional sports?" He laughed in agreement. "You don't know the man's field, but you're sure he's well-known. What were his dates?"

"Oh." My question flushed the amusement from his eyes. "He's still alive. And I didn't say well-known. I said I was sure he'd done something important. Some *real* work once." He spoke precisely if incoherently, sure that intelligibility would eventually, as with the current administration's promised economic prosperity, trickle down.

"I see." I hid my irritation by taking sparse notes. "Still living. Born...?" I finally prompted, "When?"

He thought long. Breaking through triumphantly, he said, "He is about twice as old as me. I know that for a *fact*. That means we can start in the early thirties, huh?"

I suggested he start a little higher, in the low forties, Fortieth to Forty-second, to be exact. "Sir. We're just a neighborhood branch. If this person is as obscure as you make him out, you'll have to go over to midtown."

He sensed my shame in referring him to a higher authority. "You kidding? They'd laugh me off Manhattan."

"Why shouldn't we do the same?"

"Heard you don't laugh as much here." At which, I did.

Even as I tried to palm him off, I knew I wouldn't let him go without first testing my skill. His softheaded question had a difficulty that hooked me. Solving it would be at least as valuable to the long-term survival of the race as determining Dorothy's shoe size or supplying a six-letter word for a vehicle ending in U. "All right. What great thing, broadly speaking of course, do you think he did? How did you hear of him?"

"I work with him."

It took no intuition to hear the warning buzzers. Those who want to get the drop on another—from term-papering school-children to businessmen steeped in interoffice sabotage—outnumber all my other clients. I would not be party to spying on a coworker. But just about to hand back the paper scrap, I recalled how, at the moment when this man had joked about his acquaintance straddling animal and vegetable, he had hidden his hazel-and-bark face. Rather than return the name, I stiffened and held it, implicating myself for good.

Had I paid attention, I might have been quicker in drawing connections in the days ahead. But as in most informational work, content evaporates completely before the end of the shift. Specifics disappear, leaving just the trace of categories, methods. Archivists aren't wellsprings of fact; they are search algorithms. The unfolding subway, the byzantine network of accumulating particulars—our Pyramid, Great Wall, St. Peter's, the largest engineering feat of all time—daily runs a nip-and-tuck footrace between the facts worth saving and the technology for managing the explosion. A single day produces more print than centuries of antiquity. Magazines, newspapers, fliers, pamphlets, brochures: fifty thousand volumes annually in English alone, ten times what a person can read in a lifetime. Six new books every hour, each one the potential wave-tip that will put the whole retrieval system under. Dictionaries of dictionaries, encyclopedias of indices, compression tables into microfilm windows onto text bases. Even my sleepy branch has its desktop computer—a genus nonexistent ten years ago—that scans years of periodicals by subject, title, or author, in seconds returning a cartridge that plugs into a reader that zooms to the complete article in question, assuming the high schoolers haven't wedged Slurpee cups into the mechanism. In summer '83, I had every confidence in the power of my tools to crack the script. Two years of even more spectacular advances in retrieval, and I'm guttering in the dark.

One night not long ago Ressler, Todd, and I—contents, carrier, and cracker of that first ID—sat together in the hum of the computer room, its gigabytes of sensitive data in the sole care of these two vagrants, over stale bread, grocery-store Camembert, and Moselle. Expansive in the combination of tastes, Dr. Ressler remarked that people of last century could look at a musical score and hear the piece in their heads. "Name the work; they could hum the principal motifs. We've traded that for the ability to lay hands on a recording in five minutes, or your tax contribution back." Affectionate burlesque of my trade, the one that for a moment recovered him from the heap of lost scores.

In that professional capacity, I didn't for an instant doubt I'd be able to find the nub-penned name. Even without any contribution, Stuart Ressler was somewhere in the permanent files, many times, in immense Orwellian lists. Time, resources, and brute research could extract him. I needed only decide how much effort this other man, in his twenties, with the Bonnard coloration, was worth.

I try not to second-guess the social value of my daily assign-ments. From each according to his critical needs, to each according to my best retrieving abilities. I must believe that my clients are the best judge of what information they require. My colleague Mr. Scott, advanced degrees in anthro and philology as well as library science, hovering on the brink of eternally threatened retirement, pulling volumes to prove to this year's perpetual motioneer that the latest ingenious scheme once again violates the Second Law, likes to sing the couplet:

They all laughed at Christopher Columbus when he said the world
    was round,
They all laughed when Edison recorded sound.

Skepticism sweetens Mr. Scott's countertenor: all that sad, mis-directed, highly trained skill, with only a once-an-epoch useful solution preventing his whole career from degenerating into a waste of shame. Scott, like everyone who looks things up for a living, prefers Gershwin to admitting that progress has destroyed our ability to tell which facts of the runaway file are worth recalling. Value is the one thing that can't be looked up. I myself am some-times shamefully pragmatic, cutting losses on a goose-chase, bow-ing out on diminishing returns: the awful ethical calculus that forces politicians to cut a deal, surgeons to choose which of three dying people to repair. My first impulse was to give this college boy a list of biographical dictionaries and ditch him until he'd run the legwork, by which point I would be safely over the informa-tional border, joining Mr. Scott in retirement haven. Defensible, given the opacity of the question. But pride made me give it a preliminary nudge. However ill-defined, the ID was at least as diverting as rock stars' birthdays.

We started at the top, the *Who's Who*s. The boy annoyed me completely by trotting ahead, going down the spines saying, "Tried it, skipped it, tried it...." Months later, he explained he was being funny. By then, I'd discovered that Frank Todd was a competent researcher. The only thing standing between him and Ph.D., aside from sense of humor, was excessive thoroughness. He belonged to the class that can't get started writing, paralyzed by that last overlooked source. Franker perpetually budgeted another half year to mopping up; by the end of the period, the holdouts had pro-liferated. When I accused him of playing dumb at that first meeting, making me do the scutwork he could easily have done himself, he said, "Woman, have you ever seen yourself reach for the top shelves? Choice."

I ignored him and began the elimination sieve. As I thumbed, he stood by, irritating me further by humming. His hum sounded like the vibration of the library air conditioning, so soft and sustained were the intervals. When I looked up he was standing shoulders hunched and eyes closed, conducting himself with the closed forefinger of his right hand, wrist curled in front of his chest like a gothic icon. I just made out the tune, the slow accretion of a haunting chord. Flirting between major and minor, it brushed me with the sad suggestion that I'd heard it before, something forgotten and irretrievable. It sounded like a decision I'd made about myself long ago. But I could only work on one mystery at a time and so kept reading rather than add a descant.

We came up with nothing, which neither surprised nor disappointed him. We searched the indices and traced the biographies back a decade. The mystery man had, by all appearance, written nothing of note; we combed the combined abstracts as far back as credible and came up empty-handed. The undertaking took us both—for the solo conductor at last broke from enchanted humming to lend a hand—all afternoon. I assured him that failure still taught us a great deal, narrowed the scope considerably. "We know, at least, where the mark *doesn't* live." I didn't add that we'd greatly reduced the plausibility of the original hypothesis. My client stood dumbly by the card catalog, stuck his hands in his pockets, and waited for me to say what happened next.

I in turn waited for him to volunteer the reason why this search was so important. But his patience outlasted mine. In another moment, he might have gone back to humming. I gave in, ensuring another meeting. "I can run some electronic searches. But these are expensive if you don't know what you're looking for. Every vendor has a per-minute connect fee, and if you simply instruct them to grind away on an unspecified name. . . ." He continued to smile; I wasn't sure he followed. "Then charges add up."

He spread his palms: *Pay as you go? Don't I always?* His voice dropped a notch. "All I have is yours."

I'm astonished to think how easily I slipped into flirtation. "Yes, but how much do you *have*?"

"Think Marx to Dumont on the ship's gangplank in *Night at the Opera*." Fifteen minutes after he left, I would produce the allusion.

I haven't had any complaints yet. I promised to tweak a few angles we hadn't explored that afternoon. He nodded and agreed to find out more at the source. Then he troubled his voice into greatness. "We won't give up so easily, will we? Not by a Lamb Chop." I refused to grin. He turned to leave, but just before quitting the reference area he swung to face me. In one of those unexpected shifts in tone I learned to predict, he asked, "Are you beautiful?"

The question floored me less then than it does now. "Who wants to know?" I flipped back. The professional in me beat the *provocateur,* two out of three falls. Leaving that evening, I was still working on his parting shot. Was she beautiful? I said out loud, to no one, "Let's answer the hard one first."

Was She Beautiful?

I've never thought so. Perhaps he did. Dr. Ressler lent a gracious second, always chivalrous. The whole inquiry hardly seems relevant anymore. Dead issue. Why is that answer ever crucial? Those third-party testimonials—*she's so trustworthy, loyal, helpful, friendly, courteous*—are superfluous adjective catalogs without the key commodity—*and so beautiful*. Add that, and bored listeners beg for the chance to judge for themselves. The soberest article, mentioning good looks, sensationalizes mere journalism. *She was beautiful. He was stunning.* Porcelain, startling, deep, timeless, haunting: more than cosmetic. Political. Historical.

Custom downplays it, pretends that looks are a judgment call, denigrates the superficial. But the faintest suggestion of beauty and everyone's off, Todd in the lead. A glimpse, and he couldn't help myself: pretty form clamped his imagination, a credential for inner sense. Beautiful faces kept ineffable secrets he then needed to reveal. They *knew* something, something they might tell him if he could only get close enough, inhale, smother himself in their perfection. I've seen him stopped dead by the line of a woman coming carelessly out of a shop across the street. Perfect plumage chilled his heart. A classic face carried the imprint of another time, like those garbled message-dreams that distress the dreamer but reveal, to the skilled explicator, perpetual homesickness. For my friend, it was always the first question. Todd's every ache was desire to return. And beauty mapped the way back.

Franklin suffered from uncontrollable love for lovely women.

32

He nostalgically confused the lost domain with something more visceral: yellow hair, witch eyes, a pout to the lips, tight crepe black dresses stopping just south of the hip and running up the back in little ripples. Time and again he took the hook, went for the stamp, the visible spectrum, the package job, the fatal allure of surfaces. He could not resist the *Vogue* look. His Annie was much more the homecoming-queen shoo-in than I. I never possessed glamour or high features. Not even in the ballpark. Passable cheekbones, nose a bit too Sumerian. Body sound, but a step below aerobic. After years of living with me, Tuckwell said my face had the forbidding attractiveness that announced, "For office use only. Do not write below this line."

Hair between brown and blond is my best feature; but every schoolboy knows what hair is. Given Todd's desperation for Glossy, I don't know what he saw in me worth buzzing. If I have any surface, it is anachronistic. And yet anachronism has always had its fatal Franklin charm. "I know where I've seen you before," he said once, stroking my chin, studying it in candlelight. "The Cluny tapestries. Lady and Unicorn." He meant it as a compliment. High Medieval Flemish is his chosen field. But faint praise: *he* could see something in me the herd could not. I pushed my luck by asking, "Former or latter?"

I have it on authority that Franklin, confirmed Platonist from way back, seeing women who better approximated his rage for perfection, felt, above anything, distress. When led into Penn Station by a breathtaking madonna only to have her turn and reveal a mulish forehead or mousy nose, his utter relief was like a life sentence commuted to death at the last minute. A hopelessly plain face freed him of responsibility, while agonizingly perfect physiognomy attacked his cortex like an opiate, haunted his sleep for weeks, whispered to him of missed chances that might at last have lifted the confines of the mundane.

But did I have a face that compelled that connoisseur to desire? Eyes, nose, expanse of skin to alert that stranger-stalker? His repeated insistence contradicted itself. Mine is a middle-percentile dazzle, smack in the fat of the normal curve, the not-bottom-of-a-truck woman who sits next to you on the bus, attractive but unrecognized at class reunions. What Franklin saw on second take would never have sold cigarettes or survived pastel. But in the time and place he saw me—Flanders or Artois, 1500—he insisted I had the stuff that earth's waters and wild animals wept at in envy.

33

Did *he* have looks enough to justify that gangbuster, self-conducting solo-humming? Oh, he's beautiful. Undeniably, breathtakingly, in all prosaic senses, the classic regularity of features. He claimed to be a little short, a little overweight, a little caulky. He was none of these when I last saw him, and he knew it. He hid behind a face that shone like no other.

The vertical files now contain us: clippings, grainy pictures of all four faces. They show me as a woman somewhat startled. Only the initiated would call me attractive. The Wire photo of Frank shows a young man whose face is a prism. Bent from its white light is the spectrum of every autumn day that ever hurt him. For standard beauty, he had a decided head start. And yet, all of us would grow infinitely more attractive. Even I would shoot open, turn heads like the rarest hothouse flower. Events conspired to make us all, for a moment, beautiful. His parting question, insouciant and impertinent, seemed to create the very pull it asked about. Somewhere I heard rules breaking, water trickling through limestone. Here was a man possessed of boundary-free confidence, asking not if I was beautiful but if I was ready to become it.

He's right: beauty *does* correspond to a profound secret. But there's a catch. Not the emblem of inner power, but its by-product: the last, faint track of a slowly unfolding generative order, numbingly miraculous, even in end results—mouth, eyes, hair. The epiphenomenon of desperate cells, every face forms the record of shattering, species-wide experiment. The perfect face, the one we ache inside to stand near, is just the median case. The Artist's composite criminal, one that destroys us to leave. And we always leave, once we learn its creases.

He left me that day with two unknowns for the price of one: I didn't even get his name. But he left a trace, another scrap of nub script discovered that evening before I left. When I went to update the quote of the day, making my perfunctory, usually pointless search of the submissions, I found a piece of drawing paper torn from the same notebook:

Natura nihil agit frustra
(Nature makes no grotesques)

Signed Sir Thomas Browne, although he misspelled the name. I used the quote, paying the price. Few selections have produced

34

such public bafflement. But I'd choose confusion even now, over the usual indifference of days.

The Question Board

Mother always insisted I got what I had coming. From birth, I was addicted to questions. When the delivering nurse slapped my rump, instead of howling, I blinked inquisitively. As a child I pushed the "why" cycle to break point. At six, I demanded to know why people cried. Mother launched into the authorized version of the uses of sorrow. At the end of her extended explanation, it came out that I really wanted the hydromechanics of tear ducts. By her account, I worsened with each year's new vocabulary. She finally took refuge in a multivolume children's encyclopedia, parking me by it whenever I began to get asky. I can still see the color plates: Archers at Agincourt; Instruments of the Orchestra; two-page rainbow Evolutionary Tree. But her scheme backfired. I could now ask about things that hadn't even existed before. Whys multiplied, poking into the places color plates opened but failed to enter.

So it righted a cosmic imbalance in her eyes that I ended up answering others' questions for a living. She hoped to see me sit behind the Reference Desk until I'd answered as many unanswerables as I had plagued her with all those years. To hasten that payoff, I invented a way to address interrogatives around the clock. The Question Board, with Quotes and Events, completes the trinity I used to break up the routine of human contact. Librarian is a service occupation, gas station attendant of the mind. In an earlier age, I might have made things. Now I only make things available. Another blit in the bulge of the late-capitalist job curve. Service accounts for two thirds of the GNP, with the figure expected to rise well into next century. By the millennium, half of all service professionals will specialize in processing data. My Question Board, then, is both living fossil and meta-mammal.

A portion of board duty is always custodial: disposing of "Why can't Jigs talk English?" and "How 'bout the phone number of the girl who does that shower commercial?" Eight of ten remaining requests are fish in barrels, solutions floating off the pages of major almanacs or last week's periodicals. One in ten demand tougher track-downs, sometimes lasting days before breaking. The final 10 percent, not always demanding, aren't technically answerable. For-

35

mally undecidable, to bastardize math jargon: heartbreaking, ludicrous insights into the inquiring spirit, requiring special delicacy. "Q: Is there any meaning to it all?" "A: According to Facts on File..."

Over years I've squirreled away a mass of three-by-five Q-and-A's, perpetually preparing for nebulous further reference. Backtracing, I dig up the cards displayed on the day I met Franklin. If, as all facts at my fingertips insist, I truly live at the crucial moment of this experiment, if creation itself is now at stake, it's tough to tweeze from the whole cloth the significant, saving thread.

Q: I need (desperately) to know the source of the line: "How do you get moonlight into a chamber?" *Please* find this. My life's at stake.

A.H., 6/20/83

A: Quince: Well, it shall be so. But there is two hard things: that is, to bring the moonlight into a chamber; for you know, Pyramus and Thisby meet by moonlight.

Snout: Doth the moon shine that night we play our play?

Bottom: A calendar, a calendar! Look in the almanac. Find out moonshine, find out moonshine.

Quince: Yes, it doth shine that night.

Bottom: Why, then may you leave a casement of the great chamber window, where we play, open, and the moon may shine in at the casement.

Quince: Ay. Or else one must come in with a bush of thorns and a lantern, and say he comes to disfigure, or to present, the person of Moonshine.

Midsummer Night's Dream, III, i. If we can save your life again, by all means let us know.

J. O'D., 6/23/83

Q: Got an anagram for "ranted"? "Roast mules"?

R.S., 6/04/83

A: This one took time. Unfortunately, anagrams can't be solved by dipping into *Reader's Guide.* The first is trivial: "ardent." The second took our concerted staff two weeks, although the answer is so simple any child can do it: "somersault." We hope you appreciate the tax dollars that went into these. If your efforts produce any cash prize, we trust you'll split it with your favorite library.

J. O'D., 6/23/83

Q: Where can I go live where the people are really well off, money-wise? I don't care what type of government, because I don't vote anyway.

K.G., 6/22/83

A: For sheer income there's always Nauru, a Pacific island whose eight thousand inhabitants are far wealthier per capita than the U.S. population. They make their money on one product, phosphates, which run the industries of Australia, New Zealand, and Japan. The Nauruans extract the chemicals from huge deposit of seafowl guano laid down over thousands of years. Such affluence has a price. The island is itself largely a giant guano deposit, and the more than two million tons of phosphates exported each year eat it away rapidly. While everyone on Nauru drives expensive cars, there are fewer miles of road to drive on every year. You might as well stay home and vote.

J. O'D., 6/23/83

Q: Has a woman ever given birth to the child of a goat? What was this creature called?

B.R.G., 6/23/83

A: No. But such an offspring would be a satyr—Greek mythological hybrids, man above the waist, goat below.

J. O'D., 6/23/83

This last one attracted special attention. I've marked the card for admittance into my circumspect list of all-time classics. During my Question Board tenure, I've been asked everything at least once. Which is worse, cancer or heart attack? If Chicago time gives more hours than New York time, why don't we go on it too? I'm doing a family tree of Jesus and need to know Mary's last name; was it also Christ? Three weeks in the reference section of the local public would convince even Saint Paul that *caritas* is, if anything, beside the point. Love doesn't even scratch the surface of what the species needs. Goat-people arise more frequently than anyone except reference librarians knows. I long ago stopped being astonished at the number of people unable to distinguish between whim and brick wall, who choose their newspapers on whether they are readable on the subway.

As I left that evening, I thought how the italic-penned challenge also partook of the species-wide inability to tell need from not. All the way home, walking through the enfeebling city heat, I wondered why I'd agreed to help find what could better be learned by asking the man in question. I came up with no better answer than the asker's beauty. Reaching the relative safety of my neighborhood, I heard my father—no more tolerant than my mother in answering my endless girlhood questions—whisper his old litany, "Stranger, Danger," in my interrogative ear.

Face Value

I worked for a humiliating week and a half without turning up a shred of evidence that Stuart Ressler had ever existed, let alone done anything hard. I spent more time on the job than I should have, rigor proportionate to my anger at the thing's idiocy. Half a dozen times a day, on a new inspiration, I'd labor a page or phone midtown. I was on the verge of running a bogus credit check to get his date, place of birth, and social security. Ethics and pride prevented me, but only just. The sponsor called once during that period, more out of obligation than hope. He'd weaseled some specifics from the source that he thought might help. The man was born in 1932, putting him just over a half-century. He had been brought up in the East but joked about time as a young man "in the interior." He spoke little and read perpetually, everything from throwaway fiction to abstruse journals. He was by all appearances celibate. He lived at work. "You probably can't use this," my accomplice added, "but the only time I've ever seen him show emotion was last year, when that famous pianist stroked out dead."

I brought up the matter of occupations. "I know we're after the distant past here, but it might help to know what line of work the two of you are currently in."

Mr. Todd chuckled hollowly at the other end. "We run the country, the two of us. Nights. Paper collating. Buck ten over the minimum." They were the mainframe operations graveyard shift for a data-processing firm. "Info vendors. You and me are practically kissing cousins." He stopped short of suggesting we improve relations. As worthless as the stray facts were, I learned one helpful bit before disconnecting: Todd's name. He also gave me a number where I could reach him, "any hour of the night or night."

I hit the payoff only by coincidence, after another week of ingenious, impotent search. Serendipitous discovery, beloved of science historians. The trick to blundering onto a gold mine lies in long preparation. I undertook no project without testing it for relevance. But the solution chose to arrive with such accidental grace that it appalls me. A wide-eyed schoolboy had come to the Reference Desk with a whitewashed first draft of a term paper on civil rights. Attempting to bring the movement back from gelded interpretation, I led him to primary sources, contemporary reports of 1957 Little Rock—the Arkansas National Guard confronting the U.S. Army. We flipped through a popular Year in Pictures, the ingénu discovering that this foregone event had in fact required a second civil war just before his own birth, and was not yet decided.

As I'd done habitually with every book I touched for the last two weeks, I scanned the index. Nothing. Then the next year's cumulative, reduced to hunt-and-peck. This time, beyond all hope, an entry. Refusing to believe, I pulled the citation. A gallery of black-and-white portraits accompanying an article on this *annus mirabilis* in molecular genetics carried a minor caption that read, "Dr. Stuart Ressler: one of the new breed who will help uncover the formula for human life."

That was just the first shock. I had seen the accompanying face before. The eruption of coincidence made me put off calling Franklin Todd. I woke that night from a sleep of secret cabals to make the connection: Ike's coronary specialist, the man in the pilled oxford. He was a smooth twenty-six in the photo, and over fifty when I'd met him the previous fall. But despite the intervening years, his face was unmistakable. The cell paths responsible for aging had failed to erase his particulars. Lying in bed, unable to go back to sleep, I did the long division. The NYPL has over eighty branches serving more than ten million people. The odds against a man paying my insignificant branch a visit followed months later by another who wanted to identify him were incalculable. I jumped to conspiracy: the two were colluding to test my research skills for some reason I was compelled to figure out. In the dark of my room, beside a sleeping male whose breath did not change cadence

39

as I shot awake, it felt as if Dewey had broken down: on the shelf, spine to spine beside the Biography Index where I had begun the search, came cheap intrigue.

Suspicion didn't leave me until the day Frank Todd took me to his office, that converted warehouse he shared with the still obscure Dr. Ressler. Only then did the statistical improbability work out. I laughed at my mathematical paranoia, at how I had missed the crucial, obvious splint: their office, the night watch where they nursed the machines, was four streets down from mine. I had swapped cause with effect. The two lost men were simply both patrons of the nearest public bookshelf.

Rule of Three

I've logged tonight much the same story as the one I started a few nights ago. Identical, with changes: the dead man's one theme. A life in the laboratory made Dr. Ressler see everything that happened on earth—everything that ever *can* happen—all speciation as a set of variations whose differences declare their variegated similarity. Yet in the end, the work he left behind, the bit he added to the runaway fossil record, proves that the occasional, infinitesimal difference, astronomically rare, is the force that drives similarity into unexpected places. Tonight I put the scratched record on the machine again, playing it out loud when my memory becomes too spotty to call up the melody. The same tune this evening, same simple scale as the one that a few days ago prompted me to end my professional life. But not a note of Dr. Ressler's piece is in place.

Last week, the dance seemed a duet, subtle play between a right hand too close and *courant* to hear and a left I left so long ago I didn't at first recognize it. But tonight: I definitely hear trio. Love triangle. Dr. Ressler's story is nothing if not a threesome. He loved a woman; and he loved something else, inimical. Research didn't teach me this; firsthand contamination did. I've been to the place, picked up the spore.

Coy cat-and-mouse, familiar Q-and-A game around since the dawn of Chordata. The man I loved was of a low opinion of love's predictability. I can hear him—in the same voice that wandered up that stacked, homeless chord while he conducted himself— singing, "Birds do it, Bees do it; even shiftless ABDs do it...." I loved Franklin, and it all seemed a duet once. But every late-night visit I ever had from him, every visit I ever paid, took place in the shadow of an unnamed corespondent. A third party. Every couple an isosceles.

I am no calmer tonight. For all that I've already written, Dr. Ressler's death still comes on me at odd hours. Worse, more real. I hit a sentence requiring a fact I can't bring back intact: *Ask Stuart; he'll remember*. But his memory, the finest I've ever seen, is scattered, lost in small changes. What I have in mind is no clearer now than on the day I gave notice. Half my two weeks is over, and I've still not explained to incredulous coworkers what's going on. I promise to, the moment I figure it. Tomorrow, I start my last week of work, with no plan for after. Every book I touched this afternoon seemed strange. I must have been crazy to quit. Overreacted in a moment's grief. I've thrown away what little prospect I had of making it through these days intact. And yet: hurt demanded that I lose my job. For a week, I know I must square off against quiet, coming catastrophe alone.

Tonight, at the old sticking point, I hear another voice in the bass, below the love duet. However entwined the upper lines, another figure informs them, insists on singing along. All two-part voice separation harbors a secret trio in dense fretwork. Three in nature is always a crowd. A chord. A code. If science was that man's perpetual third party, the scientist himself was mine.

Today in History

Inappropriately exhilarating to be in the stacks today, now that I'm a short-term impostor. Still, work continues until the last check. This morning, as if nothing has happened to routine, I posted for the Event Calendar:

June 28
Half a year before the United States' entry into World War II, Roosevelt establishes the Office of Scientific Research and Development. Vannevar Bush, designer of one of the earliest computers, becomes director. The OSRD coordinates U.S. scientific work with military concerns. It presides over the development of radar and sonar, mass-produced sulfa drugs and penicillin, mechanical computing, and the atomic bomb. The contributions of science to the

41

war effort are widely appreciated. But the effects war has had on subsequent scientific research are more difficult to state.

Posting, I'd already made my break with the branch. My thoughts were no longer on work, but on that other today, twenty-five years ago, when Stuart Ressler, newly minted Doctor of Biological Science, nine years old when the OSRD was born, arrived in the Midwest to commence adult life and make his crucial if subsequently forgotten contribution to progress. His bid for the *Who's Who*.

III

We Are Climbing Jacob's Ladder

From the window of a wandering Greyhound, Stuart Ressler gets his first look at unmistakable I-state phenotype: unvarying horizon, Siberian grain-wastes, endless acres of bread in embryo. The most absent landscape imaginable, it calls to him like home. Schooled in the reductionist's golden rule, he sees in this Occam's razor-edge of emptiness a place at last vacant enough to provide the perfect control, a vast mat of maize and peas, Mendel's recovered Garden. Green at twenty-five, with new Ph.D., he leaves the lab to enter the literal field.

The tedious bus haul catches him up on the literature. The *Journal of Molecular Biology* takes him into Indiana, where he acquires a seatmate whose disease of choice, obesity, spills provinces over the armrest into Ressler's seat. Three articles into the *National Academy Proceedings,* Ressler must listen to the huge stranger's invective on the perils of reading. "My father could put away a Zane Grey in one afternoon, and it got him nowhere. Never touch the stuff. You'd be wise to go easy on it." Ressler nods and twists his lips. Not recognizing the dialect, his seatmate persists. "What do?"

Quick decoding eliminates *Gesundheit* as appropriate. "I'm a geneticist."

"Oh, rich! You fix women trouble? What I wouldn't do to trade places with you. Oh *brother*. What I wouldn't do. Heaven on earth for you fellas, init?"

Ressler inspects his shoes. "Never touch the stuff." This too cracks up his fellow traveler. Fortune extracts the man at Indianapolis, and the plague of companionship passes over. Safely into

Illinois, a half hour from his new life, organics lays a last ambush. A stream of tortoises possessed of mass migratory instinct crawl over the highway in the twilight. Bottlenecked cars take turns gunning, crunching over the shells. The tortoise-trickle does not even waver. Ressler stares out the rear window as long as he can stomach it. For a hundred yards, he can make out the horror. The insane persistence of the parade holds him in fascinated disgust.

Chelonia has nothing over primates re the processional urge. Ressler weighs the similar drive that brought him out here. Four years earlier, a fellow first-year grad stormed into his dorm room waving the legendary Watson-Crick article in *Nature*. A new threshold torn open for the leaping. The awesome, aperiodic double helix—with its seductive suggestion of encoded information assembling an entire organism—spread before him at twenty-one, wider than the American Wilderness. The next day, he dropped his four-year investment in physiology to rush the frontier.

To his astonished adviser, he pointed out how much solid prep he already had for the curriculum change, how much carried over into molecular. He'd concentrated on chemistry, so the scale change would be a snap. Besides: all significant breakthroughs were made by novices free from preconceptions or vested interests. In six months of ferocious precocity, he'd made believers of everyone. Research schools singled him out as a future player, recruiting him even as he put the last touches on his thesis. He accepted the post-doc at Urbana-Champaign, guided exclusively by heroic impatience. Illinois could get him started the fastest. From the stack of invitations he selected theirs, scribbled a ballpoint signature at the bottom, and dropped the reply in the nearest box. The game was afoot; a lab was a lab so long as it was antiseptic. Hunch, induction, and technique could put even an I-state on the map.

At twenty-five with no major contributions yet, he's under the gun. Miescher was twenty-five when he discovered DNA ninety years before. Watson was twenty-four. If the symptoms of breakthrough don't show by thirty, forget it: throw in the lab coat, get an industry job. Research—America in '57—is no country for old men. Sure, his dissertation was a minor *tour de force*, but just juggled ideas evident to anyone paying attention. Quickness and insight, both necessary, won't suffice to take him where he's headed. Now he must mint, in the crucible of his new lab, hard currency. He packs two changes of clothes and comes to this outpost Eden.

He acclimates instantly to the box houses, orthogonal blocks, and infinite corn in parallel plowcuts running clear to the horizon. Urbana, at twenty thousand, is just what he needs. Stagnant backwaters are the most fecund. He needs only a steady supply of pipettes and a place to spread his bed. Stepping off the bus into the greasy station, he parses the downtown, shoos off a soliciting cab, walks to campus. All significant discoveries are made on foot. The straightedge streets of his adopted town bear ingenious names: numbers, states, presidents, and the trees slaughtered to make way for them. They swell with whitewood houses, diners, five-and-dimes. A church pokes Pentecostal finger at the nimbus of clean linen laid over it, its promotional postboard announcing Sunday's sermon: "Can the Guests Morn When the Bridegroom Be with Them?"—the "u" deleted in point mutation. The rows lining each lane seem so many complementary, self-replicating pairs—the fifties' fastest-breaking metaphor. In minutes, Ressler forgets the seaboard, the flattened Eastern affect of his childhood. He settles into this emptiness, a symbiotic bacterium in the belly of his host.

On campus, he discovers there is no room at the inn. A superannuated department secretary, predating fruit flies, scrapes him up a place in the old army barracks reprieved from destruction until veterans stop pouring back to school on the G.I. Bill. Stuart, who missed the world crisis by enough years to think that G.I. bills come from internists for services rendered, also scabbed out of Korea on dissertation deferral. His thesis drafts him into another campaign, a magic bullet as explosive as any gunner's. Fitting then, military digs: vicarious enlistment. He takes possession of one end of a single-story tar-paper triplex in a shanty called Stadium Terrace. The row huts line the colonnaded shadow of Memorial Stadium, one of the country's largest collegiate football coliseums. He delights in discovering that his cell number, K-53-C, encodes his precise locus within the village.

Cursory inspection turns up ratty bunk, gas stove, half a black-and-white print of James Dean with head on steering wheel, several septic razor blades, and a box of cereal with both flakes and enclosed coupon devoured by red ants. He needs nothing more. He unpacks his worldly belongings—a tartan suitcase of second hand clothes and a tote bag crammed with journals. Social rounds, town exploration can wait. After a perfunctory trip to the convenience grocery, he holes up in the barracks. Days he toys with the coding problem and evenings he sits on a lawn chair staring at the pie-

45

wedged fallout-shelter signs plastered over the stadium across the way. For dinner, tomato juice minus gin: alcohol is a trace mutagen and destroys brain cells. The department must wonder why he hasn't come by to introduce himself. That's all right; wonder is the trump of the twenty-three-pair chromosome set.

He remains horizontal for days, boning up, resisting the temptation to indulge in premature cracking. Feverish, unleashed vistas tempt him with fat feasibility. He must first consolidate, gather strength, quiet his mind, assemble the tools, await, without expecting, that rare, most skittish visit. Yet before insight can alight, the outside world flank-attacks him through the mail. A letter appears in his box, his first communiqué since hitting Illinois:

July 16, 1957

Dear Stu,

Heard you're in town and hope you're not waiting for official commencement of the fellowship to drop by the lab. We could use you in the Blue Sky sessions if nowhere else. No one's doing much biology at the moment, as you might imagine. Too much excitement in the air. Right now we're all thinking math and language. How are you at combinatorials? Oh for a spark of Aha! By the way, Charlene and I are having the team over for dinner and cards or something next Thursday. Do come. We'll even have the get-together in your honor, if that's what it takes.

Yours,
Karl Ulrich

P.S. Review *Adv Biol* 4:23 if you haven't done so recently, and let me know Thursday if you think Gamow's right in discarding the diamond code. I never liked the layout: too pretty; too much the work of a physicist. But too convenient if the whole pattern just coiled up and blew away.

Ressler has met his new boss only through the professional journals. A prolific writer, the man is to trees what Bill Cody was to buffalo. Ulrich, at fifty-two (Ressler's age transposed), is Illinois's grand old molecular man, guiding spirit behind Cyfer, the team of microbiologists, chemists, and geneticists who induct Ressler as new recruit. Stuart ingests the assignment in place of lunch, tracking the article down to the university library. The stacks, third-largest in the country, are, like Memorial Stadium, decorated

46

passim with orange-and-black Civil Defense pies. Ressler doubts the pragmatics of the motif. Four floors of masonry are not likely to survive an airburst. Brick and poured concrete do reduce rad passage, but story-height blown-out glass does not. And using the library as shelter until the renovated landscape returned to safe levels would require keeping survivors alive for weeks on cellulose alone.

Nevertheless, this homage to Dewey Decimal is the most impressive monument America's Breadbasket has yet shown him. Several million volumes colonize ten floors of catwalks and twisting alleys. Every deck contains, in its hectares, plumbing and facilities for long-term residents. If the stink of binding paste didn't offend, he'd go AWOL from the barracks and set up his two pieces of luggage here. A sadly vindicating tour reveals an 824 untouched since Henry James died. Humanities have clearly slid into the terminally curatorial, forsaking claim to knowledge. Ressler finds his niche-to-be, 575, by cytotropic sixth sense, tucked away in a grotto deep in the cavernous recesses, incandescence lending it appropriate spelunker's air. This rarefied branch of a specialized discipline, barely extant a decade back, now rates several shelves, swelling by the hour.

At any other time, he'd be hopelessly waylaid by 1930s unemployment lists, turn-of-the-century novels, hundred-season sets of symphony programs. A comprehensively dense map striving for perfect isomorphism with the outside world provokes his browser's awe. But commissioned, Stuart goes straight to the target periodical without cracking a spine. He's read Gamow's views on the code—one of the first formal attacks on how DNA might embed its protein-plans. But best review the physicist's retraction; its details are likely to be of more use at Dr. Ulrich's soiree than the latest Elvis or Fats Domino. *Advanced Biology* 4:23 comes off the shelf suspiciously easily, plops open to the piece in question, a penciled scrawl near the title:

JHB SZI HVA OLP GVX IKZ XHO DBN ZRU ALW WKH TVI HQQ
BTI VSR EP

Disguised messages hook him by the brain stem. The cold lure of this adept's sport, text trapped in nonsense: a face-slap, tapping impulses fiercer than the urge to pile up cars or cure the forbidding loneliness of women. The sanctioned desires of twenty-five—warm breasts and cold chrome—are mere substitutes, garbled misreadings of the *real* pull. All longing converges on this mystery: revelation, unraveling secret spaces, the suggestion that the world's valence lies just behind a scrambled facade, where only the limits of ingenuity stand between him and sunken gardens. Cryptography alone slips beneath the cheat of surface. Yes, test adrenaline, the attempt to justify the teacher's faith, contributes to this nonsense string's siren song. But this puzzle—clearly planted for his benefit—this chase, this unscrambling, waiting, working, worrying the moment when simple, irrefutable plaintext explanation descends: this (the cadence of his thought straying dangerously close to Protestant hymnody) is the reason why awareness itself first evolved out of inert earth.

Experiment *per se* has never carried any special appeal; rare steak aside, Ressler has never enjoyed cutting into any genus higher than *Anura*. But the driving design. . . . He forgets the article and sets to work on the pencil smudges. "EP," the closing, sole couplet: the initials of his antagonist, KU? He tries a few relations before hitting on a simple one. P to U is a jump of five letters; E to K, a jump of six. An incremental substitution cipher—a good, reversible garbling scheme. Seven to the final "R" yields "Y." Eight to the "S," going around the horn, arrives at "A." The last triplet comes out "day:" paydirt. The rest of the reconstruction is brute counting. Soon shell cracks and sense seeps through:

IFY OUC ANR EAD THI STH ENT HEP ART YIS REA LLY WED NES
DAY

Back to native tongue. Grouping by threes is Ulrich's hat tip to the prevailing idea that the unit in the genetic code is a triplet of bases. Regrouping reveals all.

He passes the rite of hidden passages, wins his first glimpse of the new boss. The path from discovery to tinkering to inspiration to solution takes place outside time. Returning to deck entrance, he discovers that he has narrowly missed being locked in the stacks overnight. Only when he is safely back at the barracks, flat out on the bunk in K-53-C, sipping tomatoes and savoring his victory, does he realize that he's forgotten even to glance at the article Dr. Ulrich asked him to review.

Stuart arrives at the Ulrich doorstoop on the revealed Wednesday, groomed for the occasion. The chief ushers him into the party with only a "Good job." Ressler, the last guest to arrive, uncomfortable in newly purchased suit, presents host and hostess with a box of after-dinner chocolates filled with greenish fungi. Suit and gift are both wild miscalculations; soon he'll be unable to go out in public at all, so completely has he botched the social code in his haste to crack the genetic. He makes the rounds, meets his future labmates. Tooney Blake, dark, mid-height, a youthful forty, is at the piano doing a terrifyingly down-tempo version of "Let's Call the Whole Thing Off." Only he's missed the point of the song: "Potato, potato, tomato, tomato," all pronounced exactly the same. A gracious woman with an uncanny Eleanor Roosevelt impersonation, Dr. Toveh Botkin, stands by in great pain, waiting for the promised formal feeling to come. Her accent reveals her as one of those brilliant Central European scientists lured away from the Russians in '45 by democracy and cash. Musically illiterate, Ressler can nevertheless tell by Dr. Botkin's bearing that the soiree is soul-toughening purgatory for her. She says as much in her first sentence to him, declaring with convoluted tact that the machine responsible for the apotheosis of Beethoven's *Diabelli,* not to mention the transcendent Opus 109 set, had been a sacred instrument to her until a few moments before. He nods, without a clue to what she's talking about.

Joseph Lovering, five years Ressler's senior, sits on a sofa noisily denying that he is now or ever has been a member of this or any party. He and Jeanette Koss, also near thirty, heatedly discuss some political bomb that Ressler lost track of while in grad school. These two, the only folks close to Stuart in age, more or less ignore him after the obligatory hand-grab. Daniel Woytowich, the other senior Cyfer member after Ulrich and Botkin, is at work in the corner, head wrapped in Pyrex eyeglasses, watching the Ulrichs' rabbit-eared black-and-white set broadcast Garry Moore's *I've Got a Secret.* The show is interrupted by a flash announcement: scientists have succeeded in creating today's modern aspirin, the Ferrari of the gastrointestinal Le Mans. Faster, Stronger, and now Improved. "Last year's aspirin only *killed* the headache..." When Ressler introduces himself, Woytowich tells him the panelist's secret: by marrying the mother of his father's second wife, he's become his own grandpa.

The night's entertainment alarms and depresses him: how can so human a collection hope to penetrate its own blueprint? The code must certainly be more ingenious than this crew it created.

Ressler knows Cyfer's considerable collective intelligence from their published track record. He *needs* them; they represent specific expertise in cytology, biochemistry, ontogeny, fields wild to him. Yet they sing, watch prime time, talk politics. Incredible comedown, awful circularity: no one to reveal us to ourselves but us.

The welcome-aboard party—easily his most nightmarish evening out since prom—leaves Ressler in serious need of a purgative. He pays his first visit downtown since the bus pulled in. There he indulges uncharacteristically in buying something. Spending money is not a problem; he's never been one to form emotional bonds to crinkled bits of safety paper. The wrench for him is acquiring more stuff. Since late teens, he's never owned anything more than he could carry out of the country on short notice. Now, in less than a month, he's already saddled himself with dishes, a table, even a heap of chicken-wire sculpture that charitably passes for a chair.

He buys a record player that folds up into a box with handle, a pink that has been coaxed out of the spectrum by suspect means. He is sold by a matching pink polyethylene ballerina that snaps on the spindle and pirouettes slavishly at 78, 45, 33⅓, and— whatever happened to 16?—16. Never musical, he inherited what is physiologically referred to as a tin ear. His father carried the tone-deaf gene, forever going about the house delivering a spectral version of "Get Out and Get Under." Discomfort with harmony leaves Ressler not only ignorant of music but deeply distrustful. Pitch-writing obeys amorphous, ambiguous linguistics—a dialect just beyond paraphrase. Fast and loud is more exciting than slow and quiet. The rest is silence.

He needs, without knowing, those old, Renaissance formulas equating C-sharp minor with longing, sudden modulation to E major with a glimpse of heaven. How dare an obnoxious greaser four years younger than he turn the Civil War tune "Aura Lee" into the Hit Parade standard "Love Me Tender," without a wiggle of concern for the underpinning chordal message? Either this language *has no content,* or tonal tastes have festered, fixed for 100 years and more. Both options terrify him.

He has trouble selecting tunes to keep the ballerina dancing, and Olga herself remains noncommittal. At length, he settles on an anthology called *Summer Slumber Party,* the bobby-soxer, center cover behind the pillow, reminding him of a woman he dated

50

in college. Straight brown hair and artesian eyes, she dumped him for never getting off his Bunsen. With the assistance of a sales clerk, he secures two other primers: Britten's *Young Person's Guide to the Orchestra* and *Leitmotifs from Wagner's "Ring."* The latter, still politically suspect, appeals to him from the liner description: a story told in a book-code of memorable riffs. One of these disks might contain his tonal Rosetta. To round out his disk library, in the spirit of Separate Can Never Be Equal, and knowing the tunes from his father, he buys an album of spirituals by Paul Robeson.

A summer night, the last before his marriage to experiment, and Ressler spends the few, dark, warm hours soaking in the deep evangelical minister's voice seeping in spirituals from K-53-C onto Stadium Terrace's lawn. Robeson sings, "Sometimes it causes me to wonder. Ah, sometimes." The sound ambushes Ressler, slack in his lawn chair. He watches the waves continue east at 1,134 feet per second, where they will arrive in D.C. later that evening. He hears the phrase knock at John Foster Dulles's window as the secretary of state prepares for bed. Dulles curses, shouts for this blackfella to leave him be. He's promised to return Ol' Man River's passport as soon as Robeson returns the '52 International Stalin Peace Prize. Last year Dulles told a *Life* reporter that a man scared to go all the way to the brink is lost. "Brinksmanship" is now the going word. Dulles, hands full with the Suez and Syria, his troops in Lebanon within a year, shaken by the runaway slave's son singing "Jordan river chilly and cold," shouts out the window of the State Department at Ressler to turn the volume down and have a little respect, forgetting, under stress of the brink, that democracy is the privilege of not being able to escape the next man's freedom of speakers.

Ressler, a thousand miles west, listens to the blackfella go on to sing, in resonant bass, the great ascent up Jacob's Ladder. Every rung—now the steps of the four nucleotides up the spiral DNA staircase—goes higher and higher. On the darkened, ex-army-barracks lawn, gathering strength for the work he owes the world, a physiological trick sweeps over Ressler. His peace turns to a sadness so overpowering that, before he can interpret it, tears seep out his eyes on underground springs. Avuncular defective lachrymal, until this moment happily masked, flushed by the deep voice, the simplicity of the tune, the hopeless hope of words in a world where the stadium colonnade declares itself a safe radiation haven, or just this absolute, still, summer night in a featureless

51

town. Spontaneous twitch of gland for a race capable of grabbing the next rung while simultaneously leaping for the beloved brink. Or purely somatic epiphenomenon: Robeson hits a note, springs a chord sequence that triggers solute; everything else lies outside measure. Deeply enfolded, the tune attaches to the night's lateness, and suddenly the song is real. Ah! sometimes it causes me to wonder. Sometimes.

There on the lawn, the eve before uncovering the precise, testable tape that will change the way life conceives itself, he feels the first seduction of music, his own pitiful compulsion for forward motion, the insistence that we sing ourselves over into a further place. All the while the runaway slave's son intones:

> We are climbing Jacob's Ladder
> We are climbing Jacob's Ladder
> We are climbing Jacob's Ladder
> We're soldiers of the Cross.

As rearguard action, Ressler runs through the lexical combinations biology reserves for this five-letter combination: cross stain, hair cross, Ranvier's cross, crossbreed, cross-firing, crossing over, cross matching, sensory crossway.

> Every rung goes higher and higher
> Every rung goes higher and higher
> Every rung goes higher and higher
> We're soldiers of the Cross.

To this cross list, he adds the crucial test cross, the only way to tell how he and the bass are related, to find the miscegenation harbored in their common ancestor, to trace the defective ducts. Then he hits on it, the mark, the label for the spiritual's crucifix, the deep, reluctant cross Robeson soldiers: anatomical term. Crux of the heart.

Today in History

Assisted by accident, I was out of the starting block. Given the locus—a year to peg him and a special field—I retrieved everything the limited print trail held about Dr. Ressler. Three days after

52

coming across the magazine photo, I turned up two more citations: the *Science Midwest* abstracts for the same year, and the coauthored article in *Journal of Molecular Biology* that brought the young man his first attention. I even traced, through the dense, preserved, late-fifties paperwork, his department's involvement in varied researches as molecular genetics unfolded. One colleague made important refinements in electron microscopy. Another developed a cheap way to measure cytoplasmic protein. A third cropped the copious shady old genealogical trees beloved of textbooks.

To have been a virgin post-doc then! I exhumed the Watson-Crick paper that had touched off the wholesale gold rush. The primary sources still exhale the atmosphere of intellectual dizziness, the articles thick with a sense that someone would soon crack the complete caper and seize the *ne plus ultra* of the research world, the riddle of life. I knew that every era since Anaximander and his vital moisture has tried to explain the ultimate contradiction: *living* matter. But even a hurried review of Ressler's contemporaries brought home the shock: my lifetime has seen the breakthrough moment, the first physical theory of all life grounded at entry level.

Each article, every retraction and revision recorded the heat of the exploding field. I pored over the background material—busman's holidays at the main branch—coming to know Dr. Ressler weeks before I made his acquaintance, if only a Ressler decades younger than the one I was sent to discover. How must it have felt, at twenty-five, talented but untested, to live at the same hour, perhaps even arm's length from the finishing touch, the final transcription—the first organism to explain its own axioms?

Half of what I made out about the twenty-five-year-old scientist was pure projection. I began to feel I had not lived up to my own intellect, that I'd been born too late, had taken a wrong turn, had lost my own chance to turn up the edge of the real, discover something, something *hard*. This child scientist, desperate with ability, somehow reduced to full-scale adult withdrawal, night shift labor, by something not explained in the literature: here was my own irreversible missed hour.

The race for the genetic code must have been wonderful torture for one of Dr. Ressler's abilities. By 1957, the search to describe all living tissue in molecular principles was halfway to unmitigated solution. The pace of revelations staggers even one habituated to

53

permanent acceleration. Consensus that DNA was the genetic carrier had been reached only a few years before Ressler arrived in Illinois. Its structure had fallen only four years earlier. In 1957, speculation about how the giant molecule encoded heredity became open game for theoreticians. The field is littered with articles by physicists, chemists, and other inflamed amateurs. Generations of patient fly-counters had done the legwork. The mid-fifties were set for breakout, the rush of synthesizing postulates. He must have sensed that this anarchical phase would pass quickly, perhaps in months. The prize was bare, exposed for the plucking at the top of the nucleic stair.

But something else motivates the euphoric articles, something more than self-aggrandizement, more than the desire to cap the ancient monument and book passage to Stockholm, that freezing, pristine Valhalla. The compulsion to find the pattern of living translation—the way a simple, self-duplicating string of four letters inscribes an entire living being—is built into every infant who has ever learned a word, put a phrase together, discovered that phonemes might *speak*.

As the journal evidence accumulated, it sucked me into the craze of crosswords, pull of punch lines, addiction to anagrams, nudge of numerology, suspense of magic squares. I felt the fresh Ph.D.'s suspicion that beneath the congenital complexity of human affairs runs a generating formula so simple and elegant that redemption depended on uncovering it. Once lifting the veil and glimpsing the underlying plan, Ressler would never again surrender its attempted recovery. The desire surpassed that for food, sex, even bedtime stories, worth pursuing with convert's zeal, with the singleness of a monastic, a lost substance abuser, a true habitué: the siege of concealed meaning.

The Question Board

I put off telling Franklin Todd what my search had turned up. The trail of the sure-to-be-famous youth ended abruptly, dying out in the middle of 1958. Thumbnail biographies and professional references both dried up. A void lay between the boy of twenty-five, in the middle of the fastest-breaking biological revolution ever, and the man twice that age, an obscure computer functionary. I could do nothing but confirm the same enigma that had driven

Todd to consult me in the first place. I returned to that hauntingly alien photo, "one of the new breed who will help uncover the formula...." The article bore an epigraph by Friedrich Miescher, the twenty-five-year-old who had discovered DNA in 1869:

Should one ask anybody who is undertaking a major project in science, in the heat of the fight, what drives and pushes him so relentlessly, he will never think of an external goal; it is the passion of the hunter and the soldier...the stimulus of the fight with its setbacks.

One passionate hunter had evidently been shot along the way. I would have gone on trying to determine how, even had Todd not returned. Some days after my break, I caught him hanging around the Question Board, scouring it as if nothing mattered except this discontinuous glut of fact stripped of context. As if, despite the biblical promise, the world would end in flood after all. Of information. If Todd lay in wait for me, he made no sign. "Truly amazing," he said, not even looking as I approached. "How'd you *find* all this stuff? You make it up?"

It distressed me to enjoy seeing him. I tried to pull my mouth out of its involuntary grin into disapproval. "Of course not. What do you take me for? This is human services. Not for profit. Bulk mail permit."

"This one, for instance." He pointed to the weeks-old question about where in the world people were best off. The outdated card was due to be removed; I took it down as Mr. Todd continued. "How did you know all that, about the two million tons of bird shit and disappearing roads and all?"

My M.L.S. cheekbones crumpled like a rear-ended economy car. "Nauru? Nauru is a reference librarian's mainstay. Smallest republic. Largest per capita income. Typical instance of List Mentality. You might as well ask any urban male over fourteen if the number three sixty-seven means anything to him." Cobb's average, which I verified every few months, meant nothing to Todd. He looked inquisitively at me, not yet daring to ask if I had results. I wasn't volunteering. I carried on with my work, pinning to the board the Q-and-A:

Q: Who is the head of the CIA and where can I reach him? This is an EXTREMELY confidential matter.

F.P. 7/3/83

55

A: William J. Casey, Central Intelligence Agency, Washington, DC 20505.

J. O'D., 7/5/83

Todd took two more cards from under my clasped arm, careful not to touch my side. He assisted, pinning the cards into place. It seemed we had worked together, easily and quietly, for years.

Q: What must we do to be saved?

C.R., 7/2/83

A: A tough one, but worth looking into. According to George Saville, Marquis of Halifax (1633–1695), in *A Rough Draft of a New Model at Sea,* "To the question, What shall we do to be saved in this World? there is no other answer but this, Look to your Moat."

J. O'D., 7/5/83

My new acquaintance examined our handiwork. He giggled at the first and took undisguised pleasure in the second. Then he looked at me, scrutinized my face, trying to determine exactly who worked this advice column for the fact-lorn public. "You've found something," he declared. "That much is clear."

I wanted to contradict him, but couldn't. "Like the Canadian Mounties..." I began, but caught myself before ending up in the double entendre.

"You'll have to tell me everything. Listen: turns out I'm the sole patron of a seafood dive very much ahead of its time." His burlesque was gentle, with no sadistic edge. "I'm particularly enthusiastic about their humane handling of shellfish. Want to do lunch?"

It felt good to be asked a question that didn't require a double-check. I laughed. "It's almost five o'clock."

"Almost time for night-shift breakfast. I thought lunch might be an acceptable compromise."

"You *cannot* have seafood for breakfast. I forbid it."

"I've done worse. Can we take that no as a yes?" He went on, with wondrous, unassisted certainty, to set the time and place, not to mention what I would be eating. He rubbed his hands and made a curious snapping flick with thumb and middle finger. I later learned how many different things that nervous gesture stood for. "All *right* then. Meet you there. I assume you are dependable, Ms.

56

O'Deigh?" My paranoia flared as I heard my name in his mouth. "You'll be there?" Urgent but decorous library subdecibel. "Ach, she'll be thare, laddie. Stop with yare wurryin'."

All that I know of animal courtship dances comes from *Van Nostrand's*. But this clearly was one; too much bravado and flutter to be anything else. No man had done me so elaborate a two-step in several seasons, and I let it go on, despite myself. Pure, amateur male theatrics: nothing to take seriously. While ambivalent about meeting the man outside the jurisdiction of the shelf list, I saw little danger in it. Capitulation was easier than trying to outtalk him. My own curiosity about the collapse of the precocious empiricist would have been enough to take Todd on. I wanted everything his colleague might tell me.

But Franklin Todd's soft-shoe polish also smelled of something else: aromatic locales I hadn't yet visited, the scent of travel. The man was genuinely strange. Two people, no longer young, knowing nothing about one another, their pasts sharing no word in common, meet on a day in early summer to compare notes on a third party. The scenario had all the charm of travelers' phrases, a crash course at Berlitz. Sardonic, innocent, Todd backpedaled from the Question Board. He stopped abruptly and retraced his steps. He looked me over a last time and said, "But you *are*." Contradicting all advance reports, yet firm in the face of the evidence.

"Am what? What am I?"

"You *are* looking after your moat, aren't you?" He'd meant something else, an answer to his own question of a week before, deciding that I was, after all, possessed of surfaces. And the decision surprised us both. Still pruning the board after he left, I found an impeccable imitation of one of my own typed cards hiding amid the others, one of those marvelous walking sticks or owl-imitating moths. The impostor-card asked, "Q: What is the origin of the phrase 'Make the catch'?" It had not been there before Mr. Todd's visit.

Persistence of Vision

At the time, I was not in the market for dance steps, however novel. Already involved, as contemporary idiom puts it, tied to a man in a mutually professional windbreak stable enough to deflect this new sea breeze. Staying together for four years proved our complementarity. Keith—slick, quick to anger, addicted to excitement, at times insane—countered my own reverse extremes. Together, we passed in our class and era, subtly matched opposites in a country full of couples as incongruous as Tuckwell-O'Deigh.

Keithy always made me laugh. The problem, by summer of '83, was that I'd begun laughing at his running routine despite myself. My mate's particular brand of joke had lost the redeeming secret: the trick of making disparate reality show a hopeless, bearable seam. Like everyone I know in New York, Tuckwell was a prairie refugee. Every damn person I get close to in this city—all transplanted Hoosiers or huskers. It would have been cheaper to stay home. Keith's dress, speech, and manner were compensatory— Coastier Than Thou. He could speak convincingly about everything on the island from P/E ratios to performance art. "Appraising, dear heart, doesn't necessarily require the inconvenience of knowing."

He knew the city like a cabbie. The stress of midtown at 5:00 p.m. rolled off his downy obliviousness. Keith would have sickened and died if he'd had to live anywhere else but this epitome. For years he protected me, underwrote my survival in this toxic place. Keith had dabbled in academics but soon strayed into advertising, "Needs Manufacturing," as he liked to describe it. Tuckwell was outstanding at what he did. He made pots of money without shame. But he pumped a wellspring of sardonic commentary, the progressive's estrangement from his own pursuits. "Ads," he once defended himself at a dinner full of less forthright friends, "are our supreme art, polar exploration, and depth psychology rolled into one. And the shit that keeps the GNP blooming, to boot."

We liked each other well enough. But the spit holding us together was the power of mutual facetiae to legitimize affection. Against my reference-desk reserve, he cultivated crude anarchy. He was far more comfortable in the flash of Lower Manhattan *haute Kultur,* but he had to come to me for help in navigating the boroughs, even our own neighborhood. I kept him out of debt and he kept me from starving myself. We divided the household chores contractually. I did mine in the evenings and days off; he hired outside help. Tuckwell was convinced he would die by electric shock. I milked the opposite fear of wasting away for decades in a nursing home. Our phobias and philias canceled out one another. We arrived at an equilibrium that could go on, like those fleas on backs of fleas, forever *ad infinitum.*

We conversed well, when we saw one another. Keith overheated at times, but he knew the language. People who still love words have to be forgiven everything. In what the last century referred to as mechanical transport, we were scarily compatible, even after four years. He taught me abandon. The rule was: recklessness could always be repented at leisure. With ad designer's ingenuity, he steadily introduced wrinkles into our sex life, always managing to suggest that R and D had future, new-and-improved packages around the corner.

His total shamelessness even made the awful minute afterwards almost comic. As I postcoitally recoiled, Keith, still savoring the instinctual release just served up, would lie alongside me and wail, in a perfectly timed, plaintive voice directed at the ceiling, "What is the Law?" He'd answer himself in animal sadness, "Not to eat meat; not to go on all fours...." I always laughed—the dovetail joint between need and embarrassment.

Our attraction, unplanned and mismatched, was the physics of charged particles, ions pulled toward their neutralizing *not*. He was one of the few who prance through the world with self-esteem. His absolute views on everything were manna after a day in the perpetually uncertain, qualified reference wilderness. Keith liked himself, a fire worth hovering near, trying to steal.

On the day I accepted dinner, I was not dissatisfied. I'd never been a big fan of unnecessary drama. Mr. Todd's invitation was flattering, but not enough to account for my accepting it, even under guise of business. Tuckwell and I were, in the rules of coming and going, hopelessly liberal. His work was continuous and mine too variable for us to set up the schedule that ordinarily substitutes for home life. I tried to call him that July evening to tell him I'd be late. But already half sabotaging, I didn't try his office. I rang up the apartment and listened to Tuckwell's latest tape: "Your mission, should you decide...." I then announced to the machine that I was eating with a stranger.

I remember little of the clam shack Franker took me to. I do remember what he wore—creased, formal, button-down bemusement. I remember the soulful look when he implored me to order the linguini with calamari, and the scolding brows leveled at me when I left it untouched. I remember seeing the chef hack off a living lobster's tail while the creature's front end bourréed blithely across the counter to plunk back into the tank, mix it up one last time with the ladies. "You should see him do beef," Todd said.

And I remember him quickly relieving me of my discoveries. My disclosure—the young man in the journals, teetering on the verge of significant contribution—confirming his pain. He demanded to hear, in as much detail as I could muster, about Ressler's early work and the predictions about him. Todd seemed to have suspected the worst, all that had been at stake. When I finished relating what little story I'd uncovered, I sat silent, gingerly prodding my unfinished plate like a bomb squad nudging a black satchel. When he finally spoke, it was only to repeat, incredulously, "Twenty-five! My age to the day, as it turns out." I mumbled a birthday toast, unsure how literal he was being.

I naively proceeded to hand over my entire list of primary sources without securing any return hostages. My dinner date then fell rudely indifferent. His interest in me had been entirely functional after all; despite the expertly mimicked courtship dance, he wanted no more than a research assistant. I felt abused, doubly stupid for not recognizing the trick. But watching him toy with a Parmesan shaker, I was astonished to see Frank Todd clearly grieving for a person who, given what he'd said about their working relationship, was as great a stranger to him as to me.

Sitting across from me at the hired table, morose with concern: at last, someone who I might matter to. I felt a twinge of guilt toward Keith, just then listening to my taped won't-be-home-till-late. In that one instant, Todd seemed about to fold up into himself, to drop out of sight for good. I wouldn't have prevented him. In that minute gone bad, we were an accent away from splitting the tab and quitting. We were both geared to be rid of one another when the only real coincidence of those days intervened. A fluke, outside chance yanked Frank Todd out of a reverie he would never have come back from on his own. The sawdust dive's piped music, until then an eclectic collection of Balkan reed choir, Tyrolean zither, and Memphis twang, turned abruptly and became solo piano. The boy bolted upright, listening, alarmed. He shook his head, amazement moving his lips: the inappropriate smile at hurt too diffuse to absorb. "Name that tune," he said bitterly, slamming the table. "Name it, and I'll introduce you to the bastard."

I recognized the music, having learned the first, trivial thirty-two measures as a young girl before giving up the piano in favor of pragmatics. I had even made first forays into the variations Bach had extracted from the thirty-two-note ditty. The distillation of the first few notes held all the chest-tightening surprise of unlikely

60

visits. "I happen to know the piece," I said giddily. "But I'm off duty just now."

"Name it," he shouted. Conversation at other tables stopped. I mumbled the name of the work. By the effect on Todd, I'd just guessed the one-in-five-billion secret word. We listened. A few minutes in silence with a stranger lasts a lifetime. Only after two variations did he tell me that this piece—"this *particular* recording, in fact"—was the only music our mutual friend had listened to for the last year. Todd, reanimated, described how his lone shift partner sat every night in a sterile chamber of humming processing units, high-speed printers, floor-mount disk drives, and glowing consoles, doing routine work that any modestly endowed twenty-one-year-old could do, changing tapes, running the unvarying deck of punched cards through the hopper, while all the while this set of baroque irrelevances spun around on a cheap grinder perched on top of the digital check-sorter.

"All the way through, both sides, three times a night for the last few months." Todd, the insult of care cracking his voice, fell silent as the restaurant sound track reached the third permutation, a well-behaved melody beginning all over again against itself. Two pitch-for-pitch identical but staggered parts crossed each other, independently harmonized and harmonizing, no longer one identical source of notes but two. The study in imitative forward motion, the staggered, duplicate pair of voices stood motionless at the axis of the turning world. The unison canon, contradiction in terms, left Todd morose, ready to replay the older man's disappearance of years before. He came out of his trance long enough to say, "You won't have heard the thing properly until you see my friend in the flesh." The invitation I so badly wanted.

Later, after a stop at the futuristic supermarket that, like me, had recently gate-crashed this neighborhood, I found Keith alone in our apartment, still engrossed in a lucrative day's work, sprawled on the floor surrounded by tape splices, single-stepping through a video of his latest collaborative effort: the fifteen-second story of how a young woman and her breath spray find happiness together. "Dinner OK?" he asked, intent on the frame-by-frame.

"Yeah, dinner OK. Four-B's car alarm is howling again. Buzzing like a shorted bumblebee. Nobody paying any attention. Not even the beat police flinch anymore."

"Speaking of High Security, how's my Princess Grace?"

I'd lived with him long enough to follow every free association.

61

I was glad for glibness just then and retaliated in like currency. "American film actress. Born in Philadelphia, 1927? No, '28. Killed in Monaco car crash in September 1982. Almost a year already. God." I went to the window and held back the curtain. In the street below, late-evening pedestrians worked out the details of Brownian motion.

Tuckwell gave his representative laugh: a high-pitched, uncontrolled cackle. "*Very good.* Been earning your keep, I see. The Human Reference Shelf wouldn't care to say what *day* Mrs. Grimaldi died, would she?" I sat down next to him, looking for warmth that wouldn't aggravate the heat. He gave me a kiss on my exposed collarbone. I made no rejoinder, and he returned to work, adding, "See *To Catch a Thief* for a demonstration of life imitating art."

The television was on, sound just loud enough to give voice to incestuous bad girls from Texas and tough but basically good inner-city cops. We witnessed the last five minutes of *Five Minutes to Meltdown,* where political extremists, natural disaster, and old-fashioned carelessness conspired to threaten the nuclear reactor on the community outskirts nearest you. Four young, lusty civil engineers narrowly thwarted the disaster. After, we caught the late news, fulfilling our social duty. Keith got his chance to make his favorite joke: "Twenty million face famine in Ethiopia. First, *this.*" He made running commentary on all the spots, from headlines down to the perverse, trailing human interest. As usual, during commercials he cut the sound and ad-libbed. "Terrorism: the mini-series. Thursday, right here on...." Had he thrived in another decade, his manic energy might have made him an activist.

When one network in its allotted half hour said all there was to say about Tuesday, July 5, 1983, we switched to another. The coverage was identical, a half hour later. Keith carried on his inspired annotations, even after I stopped listening and disappeared into the bedroom. There I worked on loose ends, preparing for work the next day. I glanced at the librarian's trade journal, caught up on old correspondence, and, while I had the typewriter fired up, finished tomorrow's Today in History and the unanswered Question Board questions. I rolled a clean index card under the platen and typed "A:". I remember pausing long enough to feel proud that what I was about to answer would have taken the median librarian, relying on *Brewer's, Bartlett's,* or the *OED,* considerable effort. Experience, private knowledge, could still stand one in better stead than mastery of the disjointed stockpile. I typed:

A: A "catch" is a form of musical round where identical voices enter at different times. The catch to a catch is that it is printed on one solo line. In the past, as a party game, singers would sight-read from catch collections, each group responsible for figuring out when to "make the catch," when to come in at the proper moment. Making the catch reached its peak of popularity under England's Charles II. The phrase may have originated earlier. Rounds in general are at least as old as the thirteenth-century tune "Summer Is Icumen In."

I stopped, realizing I was straying from the point, that summer was already two weeks gone. As the submitter had not deigned to sign the question, I left my answer similarly anonymous. The pair are both still on file that way. As I held the cards next to one another, checking my work, I knew I would not, contrary to all I'd ever assumed, remain a librarian forever.

Canon at Unison

My old associates threw me a going-away party today. It was, as going-away parties go, a bad mix of parting embarrassment and exhilaration. For want of a more plausible story, I spread the word around the branch that I am going back to school. Loosely interpreted, never a lie. The celebration was a sorry affair. Several colleagues brought homemade cookies, which nobody's diet permitted. We broke the rules and served Chablis in paper cups; everyone partook dutifully, in professional moderation. Separation—life's major emotion—is being slowly written out of our repertoire. A few friends will genuinely miss me, and I them. My buddy Mr. Scott, he of the eternal retirement threat, came up to me late in the afternoon, making no effort to disguise his eyes. "You beat me to it," he said, shaking his head. "I can't believe you beat me."

"I'm afraid I'm abandoning you, friend. Fight the good fight." Before I could get all the way through the sentence, he swept me up in an embrace, which we held for a long time by contemporary standards. Close to his ear, before pulling away from it for good, I whispered, "Work forever."

We all made the standard plans to stay in touch, plans we knew, even as we made them, would atrophy for no reason. As a gag gift, the collected staff presented me with a wrapped Facts on File binder stuffed with miscellaneous soap-opera synopses, gov pubs, library memos, and those You-Are-Next fliers collected from the prophets of apocalypse who hang around Grand Central. Then they presented me with my own copy of the *Times Atlas*. The combination of my long-expressed girlish delight in the book, the misplaced earnestness of the staff, and the hopeless ambition of the atlas itself—the simple description of how to get anywhere in the world—caught inside me. Seeing the effect the atlas had on me, my friends broke up the party.

As ironic token of affection, the staff let me have a last go at the Quote Board and Event Calendar. "Made me" might be more accurate. The work was more than I wanted to take on today, but I appreciated the gesture. For tomorrow's Today, I chose the Homestead Strike: the fifth day's clash between five thousand steelworkers and Frick's three hundred Pinkertons. I avoided my habit of extending the fact into exposition or mouthing my usual guarded meliorism. I wish I hadn't chosen that particular event; I'd hate to suggest that I've left on a labor dispute. But done is done. For my last ever selection for quote of the day, I posted vintage W.C. Fields:

It's a funny little world. A man's lucky if he gets out of it alive.

My final official act at the branch was to sort the unbound issues of *Congressional Quarterly,* which some malicious cit had mixed up beyond recognition. Alexandria arranged its scrolls by size— an order useless except to the initiated. The race's chief discovery may well be the idea that even a perfect stranger could retrieve things from parchments, given the sequence. Filing was a bit below my skills, but it was basically what I did for a living, until today. And in truth, returning the *CQs* to useful order gave me the thrill of send-off. I was packing my bags, feeling my freedom. I took a last look around my stacks. The collection suddenly seemed wonderful beyond naming. I had for a time lived here. Then I snapped the binders shut and was gone.

IV

Today in History

A postcard arrived today. A fifty-cent picture and message, and for a moment this morning it seemed I would not be cut off from all word from Franklin. Nothing for almost a year, then four lines of friend's postmortem. A few weeks later, a postcard making no attempt to explain the gap or give any idea of how he is. A fair sample of the man's communication. Still, I was glad for even this scrap. I remain one of those unreformable suckers who want to hear, just *hear* from time to time, even if the point of hearing has long since disappeared. The card carried a pastel foreign-denomination stamp complete with obligatory royal sovereign. Frank writes:

> One cannot, I suppose, traffic in Flemish masterpieces without a passing knowledge of Vlaams. And as a beautiful woman not unlike yourself once taught me, the only way to learn a foreign language, *natuurlijk,* is total immersion. Flanders seems the likely place. I could live for years on new vocabulary alone. *Eenvoudig* = one + folded = simple. *Uiteraard* = out of the earth = obvious. And those just the adjectives! Invigorating, learning a second tongue. (Invigorating to have twigged a first one.) The doors that new words are opening right now! This man has spent sorrows, lacks no delight, has hoard and horses and hall joys and all a lord is allowed had he his woman with him. FTODD

On the card, a late-gothic village, purportedly in the rolling geest of Northern Europe but more likely, given the crags looming in the background, situated just south of the painter's frontal lobes. Tempera and oil on panel, it has that gessoed, patient, long-

65

suffering look that only painters in that part of the world, in that century, knew how to make. Ephemeral transfusion of light through foliage, discontinuous brushstrokes, the countryside's green shading into azure and aquamarine color-freeze the village in escapist fantasy. The town is more familiar to me than my own childhood. Ground mineral, egg yolk, oil, chalk, varnish: an organic cupboard exudes a lost landscape that would be heart-balm to look at, were he not in it.

I hardly needed to check the attribution: Herri met de Bles, an itinerant early-sixteenth-century painter so obscure as to be almost apocryphal. Franklin has been trying to write a dissertation on the artist for years, searching for sufficient motivation to produce a treatise of interest only to a dozen specialists in the world. He nibbled at the project, two years stretching into four. Procrastination at last exhausted his assistantship money at Columbia. With the project still hanging over him, finance forced him into night-shift data operations.

Franker spoke of his halted work, his failed scholarly biography, the second night we went out. "The son of a bitch had a bouquet of names. Herri. Henri. Civetta. De Bles. De Dinant. At least two places of birth and half a dozen birthdates. Circa 1500; emphasis on *circa*. Half the paintings attributed to him probably aren't his while half of the ones he did paint are probably attributed to somebody else. Not a single signed or attested work. May have been a pupil of Patinir; emphasis on *may*. May have been his nephew. Christ; I don't even know if I'm dealing with one guy or three."

I watched his fingers, strangely entwined. His distress, lovely dressing, was just more flavor for that moment. "His works must be very moving," I at last said.

"Why do you say that?" At that suspicious snap, the evening changed, modulated into harsher places. Todd's unkindnesses tore down pathways he himself couldn't anticipate or steer. I learned that only by stages.

"Well, you wouldn't spend so much of your life knocking up against those difficulties if they weren't."

He laughed, rewarding me for nursing the flame of logic in dark times. He saw me as a faithful Chartres peasant, preserving the cathedral rose in pieces strewn through a thousand wartime cellars. "Sorry to disappoint, Miss. He's average. Very. Passable panels, in a relatively narrow range. A handful of awkward biblical alle-

66

gories. Impatient with human figures, dashes them off to justify the scenery. Some compositional interest, slight technical skill, but spiritually mediocre." He felt silent, the silence of ancient oracles. Finally, speaking to himself under his breath: "But *landscape*! You ought to see them." As if every contradiction could be reconciled by jagged, fantastic rose madder.

"If the fellow is as average as you say, why not do somebody more important? Someone you love. Difficult, I have no problem with. But difficult, obscure, and trivial? No wonder you can't get through with it."

"Believe me, sweet lady," Franklin shot back, affecting troubadour. "I'd kill for Brueghel or Vermeer. I'd write on the Mystic Lamb, pour out a book on the singing angels panel alone, if it were still possible. You know how much wood pulp has been sacrificed on the Ghent Altar already? You want the sheepskin, you gotta do Herri met de Bles."

"Henri," I corrected. He laughed a compensation, restoring us to other, more pressing theses in need of writing.

I flipped this morning's postcard over and read the tag on back: *Landschap met grote brand*. Knowing just enough cognates and etymology to be dangerous, I translated the title without the humiliation of showing my face at the branch within a month of quitting. Landscape with large fire. Only on second look did I notice, true to billing, near the right edge of the pastoral oblivion, something burning. The most delicate umbers and ambers twisted into plumes, shaded to grays, and slipped off into the cloudscape. Fires were, Franker told me, a minor specialty of his apocryphal painter. This one went completely overlooked, even by threatened villagers.

Todd gave no address, *natuurlijk*. I admired his poise, blowing clear of the wreck, slipping off to Europe the minute his mentor was cremated. The Grand Tour at last, as he always threatened. And making the catch, reaching the far side of the Atlantic, he caps the escapade with a postcard home. No tourist's trinket vista: that would have been forgivable. The typical Technicolor snap of donjon or belfry might have helped me imagine where he'd run to. But the fool sends a transcription, a reproduction of a painting of an idea of a place, if that.

Nothing would make me happier, even now, than to think that Franklin has at last gotten down to unfinished business, tying up the eternal loose end, spurred by Ressler's death into at last putting down the ideas he a hundred times explained so lucidly to me in private, in streetlit rooms. But the postcard makes no such claim, no word of the professor or the uses of death. The card says only that he has jumped continent and bought a phrase book. As sympathetic as I am to the scholar's need to speak in tongues, as much as I share his delight in word acquisition, Flemish would not be the first language Frank has distracted himself with. He invested years in French and German and can at least read Italian, if his pronunciation tends to scumble into sfumato.

He's told me enough of the scattering of Bles's panels to suggest that Flanders would only be stop one. To do the job right, he'll need Vienna, Dresden, Copenhagen, Budapest: excuses to stop and learn Danish and Hungarian. He doesn't need to read, see, think, or hear another word in *any* language. He's memorized all the sources already. He has the damn paper complete in his head, an inch away from written. He's practically recited it to me. He just has to work up the nerve to declare, "*I* put my name to all this. Sue me if I'm wrong." It's not even conscientiousness that keeps him from the final draft. The real impediment—one as one-folded as seeing—is Franklin's inability to convince himself that the project has any worth. A year ago, our little band breaking up, I said to him, "At least this is goodbye to distractions. Now you'll have the time to get back to Herri." His parting shot: "Why bother?"

He meant to slight more than his panel painter's technique. He meant the whole, colossal impertinence of studying Art History— the delicate, gessoed, tempera conflagration—in a world setting *itself* on fire. Franker, in the year I knew him, carried inside, wound up in his love for anachronistic art, a contempt for aesthetics that only the aesthete can feel. Every so many weeks he tried, despite his temperament, to turn himself into a moralist whose ethical code bore one criterion: use. Front-page news—the bleakest of which he clipped obsessively for months—would not allow him to indulge the pointless pleasure he needed. Headlines confirmed his worst suspicion; current events shamed panel and oil. Like an unfaithful lover, he repeatedly swore off sin and allure. But repeated infidelity made the betrayed more beautiful.

What use could new light on a sixteenth-century landscapist be to a sick, self-afflicted present? Dr. Ressler's terminal nightmare may have decided Franker on that account. His card is cheery enough; he sounds worlds limberer than in the closing weeks of love. But has he really gone to Dinant to write? Could he sincerely believe long-postponed looking might now be of some moral use? New language, *any* new language—at best, homage to a lost linguist he loved. He'll never put his new adjectives to the use he wants. Acts of care are never fundamentally useful.

At least he's made the pretense of getting down to work. I, on the other hand, entering unemployment's third week, have done nothing for days but add up my liquid assets and divide them by my spending rate, determining how much time I have before I run my life savings into the ground. Depending on the weight I assign the variables, I'm left with between forty and sixty weeks. Less than nothing and more time than I know how to fill. Weirdly exhilarating prospect: I give this week a number and begin the countdown. Week zero, getting closer every seven days, ought to put an edge on my style. Make me more supple than I've been in a while. But supple for what? Having nothing better to do, finding guilty delight in the pure, useless exercise of powers, I spent two hours this afternoon placing the allusion in Franker's card. The accents and alliterations gave me a broad hint where to begin. I worked in the sunny pleasure of my own room, combing the volumes that have grown over the years, reproducing themselves into a private reference collection. I worked—the oddest of feelings—for myself alone. No one to solve the citation for but me.

The line showed up in an Anglo-Saxon poem, one of the earliest in the language that mutated into English. A fragment in the Exeter Book called the Husband's Message. He closed with it as friendly challenge, for old times' sake: from a vanished friend to one left behind. Invigorating, to learn a language. Aside from that citation hunting, nothing. Dinner, extravagantly, at a sit-down place near Prospect Park, savoring spice and irony, paying for both with two days' worth of remaining time. The passage of time with nothing specific to accomplish makes me feel a little more blessedly, acutely free. I eat, I walk fearless in the summer air back home. I sit alone in my room, among the home reference. I now have all a lady is allowed had I only an answer. Had I only him.

Imitation of the Dance

If the forties' great debate raged over which macromolecule carried hereditary material, and if the early fifties fought over nucleic acid structure, Ressler walks smack into *the* contention of

69

1957 on his first day in the lab. Conscientious hygiene resulting from a working relationship with microorganisms made him bathe this morning before leaving barracks. A regular dawn dunking also gives him time for undirected reflection. Like Luther, his best insights arrive in proximity to porcelain. But drying his hair before setting off is time lost to superfluity. The omission puts him into the scientific cross hairs.

While he unpacks his glassware and sets up a cot in a storage room, Jeanette Koss, the woman at Ulrich's party steeped in world polemics, passes his counter and puts a discreet hand on his. The contact startles Stuart; her touch, real skin rubbing the fur of his arm, cuts—so long has he been without—like an accusation. Dr. Koss whispers, "If Blake or Lovering catches sight of you in this condition, your year is ruined."

In the same soft confidence, she lays out that Joe Lovering, her soiree spar partner, and Tooney Blake, the pianist of less than gershwinning ways, are locked in an ideological conflict about the hazards of going outside with a wet head. The two scientists share compatible lab practices and commensurate views on the coding problem. But on this matter, they are bitterly bipolar. Dr. Koss relates how Blake has devoted himself to a systematic destruction of the old wives' hypothesis linking wet hair to open virus season. For the last month he has immersed his head twice daily, once before setting off to work and once before leaving the lab. "Just a hairsbreadth," Dr. Koss confides, "between empiric physiology and abnormal psych." Lovering, on the other hand, in horrified reaction, not only maintains bone-dry hair at all times but even now, in late July, keeps up a steady regimen of preventive tonics. "You see," Koss explains, releasing him from her touch, "they have no experimental control. If they catch you like this, you're It."

He's walked into all-out inimical politics. To date, he's lain low in the exchange between lab partners Niki and Ike. But his colleagues in deciphering have brought the Cold War home. Best avoid getting caught in the draft. Ressler thanks Dr. Koss for the caveat, but that's not sufficient. She produces a supply-room towel and insists on helping him. She wraps his head in the fabric and before he collects presence of mind to object begins rubbing him gently but briskly, businesslike, from crown to nape of neck. Buried memory shoots up through scalp: his mother preparing him for church, a wedding or funeral. The wince of somatic recall—thumb moistened with saliva, rubbing raw the skin behind his ears. The woman pinches his head into sweet pain. Woytowich walks in, salutes abstractedly, not even blinking.

Koss smoothes back his hair, combs it, smiles, and crosses the room to resume her work with the vernier scales. There she carefully measures the thickness of near-invisible growing media. In a minute, nothing out of the ordinary has happened; in two, Ressler's skin forgets the contact. He'll have to make allowances for the woman in the lab. Female scientists are still rare enough to seem as anomalous as Dr. Skinner's Ping-Pong-playing pigeons. Cyfer's employing two is a statistical violation. Toveh Botkin, the team's senior member after Ulrich, possesses an antique, clinical grace that sweeps her into the province of competent sexlessness. At the welcome party, he took to the older woman and refused all but a weak smile at the lone flash of humor to come from the evening: Joe Lovering describing her life as a series of near Mrs. Dr. Koss, on the other hand, a certified Mrs. in her spare time, is not to be completely trusted. Young, still breeding-age, somewhat better looking than germ culture: might upset the pheromone levels around here from now through the end of summer.

Yet this first afternoon, there seems little to worry about on that score. Blake, by his pianistic skills, is prematurely male-menopausal, Dan Woytowich too B-complex-deficient, and Ulrich too intent on cash-raising to raise any more disruptive fund drives. That leaves Lovering, who, by the time Stuart finishes unpacking, has taken up a post by a caged pair of white lab rats, apparently more mascots than experimental animals. Crew-cut, glasses, starched white coat with nub tie underneath, Joe shouts, "Mate, you suckers." Lovering's safe too.

The lab is well equipped. The experimental world divides into steriles and breeders. Stuart did his graduate work under a breeder, a brilliant teacher whose workplace's itinerant confusion—proliferating notebooks, apparatus, scopes, and racks of flasks whose labels had soaked into illegibility—was acute torture. Ulrich, happily enough, is a sterile. Never have supply cabinets so closely mimicked the pictures in warehouse catalogs, and the entire team, from post-doc Koss through veteran Botkin, keep their rubber-glove boxes prominently displayed.

The steriler the riper for Ressler. The only antidote to what ubiquitous radio announcers call the aches and pains of today's modern living is hair of the dog: research alone will cure a world sick on the aftereffects of discovery. Empiricism is the only way

71

from ovum to novum. The panacea he has in mind requires only a lens with focal length long enough and a sterile place to stand.

Ulrich's note was accurate; the lab is between measurements at the moment. The day Ressler arrives the group is on extended leave from titrations, stains, and partition chromatography. They are after a transcription axiom, linguistic. For the rule linking nucleotide sequences to protein synthesis to be determined experimentally, Cyfer must first play with its shape, its inner symmetries. They are up against not so much the chemistry of biology as the math. Molecular genetics, stringing the fine line between experimental and theoretic, has a first shot at bridging the gap, grounding organic complexity in fundamental arithmetic. Ulrich has called a moratorium to consolidate the lightning results of recent months and formalize Cyfer's understanding of the symbolic logic that genetics has stumbled on. First vocabulary; then the generative grammar. Time for pure speculation. No more cigar butts, fingerprints: just, as the Belgian says, the little gray cells. Ressler's first day at school is a day to indulge in that old sworn enemy of experiment: reason.

The team was originally called the Ulrich Group, but that was impossible to say without coming to a full stop between words, which no one since Chargaff has had time for. The year before Ressler arrived, the team was rechristened the Enzyme Synthesis Identification Group. But that broke the unwritten rule of acronyms. At last Tooney Blake hit upon Cyfer, a compression of Cytology Ferment. While they weren't strictly in the wine business, the name was the catchiest in the hard sciences since Bill Haley and the Comets. The sobriquet even gives them an edge with grants.

A strange brew of personalities the name stands for. Toveh Botkin bicycles up on a machine that might have taken her on annual prewar pilgrimages to Bayreuth. Tooney Blake enters, abstractedly patting every empty pocket on his person. Karl Ulrich pulls into the Biology Building parking lot in a VW bearing the plate E COLI. Ressler has nothing against this bundle of bacterial joy so long as it stays in the intestines. But why dirty one's hands in the buggers when the problem of pure coding is at stake? All present and accounted for, Ressler joins his maiden Blue Sky session. The informal brainstorming gets underway, everyone tossing out abstracts of articles and volunteering to review others for the following week. Soon talk wanders onto topics that leave them sounding more like a clutch of cabalists or college of cardinals.

From their predecessors—pylons in the vast, incomplete suspension bridge between the inanimate atom and the world ecoweb—Cyfer inherits a list of numbers it must arrange into a magic square. They work with an alphabet of four nucleotide letters. These, if grouped as commonly believed into trinities of nucleotides, produce a vocabulary of sixty-four different words. These three-letter words translate into immense miracle-sentences in a language of twenty amino acid actants. Cyfer brainstorms, trying to weld together these incunabula into a grand, new gnosticism.

In this free association, they run the gamut of human failing. Joe Lovering races in minutes from embracing the newest fad on punctuation to discarding it wholesale in favor of a newer, improved flier. Dan Woytowich remains, incredibly, the last of the old guard to refuse to embrace the Watson-Crick model. His every static-sparking comment rejects the helical staircase. He declares, in a folksy singsong tailored to get on everyone's nerves, "Too simple to be all there is." Whenever anyone says anything remotely lucid or steers the group toward something they might at last get started on, Woyty shakes his head sadly and says, "We're overlooking something here. We're talking the big L, after all."

Ulrich is a bright spot in the painful group grope toward microunderstanding. Cyfer's leader runs the session as a benevolent dictator, neither encouraging nor condescending to his charges. He follows the time-tested policy: let intellect propose and measurement dispose. He fills the chalkboard with A's, T's, G's, C's, unzipping helices, decoding boxes, templates, diamonds, triangles, every model short of hex signs. He mutters out loud from time to time, as do the rest of the team. But Ulrich's mutterings hold the floor. The part of Ulrich's presentation that most captivates Ressler is not molecular, but rhetorical. To one beautiful scheme that reveals a flaw, rolls belly-up against experimental evidence, the chief pronounces stoically, "So goes poetry. Shipwrecked on shoals of fact."

Ulrich possesses that critical leadership skill in the age of Big Science: the ability to inspire others to work with devotion. Members compete to win the next stroke of praise. Ulrich makes them each sense that all of their names will appear on the resulting paper. Still, Ressler declines to put forth his private bias on how to begin cracking the coding problem. Reticence is not an issue, nor fear of bruised ego. In his freshman session at the public trading post, the small crystal of clarity he now possesses might get lost in the hypothesizing pandemonium. In a few weeks, after he learns the ropes, he'll lay out his vein, the method so new that he himself can't formulate it yet.

As Ulrich smoothly wraps up the Blue Sky session before it turns to Gray and Partly Cloudy, someone slips Ressler a note. More spectral theory, a spidery nineteenth-century hand:

> Dr. Ressler—
> Dismissals of verse notwithstanding, Fearless Leader harbors a closet predisposition to literature. Ulrich has contracted Poe's Gold Bug. Communicable, I gather.
> J.K.

The syntax seems a sequel to this session in cryptography. But the note, on second reading, begins to make marginal sense as plaintext. There already is a "J.K." in the room; no need for letter substitution. Yet the note resists ultimate understanding. It doesn't occur to him, as the brainstorm session breaks up, to ask the woman herself what she means. He watches her leave the room and looks again at the note, the first he's received in twenty years of school. He follows Dr. Koss with his eyes across the lab and out the door. Monk Mendel's chief lesson returns from first-year genetics: the rift between inner genotype and outer phenotype. Surfaces lie.

Back in his bachelor and still unfurnished flat, Ressler lies in his bunk at night, wrapped in the barrack walls, the cradling vacancy of his adopted town. The day's stimulation prevents sleep. He runs through the proposed structure currently entrancing all biology except Woytowich and a few lone holdouts. The spiral molecular staircase—two paired railings sinuously twisting around one another, eternally unmeeting snakes caught in a caduceus—becomes in his fueled brain the stairs of Robeson's spiritual: Jacob's Ladder, the two-lane highway to higher kingdoms. Angels are caught descending and ascending in two solemn, frozen, opposing columns. In his soporific reverie, four kinds of angels twist along the golden stairs. Bright angels and dark, of both sexes. Four angel varieties freeze in two adjacent queues up and down the case, each stuck on a step that it shares with its exact counterpart. Every bright man opposite a dark woman. Every bright woman, a dark man. Fitful in his bunk, in the blackness, the unappeasable modelmaking urge. Four angel varieties to signify DNA's four bases: thymine, cytosine, adenine, and guanine. Jacob's helical staircase ladder conjured out of a single strand of nucleic acid.

How indispensable models have been in the fray to date! Watson and Crick did the trick with tin shapes, interlocking jigsaw pieces that refused to combine in any configuration consistent with the data except the spiral staircase. The great Pauling's snips of accordion cardboard are an industry legend, an industry joke until laughter was hushed by the tool's repeated success. Pauling's children—molecular spheres and dowels—pop up in classrooms, raising a race of clear-eyed students whose innovative exhalations already warm Ressler's neck. All the models agree: life science, to advance at all, cannot start with big and hope to pull it apart into underpinning little. It must begin with the constituents and tease them into a structure consistent with observation. Cyfer needs a model as simple and labile as baby blocks, a breathtaking Tinkertoy indistinguishable from the thing it imitates.

Four years ago Ressler, along with every other hapless haplotype, noticed that the double-spiral staircase embodies two identical informational queues. The ascending angel order complements and mirrors the descending stream. Wholly redundant. Each angel-file sequence can be entirely recreated from the other. Bright and dark men, dark and bright women: each pair-half uniquely mated, each edge of the staircase carrying the same message. All there in Crick and Watson's tantalizing summary: "It has not escaped our notice that the specific pairing we have postulated immediately suggests a possible copying mechanism for the genetic material." The angel-files in each half-stair must somehow be capable of latching on to their proper mates out of angelic bouillabaisse. Chemical lightning, sundering the staircase down its middle, unzipping it, creates two severed parades, each capable of recreating the entire original ladder. Ressler, in his bunk, has the wind knocked out of him by the ingenuity, the *rightness* of it: a long molecular chain, stupefyingly massive but simple, obeying nothing but chemical requirements, somehow lucks upon viability—the fundamental, self-replicating machine.

Stairway replication, an inanimate molecule's ability to double, is just the tip of proliferate miracle. Somehow, incomprehensibly tortuously simply, coded in permutations of brights, darks, males, and females—four bases alone—is all the sequence needed to conduct the full angel choir. On this dream of spiral ladders, he lulls himself into brief, shallow sleep. Rest does not last long, nor does he wake refreshed. He is back in the stacks at opening, armed with the tip-off Jeanette Koss has passed him. He came to Illinois to crack the nucleic code. To date the only triplets he's gone up against are Dewey Decimal. He looks up her clue in the card catalog: Poe's "The Gold Bug." Mystery, suspense: a story in a thousand anthologies. It's been years since he's read any fiction except the Oppenheimer charges. But the library jump-table leads him to 813 as easily as if he were a regular.

Squatting between two metal shelves, Ressler loses himself in the adventure. Discovery—a piece of heated parchment reveals secret writing. Pictograph of baby goat identifies author as Captain Kidd, language of cipher as English. Simple letter frequency and word-pattern trick leads scholar to pirate's treasure. But directions to treasure are themselves a coded algorithm for unburying. Two men and blackfella servant, applying human ingenuity, measured paces, and plumb line, crack third-level mystery and uncover wealth beyond wildest dreams. Only at story's end does he emerge, shake off the fictional spell. "Gold Bug" is the ticket all right; he's come to the right place.

If he understands Dr. Koss's warning correctly, Ulrich may be in danger of confusing the *message* of base-string sequences with their translation *mechanism*. Bulling through frequency counts and base-order mapping will never reveal a simple rule equating the impenetrable archive of nucleic rungs with hair color, hand length, texture of skin. The game is immensely bigger; much more than gene-reading is at stake. To search for sequence substitution, to pan for genetic gold bugs, would be tantamount to learning a foreign language armed with only a translating dictionary. They'd get no farther than a refinement of Morgan's endless generations of *Drosophila:* chromosome bump X produces white eyes. A swap of one name for the other, no more than a means of reading individual messages without ever getting fluent in the tongue they're written in.

The heart of the code must lie hidden in its grammar. The catch they are after is not what a particular string of DNA says, but how it says it. For the first time, it is possible to do more than wedge open the door. They must throw wide open the means of molecular articulation. They must learn, with the fluency of native speakers, a language sufficiently complex and flexible to speak into existence the inconceivable commodity of self-speaking. The treasure in Poe's tale is not the buried gold but the cryptographer's flicker of insight, the trick, the linguistic key to unlocking not just the map at hand but any secret writing. Ressler must bring the team to see that they are up against something considerably larger than the pleasures of the Sunday Crossword, fitting a few letters into empty boxes. Not the limited game of translation but the game rules themselves. Sprawled between the girders of the 800s, in the summer of his twenty-fifth year, he gets his first hint of the word puzzle he is up against. He must latch onto a language that can articulate its own axioms, a technique that can generate—in the effortless idiom it models—endlessly extensible four-letter synonyms for Life.

Quote of the Day

When I left the library, I took my entire collection of index cards, the complete file of the three boards I'd established at the branch. The records would have disappeared long ago had I not squirreled them away in the first place. Still, the data theft will hurt more than a couple of old friends, who over the years have come to rely on my pocket score the way we all rely on Bowker or Wilson Line. Let them find their own materials. Yet by taking the card collection into custody, I've created my own problem. Squarely on my grandfather's desk, a private encyclopedia of three-by-fives cries out to be transcribed.

Any attempt to extract affidavit from these facts requires dirtying my hands. Franker, with his charming idiocy, liked to compare existence to a mound of potatoes: "You can't proverbially mash 'em till they been proverbially skinned." Information theory phrases the problem more elegantly but not as well. Yet the thought of putting my card hoard to account fatigues me beyond saying. A flood victim's, a chemotherapy patient's fatigue. July 15, 1985: I look over the options from the file, the day's previous incarnations. One stands out from the cycle, one that positions me on the timeline.

I was no longer fresh in the field when I posted it. Much of the novelty of the job had worn off. But I was working full time, for myself, for achieved adulthood, for the sheer pleasure of work.

The Event Calendar, my pride, had run smoothly for a couple of years. I posted everything from Savanarola to Synthetic Rubber, and people enjoyed the end results. In 1978, I took a small risk. I posted as canonical history an event only three years old. July 15, 1975: two spacecraft, each the peak technological achievement of two supernations, inimical enemies at ground level, take off from the earth. The enemy craft dock and join crews somewhere in the endless, frozen, neutral vacuum. The crews visit one another's quarters. The coupled craft float soundlessly in orbit. Back on earth, everything is, for a moment, wonder.

The risk in posting this had nothing to do with going out onto a predictive limb. Beyond doubt the Apollo/Soyuz linkup, symbolically at least, was the equal of half the revolutions and three quarters of the assassinations that mark the usual mileage posts of progress. My risk was not in jumping the canonical gun. It lay in my four lines of accompanying caption—shriller than public servants were supposed to let themselves become. I held out the hope that the event had not come too late to save us from the rest of history. I announced, supported by facts I felt no need to produce, that we were pitched in a final footrace, not between Manichaean political ideologies but between inventiveness and built-in insanity. July 15 tipped the calendar ever so slightly toward the euphoric, exploratory. The risk I took was editorial, insisting that event was real.

This was years before I met Dr. Ressler and his clear-faced protégé. That same day, six years later, for a reason preserved in artifact, I posted, as quote of the day, Aristotle's critique of the Pythagoreans in the *Metaphysics:* They say that things themselves are Numbers. The risk this time was entirely mine.

The Husband's Message

For days after meeting Frank Todd for seafood—my dinner, his breakfast—I heard nothing from him. I'd turned up the facts; our business was transacted. But we weren't done with one another. The flavor that kept coming back at odd hours as I fielded calls or directed question-traffic was the look that had come over my makeshift date's face as I told him of Stuart Ressler's disappointing early collapse. Todd had looked for an instant as if he were hearing, after the fact, the obituary of a childhood hero.

Time passed with no follow-up on Todd's invitation to dig deeper. My job was to discard the content once I'd handed it over. In those few previous instances where professional assistance had aroused other interest, I'd always nipped it quickly in the stamen. Not that I felt any need to avoid temptation. Tuckwell had never demanded monogamy, at least not overtly. Keith referred to our commitment as a "Five-Year Plan" or a "Great Leap Forward," depending on the humor his adwork left him in on a given day. If I steered a course of noninvolvement through daily contacts it was for my own sake: my research skill exceeded anything else I had to offer anyone. But Todd's taciturn courtship, comical when delivered, confused me when withdrawn. I resented that professed infatuation with my face—sheer, male data—bribery. His semantic waffle over whether I was beautiful, a question more aesthetic than erotic, was simply clinical fascination for a woman who had him momentarily at her mercy.

I had wanted at dinner to preserve my informational advantage, to surrender the hard-won facts only at a favorable rate of exchange. But for some reason I still don't understand, I gave in to pity, told him everything, bared my throat like low dog in a fight. I heard myself give him abstracts of every article I'd turned up. When all shred of danger to him had passed—one of those predators capable of remaining inert for hours as prey blunders blithely over it—Mr. Todd took the proffered parcel and was gone. My resentment kept doubling back on that moment when I'd caught him disconsolate, his confidence dropped. That quick glimpse of facial bruise told me he wanted something from me that had nothing to do with biographics. He needed what he would never know to ask for. It wrecked my equanimity: he requested less and went away satisfied.

When he called the Reference Desk again, he did not bother to identify himself. "Can we try this again? Same place and time? Round two?" I couldn't imagine his motive in calling back. No hope of anything fresh, no new esoterica. I didn't know whether to cut him or accept with pleasure. I went for a frosty yes.

I found the restaurant again, and Franklin Todd was waiting. I knew instantly the reason for this follow-up. I could tell from his posture, his welcoming grin. This date meant to erase whatever impression of weakness the first might have left. We were not to mention the case. We were to be absolutely upbeat. And afterwards, as befit cheerful strangers, never see each other again.

I confirmed that he was lamentably attractive, taller and sandier than I remembered, his light stubble two years ahead of fashion. He looked completely incapable of being devastated by the deterioration of an older coworker. But then, I did not then look like a woman capable of quitting her profession for nothing. He was in midsentence when I reached the table. "So what happened this morning?"

I was about to give the same, daily nonresponse I gave Tuckwell when, stopped by a sardonic crook to his face, I caught on. I returned the look, saying, "Spanish Civil War on the brink of breaking out, 1936. Goldwater wins GOP nomination, 1964. Apollo/Soyuz, 1975."

He beamed. "You're so predictable."

I shook my hair loose and sat down. "You know, I haven't even met you properly and already I don't like you."

"The pleasure's mutual, I'm sure." His face broke out in all the muted possibilities of the opening game. "You are extraordinary." He gave the long word an extra syllable, intoning it with the same converted skepticism he had given his measurement of my beauty. "But you suffer from this terrible twentieth-century bias."

"It's not a bias. Most of what has happened happened in the last hundred years. Any newsworthy July day is probably recent."

"I see. Current events, like traffic, increasingly clogged until one day soon some old guy's going to pull out of his garage in Iowa and poof: universal gridlock." He ordered for both of us, issuing instructions throughout the meal: "Squeeze the lemon like this. Let the taste sit on the back of your tongue while you think of Mardi Gras." The imperatives carried the inbred, dictatorial drive of males—the hand in the small of the back they always use to steer the weaker vessel. But something else in his voice too: inappropriate enthusiasm for experience that needed sharing. Franklin in no way passed for a gourmet. He sniffed the Tabasco cap and made me do likewise. "Most expedient sinus recipe known to man." He did not preach good taste so much as enjoyment. "Cut this end off. Swirl it first before dunking." Expertise acquired over long trial and error, offered up now to save me the bother of the learning curve. It amused me, his assuming I'd never eaten food before. He had the ingenuous pleasure of a novice who sees in everyone a new initiate.

We paid and left. Coming out to the street, turning into the sidewalk tide, he took my hand and shook it enthusiastically, as if

I'd been a far more entertaining guest than I had been. I was supposed to remember only this round, erase the unpleasant undertone of the first. I asked where he was headed. "My night off. Back home to the Butter and Eggs."

"You live in Manhattan? What were you doing at our branch?"

"Research."

"*I* was doing the research. You were humming to yourself, as I remember."

"There's a difference?" He smiled and left.

Another week went by before Franklin turned up again. I was cleaning out the Question Submission Box. To the query "I want to buy a microwave oven. Are they safe?" I knew both the desired answer and informed opinion. I'd been asked the question often, and I easily delivered the unimpeachable stats, adding at the bottom of my response, "Most reports concerning cooked human kidneys are urban legend." Number two was "What is the formula for figuring compound interest?" or something as trivial. "Trivial," I knew, derived from *trivium,* any junction of three Roman roads, where your basic whores hung out. I gave the formula with no editorial comment.

But the third note had been left for no one's but my eyes. It was in the same anonymous typewriting as the one about making the catch. Todd had never had any intention of disappearing. He meant to water me with a steady stream of far-ranging, restless demands for answers for every imaginable issue, however far from hand.

> **Q:** My friend and I (neither a crackpot in the ordinary sense) are in the middle of an ongoing argument that we'd like you to clear up. What is the possibility that we will someday communicate with life on other planets?
>
> F.T., 7/19

I laughed out loud to read it. I spent the remaining afternoon answering as if this were itself an anonymous hello from deep space. Not that it took that long to compose my answer. I lingered, let myself down the luxury of unrelated alleys, the side paths research always opens up when one pays attention. The encyclopedia's country lanes.

> **A:** Serious scientific estimates about the possibility of contacting life on other planets are based on the Drake or Green Bank formula:

81

$$N = R * f_g * n_{chz} * f_l * f_i * f_t * L$$

where N = number of technical civilizations, R = rate of star formation, f_g = fraction of stars with planets, n_{chz} = number of planets that are habitable, f_l = fraction of these developing life, f_i = fraction of these developing intelligent life, f_t = fraction of these with communications technology, and L = length of attempted communication. Of course, the equation says nothing about the *values* of the terms. Guesses for these are hotly debated, resulting in estimates for the number of intelligent civilizations in our galaxy ranging as high as 100,000 and as low as zero. After a quarter century of listening for messages from unknown galactic neighbors, all scientists have yet heard is a very imposing silence. Finding an intelligent signal would immediately present the enormous problem of how to respond. A two-line dialogue between sentient planets could take centuries; our great-great-great-grandchildren would have to remember what we said in order to make sense of the reply, assuming they could make human sense of nonhuman words. It is hard to say which would be more sobering: to hear someone answer our "Are you there?" with "Yes," or to learn that the whole experiment lies entirely in our hands.

Of course, the real question was not whether intelligent life existed elsewhere in the universe but whether there was intelligent life on Earth. Still, I delighted in my answer, knowing who was asking. He meant to let me know that I could hear from deep space if I wanted to. The two of them would enter and reenter my life, persistent, transposed, inverted, retrograde, spread through different voicings, announcing themselves in all contexts for every reason, sounding the capricious, cantabile motive as often as I let them.

Three answers in one day was a good haul by any standard; most people don't arrive at three definitive answers in a lifetime. And I had accomplished all three in the interstices, between the other duties demanded by one of the NYPL's sixty Brooklyn franchises. True, I had also fielded the routine phone calls: armchair investors too lazy to get off their A-ratings and read their own *Value Lines,* high school kids asking for a definition of S-O-D-O-M-Y (tape machine audible in the background), the bewildered citizens who'd crawled out of their paneled dens to request the names of senators. Those, plus the archiving, inventorying, and maintenance work, the box-piling tasks that monopolize existence.

But three for the *fait accompli* file: in that I took considerable fisherman's pride.

Back home, I found my POSSLQ—Person of Opposite Sex Sharing Living Quarters—hard at work on a campaign alerting the public to a major dental development that would, like the Great Wall of China, provide the long-sought security of Tartar Control. As I fell into the front room, Keithy asked cheerily, "So what'd she do all day?" For the first time all day, I was stumped. Coming at the end of the stack, this seemed less question than request for intimacy. And intimacy was no longer mine to give. I flopped on the couch, undid some buttons, and capitulated. The candy dish stood in for dinner. I listened to Keithy insult mankind for my amusement. "Looky here. You hate this photo? How about this text? Totally humiliating? Good. I think we've got a wiener, here."

Lying slack, I thought of something my mother said, the first and only time she ever came out from Indiana to visit me. "This is not a city," she sneered in utter distaste for the place I'd chosen as home. "This is a country. A world." I was new here myself then, and thought she was right. Precisely the reason I had come here to live. A country, a world, large enough to lose oneself in. Now I roused myself enough to look out of the front picture window onto the East River, a stunning view that cost Keith and me half our income. On the far side, the fanfare of lights, the community that was slowly killing us. From where I lay I could see my mother's error. Nothing stood between me and the insane compression of midtown. No moat, no ad-campaign misanthropy could shut out the runaway numbers, the gang rape of the place.

Keith watched with me as the lights came on—Japanese-lantern bridges, street pearls, block skyscrapers that flared as if half the executives in the world worked late. He burlesqued the view, the most overwhelming display of scale that the race has yet assembled, dropping into his smarmy announcer's voice. "Experience the charm of Halogen." He did it to relax me, but I hated him for it all the same. I picked a block on this side of the river and populated it: two souls of unfortunately high intelligence sitting alone among precision machinery, watching over the magnetic data by night, arguing, as if it mattered, over whether we were the only going show in the universe. Clear-faced Todd, obvious closet romantic, held out for other intelligent life, while his night-shift companion, a generation older, told the boy to stop kidding him-

83

self. Imagining this insignificant dialogue in this uncounted corner of a sprawl too dense to map adequately, I reversed my mother's terrified conviction about the city. This was not a world. It was an abandoned colonial outpost, a private conversation. Only the buildings were big.

Fear of scale came over me: if I lay there any longer, every uncountable block in these awful islands would become inhabited. Clicking heels and chanting "There's no place like Elkhart" was no longer an option. I had to do something quickly—leave some entry on *this* July 15—or lose myself in the cycle of torn-off days. I lifted myself like a wet foal. Without explaining, I left Tuckwell still talking to himself, in lone possession of the front room. Shutting the door with a furtive thump that echoed badly down the months ahead, I locked myself in our bedroom. I picked up the receiver and dialed the number Todd had given me. A number I'd filed for easy retrieval.

The half of the night shift I could claim some knowledge of answered. Franklin professed to be glad I'd called. "You'll never guess what has happened. I confronted Dr. Ressler with your evidence. He was greatly impressed." I waited for him to go on. Ten seconds, an epoch over the phone. How do messages travel simultaneously over phone wires without colliding? It occurred to me that while wires did not technically carry any information when both parties were mute, passed silence nevertheless required a phone.

I looked for anything to fill the gap. "I've contacted your extraterrestrials. If you come by the branch...."

"Maybe it's time you visited us here." He gave me the address, one that took my breath away. A dozen buildings from the branch. I knew the exact place, a brick turn-of-the-century warehouse that gave away nothing of its contents. The city, big, uncountably massive, had a way of turning viciously small, like Nauru, digging itself into disappearance. A range of adjoining neighborhoods that refuse to collect. Ten million neighborhoods of one. It is not skyscrapers; it is the bottoms of deep troughs, deeper than the carved canyons out west, cut from harder stone.

Familiar forward motion, bandying between the two of us: the tone of our first social phone conversation stated that it was all right to feel all right, even in mid-July, even with a bad conscience. Bad conscience has no survival value. Todd's confidence cascade gave me a go-ahead to go ahead and do what I wanted to, to indulge in whatever worked. But a slight condition, an extra saddle, was tucked away in the injunction. I could not beat this conversation in one. To give in to the rush, the thrill of voices piling up against voices, colliding over the phone wires, I had to count the thing in three. In my mind, I already stood on a July evening outside their warehouse. Keith, at last coming in to bed, found his POSSLQ lying motionless but wide-awake. He asked if anything was wrong. I answered no, hearing the word leave me, too late to retrieve. The first time I ever lied to him.

V

The Quote Board

For all knowledge and wonder (which is the seed of knowledge) is an impression of pleasure in itself.—Francis Bacon

"I only ask for information."—Rosa Dartle, in *David Copperfield*

Transcription and Translation

In those weeks when we were happiest, and well into that nightmare period when he learned what was coming, Dr. Ressler's theme was always the same: the world was awash in messages, every living thing a unique signal. We were all cub interpreters at a babble-built UN, obligated to convert the covert metaphor, tweak the tuner, read the mechanism by actively attacking its surface. The catch to this elaborate *Wissenschaft* was the active obligation to extract cache from courier. I managed to avoid that imperative, ignore the mess in his message, until Frank left, Ressler died. Now time forces the issue. Time, as the Bacon entry says, just below the quote linking knowledge to pleasure, is the author of authors. Time to start my cub translation, to learn the place, as I'm likely to be here a little longer.

The whole day free, hours without end. How hard to make anything of unbudgeted time. In my remaining free days, I've decided to learn something, become expert, exchange fact for feeling, reverse what I've done with my life to date. A needy soul once asked me, through the anonymous three-by-five, what old film had an important state secret transported across Europe via musical code. Hitchcock's *The Lady Vanishes,* 1938: a banner year for secret European messages. I remembered the question this morning, listening to that other musical code whose message our circle carried through a similar plague year. I could whistle that melody in the dark, its pleasure returned permanently to school by grief. The tune of my new career.

My chief problem is what to study. Something empirical, something hard. My prospect of success depends on where in the hierarchy I attach myself. I start with top magnification, fix my lens on cosmology. If that level remains abstract, I could drop to the step below, stop down an order of magnitude, make due with astronomy. A working knowledge of galaxies must be of some use in naming the place where I'm left.

But the light-year is too long for me to get my bearing. I must reduce the magnification another exponent, start my study with the earth under my lens. A geologist I suppose, or oceanographer. But the explanations of this critical niche are still too large. I am after not earth science but its underwriting specific. Down another order. The search for a starting point begins to resemble that painful process of elimination from freshman year, spent in the university clinic, a knot across my abdomen from having to choose which million disciplines I would exclude myself from forever.

This time I narrow ruthlessly. I sharpen my focus to the raw component populations inhabiting this planet. Zoologist, anthropologist? Neither would yet clamp down on the why I'm after. I go a finer gauge, assuming that understanding can be best arrived at by isolating terms. That means downshifting again to the vocabulary of political science. The first limb of the hierarchy that speaks human dialect: what do we need, and how best to get it? The question is powerful, but as I zoom in on the increasingly precise concern, explanations recede, grow fuzzy and qualified. A faction of me secedes, insists that political science can be understood only in terms of constituent economics. But the study of goods, services, and distribution produces more problems than prescriptions.

Herds, it seems, are hundreds of individuals. Feeling no edge, I scale myself down into psychology. Here my lens reaches that cusp magnification: one-to-one. But a complete explanation of behavior requires somatic cause. Focal ratio flips, increases again, now in the microscopic direction. Psych shades over the

87

bio threshold. The gradients, the gauges are continuous. Fields of study, like spectral bands, differ only in wavelength. No discrete moment when red ends and orange begins. Yet every constituent bent from white has its precise and particular name.

The final gloss hovers always one frame beneath. Physiology. Biophysics. Biochemistry. More light. *Molecular* biology, the transitional rung where Dr. Ressler hung. Downwards toward delineation, I consider studying chemistry. Unsatisfied, I pass another strangeness barrier, into quantum physics, beyond conceptual modeling. A push for terminal detail takes me into the statistics of perhaps. Here, in the domain of sub-subatomics, where I expect to butt up at last against fundamental phenomena, I find, instead, a field veering startlingly philosophical: eleven dimensions, superstrings, the eightfold way. Like a Klein bottle, insides twisting seamlessly onto out, small-scale physics drops off the edge of formal knowledge back into cosmology.

The whole hierarchical range up and down the slide rule of science shares one aim: to write the universe's User's Manual, to bring moonlight into a chamber. But what scale to choose? I'm thrown back on Lewis Carroll's information theory fable, the map paradox. A kingdom undertakes a marvelous cartographic project. They know that an inch to a thousand miles is too gross, giving only rough orientation of the largest places. The royal cartographers improve steadily over the years: at a hundred miles to the inch, true roads take shape. At ten per, the map navigates from village to village. At a mile to a map inch, individual structures become visible. The more exact the scale, the more useful the map. The kingdom's surveyors launch the supremely ambitious project of mapping the region at an inch to an inch—a map every bit as detailed as the represented terrain. The apotheosis of encapsulation, the supermap has only one drawback: the user can't unroll it without covering the landscape in question.

This is my problem in choosing a field to fill the ten months my savings leave me. The whole hierarchy spreads in front of me in imbedded frames. But each rung, cross-referenced, reads, "For more information, see below." Hinduism says the world rests on the back of a tortoise standing on the back of tortoise, etc. *One* of those terrapins must reach bottom. Where can I break in? What discipline will put me closest to knowing him? A year ago, when Dr. Ressler received the verdict of his cells (but not yet the sentence), the three of us met for a last evening before pulling the switch. Franklin asked if he felt any regrets about straying from his training, losing his career. "What would I be if I could start over?" Todd nodded furiously at his succinct rephrasing, so much more accurate than what he'd asked. Dr. Ressler thought in the white waterfall hum of the computer installation. At last he said, "There are really only two careers that might be of any help. One can either be a surgeon or a musician."

I set my magnification, choose my lens. Since surgery arrives too late, I'll be a musician. I'll spend what remains of my life savings studying music. First, I must tackle theory. And for a good grounding in tonal fundamentals, I must first learn everything I can about the genetic code.

On the strength of that late-afternoon decision, I rode the D over to the main reading room. There I drew up a preliminary reading list. This evening, back home, I sit armed with a stack of texts on two-week loan. I toy with this pointless bookwork as if training for a genuine career change, a way of making a living after my bank account runs out. It wouldn't be too late for such an overhaul. The field is rife with refugees, immigrants from sister disciplines and distant relations. I come across a man who began in physics and earned an undergraduate degree at the ripe age of twenty-two. Global war sidetracked his studies, stripping him of seven years in military science. After the war, he again postponed an already alarmingly delayed career to spend two years retraining in another discipline. Only at the ancient age of thirty-three did he finally enroll in a Ph.D. program in his new field. Four years later, luxuriously older than I am now, he at last filed his dissertation. But a few months before, Francis Crick had also cowritten the Nobel Prize-winning paper revealing the structure of DNA.

I set off, late, to make myself expert, with no pretense of adding to the dizzy swell, simply wanting to swim it myself. I need to know exactly what happened to Stuart Ressler between 1957 and 1983. And only a sense of the tonal variations hidden in self-replicating molecules will lead me there. Having spent my life distributing fact, it was odd to sit this evening in front of reference books, see them take on a different complexion. In my years at the branch, these works were the final destination. Now their pages seem more like customs clearance prior to departure, the last port before incognita. With Bacon still open in the quote book, I go to the well again: if a woman will be content to begin in uncertainty, she might end by drawing provocative maps indeed.

The scope of the stuff I have set myself is utterly draining. But I feel a certain excitement at the volume and novelty of material I must get through before any of it starts to cohere. A thrill at wondering whether coherence will come in the ten months left to my cash stockpile. I set my scale at the only gauge I have ever had firsthand experience of. For my attack on the life molecule, I fall back on that fine old obsolete mode of sightsinging: historiography. Tonight—the overviews, the outlines. Tomorrow, next week, a month from now—the big leap, that evolutionary giant step dear to saltationists. The jump from information to knowledge.

The Law of Segregation

Dr. Ressler and Cyfer were no spontaneous generation. The more I read of the first twentieth-century science, the clearer the chain of ideas about heredity stretches continuously back through speculation to the start of thought. The scenic overview leaves me nursing a metaphor: the *idea* of chemical heredity is itself an evolving organism, subject to the laws it is after. Or better: the field grows as a living population, a varying pool of proposals constantly weeded, altered by selection. Theories duplicate or die by feasibility. Every article floating in the journal-sea on the day Dr. Ressler began life's work was an inheritable idea-gene vying for survival.

I sift the birth records of consecutive generations. Pleasant, to disassemble this random assortment and rebuild it into a body of thought. The principal names return from college biology, supplemented by professional searches from my last ten years. I see for the first time what an undertaking the thing is, how stunning the setbacks and solutions. I begin to view it from the air. Dr. Ressler assisted in the final push to join three islands. Mendel on one, observing that characteristics in intricate organisms were preserved in patterns. Mendeleyev, with his atomic construction set on another. On the third remote tip, Darwin, whose species-

90

mad pageant was a continuous thread, a diversifying alluvial fan. Heredity, chemistry, and evolution, about to be spanned by a simple, magnificent triple-suspension more remarkable than anyone imagined.

For all its necessity after the fact, genetics advanced on the mark as shakily as nature toward fur. Every step of the way is littered with missed discoveries, untransmitted truth. Research, a poor parallel parker, needs several passes. Ressler's distant ancestor is case in point. Mendel toiled obscurely in the peapatch vineyard a hundred years before Cyfer. Devout Augustinian, hungry observer, agriculturalist, meteorologist, philosopher: variants on surgery and singing, Ressler's careers of choice. The father of inheritance, a celibate priest. Celibacy mysteriously preserves itself, passed on by paradoxical means. It should have died out long ago. But I've seen, face to beautiful face, another Augustinian pass celibacy on.

Mendel, a failure as a priest, was put to work as a schoolteacher. Capable but untrained, he twice failed the staff qualifying exam. He began research on the garden pea at thirty-four, devoting ten years to his hobby before promotion to abbot curtailed it. By then, drudgework and rare synthetic ability had led him to one of science's great insights. He delivered his results to an indifferent regional society in 1865 and published them in its proceedings. Distributed to a hundred scientific communities, his conclusions promptly sank like an oil-slicked bird, lost until 1900, when independent researchers reannounced them.

In the span of ten years, Darwin published *Origin of Species,* Mendel produced his inheritance paper, and Miescher discovered DNA. But it took a century to braid these three. Mendel's undeniable demonstration lay forgotten for thirty-five years, delayed by something dark and surreptitious. The monk's first giant step toward proving Darwin at the mechanical level was another human takedown, this time reducing us from monkey to molecule. Darwin was instant controversy; why total oblivion for the monk? Because of the revulsion produced by mentioning the fecundity of biology in the same breath as inert mathematics.

In Mendel, every characteristic derives from discreet, inheritable factors—his law of segregation, the philosophical implication lost on me until this minute. Seven years' labor in the garden overthrew Aristotle's notion of blended inheritance. Offspring of blond and brunette are not simply sandy. Rather, pairs of independent commands from each parent remain separate in the offspring, passing unchanged to grandchildren. Wildly counterintuitive: all immeasurable diversity deriving from rigid, paired packets. This Augustinian's God was more grossly architectural than the Deists'. For each indivisible characteristic we inherit two paired factors, with an equal chance of getting either half of each parent's paired set. The tune accompanying inheritance's barn dance is aleatoric, more Cage than Brahms. Individuality lies in the die's toss. The language of life is luck.

Mendel rescues living variety by noting that each gene comes in more than one tune. Some alleles for any trait dominate others. The visible result of a gene pair shows only part of the underwriting package. A person's genotype, the internal packet, is not fully revealed by phenotype, the outward form. Blond may lie hidden for generations, erupting again in unknown great-granddaughters.

I picture Dr. Ressler in his first weeks in the lab, wondering about the delicately turned nose of the woman who will nonchalantly waste him. The allele giving her bridge that innocent flip floated detached in either or both her parents. Her Myrna Loy allele might hide a matched half that codes for Irish pug: a half-breed, heterozygous. Or she might need identical alleles from each parent to achieve that cycloid dip—homozygous for profile. The same holds for the hazel eyes. The woman's daughter—I picture him wondering if she has one—might revert to any number of recessive traits: square nose, eyes drab brown. Yet even so prosaic a child could go through life a secret carrier of mother's mystery.

Mendel's Law of Segregation, not to be confused with the Little Rock affair, is itself a shade un-American. You can't tell by looking at a thing what ticks underneath. Two pea plants, both tall in phenotype, might have different genotypes—one homozygous tall and the other heterozygous. Violation of truth in advertising. The language of life is not only laced with luck. It also refuses to say just what it means. The generation of geneticists who rediscovered Mendel devised a way to determine a plant's hidden makeup. If tall allele is dominant over short, then a tall plant might be either Tall/Tall or Tall/Short. Crossbreeding against a known homozygous recessive produces four possible first filials:

	Short/Short	
Tall/Tall	Tall/Short	Tall/Short
	Tall/Short	Tall/Short

	Short/Short	
Tall/Short	Tall/Short	Tall/Short
	Short/Short	Short/Short

Descendants of the homozygous plant all appear tall, while half of the heterozygous descendants will be short. The test cross. Ressler referred to his abandoned profession by a name both sardonic and nostalgic—the irony of one no longer in the inner circle. To Frank and me, he always called geneticists soldiers of the cross.

First filial generation after Mendel had to find where these abstract inheritance packets resided. From the beginning, men hoped that genes would prove chemical, tangible. The coordinated effort reads like the greatest whodunit ever written. Blundering with desire toward fruition, as poet-scientist Goethe says. While geneticists made their gross observations, cytologists began to elucidate the microscopic ecosystem of the cell. As early as mid-nineteenth century, researchers described dark threads in the cell nucleus. Improvements in staining and microscopy revealed that the rods came in mixed doubles. During the choreography of cell division, these chromosome pairs split and moved toward opposite poles. Each daughter cell wound up with a full chromosome complement. Chromosome behavior suspiciously resembled Mendel's combining and separating pairs.

The gene factor somehow lay *inside* the chromosome, a segment of the thread: a tie bordering on magic. It must have been pure fear, to isolate the physical chunk embodying the ethereal plan, the seed distilling the idea of organism. The first link in the chain from Word to flesh, philosopher's stone, talisman, elixir, incantation, the old myth of knowledge incorporated in *things*. I can't imagine the excitement of living at the moment when the pieces began to fall into place: living design located in matter. On second thought, I can imagine. This morning's papers carried another update.

Traits didn't behave as cleanly as theory would have them. Morgan and team spent seventeen years in massive, spirit-breaking ef-

93

fort, counting two thousand gene factors in endless generations of *Drosophila*. Mendel's predicted ratios for second-generation dihybrids did not always occur. Experiment, recalcitrant, gave different numbers than pattern dictated. First temptation must have been to squash the aberrant gnats, take no prisoners. Morgan, not yet believing the chromosome theory, found that certain characteristics always occurred together. Such linkage supported the notion that groups of genes lay along shared chromosome threads. Linked traits lay on the same thread, passed through generations as a unit.

But Morgan's team also turned up incomplete linkage. Occasionally in the chaos of meiosis, paired chromosomes from separate parents cross over, break at equivalent points, and exchange parts. Half a linked group might thus be sent packing. Leverage into the unobservable: the odds of linked traits being split must vary with their distance on the chromosome. The chance of a break falling between two adjacent genes is very small, whereas *any* split in the chromosome separates the genes at opposite ends of a thread. Frequencies of separation thus mapped relative distance between genes.

The chemistry was still lacking. But chemistry would come. Ressler himself would join in the cartographic project of ever-improving scale. Inexorable, but full of halting dead ends, overlooked insights, reversals. Morgan's work too was resisted by the scientific community, while Levene's incorrect tetranucleotide hypothesis was embraced disastrously for years. Researchers have made every possible mistake along the way. Reject the Moravian monk; doubt Morgan; ignore Avery's 1944 identification of the genetic substance. Fits and starts, endless backtracking, limited less by technique than by the ability to *conceive*. How do you get moonlight into a chamber? Dress someone up as the moon.

Mendel's laws have since become more complex. Linkage, multiple alleles, epistasis, collaboration, and modifiers enhance his metaphor. But by the time Ressler took orders, neo-Mendelism was forever in place. Cyfer had inherited the idea that all of an organism's characteristics were written in a somatic language, generated by a grammar that produced outward sentences distinct but derivable from deep structure.

I live at the moment of synthesis, sense the work that is almost written, watch the structure complete its span, register for the first time how strewn with mistake and hope the path has been. This place, this night, a lamp, a typing machine, my books, my chromosomal map: I grope for my technique, my leverage into

Dr. Ressler's world. The test cross that will spring the hidden, recessive gene. How he blundered with desire toward fruition. How in fruition, pining for desire.

Public Occurrences Both Foreign and Domestic

My private life began to accelerate. Before Todd, I never thought of myself as having a private life, let alone one with a brisk plot. Opening the door a crack on that stray, I found my after-hours hinting at a first étude, a study in unmitigated motion. Within minutes of returning from what I still refused to think of as a date, I was back on the phone, arranging to meet Todd again. I rationalized the secrecy, the closed door: I didn't want to confuse Tuckwell with transactions that weren't what they seemed. Not that I knew what they were, or could pick out from my old life the complicating new accompaniment.

I'm not built for change. I work at cultivating habit. Pull out tonight's meal to defrost before leaving; turn right at third stoplight; issue the collegial, automatic greeting. Habit is an index, a compromise with irreversibles, a hedge against auto wreck or disease. The arbitrary day requires a pretense of *a priori*. But defenses atrophy in quarantine. When I felt that first symptom, I slaughtered routine before it could dissolve on me. Crazy schemes—one day deciding to knock out the living-room wall. The instant the sledgehammer splattered plaster, I knew what I'd done. But a sickening sense of relief too: I'd never again have to worry about the wall caving in.

I was sick in my stomach pit, enough to extinguish a satisfactory existence. Tuckwell and I began to fall apart, wrecked in event. We'd committed no offense except the habit of living together. But all habit ends by presiding over its obsolescence. Even as I closed the door to the bedroom to arrange my next date, I felt I wouldn't be strong enough to end my old life cleanly. If I deliberately killed the old arrangement, everything would be killable. Escape rendered escapable whatever might follow.

Everything about Tuckwell—our apartment, shopping together, our trivial exchanges—grew horribly beautiful. I'd never treated him well. We'd failed to do the things we'd always talked about. I got nostalgic about the most bizarre items: shared wine bottles, accidental tears in the bed linen, utility bills. Even before I started seeing Todd in earnest, I sank into the death-denying compulsion of the collector. Countless times at the library, confronted by a perpetual crisis of shelf space, I've argued with Holdings that thirty-year-old sourcebooks ought not necessarily be pitched just because nobody had ruffled them since publication. Yet even as my heart clamped down to protect a life that had become as habitual as circulation, I knew that the place had already gone bloodless.

Deep in humid summer I felt the shameful excitement of spring cleaning, the sensory alertness brought on by an impending death. Explosion of taste, touch, sight: colors grew subtler, smells more variegated, more exciting because of their morbid source. I profited by another's agony. Three sick weeks, laced with the flavor of discovery, loss restoring the insight that recovery subsequently buries: however much I made love to it, I detested habit with everything in me.

For three weeks, my composure rode an explosive rush. The novelty of Franklin saw me through; I could not have gone it alone. How did I accomplish those leaps, the terrible intervals of those days? All done cross-hands. Independent lines somehow crossing over. Pain and elation in a linkage group. Departure anxiety, the promise of new places intensifying the ache. Disasters stand out: an excursion Tuckwell and I made to Central Park Zoo. We'd planned the trip for one of our rare simultaneous days off. Once there, in front of the cages, we couldn't for the life of us recall why we'd come.

Committed to a formal outing, Keith and I made the rounds, although we knew in the first minute it was an awful mistake. The zoo was grayer, more decrepit than either of us remembered. As everyplace else, it had succumbed to creeping graffiti fungus, the surreal, urgently illegible signatures of the buried. Animals lay neglected in cages, sick, overfed, deflated. The few that moved traced out tight, psychotic circles. A pack of safety-pinned twenty-year-olds (although given our infatuation with extended adolescence, they could have been thirty) bounced marshmallows off the open mouth of a panting sea lion, ridiculing the beast for being too stupid to bite. "Sick, the whole lot," I whispered violently.

"It's *your* generation made us torturers," Tuckwell joked, steering me on. I couldn't keep from attaching myself to each pen, a mission of pointless distress. Why was the zoo still standing? Why this irrelevant park in the first place? Certainly not for solace. Gruesome ornament, tribute to the sadistic housebreaking of a force that long ago ceased to command fear. The cages proved that plumbing and shag were best, after all. The worst civilized annoyance was superior to the dead end of animals. I waved at the insults tailored to each genus. "What's the point? No beauty we can't humiliate?"

"Serves them right. Lower forms of evolution. They've had just as much geologic time to get evolved as we have. And look at them. Just *look* at them. Pitiful." But seeing that his patter only irritated me, Keith resorted to logical blundering. "You're mad, woman. So the place is on the decayed side. That's a problem with the tax base, not humanity." Pragmatics failing, he tried compassion. The animals did not know their suffering. And at least here they were kept alive.

We tried to salvage the afternoon by eating out, but fell into a fight over where to go. Keith had made reservations at the Chinese place in the 50s where we'd first had dinner together. He dropped the announcement on me with a now-for-what-you've-all-been-waiting-for flair. "Can't you hear the wontons calling?" I didn't even fake my usual diplomacy. "No? I was pretty sure I could hear a wonton calling. *Something* was calling, anyway. High-pitched, squeaky. Maybe it was an egg roll that *thought* it was a. . . ." Making no headway, he gave up. We began walking crosstown. After a grizzly block, he stopped and caught my arm. "I thought you liked the place."

"I like the place. I'm glad we're going there, OK?" But every concession was a refusal.

"We don't have to go there, you know. So they sue us for the canceled reservation. Take us for everything. I can get a second job. . . ." I laughed, if through my teeth. Feeling the victory, Keith chose his cadence. "Is it those punks? Forget them. Beatniks. Greasers. Whooo-dlums."

"It's *our* generation made them torturers."

"Oh. *That's* it. Sorry. You're not old enough to be their mother. Maybe a very much older spinster sister. . . ."

"Thanks, ass. That's not it."

"The animals, then? Look, you can't do anything about them. Lost cause. The least offensive of our sins. You want anxiety? Zoo animals are the last thing to get morally outraged over, at this late a date." I was still refusing to incriminate myself when we drew up outside the restaurant. Keith was near distraction. "Listen. It's obvious, even to me, that you're trying to tell me something. What's the secret word this time, Jan? I've got to guess, evidently. One assumes it's bigger than the proverbial breadbox, or we wouldn't have killed a decent day over it. Damn it, woman. Look around. We're standing in front of a fine establishment; we can saunter in and make them wait on us hand and foot. The best goddamn mu shu this side of Confucius Plaza. We're more than reasonably well off, given world per capita. . . ." Feeling himself on dangerous ground, he dropped a decibel. "We're both doing exactly what we want in life. You realize the odds against that? Look around, woman. It's your day *off*. We can do anything you want. Get a room uptown tonight, if you like. Anything. Condemned to freedom, as the Frogs like to say. A perfect day, if you make it. Unlike any other that has ever happened."

Ridiculous, I thought, even as he got the sentence out. *Seven August, one of an endless series*. Ten days earlier, I had passed over, without ripple, that landscape with conflagration, the 1976 quake in Tangshan, China, 8.2 on the Richter, killing a surreal 655,235. I'd passed it by for the Event Calendar for no other reason than my deciding that history had to serve some other cause than ungraspable tragedy. In contrast, two days before this outing, I'd posted the *Mayflower* and *Speedwell* setting sail for the New World. Honesty compelled me to add how the Pilgrims were forced to return to England and ditch the *Speedwell* as unseaworthy. Yet the abortive first run seemed the one needing commemorating. The uncelebrated cost of leaving. My own life was about to modulate to exploration, and it made me morose. Had I known the first thing about being alive, I would have made my last weeks with Keith affectionate, funny. But I've never known anything. I didn't even know what he knew: I was already gone.

After dinner, I lifted again. The sides of the absurd Woolworth Building, in low light, grew oppressively beautiful. I wanted to save all those horrid skyboxes, paint and carve them. We walked back east, and the stone and glass took on the dusk-shades of Morandi bottles glowing subtly in a chalk-and-sand rainbow. We skirted the panorama of Wall Street, the Battery, Chinatown. We walked back over the bridge, taut cables pulling the span up in the middle, a woman arching her back in animal ecstasy as her mate bit her gently by the neck. The city sat in the ocean, practically drifted out, afloat on the water. I could smell the brine and hear the surf above the traffic, as if this were not the densest collection of refugees in the world but only a summer resort, breakers and gradations of late-summer light visible from every window of the great beachfront hotel.

Night had dropped over the buildingscape, but every structure burned—cubist crystal palaces, technological Oz of local urgencies, with nobody manning the controls. I turned in mid-bridge and looked back where we had walked, saw the miles of fossil-fuel blazing, the millennia of buried plant beds going up in smoke in an endless point-tapestry of yellows and fire-blue greens and incandescent whites—a rush of unstoppable, jarring intervals. No matter how I moved or where I stood, I seemed plunged dead-set in the middle of the known world.

Today in History

Cyfer is not what it advertises itself to be. The four senior scientists and three apprentices form not so much a real research team as a loose specialist confederation. Each member pursues a personal line aside from the coding question. A cross section of disparate disciplines, they have been brought together by Ulrich for communication that could produce the hoped-for experimental avenue, give them a bead on the big picture.

Assembling such a band of crossovers initially struck Ressler as half-baked. How dare they jump headlong into the hottest topic now going, a field already filled with skilled investigators? Yet the more he mulls it over, the shrewder Ulrich's move seems. Molecular genetics, precisely because it is rapidly converging on a cross-disciplinary synthesis, requires exactly this assorted band, technically adept but without the retarding lead.

The field is dense with DPs: Gamow, Avery, Franklin, Chargaff, Griffith, Hershey, Luria, Pauling. The purebred geneticist among them is the rarest of blood groups. The coding problem can be approached from any angle: math, physics, stereochemistry. The problem in this moment of synthesis is that the mathematicians, physicists, chemists, and biologists don't all speak the same language. It's all interlingual patois. Ulrich's assembling a few native speakers of the various dialects to meet weekly increasingly seems a master stroke. The group has built into it all the expertise it needs. Ressler himself is to play a lead role: state-of-the-art liaison. The only one of them young enough to have grown up speaking *molecular*. Hell of a burden to place on a kid just out of school.

So be it. However disarrayed the sessions, they give Ressler the unique opportunity to pick the brains of experts in fields he has only rudimentary exposure to. The first four weeks of group barn-burning remain theoretical. Experimental progress must wait for the recent flurry of development to clear. The same thing that makes the coding problem the most exciting project going also makes it the most opaque. Theory permits a bewildering array of possible codes, while DNA sequence data provide no hint of regularity of pattern. This proliferation of too many possibilities gives Ressler hope that Cyfer has as much chance as any to receive the capricious break that will catapult them to the fore. The twist, always unanticipated, like the arrival of a startling bird one morning at the feeder outside the breakfast window, may pay its fragile visit at any moment. Ressler posts, by his office window, Delbruck's words: "It seems to me that Genetics is definitely loosening up and maybe we will live to see the day when we know something about inheritance...."

On an obnoxiously hot August day that melts the streets of Stadium Terrace into La Brea tar, Ressler takes time out to do a rudimentary milk run. He hits the futuristic supermarket with no shopping list except necessity. Pushing a cart with one oscillating wheel, he genuflects in aisle four toward Battle Creek, Michigan, for making survival possible. The daily cereal, consumed each evening over journals, if failing to carry him inexorably toward athleticism, has at least kept him from scurvy. Likewise, frozen juice concentrate takes one fifth the space of a mixed pitcher and requires no maintenance aside from rinsing the spoon. He ignores the taste, even enjoys it. Processed foods write the species' insatiable advance in miniature: freed from the overhead of care to get on with the real matter.

He chooses a meal that promises "Ready in One Minute," figuring he can eat it in two. Thus recovering four hours a week for his own pursuit, he swings his cart leisurely around the corner smack into none other than Toveh Botkin. The elderly Western war prize, whose protein chemistry work Ressler has studied, keeps cool in the mangle of metal. "I understand that the auto accident is a national obsession with Americans, Dr. Ressler. But don't you think this a bit extreme?" He grins and waves the curlered housewife traffic around the wreck. The two empiricists step forward to inspect the damages. The fronts of both carts are mauled. "Are you insured?" she asks.

Together they restore a pyramid of soap boxes their wreck has upended. "How wonderful!" Botkin exclaims, holding one up for Ressler to see. A green explosion on the soap box advertises the

100

obligatory miracle ingredient, Delta-X Sub-2, dirt-bursting enzyme. "Here our little group racks its brains to get enzymes out of nucleic acids, while the rest of the world is busy figuring out how to get them *into* laundry powder."

They dust themselves off, shift effortlessly into a notes session. They compare the relative merits of direct templating of protein chains on the surface of the split DNA string to some form of intermediating sequence reader. The conversation breaks off when Botkin catches sight of the contents of Ressler's cart. "My young friend. Convenience taken to its logical extreme is cowardice." She looks personally wounded. "If the universe were as convenience-minded as you, it would never have proposed so inefficient an aggregate as life."

Ressler loves this woman's speech. Worth the dressing-down to hear her perform. "Dr. Botkin," he counters. "It's impossible to cook for one."

"Nonsense. I've cooked for one for half a century, occasional dinner party aside. But if it is the motivation of pair bonding you need...." She hooks a passing young thing in white anklets and coos at her, "My dear. Would you love, honor, and obey this decent-looking young man so that he can get a reasonable meal in the evenings?"

The girl giggles. "I'm already married."

"Do you expect your husband to live very long?" At length, Ressler makes a few dietary concessions, the most important being his agreement to dine with her at least once a week. "I will introduce you to the clarity of thinking brought on by baked lamb, and you can bring me up to date on molecular mechanisms. I think I understand the part about the tall pea plants and the short, but beyond that...?" Botkin shrugs, reverence for the engine of skepticism. They arrive at the checkout behind a woman giving herself whiplash by watching the bagging and the register at the same time. What a very strange place he has been set down in, this world. He ought to get out more often.

Botkin, whatever her gifts as a conversationist, is almost as old as the rediscovery of Mendel. The other extreme in age, Joe Lovering, beat a time-honored path out of pure math into muddy population statistics. Ressler has seen the guy potting about in the lab, although exactly what the excitable kid does is anybody's guess. He looks decidedly gumfooted holding any equipment more corporeal than a chi-square. Stuart takes him to the Y for lunch, part of a court-your-resources campaign. He has the sub, Lovering the congealed mac and cheese. Hardly are they seated when Joe whips out a napkin and begins sketching proofs. He argues that the genetic code, as an algorithmic formal system, is subject to Gödel's Incompleteness Theorem. "That would mean the symbolic language of the code can't be both consistent *and* complete. Wouldn't that be a kick in the head?"

Kid talk, competitive showing off, intellectual fantasy. But Ressler knows what Joe is driving at. He's toyed with similar ideas, cast in less abstruse terms. *We* are the by-product of the mechanism *in there*. So it must be more ingenious than us. Anything complex enough to create consciousness may be too complex for consciousness to understand. Yet the ultimate paradox is Lovering, crouched over his table napkin, using proofs to demonstrate proof's limits. Lovering laughs off recursion and takes up another tack: the key is to find some formal symmetry folded in this four-base chaos. Stuart distrusts this approach even more. He picks up the tab for their two untouched lunches, thanking Lovering politely for the insight.

In mid-month, a departmental review committee spot-checks the lab, sits through a free-association session where Lovering shows the group that the translation scheme under consideration can't map sequences of four linear bases into twenty amino acids and still indicate where a gene message starts and breaks off. Since the last few weeks have been devoted exclusively to this scheme, Cyfer disbands that afternoon knowing less than it did a month ago. The review panel is sympathetic to the need for experimental interludes. Fact-gathering without theoretic guidance is mere noise. But theory without fact, the review suggests, is not science. Incriminatingly large amounts of glassware in the lab carry that See-Yourself Shine. They urge Ulrich to produce some activity, reduce the Blue Skies, begin investigating *something*.

So in midsummer, a dozen weeks into his tenure, Ressler volunteers to help set up a showpiece, tracing the incorporation of traits through daughter cells. He'll use the elegant Hershey-Chase trick of radioactively labeling microorganisms to study how certain tagged strings are passed to the next generation. His first chance to do hard science since hitting the I-states.

Ressler devises a variant on the now notorious Waring Blendor technique to test the supposition that DNA information is transcribed and read like a linear tape. But the day he goes in to set up the

102

growth cultures for his first run is a bad one for experiment. He smells aggression in the lab air, walks into the middle of a fight. He looks around but sees nothing departing from the status quo. Ulrich and Lovering are by the basins, the only two people in the room. Their conversation is subdued, their postures unthreatening. Ressler heads to his work area, lights a burner, and begins rudimentary sterilization.

Soon, however, Ulrich's and Lovering's raised voices filter into the public domain. Their words are lost in the flare of his gas jet. He assumes that the two are hashing out a labor dispute, currently in vogue. The McClellan committee investigates Beck, Brewster, and Hoffa, and suddenly everyone puts away his Monopoly set and joins the Mine Workers. It's demeaning for a scientist to argue over cash; Ressler has always solved budget problems by spending Saturday nights in the lab instead of at Murphy's—exactly the sort of chump that management loves to have in the rank and file.

A few escaping words and Ressler hears that matters are actually reversed. Joe is being called on the carpet, or the linoleum in this case. "You are forcing me to practice black magic, Dr. Ulrich. Pure popular hysteria plain and simple."

"Black magic? That's what you call a century of cumulative research, *Dr.* Lovering? Maybe you'd better give us *your* definition of science."

"What in the hell does *Salk* have to do with science?" Ressler shuts off the Bunsen. This one's a to-the-canvas brawl.

"Salk is the most systematic mind in today's laboratories. If we had half his thoroughness, we'd have the code out by now."

"Salk's a technician. An administrator. 'Thoroughness' is a euphemism."

Ressler strains to see without attracting notice. But he can't catch cither man's face from where he stands, and he can't move without getting drawn into the fray.

"You're suggesting that science is only science provided it never turns up anything practical? That's not especially rational, is it, Dr. Lovering?"

Ulrich infuses "rational" with so much hiss that Ressler slips and contaminates a petri. He looks around the lab to see who else is in calling distance. Botkin's in her office down the hall, but an old woman wouldn't be much help in pulling bucks off each other. Lovering looks about to bolt from his corner and tackle his adversary. "This is a witch hunt. You've singled me out because of my politics."

"I'm doing no such thing. You've singled yourself out, by refusing to take a proven vaccine."

"Proven my ass. Read the field trials. Where are the controls? Polio reduction in heavily dosed areas; so what? The disease moves in epidemics. It's erratic by definition."

Ulrich becomes cool, compensatory to his junior's frenzy. "Joe, you're the only one in this lab who refused the vaccine."

"You want me to take the doses and cross myself like everybody else? What's the paranoia? You've had *your* three slugs; I can't hurt you."

"You can hurt me plenty. If word got out that a scientist refused readily available precautions this late, when we're finally moving towards eradication. . . ."

"Oh! So *funding* is the issue. That's not especially rational, is it, Dr. Ulrich?"

Ressler can't believe this: the kid spits out words that could cost him everything. And the old man lets him. Ulrich grows gentler than Ressler has ever seen him. "Joseph," he says, almost singing. "Just tell me why you refuse it."

A look comes over Lovering's face: able to rationalize forever, when asked outright, he will not misrepresent. "Because my mother's a Christian Scientist. That's why." Lovering dashes from the lab, leaving Ulrich to nurse his victory. Ressler returns to experimental prep, but his heart is no longer in it. He lays out the first trial and organizes the notebook. Then he knocks off for the day. The lab is suddenly infected with labeled belief. The charm has temporarily fled the whole inheritance question.

Back at the barracks, with nothing to protect him from night's humidity except his lawn chair and tomato juice, Ressler involuntarily recalls a painful joke he himself helped propagate in grad school days: A Jew, a Catholic, and a Christian Scientist sit in the anteroom to Hell. The Catholic turns to the Jew and asks, "Why are you here?" The Jew replies, "Well, God help me, but I couldn't keep from nibbling ham now and then. Why are you here?" The Catholic answers, "I had a little trouble touching myself where I go to the bathroom." The two of them turn to the Christian Scientist. "And you? Why are you here?" The Christian Scientist replies firmly, "I'm not."

The joke incriminates him. Hypocrite: how did he fail to see in himself the same persuasion, the old blessed are those who have not seen?

VI

Cook's Tour

On August 20 I committed myself to leaving, putting together a portfolio of the day's restlessness. I began my travelogue in 1597: Dutch East India Company ships return to Europe with word of a remarkable voyage. Germ cell of the modern world, its commerce craze, engine of expansion. I added Bering's arrival in Alaska in 1741, precisely the moment—bizarre anachronism—when Bach unravels his *Goldbergs*. Another 173 years later, the Panama Canal's first week of business opens a short cut between worlds. The day of exploration seemed a cornucopia expressly for my use.

In fact, the date was nothing special. On any calendar page, exploration rolls out anniversaries on demand: take every location on the globe that produced a recorded first encounter and divide by 365. Each day approximates what it means to need to be forever someplace other than *here*. Faces pressed to the glass of cabs, a summer freight's lapsed, transfigured blast, autumn attic-rattling, the furious slam of screens in back-door disappearance. Departure was easy, commonplace, everyday.

I'd signed on for the full ride. August 20, after my shift was done and the foreign legion was just punching in, I showed up on the doorstep of the converted warehouse and buzzed to be let in. I'd discovered no more about Dr. Ressler in the interim. Harder to prove a thing's absence than its existence. But in the run of time, the evidence adds up. His work had clearly come to nothing. He had produced nothing of consequence that had entered the permanent record, at least the record I wasted weeks sifting.

His non-work began to infect mine. Life science made raids on events of the day, colored my choice of quotes. He and self-appointed sidekick Todd used my Question Board to settle running disputes—everything from that calculation about the degree of our isolation in deep space to "How far did Goebbels get with Katherine Anne Porter when they dated in the thirties?" They used the forum to communicate with each other, with me, and with a public that never wrote them, put it to work for everything from Todd's private joke about making the catch to Ressler's request for the name, lost to one of the rare failings of his memory, of the tendency of languages to become simpler—to drop inflectional cases and consolidate. I proudly produced, without revealing my footwork: A: Syncretism. The board became their private tin-can telephone, although I never saw Ressler inside the branch. He must have been by regularly, but either he calculated his visits to avoid my shift or he perfected invisibility in public.

As I learned his story, I continued to steal his quotes for my own use. Even as we set in motion our own small act of code-breaking, I posted extracts from that Poe story, the one that marked for him the bewildering human propensity for metaphor. "Circumstances and a certain bias of mind," says the cryptographer of "The Gold Bug," a coded persona of his inventor, "have led me to take interest in such riddles, and it may well be doubted whether human ingenuity can construct an enigma of the kind that human ingenuity may not, by proper application, resolve." I posted this on August 21, the day after meeting Dr. Ressler for real. Although we had exchanged only a few paragraphs, my head still spun on his long, periodic sentences, the sense underneath.

I told Tuckwell I was going out that evening with a couple of friends who were in town. The old rot about half-truth being better than whole lies. Keith was so relieved at not having to throw our apartment open to a night of reminiscence that he didn't even ask who the friends were. He gave me a blank check for the evening. I had the warehouse address and a standing invitation. I needed only walk a few streets from the branch and satisfy my curiosity, answer *my* questions for once. The nondescript reddish-brown building was flanked by two sooty, brick, cliff walls, gullies where sunlight would not shine again until all buildings fell. It was fronted on the alley side by loading docks. On the street, story-length stone-trimmed windows filled with uncooperative darkness. From the outside, it was one of those mildewed, permanently For Let places, countless late-nineteenth-century brick rectangles that I no longer noticed after my second day in the city. I thought: They've lost the deed to this place. No one owns it. A forgotten tract squeezed between forgotten tracts, stuffed floor to ceiling with wooden files from a hundred years ago, papers slowly ammoniating. Nothing could have been further from the truth. In bland buildings with concrete cornices, everything is decided.

I peeked inside the first-floor turret. I could see nothing through the smoky quartz and iron bars. In front of the main door, I scoured the buttons until I found the suitably corporate monogram MOL—Manhattan On-Line. "You can remember the name," Todd had told me over the phone, "because we're not in Manhattan and we're not on-line." I debated a last time and pressed the bell. After a second, a tinny transcription of Todd's voice came over the intercom. "Friend or foe?"

"Do I have a choice?" I heard either static or his laugh, followed by the magic buzz. I grabbed the door at the tone's order, and climbed the stairs in the half-dark. At the top of the first flight, following the quaintest layout imaginable, the stairs petered out and presented an accordion-grated service-elevator shaft, the only way higher. It violated all zoning ordinances. I pressed what passed for a summons button. Cables tensed like a surprised nest of bushmasters and a counterweight sluggishly unwound. Several seconds later, the elevator—little more than an open cage with forty-watt bulb strung through the ceiling—sallied down into sight.

The antiquated grate made a noise like an enraged myna. I took my life in my hands and entered. On the way up, I had to yank a cast-iron dial crank back and forth in its semicircle to keep the lurching car in ascent. Just as I was sure a cable was about to snap, a man's voice echoed down the shaft telling me to stop at the next landing. I eased the throttle and cruised to a halt. I'd entered the car from the north. The box's exit, however, lay to the east. To leave the deathtrap, I had to open a perpendicular grate, revealing a period-piece, dented, lead-alloy door with frosted chicken-wire glass—the non-windows once ubiquitous in office buildings. Todd's silhouette on the other side called out, "Ya gotta kick it." I did. The door swung open on a turn-of-the-century anthology of alcoves, now a functionless reception area, Manhattan On-Line being one of those businesses that never received. The dozen subdivided walls were of assorted glass, multicolored brick, and an afterthought of stucco.

"Ms. O'Deigh," Todd greeted me with a formality that might have been mock. He shook my hand as if we were execs meeting

107

over power brunch. Every time out with this fellow was starting from scratch. "Terrific you've come. I've got so much to show you." Absolutely unreadable. He led us down the hall to a re-straining door. He punched a code into the electronic lock, and we entered a blazing fluorescence reminiscent of fifties science fiction. Behind massive plate safety glass, several thousand square feet of room stood in the pallid postindustrial shimmer of night shift. The space, once tall, was now wedged between false floor and drop ceiling. The room shone as bright as daylight but with minute, maddening, near-imperceptible flickers.

Machines took hold in every niche of the place, devices in no way mechanical-looking. Beautiful expanses of metal and plastic, each enclosed in seductively homogeneous chitin of earth tones and ochers, formed a ring around the room as secret and mono-lithic as Stonehenge. Todd conducted a Grand Tour, mapping the layout. The world outside this nineteenth-century masonry held no sway here, so self-defining was this fluorescent, windowless aura. Todd took me to a console, where he issued a command to a keyboard, the rites of an inner circle closed to the uninitiated.

"Don't be taken in by the bells and whistles. We're engaged here in one of the most tediously repetitive routines known to man. The assembly line of the digital info set." He punched a few more acronyms into his CRT and hit ENTER. Behind us, discharging pneumatic libido, a punched-card reader came to life. Todd re-moved a rubber band from a card deck and dropped the packet in the hopper. "Antique input method," he apologized. The device sucked up the instructions, spat them out, and fell into cogitative silence.

I tried to study his face without staring. He was different on his own turf, but I couldn't say how. His melodic voice showed no surprise at my being here. "I get in early every evening. Kick these beasts around until two, three a.m. An hour for lunch." He smiled faintly. "Procedure for keeping the wheels grinding is absolutely axiomatic. Let me show you." He tapped a pen-and-ink flowchart taped to the side of a nearby cabinet. "We go in this funnel here. We follow these arrows. Human intervention at the diamonds. We get pissed out here at the bottom. Then it's time to go home." He meditated on the flow of control. He pointed at a spot on the chart and said, "You are Here."

He showed me the storage devices—waist-high spindles with removable packs resembling layer cakes under cover. "These boys will take an entire thirty-volume encyclopedia each. I hate to use the word 'gigabyte' in mixed company, but there seems no way around it." He showed me the industrial printer, screaming under its sound hood. He opened the card cage of the CPU. "When this little electroluminescent display flashes 'Help me, I'm melting,' you're in for a long night." He introduced me to a dozen other devices whose functions I instantly lost. Decollators; sequencers. Like one of those five-language bus travelogues through Rome— never quite sure where the guide's English leaves off and his German begins.

When Todd at last fell quiet I noticed the hum of the metal, hard at work on calculations that never ruffled the silky surface. Constant, low-level drone permeated the room. Noticing, he dropped to his knees and spread supplicant-style across the floor. He put his ear to the acoustical tile and tugged on my pant leg for me to do the same. Amazed at myself, I crawled down with him and did the Native American trick of listening to the ground. Sound rushed into my ear, a rumbling chorus somewhere between Holst's *Planets* and Aristophanes' *Frogs*. He gestured me to lift my head. "Know what they're humming? 'Wake up, wake up, wake up you.... Get up, get up, get up, get out of....' Synthetically, of course."

We left the computer room, the alphabet-lock door swinging shut behind us. The sudden cutoff of noise reminded me of Midwest childhood, the abrupt end of a cicada-storm outside my window on a summer's night waking me from deep sleep with its roar of silence. The suite extended in the other direction. "This is the storeroom. These are the day-shift offices. Here's the software vault: Authorized Programmers Only." Indeed, a check-in desk blocked a door affixed with the same punch-code lock that had allowed us grudging access to the machine room. Hidden in this hierarchy of offices, the rift between information-rich and information-poor.

"Here's the lunchroom," he sighed at length. We entered a twilit cubicle containing sink, refrigerator, table with plastic chairs, and microwave. He pointed to a sign on this last device reading No Metal. "Obscure political protest, I guess." He made me coffee and yogurt without asking if I wanted it. "You see," he wound up. "Not exactly the glamour of high tech I used to dream about in art school. I could teach you to do what I do in two nights, so come back at your own risk. We are not so much this monster's brain as its arms and legs."

"Speaking of 'we'...." The first substantial thing I'd said since arriving. The sound of my voice surprised me.

"Of course! The man you came here to meet." I protested that meeting wasn't necessary. I just wanted to *see* the man the reference works hinted at but couldn't identify, the man that could elicit concern from these otherwise self-possessed features. Todd led us down a hall that doubled back behind the main computer room and dead-ended in a fire door. He gripped the knob, looked back at me over his shoulder, and asked, "Ready?" I wasn't in the slightest.

But there was no backing out. Forcing entry, we fell forward into a black cinematic cavern blazing with point lights. Cathode rays, a glowing halo of meters, and a tower of heavily cabled boxes twinkled a christmas of continuous bit-streams being transmitted and received. Against the opposite wall was a pane of one-way glass that revealed the computer room with its gigabyte drums and its silk-smooth calculating cases. Todd and I had not done our surveying alone. I felt spied upon, violated, caught in the act of eavesdropping.

Above the hum, as the door swung shut, I heard another sound altogether. Todd had warned me, in the seafood-and-sawdust dive. And yet, each time I'd imagined these two lost boys serving their abandoned-warehouse night shift, I never once gave their isolation so ravishing a soundtrack. Aural obsession, in such astringent surroundings, was too fantastic. The music, ground from a cheap stereo that hid its low tech in a corner, was that same crotchety keyboard exploring that same eighteenth-century glaze, testing the keys' tentative possibilities. Imitative voices chased and cascaded over one another, interleaving, pausing at pivots, only to tag-team pratfall down the scale in close-interval clashes. In the dark, this finger-probing was the most perfect sound I had ever heard.

Like a shepherd's on breaking into a buried tomb, my eyes adjusted to local dark. I made out a figure, tipped forward in a tilt-and-swivel chair behind a desk littered with electronic instruments, liquid-crystal readouts, and a vast, rack-mounted technical manual that would have been the envy of Diderot and his *Encyclopédie* henchmen. I knew my man right away, although I'd seen him only once the year before and once in a magazine photo at twenty-five. We surprised him in the act of turning over pages in the massive manual, not so much looking up an error fix as reading though the entire yard-wide spine from cover to cover.

110

As we entered the confined space and stepped toward him, he stood and unfolded himself. He was thinner and shorter than I remembered; his features, not classic, by the glow of the machine diodes possessed a resignation that, like the ambient piano trickle, was consummately beautiful. In contrast to Todd's collegiate slovenliness, he dressed in coat and tie, as if some sentient presence in all this mass of integrated chips cared how he looked. Not just presentable; immaculate. Natty.

Before Todd could do formal introductions, Dr. Ressler, with a charming outdated gesture, offered me his hand. "You know who I am. But aside from the fact that you work for the public library, once considered becoming a professional dancer, and are called Jan, I know absolutely nothing about you." You've-been-in-Afghanistan-I-perceive. It came off hilariously. That slight, dry, upward curl of his thin lips convinced me that here was the last cultivated enclave in the forsaken world. I loved being in the man's presence from the first minute.

We left the control room and stepped back into the hall where we could see and hear one another. We might have been business associates who met frequently in London or Tokyo, acting together in silent consensus. On the far side of the fire door, Dr. Ressler paid me gallant attention: "You have exactly the sort of complexion required of the quintessential wronged heroine of Victorian pornographic fiction. I regret having to be the one to offer the observation, but Franklin's reading may not yet be broad enough to allow him to do likewise." This rolled out of him intact, with only the slightest ironic hint.

Todd rushed to assure me, "That's the nicest thing I've ever heard this old man say to anyone." But I wasn't at all embarrassed. And neither, it seemed, was the old man.

The instant we assembled in the hall, as if counting the seconds since his last, Dr. Ressler offered us cigarettes, which we both refused. "Am I the only one of this suspect group with an oral fixation?" He smoked, inhaling pensively and catching the ashes in a fastidiously cupped hand. It was by then the middle of the night. No one seemed in any hurry to ruin the rare visit with something so inexact as conversation. At last Dr. Ressler smiled at me. I can recreate that grin perfectly: laconic, amused, mixing its passive enjoyment with a particle of despair. The smile of a mathematician who cannot decide if his latest calculation presents him with a near-tautology or has plunged him into the heart of

111

the enigma. "So how do you two come to know one another?"

I didn't dare look at Todd. Half a dozen near-truths passed through my head, but I missed the beat necessary to pull off a plausible lie. "He came to me and asked me to look you up."

Ressler's already high hairline moved higher as he smiled. "So the fellow said himself, although not nearly so forthrightly." He finished his smoke and motioned for us to wait while he discarded the remains in a nearby commode. As he returned, the shrunken figure was picking lint off of his suit coat. "I'm not sure what anyone could possibly find to be interested in. I've had no historical import." It seemed the wrong place to argue the point, yet something in my reading had convinced me that the world of scientific research was one continuous, shifting, interdependent event, an event still encompassing him.

I can't remember exactly how I phrased the question; I probably bungled it. I was unable to make a decent sentence in his company, so self-conscious did his parts of speech jumping through hoops make me. But hook or crook, standing in the deserted hall, the *Goldbergs* no longer audible through the control-room door, I asked what had happened to strand him here. He pulled at the skin around his eyes; maybe I'd miscalculated in believing the admiration for bluntness he professed. But when he answered, it was again with that look of bemused pleasure. "Science lost its calm." He extended an arm, palm up, in a gesture indicating the renovated warehouse, Brooklyn, the entire maze of current events the meek were condemned to inherit. "And as Poe long ago pointed out, cryptography begins at home."

With that, he excused himself; the machines were calling. He hoped I would drop by again. "He doesn't deserve it, but give this young man the benefit of the doubt." Ressler: if anything, more mysterious in person than in the elliptical accounts. The riddle the young scientist had once faced—how a four-letter chemical language could describe all life—was more opaque now than when it had sent him empty away. The only thing the visit told me was why Todd so urgently wanted to turn up this man.

By next morning I'd checked out Poe. I too wondered whether human ingenuity could construct an enigma that human ingenuity could not resolve. Yet the detective in me, a hardcover strain cross-bred with hardy paperback perennial, was stumped by Ressler's ingenuity in displaying himself to us without revealing a thing. I rephrased Poe's dictum: It may well be doubted if genetic ingenuity can construct an enigma that genetic ingenuity may not resolve. His genetic code, the gradual accretion of living molecular language, had created itself out of free association. Everything derived from it, all successive mutations, recombinations, crossings over— fish in the ocean, eels in the sea, a thousand Darwinian finches, every researcher, Todd and I, Ressler himself, all natural history were elaborate permutations on an original four-base message. The young scientist left in this gaunt body was himself a product of the code he'd been after, the code that couldn't keep itself hidden from itself.

I took his paradox apart from every direction. Against my policy of not repeating sources, I hit "The Gold Bug" twice over:

> In the present case—indeed in all cases of secret writing—the first question regards the *language* of the cipher.... In general, there is no alternative but experiment (directed by probabilities) of every tongue known to him who attempts the solution, until the true one can be obtained.

There lay the rub; the language of Ressler's enigma *was* the genetic code, organic chemistry, well-understood forces. Ressler had known all that; the work of generations of whitecoats had identified the idiom the secret writing was written in. But there the man was, at the end of his working life, empty-handed, high and dry, alone at night in a dark room lit only by CRTs requiring as much attention as wetting infants.

The code he was after was not so much a message written *in* a language as all grammar itself. I felt that with my first good look at his wasted face, his intelligent eyes that resigned themselves to courteous elegance. The old vocabulary of research and exploration, the whole poetics of science still poured from the man's mouth in rolling, perfect paragraphs.

At work, the routine that had taken me into adulthood came up short. I did not want my life. I wanted another thing, an analogy. I wanted to read Poe, all Poe. I wanted to read science, the history of science. I wanted to be back with those two men, listening to the language of isolation they spoke to one another. Half a dozen sentences, and I was fixed. Was any grammar sufficiently strong to translate the inner grammar of another? Did anything in the cell, in the code itself, actually *know* the code? I needed to win this man's confidence, to ask him as much. To ask him how he had guessed I'd wanted, once, to be a dancer.

Todd had said to call him anytime. I did, in the middle of the afternoon a few days later. "Oh God, I forgot. I woke you."

"No, no," he lied groggily. "There's something I've been wanting to ask you forever."

"We answer anything."

"What is the origin of the phrase 'Make the catch'?" Half-conscious silliness: repeating the question, reproducing the round he pretended to ask about. Clear dalliance, an open invitation to come again, that evening if I wanted. I had passed the audition. I needed no further lure. I could sit in that soundproof control room behind the one-way glass, savoring the banter of people who under-stood the scary unlikelihood of speech. I laughed something back at Franklin; hard to say which of us led the flirtation walk. A step-ladder catch, second voice identical, only higher. He chases her until she catches him.

The Nightly News

Ressler accepts Botkin's standing invitation to eat with her. Food's gone by the boards too long. Over venison or Duck à l'Orange, they might even make headway on a coding angle. The elder woman's mind is first-rate; if her science isn't up to the minute, it's the fault of the discipline's runaway proliferation, not her ability to grasp essentials. He himself can't understand more than three of five articles, even in those journals devoted to his narrow specialty. He becomes a regular at her table, benefiting more than just nutritionally. Botkin too seems fond of the chance for conversation. Odd thing: talk's no good alone.

By day he frequents her office, the single place on campus providing that balance between attention and escape necessary to concentrate. Over decades, Botkin has perfected her digs. A heavy oak panel obscures the pea-green steam pipes, and lace curtains, white embroidery on white, meliorate the industrial frosted glass. University-issue khaki bookcases against one wall house journal indexes, meticulously aligned, going back into forties antiquity. Across from these shelves stands another case, a varnished turn-of-the-century hardwood masterpiece. It holds editions of Werfel, Mann, Musil, essays by Benjamin and Adorno, and other suspect tomes from the soft sciences. The spines alone qualify some as minor triumphs of decorative art. Ressler likes to heft these, examine the marbled paper. He is entranced, too, by other items on the shelf: molding Furtwängler platters older than he is, pressed, to his delight, on one side only. "So did this man collaborate?"

Botkin smiles sadly. "Half the NSF collaborated."

The lid of her centenarian rolltop desk, long stuck closed, renders the piece ornamental. Dr. Botkin now employs it only for stacking; piles of print, heaps of paper of all religious persuasions, welded into inseparable masses, ski down the desktop slope into further piles scattered about the floor. And yet, the room is meticulous, tidy. A Viennese overstuffed chair, faded but impeccable, flanges in ornate wings at the top; armrests flourish fruits and vines, and the stitchery on the back, though ghostly now, still shows the trace of a pastoral scene. The right armrest bears stains smelling of anisette, temporary storage spot for candy when the bone-handled phone demands answering. Botkin sits there for hours while Ressler lies flat out on a tooled Moroccan leather couch, as if for regression analysis. Botkin abstractly considers the skin on the back of her hand, which has gone slack and no longer snaps back when pinched. "And what is our lesson for today?"

Ressler, prostrate, grins at the ceiling. "The surface shape of the split helix. Its transcription to RNA. Energy considerations against assembling protein chains directly on the strand. The possibility of the peptide chain peeling from the RNA surface as it forms."

"If you insist," she sighs. But her imagination has come alive after a dormant winter. She once more reads voraciously, devising tests, learning, freeing herself from dead preconceptions, leaping for the first time since the war.

The room, curtained for minimum sunlight, smells of tea, rose water, hair oil, napthalene—nonspecific aromas of the past. Its scent encapsulates a forgotten ghetto—Danzig, perhaps, or Prague, though it would take a hopelessly sensitive nose to tell. Ressler can concentrate here. What's more, he can think out loud. Botkin has the intellectual chops to keep him honest. Something about the place makes it perfect for guided associating. Oriental richness, dark and full, despite a paucity of decorations. Only two ornaments grace the walls, two framed photographic prints, one of Mahler and one of the chemist Kekulé. The latter dreamt one night of a snake rolling its tail in its mouth, and woke with the structure of the benzene ring. The former composed, in already antiquated idiom, a staggeringly beautiful song cycle on the death of a child

115

from scarlet fever, losing his own to the disease shortly thereafter. The two contemporaries hang side by side, a semblance of a shrine. Near them, mounted under glass, hangs a tiny, inexplicable object that could only be a gold filling.

Gradually Ressler ventures farther afield. Dan Woytowich has him over for a nervous evening. The group's classical geneticist, Woytowich has spent his professional life raising fish and plotting their susceptibility to disease against their number of stripes. Full of promise once, by all accounts. No one knows exactly what happened. Recently, alarmed by the advanced hour and suddenly aware that his generational studies have been all talk and no action, Woyty has married a grad student in English literature half his age, a woman both stripeless and disease-free. Despite the late discovery that he would even now like to father a *real* family, Woyty's only child to date is wife Renée's emerging dissertation.

Renée describes her project in detail, after the get-acquainted conversation falls into autism: "You know Ben Jonson? O Rare Ben Jonson?" Ressler nods before she starts singing "Drink to Me Only." "Someone once told Jonson that Shakespeare never blotted a line. Jonson replied, 'Would that he had blotted a thousand.'" Renée explains; Ressler drifts, loses the thread. Something to do with her determining exactly which thousand lines Jonson wanted Shakespeare to blot.

Woytowich is reluctant to talk shop. Stuart could learn endless classical genetics from the man; he slighted macroheredity in school, in the heat of molecular excitement. But Woyty just sits taciturn throughout the evening. When Ressler catches Dan looking at his watch, he apologizes for overstaying and gets up to go. "Oh, no," Woyty laughs anxiously. "'Tain't that. Only...would you mind very much if we...?" He gestures embarrassedly at the color set, one of the first quarter million to grace an American home. "It's news time."

Ressler defers with pleasure. He watches attentively, not the new technology or today's current events, but the behavior of his colleague, a genuine habitué of headlines. Woyty sighs. "I'm absolutely dependent. Jesus; even quiz shows bind me for hours. But the *news*; God. I'm terrified of missing something. Ever since Khrushchev did his CBS interview....Christ Almighty. The news is the most gratifying thing life has to offer. Think of it; we can know within hours, things all over the globe actually happening *now*."

116

They watch in silence, the first comfortable moment all evening. The danger of the nightly You Are There. Partly developmental, like the soaps: today's police action is tomorrow's outbreak, so stay tuned. Only the stories change faster and more wildly than soaps. "Catch the broadcast about the Saigon stabbing of the Canadian armistice supervisor?" Woytowich asks during the commercial. "A real whodunit. But what happens next? Always the question. Catch Diem's visit, the great scenes of Dwight personally meeting the man at D.C. airport? Bloody hell, you know? Gets to be a problem. I mean, I could sit until the world ends before they give the wrap-up."

At the next break, fearing for the man's well-being, Ressler tries to change the topic. He describes his last twenty-four-hour shift manning the rate experiment, the isotope readings on his cultures. But the elder partner is unseducible. "Ain't that the kicker? They fail to tell you in Bio 110 just how much science amounts to jacking a knob every hour for three years and jotting it down in a journal. You ought to look into one of those portables. Pick one up on payments. Put it in your office. Go anywhere with one. Never have to miss an update."

"There's always the next day's newspapers, Dan."

"Not the same, reading about Yemen *after the fact*. Like listening to a tape of a ballgame. What difference does it make if Mays gets a clutch hit when the affair's a done deed? Give me live broadcast, the announcer muffing his words, the station disclaiming the views of third parties. Give me simultaneous report." That's it, the reason Woytowich has sunk into information dependence: if he hears an event while it's still going on, he has an infinitesimal chance to alter the outcome. Not to watch tonight's segment, even to entertain a junior researcher, is to commit a sin of omission. He's Horace Wells all over again, the man who, altruistically pursuing proper anesthetic dosages, discovered, instead, addiction and squalor.

Summer's almost gone, winter's coming on when K-53-C gets its first knock on the door. Given his utter anonymity, Ressler assumes some terrible mistake. It's the NSA, confusing him with some other Stuart Ressler of the same name, or Veep Dick Nixon on search-and-destroy committee work. What's he done recently to run afoul of the authorities? Growing radioactive microorganisms without a permit.

The visitor is Tooney Blake. Although they've worked in prox-

117

imity all summer, the two men are still strangers. Blake is a solid biochemist who has taken up partition chromatography, a six-year-old technique that, given patience and precision, reveals the amino acid sequence in a protein. He has never voiced anything but irrefutable clarities at the Blue Sky sessions. Neither brilliant nor erratic, Blake is the sort of steady lexicographer Ressler will need to pull off any *coup de grâce*. Here Tooney stands, inexplicably in the doorway on the last Friday evening ever in August '57. He has his arm around an attractive woman in her mid-thirties. Ressler can only greet the couple warmly, as if they've been expected.

"You know my lovely wife Eva." Ressler wobbles his neck. "You've met," Blake insists. "Ulrich's. Stuart, you'll never believe this. We just discovered it ourselves, in fact. We live under the same damn roof."

Ressler is lost in the vistas of figurative speech. Eva explains, "You know, K-53-A? The other end of the triplex?"

Blake takes up the slack. "Luck of the draw, huh? So Evie and I found this here bottle...." He holds it up, as if the label might persuade the fellow to let them in.

Stuart pulls himself together. "I'm afraid I haven't bought a welcome mat yet, so you'll have to take my word for it." This the Blakes do, with easy style.

Within minutes, Tooney has the *Summer Slumber Party* on the player, watching in fascination as Eva does a wonderful one-step imitation of Olga, the plastic spindle ballerina. In no time, the two of them have done Stuart's week of dirty dishes, singing descant to those teenage death songs the whole while, even getting the boy to kick in on the choruses. They graduate to the Wagner excerpts. "Ah, the hero's motif," Tooney says. "Just the tune to welcome young geniuses to town." Ressler reads the text on his tennis shoes. Inspired by the musical Siegfried line, the Blakes crack open the Riesling. Tooney proposes a toast: "May your stay here be filled with significant insights."

Noticing the empty space in the living room where a sofa should be, Eva protests. "You poor boy. Have you been sitting on the floor all this time? We've an extra one, don't we, Toon?" Shamefaced at being caught with more sofas than her share. "Don't say anything! It's yours on permanent loan."

Pointless for him to protest. Something in Eva's extreme generosity toward a total stranger—pointless, pathetically trusting—moves him to accept. Before he knows what's happening, the three of them dash down the barrack row and begin moving furniture in the Blakes' parlor. "Shhh," they giggle. "Don't wake the kid." They spring the spare sofa, trundle it across the lawns of K-53 in the middle of the night, laughing hilariously and daring all Stadium Terrace to mistake them for sofa burglars.

As they lever the beast through his door, Ressler realizes he will be twenty-six in a few days, too old for discoveries of consequence. He has done nothing to advance the project, to locate the approach that will systematically decipher nucleic acid. The three of them, gasping for breath, position the sofa to fill up as much empty space as possible and then plunk themselves down on it, exhausted. A failure, he is forced back on the compromise of companionship.

They find a deck of cards hiding in the crack between the back and cushions. "Little Margaret's been playing hide-the-folks'-stuff again." Tooney and Eva teach him to play pinochle, a game whose payoff matrices would soon addict him but for one shortcoming: the play of the cards contains no progression, no development. Each hand, no matter the outcome, leaves the play of the next unchanged.

Eva, giddy with wine and aces around, waxes astonished over the playing cards. "These things are amazing. Glossy, washable, every one different. There's a miracle for you. What are these *made* out of? Not paper, surely. Soybeans? You scientists are always making things out of soybeans."

Ressler cannot resist these two. He talks with Tooney, the only other human capable of conversing about RNA templates while the Valkyries skip their way up the slopes of Valhalla. Eva fascinates Ressler as well. Undeniably attractive, Eva possesses skills that can only be called freakish. The three of them sit outside in Ressler's favorite spot; the Blakes instantly adapt to the lawn-chair routine. The couple drink their wine and Ressler his tomato juice, with just a smidgin—make that two-thirds of a dollop—of wine at Eva's insistence. On the lawn, Blake pressures his wife to roll out her mental arsenal.

He asks Ressler to supply two pieces of paper and two pens. "Now, talk to her about anything you want, and I'll do the same." Ressler describes an article on partial overlap he has just read. At the same time, Blake babbles in her other ear about the weather, Wagner, how fine a neighbor they've discovered. Eva, a pen per hand, takes simultaneous dictation on separate sheets, without garbling a word. Right-ear stream with left hand and vice versa.

119

Knocked out already, Ressler learns there is more. "Give her a sentence," Blake urges. "Nice and long." Ressler reaches back, performs a mental feat of his own, and pulls up from God knows where a favorite quote. Flaubert, from days when he could still afford *belles lettres:* "Some fatal attraction draws me into the abyss of thought, down into those innermost recesses which never cease to fascinate the strong."

Without a pause, Eva responds, "Strong the fascinate to cease never which recesses innermost...." It takes him a moment to figure out what is going on. The whole stream, backwards.

Unbelievable. A living palindromist. "We could use you in codon transcription." For all they know, the gene might be read in either direction, both at once, for that matter. Who knows what golden patterns this woman could mine?

Eva laughs, fetchingly shy again after her bravura feat. "I've already got a job."

"Who could possibly make proper use of you?"

Tooney breaks out laughing. Eva joins him, managing to explain, "I work for the Civil Service. Processing job applications. You two think *you* have a coding problem on your hands. You ought to see ours."

"Let 'er rip," Blake chuckles. "What's the code for 'Changed Jobs'?"

"Let's see.... Applicant Changed Jobs—five point seven E."

"How about 'Retired'?"

"Easy one. That'd be five point eight I."

"Now then. How about illness?"

"Terminal?"

"Heck, why not. Live it up."

"Name your disease."

"Try cancer."

"More specific, please."

"Leukemia."

"We give that a six point six Q."

"Q? How in hell do they get Q from 'leukemia'?"

"My dear husband. There is no wherefore to the Service."

"Radiation sickness?"

"Still in committee. We lump that into seven point oh, your basic 'Deceased.'" The Blakes break off their vaudeville, noticing the unintended effect on the audience. Ressler has gone silent, the glow of the corner streetlight unmistakably glinting off his am-

120

bushed cheeks. He feels, for the first time, his mother's status, something in the 6.6 range. She died three years back, while he was in grad school. The details of the woman's decline are intact in memory; only the nightmare of not being able to name what was happening remained lost until this evening, the evening the U.S. fires its first rocket-powered atomic warhead due west of this improvised lawn party, in the empty sands of Nevada.

Only five months between diagnosis and death. He took a leave from studies to go home and sit with her through a pain that she preferred to the alternative bouts of annihilating fatigue. His role was to sit and assure her of the great strides medicine was making at that moment. He would tell her, day after day, as her hips wasted to grotesque ripples, that the most important thing was to fight the malignancy and live for the outside shot. Mind as medicine: no other course. Deny the numbers. Cancer lives for the onset of common sense. Reconcile yourself to it, and it wins.

A nursing more for his sake than the dying woman's, obsessed, all the way up to the final metastasis, with proving that mental function did not altogether dissipate, was not dispersed by illness and treatment. That *she* was preserved inside somewhere. "Read anything today, Mom?" he would lead. "Well, yes I have," she would answer, with a weak smile hinting at the miracle of deception. He never asked for specifics.

He does not hear the Blakes stop their routine. He is elsewhere, thinking how he used to sit with her on the front porch, just like this, late in the evening, not daring to hold her hand, while she said unexplainable things about the effects of her illness on perception. "Who would believe what this place *sounds* like? I had no idea nature made so much noise."

She talked for the first time about her father, the third child from the right in front of the shaft entrance in a famous photo of child mine workers. Now Ressler has never harbored closet Lamarckism; social traumas experienced by the forefathers are not visited upon the sons. But his grandfather's life underground left its imprint—the dream of meliorism that child laborers impart rose up from his mother's lungs on the warm tufts of her disease. Suffering, her last looks said to him, must be the precursor to greater things. Every rung goes higher and higher.

She died ten days after his return to school. In a misguided final tribute to her son, she left her body to "medical science," meaning, Stuart knew, that third-year premeds lopped her organs off in

121

anatomy lab. Because he never saw her body again, she did not die until this evening, when Evie Blake assigns her a number. He always knew the world would one day be like this: a night of no temperature, sitting outside with no one there any longer to call him in. Free to sit forever in the company of strangers, in the belly of a cold, formless waiting.

The Blakes, seeing they have accidentally sent their host off alone, call it a night and take their leave back to K-53-A. But they read him wrong. Ressler comes back to the lawn party, wanting them to resume the careless evening, extend it, stretch out the mixed blessing of companionship until morning. But searching, he cannot find the pointer to the words "Don't go yet." The Blakes disappear, waving, across the lawn. He cannot even find those two syllables for a departing greeting. Minutes later he remembers it: "Good night." Come back. Good night.

Landscape with Conflagration

I've reached a sticking point in my homework, the background reading that must take me inside the man. Not a barrier to comprehension: I remember, flexing my intellect again this season, that given time, I have the capacity to tackle anything, however formidable. And I have more than enough time—time spreading from sunny sahara mornings alone over onion bagels and oranges to arctic nights, postponing sleep as long as possible, armed with only thick books and a headboard lamp. I've hit a barrier not to comprehension but to credulity. How can an assortment of invisible threads inside one germ cell record and pass along the construction plans of the whole organism, let alone the cell housing the threads themselves? I've grasped the common metaphor: the blueprint gene somehow encodes a syntactic message, an entire encyclopedia of chemical engineering projects. I feel the thrill of attaching abstract gene to physical chromosome. But it remains analogy, lost in intermediary words.

The task Dr. Ressler set himself was merely—and only he could have thought "merely"—to capture the enigma machine that tweaks this chromosomal message into readability. Did he believe that nothing was lost in translation as signals percolated up from molecules in the thread into *him,* that brain, those limbs, that hurt, alert face? Searching for his own lexicon required faith that the

122

chemical semaphore could serve as its own rosetta, faith that biology too could be revealed through its particulars. Faith that demonstration could replace faith.

It grows like a crystal, this odd synthesis of evolution, chemistry, and faith, spreads in all directions at once, regular but aperiodic. By Ressler's birth, enzymes—catalysts driving the chemical reactions of metabolism—were identified as proteins. The structure of proteins—responsible for everything from the taste of sole to the toughness of a toenail—strikes me as ridiculously simple: linear, crumpled necklaces of organic pearls called amino acids. What's more, the protein necklaces directing all cell processes consist of series of only twenty different amino acid beads.

It seems impossible: twenty can't be sufficient word-hoard to engineer the tens of thousands of complex chemical reactions required to make a thing live. But lying in bed under my arctic nightlight, carrying out the simple arithmetic, I see how the abject simplicity of protein produces more potential than mind can penetrate. A necklace of only two beads, each in one of twenty colors, can assume any of four hundred different combinations. A third bead increases this twenty times—eight thousand possible necklaces. I learn that the average protein necklace floating in the body weighs in at hundreds of beads. At that length, the possible string combinations exceed the printed sentences in man-made creation. Room to grow, in other words.

The protein bead string folds up, forms secondary structures determined by its amino acid sequence. The *shape* of these fantastic landscapes, fuzz-motes as convoluted as the string is simple, gives them their specific, chemical power. Their jungle of surface protrusions provides—like so many dough forms—niches for other chemicals to assemble and react.

But if these cookie cutters—in countless possible fantastically complex shapes—build the body, what builds the builders? The answer appalls me. The formula for the builder molecules as well as its implementation are contained in another long, linear molecule. This time the beads come in only four colors. It says something about my progress in scientific faith that I accept the calculation showing that the possible combinations in one such foursquare informational molecule exceed the total number of atoms in the universe.

But I hang up on the idea of such a linear molecule encoding a breathing, hoping, straining, failing, aging, dying scientist. I find as I read that I'm in good company. If I still ran the Quote Board, I'd use tomorrow that gem of Einstein's when meeting Morgan and hearing of his project to mechanize biology:

> No, this trick won't work.... How on earth are you ever going to explain in terms of chemistry and physics so important a biological phenomenon as first love?

But I no longer run the Quote Board. I run nothing now except the Jan O'Deigh Continuing Education Project. And for that, I have only more history. When counting aminos fails to put me to sleep, I charm insomnia by reading Beadle and Tatum's 1940 work on the bread mold *Neurospora*. Only seventeen years old when Ressler got his brainstorm, it must have read like a classic to a student raised on it. While the world once more indulged its favorite occupation, Beadle and Tatum dosed mold with X-rays to induce mutations. Raising thousands of test-tube strains, they produced mutants that could no longer manufacture required nutrients. Mutated chromosomes failed to produce necessary enzymes.

With an excitement that penetrates even the sober journal account, they crossed a mutant that could no longer make enzyme E with its normal counterpart. Half the offspring had the mutation and half did not. Enzyme production precisely mirrored Mendelian inheritance. One gene, one enzyme. Each time I read the conclusion, I hear his perverse question: "What could be simpler?"

A unique gene, coding for a unique enzyme: Cyfer inherited as dogma what actually arose only through recent, bitter debate. The limited informational content of DNA—the four bases adenine, guanine, cytosine, and thymine—did not seem adequate to build the fantastically varied amino acid necklaces. For some time, the size of DNA was underestimated, and even after the enormous molecular weight was correctly determined, many scientists believed that the four bases followed one another in repeating order. Redundant series carry no more information than a news program repeating, "Earlier today, earlier today...."

DNA was long rejected as the chromosomal message carrier. Some researchers believed that proteins themselves were the master blueprint, even though every protein would require others to build it. Avery blazed the trail out of confusion. His 1944 paper showed that the substance transforming one bacterial strain to another was not protein but DNA. Inheritance was rapidly being reduced from metaphor to physical construct. DNA was a plan that somehow threaded raw amino acid beads into proteins. These protein chains in turn catalyzed all biological process. Cyfer's question—the coding problem—was how a long string of four types of things stood for thousands of shorter, twenty-thing strings.

Before the problem could even be posed, scientists had first to determine a structure for DNA that fit the evidence. The structure fell the year Ressler attained legal adulthood, one of the most celebrated solutions in science. X-ray diffractions of crystalline nucleic acid suggested a helix. The beautiful Chargaff Ratios demanded the amount of adenine equal that of thymine, guanine equal cytosine, and $G + A$ equal $C + T$. DNA presented too many structural possibilities to be cracked by standard organic analysis. By starting with the constraints in Franklin's and Wilkins's data, Watson and Crick tinkered with cutouts until the shoe dropped. They hit upon the double helix, where complementary base pairs—G pairing always with C, A always with T—form the spiral rungs.

Temperament, coded in long strings of base pairs, plays a big part in any interpretation of data. The full ramifications of the model were not quickly grasped. It followed neatly that chromosomes were just supercoiled filaments of DNA. Mendel's genes were simply sections of chromosome, a length of spiral staircase— say ten thousand base-pair rungs spelling out auburn hair. But using four letters to convey the content of all living things seemed like transmitting every *Who's Who* of this century in staticky dots and dashes across a copper filament.

How was the message read? How to determine the *language* of the cipher? Understand that question and I've understood him. Dr. Ressler, receiving intact the work of the structurists, trained his temperament on the smallest end of the genetic spectrum, the connecting link. The task given him was to determine how twin-helical sequences of four bases

...A-C-C-G-T-G-T-G-A-A-C-G-G...
I I I I I I I I I I I I
...T-G-G-C-A-C-A-C-T-T-G-C-C...

strung amino acids into enfolded protein:

... threonine-valine-tryptophan ...

125

Dr. Ressler's question was not primarily cytological or chemical or even genetic, although it was all these. Heredity's big hookup lay in information, pure form. It floated agonizingly close in the air, an all-expenses-paid trip to Stockholm taped to the bottom of some chair in the lecture hall. Yet prestige played no more than ironically in Ressler's mind. His was a drive deeper than recognition, a need to cross that hierarchical border, that edge, that isomorph, that metaphor, to get to the thing itself, to arrive at the enigma machine, reach it on pattern alone, reach down and take into his hands the first word, name it, that string of base-pairs coding for all inheritance, desire, ambition, the naming need itself—first love, forgiveness, frailty.

Canon at the Second

I know that need. It keeps me up late, reading. It ruins the best hours of the day, as I run downstairs every fifteen minutes to check the mail. But no further word from Franklin. Only that northern scene, the lovely, faraway village with the fire forever frozen in gesso, proves to me the man ever existed. The painter known only to him, me, and a dozen experts in esoterica: Herri met de Bles, Frank Todd's coding problem. How to find, in the work of a forgotten artist, evidence of that same message Dr. Ressler looked for, the same link, only from the other end, writ large in the outside world.

Frank's problem from the start was convincing himself that skill of hand and eye was its own best excuse for using it. He was temperamentally incapable of believing his own ingenious proofs. He was already in danger of disappearing before I met him. The pointless proliferation of voices, dispersed over the map, shouting, conjugating, declining, declaring nothing except *look at me, look at all this,* lost and leading nowhere except to their own noise, led him to a place where I can't trace him.

Already too long out of training, I remember I own a book that might be good for something besides proving that people I once worked with actually liked me. I go to my private reserves and pull out the *Times Atlas,* goodbye gift from my old life. I flip through the maps and locate the pages corresponding to his landscape: Dinant, the Meuse, Namur province, Wallonia, Belgium. I slip my finger up an inch, over the language line into Flanders:

Leuven, Mechelen, Antwerp, a world away. What does it tell, the geometrical isomorph, the representations drawn impeccably to scale? Does it help to know that Franklin, on 7/6/85, by the postmark, was near the tip of my fingernail?

I need more. I return to the shelves, pull out a bit of esoterica of my own. I fish about in my two-volume historical atlas for that contradiction in terms, the same place at a different time. I find the cartoons—Low Countries, Burgundy, Hapsburg Sphere. I follow the ebb and flow of colored lines, picture Herri moving through this Gobelin tapestry of economic confusion and geopolitics. But I can't recover the place, realize it in imagination. I sidetrack myself on imagining Franker in his self-described liberation of new words. I studied French for four years in school, during which time I never met a native speaker. All my classes were taught in English, and all I can remember is the cheat of making a sound intermediate between "le" and "la" and the insistence of the texts that one uses the formal form with everyone except intimates, small children, and animals.

Yet I must have retained some spark of the secret life of words, Franker's excuse for more study. Because I also remember being able to translate, fluently and without prompting, the one French sentence Dr. Ressler claimed to know. He rolled it out wistfully as early as the second visit I made to their mechanical hideaway, and he repeated it at odd moments in the course of the year I was his friend. *Je ne fais aucun mal en restant ici.* I do no harm by remaining here.

He claimed only one other standing bit of foreign-language repertoire, Bach's favorite saying: *Es muss alles möglich zu machen seyn.* All things must be possible. Tenuous assertion at best. Both Dr. Ressler and Todd sacrificed themselves to a corollary translation: All things that are possible are real.

VII

Breakthroughs in Science

The daily papers have never been kind to his field. They cover the developments well enough, in an Ike's coronary kind of way. They lay out in lay terms the birth pangs of the science, but wind up promising a bevy of mail-order life forms by the end of the decade. The subject matter itself isn't beyond reporters. The logic of inheritance is straightforward. Beadle and Tatum are more coherent than the Mideast. However complex science becomes, it remains at least internally consistent.

The trouble with science journalism lies in time scale. The average news story wraps up in a week to ten days. News confuses significant with novel. I was shocked to discover, at twenty, that news carefully culled not the day's most important events but the most alarming and unusual. Lingering separatist movements are not news, except to today's corpse. Species extinction is too mundane to report. Every "event" in molecular genetics is made out to be a fast-breaking story, conspiring toward an end. A sneak preview of a biological revolution on Monday implies that the derivative consumer good will hit the shelves by week's end.

His science has done its share to aggravate expectations. Genetics has evolved more in the three decades since Ressler worked it than in the previous three millennia. It's easy to think that discoveries will continue to pour out in saturation patterns. But journalism errs in equating development with advance. A new postulate is no more news than a new poem. What news reports as fundamental progress in knowing the world may be only a subtle rearrangement of best analogies.

A new relation is not conquistador's plunder. Science is not

128

about control. That is technology, another urge altogether. The pursuit of living pattern that possessed Ressler has nothing to do with this year's apotheosis of bioengineering. He once remarked that mistaking science for technology deprived the nonscientist of one of the greatest sources of awe, replacing it with diet as filling as Tantalus's fruit. I had only to hear the man talk for fifteen minutes to realize that science had no purpose. The purpose of science, if one must, was the purpose of being alive: not efficiency or mastery, but the revival of appropriate surprise.

Separately, the three of us relearned that truth more times than I thought a body capable. If Dr. Ressler lamented the commercialization of science, he despaired even more over the science of commerce. He told us of legislation that had come before the 85th Congress in the wake of the Civil Rights Bill—the White Coat Ruling. In the few years that it took sponsors to bail out of radio's *Official Detective* in favor of TV's *Name That Tune* they'd developed a trick that threatened the public's ability to discriminate. Advertisers found they could dramatically boost sales of just about anything by having a man in glasses and white coat hold it up for view. Weed killer, rubber tires, lipstick: a few Erlenmeyer flasks in the background, and a sales pitch became news.

A well-meaning legislator decided that blind trust was, like Robeson and Oppenheimer, a national security risk. He introduced a measure that would require every televised commercial where someone held up anything that bubbled or doodled anything resembling trig on a chalkboard to bear the caption "A Simulation." The difficulty in the bill lay in the shadiness of implication in the first place. Commercials worked because actors never came out and said, "I'm a scientist." Credentials were left to the audience to infer. If the bill passed, opponents reasoned, any endorsers who donned a smock of any kind would have to prove they weren't simulating. "It's one thing to legislate on poultry, race relations, and atomic energy," Ressler said, with that tightening of mouth muscles that passed for irony. "But legislating inference is another matter. Simulation beats legislation nine falls out of ten."

He remembered the insignificant bill with the precision that locked his half century into his brain. As he tossed off thirty-year-old details with accuracy, I felt I'd gladly suffer aphasia at fifty for a few decades of that memory. "They passed an invitation around Illinois, asking for expert witnesses to fly to Washington. They wanted white coats to sell the bill to the legislators! None of us volunteered, of course. I imagine your generation is too sophisticated to realize what a betrayal of calling it would have been then to attempt to legislate thinking. The bill eventually passed, but did nothing to stop the human mind from reifying every conceivable sales pitch." All things must be possible. And all possible things are real.

It hurt, listening to him, to think he never wrote anything but that little sampler, that one article giving so little glimmer of who he could be in speech. Starting with a Resslerism, I would search for a simulation for my day's quote:

> If we saw as much of the world as we do not see, we should be aware, in all probability, of a perpetual multiplication and variation of forms.

I used Montaigne to obliquely acknowledge that Ressler aphorism, from deep in a night's simulated conversation, too disturbing to post publicly as news, about how we differ more from ourselves than we do from one another.

Countercheck Quarrelsome

In weeks, he has struck an acquaintance with everyone on the team. Only Ulrich, like all effective leaders, remains aloof. Strange: Ressler actually enjoys the person he becomes in the company of his colleagues. He drops without thinking into a different personality with each—sardonic father to Lovering's brashness, clowning younger brother to Blake and Eva, sympathetic cousin to Woyty's low-grade paralysis, and child craftsman to Botkin's omnivorous intellect. With Cyfer's last member, Jeanette Koss, he somehow falls into awkward reserve. Not his ordinary, comfortable quiet, but incapacitating self-consciousness. Irritating to him and certainly confusing to the woman, who has gone out of her way to be pleasant.

It isn't her attractiveness that puts him off. Jeanette's features are not the sort that have ever threatened him. Her curves tend toward a topographical fullness he associates with varsity cheerleaders and nursing mothers. Those women who came closest to causing his own college coursework to suffer typically ran toward the homeless waif: You Can Save This Girl or You Can Turn the

Page. The taste may be consanguine, but was certainly in place before his mother was reduced to terminal spindliness by her 6.6.

To date, he has chosen to turn the page rather than save, although nights in the bunk in Stadium Terrace, in half-sleep, he regrets not having run the proffered experiment with a meager waif or two. These private nostalgias of desire reassure him that the clumsy cadences he suffers in random lab encounters with Dr. Koss are neither ugly nor unnecessarily indicting. He can't be hot for her. Not in so many words.

Yet it burns him to know nothing, to be in the dark about her except for the public-domain data that she is married and a few years his senior. He spends the first weekend in September raking up something substantive on her. Pickings are slim. He begs the superannuated department secretary on invented pretext to let him browse the staff files, but she will release no information without triplicate request from God.

He runs into Dr. Koss in the staff lunchroom. She smiles awkwardly at him over her coffee cup. "Keeping the head dry?" To collect himself, he smiles back, pretends to be looking for someone, and leaves. Shortly after, at a colloquium where she delivers a lucid contribution on punctuation theory, he thinks to address her in the hall, ask for clarification. But he falls back instead on skepticism: she could reveal nothing that experiment wouldn't expose more fully. He collars Blake, the closest thing he has to a confidant in the Midwest. "Dr. Toon. What do you make of the Koss comma-free code?"

"First-rate," Blake answers, grinning quizzically. "You?"

Too obvious an audit trail. Ressler swears off direct questioning and takes to the stacks. By summer's end, he has gotten adept at caterwauling down the catwalks, and the stink of binding paste no longer distracts him. He digs up her dissertation: "Simple Non-pathogenic Autosomal Mutations." He settles in for an evening with her apprentice piece. The woman describes some interesting mutagen manipulation. But the paper, while professional, contains little further interest beyond her education (Wesleyan and Cornell) and date of birth, February 14, 1929—St. Valentine's Day massacre.

A thorough search of the journals turns up references to her as coauthor on those Illinois publications Ressler already read before hitting campus. He falls back on the biographical compilations in the Reference Room, but turns up only her sterile university pro-

131

file. By chance, he finds a mention of her husband in the Local Interest area: a praise-laden entry on Koss, Herbert, in a chapbook, *Who's Who Around and About C-U*.

The fellow is a chemical engineer, a leader in local food technology. His chief contribution to the spiral of ingestibility: a superior method of getting the barbecue powder to stick to potato chips. The chapbook reports his guarded optimism on work toward a chip that will always come out of the bag intact. Their typical dinner conversation is too bizarre to consider. Battle Creek, the spoonful of frozen OJ, will never be the same.

Printed matter alone will not solve his Koss-word puzzle. As a result of killing a day and a half reading her thesis, he is unprepared to report on the article he's been assigned for the next Blue Sky. Ulrich calls on him to deliver. Ressler sputters; for the first time ever—as far back as first grade, when his teacher let him take over her abortive lesson on the language of bee dancing—he has come to class unprepared. He can admit to not having read the article, blowing his short-term credibility and profiting the team nothing. Or, knowing what he does about the authors' previously published research, the state of the art, and the article abstract, he can extrapolate a reasonable opinion. Not intellectual fraud, just the increasingly necessary short cut up the print mountain.

In the critical minute under the arc lights, Ressler decides that, Schrödinger notwithstanding, not talking about what he *can't* know doesn't in this instance preclude his talking about what he *doesn't*. He'll take a closer look at the article later that afternoon; if it should turn out that he's off base, he can give out his reconsidered opinion at the next session. Science is *about* reconsidering, revising one's position in the light of more light. He takes a breath. The description comes out easier than he thought. "I would say, tentatively, that we don't have to concern ourselves too much here with the Litner group's angle. It's ingenious in making the magic numbers fit; they get twenty out of four all right, but.... Well, I think they may be overlooking a few stereochemical constraints."

"For instance?" Ulrich looks up from scribbling, suddenly interested, choosing the worst possible moment to sit up and take notice. That's why Ulrich's in charge. Not because of the importance of his early work, but because of his intellectual aggression. Attentive, noisy, blunt: all dominant genes. The team leader hasn't shown half so much interest in Ressler's rate experiment as he shows in this almost irrelevant paper.

Ressler goes into a controlled stall. "I'd like another look at the piece before I commit, but. . . ." The whole team's attention is now alerted by that most expressive musical device, the rest. "Well, for instance . . . the article seems to me to be sidetracked on a code that isn't even colinear."

"Really?" An unexpected vocal timbre chimes in. "That's not how I read the principal thrust at all." A voice as mellifluous as a mortician's. He turns from his lame chalkboard illustration to see who could be so intent on sautéing him in public. The ID is more confirmation than discovery.

"Of course, if Dr. Koss can translate Litner's prose back into English, she's a better man than I."

The room, at a cusp of embarrassment, finds outlet in that remnant of violence, laughter. Lovering, nervous as the day Ulrich threw Salk in his stigmata, leads the way, letting loose a full-blooded cackle. Toveh Botkin, on the other hand, purses the notch above her lip crease, grim but forgiving the entire catalog of human failings. The deep-set, brown amusement of Dr. Koss's eyes flashes explicit warning: forced the issue? Gotten what you want?

Despite narrow escape, the incident humiliates him. In a few sentences, he has fallen monumentally in his own sight, if not in peer estimation. He wants only to quit this place, escape everyone, go punish himself. Succumbed to ridiculous, avoidable boy's self-deception. It disgusts him to replay the incident. Shame is not acid enough to eradicate it. Work is ruined for the remainder of the day. He smells his own unmistakable animal odor. Yes, those most capable of making some noise in the world are precisely those with the greatest capacity for shrugging off sin, for distributing their felonies sympathetically across the whole hinged circumstance of shameful existence. But in the face of his own weakness, he cannot see how to do it. The shame of false witness mars his perfect record, debases his currency. Misrepresentation of the facts: no more forgivable for being mundane. An indelible blot on the transcript: a Fail, invalidating all good faith.

Even by evening, he cannot shake the afternoon libel. He probes the ugly truth compulsively, unable to keep from picking at the wound. Far from salved by knowing how little consequence his minor lie carries, he is doubly appalled by how little it took to

133

make him lose his head. How little it would have taken to come clean, to ask for an absolution it would now shame him worse to go after.

Forgiveness requires not that he forget the crime but that he remember every other shame from his swelling past: the shop-lifted library book, the violated confidence of a friend, the broken crockery deceptively reassembled and left to break again at the next, innocent touch. Seamy little mazes of shame, not even respectably bourgeois, more disgusting for their avoidable petti-ness. He nurses the catalog, above all, this afternoon's grubby appendix. Contemptible desire to represent himself well. How much easier it would be to preempt the lie, come clean. And yet—the heart of the shame—he still could not, even now, if the whole scenario were his to correct, bring himself to reveal the real reason for his lack of preparation: I was digging up the goods on Mrs. Koss. Not even a matter of momentarily fouling the facts. He can't even bring himself to look at his motive in mucking about, much less confess it to others in good faith. He has shit on the truth.

An even more indicting memory reveals his betrayal. He re-calls, with sick precision, that day almost twenty years ago: first landmark of childhood, his seventh birthday. He awoke that morning with excitement that doubled when his father ex-plained that his present would arrive by parcel express. His par-ents' anxiety outstripped his own. Then, producing emotion difficult for a seven-year-old to grasp—awe, disappointment, alarm, thrill, and, even then, shame—the ruinously expensive set of encyclopedias arrived.

Stuart, with child's intuition, knew at once his parents' sacrifice in securing this gift. He understood the enormity the minute the delivery man arrived at the flat with four unliftable cases. He wanted to plead with them, "Oh, no, no thank you. You mustn't." Thirty inexhaustible volumes, a yearbook, and an index. His father calls to him in a voice that never rid itself of the scratch of factories, "Look here, the Ivory Coast. Isaac Newton. Phloem and Xylem. Everything worth knowing, in these pages. Alphabetical, too." Mother, father, and he sit together on the floor and unpack the treasure cases, poring over exotic entries the rest of the afternoon, the rest of remembered childhood.

An earlier edition had been heavily discounted, but Stuart's father had resolved on the most recent human understanding or none at all. His father never used the incurred debt, the years of resulting belt-tightening, against the boy. Stuart never gave him cause. The spines on every volume were broken within two years. The atlas of creases that formed along the binding—proof that the boy's precocity exceeded even his parents' guess—became his father's favorite feature of the set. He would run his fingers down the prematurely worn bindings on domestic evenings, saying, "It's all in there. Everything we've put together. Only a matter of learning how to get to it."

This is the ingenuous faith in accountability that Ressler has betrayed. For what? To keep himself from looking foolish in front of a woman for whom he cannot even plead the aberration of desire. Spirit-numbing memories follow one on another until he resurrects the summit agony. He was then twelve; the folks, years after purchase, still paying off the last encyclopedia installment. They had moved to Pittsburgh, "relocated," Dad explained, "for the War Effort." They were vacationing, camping in Maine, driving up the coast, when his father, at the wheel, in the middle of "Does Your Mother Know You're Out, Cecilia," slumped over in his seat. Stuart thought it a joke, laughed at the old man's slapstick.

But his father had suffered a massive myocardial infarction. Stuart's mother went instantly to pieces, as she could be counted on to do in the pinch of horror, the descent of real event. His father superhumanly managed to guide the car to the roadside. Stuart's mother could not have driven then even if she'd had a license. They were stranded in a remote stretch; hours might pass before they could flag a passerby. It fell to the twelve-year-old to drive them to hospital, while his mother flailed at her man's chest in a pointless effort to revive him.

From long afternoons browsing the encyclopedia paragraphs and plates, Stuart knew that the clutch was on the left and the accelerator on the right. Miraculously, from recall, he taught himself how to drive, covering the fifty miles to the hospital in two hours. Next to him on the front seat his mother huddled over the body, a perfect parody of the Michelangelo *Pietà* illustrating the article on Classical Sculpture. All the while, his father stupidly tried to get out last advice for the boy. Stuart repeatedly shouted at him to shut up, to save his strength.

He knows now what the man killed himself trying unsuccessfully to get out: How wonderful, to have had a child who might add to the endeavor. What a piece of work it all was. No sacrifice at all! Thirty volumes, a supplement, and an index. And all alphabetical.

This is what he's perjured. The world has grown another summer evening, one that seems the end of all summer evenings. He puts the *Young Person's Guide to the Orchestra* on the grinder. But neither the musical primer nor Olga's spinning convey anything to his leaden ear. Music fails him at the moment when he needs its compassion most. Autumn is here, an autumn that will spell the end of his front-lawn vigils. In town over two months; the pieces that hung so tantalizingly close to falling in place are farther now from linking than the day he arrived.

Already smelling the mixture of cold air and burning leaves that will mark the change of seasons, Ressler assigns himself penance, the only possible contrition. If one, clean, unimpeachable nugget lies anywhere within his ability to explicate, he will surrender it to Cyfer. First, the busywork rate experiment Ulrich has assigned him. Then, if chance favors, the simple laboratory technique for determining codon assignments, the leverage so agonizingly close that he can close his eyes and see it in the phosphene tracers on his lids. And not one discovery will be his.

However close he feels, he may never *be* any closer to the method than he is now, no closer than the baying kitchen mutt to the invading moon. His only means, not of adding his name to the volumes but of partially recovering perjured good faith, lies in returning to the puzzle, redoubling his efforts with focus so intense as to shame all effort he has yet made. He must place himself inside the isolated problem, feel its full, unrelenting force, cut himself off from rest, attach himself to the chance of not coming out, of never emerging from the search.

Another summer evening's knock at the door and Ressler assumes it is Tooney and Eva, through empathy of unpremeditated friendship, knowing to come and sit with him in his moment. The knock *is* them; humans are the only species that condition after one event. He stands, ready for companionship. He opens the door, jokingly asking Eva, "So what's the code for sickle-cell anemia?"

But it is not Blake or his remarkable Civil Service wife. In the doorframe stands the woman who set off this string of self-contempt. Out where the welcome mat should be, incomprehensible, stands short-sleeved, full-bodiced Dr. Koss.

Facts on File

I believe it because it's absurd: the entire *Britannica*—not to mention the stacks of my old branch as well as the entire Library of Congress—can in theory be encoded by a single notch on a rod. The whole human reservoir can be condensed to a single information-bearing groove with no loss of meaning. A trillion pages, the complete journey from Aardvark to Zygote and back, enpacked, retrievable, in a flick of a nick on a stick.

No high tech, no microengraving or fantastic manipulation of silicon. Just a twig, a pocket knife, and a grade-school ability with numbers. Any text, however long and complex, is a linear stream of characters. Letters, punctuation marks, typograhic symbols: fewer than a hundred types. Each of these hundred can be replaced by a unique three-digit number. Simple substitution cipher, the sort even small children use for urgent communications. Montaigne's brutal truth "If we saw as much of the world as we do not see..." becomes 131 006 222 023 005 222 019 001 023 222 001 019 222...

So far, even the mathless boy I loved with all my plaintext heart could take this message and, in minutes, reverse-engineer the meaning from the emotionless series. Digitization is now a commonplace, long since the stuff of grocery-line conversation. As goes Montaigne, so goes the whole *Britannica*: the entire set now represented by a huge stream of codon digits, a giant, linear, macromolecular, information-rich number.

Now the remarkable twist. If I run the triplets together and put a decimal point in front of the number, the result is a rational fraction running to millions of decimal places. But a fraction represents, and is represented by, a portion of any distance, say from one end of a stick to the other. My Montaigne number, .131006222023005222019001023222001019222..., along with my complete card box of quotes of the day for every day of the year attached to its tail, can now be committed to infinitesimally compact storage. I can incorporate my box of sayings in a discrete point a little farther than 13/100 of the way from tip to base. I might look at the mark from time to time, delighting in knowing that it encased the cycle of every famous saying ever to flesh out my calendar.

Alien, unnatural, counterintuitive. But analogous simplicity encodes a far more complex catalog. The map key, the compression that put life's *Britannica,* information intact, squarely in the palm of Ressler's hand, sweetly resembles that long, linear decimal.

Ressler himself worked out the math back in 1954, when the cell's translation game was fast becoming obvious. The math itself was easy: anyone with a little algebra could do it. DNA—a long, irregular decimal with A, T, G, and C as digits—consisted of innumerable bases lying in line on the inside twist of the helix. He had first to determine the width of the coding unit— how many digits of A, T, G, and C stood for one amino acid. This codon obviously had to be wider than one base. Codons one base wide could stand for only four different amino acids, and proteins required twenty. Two-base width allowed sixteen different codons:

AA AT AG AC TA TT TG TC GA GT GG GC CA CT CG CC

A vocabulary of sixteen was still four words shorter than required. Three successive rungs of the DNA ladder—sixty-four different combinations—at last produced enough codons to name all twenty aminos, with enough left over for start and stop codes or any other special symbols that protein-building might require. The triplet codon suffered an embarrassment of riches: forty-four more codons than amino acids. What to do with the extras became the sixty-four-codon-dollar question. More than one codon might stand for the same amino acid. Such code degeneracy might even carry potential survival value, as Ressler intuited early on.

In 1957, researchers learned how much easier it was to encode the *Britannica* than to experimentally extract from a given notched stick the particular *Britannica* it encoded. The giant informational molecule was the protein-constructing blueprint. The DNA base-pair sequences mapped out enzyme polypeptide chains. Ressler needed only intercept the map key. The unit word was a clump of at least three bases running along the half-DNA helix. No evidence strictly ruled out a larger codon, but most researchers applied the rule of parsimony. The next step was to determine exactly which triplet codon linked which amino acid to the enzyme under construction. Pure pattern-breaking attracted the lion's share of fascination: secret-message reading, ingenuity impeded by no encumbrance greater than paper and pencil.

The fearful symmetry of this structure gave a first glimpse of living logic. Ressler described to us the days on the threshold, poised on the brink of cracking the supreme philosophical crime novel. His voice rarely straying over the surrounding machine hum, he imparted his urgency for resolution. He compared his anxiety then to that anecdote about Bach entering a party where the harpsichordist broke off in terror at his arrival. The composer had to rush past his host to resolve the suspension with appropriate cadence before making his formal greeting.

"There had to be a surprising *aha*, a way we could get the cell to crack the code for us. That was my bias. It's pure torment to know that revolutionary, self-evident connections might be anywhere but here. We had no idea if a reliable method for determining codon assignments even existed. Some of us tried to tackle the problem theoretically, in ignorance of the data. On the other side of the tracks, retort heaters went about gathering data without grasping the formal problem. Like Brussels, Balzano: traffic signs so bilingually cluttered that neither camp could read them. My only advantage was that, fresh from school, I spoke just enough of both to put together something dangerous." He smiled weakly, at all that fluency hadn't prepared him for.

He told the story of a friend's short-lived glory. "Tooney Blake had been killing fifteen minutes before teaching his seminar. Doodling, he stumbled onto a stunning twist. How many one-base triplets were there? Four: AAA, CCC, GGG, and TTT. How many had only two identical bases? Four doubles times three in the last slot makes twelve. Triplets of three different bases produced four more combinations, ignoring order. He did the sum a dozen times: four plus twelve plus four, refusing to believe it added up to the magic number.

"Our chief immediately put him up for promotion. Others told him to save his scrap of work paper. Even interest in his piano playing revived. We were all so intoxicated by the dead-on simple fit that we overlooked, for weeks, the fact that Tooney's model treated the codons AGG, GAG, and GGA identically. At last one of us came to his senses and pointed out that such codons could not possibly be read the same. Tooney took the setback in stride, but others wanted to pursue the prettiness, even in the face of evidence."

Parsing was all-important. If the codons in the string

ACGGATCTAGACCT...

did not overlap, then the triplets separated:

ACG GAT CTA GAC...

But if every codon shared two bases with each neighbor, the same string would group into entirely different words:

ACG CGG GGA GAT ATC TCT CTA TAG...

This full overlap packed more information into each DNA half-strand but attached restrictions on the ordering of code words. The beauty of Gamow's diamond code lent early favor to overlap models. When his scheme failed to comply with experiment, Gamow withdrew it but suggested another full overlap in its place. But by 1957, such schemes had been all but discarded. In full overlap, every individual base appears in two adjacent codons:

CGAT → CGA GAT → x-y

A mutation altering the single base G would change *both* codon words, and thus both amino acids x and y in the synthesized enzyme. Even single mutations would then produce at least two amino acid divergences. Yet Ingram's famous sickle-cell hemoglobin structure differed from normal hemoglobin by only one amino. This argument damning full overlap contained the germ of an elegant and overlooked idea. A mutation, traced from nucleic acid to that text's observable protein translation, might be the leverage needed to manufacture a rosetta. The code could be cracked by tracing how it read its message's errors. One of the most powerful ideas in the infant science: the power of the traceable, testable blit. If the string itself was too complex to read, a small mistake in it might nevertheless show up as a discernible, translated difference.

Error lay at the source of all change, all species experiment. It was the author of all the still emerging, undesignable variations on life. Ressler's gift lay in understanding that he stood on the threshold not just of uniting chemistry with inheritance, but of joining these both to the grandiose Darwinian mutation. Tiny, cumulated, field-tested errors were all that accounted for the change from one species to another—a half-dozen chromosomal inversions between us and the nearest ape. Advance by analogy: induce a small alteration, note what value the process assigns that one ripple. The most baldly obvious idea imaginable. Yet as that most quotable biologist J. B. S. Haldane, instrumental in linking population genetics to evolution, who attributed all sonnet-writing to the microscopic speck of sex chromosome, once said: "It is, in my opinion, worth while devoting some energy to proving the obvious."

Today in History

Although I still lived in the height of summer, the days had already gone into gradual decline, at first unfelt, then undeniable, shuttling back to their opposite number. The longest day of the year is also the day diminishing sets in. In 1983, I lagged behind the official sunset posted in the almanac. As late as September, I felt the expectation brought on by sky remaining light late into evening.

Like the student who in the course of a perfunctory thesis finds a remarkable, forgotten book, I took possession of my discovery. Dr. Ressler worked his way into my daily conversation. In a slow period at the Reference Desk, I asked my colleague Mr. Scott what he knew about mutation dating. He had a master's in anthro, which suddenly seemed to me a half brother to genetics by incest. He put his fatherly arm around me and said, "Dear, I'm afraid M.S. in my case stands for Mostly Sketchy." He proposed that general imbecility might be reduced if people had to renew their diplomas the way they had to renew driver's licenses. "It wouldn't make anybody smarter. But it might slow the nonsense glut."

Not even Mr. Scott's cynicism checked my new rhythm. For events, I turned with increasing frequency to breakthroughs in science. The Question Board tracked an influx of interest in patented life. An anonymous submission of a simple penny-flipping brain teaser launched me into an aside on evolutionary statistics. A question about regional dialect differences between sodas, tonics, floats, milk shakes, frappes, jimmies, and sprinkles led me into linguistic drift and a sketch of the Sapir/Whorf hypothesis that regional word-tools predispose ways of thought.

I'd caught a salubrious dose of curiosity about the live-in puzzle

141

from nothing more than meeting a man who had retreated from it. I must have been waiting for the slightest push, for when it came, I jumped. A dozen visits to the night hermitage and the human program took on conspiratorial beauty. The science of inherited characteristics was only my jumping-off metaphor, an entrée into what until then had been neutral material. I felt the air of a new planet, the hint of unexpected links leading somewhere, things about to be revealed. I shed the curatorial, began to sense the impenetrable mechanism of mystery. Plainly put, when I woke up each morning, I knew where I wanted to be.

I had no idea whether my enthusiasm for their company was returned any way but politely. I only knew that when I visited MOL, in the presence of those two, I discovered my own powers of talk, undetected all these years. Real work was still in front of me. I had been only been resting, gathering strength for an act of connection about to become clear.

The rush of anticipation of those days lent even the most prosaic routine an edge I had forgotten. My exhilaration began to overstep propriety, at least by librarian's standards. In answering a three-by-five barely able to mask its terror about whether "secular humanism" wasn't a textbook-poisoning of the six-day wonder, I summarized the Supreme Court majority opinion, followed with *Religio Medici,* the Doctor's religion, and wound up with Haldane: asked what his work in life science had taught him about God, he'd replied that the Creator showed an inordinate fondness for beetles.

I received a formal reprimand. Unable to take the matter seriously, I replied that my answer contained no intended cheek. I was notified by committee that nihilism was out of line. I couldn't believe my ears. Haldane's beetle sass, so far from the opposite of nihilism, reveled in the force and grandeur of accidental creation, a creation following rules more remarkable than we ever assigned any Maker. The incident blew over, leaving invisible scar tissue; the hurt of misconstrual left me a little more eager for that somewhere else that MOL began to open up for me.

Within a few weeks I became a fixture in the deserted office suite. In the first throes of addiction, I saw that converted warehouse as the last endangered habitat left in my part of the world. Magic visits left me impatient when I wasn't there. And when I was, the lost digital domain filled me with anticipation. Something was at last about to happen. Something not in the least expected.

Inexplicable: how a room of indifferently calculating machines and two men on the *beau geste* shift keeping watch over nocturnal computations could stir in me anticipation profound enough to derail a life that had worked comfortably for years. I didn't know what reservoir they tapped in me, what primitive string vibrated in sympathetic resonance. And I didn't care to know.

There was the obvious explanation, of course. But an objective female jury would waffle between Todd and Tuckwell for raw desirability. Todd had the undeniable advantage of being *new:* his hair fell an unusual way across his temples, and I could watch for hours while his eyes modulated. Even level-headed women are programmed to spread themselves through every available back-water of the gene pool. At thirty, though, lust is no longer the giddy-maker it once was. Hormones will have the upper hand over me until their manufacture stops. But Todd's appeal—the reason I began to watch the library clock—was something else as well. From the moment I arrived at the MOL intercom to be buzzed in, he would pay steady flirtation. "What did we answer today? Wait, let me guess: the name for the plastic end-seals on shoe laces. No, no: how many wheelbarrows of Weimar marks it took to buy a loaf of bread." Tuckwell's manic humor made me laugh out loud. Todd's jokes, always *sotto voce,* made me ache with wanting.

He ran a continuous interrogation; I stood between him and the world. Frank's questions had nothing to do with empirical fact. His were amorphous, soft around the edges. We would sit in the corporate cafeteria while he, with a favorite skillet ported from his apartment, grilled an omelette with mace and cardamom for 9:00 p.m. early brunch. Out of the blue, he would ask, "Did you get along well with your parents?"

I'd do my best to look abashed, but he refused to let me off. Whether I answered in earnest or replied, "What's it to ya, Bud?" he would smile, ply me with requests for intimate details, and then reveal the hidden association. "These eggs, this aroma: my father's Saturday-morning ritual. Complex man, my father. Invested thirty-two hundred dollars—half his life's savings—when I was born, so there'd be something to send me to college on. When I came of age, through amazing business acumen, he had nursed the invest-ment to a grand total of twenty-nine hundred dollars. Every Sat-urday of conscious existence, he woke us up with the aroma of omelette. All we need is a little Coleman Hawkins. Loved music, my father. Brought me up to play the accordion. 'You can always make a living with one of these.'" Then, quick key change: "Could you fall for a man who played the accordion in his youth?"

The hopeless second question was indistinguishable from the misplaced, expansive first. He did not ask whether *I* could fall for *him*. He asked me to savor a sad hypothetical, a current of circumstantial strangeness. He carried on like this—questions, stories, self-absorbed silences—nothing to lose and everything to gain; pushing past the normal politeness of terms. His constant word-wayfaring was all the more romantic because it never struck him as anything but ordinary. He read wildly, at random. Dostoyevsky one weekend and *Little Women* the next. "Have you read this? God, it's beautiful! Let me read you one passage." And one passage would inevitably grow into a chapter and more, Todd reading on expressively, obliviously, for forty minutes, stopping only to feed a punched-card deck into the hopper. I didn't mind; I could spend all evening watching the further hope and hurt that all manner of words registered in his reading face. I had forgotten how one could live on just words.

Manhattan On-Line was my enclave, safe haven in the middle of nowhere. I could walk into the warehouse, summon the rickety, trapezoidal elevator, ride to an upper room where all the windows were silvered over, showing nothing of the outside but a crystal diffraction pattern of night lights—the sparkle of Whistler's nocturne. To drop out of the inescapable city from a trapdoor in its middle was like discovering a geothermal jungle at the pole that had somehow evaded all the search algorithms of man, even the ridiculously detailed eye-in-the-sky satellite maps.

MOL took me temporarily through the forgotten gate to a platform *outside,* a fulcrum. Todd became an oasis of companionship, refuting and strange. His thought was profoundly different, but not so foreign that I required an interpreter. He was capable of endless inventive talk about any subject. "You know what Nietzsche says? He says, 'Oy, this headache!' No, really. He says: if two people are going to get married, they ought above all to be able to talk well to one another. Because everything else disappears."

But Tuckwell and I could talk too, before I killed our conversation. Keith was very bright, peripherally alert. If he had lost the ability to surprise me, he could still keep me honest. But his job, his view of people, his life in the city had cut a rift between us, a gulf of getting and spending. Tuckwell was an adman, I a librarian. Should never have happened in the first place. However implausibly long our contract had lasted, all I had left to give Tuckwell was my departure. But on ambivalent days, when I remembered the woo we two too had started with, even that idea seemed rationalization.

The man I lived with, well-adjusted ambassador of urban neuroticism, used sardonic salesmanship to rouge the bruise of living here. Todd, Keith's maladjusted obverse, was sick at heart from believing that men could live in this grisly grid system as they once lived in Bruges. And yet that sad, protective urge—his coming to me to save a man already beyond repair—drew me out. I thought—incredible vanity!—I might keep him company.

"So what do all these boxes do?" I asked one night after we had solved the crossword together. We had been sitting for some time in the hum that passed for silence when I realized I still didn't know what all the equipment was.

Todd looked affectionately around the room. "My babies? Bookkeeping, mainly. Hey. Might that be the only word in English with three consecutive double letters?"

"How should I know? Stick to the point." But he was already on the phone to Dr. Ressler in the control room. Todd waved to his superior, although we could not see through the one-way glass whether the other waved back.

"The professor'll write a search routine for other triple doubles and run it on the dictionary file. Where were we?"

"Your babies."

"I call them that? Perverse. In any case, we, if I can use first person plural for a group I've only seen assembled once in my life, are what are obnoxiously called Information Brokers. A fuzzy concept. Close as I can tell, it means we provide data and services to other folks—some permanent clients, some steady customers, and a few one-shot users. I'm forbidden by Scout's honor to tell you their names, but I could spell out initials. Alternately, you could infer them through Twenty Questions."

"That's OK. I get the idea. What data do you sell?"

"Who wants to know?" He looked around furtively. "Well, we have two general categories up for auction. First, the standard numbers racket. Big-time data processing. Receivables, Payables, Ledgers, and Payrolls for a dozen credit unions, even a state office." I gathered this was the daily, repetitive processing that made up the bulk of his evening. "Second, the piece sales. Our list-crunching spins off information that either these clients, or others by the

145

same name, are willing to spend major world currencies for. Any-thing from mailing lists to...." He shrugged, suggesting that no enumeration could catch all the categories, cross-references, or calculations someone somewhere might find useful.

"The truth is, I'm not supposed to know myself who we render what services to. This whole outfit is run on distributed ignorance. A little like civics. Day and night shifts work in separate memory partitions. Analysts aren't allowed in programmers' area. Program-mers are locked out of Operations. The hardware guys are not permitted in the listings library. The software guys can't touch the machines. As an Operator, I'm not even supposed to know *how* to program. Barefoot, preggers, and harmless. But the professor has taught me a little." His face reflected that truism about the danger of a little knowledge. "COBOL's a piece of cake. No con-jugations, no cases, no inflections. Fortunately for me, I didn't mention language skills on my application."

"Officially, then, what do you do?"

"As little as possible, as you must have noticed." He took me on a second tour, one that made more sense to me now that I had visited the place a few times. "Think of us as pure functionaries. Wednesday's core routine never changes from week to week. We check the chart, any special jobs left by the day shift, drop the right card deck in the hopper, answer the questions on the screen...." He smiled empathetically. "At certain places during the run, we have to change the printer to multipart or forms. You know all those financial statements you get every day instead of letters from friends? Well, now you can think of them as personal communiqués." I wanted all of a sudden to wrap him in my arms, but because we had not yet jumped that threshold, I contented myself with pinching his shoulder.

"Then, we have to swap out packs on the drive spindles." He let me have another look into the locked bakery of magnetic layer cakes. "Each of these contains a whole shelf full of *your* pitiful excuse for a library. A group of programs or a set of data files. 'The Clients.' A hundred thousand names, but it's easy to fall into the singular. 'Put that Client up on spindle three.' Almost as ridiculous as using 'Washington' or 'Moscow' to stand for a quarter billion."

Nor was metonymy his only professional figure of speech. He called up files, spoke to the console, shook hands with peripherals, woke or retired a system partition. Programs ran and processors crunched. Names were fields and fields made up records and records were data and data came in streams, packets, or blocks. An unassuming word like "overlay" served as noun, verb, adjective, adverb, and probably preposition on a good day. The whole sport made Shakespeare's functional shifts seem like small-time word processing. Up time and down time, hot, warm, and cold boots, and the apocalyptic-sounding full system crash.

"If the runner stumbles or falls . . . then the fun starts. We're just supposed to check the hardware and resubmit the aborted job. If it aborts again, and we're sure it's not a paper jam or the wrong pack or something equally imbecilic, we're supposed to dial the field service men—the Green Berets. Big salaries, twenty-four-hour beepers. But those guys are obnoxious, and in hexadecimal to boot. So Dr. Ressler and I have gone in for a little underground education in differential diagnosis.

"Every job we submit, every command we issue, is written into a console log. Fortunately, nobody reads them. They hang in the listings library, gathering digital dust. If anybody took half a look at some of the operations we've performed to keep things running at night, we'd be in a heap of hot floppies." He shrugged. "I work. I follow the list, the flowchart. The key to the entire process, from beginning to end, even the exception handling is specifiable by exact rules. One need only know the context. Not unlike chore-ography, I suppose. 'Two pas-de-bourrées, a ball-change.' But the bit of chenille fluff in the chorus never gets to see what all that spinning is all about. It'll be Robo City in here in another few years," he said, with serve-them-right enthusiasm at the prospect. "The only thing that's prevented their introduction until now is the superstition that humans are still the only thing capable of surviving the system crash. Also, the Doctor and I are still cheaper, for the time being."

We sat in front of the console and stared at the equipment, now completely changed. The phone rang, disturbing the empty hiss. I thought: Here is one of the few places where a phone call late at night doesn't automatically mean someone has died. Todd an-swered. "That was Dr. Ressler. 'Bookkeeper' is unique. And so, my friend, is your face." I smiled, already skilled at letting his moments of confrontatory zeal fall away without crisis. "What do I do for a living? I'm not sure the question has an answer anymore. Everyone, no matter what he does, is kept in the dark about the clients."

This was the moment of expansiveness that brought me com-pulsively to Manhattan On-Line to sit with this stranger after my own shift was over. "Do you know Ben Shahn's great answer to that question? I take a guilty pleasure in the man's paintings, knowing his whole pastel, representational aesthetic has been on the outs for a decade. But his essays need no excuse. He tells a story of an itinerant wanderer traveling over country roads in thirteenth-century France who comes across a man exhaustedly pushing a wheelbarrow full of rubble. He asks what the man is doing. 'God only knows. I push these damn stones around from sunup to sundown, and in return, they pay me barely enough to keep a roof over my head.'

"Farther down the road, the traveler meets another man, just as exhausted, pushing another filled barrow. In reply to the same question, the second man says, 'I was out of work for a long time. My wife and children were starving. Now I have this. It's killing, but I'm grateful for it all the same.'

"Just before nightfall, the traveler meets a third exploited stone-hauler. When asked what he is doing, the fellow replies, 'I'm building Chartres Cathedral.'"

Home Fires

We weren't involved. I simply wanted to spend my free minutes in Franklin's company. Sitting with him while he worked felt like repatriation. Franklin, remarkably, found nothing unusual in my overnight fixation with this place. He treated both my forwardness and reserve with the same easy touch. His intimacy could go on at arm's length forever.

I felt so awake, so ready to resurrect old steps and learn new ones I'd given up on. Remorse only came when I felt how blameless I was feeling. Guilt worked its way in, however. Romance at thirty is shot through with ambivalence. I was too old to think that my liberating happiness with Todd justified putting Keithy to the torch. The pleasure I felt in Frank's company was already compromised, and I could calculate no future payoff worth the surcharge needed to reach it. But bad conscience is one of those parasites that makes its host hungrier.

The evenings when I took the detour home produced a chunk of hours I had to account for. Tuckwell's and my relationship always pretended to place no bind on one another. But even Keith's cultivated obliviousness soon gave in to curiosity. For a while I got by on transparent excuses. The irregularity of my work covered somewhat, made Keith lose track of when I would ordinarily have come home.

Hard to confess anything when I had nothing yet to confess. I had no hope of explaining to Keith a fascination I didn't understand myself. Keeping quiet, on the other hand, was evasion, and I never could skulk for long. Crawling into bed one night after my embarrassingly late return, Keith and I outdoing the other in liberal tolerance, I resolved to come clean, although I still didn't know what that meant. Copying Todd's blunt trust in words, I stoked up to make a clean break. "I've made a few friends." I thought once I got going, I could imitate Frank's easy jig. But after those six quavers, I softened the contour of the line. "Eccentrics," I added, choosing the perfect word to render them harmless. It suddenly seemed self-indulgent to concern Tuckwell with exaggeration.

My time with Keith, if increasingly infringed on, remained unchanged in all respects but the important one. We still lazed together in the front room with the panoramic vista over the river. We still watched the nightly news together. We still needled one another with need. One early September evening, out of remorse and nostalgic love, I decided to stay home. Tuckwell lay spread across the floor with a portfolio, testing out jingles on me while I did my next day's homework. Keith was building a truly bizarre strategy for selling microwave gourmet meals, using an ad I had discovered in the September 18, 1939, issue of *Time:* "Hitler Threatens Europe—but Betty Havens's Husband's Boss Is Coming to Dinner and *That's* What *Really* Counts." I had shown it to him to make him laugh, something I'd done precious little of lately. But he'd latched onto it as the perfect piece of camp with which to run a retro sales pitch. "Sick sells," he lay on his back repeating. "Not a pretty fact. But then, persuasion is not a pretty business."

I wrapped up a few loose questions. I'd chosen, for tomorrow's event, the September 3 in that year when there was no September 3: in 1752, when Britain and colonies at last adopted the Gregorian calendar. By official decree, September 3 became September 14— correcting the eleven-day disparity that had accumulated between man-made time and the seasons. As had happened elsewhere in Europe as days disappeared into nothing, the reform was met by rioting. People's already too-short lives were cheated of yet another eleven days: vanished anniversaries, lost evenings at the pub, almost a dozen nights of potential pleasure. Paid by the hour but debited by the month, tenants paid thirty days of rent on nineteen.

The nightly news was over, the set turned off, but the evening's sound track—Bartók's *Piano Music for Children*—still hobbled over fourths and minor seconds, relating strange Hungarian folktales. I closed my eyes: the music was about a forest deep in Eastern Europe where night had fallen for several hundred years. I opened them again to find Tuckwell still sprawled across the throw rug, happily destroying the evening paper. I loved the man, stayed with him because, for a manic narcissist with a fierce death wish, Keith was relatively sedate and regular in habits.

Tuckwell stood, stretched, groaned like a compromised banshee, and went and pestered the human being nearest at hand. He came over to the makeshift typing table where I worked, lifted the hair off the nape of my neck, and bit the revealed skin. Choosing not to notice how wrong the moment had become, he asked, "'Sappening?"

I pulled the first card off of the unanswered pile. Not daring to look at him, I pitched my voice into soprano and inhaled. "'Why did the Russians shoot down that airliner? Hundreds of innocent people killed. Will somebody please explain this to me?' Signed, 'A.N., 9/14.'" Facing the far wall, I monotoned, "What you got on Flight 007 today, Chet?"

"Not a whole hell of a goddamn lot, David," Tuckwell replied, but returned to the papers to see what he could dig up. I drafted answers in my head, one filled with accounts of warning shots and tape transcripts, one beginning "Discrepancies in what the interceptor saw and what the liner did persist," still another urging the questioner to read everything printed on the incident. Not one reply satisfied.

I was cut by a sharp grief, not for the 269 latest casualties in the perpetual war, but for A.N., who didn't have a chance in creation of getting a simple explanation for what was going on. It was a reasonable question, but as with the tacit prices on Upper East Side menus, if you had to ask, you couldn't afford the answer. The horrible full-color spreads, the antiseptic seal torn off of the usually restrained AP reports, the resulting global knee-jerk calling for a full accounting on the part of anonymous trigger-pullers everywhere: and then the veil of routine slamming back, once more condemning A.N. to the bewilderment of local life, while Here and Now squidded off in a cloud of ink until the next liner was downed.

Sadness doesn't capture it. I need a meatier, nineteenth-century word. Sorrow; the sorrow of press secretaries failing to explain away nations. When I looked at Tuckwell, news scrap over his lap, my sorrow grew. For the two of us—our last, ordinary evening at home. I whispered, "What in the hell am I supposed to tell this guy?" Alarming Keith more than I had in all our years of living together, I burst out in violent crying. I let Keith comfort me, talk me into giving up on answering, calling it a day. He led me into our bedroom, where he pried the typed card out of my hand and laid it to rest on the night table. It still sat there unanswered days later, on the equinox. The first day of autumn in anyone's calendar.

VIII

After the Facts

The dead airplane passengers were still on the night table on September 23. Relations with Keith hadn't steadied in the interim. There were light moments—hours as free as any we'd had. We laid into the old conversational cadences, careful to avoid irritation. But chain jumped off sprocket at the least torque. Something caused one of us to miss the pickup, and we'd be off, attacking one another in the highly civilized diction of private symbols that had caused the hurt in the first place.

Tuckwell came to bed on the first night of autumn, excited by the growing cold. I could feel in the choreography of muscle contractions his hope for a reconciling predoze fondle. He maneuvered tentatively, afraid to ask outright for a touch I might deny him. How dare he protect himself from me, blame me for refusing? Slowly enough to be above reproach, I removed by millimeters to my side of the bed. Sheer perversity; how far away did I need to be before he asked me to return?

We lay in bed, outraged in every idiom short of English. Neither of us could break the escalation of accusal. Keith flicked on the reading light and directed the spot to his side. Even politeness was a threat—the effort he took not to disturb me. He reached out for his night reading but grabbed the question about Flight 007. He slammed the card down on the nightstand. "Can we get rid of this shit, please?" he whispered, so as not to wake anyone. "I'm sick of looking at it." He went to the kitchen to fish the day's newspapers from the trash. He returned, crumpled a couple sheets for my benefit, and read: "Reasonable prospect of Navy finding black box.

Russians are sweeping for it in force. Seen dragging something out of the waters. Widespread agreement that the 747 had been over Kamchatka for some time."

I grabbed the gap widening in my face and pinched it shut, pushed it into my pillow. I turned my face sideways, an efficient crawl-swimmer coming up for air. "All right, Keith. OK."

"OK what?" Nonnatives would have heard no rage.

"OK, I'll fabricate some sort of centrist smear for this person. *Face the Nation*. Whatever you want."

"What I want is not the point. Who said anything about smear? Why doesn't this person do her *own* work? What does she want *you* to do, paraphrase the same pap she can read herself? Cliff Note the mound of crap it's already buried in?" Typical Tuckwell: whenever he attacked me, he worked around until it seemed his one wish was to protect me from assault.

"Just the opposite," I addressed the ceiling. "She wants me to shovel her out." Covered in cotton and clichés, I molded myself into the shape of the offending shepherd's crook, facing the wall. As soon as he was out of my field of view, Keith seemed the most decent human being alive, susceptible to the best of excesses. I felt him get back into bed and switch off the light. After a moment, unasked-for, denying that the flare-up had happened, he molded his body along mine. We lay flush, curled, the two fastened alloys in a thermostat coil. I neither shook Tuckwell off nor returned his pressure. If I didn't move, I might be able to drift off despite myself. But not moving only aggravated the drag holding me against the bed.

We were both in absurd occupations; that was the problem. But pressed, I couldn't place the standard blame on the office for ruining my private life. I had only myself to fault. I repeated silently, like a Baltimore catechism—*Q: Who made you? A: God made me. Q: Why did God make you? A: To know, love, and serve Him in this life and be happy with Him in the next*—the one question in recent weeks I'd managed to answer definitively: "Q: How do you get moonlight into a chamber?"

The next day, behind the Reference Desk, I typed a long, inconclusive response to Flight 007. My mind was not on the victims or the absurd geopolitics, but on the man I was downing with my own absurdity. Every time I concluded that Tuckwell and I were genuinely ill-fitted—that we'd forced ourselves together for years because we were the age when more exploration is no longer cost-efficient—I recoiled, knew I was rationalizing my own new side romance.

I could no longer tell failed imagination from realism. The day I admitted that life with Tuckwell had lost itself to familiarity, I also felt an urge to run for the crosstown and gate-crash Tuckwell's familiar office just to see him. His most irritating habit, the asymmetry of his sternum, his stupidest mannerism, the white spots under his fingernails, had been fashioned exclusively for me, and I had failed to value them.

I came home that evening intent on redeeming myself. Like a literalist from a liturgy, or coed from a cathartic feature film: nothing more important, easier than being a little kinder. Keith must have felt something similar, for we collided at the door and kissed without a crackle of static. He let me fondle him, then slipped his arm around me. He brought me to the panorama plate glass running the length of the living room. We looked down on the same life-threatening street I had just threaded. The view from here had nothing to do with the one at eye level. "Q:," he said, shaking me affectionately.

"Shoot." We laughed off the bad word choice.

"Is the world getting any better? K.T., 9/23." Last night's fight was just passing madness, the end of a fiscal quarter.

"Every day in every way," I said, silently struck by how little the billion-dollar self-help industry had changed in the half century since Coué.

"The eradication of smallpox and polio," Tuckwell offered.

"Large-scale dismantling of the old colonial system," I added. "Fiberoptics. Wide-body transport."

"The New York Mets. Frisbees." A sad joke, but our own. Keith dragged me to the kitchen in his wake. The place was a riot of dissolute Baggies and lidless jars. He was preparing my favorite of his private recipes, Neutron Chili. Beating me to the peace offering. We worked together; I spiced and stirred while he sliced and carried on a running burlesque. "I was a very ethnic child. Born into a mixed neighborhood. Democrats and Republicans...." We had both hit upon the same solution: all-out effort to save the endangered ordinary routine by doing nothing.

"Perhaps I shouldn't reveal this to you," he said, thrashing in a cabinet above the stove, "seeing as how you're in a perfect position to abuse the information. But the key to really profound chili is

154

this." He held aloft a nickel bag of cumin that had somehow evaded the Board of Health. He made for the stove, playfully chucking me out of the way.

"Keithy, stop. Wait a minute. Listen. I already put in two table-spoons of...."

"Geet otter here. What do you know from chili?" He blithely measured what he called a "guesstimate" into the stew.

"Tuckwell!" Shrill enough to draw him up short, but too far. I tripped a surprise rage in myself and could not back down. "Who do you think...? What right do you...?" I froze in his gaze: he had every right. I began again, unnerved. "Don't you think you ought to at least taste before you interfere?" Ludicrous; it was his recipe.

Still clutching the cumin, Tuckwell tried to salvage the moment. "Two people who love each other," he began mock-pompously, "who sincerely want to bridge the solitude surrounding each one of us ought to display an unwavering, unqualified trust for every-thing the other takes into mind to do. A woman, for instance, should be able to sacrifice a meal to her man's screwing about with the same abandon that Abraham exhibited in prepping the pot for Isaac, even in the knowledge that no ram will be waiting in the bushes when he hacks things up. You, for instance, should be able to watch me take this entire bag...." He started off com-ically, but quickly fatigued: if he joked me out of this, the next repair would be even more strained. I apologized, told him to do as he saw fit, and left. I looked back as I shut the front door to see Tuckwell spicing the meal for one.

Music Minus One

Jeanette Koss crosses the threshold. Ressler can neither prevent nor welcome her. Still she comes, eyes marking an astonished arc at the monkish sparsity, asceticism that registers in her eyes. Only when she leans against a wall in a girlish slump does he collect himself. "What in the world are *you* doing here?"

She takes the Ur-punchline, jutting one arm over her head and slithering a side step. "The samba." Slowly, sadly, she sings, "When you can't reproduce 'cause you've lost all your juice, It's Your Birthday," to the tune of "That's Amore," inflicting no apparent damage on the meaning of the chord progressions. She stops and examines Ressler, as if the burden of explanation rests squarely on him.

"But it's not my birthday. Not for a while." He feels his stupidity the instant he objects.

"It isn't? Damn! All the numerology worked out perfectly! Back to codon triplets for me. Here. I brought you a present anyway." She holds out a wrapped phonograph record tentatively, reluctant to give it up. Not knowing what else to do, Ressler unwraps the gift. It's a two-year-old recording of Bach's *Goldberg Variations* in a debut performance by a pianist who has the bad taste to be both as Canadian as Avery and a shade younger than Ressler. "I'm sorry if the surface is a little ground to death already. But I thought you deserved something better in life than bobby-soxers and Britten."

Ressler flinches at Koss's inside knowledge. Blake and Eva? Is that friendship, then, cozy nights made public? He wonders if this woman might also be privy to the fact that he's been afraid to put Robeson on in recent weeks. He stands paralyzed, unable to extricate himself. "I don't understand. What is this?"

"It's a record," she replies, a pouty, apologetic smile at having to do all the vaudeville. "You put it on that machine and music comes out." She lowers her arm, still thrust in pseudo-samba, and sits cross-legged on the floor in front of the loan sofa. She places her neck against the cushion, tilts her head, and lets her face go as slack as a sunbather's. She is perfectly at home in their mutual ignorance.

Ressler considers his options: deterrence has failed, and it is too late for a preemptive strike. His only chance to get his balance depends on giving Dr. Koss her own terms. He goes to the phono; for the first time since he bought her, Olga spins without a suggestion of complicity. He removes the record from its worn cardboard, experiencing difficulty finding side one. "Is your husband dropping by as well?" He tries for a neutral lilt.

"My husband doesn't care much for music. What Mr. Koss has no interest in could fill symposia." She faces him, equal parts coy, ashamed. His first good look at her. She is more juvenile, lighter than in profile. She gesticulates for him to hurry and get the music on: Why do you think I've come all the way here?

There is nothing to do except release side one, track one. He touches the needle down on the *Goldberg* aria. The first sound of the octave, the simplicity of unfolding triad initiates a process that

156

will mutate his insides for life. The transparent tones, surprising his mind in precisely the right state of confusion and readiness, suggest a concealed message of immense importance. But he comes no closer to naming the finger-scrape across the keys. The pleasure of harmony—subtle, statistical sequence of expectation and release—he can as yet only dimly feel. But the first measure announces a plan of heartbreaking proportions. What he fails to learn from these notes tonight will lodge in his lungs until they stop pumping.

If the night is complete and the train of notes advances with certainty, even formal symmetry can grow as inevitably as a living thing. The fragmented melody, the decorated trickle coming from the speakers, the lights across the dark yard (so many ships' distress signals), the pile of slip-delineated journals swelling in the corner into an unassailable fairy-tale hill of glass, the foreign woman sitting cross-legged on the floor not three meters away: everything aims this moment, indistinguishable and arbitrary, at his heart. This fluke, beautiful assortment says they are here alone. Certainly a message: the sentient musical line makes that explicit. A messenger, undeniably, at the piano. But no sender. No sponsor. Only notes, vertically perfect, horizontally inevitable.

Prompted by the aria's first octave, he at once looks through an electron microscope at a moment he will never afterwards succeed in recreating. How can he *say* what he hears? He hears a melody (it can't quite be called that) ornamented, sighing in appoggiaturas (he has never heard the word), making its stately way into frilly irrelevance. He hears something else, something substantial underneath the period piece: a bass line as patterned as the orbit of seasons, fueled by the inexorable self-burning at the core of stars.

While right hand tentatively ascends and turns, left descends in nothing more ingenious than a major scale. What could be simpler? Four scale-steps descend from Do, answered by three rising tones before a temporary return home. The aria travels only eight measures, but Ressler has come far farther. He skids across epochs, shaking loose time. The ditty insinuates itself through the most unassuming thirty-two measures imaginable: a third group of four notes is answered by a fourth, these eight together meta-echoing the initial eight. This four-by-four megameasure is answered in turn by a further sixteen—a hierarchy where each internal rung is reflected at a higher level. A pulse, a row of tones, a magic square sprung from four letters: its Pythagorean perfection holds the hint

157

of proliferation, celestial blowout of uncountable possibilities.

The scientist, until this moment incapable of hearing that every song on *Summer Slumber Party* derives from the same 1–4–5 progression as "Red River Valley," can hear in this spare, fourfold pattern potential beyond telling: answers and calls, inversions, oppositions, expansions, contractions, dissonances, resolutions. He hears all these hiding in a tune so simple it cannot in truth even be called a tune. And the variations themselves haven't even begun.

How can haphazard nubbiness of grooves pressed into synthetic polymer, read and converted into equivalent electric current, passed through an electromagnet that isomorphically excites speaker paper, sucking it back and forth in a pulsing wave that sets up a sympathetic vibration in thin, skin membrane tickling electrical nerve-bursts simulate not only all the instruments of the orchestra but this most cerebrally self-invested device, the hammer-struck, vibrating string? God only knows what those string vibrations themselves equate to. But the pattern means something: he's sure of that. And if he lets what these signal notes conceal fall back into the obscurity they have momentarily raised themselves from, a vast tract of unsuspected existence will disappear, vanish along with this woman when she stands up to leave.

Underneath the *Goldberg* aria's graceful surface is a skeleton, a stripped-down fragment, a moment not even a moment, a melody not yet the essential one. The real melody, the one that will pass with that trivial bass line through thirty wildly varying but constant mutations, is the accompaniment of desire and remorse in Ressler's listening. That bass is a mere crystal, periodic, irregular. Like all crystal instants, it seeps in both directions, back into imprecise memory of childhood and forward, in a rush of premonition, to the logical consequence of its opening phrases, an adulthood entirely unanticipated. It encroaches in all directions, a spiral architecture of sound. At the center of that musical stair, *this* moment leaves its fossil impression: a man and woman, unwitting particulars of a species frozen forever in the stillness before the historical calamity that will finish and preserve them, pressed in statigraphy, here against the Holocene floor.

Tone-deaf, he hears the tune breathing. He is inside it. In its final four bars, the bass detours back to origin. But at the moment when it must land on the octave, the delinquent line pulls one last shock. It hits and hangs on the note below, a suspended dissonance that threatens to spread indefinitely. He wonders if the chord will ever come home.

A change comes over Dr. Koss too at the music. No longer the nervous girl filled with skittish punchlines. Cross-legged, neck arched, head tilted, she sheds the sunbather and becomes a mater dolorosa. At aria's end, Ressler, scared by how much empty space has flooded into K-53-C, goes and sits next to her. His entrée to music is exactly this: wanting, just this once, without compromise, to close the curve of this woman's body, the cell surface he has not been able to forget since the moment she took his head in her hands and toweled it dry.

He does not know her, what she is doing here, why she inflicts him with this tune. She has no personality but the one she adopts this instant. Dr. Koss remains, despite his research, no more than a sketch. He needs from her precisely this refusal to dissolve into specifics. Whatever he suspects about the motive for her visit disappears. All suspicion falls away somewhere in the thirty-two measures. They sit through the first fifteen variations, rooted to the bare floor a foot from one another. When side one ends, they listen to a few revolutions of dull scratching before either can move. Ressler gets up, flips the record. The fifteen feet of floorboard to the plastic phonograph elongate epically. He fumbles with the cartridge, overwhelmed by aboriginal wonder at the device. All devices.

When he comes back to his spot, Koss reaches without looking and puts her arm around his shoulders. She touches his bone blade without hope or threat or promise. A completely unencumbered, uncompromised, just-to-be-touching touch. His shoulders support her arm as if they have known each other since the start. As if they know each other now. As if anyone ever knows the first thing about another.

The piece proceeds, with the modesty of the monumental, to launch an investigation into everything the aria, by permutation, can conceivably become. After an immense journey whose contours he only darkly traces, the piece ends note for note as it began: da capo. Once more, from the head, the delicate filigree of sarabande, fleshed out upon those four unfolding scale-steps. When the music stops, they continue to touch immaterially. Olga arabesques on in silence, not knowing the difference. The sinusoidal pulse of the needle scratching the end of the track might be surf interrogating the continental coast. Ressler is not sure what he has heard. The little air and variations, its signal now dampened, message reconcealed, disperses into noise.

A voice calls him back to the world's indifference; Jeanette Koss's, full of a timbre he has not heard until this moment. "Are you ill? You look febrile." Automatically, she places the back of her hand on his forehead. He at once burns for her to apply that ancient method, instinctive to women, of testing the fevered part with upper lip. His temperature would elude even this most heat-sensitive gauge—the burning hotel, plans lost in complexity, night, love's accident, long September, memory, fever beyond telling.

He does not look at her. In another moment, they rise by agreement and walk to the door. Their arms link a moment and unthread. At the open frame, they turn toward one another in an awkward eternity. A gulf of ignorance separates their two mutually unreadable faces. How implausible, dead-ended, and wrong any visit this woman might pay him at such an hour; he wants only to be rid of her without further calamity.

She reaches out, straightens his collar. "Whatever you think about me, try not to hate me." He cannot even ask what she is talking about. Deep in this woman, as deep in her mechanism as in his, stronger than fear of overstepping norms, than the urge to be loved or at least not forsaken, must be his own desire to stand in good faith, to do right by understanding. Do not hate me for being an experimentalist, and I will not hold theory against you. Which one of us knows the first thing about what we are after?

"I would like, very much," he begins, but breaks off in a flush of guilty well-being. He feels the warm air coming off the lawn, the light of his unfurnished army barrack at his back. How much he would like to fold himself in this woman. How beautiful she seems; how cut off, without consequence, they both are from the string of homes leading from this lot all the way to the black fields on the edge of town. He stands surrounded by danger, experience. "I want. . . ." He stops again, unable for the life of him to remember the name of the thing he wants so badly.

"I *know*," she giggles, collapsing again to the face and voice of a teenaged flirt, laughing off the game they have begun as misguided, simple eroticism. Before he can ask if the record is really his or if she wants it back, she waves him goodbye.

160

The Equinox

The day is easily recreated. Everything about September 23, 1983, is on microfiche or magnetic disk. Only ask one of the quarter million librarians in the country—85 percent women—for help in retrieving it. My log is even closer to hand. Too weak to cut himself off completely, Franklin left me a few of his beloved, unfinishable notebooks. He neither bequeathed them formally nor forbade me to look at them. Finding myself stalled after three months of memory and invention, I consult them freely, falling back on the unreliable perspective of another.

If I am addicted to Today in History, Franklin suffered from an equal and opposite addiction: History in Today. He was obsessed with proving that the atrocities of the last twenty-four hours led in a single aesthetic conga line back to the slaughter of Huguenots, the massacre of innocents, and beyond. The obsession vented itself in spurts of Schwitters-like collages, scraps of newsprint, the day at its most palpably inexplicable. Like his other notebooks, from the studious to the sheer caprice, these lasted a few weeks before sputtering out. For the last week of September, he clipped events into cubism.

I picture him as he arrived for the night and settled to work. Franklin and Dr. Ressler had to punch in, the computer's log serving as time clock. Frank would greet his colleague in one of a few stock ways, say, "Those who are about to digitize, salute you." Then he would sit in the deserted staff lounge full of jettisoned lunch bags, spread a ratty copy of the *Times* over the Formica, and cut.

On the night of the 23rd, while Tuckwell and I lay in bed, irrationally furious with each other, Frank Todd, who as yet meant no more to me than a place where I could escape the city, attacked his news. He snipped at section one with a pair of lefty scissors, gluing the composed facts into a spiral notebook. Whether documentary or artistic, a handbook for future archaeologists or a Dadaist handbill, it's impossible to say. In a neater notebook, cross-indexed to the clippings by secret numerals and Mayan icons, Franklin penned a telegraphic commentary that is now my keepsake:

Marcos getting tough with the opposition. "Extreme measures" if antigovernment activities continue. Senate Intelligence Committee (who names these things?) approves $19 million for Contras. House Foreign Affairs extends Lebanon deployment. Rooskies refuse our "appeal" to restrain Syria. French send 8 Super Etendards into Sofar. Retaliation for attacks against international peacekeepers. Who retaliation is aimed at escapes *this* reporter.

He worked into his clippings a map of Beirut, colored delicately by his gifted hand, embroidered with vegetation, serpents, spiders, deer, monkeys, savage men, and angels—facsimile of an illuminated Burgundian book of hours. Then, perhaps with a stroll around the lunchroom, a glance at the abandoned fashion magazines stinking of perfume samples and color ads of beautiful hermaphrodites stroking cars, he would join his shiftmate already at work down the hall. He would change the printer paper, mount a disk pack, check the card decks to be submitted, read the console, amend the evening's flowchart, then fire up a machine partition and leave it to multitask. He would return to the cafeteria, thaw himself an Entrée for One in the microwave. Then back to his notes.

> Things are heating up. 66% of W. Germans opposed to deployment of new medium rangers if Geneva talks stall. Chief of Soviet Gen Staff threatens "responsive measures" if they go in; shares Marcos's diction coach. Senate votes 66 to 23 to cut UN contributions $500 mil over next 4 years. "Taxpayers are sick and tired of playing host to our enemies..." says Symms, R-Idaho. What you get for bringing democracy to the provinces. In a related story... first outdoor field test of engineered bacteria allowing plants to manufacture their own fertilizer "tentatively endorsed" by NIH. Ask professor about wisdom of this. Lots of new books, movies, art, most of it blurry. Dow up 14. 'Recovery but No Boom.' Nobody died.

His script leaned to the right like a shortstop stabbing at a ball up the middle. He clipped and scrawled zealously into the journal, making love to this nonemployment. Amo, amas, amateur. Adieu sweet amaryllis.

I visited him later that week. For me, current events meant walking out on Tuckwell. I sat among the antiseptic business furnishings and related *my* news in knotted excitement. Todd clipped quietly, but bombarded me with his usual questions, that barrage that made me feel as if I might, after all, have a story to tell. Questions from succinct to silly. "Do you love the man? How much chili powder *did* you put in?"

But that night I didn't answer in the usual solitude. The last remnant of the first shift was working late. Jim Steadman, a pleasant, uncomplicated man in his mid-forties, Chief of Operations, ostensibly Todd's superior, although Franker insisted on addressing him as Uncle Jimmy. Jimmy paced pointedly past the lunchroom while I told Todd about my domestic fight. At last, hours after he should have gone home, he stuck his head in the doorway and threw on the lights. "You'll wind up blind, friend. Blind as the proverbial alley. Blind as a bat."

"Blind as the philosopher," said Todd.

"Blind as the eponymous Post Office Department," I contributed, feeling in my chest the thrill of forcing the moment.

Franklin wadded up the excised *Times* and banked it into the wastebasket. Jimmy growled, "You going to put in any hours at all this evening?"

Todd nodded. "In a minute. Almost underway, here."

"Still bothering over the news," Jimmy bitched to no one. "Counting editorials, you two'll be here around the horn again." He looked at me and added impishly, "Or should I say you three?" Affectionate, good-natured, as blind as the day shift was long. "Most men have productive hobbies, you know. Like stamp collecting, or toy trains." He crooked his thumb in the direction of the machine room. Todd smiled, sweetly obedient, but snipped on. The older man sighed and shuffled home, knowing that the late staff had long since slipped out of his jurisdiction.

Franklin glanced down the hall in the direction of his departing superior. "Long-suffering Jimmy, up solo against the technological age." This put him in mind of his shift partner, already at work, the man who remained the source of whatever pleasure Todd and I took in each other's company. Franker put his clipping away and punched in to the machine room to help the old man out. Earn his living for at least a little while.

I flip through the aborted notebooks and the days come back with precision. I turn the page to another entry:

CEASE-FIRE ACCORD GAINED IN LEBANON WITH SAUDIS' HELP
A "STEP," U.S. SAYS
Role of Marines Unchanged

In his loop-perfect hand, the impressionable interpreter duplicated the secretary of state's prediction: "They'll be a little more

163

comfortable in carrying that mission out because they won't be subject to the crossfire they have been in." At page bottom, he writes: "Interesting tidbit on computers and privacy says that Feds keep 15 files on each of us."

I try to connect those fifteen per capita files with the libraries of magnetic disks in the room down the hall entrusted to his care. One and the same, they still don't jibe. I can no more connect government electronic omniscience with the antiseptic Mylar bits he twiddled for a living than Frank could assimilate global geopolitics into a life that consisted largely of schemes to delay, another year, his masterpiece on a minor Flemish landscapist. What was Haiphong to Herri or Herri to Haifa? Less than nothing. Yet Frank, for a few weeks, turned pages and copied, insisting, against all evidence, that he and what happened all around him shared, somehow, the same substance.

> EPA scandal; Capitol Hill sets up killer watchdog, whacks it when it barks, and again for good measure when it fails to bite. "Almost 10 years after the public was alerted to the dangers of ethylene dibromide as a potent carcinogen, a Congressional subcommittee will inquire Monday into the reasons for Federal inaction on banning or restricting the substance, a widely used pesticide and gasoline additive...." Chemical "is invading food and underground drinking supplies...but the agency has yet to act." B11, for Jesus's sake. Big news was last night's Emmys.

I imagine him tending to his cut-and-paste, affecting a theatrical sigh. Every attempt to work himself into moral outrage failed to extinguish the sense of responsibility wadded up inside him. His notes filled with toxic poison, his night with the care and feeding of CPUs. But his thoughts were consumed by panel and patina, the incomprehensible landscape, the local confusion of nights when a stranger dropped by to keep him company, the chance to sketch the trivial sorrows of the nearest feminine face. Those weeks, that face was mine.

The Perpetual Calendar (I)

The breakthroughs in Dr. Ressler's science open as I explore them, like an unknown inlet that turns out to be a channel. As his post-doc went into its first autumn, partial overlap still seemed viable. If each triplet codon shared one base with its two neighbors, the string ACGAAGC would be parsed into discrete particles ACG GAA AGC. I make my own feasibility check the way he once must have. Given a codon ACG, the next partially overlapped codon must be Gxx. How many triplets possess that form? Four possible bases in the second position times four in the third gives a possible sixteen. But nothing in protein sequences places any such positional restriction. All twenty amino acids can occur freely, anywhere in a chain.

Uncanny: my first scientific deduction *before* seeing the argument in print. Of course, I wasn't first. Nor was I unassisted. But this surge of strange confidence: I have turned up a solution, attached my scent to the landmark. A cause for extraordinary muscle-flexing.

Dr. Ressler came as close as anyone I've ever met to demonstrating that saving grace of *Homo sapiens:* the ability to step out of the food chain and, however momentarily, refuse to compete. That was the quality that drew Todd and me to him, forced our love, although we barely knew him. "Nature cares nothing about the calculus of individuals." I saw him get angry once or twice. In the end, he even went after his goal with force. It wrecked him to admit that the gene is a self-promotion, a blueprint for building an armed mob to protect and distribute its plan throughout the inhabitable world.

But selflessness too has survival value. To paraphrase Haldane again, one might lay down his life for two brothers or eight first cousins. Ressler knew the calculus and how far he was condemned to obey it. But at the crucial moment, he elected for pointless altruism. Self-denial: the weirdest by-product of a billion years of self-interest. But in nature's hands, even altruism furthers selfish ends.

So I come down from my overlap conquest, return to research. I taste, after making the kill, just between the salt and sour buds on my tongue, the incomparable protein soup driving me forward: not blood. Enzyme wine.

I solve little by eliminating partial overlap. The insight, as advances do, only opens fresh cans of helical worms. I have backed into the framing problem. If a string of bases stores instructions without overlap, that long sequence still has to be framed into correct instructional bits. The gene segment ATCGGT-ACGGCCATG has three different reading frames:

ATC GGT ACG GCC ATG
xxA TCG GTA CGG CCA TGx
xAT CGG TAC GGC CAT Gxx

The string itself might carry some punctuation device, a chemical comma indicating how the codons should be read. The reading frame would then be unambiguous: ATC,GGT,ACG,GCC,ATG. But no chemical evidence for a such structure exists.

I ask all the wrong questions, raise naive, misinformed objections that would cause even that most humane educator to smile. Might certain codons chemically *fit* their amino acid assignments? How literally should I take the tape analogy? Which half of the double helix is transcribed for reading? Can the tape play in both directions? I am a rookie, a greenhorn, a tenderfoot in this new country. But so is science.

I begin to see one thing, at any rate. The chemical tumbling act is a mechanism beyond belief, a language more awesome than I suspected, perhaps more than I *can* suspect. To transpose the line of information-packed triplets into a meaningful burst of aminos is to begin to hear the structure of genes unfold over time—a virtuosic celebration of ideas trying themselves out, competing, announcing, developing, exploring contrapuntal possibilities.

As my understanding increases and my naiveté shrinks, the mechanism strikes me as unnecessarily cumbersome, inefficient. How might I build it better, simpler? I read, with distress, that ours is not the only possible genetic code, nor even perhaps the best way to keep self-duplicating molecules in production. I remember the innumerate grief of Annie Martens—an in-law, like it or not—when she heard Dr. Ressler describe how base 12 would have been a superior counting system to base 10. The woman was profoundly saddened by this irreversible impediment.

Another sadness, stronger than the code's inefficiency: it hurts to discover how much my understanding relies on analogy, pale figurative speech. My tape recorders, playback heads, builders, blueprints, and messengers. Scientific method itself—from diagrams to symbolic formulae to phenomenal descriptions—relies on seeing things in reflected terms. The gene as self-replicating organism, the organism as pan-gene, the cell as factory, the protein as robot running a program so complex that, in Monod's words, "to explain the presence of all that information in the protein you absolutely needed the code."

166

Will I ever get it? "Code" is itself a metaphor. "Cipher," the etymological dictionary says, comes from that profound mystery, the zero. A term to house my bafflement at how living things can be made up of so many nonliving parts. And if I get to the code, in the months before my savings run out, will it translate, repair the tear in my chest opened the day Dr. Ressler's instructions dispersed? One of the only sources of real company I've ever enjoyed—his gray brows, the taut, yellow smoothness of his face, the brutal, brave humor, the effortless flow of sentences—zeroed. "Dead" is too weak a metaphor. I push the barrow, sift the stone for a hint at how Chartres might come of rubble.

The first time I had a private conversation with Dr. Ressler, when my repeated visits to MOL gradually put him at something resembling ease, we sat in the darkened control room watching through the two-way mirror as Todd fired up the end-of-week processing. Ressler volunteered nothing, but pleasantly answered everything I asked. Just to hear him talk, I asked about a bank of devices, red diode lights flickering rapidly but irregularly.

"Those are modems. They translate analog phone pulses to and from digital sequences. At the other end of a phone line—who knows where—some other machine sends across a datum each time one of those red lights flashes."

"What are they sending?" I asked, suddenly seeing the spasmodic red flashes as a text.

Ressler smiled. "It could be the collected works of Shakespeare. In a single stream, four hundred and eighty letters a second."

That is the genetic metaphor that begins to suit me. Something wilder than all the plays of Shakespeare written in something as simple as blinking lights. It fails in the representation. But then, so does putting Shakespearean moonlight into a twenty-six-letter chamber. The closest we ever come is dressing someone up, calling him the moon. Clay-derived thought, capstone of evolution: I count myself lucky to achieve even that weak analogy. Where can I go tonight for conversation? He alone made me feel clever, just in unraveling his metaphors.

When I at last got out of the house today, stepped outside into the open air after ages, I bussed around Flatbush, Fulton, discovering to my senses' shock how thick autumn was in me already. Season of mists and mellow fruitfulness, to blame it on Keats. Sap consolidates; the days have begun going dark before supper. Even here, in the middle of fifteen million, colors come on, acquire

167

reputations: umber, burnt sienna, ocher, iodine, scarlet, rare earths hued to the first order. With the right formula of dry cold, for no practical reason, demure trees slip from lime to lemon, go down with all the garishness of an historical atlas. And bless with fruit the vines that round the thatch-eaves run.

Well, perhaps no fruit vines in my neighborhood. But isolated branches telegraph the first symptoms of epidemic. Trees shed brittled skin and strip down to cartilage fighting weight. Twigs scrape against phase-changed glass, followed in a week or two by tentative ice traceries, fibrous, hexagonal, the solid geometry of crystal water molecules. First day of autumn, the equinox: New Year's of Phoenicians and Egyptians, wielding symbolic power as late as 1939, when we chose the day to bury our technological message to future species.

Q: Who decided that the first day of autumn should fall on September 23? Why not the 21st, or better yet, October 1, which makes more sense? Probably invented by committee. Why doesn't the day move around, like Thanksgiving and Easter?

A: This one is trickier than it looks. In fact, the reconciliation of the solar year was the first technical bottleneck facing civilization .... The balance points, equal-nights, do move around—five hours, forty-eight minutes, and forty-six seconds each year. They do fall at odd times as the result of that committee, historical accident. Rotation divides only reticently into revolution. But then, if the repetitive calendar had come easily, we might never have developed astronomers, mathematicians, scientists, librarians.

Everything that ever happened happens at equinox. Wars start, armistices all arrive between early October and the end of the year. Symphonies begin and break off on autumn leave-taking. Governments change; the only logical time for elections (however pro forma), for mothers of four to head dutifully to precinct polls in station wagons despite a driving rain, to hide themselves behind curtains and pull the lever of choice.

Three compressed months of change write the year in brief. Plants pull back; landscape retreats into a miniature of muted colors. Tonight, where I grew up, the cicadas have their last seasonal blowout, choral storms outside my childhood window, now serving some other child in the formation of memories. Even from this distance their simmer is audible, a sex-soaked group pulse, a twitch in the dry air swelling to buzz-saw bandwidth. Wind pitches their group shout in a mechanical wave sounding for all the world like a million miniature pieces of shook sheet tin. Reaching decibel denouement the noise cuts off at the chaos instant, fizzling to a few holdouts. The signal from one swarm sets off another, a hundred yards off, flaring in pitch before it too hushes. All down the county line, the overlapping antiphony of bug choirs.

Frost stencils the hoods of cars, reveals internal cross-struts as clearly as an X-ray. Delinquent husbands return after thirty years, begging for absolution. The cheerful, hermetic next-door neighbor, receiving in his mail the most blunt prognosis medical technology can muster, turns back to his house, thinking: Just time enough to get those problem patches under the shingles. On every corner, lambent glow of streetlamps on maple limbs, an inverted carpet of rust. The moon goes gibbous, the night stars a drunken dream. Where I grew up, "Milky" is the only conceivable adjective for the spread of pebbled, intertidal autumn sky.

Combines scythe circumference swatches, close their noose around holdout corn. At the last pass, a thousand acres of trapped rats, snakes, and pheasant break from the drawn net, most mauled by indifferent machines. Sundays, as winds whip through moribund barns, harvesters meet in narthex and nave to sing how all is safely gathered in, as if they had the principal hand in bringing it off. Autumn is the note before the last melisma, the third stanza, the congregation fumbling in hymnals to read both words and music. A plenitude of pies, pride of drop-in guests, brace of hams, corsage of table settings, parliament of mashed potatoes, supplication of network sports, clatch of conversation, covey of vacation days, school of parades, volume of preserves, brood of read-alouds, keepsake of snapshots: everything running at glut, at glorious surplus.

"Healthy Midwestern girl," Todd used to tease me. "Healthy Midwestern influences." They have not helped me healthily over him. All day today, it felt as if this were the last chance I would have to remember what it felt like, in the blood, once, to be young. That synonym list of anticipation, before the business of thinning out.

Everything that ever happened to me happened in autumn. I moved away from home. I first fell in love. I got my first job. In autumn, at twelve, I thought I was hemorrhaging to death. Autumn is sea-storm warnings a thousand miles inland, everyday affairs going entirely incomprehensible, changed by the chance disaster, the autumn occurrence, the fall phenomenon.

Once I spent the wet first days of fall blowing on tea, doing a picture puzzle of Constable's *Hay Wain,* the soggy, rocking card table badly in need of a shim. Racing my mother for the obvious pieces, the wheel spokes, the stream, and leaving the uniform sky for when it wouldn't be so hard. Working alongside the woman who pieced me together, who has since put aside both picture puzzles and procreation for good.

I bought my first book in autumn, a story about three girls who swear a perpetual pact of friendship and set out to do something slightly forbidden but ultimately laudable one Saturday in September. Annually, like celestial clockwork, I acquire more volumes, seek out the great multistory secondhand dealers. Through plaster caverns damp with the aroma of disintegrating bindings, I select on size, color, the marginalia of former owners—subjects as obscure as *Guide to Fencing,* or *Tungsten Mining Commission Proceedings, 1934.* I hedge them up against winter, and toss them all out the following spring.

In the fourth grade, two weeks after Labor Day, I brought home my first instrument, a three-quarter-sized 'cello bigger than I was. I took it upstairs to my father's study, methodically ground the endpin into the lacquered floor, and touched the bow to the catgut C. A bass swell filled the house, penetrating to the root cellar— the only successful sound I ever made on the thing. All subsequent attacks on the instrument were failed attempts to recreate that first resonance. I turned the box in the following Labor Day, after a frustrating summer stuck in first position. Next autumn I took up piano. Czerny exercises (Chopin without sex, Brahms with a bad conscience) every October from then on.

September at seven, the cyclic return: government-instituted torture of youth peculiar to Western Nations. Spelling bees, closed-circuit broadcasts of space shots, oral reports, experimental alphabets, new math. At sixteen: the sweet fumblings of first sex under the pines in the dark, on a mat of needles, discovery without texts, transgressing the papal demarcation of his parts and mine. Today, years later: too late to let the season linger any longer. By thirty, autumn urgency should have run its course. The time of year for setting out, as if all summer had been only a holding pattern. The thrill of Directory Assistance, adrenaline of a toll call.

The electrostatics of wool and cold fronts, the smell of earthworms across the sidewalk, the aroma of retreat in the rain, nervous shift in the permafrost—scent of late September sets me loose. I can smell it in the center of Times Square, at Chambers Street, Rockefeller Center, uptown, all the way over the Hudson and west into the prairies where I learned it. The smell of that private, quiet secret I always had: the neighborhood getting ready for night. Night that might bring anything. Crisp, almost here: can't be far off, can't be long.

Time to dig out of storage clothes stinking of cedar and naphthalene. Heinrich Schliemann Stumbles Across Grandmother's Trunk. Did I really wear this? As late as last year? Should have bought the replacement winter coat last spring, capitalized on old stock's mark-downs. Too late now; as with fresh vegetables and apartment rentals, it's a cellar's market.

It seemed this week that sixty-eight degrees would hold out as long as its constituency. But a seasonal swing of warmth's buffer, a few dry flakes, the hint of a pressure system setting sail, and the air is suddenly cold enough for the frames of my glasses to numb my temples. The radio playing in the apartment just below runs afoul of a flux in the ionosphere, bleeding the stations in and out across the dial. Partly sunny skies, breezy and somewhat colder. Dropping by this weekend, with the lows ranging into the deo gratias of medieval monks, or the cheerful idiocy of a helium-voiced talk radio host who argues with the home audience that things might not be half so bleak as they seem. That is, only twice as bleak as survivable.

Every year, preexistent in the almanac, each day already marked out on the perpetual calendar. Light length on the downward trend, caught for a moment at fulcrum. Hours are too small an increment to think in. Clocks go inconsequential. I need a wider instrument— the click of tree branches—to measure the only quality that has ever counted. Weather is the one tenuous connection between this year and two years ago. Then too, the season slid so deep in me it seemed to change direction. Ambiguous cusp of temperature; newly bare branches identical to those on the verge of budding. With only the lightest push, tonight's temperature could easily set off in me the same cell-programmed thaw. Cells can't tell that no one is around anymore. Spark of arousal—dumb fixation, stupid holdover—while paging the atlas for him. I haven't even pinned him down to a specific city. But he's there, somewhere among the burnt umbers.

In autumn, Herri, the Flemish landscaper whose rescue from

171

obscurity will never be written, stood on a hill just outside a Renaissance village and painted the sweep of trees turning autumnal tones, harvest being hauled in, stooks standing in the vacated fields, departing vees of geese, soft rub of dusk on the contoured hills. And in the corner of the panel, almost overlooked—autumn bonfire. The only persuasive argument against living practically. The return of a familiar friend.

It suddenly occurs to me how I might fix him to a specific spot. I'm not restricted to the atlas. Perhaps that landscape—the one word he's sent since Dr. Ressler's death—never existed. But the panel itself exists somewhere, if not the panorama it imitates. The picture sits in a collection, and all collections have catalogs, compiled and archived. I've got a skill. Let me use it, however irrelevantly. However much my trying to locate him puts me on par with those birds whose apparatus does not stop them returning yearly to the unilaterally abandoned nest.

The shape of my day may already have been printed in the almanac. Sunrise at x. Sunset at y. H amount of daylight hours. The arc of prediction intercepting today. And yet: something about to give, about to happen, near at hand. Quick, close, behind the advertising, during the frozen dinner, over television, after the office politics, waiting its turn in the queue of current events. Something fundamental. Something real this time. The secret will come clean. I will not die in bed.

It's good to go to sleep with a project. Staves off winter for another week. But the day needs its quote, and one has just occurred to me. They still suggest themselves in the evenings— evolutionary holdovers, tonsil or appendix. I juggle today's for a minute, so tired I can barely spell, before I get it intact and identified. De Tocqueville's *Democracy in America*. "They are all advancing every day towards a goal with which they are unacquainted." The only direction the calendar allows, forward toward that old friend, leaving. The goal of autumn.

172

IX

Canon at the Third

Days later, Ressler still doesn't know the reason for Dr. Koss's visit. Neither seeking nor avoiding, he sees her everywhere—in the lab, in conference, in the creaking Georgian hallways of Biology. He studies her for flutter, but sees none. She is unaffectedly congenial. No secrets: so I was wrong about your birthday. He does his best to be congenial back. A week after the visit, coming out of the office he shares with Lovering, he practically knocks the woman over. Who knows how long she's been standing there. "You scared me," she says. All at once, the pound of blood pressure, hypertension bruits coming on like Mardi Gras. Excitement or fear? His or hers?

"Were you looking for me?" he asks stupidly.

Embarrassment clouds her face. She looks away shyly, confessing something for the first time since her visit. "No. Your office mate. Can you give him this?" She hands him a note and rushes off too quickly. Ressler battles with ethics for as long as it takes to peek. The message is unsealed and he kills no cats by looking. It's nothing; a reminder to Joe to get his paperwork in. The man has a mailbox for these things.

She's taken to dressing differently, but he can't say how. She seems airier, her walk a brisker cadence, her shoulders buoyant. She no longer fits the make he'd assigned her. She can't quite make the flamboyant smartmouth stick. He has no idea how to classify her, let alone interpret her late-night light arm around him the week before. Only her gift—those vinyl keyboard variations—proves irrefutably that she really dropped by. But that piece is the most ambiguous code wheel of all.

173

He needs real work to distract him from speculation. He throws himself into the rate trials, promoting them from the make-work they were made for. He visits Ulrich's office without appointment. Rousing the team leader from a pile of papers, he feels the force of his ludicrous mission. Low man on the totem, with no productive work to speak of, asking a man of thirty years his senior to humor a proposal he hasn't even formulated. He sits nervously. "Stuart?" the chief asks, affecting pleasure.

"Dr. Ulrich, I...." He seizes up, choosing just that moment to remember Koss's departure at his door, his trailing *I want*, which he now can too clearly name. "I think we ought to leave amino sequence analysis to the chemists."

Ulrich smiles at the boy's diplomatic choice of words. "How do you suggest we get to the translation without the ciphertext?"

Ressler knows Ulrich to be intellectually capable of grabbing the heart of things. "There must be a way to determine the codon-to-amino map without pacing over every inch of resulting print. The thing's too dense. We'll be forever."

"I agree." Ulrich lets the full weight of silence spread without comment.

Ressler fights the urge to run. After an agonizing half minute, he tries feebly to elaborate. "The sequences on both sides are too numerous and complex to correlate without a key."

"You'd like some kind of Rosetta apparatus?"

"The *cell* is our Rosetta."

"Hmm. Have you any argument other than analogy?"

"No."

Ulrich forgives the antagonized monosyllable, remains the understanding boss. "Interesting. But let's follow through awhile longer with what we have. After the write-up on your trials, we'll see where we stand."

Hot-faced, humiliated, Ressler leaves. Yet in losing his discussion with Ulrich, he's gone a small step further in the elusive process. The cell itself as Rosetta. Feed it the barest theme.... He lavishes attention on the radiation-doped microbes in his care. He hangs about the lab, isolating, repeating, recording, filtering for telltale mutants that might surprise, prove him wonderfully wrong. He fishes for results that will buy him time to consolidate, gather strength, coax the next hint into place.

As he shepherds the petris, almost contaminating them with overcare, Ressler replays that day, ancient history, when Dr. Koss made him bend and surrender his head for toweling. The imprint will not extinguish. His temples tense under the contour of her recreated fingers. He maps his own, slow, reciprocal finger path over her head, the bridge over her eyes, the gentle ridge running along the sides of her skull to its crown. Her skin's capacitance courses down the length of his arm into an endocrine reservoir filling his abdomen.

These buzzers set off others, until he cuts the chain reaction, recalls another day when a clue from Koss sent him into the stacks in search of the gold bug. One deletion, one insertion, and one substitution brings him to goldberg. Too near a variation to be accidental. Koss, yet another code thug, infects him with some viral mess, injects him with some vital message mutation. Before his paranoia can flail out, finding hidden significance in every co-incidental letter-string, another message arrests him. A clipping left on his desk: a cartoon of a marvelous, machine-age invention employing two dozen elaborate programmed steps to butter a piece of toast. The contraption is pencil-captioned, "Goldberg Variation #?" Lovering saunters over from his side of the office. "Dr. Koss left that. Said you'd know what it means." It means the woman likes puns. That he's been a first-class goldberg rube.

When the Blakes invite him to dine at K-53-A, Ressler gratefully accepts. He never imagined human company could be so welcome. Evie greets him at the door with an elbow squeeze. "I've prepared something incredible: a baste-a-bag turkey that ejects a little flag when done." She leads him into the kitchen, where the rest of the family peers intently into the oven. Tooney introduces him to Margaret, a seven-year-old marvel of precocity and miniaturization. "I bet it's a tiny Union Jack," Blake baits his daughter.

"Don't be silly," Margaret says, shoving him. "The bird's from Virginia. A Stars and Bars." With no trace of shyness, she commands Ressler, "Watch! Fowl in a flag-bag. It's going to wave when it's cooked."

"Maybe it's a white flag. Surrender?"

The kid rolls her eyes. "Funny friend you've got, Dad."

Ressler wonders what role Herbert Koss, the man who put Champaign-Urbana on the Food Technology map, had in developing the self-semaphoring bird. The family sits down to eat, making an unbelievable racket for a trio. Blake begs everyone's silence, then drops his head. "Bless food thank Lord selves service." High-speed blur. Ressler is stunned; is the man truly devout, racing

175

through the prayer for the visiting agnostic's sake? Or is the rapid-fire benediction for his amusement?

He looks at Eva, but she just mugs back pertly. "Service selves Lord thank food bless!" Retrograde grace, in Eva's mouth, the purest thanksgiving imaginable.

Little Margaret giggles and adds, "Amen. Dig in."

The invocation wrecks Ressler's appetite. "Dig in" these days has other connotations altogether. Home shelters, advertised in the backs of magazines. If the race knew the rads they've already released it would roll over and give up, adrift in a sea of brave new mutagens. Only this family's free affection keeps him from the thought. He and Tooney swap anecdotes about their colleagues. Eva entertains them with more Tales from the Civil Service. "I have the sneaking suspicion that despite the upward spiral in the standard of living, we're all getting poorer."

"Come again?" Ressler says.

"You realize my wife hasn't really quantified this."

"You should read some of these applications. 'How are you qualified for this position?' 'I need it real bad.' 'Why did you leave your last job?' 'False pretenses.' One fellow filled out the space Below the Dotted Line reserved for previous employer's comments: 'Would you hire this worker again?' The guy wrote, 'Yes indeed.' Only he misspelled 'indeed.'"

In the general hilarity, Ressler leans over and whispers to Eva, soft enough so the kid can't hear, "You have a beautiful child. Mail-order."

Eva claps her hands. "No, I assure you we got her through the conventional channels. Oh! That's rude, isn't it?"

"All right, short stuff," Tooney says from the head of the table. "Do your thing."

"Have to?" Both parents nod gravely. The child groans, clearly delighted. "'Margaret are you grieving over goldenglove unleaving?' What the heck is a 'goldenglove,' anyways?"

"It's 'Goldengrove,' sweet," Mother corrects. Eva, with her ambidextrous brain capable of retrograde inversions, must have a soft spot for postromantic poetry. "As in groves of plants that have lost their green."

"Oh. I like 'goldenglove' better. As in golden glove."

"So do I," Ressler concurs.

"Get on with it," Tooney mock-growls.

"'Leaves....'"

176

" 'Like the things of man. . . .' Come on, girl!"

" 'Leaveslikethe things of man you with your fresh thoughts care for can you? Ah! As the heart grows older it will come to such sights colder by and by.' "

As recitation, the half-dozen lines are mediocre at best. But the child cuts Ressler to the quick. To a scientist habituated to the microscopic, her snip nose, proto-mouth, tiny eyes that actually focus and see are miracles. Blood courses through Margaret as she recites. Lungs pump, kidneys filter. Systems and subsystems weave an intricate, interdependent free-for-all. Her nervous system, a fine spray of veil, a cascading waterfall of paths and signals, subdivides into web-bouquets, structures more elaborate and beautiful the more he imagines their constituent firings.

This is the awful northern face that molecular self-duplication must scale, an ascent as unlikely as the climb of chemicals out of the primordial soup of reducing atmosphere. The superstructure alone is inconceivable. Just the thought that a single zygote, in less time than it takes the average Civil Service gang to dig a bed for a mile of interstate, differentiates into vertebrae, liver, dimpled knees, and ears complete with recording membrane is enough to knock Ressler flat on the metaphorical mat. Yet nucleotide rungs alone curve this child's cornea, curl her lashes. Nothing else needed; he's sure of that. The entire, magic morphogenesis is explainable as terraced chemical mechanisms.

This *machine*, this polyp, this self-assembling satellite of two parents with no special technical ability outside of inserting complementary parts inside one another, this self-governing bureaucratic republic of mutually dependent parasites (every one incorporating a transcript of the master speech), has mastered speech. Mimicked language. Biggest of the big L's, from fist to lash, the real tissue. Margaret's cells have found out how to say what they mean, or a rough approximation. Her hierarchy of needs insists it is more than chance initiation.

This child, all of seven, creates, in a few phonemes, real grief, the shorthand sequence until then only metaphored. The metric, or rather Margaret's meter, invokes the strangest insight: this morphologically perfect package is not a little girl, but a chemical unknown putting itself through reduction analysis. Her life is the task of isolation, the desperate longshot of learning. Margaret's virtuosity denies objective treatment; he gets sucked into the shape of the line, the precocious musculature, the labial coordination.

177

He stares at the juvenile a nanosecond longer than is appropriate, begins to see in that self-delighting, self-affrighting library of sentient routines a thing to spook the strongest empiricist. Design without designer. Effect, perfect and purposive, without even casual cause.

The child—with that sensitivity, like linguistic preknowledge, built into children—picks up on his fear. Half into "by and by, nor spare a sigh," she stops. The silence does it: his nose flares, blood flushes his cheeks, his glands secrete. A reaction mechanism, one of those instincts that puzzles the issuing organism as much as anyone. Margaret shoots a pitying look at him.

"Peg, my leg," Tooney jokes. "What's up? Why heck you stop?"

"That man is crying," she whispers, suddenly no more precocious than her years. Ressler looks away, unable to evade this minutest observation. He has somehow grasped her, not as a performing child, but as *this trial run*. The helix's experiment.

"Well, maybe this poem is sad. Did you ever think of that?"

She looks at Ressler, eyes huge: can this be? He makes no denial. Incredulous, danger past, racing through the syllables for sheer love of the sound, shooting out of the gate again in amazing breach of decorum, in that elaborate, cumbersome, ornate, mathematical, obsolete, and hopelessly contrapuntal ritual of rhyme, she shouts, " 'Nor spare a sigh though worlds of wanwood leafmeal lie.' " "Wanwood leafmeal" cracks her up. She cannot keep a seven-year-old's smirk off her face as she finishes the postponed feat. And yet you *will* weep and know why. " 'Now no matter, child, the name!' "

But Ressler no longer listens, let alone cries. He knows the name. He was that little girl's age once. He knows the layout, the mortgage of that miracle—the process that has coarsened features, thickened spirit, and slowed joy while leaving him a perverse window through which to see the place he has left. He was himself that exploration once, despite his mother's repeated objection "You were *never* a child."

How could the enormous head, passing only with agony through Evie's conventional channels, a design resulting in years of dependent helplessness—the longest adolescence in the animal kingdom—ever have been selected for? A liability for millennia before earning anywhere near its keep. Yet that outsized organ is his biome, his stock in trade. He was the prodigy once, not much older than this girl. He lavished this precocious love on the home nature museum—a walk-in catalog of the planetary pageant. Every

Saturday he redrew the floor plan: protective coloration got pushed against the kitchen wall and the ant colony went into the living room, clearing the place of honor in the front foyer for this month's *cause célèbre,* the struggle between Allosaurus and Triceratops, in 3-D.

His parents suffered the formaldehyde stench in happy silence. While classmates spent their energies on kick the can, he curated. It took him until sixteen even to consider running away, and then it wasn't to join the circus but Byrd. Yes, like the rest of his peer group, he avoided sidewalk cracks. But he kept to the clear concrete on account of Pascal's Wager: the consequences of coming home to find the ambulance carting off broken-backed mother prohibited taking the infinitesimal chance.

His protoself, a thing independent of who he has become: a boy completely, passionately in love with links. The more esoteric the system, the more ecstatic his pleasure in tricking out its hidden form. His sixth-grade math teacher, introducing summation notation by brutal means, made the class add up all the numbers from one to a hundred. The plan was to imprint in the half-shaped charges how trivial the task was once one had the formula. But a few seconds into the assignment, while the rest of the poor slaves labored to total their columns, little Stuart raised his hand. "Sir?"

The dumbfounded educator listened to the preteen derive a perfect copy of Gauss's great work. "Look: one plus one hundred is one hundred and one. So is two plus ninety-nine. See the pattern? If you split the numbers in the middle and reverse the second group, you get fifty sums of one hundred and one. Instead of a hundred hard additions, one easy multiply."

"That's . . . right," the teacher whispered, going pale. Original thought, the once-a-generation find, in *his* classroom. Stupidly, he asked, "And what exactly *is* fifty times one hundred and one?" As if the answer mattered. But this simple product was beyond Stuart. Adult Ressler still takes a minute to get it. Once he'd rediscovered Gauss, the problem lost its interest and he went on to calculate which two rings on his wooden desktop he'd been born between. To figure the weather that year, by ring width. Teacher could solve the multiplication for himself if he tried.

His whole childhood was an unsuccessful effort to show various instructors that the crucial thing is not fifty times one hundred and one, but how one got those terms. Not what a thing *is,* but how it connects to others. In the second grade, shown a card with the words "little wind how today Mr. ask," and told to make a sentence from them, he wrote: "My teacher has a card with the words 'little wind how today....'" The following year, he discovered that when one flipped one's tongue over, a touch applied to the bottom seemed to emanate from the top. By junior high, he had proved to disbelieving high schoolers that almost all possible numbers have an eight in them, or a seven, or nine, but an infinity of numbers contain none of these. In late teens, he announced to an uncomprehending English teacher that the word "couch," repeated a thousand times at high speed, deteriorated into semantic nothingness.

Each thing is what it is only through everything else. Life is a crystal, combinatorial. A surreptitious system. Feel the pull to uncover it while still a child, or that pattern will never, not even in the cells' collapse, open its hidden order. Ressler remembers this boy, how he usurped Western Civ from Mr. Jameson, scorned the Safety Patrol, barked about some ship called the *Beagle,* and corrected Mrs. Rapp on the bituminous/anthracite debacle. Even his mother gave up trying to teach him anything outside of never to wear blue with brown.

He's paid the toll in playground hate. Hate of his memorizing *and* explicating the Gettysburg Address overnight. Hate of his never, not even in the face of electrons, Greeks, and other hopeless abstractions, getting flustered. The annual resentment of a new crop of classmates at his hearing sounds and sweet airs of the sweetest simplicity, a whole home nature museum of shifting voices, each claiming to be the melody. His learning everything from scratch. Everything connected; all classroom assignments, aspects of one theme. He heard what the rest of the percentiles had to take on faith.

This Margaret already suffers the same exile. He sees it in her anxious face, her rapid flashes of recitation. They two are of a piece. Out of the ubiquitous, sick anxiety of childhood, he and this girl, skipping past those classmates blundering through the accepted steps, are off on their own, cataloguing, curating their own internal, interwired discoveries, attempting to dance, as fast as lips and breath and understanding can.

After Margaret goes to bed, the adults spend the remaining evening pleasantly. Suffering community with the Blakes is vastly superior to another evening of overloaded solitude. Since Dr. Koss's visit, he has lost his capacity for productive isolation. He finds himself driven to company, not sure what exactly he hopes to find there. They gravitate to the front lawn, stroll down the street toward the university. The air is brisk. Students have poured back to campus, in the erotic uncertainty of a new term. Eva relates her latest cerebral misadventures. She has just mastered the trick of delayed dictation. With her right hand, she jots down whatever someone is saying; with left, she writes the previous sentence in the past tense. "I'm not sure what practical advantages this has," she says, smiling fetchingly in streetlight.

Tooney puts his arm around his wife. "Do you know that we are walking in the presence of a woman who does crossword puzzles in *pen*?" Blake shakes his head. "When I first discovered that, I knew this was the sexiest woman I'd ever meet. I had to marry her."

The rhythm of the evening, the pitiful, arms-flung attempt to articulate the thrust, is drowned in cicada swarms. Ressler is shot through, unable to rid himself of the idea, the face, the scent of that woman who has attached herself to his brain like a water parasite. Why isn't she here? She is at this minute home, with her husband, while his thoughts are thick with her shape and spore. He grasps the slack truth: he is already lost, the one person alive who knows he isn't a native speaker. Ressler smiles as Tooney relates his own courtship. He watches this man and wife, such obvious mates, and suddenly decides to risk the infant friendship on an outside chance that can tell him nothing except how lost he already is. "Your wife is phenomenal," he blurts out. "I'm in love with her."

"Terrific!" Blake shouts, shaking his hand. "Hear that, wife?" Eva blushes. "See that? She thinks you're neat too."

"I mean it. I want to have an affair with her."

"Don't blame you in the least," Blake chuckles. "But I ain't gonna letcha, lecher." He cuffs Stuart's ears, rubs his hair with his knuckles, dangerously close to a hug. "You may kiss her good night, when the time comes. But no tongue!" Both cackle nervously, good-naturedly. The woman in question pretends outrage, but shoots Ressler a look that says, *Well, we might have been an item, you and I, in other circumstances.*

"Suppose it *were*," he persists, but the experiment is ruined by descent into hypothetical. "Suppose it were Eva. Magnet, built in, like migration. That I had to come back to her, to *that* beach, even the first year, never having seen it. Suppose it were Eva. And

181

everything depended on my making Margaret." Ressler rubs his neck, embarrassed. "You have an amazing child."

"That time of year, is it? G'wan. Get married. What're you waiting for? Can bachelor days last forever?"

"Does ripe fruit never fall?" Eva adds, her quota for the day. "Do, Stuart! Not even science compares with parenthood."

"Seems irreversible at first," Tooney says. "Terrifying. You look for the sign that she, out of every active genome in the species, is the one you're after. But the one you are after. . . ."

Eva interrupts him with a nod toward Ressler. Tooney, noticing, clams up. Ressler announces quietly, "The one I'm after is already married."

"Stuart, I'm sorry." Eva takes his arm. "We're so *stupid*. We had no idea."

They walk another block, then circle back. The Blakes ask nothing, probe no further. How much has Tooney inferred? Ressler's been here but months, is a notorious hermit, knows no one except the crew. He can't believe how obvious he has been. He's just been waiting for the chance to commit this carelessness. They wind up back at K-53-C. Nobody is ready to break up the company, but the night is clearly over. "Can I still get that kiss good night?" Eva takes him in her arms, shoves her husband away.

"Deep and lasting osculation," Blake says, as his wife and this stranger kiss fully on the lips. "Nothing like it."

Ressler turns his back and lets himself into his apartment. Closing the door, he enters a vault, a time vacuum. He feels the first seed of what could easily become panic if he nudges it. He goes to the record player. But the flowering, formal perfection of the music is so close that he rips the playing arm off the motionless canon. The needle lurches hideously across the vinyl. He flings the record into the corner and with the same violent, emotionless wrist twist puts the banished Robeson on. But spirituals, smacking of theology, only intensify his shakes.

He digs in, steadying. Fear? Grief? The intrusion registering down his nerve sheaves, the radical dissection has its root somewhere before words: in the self-describing semaphore. The home nature museum. The work undone at the lab. The fallout shelter signs on stadium and stacks. That syntax-generating syntax. Jeanette's genome. The code bug. Now no matter, child, the name. Sorrow's springs are the same. It is the blight man was born for. It is Margaret he mourns for.

Program Notes

A handful of visits to Manhattan On-Line revealed that the night staff were not completely cut off from the rest of the firm they worked for. There really was a business behind them. If I came early enough in the evening, I caught the remnants of the swing shift who enjoyed hanging around after hours, avoiding rush commute or baiting the company recluses.

Jim Steadman was a regular, always late punching out. He had ostensible business: "Transfer of power, Ms. O'Deigh. Somebody's got to steer this pitiful ship." But Jimmy's nautical function was, if anything, ballast. Compensating for a lack of skill at the helm, he tried to run things by the manual. With those two on night watch, that was impossible. Jimmy was dear: he rarely transcended the accidents of his life and time, but was squarely in the camp of good men. Franklin had trained under him and took to calling him Uncle within days. Uncle Jimmy never objected to the sobriquet, although he was only a dozen years Franklin's senior. Avuncularity sat on his chest like a Good Conduct medal. The man would have made a great counselor, or one of those folksy district representatives, prematurely senile, whom the constituency returns term after term because he's a harmless institution.

Convinced that Chief of Operations included the duties of utility fielder, Jimmy patrolled the grounds, did minor maintenance, set rat traps in the attic, swept the stockroom, cleaned the corporate fridge, and managed to run the computer in only three or four times what it would take a teenager who stuck to the task. He would come in early, kill the morning, gossip with the keypunch girls. He would frequently still be there in the evening when Todd and Ressler arrived, modestly martyred by the OT, with horror stories about how he'd been checking the circuit breaker when he somehow brought the shop to a standstill just as the machine was closing out totals. The three of them would spend hours restarting the process from the top. Jimmy would stay on happily, around the clock. The computer room was his home, the staff, his family.

He flirted outrageously with all females, a snips-and-snails teasing. Jimmy had no wife or girlfriend. Shyness made him clownishly aggressive. He was sweetly overweight, suffered from an emotional skin condition, and nursed a "bum leg," a circulatory symptom telegraphing an advance notice nobody paid attention to. He lived at home with his widowed mother. He called her each evening just before leaving. Presumably, this mobilized supper or instructed her to call the police if he wasn't home within the hour.

He struck a wary symbiosis, a nonaggression pact, with the system. He did not trust the machine but treated it well and hoped for the best in return. He had no explicit grasp on what the computer did. It seemed to run itself, a part of the mundane miraculous. He liked to take me aside and inform me confidentially about the little men inside the CPU, at the consoles of their own little machines, which they, in turn, did not entirely understand, but which kept the whole she-bang going.

Todd and Ressler got along with their colleague, even liked him. But they couldn't help treating him as a young Walter Brennan, lost in the vast backroom poker game of the Information Age. Jimmy would sit in the lunchroom at ten to seven, eating his neglected bologna with mustard and browsing the *Daily News* as Todd clipped current events, waiting for the system to do the afternoon's General Ledger, which Jimmy should have finished by five. He'd limp to the computer room, punch the code into the electronic lock, rush to the printer, and discover that it had jammed at the beginning of the run. At this setback, he'd offer up an oath on the mild side of "Oh, nuts!" Todd insisted that Uncle Jim would not say shit if he had a mouth full of it. Jimmy would return to the cafeteria, throw up his hands, and half-happy, say, "I give up. Gonna quit and start that chicken farm."

He was an affable, engaging, hopeless plodder who talked in homilies. After a dozen truisms, winding up with "It matters not how strait the gate, how charged with punishments the scroll," he'd head back to the computer room and rerun GL, bloody, but unbowed. Todd would match the man's Victoriana, remarking, "We wander between two worlds: one dead, the other on the critical list." Unimaginative, dedicated: in short, the ideal operations manager. Todd always said he would die one. Still, for all his happy ineptitude, Jimmy could point to ten fully vested years without failing to bring his machine on-line in time for the next shift. Franklin had failed twice already by sophomore season.

Other hangers-on sometimes strayed into the late show. Occasionally, an upper-middle exec in full three-piece regalia worked late, auditing some process or another. This was my cue to pretend I'd only dropped by to deliver a message. The office also employed a succession of earnest teenagers, their eyes on Wall Street, to collate and sweep up. A knot of females sometimes stayed late to offer Todd bits of their unfinished lunches. "The Frank Todd Fan Club," Uncle Jimmy enviously called it.

In the second month of my regular rounds at MOL, Dr. Ressler buzzed me in one evening. He met me at the door, as charmingly distant as ever. "Ah, a familiar face! May one presume to call you Jan, after this length of time?" I nodded enthusiastically. Although now on first-name basis, I was afraid to say anything, lest I scare him off. "What is Jan short for?"

"I'm afraid that's what's on the birth certificate." I still knew little more about him than on the day I made my photo discovery. His mystery had drawn me here in the first place. I felt shame at how easily I'd dropped pursuit, distracted by more immediate pleasures. I suppose I thought: He has taken decades to get this lost. I have time to find him at leisure.

"On the topic of birth certificates," he said, grinning in advance at his own Byzantine connection, "I suppose your expertise makes it an easy matter for you to identify what was born today, twenty-six years ago?"

I waved my hand for time, but didn't need it. "Sputnik." My pulse picked up: an event from the year that Todd and I would have given anything to hear him talk about.

"On the nose! A quarter century after the first transpacific flight. Five years before Wally Schirra. It would be tough to measure that kind of acceleration in G's, would it not, Jan?" The sound of my name in his voice froze me. Dr. Ressler took my fluster in stride. "Your friend is in the machine room, with an artificial moon of his own." He left. But not before I'd talked to him, come within a syllable of his past.

Outside the computer room, I stopped at the punch-in lock, although I knew the secret letter combination. Through the plate glass, Franker entertained a woman in her early twenties who I could not stop looking at. Frank must have been at his most charming, as the woman kept hiding her face in her hands. In a minute, he saw me and waved me in, a look of irritation asking why I was hanging around waiting for an invitation. "*Bon soir,* bud. Where you been?" He grabbed my hand and pumped it, as always. I was slow returning the pressure. He smiled and said, remiss, "Ms. Martens, Ms. O'Deigh. Vice versa." I don't feel especially attractive, remembering the introduction. "Annie here is an affiliate of MOL.

185

A teller for the Mother Ship." The bank that was parent company of their firm. "While Jan-o...."

The beautiful girl cut him off. Her eyes lit up as if she had just met a celebrity. She smiled, clearly seducing me with an innocent display of unearned affection. "You're the one who discovered all about Stuart."

I shot Todd a look. He shrugged. "I wish I had," I said.

Annie Martens looked puzzled. The dazed confession of missing something—her "frog face," as Todd called it—came on her often, but never for very long. "Franklin thinks so much of you," she said, eager to start again.

I'd think highly of him, too, I thought, if I knew the first thing about him.

Pocket Score

No climate can resist colonization; the city seeped into even that remote outpost. But *my* MOL, the place's true state, started around nine at night when the supporting cast cleared out. (I say mine, though I won't be going back.) Only after nine did my adopted electronic cave take on the full flavor of dark. For an hour or so before I had in all conscience to return home, the deserted office bloomed.

Their work, starting when most of life was knocking off, was as aloof as a deep-space probe. The almanac says that a sixth of the employed population of industrial countries works other than standard daylight hours. But even in a city notorious for staying up around the clock, the derangement of late shift put them outside the frame. They moved about in a world after the long-expected evacuation, inhabiting one of those heavily worked mezzotint prints of vine-covered ruins, two rococo foreground figures with walking sticks.

Only people who wake in late afternoon and spend their lives in polar dark glimpse the place as it really looks. The nocturnal world disperses light's artificial still life. Dark does something to perception, baffles the rods and cones with a color-flat landscape where touch becomes the chief navigation, even in a room blazing with fluorescence. Certain mood disorders are brought on by reduced daylight; some sufferers of acute depression respond to houseplant UV. Prolonged time in the dark casts the imagination

186

off. Everyone who lives in it ends a romantic, permanently jointless, unappeasable.

The graveyard world is as big as day, but abandoned. Inhibitions are at best irrelevant. Conversation gets strangely quaint. All earth's supervisors are in bed, narcotized. Only the outcasts are up and about, pretending production: decoupled old Belgians in the Congo after colonial withdrawal, playing squash on concrete as lichened as ruined Mayan ball courts. After nine, Todd and Ressler could choose any path they wished, providing the disk packs were processed and the reports in the bin when the morning shift punched in. The office was theirs to use as they pleased: candelabra dinners, masques, music.

And music first persuaded Dr. Ressler to open. Frank was sitting with Annie, on another of her late visits. I joined them for half an hour before heading down the hall on an uncharacteristically bold, dark-inspired whim. I found Dr. Ressler where he always spent the first hours of the shift: in the cramped control room, the closet of consoles and flickering modems. I listened at the door, although I hardly needed to: on the far side, the same music that had been playing the day I met him. I knocked, not even hoping he'd let me in.

But he did, as genteelly as ever. I'd already discovered that frontal assaults would not overcome his privacy. When I'd confronted him point-blank with the printed proof of his earlier profession, Dr. Ressler responded only with amusement. "You can't be interested in such inconsequentials." That night, I easily might have run into the same impasse. He asked with a concealed smile how the news scrapbook was going, then scowled when I told him Todd had already lost interest in the project. "Our friend's cultivated character flaw," he said, "is a refusal to finish things."

He was attentive; he several times asked if I would prefer the swivel chair, if I would like the room a little warmer or cooler, if the music bothered me. But he just as easily fell into unselfconscious silence, and he never once asked why I'd dropped in. We might have sat mute all evening if I hadn't at last said, desperate for a topic, "I used to play these things once. In my teens."

He sat forward as if slapped. "You play?"

"'Played' would be closer to the fact. I haven't touched a keyboard in years."

"You were good?" he asked, gesturing to the pealing from the speakers. "Good enough to play these?"

187

"That was part of the problem. I could play the easiest of the set. With a few, I even reproduced something more than the notes. But the harder ones...." I imitated his wave, not knowing whether to direct it toward the speakers as he had, or toward the turntable, where the generation was taking place. One of the more demanding variations was in the air, a juggling act demanding three separate hands each under the control of its own brain.

I kept talking, not wanting to do anything to endanger his alertness. As with stalking, smooth motion seemed better than sudden, even sudden freezing. "There are two sorts of piano students. The first is proud of the piece she's just mastered. The second hears the next piece snickering. I started out as the first, but drifted into the second."

"I know," Dr. Ressler said. He'd grown as effusive as a boy on a first date. "Oh, I can't say I *know*. I've never taken a music lesson in my life. I am your classic, digital autodidact. I can clunk along on a keyboard fairly grammatically, but with the thick accent of a Pole who has learned to speak English through books." He looked at me, and his eyes shone. "You give me a chance to learn something from a native speaker." I demurred, but he took no notice. "As a self-taught listener, I've often felt, as you describe, pieces snicker at my inability to hear a fraction of what's going on in them." This time he didn't bother to wave at the offender.

We listened, quiet in the exertion. Even his silence seemed preparation. "Certain pieces," he resumed, "have to be put away for a long time. I can't listen to them; they're too evocative. They possess an intensity incommensurate with everyday life. But when I take them out again from their place in the back of the closet where they've waited for years, I can't stop listening." I couldn't stop listening to *him*, to what I'd first haunted this place hoping to hear. "Not long ago, around the time your friend took up as my shift assistant," he grinned, "after several years of not being able to bear it, I found I wanted to study this set again." He contracted his mouth into a grimace: the architecture of the sound, despite his best effort, still held his ears' ability in joyful contempt.

I took a chance. "You've studied them before?"

The grimace broke into a full good humor. He knew I was fishing—the same pond I'd pointlessly trawled a few times before. He was no more eager now to grant an interview, but as someone who might be able to tell him something, however modest, about keyboards, I had him over a barrel organ. He might never have talked so easily had Todd been there. Maybe he considered me a cousin who had also failed to end up in her chosen field. Maybe he saw that I was ready, after thirty years, to begin my education in information science.

Whatever his reason, Ressler told me a story. He spoke of a series of nights as a young man when he first discovered the *Goldbergs*. A week of concentration, when the closed code of music at last broke. "Dangerously close to turning twenty-six, paid to do genetic research, I instead spent evenings lying in an army barracks bed, listening to that aria over and over in my ears, eyes, throat, and head. I was trying to discover why the thirty minute waltzes reduced me to hopeless emotion, to neutralize them through overexposure so I could forget them and recover an even emotional keel.

"I had secured myself a pocket score. You must understand that as late as my mid-twenties, I could detect little more in printed notes than inscrutable black bugs crawling across the bars of their prison. I'm still illiterate, to some degree. Some things one must learn before five or they never come fluidly."

I had a hard time imagining this man as illiterate at anything. But I didn't dare contradict; he was venting decades of introspection, and I wasn't about to stop him for polite objection.

"Who knows? Perhaps I have repressed all memory of an unspeakable grade-school accident involving an unmarked glockenspiel that left me unable to listen to rhythmic pitches without suspicion." He checked my face, to see if he had lost the cadence of humor. "But oddly," he went on, shaking his head, "for some reason I am still trying to puzzle out, from my very first listening, this piece seemed to me less like music than a rescue message. Word from a place I had lived once, but could not find my way back to. That sounds ridiculously romantic, especially for an eighteenth-century piece! But after uncountable listening to a beaten-up copy of the variations lent me by a labmate, I began matching aural events in the rush of notes with the complex symbols standing for those events on the page. The day I finally figured out how the correspondence actually worked, it took the top of my head off. Incrementally, over hours of effort, I found one night that I could actually *read* the score. Incredible! Without actually playing the record, I could transcribe the aria from the page to my head. I could hear the chords themselves, just as if the *Wunderkind* on the recording were in fact playing it. That, young woman, is power."

He paused long enough to shoot me a playful look. "As you know from bibliographic snooping, I was then engaged in tracing the exact mechanism by which macromolecules code for inherited traits." He took a breath. For a terrible moment, I thought he was about to choke. "A big project. Several of my colleagues are still at the task. Their offspring will still be at it. We had arrived at a cusp. We knew a little; enough to know that further extrapolation would require a whole new zoo of relational models. Certain things we already suspected: a long, linear informational string wound around its complement, like a photo pinned to its own negative, for further, unlimited printing."

I had only a dilettantish idea what he was talking about, a modest background from answering a rash of alarmed questions about patented new forms of life. I'd been proud of the bit I had mastered until that moment, when I saw it would not be enough to carry me through this discussion, let alone this decade or the approaching millennium.

"We were looking for the right analogy, the right *metaphor* that would show us how to conduct the next round of experiments. We were in a furious, often-mistaken model-building stage. Exciting—unmatched for human effort, as far as it went. But slippery. You see, DNA is itself a model, a repertoire for proteins. And the convolutions of protein shape are themselves analogies for the processes they facilitate. In programmers' terms. . . ." He gestured through the one-way glass to the computer room. On the other side, Frank Todd stood on a chair, making sublime, exaggerated, Buster Keaton gestures for the entertainment of Annie Martens. She was trying to leave for the evening, and he was clowning her into staying a little longer. I watched as he gave up, thumbing nose at her. She laughed and waved goodbye.

"You're not supposed to know how to program," I objected.

Ressler smiled. "In programmers' terms, the incredibly complex chemical routines of the cell blur the distinction between data and instruction. All this is an overly long digression to give you some idea of what preoccupied me when I first heard Bach's solution for recombining his modest aria. I lay there in bed, concentrating on a line in a particular variation. Say, the first entry of a canon, although I could not at the time have told you what a

190

canon was. After intensive, repeated listening, I could hear the first suggestion of what had covertly fascinated me. The strain separated like an independent filament of DNA—part of the melodic line, but simultaneously apart. I made the momentous discovery that it was a note-for-note transcription of the master melody. My little fragment played against a copy of the musical idea it had just been, a moment before. Disengaging my focus, transferring it from the first to the second voice, I could hear the same fragment matched against the shred it would in the next moment become. When I shifted awareness like this for any length of time, the whole variation, at first inscrutable, dissipated into crabs crawling over each other in a bucket. Just as my ears got hold of the rhythm, it would strobe hot potato with the motive. The two lines would twine themselves back into a double strand. I had found my model for replication."

Dr. Ressler pulled on his earlobes, a characteristic gesture he used whenever he caught himself being inexplicably human. "I thought: 'No wonder this Bach fella is so great a composer. He anticipates Watson and Crick by two hundred years.' Idiot! And I grew worse with the piece before it was all over. It didn't take me long to discover in the music all sorts of outrageous parallels. Nor was it all my fault. The piece has the same numerology as the systems we were working with. Do you know how the variations are built?"

I shook my head. Music had never been a formal thing to me. It had always been a run of expressive moments—urgencies that words only interfered with. But I watched in fascination as Dr. Ressler stood and walked to the turntable, curtly jerked the needle. He placed it back down on side one, track one, and to my astonishment, when the music started again, he began to sing. But not the melody, not the right-hand filigree I had concentrated on when learning to hack out the little aria. He sang, instead, the simple sequence spelled out in the bass. "This," he said, "is what the composer will vary through his gigantic construction. Not the melody; the harmonic sequence. The first great analysis of the piece, written at the moment of Mendel's triple rediscovery, set a precedent by calling this theme the Base. Handy English coincidence." He sang, batching the Base into four-note blocks:

191

He launched into numerology: triplet triads over each theme note. Superimposed over those first four triplet rungs, a diversionary tune that, with grace notes, contains twenty tones. Two halves of the aria, each sixteen bars, both scored to repeat, totaling sixty-four measures. He went to his earlobe again. "All the numbers we were after. The coincidence meant nothing, of course. But to a snot-nosed kid of twenty-five, the exercise was invigorating." To an old woman of thirty, too. It brought out the closet gnostic to hear him talk. Not for the correlations themselves, at best novelties, but for the look at a mind that years of night shift had not put to sleep. One that still drew connections between all things, if now only with embarrassment at its own profusion. A mind that looked for the pattern of patterns, the structure that mirrored mind itself, gave it something to recognize in the landscape around it.

This was my first introduction to musical experience I had not even suspected existed. As Dr. Ressler sang along with the record player, I began to see that he listened to these variations not as if they followed one after another, but as if they stacked up simultaneously, sounding all at once in an unhearable polyphonic chorus. He listened to the world, more attuned to its awful fullness than its expendable melody: a set of variations all based on one, simple, thirty-two-note ground bass; a giant passacaglia preserving the harmonic structure of the original, fleshing it out into every conceivable design.

My hush made Ressler self-conscious. He snorted. "As you can imagine, I fast approached the conviction that either everything in the universe fit into a regular pattern or that I was, at my tender age, perilously close to a weekend at what people in the late fifties were fond of calling the Funny Farm."

I looked away from his self-deflation, through the silvered glass at Todd, preparing a night's work in the other room. Although he could not see us through the mirror, Frank now and then looked up at the room where his delinquent shiftmate sat talking. Ressler, anxious to join him, wound up with that favorite expression of Bach: All things must be possible. A pedagogical goading-on to performances that lay just outside the fingers. What exactly did the phrase mean? "Everything that *is*, is possible" was possible, if redundant. "All things that might be, can be" rubbed up in my mind against unlikelihood. Yet an evolutionist might say the same. All permutations on an amino acid theme are possible; given sufficient time and the persistent tick of the mutation clock, everything might be tried, with varying success. Not every experiment will fly; but every conceivable message string is—whatever the word means—possible.

The mind, emerging from blind patterning in possession of catastrophic awareness, condensed the eon-work of random field trials into instants. Did Bach's baroque ditty harbor the political horrors of Ressler's own lifetime? Everything that humans *can* imagine *will* be implemented. Bergen-Belsen, Nagasaki, Soweto, Armenia, Bhopal: he had lived through all manner of atrocity. These mutations too were built on the little phrase, and then some. To listen to a theme and variations, he suggested, one had to be prepared for dissonance severe enough to destroy even the original theme.

"You see," Ressler at last broke our moratorium, "once the experiment gets underway, all possible outcomes are already implied." He spoke with a spittle of fear in his throat. "The impossibly delicate pineal folds of your ear, for instance. Just one of the infinite ways a child's ear might unfold." He winced, as if at the memory of a specific child. He ended our first lesson by returning to the phonograph and lifting the needle. "I listened to these miniatures for a year, pulled out of them the most marvelous genetic analogies. But at the end, the music refused to reduce, and it hurt worse than before. I was a good empiricist, and just as causality was forbidden me, so was prescription. All an empiricist is allowed to do about terrible possibility is describe it. All things being possible, description is everything."

He grew curt, perhaps ashamed at choosing this moment to break so long a silence. He asked forgiveness with his eyes— ridiculously inappropriate. Only with a woman twenty years younger, one he'd known just weeks, could he reveal his ambivalence toward human company, the host in the hermit. Quietly, his back turned as he punched a few console keys, he asked, "Do you think it would cost you a great effort to recover what you've lost?"

I couldn't for the life of me make out what he was talking about. Then it hit me: my piano skills, never more than modest. He wanted someone to play for him. "Do you two have a baby grand tucked away in all this electronics?"

"I'll get one tomorrow." He laughed, a sound that went straight into my chest.

Time passed before Dr. Ressler trusted us with the rest of the story; he'd dug a great deal more out of the sarabande than a handful of genetic metaphors. He had discovered, in the most painful way, why the aria and its wayward children made unsponsored appearances in his mind's ears, keeping him awake in his barracks at night. It cost him considerably to find out. The music would remain unlistenable for decades. Love was long over, but what was lost to him he still loved so harshly that it prevented him from listening even to its trace.

I would never get from him, in so many words, why he chose the moment of Todd's arrival to return to the unlistenable piece. Why take it up again, just then, obsessively, once more finding in it more than he suspected? Perhaps it had something to do with the incurable Bach's other favorite quote. Asked how he made the keyboard perform miracles of interchanging voices when he possessed only the same finger-bound hands as the rest of mankind, he would say: It's simple. Just hit the right notes at the right time, and the thing virtually plays itself.

Double Check

Three months under the bridge; with frugality and luck, eight more in front of me before I have to hit the classifieds. Sickening to consider, so I won't. Human prerogative. Still: three months of reading, jotting, recalling. It feels as if I quit yesterday, that I'm on that most contrived of civilized symbolic stopgaps, a vacation.

A quarter year of unbroken booking and I begin to acquire a layman's understanding of mutation at the molecular level. Information in the nucleic acid string is carried by the order of base pairs, the sequences of genes. The sum of gene messages—the tangled program of genotype—expands from single egg to runaway cell civilization. The same linear long set (more possible messages than atoms in the universe) chemically juggles the whole fantastic hierarchy until at last it impairs itself with old age and dissolves.

I have a rough analogy of the master plan. Each DNA spiral is *two* chains. The rules of complementary base pairing and the undulating regularity of the molecule give each half-helix the ability to act as imprint for the whole. This trick of molecules to sort, arrange, and assemble odd parts of random world into copies of themselves arose spontaneously, from the early chemical mix and

194

the energy of an electrical storm. Miller produced the essential building blocks by exposing hydrogen, methane, ammonia, and water vapor to electrical discharge and ultraviolet light. By 1956, Khorana had synthesized polynucleotides in the lab. Ressler was then younger than Todd is now, and I was a toddler.

Replication is simple enough to model with a drawing. The split strands separate, each becoming a template for duplication:

```
                        ATTCGAGCCT              ATTCGAGCCT
                        : : : : : : : : : :     : : : : : : : : : :
ATTCGAGCCT                                      TAAGCTCGGA
: : : : : : : : : :    ⟶                      ⟶
TAAGCTCGGA              : : : : : : : : : :     ATTCGAGCCT
                        TAAGCTCGGA              : : : : : : : : : :
                                               TAAGCTCGGA
```

The two daughter strands are identical to the parent. One third of the great bridge: Mendel's factors, *embodied* in a self-perpetuating molecule. That length of string—TAAGCTCGGA, plus hundreds more bases in strict sequence—encodes particular inheritable traits, say smooth seed or wrinkled. Molecular neo-Mendelism is consistent with the rules of gross segregation and assortment, requiring no metaphysical rules—just the constraints laid down by chemists: purine with pyrimidine, electrons in the lowest energetic state.

But that "just" is enormous. Genetic mechanism contains nothing transcendental. Cell growth, organism development conform to the principles of undergrad chemistry. The grammar does not change from generation to generation—only individual sentences do. A simple lookup table, one or more triplets of nucleotides to each amino acid, is universal for all life. Yet to get hold of this, to learn what it means, I must look into a creation story more miraculous than any human genesis myth.

I try to imagine a machine that, through a design stumbled upon by trial and error, has developed the ability to sniff out compounds that it then strips and welds to create another such machine. I cannot. Then I can: deer, euglena, snowy egrets, man. Self-replication is the easy part of the story, the simplest way that the purposive molecule arranges its environment. The sequence of bases in a gene is nothing in itself. Not phalanx, strut, tooth, claw, or eye color. Merely a mnemonic for building

195

an enzyme. The enzyme does the work, steers the shape and function of the organism. The gene is just the word. I must follow it down, make it flesh.

I begin to understand how the real power of this self-duplicating machinery lies not in how perfectly it works but in how, incredibly rarely, it fails to work perfectly. If inviolable process allowed the magic crystal to seed itself in the first place, occasional fallibility permits life to crack open the sterile stable of inorganics and scream out. On the order of once every million replications, something goes wrong. Perhaps a base in a daughter string pairs with a base other than its required complement:

		ATTCGAGCCT		ATTCGAGCCT
		: : : : : : : : : :		: : : : : : : : : :
ATTCGAGCCT				CAAGCTCGGA
: : : : : : : : : :	$\longrightarrow$		$\longrightarrow$	
TAAGCTCGGA		: : : : : : : : : :		ATTCGAGCCT
		TAAGCTCGGA		: : : : : : : : : :
				TAAGCTCGGA

A mistaken daughter: *C*AAGCT.... Who knows what this new chain might mean? Slightly different from its parent, it may produce a different enzyme, an unexpected convolution in the unfolding ear. I draw the repercussions, repeat the replication process with the impostor cytosine going on to pair with its normal mate, guanine. One of the four granddaughters differs from all the other copies. Noise invades the system. One bad pairing alters the gene's original message. Unlike the surnames of American daughters, the change need not be lost in generations. This aberrant offspring—with a new arsenal of enzymes—may be more successful at making further copies than her dutiful sisters, though the odds against this rival the odds against mutation in the first place.

Now I must link Darwin and his riot of proliferating solutions to that one-in-a-million molecular mistake. I must trace how chance static—a dropped, added, or altered letter in the delicate program—can possibly produce the mad, limitless variety of the natural history plates. That forethought and design could come of feedback-shaped mistake is as unlikely as the prospect of fixing a Swiss watch by whacking it with a hammer and hoping. The element I lack is the odd eon. I have eight months. The world has all the time in the world.

196

Whatever works is right, worth repeating: not much of a first principle. How can blind unplan produce a string thick with desire to reveal its own fundament? Where is the master program he was after? Somewhere in the self-proliferating print, the snowy egret, a keyboard that plays itself when you hit the right notes. The theme Ressler hoped bitterly to forget urges me on, whispering in enzymes to rebuild the buzz all around him.

The Question Board

Q: There is an enclosure with ten doors.
When one is open, nine are shut.
When nine are open, one is closed.

A: Once we held metaphor cupped in our hands. But it's foreign to us now, the riddle, lost to our repertoire except in the short span of childhood and the handful of adult months when we recover a glimpse of where we're going. We can predict, measure, repeat our results better than anything that has ever lived on earth. But we cannot answer this simplest of games.

Its beauty is verbal ingenuity: how well the hidden comparison fits. The sorrowful romance of three lines says more in hiding than it would by spelling out. But what *good* are riddles? Why bother with them? One might as well ask why bother with growing old. They are ways to begin to say what wonder means.

But my lost friend, this one is easy! One needn't be Solomon to solve it. When the umbilical is open, all other ports are still sealed. But cut the cord, and the stitch in time opens nine. You have one, proved by your effort to escape it. I have one, a full complement of symmetric parts; you knew it intimately once. Forgotten already? There is an enclosure with ten doors. We are each locked up in one for life.

J. O'D., October '85

197

X

A Day Without the Ever

Todd would choose mornings like this to show up downstairs, ring his private signal—a monotone but unmistakable rendition of "La donna è mobile"—and insist that I come out to play. "All systems go. The dissertation's in hand. Ready for committee in six weeks," he would say, tossing me a softball when I opened the door. "How's about a little fungo?" Unflappable in the face of adulthood. This morning, I'd close his batting hand in the doorjamb. Just once, I'd leave him something he might feel for longer than the usual afternoon.

The date on his Greetings from Europe leaves him at most a few weeks to have stood still and grieved. He never had any trouble feeling deeply. Just broadly, for any length of time. Ressler's lecture notes will never be made good. The ludicrous old stereo has been farmed out to Goodwill. The rooftop garden in Lower Manhattan that kept us in tomatoes all summer has run to seed. And Franklin's moved on to the next feel.

Why waste my limited time narrowing Todd down to a specific atlas spot? He is unreliable, skittish, more changeable than the seasons. But he is the only other person who *knew* Ressler. The only person I know who, even now, I might speak to. If I find the museum that houses met de Bles's panel, what will it tell me? Nothing guarantees that Todd stayed in the neighborhood more than an afternoon. But a start. Something to use my training on. Odd comfort, to know the exact town he was in on 7/6 . An anchor spot. A day like any other.

I start with the obvious: the Low Countries. Aided by art catalogs, I search through northern Belgium, the Dutch Rim Cities. For a minute, I think I've pinned him down in Rotterdam. There, in the Boymans–van Beuningen, a picture that might have drawn him: one of Brueghel's two great Towers of Babel. The painter and subject matter he really wanted to write about. But no Herris. I find a Bles panel—*Paradise*—in the Mauritshuis in The Hague, and another in a regional museum in the south of the country. I am dragging my heels, pursuing the unlikely. The stamp on his card was in francs, not guilders.

I cross the border, no *douanes* to trouble me over undeclared baggage. I find nothing in Antwerp but an afternoon of fabulous distraction. Ghent is a dead end; the altarpiece must have brought him there, but I have no proof. No clues when. I save my chief suspect for last. Brussels. French-speaking enclave in Flemish countryside. Musée des Beaux Arts. Voor Schone Kunsten. Brueghel's *Census at Bethlehem,* his *Fall of Icarus.* Indifferent, irrelevant, overlooked, unbearably mundane suffering, depicted dead on. And for a moment: electric connection. Three bona fide panels by Bles. But the two landscapes do not match the view I'm after, and the subject of the third is all wrong. This painted apocalypse is of flood. The world I'm looking for must end in fire.

The Date, No Longer Off

Todd was never sufficient motive for overhauling my life. I knew nothing of his private affairs, his prior commitments. No matter; I simply liked to be with him. Time was wide, broad enough for all manner of RSVPs. All his solicitous attention made me feel unique. The decorous handshakes and hugs—generations out of date—the barrage of personal questions, the liquid forest-animal eyes, the detailed monologues about his father's Saturday ritual or Northern Renaissance painters made me feel that I brought about a reciprocal cold alertness in him, the suggestion of imminent ocean crossing.

Five minutes of seeing Todd, through the one-way glass, smother pretty bank teller Annie with the same courtier's attention should have brought home that his flood could engulf anything that would hold still long enough to get wet. Sometimes in the early evening at MOL, the phone would ring with acquaintances eager for a share of his voice. Frank would greet every obscure claimant at the other end like a childhood blood brother lost for decades. A thousand people in greater New York considered him their best friend. Only he was on this island alone.

With only the slightest encouragement, I was prepared to jettison Keith, the apartment, our circle of mutual dinner friends—to slash and burn them all, rewriting the past with brutal efficiency. For a moment before consigning the old letters to the bin, I hesitated. Some nights I fell asleep swearing it would be tomorrow. But in the morning, the thought of splitting up the end tables we had bought as a set struck me not as clearing off deadwood but as torching the living tree. Tuckwell, sensing the lumpectomy might yet be avoided, played on my remorse. Fighting to keep me around, he put on a heroic show of lightness, as if that quality would awaken my fullest nostalgia for him. In October, the air took on unbearable, crisp clarity. It was waiting for me. The solid blue of the sky, the smell of dead leaves insisted that courage was a little thing. Slight. Easy, in that time of year when everything happened.

I was then on weekend rotation, two days off in midweek. Keith's willingness to market anything to anyone had landed him in court. An exporter and a manufacturer of an ultrasonic antipest device for whom Keith had done a brilliant multimedia campaign were suing one another for fraud. Each had led the other to believe that fortunes were to be made selling the killer sonic machine in Australia. Following bankruptcy, both held the other responsible for failing to determine that the top three Australian pests were deaf. On one of my free mornings, Keith suggested I join him in the civil courtroom where he was performing. "An especially interesting item in the docket today. An animal psychologist who specializes in vermin defense mechanisms. A must-see on anyone's judicial list."

"Keith, I'm not up to it just now. Besides. . . ."

"Come on, woman. This is just what you need. Lose that long face. We're talking major Constitutional implications here. Democracy in action. The unmistakable element of human pathos." The couple that litigates together, mitigates together. Whenever the *tertium quid* settled down between us, he began to practice an ivy-league irony that made fun of everything he did for a living.

"I can't. I have to meet a friend at the Met."

"First I've heard about it." It would be the first Franker heard too. Todd had extended a standing invitation to look at paintings together any daytime I wanted. That afternoon, I wanted. But

200

unable to move from one life to the next, I took to deception. To compound the ugliness, I blamed the need for deceit now on Keithy. But skulking had started all the way back with that first dinner date. I'd thought that for me to call Tuckwell and tell him "I'm meeting a man for dinner" would have been like the secretary of state announcing, in front of that bas-relief, briefing-room, world map proclaiming this country's perpetual escapade in high seriousness, that we have no immediate plans for amphibious invasion of this week's hot spot. Tuckwell and I had always danced warily around formally fixing the contract. We lived on a perpetual option to renew. My coming on with the threatened leverage of a stranger would seem to telegraph the conventional dictate "Marry or get off the pot." This I refused to do. So I withheld the facts, and withholding, week by week, grew progressively easier.

By that October morning, I was positively skilled at fabrication. Truth seemed so small a thing, against such overwhelming odds. Lying about plans for the Met had an aura of novelty, as exciting as hearing the mailman downstairs. As soon as I invented it for Keith, my faked afternoon date took on a sweepstakes feel. Bold and violent decision, the scent of spice islands.

I refused to justify my day's plans. Keith repeated, "Come on. You'll love this. The technology, the untapped continent, and the men who dared rid it of its lower forms of life. The shattered dream, the falling out of friendship, and the judicial system that reconciled them. And it's free. Can the Met offer you even a fraction of that?"

For years, his ability to stoke up inspired silliness on demand had saved me from myself. But today, that was history. "Not very attractive, Keith."

"Pest eradication prosecution seldom is, dear one."

"Stop it!" I scared myself with the volume. "It's all a big burlesque, your life, isn't it? But you keep putting on the power suit every day, don't you? You jump through the same hoops as any other little zealot. Then you parody it all for your friends, so we'll all know you're only an observer."

Breaking loose, but in exactly the way I didn't want to. Keith closed his eyes and got infuriatingly calm. "OK. Easy, sweet. Let's do a little breakfast before we get too far into this. We don't want to start a catastrophe simply because we skipped today's E, hmm?"

After a healthy dose of vita-look-alike, I still declined to come watch the system in action, if more affectionate in my refusal. To

201

fault Tuckwell for hypocrisy was even worse. Keith, private maniac, professional fair-haired boy of the senior partners, the perfect adaptation for steel and glass, was simply more honest about living the split than I was. The moment he walked out the door, still trying to seduce me with the ludicrous court battle, I was on the phone. By the third ring, I was about to hang up and disappear into telephonymity when he answered. "Museum?" I asked, aping his trick of plunging in *in medias res*.

Franklin answered, "Museum," enthusiastically on the downbeat, although sleep still coated his voice.

Hunger Moon

Even the Biology Building is lately promoted to Shelter Status. The need to imagine safe havens has become epidemic. Ressler's isolation in recent weeks—winding up his rate experiment, avoiding the distraction of his colleagues' company, exploring in the evenings that inscrutable musical code—has been so complete that he has not heard the world-changing news: the Russians have launched an artificial moon. For the first time since the first star maps, a new celestial body circles the sky. Everything at launch level is changed utterly. For a moment, the planet discovers itself on the edge of unforgiving space. Fear is electric: we've escaped the pull of the world.

Western alarm is worse, deafening. The Russian scientist's legendary backwardness is wiped out in one shocking headline. Stalinist science has produced its notorious monsters, notably the state-sponsored revival of Lamarckism. A body's ability to develop and pass on beneficial mutations was deemed ideologically appealing enough for the party to overrule the demonstrated direction of genetic translation. Forced by political dictum, Russian scientists wasted decades hunting the pangene, proof that somatic cells could alter the organism's gametes. When Uncle Joe died in '53, his Acquired Characteristics died with him.

But the West's own search for the genome might itself be biased toward a representational democracy. Ressler loves Haldane's quip about terriers growing tails despite generations of clipping: "Yes, there's a divinity that shapes our ends, rough hew them how we will." But on humbler days in the sophisticated West, he recalls that field evidence for the neo-Darwinian synthesis is itself equivocal. That some bump, not yet a functional eye, can be promoted for generations before it can see is at least as implausible as molecular-environmental feedback. Chance and necessity differ only by degree.

In labs across the country, the "What do you get when you cross Stalin with Lamarck" jokes are hushed furiously this week. A new respect for Soviet science emerges in 100-point type. They've made a satellite, while the brightest stars on our technological horizon are the exploding Vanguard and the Edsel. The blow to national pride is a mobilization call. In one night, science is promoted to unchallenged prominence. Shaman status, educational rage, patriotic and pragmatic. The once-revered business career slips to a distant second in immigrants' dreams for the perpetuation of their genes. Stuart's folks' vision is vindicated.

Where the public feels knee-jerk fright, Cyfer expresses hushed elation. Koss, usually caustic in groups, opens the first Blue Sky after the launch. "How does it feel to be alive at the first groundbreak since Columbus?" We've left the planet. Now there's no stopping.

Joe Lovering, misreading her amazement, scoffs. He can explain the Soviets' beating us to space. "The same thing that got them our A-bomb so fast. And the Super, just one year after us. We let them capture too many Nazi profs."

The lurch into the Space Age will make that last jolt from Stone into Iron seem like a pothole in the road. The dazed, mismatched layman's response to the alien new place follows the second Soviet launch. Laika, first dog in space. The papers demand: Are the Communists just going to let the poor thing die out there? They forget that the ongoing experiment has already taken its every living victim, each step along the way.

Sputnik and the space race make less of an impression on Ressler than they might. He stands on the threshold of news that could rival the Russians'. After a bout of intensive lab work, sleeping little and eating less, he concludes the radioactive trials Ulrich assigned him as busywork. His results fail to support the phenomenon they were looking for. Yet—basic paradox—the unmitigated negative result reveals more than any qualified positive could. The nonresults tell Ressler something serendipitous, critical.

He can't quantify it yet, but certain phages remain partly functional even after mutation should have wiped out enzyme activity. This degree of mutation survival may confirm that the gene is read like a linear tape, that the gene has error tolerance built in, that the message is more flexible than anyone suspects. Suppose a codon in the base sequence mutates from GCT to GGT. If the enzyme synthesized by the new codon is still functional, then perhaps GGT and GCT code for the same amino. Those extra forty-four codons that have been troubling everyone could reduce the chance of error. Redundancy may itself be useful.

He deduces this much from his data on enzymatic persistence. But another unexpected result suggests more. As widely grasped, individual mutations—insertions, deletions, or substitutions of base pairs—garble the stretch of affected message by rearranging its letters. But as little as a single deletion near one end of the asymmetric gene can totally destroy the enzymatic function the gene codes for. Conversely, a deletion near the other end leaves the gene function largely intact. An enzyme produced by a gene with a single dropped letter at the tail end remains chemically similar to the one produced by the original gene.

Ressler infers something Cyfer until then only supposes: the code is read from head to tail. An error at the beginning of the tape throws off the remaining reading. But an error at the end is translated only after most of the enzyme has been built. The metaphor fits, substantiates the model that Ressler has been working on in mental privacy. More important, in the course of the experiment, he's come up with a technique that may help him assemble his Rosetta. He has learned to use acridine compounds in a way that lets him control more precisely just where he places the garble and what shape it takes. One of the first impediments into the codon substitution table vanishes overnight.

Three quarters of the methodology he needs must be out there in print somewhere, public knowledge. All he needs to do now is collect the leads from divergent disciplines and work them into a coherent whole. Nobody has yet assembled the pieces, although he feels the entire field teeter on the edge of the simplicity just beyond their mass conceptual block. His head spins with the immediacy of it: a simple, experimental means of inducing controlled mutations, the tool that will permit them to determine the codon/amino assignments. Selective garbling can tell them everything. Inducing mutations, introducing bits of nonsense into the gene's message, can force the code to reveal itself in entirety.

He sits on a code mine. His mind races to the choices available should the method lead into the vein. He can keep the method in-house a little longer, surrender it to Ulrich, announce the results to the team. But as much as he'd like to, he can't keep mum for long. He must publish the results from this experiment, hastening the pace of the accelerating field. He can't refuse to testify, however much time it might buy. He feels a strange euphoria, an over-whelming sense of inevitability. The thing about to make its grand entrance surprises him by its uncanny *familiarity*.

Leaving the lab in late evening, he fails to recognize the outside, so deep are autumn's inroads. He heads to Stadium Terrace, ex-tended concentration catching up with him in mild hallucinations. Passing the sewage facility, he transposes two letters in its sign: "Flirtation Plant." He hears his name in a distant car horn. The columns flanking Memorial Stadium, in inflamed peripheral vision, become a chorus line of Nike-Ajaxs in launch position. He knows what causes the phantoms; he even understands a little of the physiology involved. That doesn't make the tracers any less real.

He recalls his meeting weeks before, his fumbling attempts to convey the idea to Ulrich, who instantly intuited how little Ressler actually knew of his target. Weeks have slipped by, weeks of self-exile. He longs reluctantly for friendship with team members, con-versation, any conversation, even shared silence. What is it that makes it so urgent to sacrifice the pleasures of inconsequential contact, to get to the *insight*, to be the first to announce a rear-rangement of thought? He is more driven now than ever. The means are nearer than he imagined. He needs only another few months. Time to verify, hunt down obvious oversight. Flush out the variables. Add the imminent last links. But can he take that time in good faith, or is he merely drawing out, delaying?

At home, in the dark, he feels why he needs to race this thing, prove his own intellect, assign a portion of the unmapped world a fixed, unambiguous valence. He knows the cause, but he will not say it. At night, in the dark, he lies in his bunk and listens to a brilliant keyboard strain that will never again sound as it did. The piece flies along under his fingers, in his substrate. Even repeated exposure leaves him with no resistance to her code bug. He imag-ines the woman's face an inch from his. He reaches out, takes her head in his fingers, runs them over her meridian lines and ridges, around her ears, down to the slight flip at the base of her skull, back up to her crown. His innermost cells want to force up against hers, fuse, intermarry. He wants to fight for her, beat experience, propose himself as the best of all fits, the surviving solution. Yet part of him—the most recent addition to that composite surviving act—knows that knowledge this critical must do more than survive.

He is virtually *there,* on the threshold of a barrier-breaking as great as earth's first artificial moon. For the first time in the procession of biosphere, some part, some chance permutation threatens the technique, arrives at the place where it might reach down, feel its own material base, place its hands on its own mechanism, its own *inheritance,* grasp it as deeply as it can be grasped. His own contained code can synthesize the last span. But how can he begin to press his hands through if he cannot extract even the information in this breathtaking tune?

Night Music

A neat trick fires my imagination all afternoon. One lovely demonstration proves that the genetic tape is indeed written in triplet codons. I seem able to catch these things only in rough analogies. I imagine the string of letters:

YOUCANRUNFARBUTCANYOUFIXOURBADEAROLDMAN

In that form, the string conveys little. But if I know the cipher's word length is three, sense springs from the foliage:

YOU CAN RUN FAR BUT CAN YOU FIX OUR BAD EAR OLD MAN

The sense is still a bit cryptic, but I've shed enough noise for the emergence of message. Suppose something damaged this string as it was delivered. Parsing the letters into groups, I accidentally drop the first C:

YOU ANR UNF ARB UTC ANY OUF IXO URB ...

Except for stray coincidence, the line now yields only nonsense. More gibberish results if I drop two letters near the beginning. But deleting three letters near the front produces:

YOC ANU NAR BUT CAN YOU FIX OUR BAD EAR OLD MAN

The message momentarily crumbles, only to rise again into sense. A single deletion near the beginning of a gene destroys the functionality of the synthesized protein. The same holds true for two deletions. But surprising modulation: three successive clipped bases partly restore the nature of the original protein, experimentally supporting a reading frame of three. This result, when combined with the sequential tape metaphor, provides a clue for solving the framing problem. If, in the catalog of sixty-four possible codons, one triplet stands for the start of the gene's message, such a marker would not only separate genes but would also establish the gene's word-frame.

My hunger for proofs grows as I consume them. I feel an unearned pleasure in tracing them, as if I were the first to haul them to the surface. As I catch the formal bug I begin to follow, in analogy, the cold joy, the distinction that had made Dr. Ressler seem so alien. The simplest, most childlike passion: he believed in readability—patterns connecting patterns—long after the age when the rest of us resign ourselves to adult confusion.

That triplet trick returns me to an evening Todd and I spent listening to the great tenth variation with him. Franklin should have been finishing his end-of-day processing. I should have been home, picking up the pieces of my domestic wreck. But neither of us could budge from the room, the formal spell Dr. Ressler had thrown over us. We'd been having an armchair discussion of current events accompanied by the standard background music for those parts. When the fughetta began its four bars of foreshadowing, Dr. Ressler broke off in midsentence. He announced, "Bass entry," and pointed to one corner of the room, as if the piano producing the line hid there. Thus instructed, I heard in the phrase an ornamented descendant of the first four notes of the sarabande. Not as they occurred in the original, but as sent out into the world, harmonically:

A second voice entered. "Tenor," Ressler commanded, pointing his other hand into the opposite corner. I heard the new voice chime in, duplicating the first, a fifth higher. Two more lines entered, question and answer, tonic and dominant, building up a complex clarity of texture. Ressler announced both in turn with near-shouts, "Soprano" and "Alto," cueing each voice, pointing a finger into the room's remaining corners.

At the edge of overflowing, the piece's motor rhythm stopped. The break lasted less than a breath. Immediately, a new harmonic variant on the four-bar subject made its way through the four-voice rotation again, this time rearranged, accompanied by a counterfigure. "Soprano," Dr. Ressler called out from the top, flipping toward the corner where he had first consigned that voice. "Alto," answered right hand with left. "Bass," he cued. I caught his eyes as he called out, "Tenor!" They were full, liquid with a throat-stopping delight.

When the fantastic construction dropped off into random silence, I looked over at Todd. He too, under the persuasion of Ressler's four spatially separate pianos, had heard something. He looked at Ressler imploringly, the way a child looks to a parent to explain the latest infecting crisis. But Ressler was off elsewhere, remembering, after three decades, his search for the underwriting metaphor. "Four-measure bass, four-base measure," he said, to no one in particular, as variation eleven already took the matter further. "Extraordinarily clever fellow, Bach. Ahead of his time."

Only tonight, my head full of mutation tricks, do I begin to name just what I heard, what connection Dr. Ressler mumbled about. Four voices, at four measures for each subject entry, the whole turn-taking undertaken twice, yielded thirty-two measures, a map of the thirty-two-note parent. Not a breath wasted. Nor did the three of us waste ours for catching it. With Dr. Ressler pointing them out, I heard the successive reentrant voices, layering one on top of another, musical analogs of those plastic anatomical overlays in biology books. Each transparent sheet contains its own, separate hierarchies—circulatory, skeletal, nervous. But each overlay, flipped on the stack, adds its system, compacts its parts into a surprising, indivisible composite.

Hearing that much, however modest, was a small triumph. I knew that fugues—while most not as compact as this one—did not necessarily require enormous musical gift to create or hear. Marvelous in my ear, and yet, every note just as it should be. But that much was just the surface of the form, one that went all the way down, as far as I chose to follow. Listening to the cyclical subject-passing entrances, I all at once heard something else. Something going on in the lines after they'd made their grand, identical entrances. In between the formal constraints of fugal entry, percolating up through the piling voices, was the outline of a musical idea I'd heard somewhere before.

My ear flipped back and forth between figure and ground, focus and periphery. What was the bass doing in the second four measures, when the tenor has the subject? Or the bass and tenor, in exultant dialogue, four measures along, while soprano took up the fugue? I heard it in a single stroke, endowed with new ears: the growing braid of free voices sang out nothing short of a mutation on the Base, the original, template theme.

The music ran beyond cleverness, outside admiration. According to my scholarly reference, it follows that fugues, because the same subject enters slavishly in each voice, however brilliantly carried forward, are more or less determined by the thrust of the subject itself, in this case, the fughetta's first four bars. But holding both vertical and horizontal at the same time, I heard that theoretical limit being shed, left behind like a spent chrysalis. Packed in the thirty-two measures of information was a harmonic structure informed by but also perpetually advancing the original aria from which it was merely descended.

The compositional triumph of the piece, both for Bach in the eighteenth century and the three of us lost in the twentieth, came eight bars from the end. The bass, taking its turn with the second fugue subject, extended the harmonic progression and completed the constraints of variation in the same four bars. Breath of air, genuine surprise although absolutely predictable. Rigidly perfect, but moldable to all the nuanced sworls of living ears.

The whole piece, as well as my brief understanding of it, lasted forty seconds. How Bach could meet both horizontal and vertical constraints with such efficiency of material, how he could add insight to inquiry without showing either seam or sweat left me in awe, even after my ability to hear it died away. During those forty seconds, I first felt the resonant, connecting joints holding together this experiment in reversing the randomness of inert matter. I heard the sound that caused Dr. Ressler's eyes to water, the sound that had once vibrated in the tones of scientific reductionism. Pure analogy. No, I need a better name for being unable to tell where I left off and the piece began. I heard, for a moment, the explosion of shape, the diversity of living awareness, dovetail into one simple, accidental, but necessary and breathtaking generating form. For forty seconds, I understood that all evolution was accomplished by juggling only four voices. In the fughetta:

SATB. In us listeners, in the fughetta-writer himself: GATC.

The three of us stopped conversing long enough to follow the shadow of technical virtuosity at patient work, to listen to the fughetta map its own grateful ability to map at all. We eavesdropped, undetected for an instant, on a discussion supremely urgent and articulate but entirely without content. That sound took us, for forty seconds, beyond the point where experience commonly defers: beyond cleverness to joy, outside admiration into understanding, rubbing shoulders against wonder. I heard, in a word, my first few measures of music.

The Enigma Machine

A line runs down the office he shares with Lovering, straight as a surveyor's cut, an osmotic membrane separating the organization of Ressler's area from the entropic mayhem of his office mate. On Lovering's side, arboreal colonies of books, lush, vegetative pools of mimeograph, and ruminant herds of manila-enveloped crap creep up to the divide and abruptly drop off. On Ressler's side: the formal gardens of Versailles. He'd feel better if the barrier were physical—firebreaks, barbed wire—instead of nothing more explicit than mutual goodwill.

His office mate's filing system for the proliferating piles is astounding. Asked to retrieve any paper that has ever come into his possession, Lovering can pull it from the papyrus morass. Nevertheless, the watering hole gives Ressler the heebie-jeebies. He finds it hard to think, seated at his desk; he can feel *tinea corporis* in the damp air, jungle rot crawling behind him, tendrils sucking him into Lovering's data sprawl.

This afternoon, he can avoid the place no longer. Ulrich distributes progress-review forms to be completed by semester end. He must describe all lab activity in the last four months. His one experiment—with its blaring negative results—must be reported with great care. He heads to his office, breathes deeply, and enters. Lovering sits at the desk opposite, red-lining, dispersing professional confetti. "Stuart Ressler! You still on the payroll? Thought you'd skipped town."

"Afternoon, Dr. Lovering," Ressler replies, affable emphasis on the title. "I've been around. Lab work." He keeps his eyes diverted, lest they register the excitement of what he's stumbled upon. Head down, he cuts a path to open spaces.

"Work? You know what the good Dr. Freud says about work?"

"N-no." Ressler sits gingerly on the edge of his chair and eyes the border for any recent incursions. He spreads the form in front of him. "I can't honestly say I do."

"But you do know what Saint Paul says about marriage?" This delivered with sly, shit-eating grin.

Quietly, placidly, Ressler resigns himself to the reproaches of conversation. "What's that supposed to mean, Joe?"

"You know damn well!" Lovering rocks dangerously back in his chair, arms all over the place. Suit jacket and tie are suddenly belied by hayseed, goofy, boys'-locker-room intonation.

"What do I know damn well, Joe?"

"Poontang, my friend." Lovering shakes his head, laughs. "You dog! You animal!"

Ressler does some rapid cryptography. "Oh, no. No, Joe. Really. Believe me. It's nothing like that."

"It's something, then!" Lovering proclaims, as if verifying another organism's distress were cause for publication. "Now we're making headway. Come on, man. What else could it be? You found a little something? No, you haven't. That's the problem. No *poontang*!"

"Uh, Joe. Would you mind keeping it down? This is a university."

"I *knew* it! How could you hope to keep anything like that from your close office mate?"

How indeed. "No, Joe. Really. It's not . . . loneliness. I've just been winding up. . . ."

"We're not talking about *loneliness,* Stu. We're talking about the hot-to-trots. The savage scrotum. Your balls're backed up. Nothing to get embarrassed about. Wouldn't be surprised if the compulsion were programmed into the old transistors at a fairly deep level." Lovering, smirking, tapping a retort rapidly against an ashtray, enjoys himself immensely. Ressler wonders how a nervous distraction he has just identified himself can already be public knowledge. For a professional decipherer, he's shy on a few key secret-communication commodities. "Fortunately, there's a fairly specific treatment," Joe insists. "You just need to find a chick who'll sully herself with you. Barring that," Joe holds up his hand and wriggles his fingers, "there's always the lab assistant's assistant.

211

Blood pressure is entirely incapable of telling the difference."

Ressler sits mum as a skewered saint, nauseated by this crowing cockdom. Even pretending to the ugliest mechanical bias, Joe lies to himself about what blood pressure is after. There is a gene, flexibly distributed throughout the pool. It codes for a protein.... How to put this? If rutting truly drives each organism—and doubtless it does—not even vilest desire, aroused in violence, abuse, or smudgy photos, is free of that linked factor. How did awful tenderness take hold? What possible survival value has it? Lovering's enlightened smuttiness is faked. Heat is by far the easier half of the linkage to admit. Lust does not exploit tenderness; tenderness manipulates lust.

Lovering reaches the heights of confidential repulsiveness. "See, Stu, I have this...." He beams, a boy bringing home a gold star. "I guess you'd have to call her a mistress." The disclosure promotes him to King of France. "Her name...I shouldn't be telling you this."

"You shouldn't be telling me this, Joe."

"Her name is Sandy. A remarkable woman. You know Marie Curie?" Ressler doesn't bite. "Well, she's nothing like Marie Curie. But that's Pierre's loss. Not to say Sandy's a dumb bunny. She knows Diffy Q. But let's face it: if you could bed down the most brilliant female yet produced by evolution, or have your fly zipped for three seconds by Kim Novak, I mean, tell me...?" Ressler rustles his report, but Lovering perseveres. "That's where Sandy comes in. One month ago, after much open and healthy athletic debate, I finally managed to persuade her to bestow upon me all the corporeal benefits of holy matrimony without the contractual obligations. A mere Miss Demeanor. I'd feel like a heel if it weren't for one thing. She *loves* it. I can't come through the door without her...she's an altered personality. Crazed. She *shivers,* for God's sake. She gets, like, surgically grafted.... Let me tell you, the word 'stamina' has taken on entirely new threads to me. On top of that, she can turn stale shrimp into Lobster Newburg."

Almost to himself, Ressler asks, "If she's got all that, Joey, why not marry her?'"

"Where's the crime in that?" This self-declared fling, the prescribed male bravura, renders Lovering so heartbreakingly pathetic that Ressler cannot abide the office another minute, even if leaving means abandoning Ulrich's progress report. Lovering holds forth:

"Come on! You've read Frazer! That's science, too. Soft, maybe, but hey? Tilling the ol' fields?"

Ressler mumbles apology and retreats to the hall.

He arrives without plan at Botkin's office, knocks and enters. Toveh stops her patient exam grading to greet him. "Well! Here is a face absent for too long. Have we clarified some further coding mechanism?" Ressler glances at her, startled. But she's simply making conversation. Alarm unnoticed, he takes his traditional place on the leather couch, psychoanalytic-style. Botkin smiles at the familiarity. "Well then. Today's lesson?"

Ressler raises only a weak, pained grimace. He folds his hands. "Tell me everything you know about music."

"So I'm in charge of the lecture, today. Student teaches teacher, is that it? Such a topic!" Concern crosses her Alpine face. She presses her eyes with the heels of her palms. Her accent spontaneously thickens. "One must learn a language at a very early age in order for it to stick." Ressler, prone, does not move. No point in her asking the source of this sudden cultural interest. Without further objection, Botkin rises to the challenge of condensing the complete procession of Western music into an hour. Assisted by her archive of 78s, she conducts the tour in the hushed monotone of a cathedral guide who tries not to disturb the sanctuary: thorough, succinct, amazing herself by what she says, embarrassed by the desperate variety of ways of singing.

She begins as far back as she can touch, in the incense-dosed anonymity of the Middle Ages. The world as deceptive epiphenomenon. She sings a few bars of plainchant in a rich contralto, unaware of the prohibition against public singing. The mournful intervals of Pope Gregory turn her Edwardian cubicle into a Romanesque-capitaled, monk-infested crypt. She adds two parallel parts to the plainsong and arrives at Organum. From the Notre Dame school, she glides across open terrain, resting momentarily at Conductus, Ars Nova, an excerpt from Machaut's eerie, unrelenting mass. She flowers forth into the Renaissance, demonstrating the startling development of imitative polyphony with the assistance of her disks. She speaks of a new expressiveness, an emotional molding of discord. Music divides into cold North and sunbathed South, remote England and dazzling Italy, although the Venetian school is overrun by defecting Dutch contrapuntalists. Proper names begin to serve as post markers: Palestrina, Monteverdi, Gib-

213

bons, Byrd. Serious music strays out of the church. She plays him that party craze, the madrigal. April is in my mistress's face. And July in her eyes hath place. Within her bosom is September. But in her heart: a cold December.

The monodic revolution saddens Ressler, as does the advent of opera. Both, he feels intuitively, are wrong turns, apostasy. The sensuous music of France and the striving for new complexity in the Netherlands and Germany console him a little. Botkin maps the rise of the fugue through the Northern Baroque masters, all of whom were required to have names beginning with "Sch." The late Mediterranean Baroque is lost on him, tinkled away in ornament. She talks about the emergence of a cryptic system called tonality—a set of rules, mathematical equivalences and prescriptions. Her language becomes laced with arithmetic relations. Reaching Bach and Handel, Botkin forgoes any hope of wrapping up the outline in an hour. Rather, lecturer and audience lose track of time. She stumbles, unable to sum up this first great watershed. She mumbles a few words about the High Baroque rage for unity.

Mention of the Leipzig cantor throws him into nervous agitation. "More on Bach," Ressler shouts from the sofa. "What do you know about this man?"

"Bach?" Botkin remarks in surprise. Not the usual starting point for novices. "Of all the composers in the tradition, Bach is by far the most..." She looks for the appropriate hyperbole. Nothing transcendent enough. "Bach is the most likely to offer to help wash the dishes."

"More Bach," Ressler insists. She plays him the most awful moment in auditory art: the Barabbas chord from the *Matthew Passion*. "More Bach." She plays him the last movement of Berg's Violin Concerto, where out of the abject, serial mass of twentieth-century dissonance arises first the agonized tritone, then the whole Bach setting of a resigned chorale. *Es ist genug; Herr, wenn es dir gefällt, so spanne mich doch aus.* It is enough; Lord, if it pleases you, simply unharness me.

She pursues doggedly—the rococo, the classical homophonic reaction against the spent baroque. The issue is not progress or even advancement of technique, however tenuously that might be defined. Motion is not forward, but concentric: restless rearrangement of styles oozing into every open cranny. She draws him the floor plan of sonata form, its tug between tonic and dominant, symmetry and surprise. Ressler wonders if composers are made to study algebra and architecture before being allowed to play with tunes. The joking grace of Haydn prepares the way for the aerial escape artist Mozart.

She plays him the *Jupiter*. "Listen to him combine the old fugal with the new sonata form; as close to sublime as human engineering gets." Ressler hears, but dimly: faraway sounds from the next town over. He feels the essential oddity of this moment—a young man, hungry for a vocabulary that can contain him, reaching in progressive restlessness back into time to revive an archaism, pouring a *tour de force* effortlessly out of the orchestra like water over stones in a brook, proving that no ear had ever really heard the idiom before, even when it was given up as exhausted. He needs to locate more notes. To detect with more precision the relations of time and pitch that evade him. His clay ear calls out for schooling. But can one learn to hear?

Beethoven, Olympian peak, shakes his fist, cracks a punchline, storms heaven by force. Botkin does Opus 18 Number 1, Opus 59 Number 2, and Opus 133, the *Grosse Fuge,* three string quartet landmarks to give a blurry route description of that lonely launch into the unknown. She mentions the famous intrastaff annotation— *Must it be?* "Either a rage against fate, a rejection of metaphysics, or a reference to his landlord on the doorstep again demanding the rent in cash."

In Botkin's version, this flinging wide of sound's expressive possibilities—contrasting keys, intensifying form, expanding tonal vocabulary—paradoxically spells the beginning of the end of concert music. As with a tumor that initially stimulates a patient into rosy vigor, self-destruction hides in the richest profusion of musical invention in history. Undaunted, she takes on the unmanageable rash of romanticism. She sings with Schubert, Mendelssohn, and Schumann, indulges the introspection of Chopin and bravura of Berlioz, puts up with Lisztian pyrotechnics, and arrives too quickly at Brahms, the most unbearably beautiful of all. "Then we have two towering operatics who might as well have lived on different planets. The first is Verdi. You know all his tunes already; you just don't know they are his. The second, undeniably a genius, I'd rather not go into just now."

"All right," Ressler guesses. "We skip him. Who's next?"

"Well, music gets mixed up in nationalism. Every land its spokesman: Norway, Grieg; Slovakia, Dvořák; Finland, Sibelius."

"I get the pattern."

"The names start shrinking and clumping in groups. The Five. *Les Six.*" She concedes a few more individuals: Tchaikovsky, Rachmaninoff, Debussy, Ravel, Bruckner, Mahler, Schönberg, Stravinsky. "More continuously than most realize, post-romanticism shades off into the eclectic anarchy of the twentieth century. And here we arrive at the far end, writing pieces of unhearable symmetry on one extreme, and on the other, picking notes out of a hat." The thumbnail trip has lasted all afternoon. Outside, the first negative traces of dark. Botkin, hearing herself compress the whole story into a few hours, is bewildered at how a race with fixed needs could get from Machaut to Milhaud in so few breaths.

Ressler feels her displacement, the little light that has gone out in her tent. But empathy makes him suddenly impatient. "What incredible sprawl. The stuff makes no sense. How can I be expected to remember all this?"

Botkin turns to him pityingly. "How do you remember your stereochemistry?"

"False analogy," he snaps. "That's a system."

"History is a system too." She returns to the dry tone predating their friendship. "You might try taking a few decades to study it."

"Too cluttered. Too many names...."

Botkin snorts. "You want a short list, I suppose? Tops of the Pops in each critical period?"

"Yes. That would be fine."

"You Americans are all the same."

"So: all those fellows in the Dark Ages and Renaissance...?"

"Give that to Josquin, with Monteverdi the transition."

"Baroque?"

"Bach. We want help with our dishes, do we not?"

"Classical's clearly Mozart. Beethoven his own class, I suppose."

"Has anyone ever told you that you are a quick study?"

"Romantic? Brahms?" Botkin doesn't answer. She is hearing a light in the night. "And beyond?"

His tutor returns. "Post-romantic... Mahler, definitely. Twentieth century...." She drifts into silence that lasts so long Ressler thinks she has forgotten the question. As he is about to suggest they quit for dinner, Botkin smiles. "Our century: Adrian Leverkühn." He won't get the quip for decades.

"Maybe I'm not after stylistic history, *per se*. Not names themselves—not even the short list." He smiles affectionately. "I need to locate the musical message. Do you know what I mean?" Botkin shakes her head. "Can you look at a score and tell... simply by the pattern of notes, whether the composer has uncovered something correct?"

He has not said what he means; so not surprisingly, she misunderstands him. She tells of Mahler applying for a conducting job, lying about his knowing an opera he'd never heard. "He was hired, spent an afternoon with the *full score,* and conducted the piece that evening, from memory."

She tells the story with such passion that Ressler asks, "That man moves you?"

Botkin laughs. "You have discovered my surreptitious character flaw. Have you any idea what it means to be in love with turn-of-the-century suspensions in a world fixated on drums? Despite effort, I cannot assimilate to the North American ethos. Do you recall that supermarket where we ran into one another? They have, this week, at every checkout, a tabloid reading, 'Millions Dead in Epidemic.' I saw that yesterday and thought: 'So we've brought on the end.' It did not cheer me to discover that the article was about the Bubonic Plague.

"Unquestionably, the music we're talking about is dead. I will not inquire into the source of your sudden surge in interest. Perhaps you shouldn't get started with it. Surely you realize the extent of the transistor age, and where it must lead. I can forgive the children; somehow, they understand the deliberate decision to permanently militarize the world. Even our old refuge science— older for some, granted—is conscripted. So: an eighteen-year-old needs music that can be listened to entirely in three minutes. Just in case.

"And yet, if we're to be saved, the prophase must do the saving. Youth. You've read von Baer, Haeckel, the developmental homologists?" Ressler shakes his head, says he knows "of" them. "My God!" Botkin cries. "Don't tell me they've dropped 'ontogeny recapitulates phylogeny' from formal training. Perhaps they still read Rilke, in any case: *'Glaubt nicht, Schicksal sei mehr als das Dichte der Kindheit.'* Don't ever think that fate's anything more than the condensation of childhood. Champaign-Urbana, with more engineering buildings than pizza parlors, is already a lost cause."

"But music," Ressler reminds her.

"Exactly. But music." She plays him the first hundred bars of Mahler's Ninth, that premonition of wholesale disintegration of the dream—the abandoned condensation of childhood. She tells of

217

the composer's anguished marginalia—the "Oh Alma!" penned into the score upon his discovering that his young wife was copulating with another man. She describes Mahler's session with Freud, how the composer lay prostrate on a couch in Leiden in 1910 for four hours, as Ressler has lain all afternoon. "I picture Freud taking the score of this symphony, studying its figuration, seeing, as you suggest, even as an amateur, that the composer has revealed something terrible, real, and saying to his patient, 'Don't let me cure you of *this*.' That, my friend, is your musical moment. But we're wasting our time. Come. Let's go have a meal. There is still eating, drinking, good talk."

They walk through the deserted corridor, leave the building, lock it behind them. Halfway across the quad, Botkin stops. She turns on Ressler fiercely. "You've worked in a lab, you've scribbled in enough notebooks to know better. I tell you, the world is not modulations and desire. It is stuff, pure and simple."

The attack floors Ressler. He can't think why he deserves this dressing-down. A minute later, Botkin is pleasant again, discussing the choice of restaurants. Over ordering, she speculates, "Your 'musical message.' I've always been partial to text. I don't mean opera; I've never liked flailing. But let me tell you two litanies, late mutations on the Viennese tradition. The first arises in Mahler's *Resurrection:* 'What you have loved and striven for is yours.' I would love to believe that. The second, more realistic, is from a Webern cantata. You admire the compaction in a nucleotide sequence? This man's Opus 21 is a perfect palindrome: a symphony that reads the same forward and backward, entirely generated from a densely threaded theme. Of course, the ear can't hear that perfect order. As far as the listener is concerned, the piece might as well be random! But his text. His 'message,' as you so wonderfully and naively put it. I paraphrase the cantata: 'Keep deep down, for the innermost life hums in the hive.'"

The Enigma Variations

I find a footnote to the race for solution in his day, the story of Beadle's 1958 Nobel Prize for the elegant experiment equating one gene with one synthesized enzyme. On winning the prize, Beadle received a cable from Max Delbrück, a later prizewinner, reading:

ADBACBBDBADACDCBBABCBCDACDBBCABBA
ADCACABDABDBBBAACAACBBBABDCCDB
CCBBDBBBAADBADAADCCDCBBADDCACA
ADBBDBDDABBACCAACBCDBADCBDBBBA

The question could have sat unanswered on my board forever.
I get out my decoder ring, put together everything I know about
Beadle's and Delbrück's state of knowledge in 1958, and set to
work cracking the telegram. I break the string into triplets. By '58,
even post-docs knew to begin there.

ADB ACB BDB ADA CDC BBA BCB CDA
CDB BCA BBA ADC ACA BDA BDB BBA
ACA ACB BBA BDC CDB CCB BDB BBA
ADB ADA ADC CDC BBA DDC ACA ADB
BDB DDA BBA CCA ACB CDB ADC BDB BBA

The message still means less than chance to me. But in the noise
of these codons is a tip-off, an improbable distribution, something
designed. The four independent letters appear freely in each position with one exception. The letter B occurs in the middle of
only one codon: BBA. The unique nature of this most common
trio suggests a special function, perhaps framing. I try a space; the
message splits revealingly:

ADB ACB BDB ADA CDC   BCB CDA CDB BCA   ADC ACA BDA BDB
ACA ACB   BDC CDB CCB BDB   ADB ADA ADC CDC
DDC ACA ADB BDB DDA   CCA ACB CDB ADC BDB

Three words end with BDB, the most common remaining codon.
Taking a tip from Poe, I bank on this one standing for "e." The
two-letter word affords another entrée. A list of common English
digraphs and a little knowledge of combinational restrictions make
the nonsense spurt sense: "or," "code." I push on, lost in a perverse
pleasure. The flush of success makes me feel strong, attractive,
erotic. Suddenly, it's over.

BREAK THIS CODE OR GIVE BACK NOBEL PRIZE

Nothing compared to coaxing the truth out of *Neurospora,* yet
the Nobel nominee needed help in the cryptanalysis. Beadle re-

219

taliated. He sent Delbrück a comeback code of *his* invention, which Delbrück also needed help in cracking. But Delbrück got in the last word. Beadle's scientific address before the awards ceremony in Stockholm was interrupted by the confused delivery, in mid-speech, of a package air-mailed Urgent. Beadle opened the crate to reveal a toothpick sculpture in the shape of a giant double helix. The tips of each toothpick were painted one of four colors. The pattern was irregular with hidden information. When Beadle's lecture broke up, the roomful of premier life science brains pushed up to the podium, studying the color sequence, speculating, testing propositions. At last someone—or not someone, but that collective twentieth-century organism Big Science—hit on the solution: I AM THE RIDDLE OF LIFE. KNOW ME AND YOU WILL KNOW YOURSELF.

Both Delbrück codes are curiously self-referent. Break *this* code. *I* am the riddle; know *me*. What "me" could possibly proclaim itself the riddle? The cipher? The plaintext? The coding algorithm? The riddleness in the coder himself? What part of the DNA sculpture has the audacity to call itself "I"? The Delbrück code, the one inside the codemaker's "I," modified by no criterion except survival, grows miraculously capable of games. The I's have it. Know me and you will know yourself. I spend the afternoon playing with messages, and on no proof but my pleasure, feel as if I'm closing in on my discovery, me.

The Census

At night, I put away the substitution ciphers and return to the painting index. I search for that particular oil-on-panel. But only Brueghel surrenders to me. Pieter the Elder: the man who was what Bles might have been, had the lesser possessed the passion of ordinary events. In *The Census at Bethlehem,* burghers in a wintry, sixteenth-century Brabantine town go about their business—men carting cargo, women slaughtering animals, children playing furiously on lake ice—without noticing the holy couple queuing up in the foreground to be numbered in obedience to Herod's order, unaware of the coming slaughter.

> Believing what we count, counting what we see:
> A fistfight; gathered firewood; gutted pig-

220

grease caught in waiting pan. These things
are here at hand and present endlessly,
an endless repetition of infolded theme.

What was it that we hoped to settle on
by census, counting, inventory, roll?
While earth runs to frozen iron ball
we number Now as if already gone.

This time we say we'll get it straight
sum the total, number all the fear
that snows the town in at the end of year,
the spur, the memory that drives men out

onto the frozen sea to map its edge
for clues to the mystery that was here
all along sends children out on sleds
with their own keen sense of the contested game:
Believing nothing lost that's lived, counted, named.

    Today the Pilgrimage of Grace occupies York, thirty years before
Brueghel's census. Religious sectarian revolt, same genus as the
violence daily sweeping the Near East to my absolute bafflement.
Today is the first newspaper to be printed regularly in New York
City, 1725. The first of those loose-leaf folders filled with Bruegh-
elian specific figurescapes whose holy historicity no one ever manages to feel. Today is a town square packed with people: Marie
Antoinette guillotined, 1793; battle of Leipzig, 1813; first use of
ether in surgery, 1846; Harpers Ferry raid, 1859; excavation of the
Cardiff Giant, 1869; British halting the Germans at Ypres, 1914;
1,200 killed in Yangtze troopship explosion, 1926; Bengal struck
by cyclone, 1942; China's A-bomb, 1964. Anachronisms as persistent as the Flemish church in the background of a scene showing
Mary and Joseph's arrival in Bethlehem.
    "I have this persistent fantasy," Franklin told me, holding the
cold bed linen to his neck as he spoke. "Met de Bles seeing that
incredible panel, from the far side, a dozen years after his death.
Knowing at once that his compatriot has spelled out in specific,
radiant, complex, floating detail the nomenclature of human ecology that Herri himself had been born to describe, but died unable
to articulate."

Near Where the Wheatfield Lies Cut Down

I met Todd on the steps of the Met, sitting in the middle of a Brueghelscape of tourists, pushers, impoverished art students, culture vultures, religious questers, Van Meegeren society frauds, footsore pedestrians sitting a minute, delinquent office workers taking a late lunch, and the occasional pilgrim of grace who simply liked looking at paintings. Frank stuck out of the assembly, even a block away, the one anomaly in the packed crowd. The first time I ever saw him in broad daylight.

Incredible weather, a June detour en route to November. I'd walked from two subway stops away, to discharge the jitters and give myself another chance to back out. Walking, I saw Manhattan as I hadn't for a long time. I remembered why I'd come here—the epitome of epitomes, the most convoluted, aggressive, over-stimulating *tabula rasa* imaginable. The place was just bizarre enough, packed with sufficient diversity of neighborhoods, for me to make of it anything I wanted.

I saw him from a block off—outside the cave. He was exhilarated by the crowd. Here, in midday, he had lost nothing of the air I'd assigned him at our first meeting. He met me halfway down the steps, pumped my hand vigorously. "Great idea, this. Haven't been here since late last week." He rushed ahead and paid our admissions, over my protest. Then we fell into the quiet of the galleries.

We could head down any corridor of this maze, choose our century, school, bias, genre. We could buzz through, a masterpiece a minute, or stand all afternoon in front of one portrait. With every imaginable way of seeing to choose from, we made no choice. We wandered, letting each step determine the next. Franklin knew the galleries by heart. He could set in on a topic, wheel slowly around a corner, and land us in front of a picture that I'd realize had been the topic's inspiration, even from the previous room.

Sometimes he was all formalism, tracing a lazy zigzag in the air in front of a Claude Lorrain, the rigid design of seemingly languid figures in landscape, a pattern glaringly obvious once pointed out. Sometimes he was all association and shameless indulgence. "Look at her gaze," he whispered, nodding at Vermeer's *Head of a Girl*. "A solitary locked gate, with no adjoining wall, in the middle of nowhere."

Sometimes he told unrelated anecdotes. "When Renoir became too crippled to hold a brush, he painted with one strapped to his forearm." His praise was all in his eyes, and his criticism was so gentle I sometimes didn't realize what it was. "A skilled painting; blameless to a fault." He was too funny to be pedantic. We stopped in front of a cryptic contemporary piece in the American wing. "Don't look at me," Todd mugged. "I got a B in Zen Buddhism." Gazing at one of those baroque hyperrealist spreads where you can count the cherubs' lashes, he smirked, "You know what this painting says to me? It says, 'Press on.'"

"Ain't nothin' here I haven't been drilled on," he drawled. "Would still be drilling today, if the alma mater hadn't pitched me out on my severed ear. Seems they have a business to run; actually expected me to turn out some finished product." He tsked at the academicians' psychological naiveté.

We arrived, as if by chance, at an enormous gold resonance, a wheatfield being harvested. In the foreground, among the stacked sheaves, by a tree, people sat eating. One exhausted figure lay sprawled asleep under the tree, breeches loose and abandoned. Todd would tell me nothing about this work, but the length of time he spent looking at it made me realize he'd been steering us to it all along. Brueghel's *Harvesters*. One of a series of Months, depicting the run of the year. At last, Todd spoke, bitter with fullness, out of the corner of his mouth. "If by some accident we get separated," he said, "meet me back here."

Under the persuasion of my private guide, I realized that my own modest understanding of painting had gathered nothing of the unlimited vocabulary of sight. I had never seen paint before; I had never *seen*. Not that I saw any better then, but I began to feel that I might. Shape and form began to seem dialects of desire. The desire I started to see between Prussian blue and cyan owed much to the way he kept his voice low, came behind me, placed his head on my shoulder, moved just enough air to register in my ear: "See the line of that mountain, how he mirrors it in that tree limb?"

Slowly, deliberately, I let my focus slip from the paintings to his descriptions. I gave in to heat; I hurt, slack across the slope of my chest. I arched involuntarily from the small of my back. I could discriminate every hue, every brushstroke he mentioned. I had dressed up, made myself a visual lure, come down here expressly to let this stranger pick me up, undress me with art lecture. I knew

223

then that I would leave Tuckwell, that I would tell him that evening.

I tilted my face toward my private guide, pulled his ear to me.
"Could we see?" I said, ashamed at the femininity of the request.
"Could we see the costume collection?" We went downstairs together. There, amid a fabulous fetishistic compendium of Belle
Epoque embroidered underclothes, he at last smelled the rearrangement going on in me. Having done nothing but brush hands
since the day he first accosted me, he leaned down toward me,
announced, "I think it's time," and kissed me. I knew it was coming,
I had solicited it, but for some awful reason, my mouth ossified.
We kissed like two planks being nailed together. Todd straightened
up with a blameless smile and said, "I think it's not time." But it
had been. Only, in the moment before our mouths grazed, I saw
myself *there,* near where the wheatfield lay cut down, waiting for
someone I'd become inexplicably separated from.

XI

I Sit Still and Wait for Cloudburst

Q: And after the private gallery tour?

I went home and told Tuckwell. It was eerily easy. After months convincing myself I could never go through with it, molting, when the time came, was far less traumatic than the preparation. Avoidance is always a dry run. Keith, too, had prepped for the inevitable. He met my declaration as if he'd engineered it. When I entered our apartment fresh from the museum, Keith sensed something. He said in emcee's voice, "If it isn't the Jan o' the Day." He rushed at me, hunched over in playful wrestler's crouch. I gave in to the squeeze. Then I calmly dropped my clinch-breaking clincher. A tiny, pro-tem stem of brain took over, and with a quiet final whack of the gavel, I announced I was withdrawing from the Five-Year Plan as soon as I could find a place.

Keith and I had met years ago on a downtown E that had stalled. For the dubious entertainment of the whole hostile car, this lunatic in three-piece suit began telling a story about a Beechcraft Bonanza amassing a lethal charge while passing through an electrical storm. The passengers and pilot had no idea of the potential they carried. When the plane touched down on a wet runway, they were all electrocuted. The train lumbered back to life and coughed us out at West 4th. Chance put me behind the stand-up act, and as he touched foot to the concrete platform, I goosed him in the ribs and shouted, "Fatal discharge!" He practically shot up through the sidewalk.

We had dinner together, discovering we'd been virtual neighbors before transplanting. I asked him how a good Midwestern boy triumphed over regional reticence to tap-dance for whole trains full of angry urbanites. He stuck by the story. "That's how I'll go. I know it. You're looking at a man who has a standing date with electrocution." Foreknowledge of what waited if he ever came to a full stop kept him on the continuous insulated ride. We left the restaurant, and he kept at it: everyone we passed was either a massive anode or cathode; one couldn't tell, just by looking, which. "A pasty-faced World Trade exec and a punk, spike-haired bohunk might carry the same charge. The two of them can shake without fear of instant annihilation. But you and I might be dosed with opposite capacitance. Brush shoulders, and we're a spent commodity. Null and void." No more fitting an exit than to go up in a spurt of acrid smoke in the middle of pedestrian traffic on Avenue of the Americas. But that end, however much it might have appealed to him, didn't arrive that first evening. Not until we stopped touching, grounded.

As he raced to embrace me, wanting forgiveness for the tiff that morning, I limply let him pin my limbs to my body in comic wrestling. Then I discharged. He dropped me, burned, and sat down with a look I'll never forget. It crossed our minds at the same instant—that ancient silliness neither of us had thought about for years. I'd confirmed him at last. He put a hand to his head, shook it, smiling: *I always knew it would be electrocution.*

It was easy. I said, "Keithy, I have to look for a new place. You know I do."

"Sure you haven't found one already?" He looked away and said, "I'm sorry." He fiddled with a piece of visual camp he'd found somewhere—a stiff cardboard print of the Virgin making a curtain call at Lourdes. He fanned himself with it. "Go on."

"I don't know how to, quite." I felt alert, autumn soaking my receptors. "We haven't been. . . . We haven't really liked each other very much lately."

"No."

"What do you mean, *no?*" I shouted. When he laughed, I felt everything I'd ever loved about him return in one instant. It had been forever since I'd dared joke. Imperceptibly over time, we'd paralyzed one another. But he was willing to laugh when I most needed. That hurt. Tuckwell's aggressive punchlines—his every affectation of mean spirit—sprang from love of human absurdity. I owed it to him to pack my bag and leave quickly.

It was automatic, once I gave it the first push. We hardly needed to hash out logistics. We agreed we were both too expert at ra-

226

tionalization to benefit from institutional attempts at patch-up. "It does seem somewhat presumptuous to show up at a marriage counselor without a license." In truth, there was no therapy except quitting. We both knew that trial separations are rigged—self-fulfilling equation in two unknowns. All separations were final. Our mating simply had not lasted for life, per our inner instructions. I felt the residual mammal tract, the pair bond, torn from me. But it wasn't my mate who was disappearing.

We worked out the particulars, adultly arranged the furniture deeding and cash transfers. We set a timetable of target dates. The more painful the depreciation, the more effortlessly I wrote it off. I looked for signs that Keith was relieved as well. But he remained subdued, neutral, if not unhelpful. We talked through the news hour, skipped dinner, at last called the day on account of darkness. But before we climbed into the now awkward bed, Keith revealed himself. He cut through my anesthetic, scraped the nerve he could not have gotten to deliberately. "Can I ask you one thing?" he said, lying on his back, examining the road maps in the plastering. "Let me look over any place you find before you sign anything. I don't want you to get stung."

I grabbed his shoulder, forced him to face me and accept my embrace. It had been months since my cells had felt so exhilarated. Then I saw his mouth pasted with the death smile, a sickening look of failed bravery, that amused lip-pinch of confusion when receiving news too appalling to put together. *Your parents both died.* Broad smirk. *You have inoperable cancer.* Warm grin. *I'm leaving.*

Q: To whom could a body turn?

We'd lived so professionally that our friends came mostly from our respective offices. Socializing with already incestuous work acquaintances is so widespread that it must be a capitalist trick to increase productivity. All jobs are surrogate families, complete with oedipal urges, sibling rivalries, and the ugly rest. To occupation and family, add primary social contact and recreational outlet. In another fifty years, we'll have returned to the medieval apprentice system, with parents selling their ten-year-olds into careers appointed by benevolent aptitude test.

Sure, Keith and I saw a few people regularly simply because we liked them. But those we saw most easily were those already in tune with who we were all day long. Keith felt no need to advertise for friends when he had friends in advertising. And I could imagine

227

no periodic contact that would require me to cross the Wilson Line. As such, we each had to go on working inside our social circle after we separated. Neither half of our partisan friends was much help in the massacre.

I had two or three major moorings, each in her way having come, once, closer than words commonly allow. Had any of them asked, I would have hopped a jet out of La Guardia on a moment's notice. But they never asked. In fact, they called only around holidays, never with a trace of desperation. That made it impossible to call them now. I also had my share of lighter long-term friends whom I might have called for steadying: college chums similar enough for some intimacy, a cast-off amour who had stayed in touch out of decorum. I'd made these friends when young enough to risk friendship casually. I lost that ability after twenty. By thirty, acquaintance-making had become a formality with diminishing return.

I called an old girlfriend in Indiana, just to tell someone I knew how I'd smashed domesticity into little bits. In the back of my mind I had the regressive idea of talking her into coming out and sharing an apartment. She upstaged my news: "How did you know to call? I just found out I was pregnant."

Had it been death, I would have had dozens of names to contact. But no one had died, Tuckwell's smile notwithstanding. I was just clearing out. Still, I needed to tell someone closer to hand. Not for emotional support; I just wanted to go public so I couldn't back out. But who to announce to? My regular social contact consisted of checkout clerks, the muffled sadism from upstairs, and a host of cheerful, limited-time phone offers.

Q: What about the third party?

He didn't even know he was one. Franklin was more self-sufficient than I would ever be. It colored his conversation—that inappropriate bravado, the ellipses of a person too long talking to himself. I saw him charm cashiers, elicit from news vendors long stories of their boyhoods, wield phone-devotion over who knows how many fellow alums, even—how could I fail to see it?—ask anonymous librarians out to seafood breakfast. Of the scores who unrequitedly counted him among their friends, he must have had a genuine confidant or two. But Todd stuck to only one other man I knew: the only man on Manhattan more alone than he.

I was the woman who had brought him, however humble, the contents of Dr. Ressler's file. That was enough to earn me visiting privileges. And visiting, up to the moment when I had the history of art etched onto my eye with Dürer precision, sufficed to show that Franklin's days of socializing had ended with the B.A. He'd hinted as much over our first date: the look that came over him at the piped music, the defensive posture he unconsciously assumed as we stepped into the street, even his stoic suggestions for quotes. Franklin's favorite take on companionship came from Melville. While survival might force one into bedfellowship with a Queequeg or two, "truly to enjoy bodily warmth, some small part of you must be cold, for there is no quality in this world that is not what it is merely by contrast."

North East West South

Q: How did he respond to the news?

The same way Franklin responded to all news. He clipped my announcement and added it to his collage. After the day in Brueghel's wheatfields and night lying alongside Tuckwell's death grin, I stayed away from MOL for two weeks. After making the declaration, my conscience didn't even allow me to call. Predictably, Todd did not call me either during that period, not even to see what was up. Nor did he come to the branch, although we were just blocks away. His signal was always the rich, ambiguous, low wavelengths of silence.

I wanted to move out without profit, to get by happily alone, assuming the worst case. In fact, the prospect of solitary evening meals, putting anything I wanted on the radio, warming the linen with my own legs was all I hoped for. But after two weeks, I had to deliver my news. The more I tried to ignore my need to notify the MOL-men of my decision, the crazier I became to see them. I was consumed by outlandish fear; their suite, in which nothing had happened for years, might have gone up overnight in smoke. Or perhaps the antique bivalve elevator had snapped. Perhaps Todd, fired with dissertation at last, had given notice. Perhaps Ressler, so long in the process, had dissolved.

On the first day in November, after two weeks of determinedly not thinking about the two of them—*fifteen days,* to paraphrase Todd's favorite joke, *but who's counting?*—I could hold out no longer. I had done nothing at all that day. My contribution to the molecule's three-billion-year attempt to name itself was exactly nil. I'd had one request all afternoon, for an indifferent statistic, and had directed the questioner to the PAIS. "The what?" Pointing out the table where we kept the service was not enough. My patron looked aghast at the thought of combing the binders herself. I bit my lip and did the lookup for her. And as I flipped through the cutaway grand canyon of back issues, I remembered how arbitrarily Franklin had first descended upon me with his plea for information, a difference that might make things different. Pathetic, pitiable, wonderfully smorgasbord, his insisting that an unknown man had once done something worthy of print, on no stronger evidence than the man's face creases and his command of diction.

Remembering how furious Todd's italic name had made me, I needed so badly to see him, talk to him, tell him my irreversible step, that I did what I'd never done in all my years at the branch: I left early. I left Mr. Scott to field any residual Oscars, walked down to the warehouse, and buzzed my private signal. The door barked without a word, and I rode up in the accordioned freight hauler, blessing the winch-and-chicken-cage for still going through its paces. Jimmy Steadman greeted me at the top of the shaft, having just punched out. He shook his head sadly and said, "I sort of hoped you'd outgrown this place."

"Why, Uncle Jim?" I asked, touching him on the arm as we swapped spots. Everything made me happy—the elevator, the cartons of three-part paper, this prematurely old man.

"Because one of these days, these electronic brains are gonna launch Operation Rude Awakening." He pushed his glasses up the slope of his varicose nose. "You don't want to be around then. You won't want to admit knowing any of us." Jimmy waved good night and swung the iron lever around its semicircle. The grate swung shut, the car descended, and I was alone in a silence so great I could hear it coursing in my ears.

Franklin was in the cafeteria, taking his time before commencing his share of the GNP. Dropping to my knees like a recruit in basic training, I crawled unnoticed to where my consolation sat. Only when I lowed did Frank rock upright, surprised but not frightened by another sentience in the room. Seeing it was me and not a dazed seven-point elk wandering down from Canada, he laughed explosively, grabbed my head in his arms, drew it to him, and nuzzled my neck. This time, no crossed choreography. "I'll teach you to stay away so long," he growled, shaking me by the rib cage and sinking his teeth into my shoulder. The man was unreformable.

230

But from that moment, visa granted, our way of being with one another changed. From then on, we could not be in the same room without resorting to the etymology of touch.

I rabbit-punched my way out of his rib-grip and straightened. Fighting to keep the guilty triumph out of my voice, I said, "It's been an eventful two weeks. I'm making a move. Looking for my own apartment."

Todd brightened vicariously. "That's great!" he shouted, cuffing me again by the waist. Then, realizing, he whispered gingerly, "Isn't it?"

I looked at him and decided. "Yes," I said. "I think it will be."

Todd turned back to his notebook, and for a minute I thought he hadn't understood. When he spoke, I saw that he knew everything, even the part he played in my decision. "We must make sure both of you get through this all right." As if he were my agent, manager, chargé d'affaires. He asked me a hundred of his patented questions that evening. Was I ready? What did I hope to get from it? Would I go on seeing Tuckwell? Did I have a bad conscience? Did it help to talk? This last, at least, I answered unequivocally. Despite the attention he lavished on me, our new intimacy, he looked at me the way he had stared at that Vermeer *Head of a Girl:* urgent, quizzical, separated by centuries. He listened to every detail of my last five years. And it all went into his new pet journal.

Q: What was he so intent on?

As we talked, Todd labored with colored pens, scissors, glue, and bits of postcard. The pages he made were so full of hue and texture I thought they must be visual studies. When I caught sight of reproductions of two paintings we had seen at the Met, I thought he'd at last begun the postponed apprentice piece he'd once described as the bane of a decent computer operator's existence. I imagined our private art tour had at last brought him to it. "I see I'm not the only one setting off," I said. Even as I clamped down, I couldn't hide my happiness. But Franklin looked up, confused.

"Oh, you mean this." He gestured defensively at his handiwork. "Scrap, actually. Stupid." He flipped a few pages, skeptically. "Here we are. Four weeks ago. Old enough for aesthetic distance, hmm? Well then. You explain this to me." He held the page open for examination. At the top, he'd emblazoned the date in parodic gothic. Below was no dissertation, no visual study. It was a base of news copy run into a Rauschenberg combine, one of those bric-a-brac assemblages that accumulate outside the grottos of Spanish

231

saints. Prominent, *en face,* he had pasted two front-page columns, set in the same typeface: "Missile Issue: 2 Perceptions," and "America's Cup to Australia II as 132-Year U.S. Reign Ends." The two headlines were indistinguishable in emphasis, except that one had a secondary head claiming "Each Feels Other Holds the Advantage."

"Exactly how they appeared in the paper. All I've added is the paint job. We're to read them both as *news,* although only the boat race passes the novelty test. And look! This one was wedged in the middle, begging to be overlooked: 'Beirut Premier Offers to Resign in Truce Accord.'" He spoke in the same voice that had whispered the secrets of canvas in my ear. But the accents of incomprehension, which in front of the wheatfield had ached to take in, applied to Beirut—in light of subsequent events—registered only bitterness at being held forever in the dark. Event was clearly there only to carry the ads. He had worked other message-threads into the collage: "Slow Start for Weinberger in Peking," "Nicaraguan Rebels Fail in Effort to Seize Large Town in the North." But the text trim, now smoke screen, debased to diversion, was just the thin excuse for a profusion of visual quotes—Rembrandt, Caravaggio, his own inked labyrinth.

We sat, Todd cradling my upper arm, rubbing it gently to revive feeling. At length, he relaxed into my arms and kissed me where the collarbone turns to sternum. He came up without apology and asked, "What would it feel like to wake up to an evening edition finally announcing that something definitive had at last happened? Something *real?*"

No matter what my failings as a mate, woman, daughter, or friend, I've always held up my end of a conversation. I answered, "November first. Pompeii buried by Vesuvius. Lisbon destroyed by quake; sixty thousand die. First H-bomb explodes at Eniwetok. Jan O'Deigh walks out on lover, unprovoked."

"You've landed fortuitously in my lap. A woman who already knows what's happened today." He looked at the cafeteria clock. "And here we are, with two hours left." He took both my hands between his. "I've been very rude. I'm sorry. I know where you must be, just now."

He was obligated to complete *something* before the day shift returned. But before he set to work and I returned to what was no longer my apartment, Todd showed me one more page of that new journal, the destruction of his careful clippings under rococo

232

stuccowork. He explained why he had given up on the text, buried it under a wedding cake of filigree. "Most people who pull apart the *Times* aren't looking for the millennium; they just want to explain the roundup in their corner of the panel. Everyone has his own port of entry: Business Day, Style, Science Times, the classifieds. Mine used to be page one. Quidnunc, ambulance chaser. But that was last month. You get tired of that. Look here."

He retrieved a story, buried alive under anatomical drawings so expert I was shocked to realize he had drawn them himself. This page of his *belles heures* carried as background "Youth Advises House on Computer Crime." Teen tells Committee on Science and Technology how he tapped into secret records stored on mainframes at Sloan-Kettering and Los Alamos. These ultrasensitive systems still used the passwords they were shipped with, unashamed log-ins like "system" and "test." I could not read the story, as it was lost in vineyard rows creeping up a craggy Rhineland castlescape. Todd paraphrased, barely concealing his delight in the child's ingenuity, the celebration of American frontier. He recited half from memory, "When asked at what point he questioned the ethics of his actions, he answered, 'Once the FBI knocked on the door.'"

Todd smiled crookedly in the direction of his own mainframe. "The problem with living in the land of self-reliance is that a fellow has to do everything himself." I look at the artwork again tonight, yellowed by two years. Reportage transcribed to raw color, Franklin's latest attempt to bring newslight into the abandoned lunchroom. Shortly afterwards, this variant too broke off in favor of a new one. Operation Rude Awakening.

Todd grabbed his workbook from my hands, flipped violently through the pages. "Lots of fertile stuff here. Two hundred marines killed by truck bomb. Invasion of Caribbean nation. Big-time visual potential." Under his thumb, the illuminated calendar shot past like those children's animation tricks. "After a little time for aesthetic distance," he breathed. "Do you think," he turned casually, "there is something in the air?"

Q: Is there something in the air?

I asked him what he meant, but he took me to him again, half-tickling, half-measuring the flesh of my back. We had been on hugging terms forever; I'd never touched anyone before. He walked me to the elevator, waited, deposited me into the box, planted the softest, most fertile kiss cleanly on my lips, and pulled

233

the grate shut as if tucking me into bed. But before I threw the lever to descend, he called out, "What day is today?"

Q: What day is today?

My answer was immediate. The day I at last left home. November first. Perpetual madness. I called out, halfway down the shaft, "All Saints'."

In the Archives

My father died when I was twelve. I remember nothing about him except my suspicion that he would have preferred that I'd been a boy. But I do remember how in every situation, he'd say that one needed "the right tools for the job." At the risk of having my old instructor in Research Methods revoke my degree *ex post facto,* I admit I haven't had the right tool for the job until today. I am looking for a town where he might be, a painting that might lead me to the hiding place. Until today, I've done this absurdly, museum by museum, from a handbook for art hunters making the Grand Tour. Trying to determine who lives at a certain address by using the phone book. I've willfully ignored the capstone of civilization—pointed arch, vault, flying buttress launching man's assault of the vertical—the cross-index. The higher the indexing level, the higher the civilization. From the recesses of my dusty reserve, I remember the cross-index for what I'm after. A two-volume, compact ordinance survey of the painted world.

With the right tool, the job is trivial. I look up met de Bles in the Painters volume. On demand, a complete list of everything the compilers know him to have painted: *David and Bathsheba, Copper Mine, Adoration of Magi, Mountain Landscape, Village Landscape, Landscape with Iron Foundry, with Flight into Egypt, with Good Samaritan, with Banishing of Hagar....* One of these landscapes must contain my conflagration. The titles give entry into the Names volume. There, amid the collections of Florence, Dresden, Belgium, I find a landscape matching my description. Even before my eyes confirm it, I know where the panel hangs. Museum of Fine Arts, Boston. As in Mass. USA. Idiot! I was there when he picked the postcard out. I stood looking at the scene with him for almost half an hour.

Todd sent me the scene to elicit a very specific association. In the depths of winter, in early 1984, he badgered Dr. Ressler and me to make a trip to New England. Pivotal visit. Franklin and I, in that woods cottage, reached a pitch of intimacy that could survive every climatic catastrophe. Dr. Ressler, coerced into the adventure, trapped with the two of us, at last told us the details of how he had fallen through the biographical safety net. Two timeless days together, isolated in the solitude only snow can bring on, tracking, talking, singing, solving mysteries late into the night. A community of three. For a moment it seemed we would never return to the city to need.

On the route up, we'd stopped in Boston, the Fine Arts, expressly so that Franker could see the panel. A research stop, he called it. He must have thought I would recognize it at once, a telegram of nostalgia held at arm's distance. Cursed with my visual illiteracy, I never connected the two images. He must have carried the artifact with him across the Atlantic and posted this emigrant Herri back from its native Flanders. It certainly came from the Low Countries; not even a draftsman of his skill could have forged that stamp and cancellation.

Now no cross-reference in the world will give me his coordinates or tell me what he's up to. I'm thrown back on that synthetic task of *building* the index. But how? In one of his few unguarded moments, Dr. Ressler confirmed my father on this one: one simply needs the right tool for the job.

"In the case of science," he told me, "the brief euphoria of slipping confusion's straitjacket reconciles you to a life spent washing beakers and sweeping up rat feces. Read the accounts," he urged, trying unsuccessfully to look grim. "Twelve milligrams of estradiol from one point five tons of mashed hog ovaries. Neurochemicals extracted from ten years' work on five hundred thousand cows' brains, at six cents per. *Imagine.* Someone carries each one of those lumps up three flights to the lab, enters them into the tedious ledger." In the end, that's why I loved him. Ressler knew how incalculably unlikely it was that a molecular duplication trick could hit upon a structure complex enough to probe its own improbability, willing to spend a life of profound tedium toward that end. To live the dull thrill of indexing.

I stayed in today, no leads on Todd's whereabouts, no tools for attacking the mound of scientific treatises that get harder and take me nowhere. I would give it up, were it not for the pain inside, remembering Ressler's dazed acceptance of long odds. "I have nothing now to give up, of course. But I would give everything for the chance to work a little longer."

The Polling Problem

She is a natural history, a sovereign kingdom, a theory about her environment, a virtuoso pedal-point performance. She follows a curve, a cadence, an animal locomotion he cannot help but lose himself to. Jeanette Koss is her own phylum. He admits it at last. No sense saving dignity in the face of onslaught. The moment the woman slips into the lab, everything Ressler is after—all careful simulation—is enveloped. He can attend to nothing, nor concentrate. She displaces with her texture, the frank affront of her skin, the arpeggiated toss of her hair. Dr. Koss walks across the lab to the dissection table, her legs inscribing a counterrhythm, the high arc of her collarbone floating in contrary motion. He is hypnotized by her approach, his pinch of chromatic pain enhanced to ecstasy at just being able to see her, look at her, taste without touching.

How can he remain impassive, give this woman no clue that *she* throws out his method, corrupts his buffer rates, soaks his equilibrium with a wash of chemical maydays? He has spent weeks ignoring her, but extended indifference only obsesses him further, ensilkens her smooth fur, enriches her odor. He probes, fascinated, cannot help but palpate the pain, the ulcered place. Oh, the blot is there, and not at all deep: the animal inkstain.

She gives no sign that she has guessed. But how could she not? The bend of her limbs, her least motion, her mere presence is paralyzing. All he can do as she enters the room is look away, keep busy, breathe quietly. Press his informant hands against the Formica. He examines her secretly, minutely along her entire length, to see if he might not have made some mistake, some enhancement of memory belied by empirical fact. But searching for repulsive detail and finding none fixates him further. He watches her gingerly pour the chloroform, pick up the stainless recurve blade as if puzzled by how knowledge always requires this preliminary killing.

Jeanette, all in white lab coat, a cat burglar working the day shift, is utterly altered from that irreverent sass he met at Ulrich's soiree. Could she always have walked like this? Is that her same sweep of cheeks, nape, thigh? He cannot imagine when the new

236

signal has taken her over. With a subtle muscular refraction, an imperceptible lip-twinge not directed at him but still returning his, she gives him the slightest, recursive suggestion of mutual cueing, letting him know *she knows*. There; it is out. She concedes. For an instant, she looks back. *His* silhouette is under examination. There, clear: she examines him for trace imperfections that will save them.

Or did he project that glance, erased in an instant? He can no longer distinguish prey, no longer say precisely who titillates whom. In the tag, the tangled affinities, her every labcoat adjustment, her avoiding friendly greeting is tacit admission of complicity. Their each move changes the other's. He studies her technique, indifferent to how the lines between them separate, oblivious to which of them is tagger, which taggee.

Dr. Koss puts the injected, virally mauled animal out of its misery according to procedures. With smooth filleting swatch, she removes the skin and bares the soft tissue. She locates the organ she is after, removes it, makes a light mash, centrifuges, titrates it with reagent from a burette. At stopwatch intervals, she prepares a time series and labels each slide. What is she up to with this experimental detour into higher animals? Does work in autosomal inheritance truly necessitate such efficient rodent murder? Her method springs from facility.

When she turns to leave the lab, he can't help himself, doesn't even *want* to. He's compelled to turn his head a fraction, glimpse her lovely leave-taking. Dr. Koss chooses precisely that instant to pause, turn her own wide eyes in time to catch him in the act of looking. She turns at the lab door—unforgettable!—inquiring, challenging, yet timid. They turn simultaneously to inspect each other. Undeniable public confession: he heats and distresses her as much as she does him. There, the guilty exchange, admitted in her eyes: he opens analogous gateways in her senses, awakes her longing to travel beyond the courtyard, to recite the words that will throw off this walking trance, the sleeping-spell of mind.

Then she is gone, leaving him alone in the lab with the apparatus he has been bludgeoning incoherently for the last hour. His viscera hold the impression—her turning pertly on that strategic threshold to announce that, yes, they are together in a hopeless impasse. He circles the recalcitrant fact. The woman is *married;* she made her selection long before he arrived on the scene, chose the display plumage of the man who finally got breakfast cereal to talk when you pour on milk. Herbert Koss: dependable, well-off, patient, kind—all those desirable qualities of mate- and fatherhood Ressler himself lacks. He can beat the man nowhere; he has no caught creature to lay at her den door as dowry. None except—it gives him a guilty rush—a crack at the secret of life.

He slows, tries once more to back down into the reasonable. He is happy with lab bachelorhood. She has every reason for sticking to her field-tested bond. There is no forgivable reason to tamper with what isn't broken, no possible attraction to exercise over one another. And yet, there *is*. Is one. It alleviates nothing to call it enzymes. Obscene cat-and-mouse, one that, if they can just this once transcend the way of the race, ought to remain cat-and-mouse forever, never developing into the thing it is surrogate for. Hot, gratifying confirmation fills him to recollect her hurried, questioning eyes. It maddens him, the extent of pleasure in this prolonged fiction, swarmed with all the alarm of the event it must never indulge in.

She leaves him alone in the lab, abandons him to the old detective story, the sober mystification of the bug. Yet Jeanette—fawn legs, down-scaped neck—has clearly announced a catalog more inscrutable than the sixty-four codons. Nature's ciphers are at least objective, potentially solvable. But Koss is a thing apart. What the two of them do to one another may be no more than a complex-carbohydrate tease, cybernetic systems feeding back into each other, an infinite Do-loop, a sentence grammatical but out of syntactical control, whom looping around to subject subject who. The moment arrests him all afternoon: Jeanette, arched, aroused, frozen at the door in fight-or-flight, scared nocturnal mammal caught in the light. What frightened her? It could only have been him, his own cross-hands panic, his broadcast desire.

The marathon sessions with the rate trials are over; he has verified them with all possible precision. He must now present his findings—the survival-value enzymes—at the next Blue Sky. Cyfer will appreciate the implications: a colinear, unidirectional, non-overlapping, redundant triplet code. They've suspected, but he has demonstrated it, assembling the facts in a configuration not entirely anticipated by anyone. He has checked and rechecked for coherence, consistency with the literature. The model is airtight, obvious in retrospect. His bit of crucial synthesis will in a few days become public currency.

He has delayed, savored the edge his extra lucid pieces give him. By month's end, the world will have everything he has, all the cards down. He must lay out his technique for controlled point mutations, selective garbling. But is he ethically compelled to point out that this technique, even more than the nonresults, holds the possibility of wrapping up the rest of the puzzle? Is he honor-bound to harp on a hunch, tip them off to his own intuitive certainty?

He looks up to see Dan Woytowich lugging unusual equipment into the lab. "You know, they bill this as a portable, but the damn thing's twice as bulky as a sewing machine." He sets up the TV in a lab corner, where it blends into the background instruments. The tube is the size of the Svedberg centrifuge and chromatography equipment combined.

"Dr. Double-U. What's new? How's the wife?"

"Renée's fine. Almost done with the dissertation. She's blotted more than nine hundred lines of Shakespeare to date."

"Great. Just a hundred to go. Has she tried *Titus Andronicus*?" Woyty adjusts the dials, fiddles with the rabbit ears, and in a flurry of static (residual background radiation from the Big Bang), Ed Murrow springs On the Air. The invasion of outside news seems a violation of laboratory controls. The two of them sit entranced, Seeing It Now, Person to Person. Ressler must at least ask. "Not your ordinary piece of test apparatus, Dan. Are you working on something arcane?"

Woyty doesn't hear. He is submerged, watching Dulles announce that he won't give Eleanor Roosevelt a visa to visit China because China doesn't exist. He surfaces long enough to unload out of left field. "I think we ought to quit calling what we're doing here 'decoding.' Technically, 'decoding' is restoring a coded message to plaintext by someone who already has the key. What we're doing is 'cryptanalysis,' since the genetic code is probably not a code at all, but a cipher. Distort the description, and you distort the thing you try to describe."

Ressler listens to this impassioned plea for linguistic purity. He may be witnessing the first stages of total organic dissolution here. Woyty doesn't blink; he gestures at the set, where the *You Bet Your Life* birdie descends on its wire like a dove ciborium, bearing a piece of paper around its neck reading "Grace." "You know, I dreamt I was a contestant on *What's My Line?* From the studio wings, I could see the panelists put their blindfolds on. I went up to the chalkboard to sign in, but instead of writing 'Research Biologist,' I wrote, 'Crypt Analyst.' Then the panelists grilled me about my profession. Get this: their questions were in code."

The news comes on, and Woytowich sits pasted to the tube. The top embalmer in the state could not have waxed the man better. His full-blown mania for current events must be linked to this other defect, free association. Ressler, his own work impaired by the electronic anesthesia, makes one last try. "Why have you brought a television into the lab?"

Woytowich mumbles, "I've some trials that need attending."

"So do I, sir." After an afternoon's glance at eyes hazel and moist enough to explain why he has been taken out and dropped in this forsaken place, the last thing Ressler needs now is Beirut. Berlin. Woyty sighs and shoots Ressler a strained smile suggesting that the youth is not seeing him at his best. Dan, Ressler knows, is a brilliant technician with every right to be alienated. The sober, classical generational studies he's produced for decades are enough to bore anyone to tears. A now ancient paper, written when Woyty was a baby post-grad, cried in the wilderness against the protein-as-gene climate. Vindication did little to rehabilitate him with the old guard he'd untimely challenged. In the early fifties, Woytowich, churning out disease patterns in fish family trees, experienced a short-lived rebirth. He reportedly combed the building for days, telling anyone who'd listen about a strange "jumping inheritance" which he could not duplicate or explain. Three years later, someone else published the complete mechanism. By then, Woyty had become an antinomian pariah, producing the barest minimum research to survive. Yet he never once violated the Lafayette Escadrille code of honor by claiming he'd almost been there.

"Were you by any chance watching last year," Woytowich wanders off irrelevantly again, bringing a blush of shame to Ressler's cheeks, "when Ed Sullivan went on his Really Big Shoe and asked his audience whether they should allow Ingrid Bergman to appear on the program?"

Ressler shakes his head quickly. "No set."

"No? Of course not. Well, it was the low point of modern opinion polling. Granted the woman is controversial, leaving her husband to take up with an Italian and all. Seven years of political exile, denouncement on the Senate floor, all for falling in love with someone other than her husband." A pause sends shimmies up Ressler's spine. "I never thought of our witch hunts as anything other than pubescent acne, aberrations caused by moving too quickly into the Data Age. Now I'm not that far out of the mainstream, and I've never given the green light to extremists, and as far as I'm concerned, we ought to send nuts like Lovering into Minnesota exile." He snorts a laugh when Ressler doesn't. "But imagine: 'If you want to see this adulteress on the show, write and tell me.' Not exactly a controlled survey."

Woytowich comes over to where Ressler finishes the beaker-washing he'd get a post-doc to do if he weren't the post-doc. The way Woyty picks up the electrophoresis strips and raises his eyebrows suggests that the difference between cueing an audience and confirming an experimental hunch is a question of nomenclature. "I guess I don't see how Miss Bergman's problems lead to TVs in the lab."

Woytowich turns away. "It is just for tonight."

"I'm sorry. I didn't mean. . . . I'm just curious."

Like one of his dazed fish doing slow loop-the-loops in the tank, Woyty circles Ressler's table. "I'd like to tell you something I'm not allowed to tell anyone. That I've kept to myself until now." Ressler waits until he realizes the request wasn't rhetorical; Woytowich really wants permission to tell. Stuart nods. "Renée and I . . . are a Stainer family." Ressler laughs out loud to put it together. The Stainer ratings. Stainer, the national pollster, with his legendary secret sample group perfectly representing America in miniature. Woyty a Stainer voter? Ressler has never met anyone like Woytowich in his life. And yet: *someone* has to stand, in those endless polls of taste that run America, for every mephisto variation in existence. "I know it's ludicrous. I was selected in my late twenties, shortly after my appointment as assistant prof at Illinois. Renée became royalty by virtue of marriage."

"Couldn't you decline the nomination?"

"Can lab rats turn down their boss's NSF grant? A median citizen does not turn down nomination to median citizenship."

"It doesn't pay, does it?"

"Actually, being a responsible sample group member has cost me considerably over the years. No prestige, obviously, as we're sworn to solemn secrecy. Knowledge of Stainer names would be golden." Woyty gives a hapless look laced with irony: I've perjured myself to tell you this.

"I don't understand. Why put up with it, if it's a burden?"

"Think about it. There are only fifteen thousand Stainer members

241

nationwide. Only one per ten thousand. We're in the unique position of rating every televised message to enter the American home. If a show passes our chi-square, it becomes the law of the land. National sacrament. In its own peculiar way, undeniable power."

So it's more than lack of collegial support that has kept this man from realizing his potential. Woytowich's social obligations have for some time been tinged with the moral fervor of a Mormon setting out on his two-year missionary stint in the Third World. Woyty's ethical compulsion to influence the sample mean mimics the first principle: go ye therefore and replicate thyself, and may the most persuasive opinions live. His peculiar polling position has made him purposive, a thing no scientist can afford to be.

Woyty breathes deeply. "The way I see it, in an industrial democracy the size of Americorp, the vote is pretty much ceremonial privilege. Your state representative? Tribal holdover. More an after-the-fact efficiency check on mass manipulation. A ballot in the Stainer ratings, on the other hand, gives me a chance to manipulate the manipulators. When I rate, the boys on both seaboards snap to attention."

"But wait...."

Woytowich aggressively cuts him off. "I know what you're going to say. The small-denominator fallacy. Well, you're right. *My* proxy vote for ten thousand people has no more significance in the sample of fifteen thousand than the votes of the ten thousand Daniel W models from whom I am indistinguishable in taste in the hundred and fifty million nation at large. And yet," Woyty smiles sadly, imparting the latest unsupported dead-on prediction of his scientific career, "the world is not a linear equation. Big changes come from small initial differences. You are a good enough scientist," he accuses, "to know that all polls are, to a certain degree, self-fulfilling. Methods of inquiry create possible outcomes. The great difference between the Stainer ratings and Citizen Rule lies in the results each is after. Ike, Stassen, Truman, Stevenson? Jesus, who *are* these guys? Epiphenomena, emblems of the homogenation of taste, the by-products of mechanization, not the actors upon it. But ask a fellow—OK, fifteen thousand fellows—to judge *Gunsmoke,* and you start to zero in on the real substrata of civilization."

So this is who Dan really is. For the past several years, he has gone about in secrecy, unknown even to his team members, doing his bit for the elevation of the species. He has had to be perfectly informed, both about world events and the hydra of churned consumer culture. Somewhere last month, last year, he passed the point, without knowing it, where he no longer simply sought the up-to-the-minute. He needed it. Like enzyme-deprived mutations, Woytowich's system can no longer function without a steady source—a glut—of broadcast.

Woyty returns to the set, adjusts the aerial. "The problem with swaying the median is that I must move selectively, a blow here and there where it counts. Stay within the standard deviation. Guerrilla war. Dienbienphu of shrewdery against prevailing tastes. To use one's Stainer vote to subvert popular culture for the better, one cannot saturation-bomb. Three votes in a row for the high-foreheads—be they ever so humble—and Stainer would dump me as an aberrant ringer."

"Dan, I had no idea. What's the battlefield tonight? *This Is Your Life? Queen for a Day?*" Two doozies of terminal civilization built on the premise that sadism is simply loving attention to one's neighbor's masochism. Both trace case histories of individual agony and ecstasy in tortuous detail, elevating the home audience through the triple intercession of identification, catharsis, and aesthetic distance.

Woyty's elbows jerk as if struck by the examiner's rubber tomahawk. "Not exactly. I did those two, months ago. My first urge was frontal assault, pan them both. I see no redeeming civilizing value in the public audit of a guy who is forced to relive through audiovisual aids his divorce, a bankruptcy suit, and two years in Sing Sing. But rating them was problematic. Whatever their faults, *Queen* and *Life* are at least tenuously nonfiction. Healthy counterbalance to *Lucy,* where the end of the episode always reveals the world to be everybody's favorite crazy uncle. So let the woman who in one week accidentally poisons her kid and contracts leukemia wear a fake crown and scepter on network TV. I gave the shows a four point five and a four point two. Low enough to show I hate them, but high enough to indicate that I prefer them to the alternatives. Coincidentally, those were close to the Stainer norm. The more I strike against the status quo, the closer I fit the mode."

Woyty gives the set a palm-slap, tuning it in. "No. Tonight, we've something a shade more significant." Just then, the familiar features of Edward Teller, father of the H-bomb, emerge from the electromagnetic gray scan. Teller, brilliant, mad Hungarian émigré, testifier against Oppenheimer at the government's *This Is Your Life,*

243

argues heatedly with another world-class mind whose face Ressler recognizes: Linus Pauling, Nobel laureate, supreme figure of American chemistry, he of vitamin C and the covalent bond, structural elucidator of any number of organic molecules, and nip-and-tuck runner-up to the three-dimensional solution of DNA.

The two sit in a San Francisco studio, battling toe to toe on the feasibility—no, the desirability—of a comprehensive nuclear test ban. "For those of you out in the home audience," Woyty editorializes, "these men are not paid actors. They are two giants of modern science, delay-broadcast, of course. Any hair-tearing or tossed water glasses long since edited out."

Ressler wants the man to shut up so he can hear; he can't believe it's happening. The scientists both smile disarmingly. There's a lot of heavy eyebrow work going on, and a good deal of finger-pointing as well. Teller's deep, black eye sockets versus Pauling's shiny pate. Incredulous, Ressler looks from combatant to combatant, trying to follow their reasoning. Teller seems to say that there would be no way of knowing how effective or reliable a device would be if testing were eliminated. Pauling shouts that that is precisely the point.

Ressler studies the hook-nosed Hungarian. Like everyone else in science, Teller has recently tried his hand at the coding problem. Ressler read the paper, and concluded that the moonlighter ought not to give up the megaton day job. He wonders how this man can be a devotee of the same crystalline bracer that has recently awakened him to the uses of music. Teller's adoration of Bach is legendary; he reportedly forced fellow members of the Manhattan Project to listen to poor recordings and passable personal renditions in labs ranging from Columbia to that New Mexico mesa.

How can these men, researchers of the first rank, no matter what their politics, take the debate of so nebulous an issue out into the public forum? It violates positivism, the ban on discussing things one can't know. Their sinking to the fallacies of politicians horrifies Ressler, grates against his belief that "is" and "ought to be" are and ought to be separate. He follows the debate, a glutton for revulsion. But before he can name the nausea in this public screech of intellect, Woytowich intrudes. "Stainer is canvassing this event heavily. In addition to figuring out who and how many are watching, they want an evaluation from any family that does tune in. They've sent out that favorite soft-science tool, a questionnaire.

Seems they're trying to determine if there's a market for reality. If there's any future for world-saving debate on television."

"World-saving?" Another defection. "You too...?"

Woyty fails to notice Ressler's crisis of conviction. "Of course. This is the Big One. The one I'm been rotting my mind on countless years of *Wells Fargo*s to preserve."

Ressler watches aghast as the two debate safety, flipping the hot potato between their four hands as if the quarrel is just its subject matter. It's agony to see Pauling, agent of so many discoveries, talking with such passion about so messy and unqualifiable a term as morality. It hurts the way a sports hero's sellout to soft-drink vending hits a ten-year-old. Even Ressler can see that verifiability isn't the real issue. If we can build the things, we can find a way of telling whether or not they're being tested. The issue is, once set in motion, whether we *want* to rein the incredible apparatus in. What'll it be? Turn back or get on with it?

In disgust, he feels a gut-tug toward Teller. We're condemned to test, to develop. How else can we know the desirability of an experiment unless we've run it? No ignorant constraints on knowledge. Yet something deeper swings him toward Pauling, the better scientist: aren't we graced with some degree of foresight? Is what we can do always what we must?

"We've got a problem here," Woyty says. "Do I do my ineffectual bit for history? Pull out the stops tonight? Give my all to the cause? Slap the show solid nines across the board and risk instant ejection from Stainerhood? Or appease the testors' expectations by turning in scores only a little above normal, seven point one or thereabouts?"

Ressler's problem is worse. Until this moment, he was certain that the highest obligation of science was to describe objectively, to reveal the purpose-free domain. But here are Teller and Pauling, carrying on on national TV as if some things were more urgent than truth, as if we're condemned always to fall back on the blind viewpoint of need. As if observation—the dismissal of final causes necessary for any solution of the physical world—can solve everything except ethics. As if exploration without ethics were no better than data without theory.

Woytowich runs on. "The secret word for tonight is seven point seven. A rough mean between what I want to give it and what I can afford to. Hover around a plausible pip, win an all-expenses-

245

paid reprieve from responsibility. Escape a near-brush with commitment this time around, live to fight another way. What do you say, friend? Pick a number. Vote for me."

At that moment, rasped by this unexpected irritant, the next piece in Ressler's maturing experimental procedure falls into place. Something's been missing from his model of chemical inheritance. Obvious, now that it's here: the coding problem is *de facto* a polling problem. Nucleotide triplets, wrapped in a supercoiled string, are not inert, static, informational bits. They are a referendum, a chorus of self-serving, purposive voices, a proliferation of experiment whose electoral outcome of enzyme behaviors decides their fates.

If he can't read the impossibly complex code directly, he can at least poll the encoder, map the mechanism by submitting it to ballot. Ressler walks quickly out of the room. Another word will jeopardize the fragile, crystallizing notion. Woytowich, looking up from the set, sees his junior partner disappearing down the hall. He misinterprets the flight. "Abstaining is still voting," Woyty calls out to the vanishing back. "No vote is still a vote. A man's gotta vote."

Ressler, not yet out of earshot, ignores him. He converges rapidly on an idea so beautiful that it needs his full attention. He can't foster the notion alone. He needs to speak it to someone who can follow his thought, add to it. He races down the Georgian corridors to his office. He fumbles with keys, throws open the door, a sea of Lovering's papers scattering in the gust. He blesses Joe for choosing that moment not to be around.

He sits at the phone, runs a shaking finger down the names in the staff directory, picks up the receiver and dials. When the voice connects, pastel and alive, it shocks him to hear who he has called. He cannot talk, so amazing is the spectrum of composite pitches in that voice at the other end of the wire. "Hello? Is someone there?" As he places the handset back in its cradle, Ressler distinctly hears her catch her breath, whisper, "Is that *you*?"

XII

The Natural Kingdom

11/3: Arrived again in November. Just being alive this late in the year is not in itself proof of having hit on a solution worth preserving. Here, now, as professional cold sets in in earnest, all the anticipation of autumn comes to this: surviving in changed conditions. New strategy for a new climate. I have twenty-five weeks left, twenty-seven if I shower with cold water. What to show for the months already spent? Only the months themselves. I've dabbled in the hard sciences, picked up a hint of chemistry. But I'm no closer to recovering that tune I dreamed myself inside of the night I heard of Dr. Ressler's death. No closer to recording that score, the dance step that made me quit the working world.

I've learned that the one panel Todd has sent me since running away did come not from over the ocean but from up the coast. The definitive cross-reference proves he brought the landscape along with him, knowing in advance not to leave traces. QED: I am here alone. And that's best, when all is figured. Alone, flat out against myself. Close to the grain of the neighborhood, no motive except making it to the next calendar island. My days familiar, but flavored strange again. The closure of solitude, the only way of knowing I am here again in wet November, still imprinted with every shed skin.

I now know the problem Ressler was after. He wanted to determine how clusters of inert particles able only to roll down potential-energy hills could stack themselves into grammars, loaded configurations readable and enactable: blueprints for assembling and regulating other clusters themselves capable of erecting, dismantling, rearranging, and elaborating every strategy that

247

has ever emerged on this sliver of rock. A modest problem for a by-product of those same, inert particles.

11/4: I've learned how the molecular archives are written in sinuous ribbons tightly packed into each cell nucleus. How these chromosomes are demarked into discrete sentences. My file proves I've actually *relearned* this:

Q: How many genes do I have?

L.N., 3/23/78

A: This number is not likely to be determined with precision anytime soon. The order of magnitude is 100,000. The complete genome of a human being is written on almost 7 feet of microscopic thread. Every human cell contains 3–6 billion nucleotide pairs.

J. O'D., 3/25/78

I've gotten a first sense of the tetragrammatonic golem recipe. I've won an analogic understanding of how seven feet of aperiodic crystal unzips, finds complements of each of its billion constituents, integrates them perfectly without tearing or entangling, then winds up again into a fraction of a millimeter, all in two minutes. I grasp, barely, that this process is taking place all over my body at this instant.

I see in rough outline the dogma Ressler was out to extend: one gene, one nucleotide sequence, one synthesized enzyme, one chemical reaction, one inherited quality. I accept that synthesis takes place at the speed of two amino acids per second, constantly, for countless enzymes in every cell. I can, in cartoon, conceive how this codex might be read, how merely speaking its words creates three-dimensional globules whose folds make each a miniature chemical computer. I grant that one enormous concatenated clause of A's, T's, C's, and G's is the plan for hemoglobin and another, every bit as inanimate, for insulin.

But I lack the critical keystone in the arch he was after: I cannot see how form emerges from the same mechanism. When to make bone, when pancreas, scale, hair, skin, or bowel? How large should the heart get? How to start it pumping? How indicate a heart at all? Take a broad, leafy, sun-spreading tuber factory, root, plumule, stolon: does the blueprint read, "Sprout a villus in the ileum; lace it up with veins"?

Pattern-juggling pattern actually makes life. From brittle and

248

spiny to sleek and silver: an impossible spreading text for four letters. Even crisp illustrations, the bright primary pastels by the Herris of natural history, their unambiguous lines running from luxurious organ encampments to the affixing term—"cilia," "thorax," "vascular bundle"—cannot convince me. How much worse, a millionfold more incomprehensible, the passage from monocot to monogamy.

I find the evolution of eyesight remotely credible, but the production of *perception* from those same four letters baffles me. Behavior: the retreat of a sensitive plant from touch, phototaxis of plankton, nyctinasty in the morning glory, the butting of rams' horns, neo-Palladian mud-and-twig palaces, the engineering monuments of colonial insects, the clicks and whistles of distress, the motor rhythm of walrus sonar (irresistibly sexy to their opposites), *speech,* for God's sake? Are these enormous structures somehow *in* the invisible code? Can all this babel come from the same idiot idiolect?

11/5: And that catalog is a mere draft, no, the draft of a draft. Years ago I received a scrawled Question Board submission, unsigned: Q: How different can you get? Inside joke, private incoherence. As it was anonymous, I felt no obligation to answer. But ever the compulsive collector, I kept the card, a record of what elbow-nudging humanity, Brooklyn branch, wanted to know in the late twentieth century. Now, five months since I've set foot in my old haunt, I've read enough to propose molecular biology's stupefying solution.

First, in a seven-year-old *Scientific American*—already fossil artifact—I learn that for an average human, almost every characteristic is homozygous. Only 6.7 percent of human genes are composed of different alleles. From that small fraction, all variability in legacy arises. How small is small? Taking 100,000 genes as a ballpark genome, 6,700 will be heterozygous. That gives 2^{6700} ways of shuffling divergences—a number of more than two thousand digits—to pass on to a child. The growth of genetics has been the growth of realizing how huge the gap between individuals is.

By contrast: the human genome, considered as a whole, represents only the slightest divergence from the closest living trial. More than 98 percent of our DNA is identical to that of both chimp and gorilla. Less than 2 percent of that seven-foot text is proprietarily human. The incredible conclusion is that two children of the same parents differ more from one another than *Homo sapiens*

249

as a whole differs from the apes. Superabundance of intraspecies diversity holds across the spectrum of all the few million species nature is currently testing. The ways of varying the original life molecule have multiplied beyond any ability to conceive of them. How much do species themselves differ? I have only to look. Eel on one hand, elm on the other: two recombinations on the same letter set. How many different yous can you have? How different can you get?

11/6: So different I can go no further on the coding problem until I narrow down my intended landing spot. If I'm to cross the bridge he was building, I've got to begin anew, with the question of what, if anything, all those coded strings are possibly after with their unbounded text scrambling. I accredit the ability of inanimate molecules to arrange themselves in configurations capable of coding. But I need to find why they go on coding for ever more elaborate configurations.

I must return to the macroscopic world, to Darwin's tautology. Survival of the fittest—Spencer's phrase—has a definite ring. But can it explain that superfluous explosion of self-generating programs? Is the famous, world-altering phrase really a "law"? Survival of those who survive. Disappearance of those who disappear. After-the-fact synopsis of species drift, missing the driving undercurrent, the molecular surge toward diversity as a way of staying around, producing more of the same.

On second look, I see I've misunderstood evolution as badly as my schoolgirl botch of Mendel. Education is wasted on those of school age. Now I find that evolution is not about competition or squeezing out, not a master plan of increasing efficiency. It is a deluge, a cascade of mistaken, tentative, branching, brocaded experiment, secrets seemingly dormant, shouted down from the past, wills and depositions hidden in the attic, how-to treasure maps reading "Tried this; it worked for a while; hang on to it," program-palimpsests reworked beyond recognition, churches renovated so often in a procession of styles that it's impossible to label them Romanesque, gothic, or baroque. It is about one instruction: "Make another similar something; insert this command; run; repeat." It is about the resultant runaway seed-spreading arabesques, unrelated except in all being variations on that theme.

"Struggle for survival," red in tooth and claw, is misleading; low-profile passivity is the strategy of choice in at least as many niches as aggression. "Struggle" carries too much individual emphasis. Selection deals in the economy of individuals, even individual traits. But evolution deals only in populations, demanding not that they struggle but just that they procreate faster than they perish. No upward march, no drive toward perfection. Evolution's move is lateral, spreading out, diversifying until every spot on the nearest-fit curve, every accidental juggle, has been auditioned against experience.

A day's reading makes plain that evolution is profoundly conservative. A species, on energetic grounds, stands to gain nothing by invention. Payoff lies in stable maintenance. Diversity, even more paradoxically, is born in preservation. "Natural selection," like the chemistry of self-replicating molecules, needs fleshing out, bridging. Evolution is circular, *post hoc* until I can underpin it, link it to the same coding problem I've circled around for months.

11/7: I read about barnacle geese. Beautiful creatures, larger than they should be, aerodynamically improbable, breathtaking in formation flight. Annually, their goslings pay the price of the safety of cliff nests. The flightless chicks throw themselves onto the rocks below, shielded by a centimeter of fluff. A few fledglings survive the massacre, perpetuate the behavior, build new nests next year in the fatal altitudes.

11/8: Exhausted, I watch a nature show shown late enough at night to ensure that only the already disenfranchised fringe will be disturbed by it. The film documents a slime mold so startling it needs seeing to be believed. A single-celled creature coats ponds in green scum. But when its food supply grows scarce, the particles transform. The cells congregate in huge colonies, differentiate, form the parts of a composite beast complete with head and body. The body grows spore cases that crack open and scatter single cells. The show cuts to a squid whose outer skin is an animated Kandinsky, awash in chromatophores that skitter across it in pigment ripples. The voiceover explains, in scientific baritone, that this fluctuating array is a map of the creature's brain activity: a visible neural analog.

Evolution becomes, on second look, an intricate switchboard, paths for passing signals back and forth: generation to generation, species to species, environment to creature, and back again. Life as exchange of mail. I think of the medieval bestiary, Frank's beloved illuminations, circulated in hand manuscripts—the journals of the day. That interpretive system seeing the spectrum of natural form as a mirror of God, eager to alert us to His nature through every living, loaded semaphore in creation:

> The leun stant on hille & he man hunten here. Alle hise fet steppes after him he filleth. . . . The lion stands on hill and hunts man here. Fills all his footsteps in after him, drags his tail over his tracks so he can't be found. When he sleeps he never closes his eyes. Why? Welle heg is tat hil that is heven riche. Ure louerd is te leun the liveth ther abuven. Well high is that hill, that is heaven rich. Our Lord is the lion that liveth there above. No devil can find him; he never sleeps.

The medieval natural kingdom was not indifferent object but pointed symbol. How else to explain the obvious interlocked design? Even its descendant science, stripping the world of every motive, reads like allegory. Even "nature," "evolution," still flirt with immanent purpose.

11/11: I begin to see science as a natural selection of species' postulates about the environment. Today: first U.S. patent for telescope, 1851. Tomorrow: Hooke appointed Royal Society Curator of Experiments, 1662. Empirical survivals for every port of call in the calendar. Survival of the fittest. Die-tosses developing goals; restless invention searching for application.

11/13: I spend the day among the ants, appalled by the Bulldog variety. They feed their sterile workers' eggs to larvae and queen. The queen mates for a day, storing the semen her whole life, from which she produces the entire colony. The Weaver, a near relation, is a bio-universe away. This strain uses its larvae as web spray guns, clasping the grubs in their jaws, coaxing them with antennae, pointing them to spots to sew up. Weavers raise Blue Butterfly caterpillars, nurse them to adulthood, protect them, sacrifice guardians as caterpillar feed, all for nectar emitted by the monster babies.

Flowers inscribed with ultraviolet runways, detectable only by particular bees. Wasps that live parasitically in bee bodies. The Bauhaus finesse of trapdoor spiders. Other spider strains that fish. Fish that shoot insects with water streams; fish that fish with electroluminescent bait. Two-pitch frog calls where males hear the low warning, females the high serenade. More bizarrerie than dreamt of in any bestiary. A species for every conceivable emblem.

I feel the outrageousness of what Dr. Ressler was after: a simple generative axiom telling where all of this comes from. Macromolecular feedback supplies the how without recourse to metaphysical why. Darwin gives the first internally plausible explanation not requiring a leap of faith. But gaps in the fossil record leave incomplete the account of how variety itself comes about. How can pruning produce the irreducible width of the world lab? That's where my friend came in. Ressler was after no less than ancient myth: a physical explanation of variety. How the creatures got their nature. How animate arose from inanimate. How different one can get.

11/14: Monod, Jacques: *Chance and Necessity,* page 48 of my dog-eared paperback: "[T]he prodigious diversity of *macroscopic* structures of living beings rests in fact on a profound and no less remarkable unity of *microscopic* makeup." Many from one. Complexity from the simple first principle. The living world as single event. Speciation is stranger than I've guessed: unstoppable, incoherent, continuous. All the parts of speech proliferated from the first verb. How can that be? Each copy grown precise in design, everything recorded within it geared toward undeniable ends driving every cell, each organelle. How can such clear, formal purpose arise without a purposive designer, no plan more steeped in necessity than chance?

11/16: Twenty-three weeks left; twenty-five with cold showers. Six months to discover how different you can get. To uncover the answer alone, in the seed-spreading core of the self-extending program. To validate that great tautology: survival of those who survive.

Canon at the Fourth

Ressler replaces the receiver even as she identifies him, picks his voiceprint out of a field of ambiguous noise. She guesses what he called to ask, and why he cannot. Koss. He grows frantic for communication. Woytowich's polling problem triggers an infant connection that he must run past someone. If he cannot find some safe other with whom he can coax it out, the link struggling to the surface will be lost. But he cannot call Koss back; the first phoneme of her voice already trickles with forgetting.

He rushes from his office to Toveh Botkin's Viennese study. Her door is unlocked, but Botkin is not there. Ressler scans the lavender, heavy furnishings and thinks: She will be dead soon. Her century of science will stop. She will disperse into ammonias, hydroxyls, aromatic hydrocarbons. Rilke and Furtwängler will scatter in auction. A regret passes through him that he cannot stop and predicate. No one at all in the building. He remembers: nighttime. The ordinary world goes home. Ressler runs out into the autumn air, following the route by heart. He reaches Stadium Terrace, K court, then 53, but at that gauge, his internal pointer veers toward A, the Blakes' end of the triplex. Ressler has not visited Tooney since the night he was shaken by child and wife. But he needs his neighbors now, needs to sound them out. Only words will get to the issue, however much he distrusts the medium. He rings the bell, stands on the stoop listening to the muffled sounds of surprise on the far side of the door. While the porch light floods on and the door lurches open, a shock of excitement stretches over his chest. The world is continuous, unlimited rearrangement: Jeanette knew his silence.

The Blakes greet him with great huzzah. Ressler, here on their turf, so late, uncoerced. Margaret cheers the reprieve from bedtime. "Hello," she greets him, wary with memory.

"Hello," Ressler grins. "Know any new poems?"

Little Margaret turns her face into her shoulder. Ressler pecks Eva on the cheek shyly and pumps Tooney's hand, grateful that the man has survived to be here at this moment. "Drink?" his host offers. "Eat? Be merry?" Ressler shakes his head. Blake, nonplussed but delighted, leads him into the front room.

They barely sit down when Ressler bursts into things. "Tooney. What, in your opinion, have we been up to?"

"Don't know about you. I've been putting the kid to bed."

Ressler doesn't even break stride. "Cyfer. These months. Trying to solve the coding problem by equating specific base sequences with amino acid arrangements in protein polypeptides."

"Now you tell me." But Stuart's excitement is contagious.

"And how have we gone about it? Like bloody Poe. Studying all known enzymes. Looking for patterns. Letter frequencies. Clumps where we might wedge a lever of correspondence. But we're making one, glaring, freshman presupposition."

"I give up."

Ressler is too fired up to be disappointed. "We're combing amino sequences for some evidence of prior necessity. Why? There is no codemaker, Toon." Ressler speaks as if bluntly urging a child to shake off a scrape.

"All right," Blake says slowly. "Assume I follow. I'm afraid I don't see the ramifications, except. . . ."

"Except that we've been attacking the problem ass-backwards." Talking to another is still superior to talking to himself, even if he must explain everything. "Listen, Tooney. I've got to talk dirty for a minute."

"Wife! Leave the room."

Eva, *in* the other room, hears her husband bellow and enters just in time to hear Ressler say "In vitro."

Eva laughs and says, "*Et in terra pax.*" Ressler, Lutheran, looks blank. But he latches onto Evie, her unspecialized ears every bit as helpful as her scientist mate's. He explains the vitro/vivo dichotomy. To Eva, the difference between running an experiment outside rather than inside a living system seems functional. "I thought y'all did everything with test tubes," she drawls. "Don't you choose the most convenient method? Careful isolation under glass. . . ."

". . . can stand in for runs on the real thing?" Ressler informs her of the hitches. He feels renewed need to make the point hurriedly. "In vivo—testing with living things—is like Murrow's report from a street under fire. Firsthand information, but chaotic. In vitro gives a coherent but dangerously simplified recreation, from the calm of the studio. A whole new can of helical worms."

Blake whistles. "You want a cell-free system."

"Exactly," Ressler shouts, jumping up. A moan of resigned fear comes from the just-dozing child in the next room, and he lowers his voice. "I knew you would come through." Blake has supplied him with the thing he was after. A name.

"Stuart. I don't know. Even supposing that synthesis behaves no differently outside the cell than in. That a reaction's a reaction, that living things form no special domain." The whole point of the last hundred years. "Still. . . ."

Stuart waits for the objection, the use of talk. Blake thinks in silence, knowing what's at stake and measuring ambiguities the best he can. After some seconds, he says, "In simulating the translation reactions outside the cell, reducing the case to manageable proportions, we might. . . ."

"Yes?"

"I don't know. Violate the complexity threshold?"

"The *what?*"

"I know. It sounds mystical. But can we be sure that reduction to constituents won't strip out emergent phenomena?"

"Is there such an animal?"

"Jesus. Maybe I'm in the wrong line of work." Eva sits next to her husband, squeezes his feet. "In vitro," Blake works out tentatively, "might give us repeatable evidence. But would it ignore some cellular interdependence?"

The two pore over the new angle while the third party sits by, asks for occasional clarification, keeps them honest. They push on the problem into early morning, hitting a hard spot that won't budge. Tooney looks at his watch, laughs, and announces, "I have to drive to Chicago in five hours." Ressler apologizes, Blake waves him off, and they tap the matter another fifteen minutes. It's impossible to say, as the meeting breaks up and the Blakes lead Ressler to the door, how all three know that this talk, so highly charged, innocent, irrepeatable, will be the last of its kind. Blake walks Stuart across the lawn to K-53-C.

"No coat?" Ressler asks, solicitous in the crisp air.

"Don't you start now. You sound like Lovering. Have you seen that pup recently? The man is so convinced that cold germs are gunning for him that he won't even shake hands. It's one thing to rage against a wet-head. Another to run around in permanent parka. I saw the madman yesterday, wearing gloves, *indoors*. He refuses to take off his muffler even to talk. And here it's still practically summer."

"Tooney, it's getting cold. There *is* a flu virus going around. I can sympathize with Joe's desire to keep a distance. The idea of a packet of DNA attaching itself by landing gear on my cell wall, injecting me with alien nucleic acid, using my cell to reproduce itself by the hundreds, and then blowing it up in a grand exit is not especially savory."

"Tell me. But don't you see how he practically forces me to bike to the lab in bermudas? I'm fatalistic about disease. I mean, if a virus has your cell's name on it.... I always say anyone can have Tea for Two, but it takes phage to make T4 tumor. Heard the one about the Cysteine Chapel? I gotta Millon ovum."

Ressler draws up short. "'If a virus has your cell's name on it...'?" But the idea, too far ahead of its time, is lost to a failure of concentration. They stand outside Ressler's door, waiting for the vagaries of inspiration to visit once more in the pre-sunrise.

"You want to trace protein synthesis *forward?*" Blake asks, summarizing, although the point is long since solidified. Ressler nods. "In a cell-free system? But *how,* man?" Ressler shrugs. He feels the answer inching on him, as inevitable as infection.

Once inside the door, he dusts off the *Goldberg* disk and returns it to its absent place on the player. The music radiates again, with only a few additional scratch-induced mutations on the vinyl to record his fit of a few evenings before. The tune, suddenly exuberant this morning, confirms him that a method exists. An alternative, close to the beating heart of translation. In the precision of harmonic structure, he hears his own conviction that the coding problem rests on a simple look-up table—at ever lower levels, a mechanism to explain cell growth, viral piracy, symbiotic coalition government of organs, the origin of species, phone impulses broken off in panic, inexplicable behavior late in the year, fitful inspiration, the continuous cold modal rapture in chords, in vivo.

He wakes after two hours and walks to the library, Saturday morning, bucking the current of fifty thousand Memorial Stadium football fans. Deep into the season, he still has not acclimated; getting from Stadium Terrace to the stacks against the crowd takes twice as long as normal. Inside the informational Fort Knox, he pores over the periodicals in a spiral search back into time, not knowing what he is looking for but certain he will recognize it when he sees it. He is skimming the *Journal of Biological Chemistry* back to the early 1950s when he is suddenly frozen by a muted roar—a tsunami coming from some distance. The sound flashes through him, followed by instant realization: this is it. The magazine ads for fallout shelters with plush carpeting and Scrabble sets, the sad government films teaching kindergartners to survive an airburst by popping under their school desks: the age of information has caught up with itself.

But just as quickly, the collective howl collapses into silence. Ressler waits for another muffled announcement but hears nothing. Then the leap of inference: the home team threatening to score. All politics are local. Curious, he climbs to deck ten, looks out from this aerial outpost through the side of the stadium, between the banks of colonnades. There, a mass of fifty thousand particles forms a single, eukaryotic Football Fan. Waving, pink arms become the manifold cilia of a rotifer rippling across the membrane of this cooperative cell.

Ohio State takes the local boys through a clinic, as they will

down the years fading into time imMemorial. Watching this remarkable exercise in collective stimulus and response, the fifty
thousand organelles testing and responding to their environment,
he resolves to differentiate himself. He will give in to the pressure
of selection, employ the one weapon he has for obtaining the one
thing of any consequence to him: Jeanette Koss—tasting, achieving
her, pressing, infecting, taking, joining, learning what she is. He
will overwhelm her by sheer display of lovely force, of preening
genotype. He will bring her an incalculable prize, like those
chocolate-box corpses certain spiders bring their loves, proofs of
potential that also shield the suitor from serving as meal.

It relieves him to choose. Weeks he has held off, waiting for
this impossible complication to become the first of simplicities.
Now he will prove to her that he, of everyone she has ever met,
most merits the selection of love. He will give her the most beautiful bouquet imaginable—objective, freezing, clear: the top rung
of Jacob's ladder. Half blind to their contents, he checks out a
dozen bound journals and carries them back to his den. On his
way, the collective supercell, its function over, lyses. He stands
helpless, feels the crowd sweep over him. The walls of the stadium
explode, issuing fifty thousand viruses into the air. Epidemic this
time of year.

Learning the Irregular Verbs

I stopped loving Tuckwell and started resenting him. No reason.
The same reason I first loved him. I can't imagine how I ever
thought my love might make a difference to him. Irrational arrival,
irrational exit. I asked myself thirty times a day why I was trading
him for an excellent shot at nothing. I wasn't even trading. Nothing
mercantile about it. I was giving him away. Throwing.

In bad moments, I blamed advertising. It had always depressed
me: form without substance, noise parading as sense. But in fairer
intervals, I knew Keith only did what most of us do for a living:
he sold things, only a little more honestly than most. He ridiculed
his career himself: "The art form of the century. Concert, gallery,
and holy writ in one convenient package. How to say 'Eat Multinational Carcinogen Patties' appealingly. How to convince the
overcashed that all they need for happiness is leg weights. Mind-
forged manacles."

For four years, he had shown me every ad campaign he did. Not for approval—to ward off boredom, keep us from drifting into different dialects. In the end, I chose one of his major accounts to throw a fit over. We were cooking dinner together, a familiar menu of acquired favorites. By tacit agreement, we did not talk about my plans to move—how far they'd gone, where I stood. We'd made that mistake twice since it became reality, and now cut the topic a wide berth. By dessert, Keith cracked his affectionate parody of my day at the office. "Question," he said, mugging for my benefit. "Is the Human Bean getting any smarter?" Nostalgic lost offering, reminder of everything we'd given each other. He put it forward resignedly, but with an element of outside shot. After all, the old joke had always worked before.

But not that evening. "Answer: If you have to ask. . . ."

"Supporting documentation, please." Behind the burlesque, Keithy was trying to save us. But I didn't feel like playing. He spread a roll of paper towel and tried to amuse me by drawing a timeline of meliorism, marking pyramids, cathedrals, flotillas, railroads, and particle accelerators in little dots that broke out in a rash over the right side of the continuum. I ignored him, clearing dishes, putting up the leftovers.

"Einstein," he chuckled. "Lord Keynes. Pretty heavy hitters in recent generations. The semiconductor," he challenged, drawing one at the far right, in a halo of stars. "Quantum electrodynamics. Got you there!" He drew a triumphal arch for each one. He caricatured a baroque staircase leading from midcentury ever upwards off the map, bearing a little sign reading "This Way. Watch Your Step." He would have broken my heart had I let him.

"This is absurd," I said, level-voiced, ready for violence. "Love Canal. Ozone depletion. Tropical rain forest the size of Connecticut destroyed annually. A hundred thousand species extinct by the time we retire. How smart can you get?" Keithy diluted the silence by a low whistle. With a few deft sketches, he infested his staircase with cracks, broke it off in a shower of mortar and falling bodies. Mounted sideways on the resulting chasm, he hung a sign pointing downwards: "To Holiday Inn." He waited for a reaction I wouldn't give. "That reminds me," he said, leaving the room to fetch his portfolio as I used the timeline to wipe the table. He returned with the boards for a national campaign and ran them past me for approval.

I must have thought to make things easy for him by making

myself ugly. I still loved him that much. But real connection between us died the moment I tried to protect him from what was
happening. I flipped through his pictures, written in the world's
only ubiquitous language, its syntax carrying the cozy, intimate
delusion of tin-can telephones. I read his copy with the feeling
that none of it made any sense. I understood the message. But his
whole campaign didn't *mean* anything. "Keith, you say 'safer' here,
but you never say safer than what."

"Hm. Fiendishly clever."

"And what do you mean, 'We make things right'? What things?
How right? Who's this 'we'? There are twenty-five hundred of these
places across the country. Am I supposed to believe that all the
wes do things one way and all the theys do it another? Grant me
some discrimination."

He began smiling the death smile. "Aren't we being a little
willful? It's a time-honored, universal tradition. 'Your Driver'—
insert nameplate here—'Safe, Reliable, Courteous.' Semiotics,
woman. We're not *communicating* anything. Folks don't care
about facts. They wouldn't believe them anyway. They just want
the promise of friendship slipped into the sale."

"And they believe that?"

"Who's gonna lie about friendship?"

" 'We'll love you. All twenty-five hundred of us.' "

"It's commercially viable."

"Is that right?" I asked quietly.

"Yes. That's right." Still smiling, he knew we were lost, that I
wanted it that way. I kept flipping through the boards, as if we
weren't in the middle of the last square-off. One thing I still admire
about Keith: despite my encouragement, he never stooped to killing as a way to preserve things. He never pretended any degree
of attachment less than he had. Just as I was on the verge of giving
him further cause, the phone rang. Keith bounded out of the room
to answer it. I heard him from the bedroom, just short of abusive,
asking, "Who's financing this? Who pays your salary? Who do I sue
for breach of privacy?"

He hung up and came back looking beautifully sheepish. "My
poor relations in the phone solicitation racket. Turns out our name
has been chosen at random to receive a book of coupons worth
several thousands of dollars, free, at only twenty-nine ninety-five.
Dante placed those people one circle below real estate brokers.
Where's that timeline? Gotta make some emendations."

I went to him and put my arms around him. After a long time, we separated, embarrassed. I mumbled something about going to bed. He didn't move. I went into the bathroom and ran the water. I heard Tuckwell let himself out the door and lock it from the outside. He went down the stairs two at a time. I went to the dark window and watched until he came out on the street below. I saw him safely to the next block. He turned north, cutting a swath toward the bombed-out blocks. Everywhere, shops had battened down for the night, the day's refuse and rinds rotting in the gutter. In the two and a half blocks I tracked him, amorphous outlines threatened from doorways, bumped against him, suggesting obscure exchanges. Keith kept up a clip that convinced the wasted, substance-dependent figures that he was in peak health and not to be messed with.

His dependency was the city itself: male addiction to the unpredictable. Covert dangers of an evening walk through the neighborhood, *sotto voce* threats implied and periodically acted out, had led him from the lazy Methodist interior where he had been raised. The instant the umbilical snapped, he'd buzzed to the coast, first to a fine arts school in Rhode Island, a state whose motto, and not Colorado's, he insisted, should have been "Nothing Without Providence." Then Boston for a year. All staging ground for New York, shooting into Manhattan's drag like an ion from a Tesla coil. He had habituated to life and needed a higher throttle. In North America, NY, NY was the most potent over-the-counter drug available. The city sucked him up as it did all insomniacs. But even here, familiarity tracked him down. After five years of Brooklyn, he talked about moving to the Lower East Side, the South Bronx. Calcutta perhaps. Someplace a body could feel.

But I moved first. Ironic: I couldn't think of the two miles' sickening diversity between the South Docks and Prospect Park without admitting I didn't belong here. One look at my clothes, one syllable of accent gave me away. And here I was, combing the neighborhoods for a place as if it were coupon-doubling day at the supermarket. For the past week, I'd had to keep myself from renting every slum I looked into, they all, overnight, seemed so full of promise. The hint of sea change was enough to make the familiar, forsaken rat warehouses show overlooked inlay of shining stone.

I watched Tuckwell until he ducked down the subway—the same route that took him each morning to his International Style

261

steel-and-glass vertical trailer park. I would never visit his office again. I pictured him boarding the car, the adored public transportation, his favorite contact sport. A subway car could always be counted on to provide the thrill of confrontation. The face-off he needed that night.

I was asleep when he returned. For the next several days, we maneuvered around each other. We ate at different times, arranged our schedules to diverge. Only before sleep did we talk. We slept six centimeters from one another, sometimes in sleep closing even that gap, pressing against each other, licensed by the confusion of night. At week's end, I told Keith that a library friend was marrying, looking for someone to adopt her place. The end of our post-mortem existence.

"Have you signed?"

"I've arranged with her."

"You agreed to let me have a look before you did anything."

"Let's go have a look, then. I can still back out." But we both knew it was a done deal, that I had reneged on the one condition he'd set for our breakup.

We walked to the new neighborhood. Keith inspected the street and nodded. "A little closer to the branch."

"It feels like home already," I said, grateful for the sign of acceptance. He winced. Too late to apologize. After four years of conversation, we'd lost the phrase book. Every word now was in pathetic talkee-talkee, creole.

"It's on a corner," Keith said apprehensively. I was forced to agree. "It's over a dress shop," he observed.

"Antiques," I equivocated. We got the key to the upstairs from the landlord, also the shop proprietor.

"An efficiency," Keith said, attempting to approve.

"I wouldn't call it that, exactly." Semantic quibble.

"Nice. Clean. Quiet. Rent-protected?" I mentioned the figure. Keith's brow cowered and his cheek pulled, protecting the side of his face.

"I can pay it."

"Not within the old quarter-salary rent rule." I thought: Nobody on the Eastern Seaboard has followed that budget since 1940. He checked the fixtures, outlets, jambs: a pantomime we saw no way to avoid. The warrant of his solicitousness was not about to let me hurt myself for his sake. Now that I was absolving him from liability, he no longer had the luxury of letting me hurt myself.

262

He sat on the bed and pounded the mattress. "Strong enough?" I said nothing. "When do we move your stuff? Not that I'm rushing, but. . . ." He drummed his fingers impatiently.

I sat down next to him. I wanted so badly to ask him if he would come visit me here, once I'd put everything right. But I kept from sinking to contemptible. After a moment's looking around the room, Tuckwell reached and pulled my elbow out from under me, controlling my roll and bringing my head down into his lap. He stroked my temples, his lower lip pushed slightly to the side in subfarction against his upper. Tell yourself whatever you need to, but don't look for confirmation.

I reached toward his face, thinking to grab his nose between first and second fingers, an old game meaning almost anything. But he moved unexpectedly and my motion carried my hand into a punch. In a flash, the whole hierarchy of second-guessing fed across Keith's face. He squashed it, but not fast enough to escape mutual knowledge. He grabbed my hand, automatically restraining. Seamlessly returning to decorum he twisted my wrist and gingerly inspected my watch. "Yikes," he said, slightly flattened affect. "Getting late. You're coming home at least tonight, aren't you?"

I had no change of clothes, linen, toiletries, towel, toothbrush, or pillow to give my neck that civilized sleeping crook, no food nor anything to eat with, very little cash, and nothing to gain by staying. But his calling the other place home made it impossible to return to. I shook my head; Tuckwell, disgusted, didn't even attempt the obvious argument. His shrug disowned me.

"I'll be fine. Camping without the poisonous plants. I'll come by tomorrow to grab some things. Take what's left. It's yours. Sell it to that fence on Eastern Parkway."

"No way. I'm through with your liquid assets, lady." I walked him downstairs, waved as he left, then turned back inside where my new landlord, uninterested in my private fripperies, frittered in his shop. I bought a matched set of Hayes-era curtains and bedclothes for nothing down. He was delighted to start a tab. I feasted on crackers and fresh fruit from the greengrocers, which I ate slowly in invigorating silence. A bare apartment: my senses were never so awake. I took a scalding bath, soapless, squeezing the water from my skin, standing in the dark, fanning dry. I took care of my arousal in the solitary room. I had never before seen it: happiness required only that I rid myself of all distraction. I went to sleep against the antique sheets, feeling parts of my body

I'd forgotten existed. I slept the best night I ever slept in my life.

I dressed in yesterday's clothes, finished the cracker box for breakfast, ran my fingers through my hair (a surprisingly reasonable comb), and walked, in the changing November, to work. The branch seemed a different building, my coming upon it from this direction. Delicious disorientation: I felt I'd changed jobs. I must have looked appalling. But of my colleagues, only Mr. Scott remarked on my appearance. "My dear, you look like you could do with a little retirement. Care to join me?" I told him I'd never been more sure: the Reference Desk was how I wanted to spend the rest of my life.

I moved my things gradually over several days, dragging my heels in a flare-up of empathy. Keith helped carry, by turns grateful and exasperated at my drawing the process out. Already gone, I had the luxury of loving that old life again at a safe range. I stayed over, slept once more with Tuckwell: a slow, sad night retracing, committing the cadence of one another to memory, realizing we had gotten it all wrong somehow, but that it was too late to go back and erase the maps, restore the white spaces.

I didn't contact my friends at MOL once during that period. My move had to be a moratorium, proof that I'd made the break, done the pointless violence for unimpeachable reasons. There had been no trade. Isolation was its own best reason. I worked at the branch, and in the remaining hours decorated the nest, wallpapered, trimmed. On days off, I learned the new neighborhood. I was determined to live as if the move were self-motivated. But I was sustained by undeniable expectation. Even the air had a scent of something imminent. *Of course* solitude was exciting—how couldn't it be? Crisis couldn't touch me. Loneliness, no loss, was something to covet. The erotic dress-up at the bottom of the cedar chest.

Strange place, Brooklyn. Not a place, a thesaurus of neighborhoods. I never belonged in any of them. Had things gone differently in local politics, we'd all be speaking Dutch. I'd be pinching my guilders. Todd would have had only to slip across New Amsterdam to the next colony in order to learn his latest irrelevant foreign language, English. Strange place, Breuckelen. Hudson sailed past fifty years after Bles's death. Two journeymen on the same enterprise: the pursuit of panels perfect for getting lost in. The elusive Passage, spice routes, epochal expansion. The world is too well mapped; quadrants capture it all. Alchemy's four elements, psychology's four humors. What can a body do in its quartet of seasons but set fire to the familiar, take off on the numinous half-moon?

I wanted Franklin, beyond a doubt. I could feel, in bands of tissue under my skin, the precise place that want had set for him. I wanted his field, his detached, unbearably patient art history. I wanted to *see* this place that I didn't belong in, its cross-sectional pigments, each assay suspended one on another, successive approximations. I wanted to recover that landscape, the place I'd forgotten as I got too good at describing it. I went two weeks without seeing him, two weeks at my new colony. One Friday I walked from my place to theirs. It seemed a miracle to be on foot. The blocks between did not seem so dangerous as strange, misunderstood. I buzzed, heard the voice thin, tinny, treble in the speaker, backed with a flack of electric static, but inimitable. He sang a ludicrous parody of a housewife's guarded "Who *is* it?" He knew full well who it was.

"It's me," I said, burying grammar. "I think it's time."

Perpetual Calendar (II)

The simplest of devices, a model of informational economy, it fits completely on a single page. You can take the magic square and palm it, hide the device in one hand. Even a small hand. The perpetual calender exists because the year has only fourteen possibilities. January 1 can fall on each day of the week, and once around again for leap years. The rest of the cycle—days when everything must happen—falls automatically, redundantly, according to compact pattern. 1983 starts on a Saturday. So do 1938, 1898, and 1842. The years of Sudetenland, of *J'accuse,* of von Mayer's first thermodynamics paper duplicate the same dates as that year when a lost woman of thirty moves across town. How does it work? A lookup table lists the years, keying them to a long, repeating series of fourteen templates for the only possibilities going. The perfect reference tool: infinite sequence reduced to formula.

The cleverest child in every neighborhood, at fourteen, discovers this table secreted in the quartos of her parents' bookshelf. Appalled, unbelieving at first, she warms to the idea of a compressible eternity. Soon, she uses it to consolidate a shaman's control over the block's information-poor. Hiding the device behind

cupped palms, she calls out her privileged, inside track to a spell-
bound audience in the back alley: "You, Pete, were born on a
Wednesday. It will be Wednesday again in 19. . . . Here's something:
ten years back, it was Sunday today." It will be years before she
knows that these facts, in demand, clean and elucidating, mean
nothing. For her clincher, she claims: "Today was exactly the same
as it was one hundred and eighty years ago." Two years, twenty
years ago, on this day, that child was me.

XIII

A Young Person's Guide to the Orchestra

He reads the stack of journals until the type decomposes into runic scratchings. He half dozes, swims awake, is washed under again for a few minutes, for hours, in tidal semiawareness. He gives the technical data rein to assort into spontaneous visuals—unzipping ladders, blueprint-imbedding blueprints, complex wartime gear-machines, families of trapeze artists linked in aerial streamers. In his reverie, the edge of biological thought is a continuous showing of jerky one-reelers. Every so often, an image-analog jars him awake with recognition. Bold simplicity of design knocks him conscious. Lucid, he sees nothing in the models but comic, clumsy, cartoon inspirations. Each time he comes to, Ressler cracks the journal repository for something he's missed. He loses consciousness again two or three articles down the pike, returning in the middle of the fourth, blindly turning pages.

He keeps up this routine—reading, dozing, imagining—for days, paying no attention to the passage of daylight. He finishes the juice concentrate and peanuts left in his fridge from a shopping run ages before. When the last remaining milk spoils, he makes cold cereal with water. The phone rings, but its bell goes languid each time he fails to answer. At odd hours he saunters to Olga, his heart full of gratitude at her patient, permanent Fourth Position stance. He listens to the independent variations, the record of that unbirthday visit. The same record, but different in every particular, just as the woman herself is now unrelated to the one he met on first hitting town. Steeped in the music, he teaches himself a vocabulary to describe what he hears in the profusion of notes. He borrows those terms he is most familiar with. Canon and imitation, audible even

267

without names, become transcription. Phrase and motif become gene. He hears polypeptides in a peal of parallel structure, differentiation in a burst of counterpoint.

Days into his journal binge, intent on latching onto the remaining piece in the synthesis, Ressler returns to the musical set to test a bizarre hypothesis. For weeks he has assumed that his lack of training would forever preclude his hearing how each single-minded permutation was a variation on *anything*. But recently he detects an unexpected pattern. The theme he begins to hear—the element drawing all filial generations into a family tree—is not a theme at all. It is a determining genotype. The existence of the Base is still a hypothesis. He will not swear to it until he hears it underwriting each of the aria's progeny. Testing the idea takes time. But listening is exactly the focused release he needs.

He began scientific life—natural history's home museum—a closet Laplacian: solving the real world required only a set of differential equations defining the movement of every independent piece in it. But a few days into his marathon session—never once leaving K-53-C, alternately sampling Bach and teasing protein synthesis—he scraps the engine. All measurement is not inherently valuable. Science is choked by unrestrained data as a pond is by too luxurious plant growth. Cyfer has attacked the coding problem by attending to every amino sequence ever unearthed. Given an English library and an identical, jumbled collection in Bulgarian, they've tried to write a bilingual dictionary by reading every book in both sets, tallying tables larger than the two libraries together, searching for spurts that correlate. Brute tabulature might work, if the underpinning translation were preordained, symmetrical. But there's no guarantee the runaway data enfold formulaic simplicity. In fact, just the reverse.

If nature is truly objective, as the entire scientific project must assume, then science can prove nothing except that we don't speak the same language as the outside world. Still, the double helix is a better map than the old homunculus or arcane pangene, which are both in turn miles beyond clay and *spiritus dei* for correspondence. Man may understand only artificial shorthand and nature speak only in innumerable instances; dim Berlitz phrases may never *be* the thing they describe, but they're the only visa available.

Three quarters of his reading aims not at throwing open the window but at stopping down his aperture. First, he discards the idea, plaguing the symposia since mid-decade, that specific enzymes are required to thread each amino onto each terminus of a growing bead string. Each of these joiner enzymes, themselves amino acid strings, would require sufficient enzyme-synthesizing enzymes to synthesize it, and so *ad infinitum*. Regress: he remembers the lullaby his mother used to sing, about how she would sing him a lullaby if he stopped crying.

Dispensing with enzyme-dispensing enzymes, he reviews the possibility of direct template synthesis. DNA might split, exposing a half-chain plaster cast where aminos line up into proteins. The idea is pleasing, but the chemistry is wrong; the bases don't have the right shape to distinguish among the twenty amino acids; a codon and an amino acid aren't even the same size. Yet just as clearly, some templating takes place. DNA doesn't leave the nucleus, and proteins are synthesized outside, in the immense cytoplasmic sea. Some intermediary must reproduce the DNA codon arrangement and carry it out of the nucleus. He goes to Olga, dips into a variation that confirms, in a burst of quavers, the only possible mechanism: transcription. RNA transcribes DNA, ports its message away for translation.

At intervals of a few hours, Ressler gets impatient with himself for belaboring the obvious. But cobwebs are only obvious after they're cleared. He smiles, recalling the Von Neumann anecdote, repeated endlessly after the man's death earlier this year. The cybernaut, considered by some the century's most intelligent man, while deriving a complex theorem on a chalkboard in front of a class, skipped a step, saying it followed obviously. A student said he didn't see how. Von Neumann scratched his head, stared at the board, set the chalk down, left the room, came back minutes later, and declared, "Yes, it is obvious," and carried on with the proof.

By forgetting common knowledge, by starting again with only the proved, Ressler begins to hear with new clarity the composition he is after. Transcription only shunts the problem of translation from DNA onto RNA. He must still make a rigid distinction between code *text* and code *book*. He goes to his door for a gulp of fresh air. Deep, metallic cold in the lungs might even be healthy. He stands on the threshold, sucking in vapor that condenses in each exhalation. He turns to go in, tripping over a basket on the stoop. Cold artichoke with hollandaise, two chicken piccata breasts, and a bottle of Médoc. He carries it inside, where he reads

269

its attached note: "Inform us if the matter breaks. Remember the essential trace elements. We are all beginners in our own lives. Best, T.B."

Ressler smiles, breaks to eat, wonders how long he has been away, then returns to the publications, searching for evidence of an intermediary molecule, a translator that might align with the transcribed RNA codon and attach the correct amino acid into the growing polypeptide. At the back of his brain is an ironic hint about the most likely class of molecule for such a go-between, one capable of reading the subtle, raised-dot Braille of the nucleotide sites. Finding such an intermediary is prerequisite to his process, still only a matter of faith, for determining codon assignments. If he is to find it, it must be soon. The field is heating up. Insights are going public. He might pick the next journal off the stack and see the first islands of the transcription table drained of their opaque, deep-water enigma.

He bathes. The hot bath scalds his few fleshy parts a pale rose. Tub thermodynamics—heat loss, entropy, the chaff of the system—is hindered by a nineteenth-century slant: bath as steam engine, body as conditioned caldron of excess libido, cathexis cathartized. His bath cools like soup in a blown-upon spoon, the water's heat gone as random as recessing schoolchildren, too quickly for thermodynamics to explain. It cools only to him, would still surprise the outside touch. The analgesic property of hot water is a message, an instruction in warming. But the text evades him as he adjusts to reading it. The code is dimmed to the immersed, but will spring scalding to the unaccustomed hand. How to leave the water and still feel? The question is as still, as paradoxical as any aria. His skin burns with the fluid's prompting though the tub is already cold.

He sleeps a few anemic hours, a dreamless carpet of feral activity, a tapestry-forest that proves, on close examination, rioted with animal communities. Asleep, he thinks: nothing in the cell *knows* the code. Neither nucleotide nor transcription nor the hypothetical reading molecule nor the target enzyme contains anything resembling the codon table. No part of the code, not even the entire assembly, can say what it is. The triplet ACG could paint cysteine or arganine or any of the twenty, or even nonsense, and what difference would it make? What code are they after, after all? Where does it reside? In what level of that steep hierarchy of cells,

270

the aggregate organism where every level depends on the one below, and all depend on the ineffable?

And should he be still—astonishingly—alive when the secret words are at last uncovered, should *he* of all searchers be blessed to find it, what will this self-generating, self-defining system—residing nowhere, unknown by any of its constituent parts—what will the assignment of CAG to glutamine lay open? What relation, what revealing rule? Will it be, after all, the first small link revealing how this flourishing, odds-prohibited architecture can come about, flower into militantly uncountable variety, build itself blindly into ever more complex communities of communication, all cooperating under the aegis of that never-itself-comprehended code, achieving more precarious orders of order, culminating in a construct that may just now be growing capable of a grammar able to articulate, to speak, to *code* a rough symbolic analogy, a name for the Code?

What name? Not nucleotide sequences; not the codon catalog; not any of the reading machinery; not the enzymes. Not even the cell is the code. It is just its working out. The code is—so near as he can figure—a figure. A metaphor. The code exists only as the coded organism. There is no lexicon or look-up book. Not in the molecules, nor the cell, nor anywhere else but in that place—unnameable except by comparison—that houses all translation, all motivation, all that self-propagating structure that only by rough analogy and always in archaic diction (but not yet in his own words) can only inescapably be called desire.

The Food Chain

A knock at the door awakens him. After a moment, he establishes the approximate time of day: late afternoon, deepening sun. He thinks first to ignore the sound, stay away from the windows until it goes. But the knocking persists; perhaps he is due the intrusion of humanity on work that for the last several hours has made no progress at all.

Ressler opens the front door and sees no one. He is almost ready to accept the knocking as hallucination when he looks down and notices a miniature human on the stoop. Little Margaret Blake, trekked over from K-53-A for unknown end to stand on Ressler's

271

stoop, motionless and martyred, as if the world were already lost despite her pilgrim effort. Ressler is taken aback. "Hello there, little cowgirl," he opens tentatively.

"Will you let me in please? It's very cold out here."

"Your dad doesn't think it's cold yet."

"My dad is a pacifist."

Ressler bursts out laughing and lets the child in. Margaret investigates the place, awed by an apartment almost without furniture, decorations, the usual adult totems. "Wow! Amazing! What do people sit on?"

"Same place they always sit on," he says, making as if to spank her on that spot. Margaret collapses in a heap of giggles. When she sobers, Ressler asks, "So, little lady. What's up?"

"The sky." This time-honored comeback sends her into another paroxysm.

He feels the unforgettable first signs of a playground pit in his stomach. Terrible at taunts, he never understood the oppressed dialect of children, even as a child. He rejects *Wrap your head in bubble gum and send it to the navy* as an appropriate rejoinder for a Ph.D. "What's the matter?"

"With who?" Her giggle is nervous this time as she tests his face. She stops goofing and works herself into righteous indignation. "Bruce Bigelow."

The name signifies little to Ressler. It sounds vaguely familiar, so Bruce is either one of Stadium Terrace's preteen terrorists or the secretary of the interior. He's had a bad dose of Jesse James Clerk Maxwell Taylor Caldwell syndrome lately, all personalities, public and private, fusing into each other, indistinguishable flip sides of a common entity. "What about him?"

"He is Ass *Hole*."

Ressler snickers. "You've got to say, 'He is *an* asshole.' But don't say it, OK? You have to go through puberty before you're allowed to say that."

This sets Margaret to crying, perhaps at the thought of one day having to deal with puberty on top of that asshole Bruce Bigelow. Ressler looks at her flushed cheeks, the hot springs leaching to the surface under her lower eyelid, and recalls the child's virtuosic sprung-verse performance. He frowns, chides, "Margaret? Are you? Grieving?" She smiles in mid-sob, gasps for air, coughs up a little sputum-laugh at her own ridiculousness. "What exactly did this Bruce so-called Bigelow do, woman?"

272

"He loosened this tooth. See?" She wiggles a canine whose time on this earth had come anyway.

"So what? Don't you get tooth-fairy payola for that? You ought to cut Brucie in for ten percent."

"You are Strangeness, know that? Strange Ness." The phrase *I'm rubber and you're glue* flashes through his mind, but he doesn't commit to it. Margaret, matter-of-fact, asks, "You know how to fight? You've gotta teach me."

"Oh I do, do I? Why me? Get your dad to teach you."

"My *dad*? Didn't you hear me? My *dad* believes in nonviolence." She sighs, a mix of incomprehension and pity.

Ressler laughs to recognize Tooney from this angle. "Ask him for a few lessons. Tell him they're *hypothetical*."

She doesn't even flinch at the word, but only shakes her head sadly. "He won't budge. He says, wait a few decades, and Bruce will die all by himself. You don't know how to box either, do you?"

"OK, kid. Them's fightin' words. Put up your dukes." Against his better judgment, he raises his palms and presents them to the little girl for target practice. Margaret jumps up in delight, claps her hands, rushes at him as if to kiss him in thanks, and takes a swing.

"Not too wild. You're leaving yourself open. Keep your guard up. Don't lead with your right all the time. Confuse him. Save your secret weapon. Left, left, left, *then* come in with the roundhouse. Shake 'im up, shake 'im up, then knock 'im down."

The phrase startles him. Perhaps his father taught him the cadence, but he has no memory of learning the words. They spring unsponsored from some antiquated chunk of neurons in the limbic, reptilian segment of his brain. He has always looked on all physical combativeness short of card games as evolutionary regression. He has never fought for anything in his life. That is, he has never applied overt violence to achieving his ends. Now the ancient formula of force, the somatic record of every successful bash that brought his forebears along their way upright presents arms, ready to address not only little Margaret's self-defense but his own akossting.

Over eons, undeniable advantage has conferred the Brute Force gene pretty ubiquitously throughout the population. But the last few millennia have produced a wrinkle—too soon to say if it's a true evolutionary variation or just a dress-up game. Capacity for violence—as unshakeable as any of the body's track record—has found a way of making itself even more propitious for survival by remaining latent. He can't take a poke at the chops of the editorial board of *Nature* in order to persuade them to accept the paper on the rates experiment he is writing up. Yet the paper is a way of going twelve rounds with Herbert Koss without ever once declaring himself in competition.

Werewolf, apeman, creature from the lagoon of lost souls: the killer instruction set still rattles loose in there. Locked in mock violence with this laughing little girl, her fists flaying at his palms as she picks up the trick of bodily injury, he sees that the unique achievement of this species, the thing that recursive consciousness ultimately permits, is the pretense that one does *not* actually manifest a trait even when taking maximum advantage of it. Everything the hominid branch has achieved—every treatise, tower, or diatonic tune—came about from surviving two out of three falls, prettying up the results after the fact. Jacob, after all, went all night against God's palooka, winning himself a *name* by avoiding the angel's pin. Shake him up, knock him down, do him in.

Man will never be anything better than a clever boxer. Maybe one that wins by footwork rather than punches, but still a creature always accountable to the win. The realization sickens him: advantage, self-interest, short-term gain are the only forces that carve a population. Every rung not higher, but shrewder, slier. The logical extreme is a species so clever it overruns its niche, bringing down the whole round robin. He quickly drops his target palms, timing it so that little Margaret's latest playful jab slams an uppercut to the kisser.

His lip breaks open. The child screams a terrified apology. Ressler comforts her, assures her it was his fault. But he is as shocked as the little girl. He puts a dishrag to his mouth to stanch the blood. How did that slip in? How can natural selection make room, in this advanced a model, for such a pathetic, pointless, destructive little *hit me* of contrition? He clots the bleeding and calms Margaret by letting her eat cold cereal dry, right out of the box. Distracted by this novelty, she forgets the tragedy in minutes. "What do you do?" she asks him, munching happily.

"You mean, for a living?" She nods her head gravely. He thinks for a minute, helpless to remember exactly what he *does* do. "Same as your dad," he says.

"N-no," she says, curling her lip and shaking her head skeptically. "No. You don't do that!"

Ressler would laugh if it didn't sting. He can't imagine what

Tooney has told his child he does. "Here," he says, getting an idea. "I'll show you." He goes to the side of the sink and takes the long-empty paper-towel tube off its holder. He tears it down its spiral seam from one end of the coil to the other. A three-dimensional helix, possessing all the magic geometry of the original. He shows the child the properties of the self-duplicating curve, all the while proving there is always an intermediary analogy between us and substance, always a messenger between the mass we are after and the message it embodies.

"You study these things?" He nods, asks her if she knows what cells are. "Of course. Don't be dumb."

"You have a billion cells in your body, and each cell has masses of these."

She takes the dissected tube, spins it around, hands it back. "Scratch it. No deal. This thing? Billions? Me?"

"Yes, you."

"Can't be."

"Then who?"

Margaret jumps up, her eyes saucers. "You *stole* that! How did you know that?"

He doesn't have the heart to tell Margaret that every secret incantation she has ever recited has been around for generations. He looks at her and wonders: Why Brucie? Well, at least the kid loosened her tooth. Why Koss? He has no good data, knows nothing about her. She has never harmed him, to the best of his knowledge. She showed signs once of a bitter sense of humor, but even that surrogate sparring has quieted. She does not possess Toveh Botkin's strong moral sense, with its species-wide, if not individual, survival value. Her contributions to the Blue Sky sessions are impeccable but hardly adventuresome, barely cerebral ballet. She lacks too the older woman's indiscriminate kindness, a trait conveying no survival value, a liability in fact, unless, like the antimalarial quality of sickle-cell anemia, it contains, for certain climates, some hidden side effect that outweighs benevolence's impediment. Of course, the whole comparison is moot, as the older woman has already committed the sin of aging. Whatever pleasure Ressler enjoys in her company will remain nothing more than irrelevant. Kindly.

But Jeanette: undeniably topical charms. Her shape, skin, coloration once upon a time had not been to his taste. Now her smallest arch obsesses him, even as he finds the full allure somehow repelling. How could he have let himself in for her when she remains unachievable—as pointless to fix his unappeasable, sharp, lost affection on as she is to covet, lust for, crave?

Little Margaret makes to punch him for stealing her secret verse—a slow-motion, platonic archetype of a punch. He intercepts its parabola and demands, "So how are you going to pay for this boxing lesson?"

The child smiles shyly, looks away. "I learned a new poem."

"Well? What are you waiting for?"

And little Margaret begins, disastrously, sing song:

> "When you are old and grey and full of sleep,
> And nodding by the fire, take down this book,
> And slowly read, and dream of the soft look
> Your eyes had once...."

By the second line, Ressler sees it all: he has built her from scratch, in the lab of his own imagination. He has dressed her in clothes that she fits, fills out unforgettably. He has invested Jeanette Koss with every quality that might pin him hopelessly to her hem. And now she *has* them all, possesses them in flesh, cannot be divested. He has taught himself to see her, has named that recessive allele that manifests itself only once every hundred generations. Uncontainable mystery. He has frightened them both into noticing, and now they can't look away.

Margaret reaches the part about how one man loved the pilgrim soul in you. He cuffs her gently. "Enough, short stuff. You're terrific."

"And loved the sorrows of your changing face," she races to complete the rhyme. She struggles free and throws another slow punch to his midriff, stopping short at the skin to tickle him. "Shake him up. Knock him down."

"That's two 'shake him ups,'" Ressler says sternly. "Make sure to count." The advice sticks in his glottis, coming up. The homunculus giggles and is gone.

He toys with his paper-towel tube for some time. When night comes, he wonders if it might not be time to get back on diurnal schedule. He lies in bed, disembodied underneath the covers. The space in the room around him does not touch him. November; he smells the remote aroma of a disappearing fall in the accumulation of heating-degree days. He feels his hands because they are not

276

his arms, his torso because it is not his legs where they rest under the sheets, his legs because they do not touch hers, and her, because she is not any of this, not his, does not touch any of these parts that can *feel* her imprint, so conspicuous is her solidity in its absence next to him.

Not this nor this nor this. But before he has power to say behold, lyrical awareness is lost to that sweet, sorry, one-word contradiction in terms. Nothing in his analogy for himself *knows* where he is. He can get no closer to the idea he is after except through contrast. Except through analogy. Except through already knowing. Sleep is as unreachable as the woman. He has not seen her for weeks. Not in flesh anyway; he sees her analogy everywhere. He cannot step out of his barracks bunk without imagining that some fall of a sheet or turn of a lathed chair leg holds the revelation he needs from her curve.

Has she thought of him in the last several days? A letter in his campus box, a casual inquiry at his office? Has she noticed his absence? That one look at the lab, the backwards glance they caught each other in convinces him that the awful hook is also barbed at the other end. One of those ignored phone calls could have been her. All of them. She *must* think of him.

He raises himself from bed. By feel, he retrieves his shirt and trousers from the back of the chair. Soundlessly in the dark, he dresses. He returns, by homing instinct, to the waiting stack of journals. The coding problem again possesses him. He smiles in mid-triplet-fiddling: I am only doing what any childless male is programmed to do. An alternative means of replication. Oblique, sublimated—pencil, paper the international chemical symbols. But he's definitely after a self-perpetuating, thriving, surviving genome with his name on it.

The search continues without sound. When the spell is broken, it's from the outside. He looks up, suddenly aware that extended sleep and food deprivation have put him in a state resembling those mind-alterers the DOD is perennially testing. The frame flickers, and he is startled to see Jeanette Koss letting herself in through his front door, a thief in the night.

He assumes—Occam's razor—that the vision is just neurons mis-synapsing. Extended fixation, never far below the surface of his work, relaying the millisecond message that the folds of his foyer lampshade are the coils of her hair. Then the apparition moves. "Are you all right? Where have you been?" He hears her exhale fright on coming close enough to see his face where he sits reading in the dark. "What have you *done*?"

Before he can put his hands up to defend, she reaches and touches his lip. He remembers now how badly it stings. She withdraws her hand, shows him the fresh blood. It has broken open without his noticing. "Oh that." He cannot keep from grinning, widening the cut. "Beaten up by a reciter of verse."

Today in History

She sponges the swollen split. He relaxes his face, neck, torso, dropping the journal at hand. If she chooses to kill him, he trusts she will at least use the swift skill of the professional vivisectionist. "This poet," Koss says skeptically, placing a hand under his neck and daubing, born to the motion. "Female?" He can't even smile without wincing. He closes his eyes, resting his head in the unknown quantity of her palm.

Nurse's talk, vessel of calming distraction. Is this some skill on that fraction of chromosome his half of the race doesn't receive? Where has she learned to move with such certainty? He sees through closed lids her ironic delight at her unexplained presence here. She sponges in delicate spirals, and he forgets all else.

"I assume it is pointless to ask for disinfectant in this part of the world." She searches the bathroom for an analog, returning empty-handed. "Your immune system is on its own for this one." She roots in her handbag for a kerchief, unused. Before he can object, she presses the fabric to him, lightly as leaves falling to earth. She holds the bandage to his broken surface, making no sound except breathing. Her fingers, fine instruments, test the damp cloth for clotting. All time's unraveling advance affixes to that square of linen, his lips on one side, her fingers on the other, his corpuscle stain sucked into the fiber capillaries like chromopartitioning. The blood that she dams by this tear pauses in the loop before its appalling haul back down to the pump.

Gauging the moment of drying, Dr. Koss lifts the linen away. She touches the congealed spot, brushes a few dry grains, shows her fingers to prove that the wound has healed. Then she leans in the most continuously smooth cycloid descent imaginable, draws herself flush to his body, and in one medicinal motion places her mouth—a mouth on the verge of saying, already forming the word—over his just-sealed scar. A sound escapes from her—threatened, mammalian. Ressler surrenders completely. He can do no other.

Jeanette changes: complete, fantastic reforging, and Ressler is inside the chrysalis with her. Unbroken, moldable expanse: moist, circulating tracts just inside her mouth attach to his awakened cell walls. The largest, most implausible living organ, the single membrane without edge, protective barrier, inescapable border, soft, semipermeable, resilient, impossibly strong for its thinness, her interface melanin prison, her—he dredges up the word: her *skin*. He feels himself dragged toward the cutoff of control. He looks over the drop in front of him but cannot measure it from cliff level. Then her mouth moves a certain way, spasms in a victimized twitch, and at once he no longer *wants* to measure. He can want nothing but to moisten her in return.

He tries to slow. A return kiss: nothing compounded. They've gone that ill-advisedly far anyway. Irreversible. They reach a place where he can level off for a moment without betraying further. Let this much be enough. More than he ever thought possible. Stop. Soon. At moment's end, seeing as they are already there.

Jeanette draws away first, changing partway back, retracting as much as possible from this melt. She stiffens her elbows and puts a hand to her head—frantic recollection, remorse past appropriate now. "I'm sorry," she whispers into the night room, the apology lost on air currents. "This doesn't help things any." She turns back toward him, touches his mouth, as if she meant the cut. "Not what the doctor ordered."

The cut has remained remarkably self-sutured. She tries to laugh, but the sound deflects in a flush of excitement and regret. Ressler makes a place for her among the piles of periodicals and she lies down next to him, holding him sadly, in mutual perjury. They say nothing, nor need to. He laces his fingers behind the base of her head, having known this shape always, how it fits in his hands, draped in this shock of hair. He *holds* her. The surf of his own circulation sluices inside him. He slips into that unforceable place free from the impulse to interpret. In that briefest space, nothing signals anything but itself. Dr. Koss answers silence with silence, the only explanation of her presence here. Her scent and bending is fact enough.

When it no longer is, they return to the nervous community of words. He extends the silence a little by reaching over to the record player, for days kept perpetually within reach. He chooses indifferently. He would fill the room with slumber party or young person's guide—anything except speech. But to do so without standing up, he is confined to the grooves already on the turntable, sound no more significant than the library of variations he has listened to continuously since the onset of his retreat. For lack of a gesture neither brutal nor clumsy, he lowers his head into her lap. She loosens her legs, makes a pallet for him in the softness of her thighs. She bends and kisses him, now briefer, drier, shallower, not so felonious. While she cannot claim that the first was an accident, it may have been an error in degree. A miscalculation, intended more *so:* quick, pertinent, almost acceptable among straight-ticket, Stevenson voters, virtually businesslike, therapeutic, preferable to the health hazard of complete repression.

But her recantation will not wash. She knows her transparency and smiles in shame. She reaches down, kisses him a third time: full again, but wary not to approach the extremity of the first. In the calculus of the permitted, everything less than what they have already committed cannot, they whisper, add to the sentence they will be slapped with. But they do worse with less. For at reduced volume, they admit to an eagerness more faultable than desire.

"I've created a monster," Jeanette says, breaking the embarrassed silence.

He disengages, reinstating the protective empty inch between them. "Wolfman?" he says, straining for joke inflection. "Me?"

Dr. Koss shakes her head, laughs shyly, tentatively recloses the gap between them. "Not that! I mean...." She relaxes her focus to infinity, lifts her eyebrows on an abstraction, pattern, airy nothingness. On the music.

"Oh. I'm afraid I *have* gotten a little obsessed. They help me think. Or at least distract me productively."

"Were they that scratchy when I gave them to you? What do you play them on, a Mixmaster?" A flash of the old caustic. The biting, brittle, almost forgotten woman thrashing in the wake of frightened tenderness. Everything she has tried to be—cold, self-assured, professionally fond—all the blind come-ons, covert glances, suggestive sarcasms, concealed double crosses, casual, intermittent droppings-by, are not yet her sum.

"Oh, those," he says. "I hardly hear the scratches anymore. Surface mutations."

"An ACA triad in the original becomes ACG in the copy?" Ressler nods, inches away from her enormous eyes. The skin beneath is cream-tinted gold leaf, freckled, fetching, heartbreaking. His nod turns to a quick exam: how much has this woman assembled of translation? Can they help one another to the construct? He has sought the code in order to seduce her. Now, with the first taste of the prize wrapped gently around him, *she* seems the recruit to enlist in the wider campaign.

He turns from that height of cheeks, focuses on the music, the surface blips. He understands, in panorama, the process of aging. Every cell division, each mitosis—how many going on each moment?—is subject to some small chance of mutation. Each of these mutations slightly degrades the command set. The more divisions, the more fouled with accidents the cell information. The piece decays, variation by variation, performer to performer, by ear and word of finger down the intervening years since composition; it loses its accuracy, laced through with mistakes. Age might be the gradual accumulation of noise in the signal. Static-rich, mistaken; old, gray, full of sleep.

He uncoils from his cradle and stares at this woman in self-defense. How will she age? Will he be allowed to see her? The cream will have crusted. The soft patina, the brown, feminine freckled edibility will be lost in slack pores. In time, the look will be obscured altogether, not even preserved in memory of this unforgettable evening, a guest register smudged beyond recall, lost to the accretion of mistakes.

Until that moment comes, he can try to keep deep down, duck the breakers of adrenaline, stay stock-still and live whatever minutes of impossible visitation might be granted him. Her body, the blank subjunctive tense that he has conjugated in a thousand unsupported persons, has walked through his door tonight. For the first dozen variations—her tender strokings, their skittish explorations of mouth and neck and shoulder salient, surveys afraid of the data they are after—he finds relief from the relentless organic trap. Her simple *being here,* their simultaneous confession of the patently clear, is somehow blessedly enough.

He wants only her safety, her survival. He will do anything to ensure it. He would even now perjure himself, petition that tired, old anthropic metaphor—the bearded, wish-fulfilling bureaucrat in charge of the mesh of metacycles—to keep her from harm. But

281

first he must learn what so badly needs saving in her. Her arrival, so long willed but never dared hoped for, at last presents the chance to discover.

"Your husband...?" He can go no further in naming the conspicuous Other. He's met Herbert several times, before the man meant anything to him. He has seen the other half of the Koss twisted pair slumped behind the wheel of a finny ballistic shape, waiting to ferry his wife to and from the laboratory, her real home. Jeanette looks down, hair red in the lamp halo. She kisses him on the clavicle, grabs the small of his back, moans a little. But except for the contortions, no answer. "Does he know you...?"

"Finish what you're...." Her posture goes insouciant. She removes her hands and looks so genuinely abashed that were his head not still in the nest of her thighs, he would think he has been wildly mistaken, that Dr. Koss's reason for dropping by was to discuss organic chemistry. She compounds the doubt by producing from her bag a copy of *Biochemistry Society Symposium*. "I came by to return this."

Back already to optative evasion? He feels her preparing to revoke, to claim that the confession was extracted under torture. He begins to jettison everything, everything. He is almost ready to dismiss their starved kiss as a miscalculation brought on by extended overwork, a psychosis she was too polite to rebuke. And yet, he clearly recalls her suckling fast to him. He stares at the journal she hands him. His eyes well up, stung. He loads his voice with the simulation of adulthood. "I'm sorry, but I don't remember ever having lent this to you."

"You didn't. But at two in the morning, I needed *some* rationalization." She laughs wildly, claps a hand to her face. She prods him under the chin, forces his eyes to gaze squarely into hers. She rebukes him with a look: Don't be stupid. We are lost, hopelessly lost, together in the thick. We don't even know each other, but in seconds, we have confirmed the predetermined fit. Irrefutable proof that we'll never be able to publish. As he shifts to restore blood to tourniqueted limbs, she adjusts accordingly, perfect ballet of self-communicating touch. They join again, flush, and the joint between them disappears. Organic chemistry indeed.

In the next rushed second, it is *her,* Jeanette in the flesh. She will never again be able to deny her signal. She shoves her face to his in breathing arrest, fixing to his lips as if to an oxygen mask.

She pulls away at last for real air, her heart racing. "I knew you would never come to me."

"How could I?"

She unbuttons him to the waist, not going anywhere, just looking, marveling at the chest she uncovers, the person she reveals. She shakes herself, starting with her head and graduating hipwards. "I was waiting for you." Silence, carefully measured, in the half-articulate rhythms of distracted desire: silence at her first glimpse of his bare ribs. She puts her head to his torso, opens her mouth, takes in his breast. She nuzzles him, running her teeth lightly in his fur, eyes closed and head rolling softly from side to side as if his body were some obstacle. She gnaws, kisses, works his flesh. She has been waiting for him to come back from the mazed pursuit. Waiting all along for him to return to where he never should have left, to recognize the place at last, to return home, to rest, to her.

They overstep, accelerating into inexcusable touch. They could still stop, save the situation. To kiss a face, even unbridled, is still an adolescent sin—pretty, forgivable fantasy. To gnaw another's chest is another purpose. At this instant, they are still one another's innocence, a place in cut grass, an orchard under the rushing in of dusk. In a moment, if they do not stop the accelerando of friction, they will be one another's spent attempt, post-coupled, unrealized, unreachable.

He lifts her away, laughing desperately, limping across her face with little diffusing kisses; it takes the last of his internal monologue to remain even this much in control. "You're right," she says weakly, brushing hair from her mouth. "This isn't making matters any easier." She wraps herself into his arms quietly, content, as if she has had twenty easy years with him in which to grow aware of his every nuance of mood. "Change the subject," she orders him, eyes closed, smiling mischievously, as if his failure to do so will mean she will have to return to gnawing. "Tell me what you've been working on." Listening furiously to the last of the variations, he cannot, for a moment, choose between telling her about the in vitro idea or explaining his theory on how these musical condensations are all variations. The two proliferating patterns seem flip sides, hiding the same hermeneutic.

The vast, macroscopic architecture of the piece flashes into his head. The music, as familiar to him now as his body, reveals, in shadow, part of its design. The infolded Base presides over its independent progeny, rendering them congruent, concurrent, a family tree without clearly defined root or branch tip, a simultaneous as well as sequential ontogeny, profoundly felt, radial: each moment of the huge movement resembles the whole. The strangely beautiful, mathematical relation rings through its tonal changes. The Standing Now of the piece is more being than becoming. Its self-resembling perfection moves forward by a germinating process of periodic imitation he begins to detect but is still years away from naming.

"Listen." He glances down at Jeanette's face, searching for verification. The half-light molds her features into an empty flask. His mouth works up syllables, silently, struggling to hold that stationary morphogenesis he has at last found a name for. But he sees a different piece in her face. The form becomes a presage, information from a reliable source, a prediction of future news. The music remaining in the air after all sound is gone retains the first hint of sadness carried in the aria itself. Begun in too narrow terms, it must broaden into numinous sorrow, making the rounds of every village between here and the edge of dark.

He can no more hope to understand why she is here in his living room at night than to understand why *he* is. She waits on this platform, for this transfer. His head has lain gently between her legs. Whatever her motivation—unbalanced brilliance, crass calculation, random desire, love of intrigue, compassion, neurosis, retaliation, pity—this woman cradles him. And that lies as far beyond explaining as this whiff of modulation. Something sits hidden, still, in Jeanette Koss. She is more mysterious here beside him in the dark than on that day when she toweled him dry. He cannot reach her, put his hand on that mystery, the potential changes in her first four notes.

The notes are the song of children inhabiting the dark yard a minute more, inventing one last game even after being called to bed. They both hear, in the stillness, how the notes code the shared speechless intimacy of this instant, made complete by apprehension of its inevitable pain. It is, say, five o'clock in the morning by the sky. She's been here hours, hours that have evaporated in mutual nursing. Neither of them has said much of anything. But both have heard the functional poignancy harbored in the first, muted strains of sarabande. Half of the heart-pounding from the moment she slipped through his unlocked door was foresight of the payment they will, one way or another now, be forced to make.

284

Their silence is not the shyness of setting out but the stunned assemblage of memory after a decade of separation. They have known one another longer than either guesses. They parted bitterly, years ago, in mitotic anger, broke off all communication. Now, they have rejoined, discovering their utter failure of imagination then, recovering it in silence and waiting. She strokes his bare back. The touch opens a strange, two-way mirror between her fingers and his spine. Her skin signals to his what it's like to feel itself from the far surface. His back reaches and returns her fingertips' touch. The double-stroking goes on, difficult to say how long, as the only delineations of time are the irregular strokes themselves. In this quiet way, the two bring themselves dangerously close to believing that a discovery of the other's axiom might indeed be possible. A matter of working out the transfer in vivo.

She breaks off stroking. She wraps herself around him as if already for the last time. "Forgive me. I had to know."

He rolls over, catches her ribs. *How could you not have?* He ruptures his lips, grinning helplessly. "You know." It will soon be daylight. Neither has closed an eye, except to concentrate more fully on the feel of the other. In all but the colloquial sense, Jeanette Koss has spent the night. And yet, as she has just said, it was all heuristic, hypothetical. She simply needed to verify the suspicion. Every pleasure of contact has known it can go no farther. Nothing can come of it. Nothing. The thought makes him rise up and begin to undress her.

She sinks and yields a moment, proof she would in a different world. Proof she wants where he is going, but cannot. She places a hand on his, bends it to a more innocent place of hayloft and pine, a quick foray of unrealizable possibility, all that can obtain, here, just yards from the inhabited picnic ground. She is right. He catches himself, slows. But each restraint revives something more dangerous, the sense of all that the other deprives herself of. He holds her cheeks between his hands and places the smallest, seismic probe on her closed lids. "Well," he breathes. "What are we supposed to do now?"

She looks at him, apologizing, self-castigating. She touches the flare of his nose in wide-eyed wonder. They have already had more than either thought possible. A half-dozen hours flush against one another. She shakes herself all over, and tickles him. "Breakfast!"

Ressler groans. "It would have to be that. I'm cleaned out. We can't very well go to the Pancake House together. Imagine getting caught without having committed the felony."

She nuzzles against him and sighs. "Mm. You know, maybe you're right." He laughs in agony. They get to their feet, unkink. She falls into his chest, stretches her every cord, then goes limp. He has never felt anyone relax so totally. "You're the man," she says dreamily. She nudges him. "Go bring home the bacon. Haven't you ever played house before?"

If she has meant, by spending the night without cost, to work some crazy blackmail, she now has the goods. If she means to hurt her husband, retaliate for past infidelity, she has accomplished that, too. If she planned by feigning heat to reduce him to an emotional appendage, exercise her female rights over the drone half of the species, she has handled that much handily. He doesn't care about her motive anymore. The lie is enough. Jeanette herself, these unexpected minutes suffice. He dresses slowly, lingering over his winter layers at the door. She comes up beside him, crawls in under his coat before he closes it. He grabs her shoulders, holds her at arm's length. "Promise me."

She raises her right hand. "I'll stay put until you get back." They laugh, and he falls outdoors. He has forgotten how weird the world is, the man-violated world. He wanders the few blocks to stores that might be open at this hour, collecting random provisions— coffee, fresh fruit, obscenely glazed doughnuts she might find funny. Giddy, he asks the grocer what women eat for breakfast. He gets a look: why do nuts always shop at the crack of dawn? He sees a newspaper on a stand. He picks it up, unable to believe this wonderful, forgotten artifact. It opens like Tut's Tomb to every-thing that happened yesterday. "Can I buy one of these?" He over-pays, folds it like a precious magna carta.

He returns home with his treasures. She has waited. She is sitting on the floor, surrounded by his periodicals, reading the notes he has scribbled into several canary-yellow legal tablets. She looks up in alarm as he slips in, an exact inversion of their positions hours ago. Her eyes hold a new admiration, a new fear. "You never told me you were this close."

Ressler comes over to her, combs his hand into one full lock of that swirling rose hair. He holds the hank as if it were the leash of a seeing-eye dog. For the first time since it became light enough to see, he looks into her face. Her features, malleable enough to disguise their beauty, are now smashed into the code for unmit-igated anxiety. He has his first real look at her. She is a scientist.

Her eyes drink and live and address the code—the latest twist of the tumbler puzzle. *Close,* he wants to say, is not yet there. There is no more dissonant an interval than a semitone. We can be *closer,* he wants to tell her. Work with me. Let me spread the plan in front of you, for your appraisal. But all he can manage to get out is, "See what I've brought you. Coffee. Fruit. A paper!"

She takes the provisions from this helpless boy's hands. She looks at him oddly again as she moves to the kitchen to prepare their meal. "Have you a knife? Thanks. Now tell me everything you know."

He does, willingly, with growing relief that someone else is now in part responsible. His entire stockpile of insight is remarkably compact. "There must be a messenger molecule, to get the message from the nucleus into the cytoplasm where translation takes place. The messenger must have stereochemical properties analogous to the master library. Thus, RNA."

Jeanette stops slicing fruit, grabs her elbow, bracing for a fall. "What is it?" he asks. In all his dictating to the cell what it *must* do, has he overlooked what it does? She tells him to look in the journal she brought as a visiting excuse. Prominently featured, a beautiful article by Crick lays out the same inescapable conclusion. He scans it, knowing what it will say, and sets it aside. "That's all right. We're still OK, here. The idea's in the air. I've traced it back a *decade,* in fact, and nobody has gotten any farther. It's welcome confirmation to hear Crick behind it." He pauses and giggles nervously. "I think.

"Combine Ingram and Neel. A change in the gene *is* a change in the enzyme. It's all sequence; we know that. There may be an intermediary, a mechanism that reads or decodes or assembles the protein globule. But it's informationally inert. The information we're after has nothing to do with anything except translating one linear sequence into another. That's where we must start. Look. Siekevitz, 1952. 'Uptake of Radioactive Alanine in Vitro into the Proteins of Rat Liver Fractions....'"

"*Please.* I'm making breakfast." But Dr. Koss sets the knife down and turns, comprehension spreading on her face. "Do you mean we might be able to synthesize proteins in a tube, without any cell, from raw homogenate? Get the mapping that way?"

He looks directly into her, eyes sunk in eyes. He walks toward her. She turns, putting up a weakly protesting arm. He moves against her backside, puts his hands on the muscle just above her breast, saying, "You are not only beautiful...."

"Mm." She rocks imperceptibly up and down on her heels, her curve against him. "If you don't stop right now, neither of us will live to regret it."

They sit to eat. She plies him hungrily for the next step. "Sorry," he says. "That's the missing bit."

"But what you have already! It feels so...inevitable."

She is of a piece with approaching winter, wanting and postponing, failing to render the world perfect, palatable, and so choosing to wrap it under an unbroken blanket of snow. In a moment, their time together comes to an end. She must leave. Jeanette's anxiety smoothes out into her former, familiar, steady-state equilibrium. The face put on for departures, the look he already knows, the not-her look of sterile good humor. He wraps her to him, arms full with her, but feeling her already halfway out the door.

He finds his voice and says, a little rusty in the cords, "What can I *say*?" Not what is there to say; what is permitted. "Just tell me one thing." But he cannot ask it, and so demands, "Are we dead yet? Does your husband...?"

Jeanette laughs bitterly. "It's as sordid as you think. Mr. Koss is where no word of his wife's meanderings can reach him. The Processed Foods Convention, Minneapolis–St Paul."

He holds her pityingly. The strength of their restraint, their intended decency, will never be known. "You know, I think you ought to stay here. Longer." She shakes her head against him. "More often, then." No again, without looking. "Once more." He stops short of pleading, of asking everything that pushes its way up to his still swollen lips. He understands something he has forgotten countless times since birth. All talk is in ciphers.

Dr. Koss mumbles from her hiked-up coat collar. "See you next year?"

"Tonight," he coaxes. She goes limp. "All right. 'Soon' is my final offer."

"Stuart." Shocking, the name come out of her like a violation of taboo. Her mouth, now fouled, goes straight to his, where it is wild to throw off its mistake. Her hands are all in his clothes, and his under hers, deploying such violence over each other that it takes the application of an equal and opposite intellectual violence to break them from mid-doorway debauch.

"Oh!" Ressler says, separating, understanding where they are left. "Heading toward serious trouble, here."

288

"Yes. Trouble. I'd like that very much." But Dr. Koss quickly changes cadences, urging Ressler to present at the next Blue Sky everything he has collected. It's beautiful, she assures him. Comprehensive, internally consistent. In line with the data, inviolably clean. The remaining block, with sustained effort, must soon fall.

He watches as she goes down the walk, thrilled to be present at the day of creation. She turns, walks backwards like a schoolgirl, waves to him, indifferent to whoever else might watch. He is irreversibly in love with her. She is not yet gone and he wants her back. They were insane not to force the issue, to throw everything else away for the thirty-second crest. The chance will never come again. The gene has failed of its own cleverness. It has believed its own trick: the ruse of care, doomed affection, decency, that desperate simulation.

XIV

Desire per Square Mile

This time Todd waited for me at the top of the antique shaft. He leaped on me the moment I opened the accordion grate, my return promoting us to deep intimates. And I kissed back. Everything had changed between us; I lived in a new place. He greeted me after long absence with effusion, offering whatever salve was his to give. Even as I touched him, I thought of that advertising precept of Tuckwell's: nothing obligates more than unilateral kindness.

After a friendly feel, Franklin partly released me. Our hands remained in contact, threading aimlessly with each other's from that moment until the day he withdrew his. Where had I been? "Since when?" I asked. He laughed, kissed me again, and tugged me into the fluorescent computer room. My pupils dilated in the weird, familiar light of the old neighborhood.

"The Old Man will be delighted to see you," Todd said. "He's asked about you several times since your last visit."

"Don't mock."

"It's true. He seems to have developed a genuine fondness for you. Lord knows what the appeal is." I threatened the power switch on the nearest writing drive, ready to wipe out the evening's work. "Wait! Let me rephrase that."

Todd, I now see, wanted me only for my ability to tell if he too was destined to disappear in late twenties after a passionate start. I would always be subordinate to the research that had brought us together. Ressler had from the first been our matchmaker, awful confirmation of how many million more ways there are of being lost than of being found. Frank was overjoyed I was back, but the spark was the spark of salvage, the revived hope of explication.

He led me down the aisle of tape drives, past the line of printers under their sound hoods, a deafening collection that had multiplied since my last visit. As we approached the console where Dr. Ressler worked, my impression bore out Todd's account of a winter softening. Instead of delivering one of his restrained politenesses, Dr. Ressler broke into a warm smile of recognition, and welcomed me with, "Ah! A friend."

The three of us shared that unrepeatable evening as if I'd come back from years overseas. Todd ran out and secured our ritual provisions, pâté on saltines and grocery-store wine in paper cups. This would be our standard until Uncle Jimmy, discovering crumbs in the card reader, read us the house rules in his inept, egalitarian way: "You folks want to ruin everything? You realize that one smudge of mustard could wipe out ten thousand credit union members?"

That night was my homecoming. We went round the ring, toasting silliness, clinking paper rims. Todd proposed, "To the return of the native." I toasted Mylar, the stuff that allowed the two of them to make a living. Dr. Ressler thought a minute and supplied, "To Antarctica." We clinked, sipped, and demanded explanation. "The anniversary of a twelve-nation pact turning the last continent into a scientific preserve." In toasting the expanse of glacier and penguins he eulogized the decimated six other landmasses. But that night, the three of us set up base camp on the Ross Ice Shelf. The digitized warehouse became a sovereign, unreachable polar province, a fair chunk of the world set aside for responsible experiment.

God! What a few months. For the first time since sixteen, I unfolded into the available panel. Still regretting the mess I'd made of things with Tuckwell, I felt remorse scatter in instrumental brilliance, bravura trills, shakes, flourishes, demisemiquavers. We were a self-governing, city-free zone. What other way is there to survive the place? The last holdout habitat will be such a niche of charity. Life at the megapole required that I decide how many of the fifteen million adjacent catastrophes I could afford to feel. In those days—the brief bloom following a desert flash—I set my empathy at three. The calculus required consigning entire boroughs to misery beyond addressing, stepping gingerly over a base-ball-batted body at the top of the subway stairs on the way to sharing whatever small delight one can save from mutilation. Those

291

months, running at surplus, meant claiming the criminally privileged birthright of well-being. In fact, we all knew that a five-minute
stroll from the converted warehouse proved the impossible mismatch of happiness.

Once, at late rush hour—his midmorning—Todd and I, prowl-
ing New York as if it were not so much death camp as theme park,
rode to Chambers Street, the underground mall beneath two buildings that alone housed a midsized American city. We stood watching the nine-escalator bank that, for half an hour, spewed a
shimmering waterfall of human foam. Frank's fascination with the
ant farm was not Tuckwell's; New York was no thrilling Indy,
adrenaline smorgasbord, buffet of ways to get killed. Franker
sought the consolation of having one's worst suspicions confirmed.
We stood at this lookout until the human platelets threatened to
burst their capillaries and flood our high ground. Franklin turned
from the scene with a gratified shudder and headed back to a night
job where he made up half the known world.

Our happiness was pathetically outscaled: forty thousand homeless; three quarters of a million addicts. Four hundred radial miles
of contiguous squalor, a deep brown demographic smear, a disappointment per square mile that left the three of us several digits
to the right of significance. Still, exile to expendable stats freed us
to do what little we could to rig the numbers game. The globe
had never been closer to complete capitulation. The dozen regional and religious wars, delineated "shooting" to distinguish
them from the ubiquitous conflict, the daily embrace of toxic spills,
the gaping holes in international economics, irretrievable loss of
a century's topsoil every ten months, continuous corruption trials,
Esperanto chatter of terrorism: only the mildest symptoms of a
world unaware of its watershed moment. But in our neck of the
nature reserve, we three breathed the air of a new planet.

The secret, sustaining garden, my illicit fantasy having nothing
to do with lucre or lust, was that by tweaking a few knobs, by
having just these two friends, by clearing a space as wide as possible
in my unstretched heart, the last living woman in Brooklyn Heights
might contain multitudes, might grow to fill the dense bruise of
killer buildings carefully designed to eat me. Might even (how
could I have imagined?) pay back into the general healing fund. I
made the dangerous assumption that goodwill was somehow
enough.

I lived by myself—yellow glow from the second-story window

over an antique clothing shop. I could do what I wanted with my free hours. I chose to spend them in Antarctica, picnicking by the punched-card hopper, getting my first lessons in programmable machines and the people who run them. I don't know what catalyzed the reaction, but we fed off one another. I was learning again, steeping myself in company. I rediscovered the strangest aspect of mystery: how much of it is temporarily knowable, how it chooses the off moment to come clean.

Who knows why Dr. Ressler chose late autumn of 1983 to thaw. I liked to think we brought him out. Perhaps Todd and I reminded him of discounted possibilities. We in turn, scared by his return just before the onset of winter, waded deeper into mutual care. Dr. Ressler was instrumental in these evenings. His approval was everything to Todd. Franklin brought the man articles, told him anecdotes, sang him little snippets of absurd radio songs. Every trick imaginable to engage an intellect that we'd seen only in concealed bursts.

At times Dr. Ressler would slip back into his native condition. Feeling the man drift away, Todd would throw himself in after, like the boy in the news accounts who always happens along at the instant of the ice pond disaster. "Did you know," he would ask when comfortable silence slipped into the wrong meter, "that Brahms and George M. Cohan were contemporaries?" He would look to me for covert confirmation, ready to recant as a joke if the guess proved mistaken. Ressler invariably smiled, less at the invention than at its motive.

But sometimes, seamlessly, Ressler seeded *us,* hosting rambling round tables starting with the prospects for artificial intelligence, veering toward the impasse in Namibia, and winding up with the Pythagorean relations or plate tectonics and the Mid-Atlantic Ridge. With his quiet encouragement, we could talk all evening. He never let us equivocate or waffle. No matter how far afield we wandered, he would call us back with a rounded predicate. Franklin credited me, some obscure reattachment therapy I worked on the man. Dr. Ressler liked me, spoiled me with attention. He treated Jimmy and Annie Martens affectionately too. If he was a shade warmer with me, perhaps it was only that I stayed later into the night.

The elegant court Dr. Ressler paid me as our familiarity took hold thrilled Todd. He at last discovered in me the seed of the erotic. We kissed constantly, a running, surreptitious feeding fetish.

293

By the elevator shaft, in the foyer, through the main office, on desks where aides-de-camp of industry had drawn reports only hours before. A quick slip beneath the blouse in a dark utility closet. Hair, hands, neck, lip: one continuous tasting, sixteen without the giggle. How long could we prolong the extended adolescent feel? What came next? It didn't matter: after evenings of verbal invention, we needed something for our mouths to do when they paused to repair.

He kissed me through the accordion grate on my way home late one night—a last freight inventory after hours of polymath, polymorphous perversity. "Come tomorrow. Early, this time."

"All right," I said. "But I have to tell you something. Neither of us is twenty anymore."

"Remind me to teach you how to count in hexidecimal."

I cranked the lever to descend, but stopped at his shout. I set the dial to climb and came back level. "I have a great feeling about us these days, Janny." He gave it just enough time. "It's called lust."

If I missed two days in a row, Franklin would leave me notes in the question submissions box.

Lovely O'Deigh—
Come out and Play? Limber those lanky researcher's limbs? I will wait under the streetlamp at the library NE corner from now until you show. If you fail, I will be forced to stand all night and the following day and miss work and be fired and waste away, massive species die-off or worse. I have a thought for no one's but your ears. FTODD.

FTODD, his system login, doubled as personal signature. As if shorthand genus and species were necessary. As if anyone else in this spreading stain of fifteen million had used the word "lovely" since the Somme.

He came to my place, appraised my rooms. I had by then outfitted them with odds and ends from my antiquarian landlord, indulging myself, giving over to darkwood and damask. "This place is beautiful," he decided. "Did you dream all this up yourself? Amazing antimacassars. You're one player piano short of a New Orleans cathouse done up by the Rossettis." He loved coming over, sitting for hours in a rocker, being read to in embroidered darkness the reverse of the fluorescent flicker where he spent his waking life. But when he took to courting me in force, it had to be outside, in the open air, grabbing the last December light, the late heat of months holding on eerily long after the season. He wanted *outside,* every possible moment, as if only by being there at the instant the change arrived could he read the encyclopedia of the year in brief, the masterpiece of condensation, the backlit landscape, that gessoed, verdigris panorama.

Early December suggested that this would be the last chance either of us might have to remember what it was, in the blood, to be young. The day now went dark well before supper. It seemed an irritant to him, a command to hold more, soak it up until saturated, walk another block in the dark. Tomorrow would be too late. The smell of dry first flakes carried the weight of de-nouement, revelations to secure, sap to consolidate while the neighborhood got ready for night. Your rooms are beautiful; but friend, let's go out while we can.

Sometimes he would not even come up, but would shout from street level. Come play. Unlimber. Northeast corner. For some reason, I always came down. I had reached the age when I could no longer resist the fantastic, especially when carried off with authority. If his message was for no one's but my ears, what would become of it if I failed to listen? I would dress and undress several times, trying for an effect I couldn't satisfy, settling on not-quite: linen, a mid-calf wraparound, and shawl. He was always under the streetlight when I arrived. I could make him out blocks away—confident, calling from a distance, as if I might lose my way at the last moment. He dressed up too, after a fashion: straight-legged gray pants and a maroon pullover. He would talk without topic, give me the most forlorn fondle: he liked the small of my back, my fingers, my neck. We would find a spot in the park, abandoned now by even the most desperate adolescents, and place damp, guarded kisses in each other's mouth until we lost the easiness of virtual strangers.

He would walk me dutifully back to my rooms, making me promise to visit him at work, as if I were the undependable one. Once, when we reached the door of the shop that still surprised me to come home to, he said, "I'm glad you came out on such short notice. Ninety-five out of a hundred women would not have."

"Private poll?"

"Ha! That reminds me. Last night, Ressler defined the difference between pure and applied science: pure science was applied science the Pentagon won't pay for."

"Don't change the subject, creep."

"What? It's all the same subject. Data gathering." He looked in my eyes, deep and long, fields for future study. "Kiss me good night?" he asked, clinically.

"I suppose. Just this once." The next fifteen minutes lost to oral exploration. Ninety-five out of a hundred women in their right minds would have known better.

When I woke mornings, a sweet, forgivable embarrassment infused me, not a little secretly pleased at still being able, this late in the season, to do something that would be prohibited in another month or two. The way I was behaving was its own sponsor, insisting that my body had not changed all that much, that it still carried its old shape and solution. Every turn it had taken since twenty had been to some extent wrong. So how could I pass up his notes, his invitations to be wrong again?

I had no reason to feel so excited, considering what I'd spent to get here. Each morning's anticipation was thick with anxiety. I was the debutante on the evening of her coming out who, after three weeks of screaming adrenals, thinks it might be easier after all to stay home the night of the ball and stick to baking gingerbread for the rest of her life. That waking dream where one finds a dozen new rooms in the familiar house: it brought on dry heaves of expectation.

Sometimes during the day reaction set in. I spent my working hours answering questions as remote from my evenings as I had grown from the lost cause of politics:

Q: How long would I have to play continuous Ping-Pong to make it into the national record books?

Q: Could you please supply the words to the third verse from the theme song of *Branded*?

Q: Who's the most eligible bachelor in the developed world?

However numbing the day's list, I took pains with it, shaping my answers with the care of a potter to whom nothing mattered except creating the perfect vessel for today's flowers. I sculpted every response as if by outside chance it might signify. However ludicrous or heartbreaking the three-by-five, an accurate reply carried some small possibility of redemption. I did not imagine myself a pragmatic force, or even a moral one. I was simply an agent, assuming that what people wanted to know, they *needed*. If I kept my head down, maintained the path between inquiry and fact, human curiosity might rise to its subject matter.

Q: How does the government calculate poverty level?

Q: Are there places on earth that haven't been surveyed?

Q: What is the Lithuanian for "I need you"?

Q: I have heard of creatures that take energy directly from thermal vents on the seafloor. Nothing from sunlight at all? How could they have begun?

The instant I turned up one of these I felt recognition, a reminder of what I was doing. One of them redeemed a week of compost. Each betrayed the interrogative passion built into grammar, fueled by that thermal vent just under the crust. Each looked for an answer that would keep them from the absolute zero of blanketing vacuum. Yes, Ishmael again, in that rented bed in a coastal inn just before setting off, proving to himself, by feeling his nose freezing, that he is "the one warm spark in the heart of an arctic crystal."

The Amateur's Almanac

I learned then how shrewdly stable the forty-hour work week was. Any longer, and corporate time chokes the off-hours. Any shorter, and we might actually sustain a thought, satisfy ourselves. Either would be societally fatal. What allowed my friends to escape the net was how little MOL asked of their attention. Once a night Dr. Ressler would put up a File Repack: a massive process where all the Clients would be collated, reconditioned, squeezed, reindexed, and streamlined. The repack required so many spindles and so much processing time that the system was committed for the duration.

While File Repack ran, those two could do whatever they pleased—kick around the innovations that daily made a liar of Ecclesiastes. Recent sighting of the W particle. Stone Age tribe hitherto escaping detection. Pioneer 10, passing Neptune on its

297

way to being the first artificial thing to quit the solar system. When the day held no particular revolutions, Dr. Ressler whipped us into silliness by making us sing ridiculously long three-part rounds in polytones until the last cat was gutted.

We saved no lives on the night shift. But then, we didn't take any either. It all seemed happy once. A nightly exercise in the quick improvisation that had brought us together in the first place. Ressler puttered with print ribbons and decollators. Todd sketched perpetually into ragpaper pads, pads that grew thinner as he filled them. Late at night, hours of work still ahead, my friends sent me home with a handful of curiosities to verify before the next evening, threads we never seemed to close out. A renaissance of contentment. I found myself in a place where words regained their campfire importance, explanatory, incorruptible, above suspicion. I talked myself into thinking that Todd and I helped repair this diverted man's considerable gift. Every curve of clavicle Todd caressed said it was all right to think so.

"Tell me everything I need to know about you," I asked Todd one night. He sat at his console, shuttling bits of magnetic flux on distant drive packs through the intermediary keyboard. Dr. Ressler was in the control room, soundproofed. The two of us were alone, discounting the obedient machines.

Franklin faked a theatrical shudder. "Brr. Jeesiz. At last it comes to this. I thought you were the reference. What do you want to know?"

I sat by the console table, legs up. I leaned over, took his arm, placed his fingers high up in my folded lap. We both felt the professor's presence on the clear side of the two-way mirror, but the obstacle itself was provocative. "Tell me, if you don't mind, how in the world you managed to get *here*."

"Well, my mother and father loved each other very much," he said, clandestinely stroking my thigh.

"Ass. Who are you? Where did you come from?"

"Dunno. 'Sconsin." I refused even to grimace. Franklin sighed. "I was wedged in the middle of a heap of kids. Must have been a half-dozen of us. Doubtless where all the trouble started. Family wanted me to be an oceanographer. Went on to college, did a couple years in physics. The universe as we knew it was too small. Ended up art history, ABD." He shot me his most opaque grin. "All but Dissertation."

298

He would answer my questions but only to the letter. "Come on, Franker. That's not a curriculum vitae."

"What are you after? *Chambers Bio*? *American Art Directory*? I don't qualify."

"How did you get so damn alienated?" The closest we'd come to friction since our first meal. I felt a sickening urge to push until something broke.

"I'm not alienated. I am a United States citizen."

I couldn't help but laugh. We had such divergent senses of humor that he sometimes reduced me to giggles just by losing me in translation. He loved inadvertent slippage. I once found him chuckling alone in the coffee room at a flier announcing: "Power Saws Cut 10 Dollars." In time, I recognized a Todd ambiguity at first glance. For several weeks he enshrined on the side of system A's central processor the headline I'd brought him proclaiming, "Incest More Common Than Thought."

I kept after him. I wanted something that had nothing to do with personal data. "Where did you learn to sketch?"

"You presume I've learned. You haven't seen my work."

"Is that an offer?"

"In lectures," he said, choosing the lesser of two cooperations. "'New French Naturalism to the Present.' Irresistible: huge, scooped halls; faces from every aspect. I spent genre after genre just sketching. Problem was, the professors kept turning the lights out to show slides. Even now, I draw better in the dark."

He was telling the truth. I'd seen his hand skid across a tablet at high speed. He drew while talking, a nervous muscle-jitter while his mind was elsewhere. Hatches, shades, and crevasses sprung up from a hidden plane beneath the paper. He did not draw, he dusted: the flour spread over the smooth stones in a church floor that magically raises the pattern of gothic letters lying invisible across a worn-away tomb.

"I'd start each term in the first row on the far right aisle. Then I'd discover a perfect Pisanello in the upper middle, and I'd change seats. But there were only so many interesting faces in any given neighborhood. Had to go track me down that Memling. Seek out new blood."

He fell quiet; I'd accidentally sent him back. His hand played nervously over the function keys. All at once I received a tremendous jolt of who-cares courage. "I want my portrait done."

He looked around agitatedly, bluntly examined me up and down. Just as bluntly, I let him. He squinted, and after an awful hesitation, clapped his hands. "Why, you're the same woman who was here last night!" He took a soft pencil, the same pencil he used to mark off the Processing to Do List. He flipped over the nearest green-striped printout and unceremoniously began that oldest form of programming. When he came to do them, the hairs on the back of my neck moved at his pencil touch. I felt him locking in to the layout of my bone. The way he drew me, what he saw there, redefined my facial lexicon. Terror made me a good deal more striking then than I am. But he wasn't after symmetrical features. Not the pretty composite, but mystery. And the only way to keep that quantity intact was to transpose it to a distant, more mutable key.

Several minutes passed. We talked, as always, as he worked. As always, he didn't care if his subject moved. When he finished, he set the pencil down and said, "Missed it again."

"Don't I get to see it?" Faithful to the strict phoneme, he seemed genuinely surprised at that clause hanging on the end of the bargain. He handed the document over, a contractual captive. I took it, but couldn't assemble what I looked at. Both a recapitulation of the Vermeer *Head of a Girl* we'd stood in front of at the Met, and a dazed, physiognomically unmistakable thirty-year-old, 1983, who showed in her penciled eyes that she did not quite know what had happened, today in history.

"We do all styles," Franklin explained. "Giotto to Gleizes, inclusive." I could only stare at the image. "I told you. I picked it up in a lecture hall. Subliminal seduction. 'Learn Mandarin Chinese in Your Sleep.'"

"This is astonishing."

"Ha! Leonardo, Rafael, Agnolo, and me."

I demanded the portrait. It was already mine. Despite a stylistic anachronism that made it unacceptable to anyone except an historically indifferent critic, the sketch betrayed such incredible draftsmanship that I was furious at him for never cultivating it.

"I need it back. I have to submit the printout."

"You can't. You aren't going to turn over this report to some, some accountant in city government with *my face* all over the back of it?"

He took the page and shrugged. "Don't worry. Nobody ever listens to side B."

"Give me something from your tablet then. Compensation. Something of Dr. Ressler. Of both of us."

"I dispatch those suckers, soon as I make them. Can't stand to look at them after a day or two."

"You *what*?" Destroyed sketches of incredible draftsmanship: it was like news of burnt Alexandria, or jerky footage of the last marsupial wolf. I shouted, "Systematically trashing art!"

Franklin shook his head rapidly. "Don't *ever* confuse art with Draw the Pirate." Precise, vehement. "I have a steady hand, am a competent enough imitator. But no compositional sense. Incapable of making anything original."

"And you're a feeble liar to boot." I'd watched his hand. "Your sketches make themselves."

He twisted his lips. "My point exactly."

"Well, if you aren't ashamed of seducing public librarians, you should be ashamed of squandering a genuine talent."

He froze, turned to face me, and said the cruelest thing I ever heard him say to anyone: "I thought you were supposed to be well-informed." He apologized by grabbing my knees and pressing them for forgiveness. I gave it to him, took his hands and pressed back, as I would now if they were in reach.

"You see the problem," he said. "You've followed the cult of originality since autographed toilets? The straitjacketing Neo-ist canvases full of original black paint? The original razor blade and follow-up hot bath?" I didn't catch his references, but he seemed to mean that we'd reached a moment in our visual lives when innovation was itself derivative. All that was left of the painted portal sat in galleries in Soho, intelligible only with the aid of program notes. "A fellow is left with few stylistic alternatives aside from 'Divest now.'"

I said nothing in defense—I hardly felt qualified. Had I words, I would never have stopped arguing that whatever a person did well, if it promoted possibility, was worth doing. Anything that added to the heft, texture, and density of the card catalog. I had no technical basis for debate except conviction, and so I only said, "But you are good."

I meant to say something else—"adept," or "gifted." Even those would have been less than I meant. Todd *knew* what I was after. But a look came across his eyes, and he refused to forgo the chance to savor another slippage. "I don't see what my moral conduct has to do with anything."

To find a person both fine and infuriating, and inside of minutes: I'll never feel that again. Such a spread, in one evening. It throws me even now, long after he has—hardly originally, but with excellent draftsmanship—divested.

Quick Sketch

Those few days before official winter were our walking tour of the known world. We walked everywhere, at any hour. I was free in the city in a way I'd never been before. When we cut our walking to a third our normal speed, the particulars of neighborhood took on specific mass. I tried the experiment again this evening: walked a block as slowly as I could without attracting the attention of unmarked cars. A slow walk—too slow to be going anywhere—changes the way everything around me holds itself.

I didn't care where we were going. We were there already, under the shed sumacs, standing a fraction of an inch closer to one another than ambiguous. The game developed unspoken rules: we couldn't say certain things at certain times. We dressed too lightly for the weather. We spent minutes looking up into the bone filigree of tree branches, whose lacework against the winter sky became brilliant as stained glass. Sometimes on those walks with Franklin, one-third teleological speed, I stopped moving altogether, needing to fix this, to find an outlet for the clarity springing up in me.

Todd still reached out at odd moments, took my hand, and shook it in both of his. He grabbed my fingers for no reason, his equivalent hopeless search for that unreachable fixative. The most he could convey of that one-word contradiction in terms was affection. He *liked* me; at the handshake instant, he again discovered and meant to take credit for me in our hands' press, the slow walk still ahead of us.

We favored a playground three blocks from the warehouse. By the time Todd took his first nightly break, the terrain was a children's Pompeii. Sometimes we tried the slide, hopelessly slowed by an autumn of tree gum. We compared old recipes for greasing. His involved sliding on squares of waxed paper, and he was on the verge of routing us to a store eight blocks away to buy some when I talked him into sense. More typically, we drifted instinctively to the swings. Expansive or expectant, however quickening the night, swinging seemed the thing. I would rock on mine, hardly kicking, dragging my feet in the gravel beneath. Franklin, male, shot for escape trajectory.

We would chatter or keep quiet—in those days they meant the same. One emblematic evening I watched Franklin pump to apogee and bail out, no doubt escaping one of those avuncular Flying Fortresses on a parachute that thighs sacrificed their stocking silks for. I calculated the parabola that had landed him between conflicts. We had a completely distorted historical view, he and I. By accident of timing, we thought this playground peace was the status quo.

Without Todd's weight for pendulum bob, his swing dampened to a stop. He got back on and called to me, "C'mere. Show you something." I hesitated, knowing the escalation. He motioned me into the sling, each leg over his, inside the chain. He helped my legs through, touching them with mute amazement. "For some reason shrouded in mystery," he explained, trying casually to pretend our thighs weren't touching, "this is called 'Swinging Double Dutch.'"

"You think you're teaching me something?" I challenged, pressing myself against him. "I was *born* knowing this." I relaxed and straddled him, looked deep into his face. Neither had done this before. Not since it started counting. And it hadn't counted until then, that moment of fragile pressure.

"Oh yeah? I learned how...." He fought to remain clear-headed, articulate, but even pretense took his breath. "I learned this... how to...before you even got your first inflatable slip."

"Right," I said, adjusting myself just enough to shatter his equanimity. He rolled his eyes at my little flick of friction. We synchronized our kicks, swinging in tandem, slowly at first, gradually gaining momentum. I could feel my vee riding a fraction of an inch above his. At the top of each arc we would press, pretending innocence, ignorance of contact. I kicked in rhythm, climbing a sapling on each upswing, and on each swing back, the sapling me.

At that moment, I would gladly have gone down onto the freezing grass and lost my last ten years all over again. I felt myself at my coat cuffs, against underwear, inside my silk collar come within seconds of anything. Cut loose, I was closer than ever to learning who this boy was. Rocking and straining, folding against him to our pulse, I had the chance to find out.

I felt it irresistibly unfold, but was surprised by the rapidity. At our arc's height, he kicked when he should have drawn in. A slight stiffening ran up his arms where I held them. Warm oscillation rippled across the gap to me—unforced, unconscious. A rush of conductance, animal-perfect rubato. Backwash erased all difference between us. No burst. Just sweet, spreading infusion, for one instant complete.

We went slack. Without kick-physics, the swing settled. Our pulse-pound, synchronized so briefly, fell into diffraction, dissipated in moiré. I couldn't begin to guess what was in his heart at that moment, let alone my own. I climbed off without being asked. He said, "So they swung Double Dutch in your neighborhood, too?" He didn't dare look at me in the dark. Every second I spent with him was, even in the absence of hard fact, another slow assembling of artist's composite.

We turned back, the silent tactic. By the time we arrived at his machine warren, I was alone. He was attentive, arm around my shoulders. But back at the warehouse, when Dr. Ressler greeted us, a sign of collaborator's embarrassment passed from Todd to me: I had brought him over the edge with nothing but my body's graze through winter clothing, the rocking of a swing.

When I left, he rode the lift with me down to the street. The night ended like all its ancestors: a handshake, the only fingerprints he conceded. He was turning back to the office when I panicked. I grabbed and spun him by the elbows. He must have thought I was trying to embrace him, for he took me up, scolded me with a dismissive kiss. "So passionate as that?" He held me, resigning, admitting. His mouth near my ear, he spoke, incredulous. "Here again. At the mercy of strangers."

The Console Log

By then, I came and went as I pleased. Frank gave me a copy of the front key on long-term loan. Without incriminating anyone, I stole the sequence for the computer-room lock—the four letters M-O-L-E. I used the password freely until one evening, punching myself into the inner sanctum I was met by my sheepish friends and an angry Uncle Jimmy. Given his older cousin's crush on me, Jimmy would probably sooner have entrusted the company's safety to me than to Todd. But he was Operations Manager, and this was a clear-cut violation of, be it ever so ludicrous at this outpost, corporate security. He demanded to know how I knew the combination.

"I peeked over somebody's shoulder. Jimmy, it just seems silly to make them come punch me in."

Jim's bureaucratic bluster was undermined by recalcitrant kindness. "With the customers we have, if it had been anyone but me in here when anyone but you came in like that unescorted, he or she'd have put her or him in jail by now." I apologized, and Jimmy barked acceptance. He went through the apologetic motions of chewing out Dr. Ressler, the Night Manager, exacting a promise to change the combination right away.

When I showed up the following night, I buzzed for Franklin, smiling at the ridiculous return to *pro forma* propriety. Frank came to let me in, wearing that smirk beloved by mass murderers and the foreign service. Just as he was about to punch in the new code Dr. Ressler had set, he stepped aside. "Go ahead," he said. "I know you're dying to see how good you are."

I hadn't the first idea where to begin. Another four-letter word, reducing the possibilities to twenty-six to the fourth power: roughly half a million candidates. I had only two clues. Dr. Ressler was the designer. And Frank believed I could guess it or he would never have set up the riddle. It also helped to have him stand by humming the intervals that have run through Western music from Art of Fugue to Schönberg, with stops along the way at Beethoven, Mendelssohn, Liszt, and others. Down a minor second, up a major third, down a minor second. I cupped my hand over the keyplate, guarding my guess. I punched in the four letter tune, transcribed from German notation, and the lock sprang open. Todd emitted his high-pitched trademark laugh and cuffed me admiringly. He trooped me into the computer room and paraded me before Dr. Ressler. "She's broken security again," he reported. "She's unstoppable."

"You may find the punchline to this in your notes file," Ressler told Todd. Franklin cleared the nearest console. The screen returned with its eternally patient prompt:

Command?

Two-fingered, amateurish, Franklin typed NOTES and hit the Return key, that quintessential late-century punctuation.

NOTES RECVD: Read (y or n)? y
Note from jsteadman, @ 12/06/83, 16:14.

Take a break! This means you! Ask your woman friend out for dinner at the Rusty Scupper. That heap of bolts won't run any faster with you watching it! Uncle Jim.

"Heartbreaking," Franklin laughed. "The man apologizes for giving us a deserved dressing-down."

"I received a similar one," Dr. Ressler said.

Todd turned to me and howled. "And what do you do first thing upon returning? A shame, for women to speak in church!" He turned back to his dialogue with the CRT.

Note @ 12/06/83, 20:23 to: jsteadman

Jimmy, We're sorry too. Even the woman friend. Her only offense is pride in ingenuity. But I think we've caught her in time. Love from everyone, FTODD

Note sent.
Command?

Todd looked up from his typing to the man whose opinion meant everything. "What do you suppose Uncle Jim would say if he knew you were in possession of every combination in this joint?"

Dr. Ressler shrugged painfully. "Passwords are trivial. How many words are there in English? How many in Indo-European, including all forms and proper names?"

Both men looked at me. A hopeless task, even to estimate the order of magnitude. I tried a rough, running total, falling back upon the technical reply, "Lots and lots." Ressler's eyes flashed; it was bliss to see him happy.

"And folks don't restrict themselves to meaningful combinations," Franklin objected.

"Nevertheless, passwords are trivial. One can employ the brute-force solution. Use one computer to generate all possible combinations of letters in words of given length. Then pipe the results to the computer demanding the password. Such a solution is not elegant but is as inexorable as death."

I thought out loud. "Every possible combination? Wouldn't writing the program be prohibitively difficult?"

Ressler smiled at my impeccable novitiate's thinking. He liked being reminded of the old place. He shook his head and said, "I could write that program in a dozen lines."

Todd clapped his hands. "Go to it." Ressler scribbled on a sheet of scratch paper, then showed us his handiwork:

```
For first letter from A to Z
    For second letter from A to Z
        For third letter from A to Z
            . . .
            Word = first letter + second letter + third letter...
            try word
            . . .
        Next third letter
    Next second letter
Next first letter
```

I looked at his program, feeling the rush of forgotten terrain opening. He said, "The ellipses are for longer words. In the loop, one could start with blanks instead of A's, to include all words shorter than the number of imbedded cogs. You see...." And I did see; my first glimpse of the synthetic achievement of language. "You see that the nested loops produce words in simple combinatorial order: AAA, AAB, AAC, and so on."

"How long would it take such a program to run?" I asked, the cumbersome coordination of loops within loops dawning on me.

"Some time. Lots and lots."

"That's why God invented operators," Todd contributed.

"To speed the search, you could pipe likely lists—say our on-line file of the hundred and twenty thousand most common English words. That's a gamble, however. If the word is not on the list, you're left with no systematic way of picking up the pieces." At that moment, I saw in the exhausted face a look so unlikely I almost missed it. Gratitude at the chance of exchange, at stumbling across a listener after years of having no audience but himself. A look full of wonder that he was being thrown back, after everything, on the shifting ambiguity of first letter plus second letter plus third. He motioned toward the console, asking Franklin, "Do you have anything running at the moment?"

"*Work,* you mean? What a curious idea." Franklin turned to the keyboard. At the system prompt, he typed the command LOG.

20:36 Dumping console transactions to log. Mode brief. Begin when?

"What time did I show up tonight?" he asked Ressler, his eyes on the monitor.

"As I recall, you were here ten minutes before closing, camped over the terminal, waiting eagerly for the last remote teller to log off so that you could bring your machine down and begin the end-of-day processing." Todd winced at the portrait and typed a time. A thermal printer embedded in the tabletop began bruising a roll of paper, producing a printout that varied only in detail from the scraps that, hopeless pack rat, I scavenged for inclusion in the capsule.

Command? EOD
18:37 Begin end of day processing. Mount Sys Pack on Spindle 1, Master Client File on Spindle 2, Client Backup on Spindle 3, and scratch on Spindle 4. Oldest cycle date tape in tape drive. Hit any key when ready?

18:43 End of day underway; backing to tape...

18:58 Backup complete. Rewind tape and unthread.

19:01 Conditioning Master File...

19:20 Master File conditioned. Merging transactions...

19:42 Transactions merged. Ledgering new trans file. Running new-acct. Running purge. Running trial balance.

19:46 End of day complete.

Command? PAY

19:46 Begin Tuesday pay cycle processing. Thread payroll tape, General Ledger pack on Spindle 3. Position checks in printer. Hit any key when ready?

The latest fable from *Homo fabulus*. Todd whistled at the history of his evening. "Do I really live this way?"

"Check your partitions," Ressler said.

Command? TASKCHECK

20:38 Partition 1: Payroll check ok.
         Partition 2: Report Generator check ok.
         No other partitions active.

"Steady as she goes. What do you have in mind?"

"Open a third partition. Give it a half a meg."

Todd gritted his teeth and shouted, papier-mâché-set style, "I don't know if the engines will stand it, Captain." He tapped a few keys. "*Et voilà. Bitte*."

"Now. Do a part reset."

"Don't know how."

Ressler hit a key combination I missed, and the screen read:

Sys 1652 Exp Ver 4.2
partition reset
login:

Ressler typed FTODD. The screen prompted for a password. "Turn around," Ressler said. Seconds later, he called, "Done."

password: xxxxxxx
System Date and Time: 12/06/83 20:40.45
User ftodd logged in.

"American Satan!" Todd shouted. "You couldn't possibly have learned that by brute force."

"No, sir."

"Selected list?" I suggested, and was rewarded by a warm no.

He let us savor the trick before confessing, "I have to admit to charlatanism here. I did not actually crack your password. I simply jumped to partition two, called up your record page, and blind-piped your password from the user profile to the unsuspecting partition."

Even his charlatanism was clever. Todd was greatly amused by the piracy. "What would Uncle Jim say if he knew you could kick this machine around?"

"Now *that* is more dangerous to corporate security than knowing a few passwords." He turned to me. "Your friend turns out to have an interesting password that you might be able to hit using the Short List." Just as I was about to pump him for data, Todd shouted from his place at the keyboard. Ressler gave a yelp and lunged to prevent Todd from punching any more keystrokes. But it was too late.

Command? EDIT
20:45 Entering editor in partition #3. Files belong to user ftodd: pnotes eoderrors daybook herri

Enter name from list or new file to create: security

20:45 Opening new file: security
File creation error.

Command? EDIT

Command? WHAT GIVES?

20:46: Command string not recognized.

"Interesting," Todd said, giggling nervously.
"Indeed," Ressler concurred. "Promises to be a long night."
I had no idea what was going on. I looked from one to the other. "System crash," Todd explained curtly.
Ressler pulled on his earlobe. "Yes, we have once again done what the three-thousand-page user's manual insists is impossible." He led the three of us into the command room, where the twinkling LCDs had frozen solid. He looked at Todd, shook his head. "I'm mortified. Apparently, one can simulate a duplicate of oneself, but one can't actually be in two places at the same time."
"My fault for keying away blithely. What about the Report Gen?" They looked through the two-way mirror. The printers were drifting dead in the electrical current. "And Payroll?"
Dr. Ressler scratched his head. "Fairyland."
"The long chunk it had already finished?"
"I think, friend, that as things stand, we'll be lucky to rebuild the Master File without a cold reboot."
Franklin whistled. "Well! I'll take a good system crash over a crossword any day. That's why we're working for the military-industrial complex in the first place. Right?" The two fell into flowchart, Holmesian deduction, tapping panels, toggling switches, volleying terms, injecting patches, and cross-referencing their way through the massive metal-bound manual with masochistic relish. As I couldn't contribute, I was forgotten in the intellectual ex-

citement of the fix. They were an unlikely pair, never more at ease with one another than at this crisis moment, with a hundred essential financial trails teetering on the brink of the ether. In the unreal solitude of their shift they were at peace, cut off from all others. Even I was at best a registered alien.

I went and sat in the lunchroom, glanced at the day's paper, which Franklin no longer shredded. I sat quietly in the dark, trying to recover that spark I'd felt on receiving my first introduction to programming. Within my lifetime, we'd built the first prototype animal capable of behaving like any other—the universal simulating machine. The complex behavior of Todd and Ressler's computers floated on a sea of self-organizing ands, ors, and nots: a circuit-medium of living language. Strange slippage: language itself was the computer; metal and silicon were just ways of marshaling the syntax. If the driving language were properly designed, it might provide a complete, enumerable description of everything there was. Not just a description, a semantic table that animated itself. I tried to formulate, without sufficient vocabulary, the odd, momentous identity at machine level of information and instruction. Every "Thus it came to pass" harbored a secret, equivalent, "Go ye, therefore." One of the great, isolate, alert moments of my life.

In a while, Franklin came to find me. "Uncle Jimmy was right; I should have asked the charming Ms. O'Deigh out to eat. Listen to one's elders; everything they tell you is right."

"I'm not going anywhere," I said.

"It's digital devastation in there. Don't look! Think the Bosch nightmare of your choosing. I might get out by nine a.m. If I'm lucky." He was in no more hurry to go home than he was to die. He never finished on time anyway. His second-shift vocation was innate, self-inflicted, a desire for perpetual distraction from real work, the thing calling out to be done. "A shame, too," he said softly, tilting my head back. "I'd thought I might be able to visit, tonight."

"Come by whenever you feel like," I said, deliberately misinterpreting. "I'll be awake."

He shrugged; the matter was digital, out of his hands. He let me out by way of the fire exit, disabling the alarm behind me. I felt him, his split, how much he would have given not to hold back. He restrained me at the door. "Got an exit visa?"

"Passwords are trivial," I said, kissing him good night. The kiss lingered, a simultaneous interpreter between visiting heads of state. It contained whole grammars, self-generating syntaxes. No longer just a description; it lived like a command.

Quote of the Day

In the expansion each day brought, I had little time for reparations. I visited Tuckwell one Sunday. Overdue, unable to put it off any longer, I returned to the old apartment for the first time since clearing out. I couldn't believe I'd lived here recently, come back every day to the settlement. I found Keith in the posture of eighty million other American males at that moment: crapped out in front of the football game. Apparently, nightly news no longer produced sufficient threat to satisfy his addiction to event. He was talking back to the set, also a national prerequisite. Only Keithy performed the pathetic act in a style all his own, turning the sound off and delivering his own play-by-play into the roarless apartment.

"Ol' Staubach ran for daylight as if an entire detachment of Mujahadin were on his ass. Secondary's fallen apart. The best lack all conviction. This is the moment when the entire offensive line must look over that brink at the inner bogeyman. Of course, none of this has any bearing on reality. All Ethiopia could live for a week on these teams' boiled shoulder pads. You think that troubles Roger? Nope. The old pro sacrifices his body, plunges ahead for no gain."

"Hi," I said. He studied the play. "I came to say hello. Roger Staubach retired four years ago after playing eleven seasons."

Keith gave me a suspicious look. "How can you be sure?"

"Forgotten already? Forty percent of my livelihood is sports trivia."

We couldn't talk there; the place was too loaded. I hauled him out of the apartment, hanging on to keep him from breaking away. We ducked into the nearest greasy spoon. He was in bad shape, worse than I had thought. We ordered coffee. Tuckwell floated unopened sugar packs on the surface of his. He waited, made me ask him how he had been. At length, he gave me a manila folder he'd brought along. "Birthday present." he claimed passively; it wasn't my birthday. The folder housed a mounted ad: a grainy aerial photo that Franklin could have drawn freehand. Photo-realism from his No. 2 pencil was child's play.

On second look, I recognized it as a vaguely familiar military document I'd seen reprinted. Tuckwell wouldn't identify; he wanted audience participation. Given the time I'd spent on Twenty Questions in my life, I had no patience for it then. But I'd long ago learned that when Keith got a bee up his ass, all I could do was let it cross-pollinate. I set the image on the table: a construction site, an empty lot a week before the circus comes to town. Muddy ground recently torn up, with man-made craters filled with water. A few pieces of blurry equipment, corrugated tin sheds. Super-imposed on the photo was a system of arrows and Acronymese. I managed to ignore Tuckwell's pointed silence long enough to concentrate. Aerial view, construction site, strategic arrows: I did my quiz-show contestant stint. "U–2 shot of Cuba, twenty-one years ago."

"Very good. Natural-born uncoverer. And what do you remember about said incident?"

"Keithy, I was just nine years old. I swear I had nothing to do with it."

"Don't be a Hoosier." We sat and looked at the icon, knowing that another word would spell disaster. To self-conscious effect, he took out of his rucksack an acetate overlay. He handed it to me, saying, "Forgot something." I spread the overlay over the photo, and the scene was transformed. It now read, in fancy, living color, 40-point type: "DO YOU KNOW WHAT THE OTHER GUY IS UP TO?"

Keith was wired by now. A wrong guess was worse than none, so I set the composite image down and folded my hands. He explained that his outfit had been hired to free-lance this ad; it would hit the stands in three big-circulation glossies next month. His eyes gleamed. "The bastard will *sell*," he chuckled. "Apotheosis of vending by fear. Paranoia—our supreme erotic desire. Everyone secretly adores having his worst nightmares orchestrated."

"I thought we bought things we liked."

"Wake up, lady."

"Who's the client?" I asked. "What's the product?"

"God *damn* it, O'Deigh. Who in hell *cares*? Haven't you figured this game out yet? Nobody sells products. They sell *slogans*."

He was right: I thought of all the times patrons had asked me to identify forgotten commodities by dimly remembered sales pitches. The best display in adland, the *ne plus ultra* of mottodom, was: "The Best Motto Money Can Buy."

We stared at the reconnaissance, pretending to sip at our tepid,

313

distracting narcotic. I could stand it no longer. "A beautiful lettering job. The layout's nice. What would you like me to say?" I had come to try to be kind, but was not prepared to find kindness so messy. I could think of nothing to say that would extricate us.

But I had misread Keith—flunked the economics of compassion. Before I knew what was happening, he was hissing at me, "You want me to quit my job? Make some difference? Go chain myself to the fence at Lawrence Livermore?" He began racing along a mental tangent angle I could not intercept. "You think I don't know what's at stake? *You're* the one; you don't have the slightest sense of what we're up against. You, with all the facts. You won't *sum them up*. Look at this." He smacked the photo with a violent backhand. "'Twenty-one years back.' You *still* haven't the slightest idea what we're looking at."

I knew I was looking at a triumph of late-day, calculated despair. I knew the sort of product the photo promoted, the market distraction we have inserted between every desire and its itch: the ultimate bottled water, a salt elixir that creates more thirst than it gratifies. I'd heard him deliver the same speech when we lived together, but never so distraughtly, never with such solid supporting evidence.

The waitress's hovering maddened him. On the woman's third return he said, "You want us out of here? Why not put a taxi meter in these booths? Or I can leave a bunch of quarters on the edge of the plexi here, and you can come by every ten minutes and pick one up." He was pacing in place, poking the slots on the napkin holder, squeezing the mustard pump, spindling the straws. I took his hands and held them steady, more wrestler's pin than old flame's cradle. He turned on me, gave me the most menacing smile I've ever seen: "You still don't know the secret word here, do you? You think the issue is apocalypse? The missiles are nothing, dear heart. *No-thing*." He looked at the photo as if he'd forgotten what the issue was. "How you supposed to take arms against something like this?" His laugh was desperate, falsetto. "Picket?" His voice popped, like a teenager learning to drive a standard transmission. "The product is electronic mail. The advertisement is a finalist for a national award."

I knew that such things existed. But I'd never taken them seriously. "How? It hasn't even run yet."

"Novelty is all. These folks are on top of things. I have to fly to

314

LA next month, because...." He looked at me with caustic pride. "Because the awards are being *televised*."

"Who's the sponsor?" I risked. Keith cackled.

"Brought to you by the folks who left you sponsorless." He breathed, clearing an aisle down the minefield between us. "Thing is, I could use a stunning, statuesque, killer beauty in black elbow gloves to drape over my arm." He waited until I could no longer accept gracefully. "Care to help me find one?"

I took him home, where he began communing with the remote control before I was out of the room. At last I asked him what I had come to ask, a question no answer could satisfy. "Keithy, will you be all right?"

He shut the sound off and stared. "Why did you move?"

I manufactured something about room, adulthood, self-reliance, the need for perpetual experiment. I didn't try to explain that I was after the one thing I already knew would not be left me at the end: what it felt like to be alive.

Books

I went through my library this morning, searching for books I might be able to peddle secondhand. A bit histrionic, perhaps. Premature. I still have cash left, if none coming in. Haven't yet been knocked back onto necessity. But for a minute this morning, I got obsessed with the idea of efficiency, the political economy of plants: capture the energy I need to build just those structures that will let me capture all the energy I need. I forgot for a moment how inept and archaic nature really is. Grotesque encumbrance of peacock tails, koalas' dependence on a single leaf, inexplicable energy cost of narwhal horn: efficiency belongs only to ingenious naturalists.

This morning around ten, I ran out of sentences. It became impossible to type another verb. So I attacked my library, thinking to pare it down. I didn't need both the *Times Atlas* and my schoolgirl *Hammond;* I could part with the older almanacs; my *Spotter's Sailboats,* acquired who knows where, had stood me in all the stead it ever would; I could ditch either *Bartlett's* or the *Oxford Quotes.*

But in choosing between these last I rediscovered just how

differently two identical purposes could be met and also, indirectly, the source of the note that first persuaded me to come out and meet Todd by streetlight. Running my finger down the entry "Ears,"

    hath e. to hear
    high crest, short e.
    I have e. in vain
    in e. and eyes to match me
    'Jug Jug' to dirty e.
    leathern e. of stock-jobbers

I was struck by the ears that were missing. If not here, then I would need to check one of those great compendia the rearguard guerrilla actions against the scattering of world's word where he cribbed all his love notes. I found them in "Adam's Curse," by Yeats.

    I had a thought for no one's but your ears:
    That you were beautiful, and that I strove
    To love you in the old high way of love;
    That it had all seemed happy, and yet we'd grown
    As weary-hearted as that hollow moon.

The lines turned up in a superfluous anthology I'd ear-marked for sale. The note that had stolen the verses returned to me intact, and with the note, Todd—more real, less efficient than I've yet made him out. And with him, I had what I was after, and my sentences came back all afternoon. And I vowed not to sell so much as a single, redundant letter.

XV

The Natural Kingdom (II)

Q: How big is the biosphere? How high? How wide?

R.G., 5/12/81

Q: What is Life?

E. Schrödinger, 1944, J.B.S. Haldane, 1947

Q: Is not the life more than meat, and the body than raiment?

Matthew (?), ca. 80 (?)

A. *Classification*

Books may be a substantial world, but the world of substance, the blue, species-mad world at year's end outstrips every card catalog I can make for it. If I'm to locate Ressler's code, I must step back and see what the nucleotides are after at beast level. But every system for listing life that I come across is a map at least as unwieldy as the place itself.

In the first nomenclature, what Adam called a creature was what it *was*—an exact lookup table for the living library. But that perfect equivalence between name and thing was scattered in ten thousand languages, punishment for an overly ambitious engineering project. Schemes to recapture the Ur-order go as far back as I can track. Theophrastus classified plants by human use, not an auspicious second start to naming, but a popular one in the centuries following him. Color, shape, feature, habitat, behavior: successive methods cast makeshift classification nets over a school that will not stay still long enough to be drafted.

I'd thought the gross macrodivision, at least, was secure, until I read of unicellulars neither animal nor plant. A nineteenth-century patch job, Protista is a category so diverse it hardly helps. I watch a fourth kingdom secede: Monera, cells without nuclei. But subdividing still doesn't suffice; later treaties draw up five or six domains. And all this splintering takes place while I'm still at the top of the classifying pyramid.

Descending into phylum, class, and order, I'm swamped in ever more controversial flowcharts. Strata shade off into suborders and superfamilies, overrunning the borders. Seed-bearing plants alone number 200,000 species. At the third rung, a single class, Insecta, exceeds three-quarters of a million species, with thousands more added every year. Tracking these figures for no one's but my ears, I realize that I'd stopped asking, for years now, that first question: how many ways are there of being alive? What is this place? How can I say it?

Bat to banyan, bavarian gentian to baleen whale: I was expelled from childhood the day that living strategies began embarrassing me with their ludicrous profusion. Too immodest, teeming: I could memorize a hundred species a day and die not yet scratching the collection's surface. Species laugh off the most rigorous hierarchy. My Baedekers to the biosphere, government offices packed to exploding with print, strain under the weight of this wild violation of the paperwork reduction act.

A year too late, a life since I last bothered to ask the only thing worth asking, I feel strong enough to take on natural history again. Girlish-strong, discovering that the catalog can never be complete. Made strong by desperation at what's come over the list. However impaired my vocabulary, however late my start, I must have a quick look while there's time. Something's happened, yesterday, this morning, something threatening the whole unclassifiable project, changing the rules of the runaway gamble forever. Something all my reading leads to.

Here, in the isolation of my books—clunky classroom translations of the original—I learn the first principle of natural selection. Living things perpetuate only through glut. How many ways are there of being alive? My answer lies in a block of code programmed to generate more copies of itself than are lost to execution. Speciation, fracturing into every subniche and supercranny, depends on surplus of offspring in every breeding creature on earth, the prodigal gene.

If the volumes are beyond listing, I try at least to locate life's bookends. How large is the envelope? Living cells have been snagged miles high in the stratosphere. Dives into the deepest sea trench, under several atmospheres, turn up diaphanous fictions that explode before they can be brought to the surface. Bacteria thrive in ice currents and boiling ripples. I look for inhospitable places where living things haven't penetrated. Even in the Sahara's desiccating winds, 4 percent humidity, and 33°C daily temperature swings, scrub dots the dunes, roots descend fifty feet into sand, grains swarm with microorganisms.

North of permanent freeze, caribou run in herds, rabbit and tundra fox find growth enough to gorge on. Extreme south swells with seals, krill, birds. Inland Antarctica, the least habitable place on earth, has its wingless insects, lichen, mold, even two flowering plants that wait the narrow window of weeks when they can colonize this waste. Living membrane can withstand the absence of energy: nematodes have been kept for days close to absolute zero and thawed out happily.

Newts requisition caves, go pink, lose their eyes. Lungfish solve the formidable flux of tidal flats. Seeds carried in the intestines of migratory birds convert virgin volcanic island. Life lives even inside other forms of itself. Large mammals are walking bestiaries of fungi, mites, fleas, bacterial colonies. A single square inch of my skin hosts ten thousand cells of one bacterium alone. Life survives even my killer city. Dozens of houseguests rustle my cupboards, spread across the shower curtain, bless my bed, raid a refrigerator designed to deny entry. Marsupials knock over my trash cans at night. Peregrine falcons nest under the Verrazano-Narrows.

Some variant of the self-rewriting program succeeds everywhere. Imperialism lies at the heart of my classification problem: life is as particular as each locale it has a foothold in. Any nomenclature I consider founders on the cartographer's one-to-one-scale solution to "How many places are there?" The program ports itself to all four corners, stopping to seed every intermediary, driven by the universal firmware kernel buried inside it. Nothing exceeds like success. Excess of issue. Surplus of offspring. More applicants than vacancies. Overproduction—duplicate, superfluous: waves of generations testing themselves against the landlord. The milt of trout turns whole streams milky. Shrimp are hauled from the ocean in solid blocks. One male ejaculate—on the swings in a dark abandoned playground—releases 300 million half-lives.

I'm convinced of an infinitely moldable instruction set. Shape may be an artificial classification, but how many forms can duplication take? What range of phenotype? After long abstinence, I rediscover the organic paradox, the extremes of living design. Blossoming chaos: a rough estimate of chestnut proteins runs into the tens of thousands. But no algorithm, however long, begins to describe how this tree branches.

Radial, bilateral, transverse; symmetries that change over a life; radical asymmetries. Sea shells unfurl by Fibonacci. Horn, bark, petal: hydrocarbon chains arrange in every conceivable strut, winch, and pylon, ranging over the visible spectrum and beyond into ultraviolet and infrared. Horseshoe crab, butterfly, barnacle, and millipede all belong to the same phylum. Earthworms with seven hearts, ruminants with multiple stomachs, scallops with a line of eyes rimming their shell like party lanterns, animals with two brains, many brains, none. Trees whose limbs root, whose roots blossom, whose leaves become needles, beakers, flesh traps, detachable emigrants. Animals that expel their organs to eat, that— split down the middle—become their own Siamese twins. Organisms that bud, divide, cross-pollinate. Sedentaries that sprout free swimmers that mate to make sedentaries. Things that breed once and die, that birth perpetually even as they sleep. Females that grow up to become males. Males that convert to females in hard times. Dwarf males that live in the bellies of their mates. Males that bear young. Hermaphrodites.

Extremes in size? I find a figure for my own class: weight difference between blue whale and pygmy shrew. My desk encyclopedia says that *Balaenoptera musculus* reaches 600,000 kilograms. *Suncus etruscus,* on the other end, must eat constantly to keep up its gram and a half. The largest mammal is 400 million times heavier than its smallest cousin. And there are creatures 400 million times smaller than the pygmy shrew, smaller than the wavelength of visible light, detectable only in the scatter of electrons. Several thousand could fit inside one human blood cell. Giant sequoias, excluding the immense roots, are three and a half times the longest whale. The Great Barrier Reef is longer than Europe: a composite mass of two hundred species of polyp a fraction of an inch long, a living superspecies spreading in sovereign continent visible from outer space.

Genomes range from a few thousand base pairs for the simplest self-replicating element to a few billion for humans. Genotype spread, less extreme than phenotype ratios, is more dramatic. The length of the program does not express the ripple effect of increasing complexity. The entire genome of a bacteriophage—so simple it only just slips into the most liberal definition of life—could be printed in a book the size of a grocery-store romance. Yesterday, I thought it would be only a matter of time before we mapped out the entire program of such a creature. Today, I discover the feat is already years old: Sanger *et al.*, 1977: the complete 5,375-nucleotide text for the φX174 virus deciphered. The simplest-known, perhaps the simplest-possible living program, but a universe beyond the most complex inanimate matter. Nine proteins long, the viral bible is written with an ingenuity beyond the most sophisticated human hackers. The sequence coding for one protein hides the sequence for another, the way the phrase "a lisp in a chromosome" embeds the name of a leafy green.

How much more complicated can the card deck get? My molecular research only begins to hint. Bacteria trap energy, metabolize and manufacture compounds, sense their environment, go dormant indefinitely, synthesize their own enzymes, Xerox *themselves*. Their leap beyond viruses is larger than viruses' from inanimate compounds. Larger than the leap from my amateur's notes to Ressler's knowledge.

I read how cells develop distinct nuclei and organelles, acquire the trick of mashing other cells and recycling their parts. I struggle with an unthinkable threshold: the formation of limited partnerships, shared responsibilities. You float, you sting, you prop, you flex, you digest: we feed. Geometric increases in complexity: anagenesis exists. Something rises, flies in the face of entropy. Not better or wider or finer fits; bacteria can already live locked in ice, hot springs, even stratosphere. The code simply learns to *do* more with the place.

The arrangement of cells into bureaucractic corporations takes me two tiers above φX174, itself nine proteins beyond my comprehension. I move into a mystery uninterpretable even in outline. Form—the ravelins of a starfish, the rococo redundancy of crabs—reveals itself as mere vessel for behavior, infinitely more varied. Evade this stimulus. Fly in this formation. Migrate at this moment. Build this burrow. Train your young.

The message, which at the low end of taxonomy began as a

simple impulse toward excess, learns to communicate, first to constituent parts, then to coordinated cells within an organism. Up a second slope—classes, orders, families of behavior—the text learns to pass itself between organisms. One more minor magnification lights upon language—a newcomer in the garden dashing off transcripts, elaborate travelogues to no one.

Maybe I'm not congenitally adrift after all. I watch a videotape of the famous gorilla Koko reading a children's book, signing learned hand-words into the empty air. Signing the way I scribble here, for an audience long gone. These notes, my evolving, catch-all phylum, live and die, propagate their own excess. I arrange them, perpetually revising, inventing writing as I go, assembling a classification system large enough to name what Ressler already knew.

How high is the biosphere? How wide? I list degrees and kilometers. I'd do better to steal from Wallace Stevens; classification, after all, is just a record of neighboring plagiarisms. "Life consists of propositions about life." Shape and behavior are guesses at the place where they've been set down. Eons-long accumulation, the organism itself is only a theory of what it might still be. My hyperactive classroom screams out its answers, constantly recanting, amending, reaffirming, anything but silent and archived, fired by the same single fact that keeps me revising. However many unclassifiable ways there are of being alive, there are infinitely more ways of being dead.

B. Ecology

Death too, at the heart of variety. Every message I turn up whispers it in code. There's only so much to go around. The splintering catalog rushes after the same circuit of available energy. Not all miracles make it. Each excess program copy is shaped by limit. Checked by scarcity, populations are pruned in constant edit. And pruning makes the garden proliferate. Death is the mother of experiment.

The earth is a differential engine—gradients of heat, cold, dry, wet, fat, lean. Some terrains snicker at all hope for a meal; others rain continuous free lunch. Even this asymmetry shifts. Currents churn up cold; mountains buckle, wear down in an era or two. Seas recede; poles reverse. The pool is played on a table so warped that players can either shoot or wait for a change in the rules.

The game, I figure out, is to figure out the game. My runaway catalog's every proposition is *about* the propositional calculus. Two strange succulents, one African, the other Arizonan, converge by distant routes. Each is a lab transcript, a probe of local conditions. Living diversity maps the diversity of available space. The race for the curve of best fit fractures at every rapid into an alluvial fan.

I pose the naif's Q: Which of these million unclassifiable experiments is the most successful? A first, satellite glance gives the hat tip to my own chromosome set. Five billion, from Sahara nomads to Antarctic scientists. Flexible, omnivorous environment shaper, top of the food chain. But almost upon arrival, it crests in oversuccess, chokes on its own effluent.

My second candidate is grass. As widespread as man, greater in biomass. And it rarely annihilates its own niche. A good enough solution to have diversified into five hundred genera, five thousand species: corn, wheat, rice, bamboo, sorghum, reed, oats, timothy, fescue, Kentucky blue. It encourages others to cultivate it, the sweet, sugarcane smell of global success. But even grass is colossally one-upped by Insecta. I trace a range greater than grass and man combined. Undivertable clouds, a single species can outnumber all humans a hundredfold. And Insecta contains as many different species as there are humans in Lower Manhattan.

Then I discover bacteria. They coat every cubic meter of the planet. A gram of soil can contain 100 million. Every cycle required for life involves them integrally. They have remained essentially unchanged since emergence, three billion or more years ago. They make their way inside every large organism. The successes of the pyramid's cap depend inextricably on success at the base. Their success *is* the success of the animate code, the living engine's linchpin. Supremacy of the sheet of cells spread passively over earth's surface is measured in tens of thousands of duplicating tons per second.

"Success" mutated from Ur-roots *sub* and *cedere,* to follow after. Its hold on my English mind is a loaded model where B competes with, bests, and replaces A. The word warps my research. Scarcity undeniably demands competition, but living success does not mean beating out all comers. Cooperation of ever tighter skeins ties the web together, interanimates the nets of success. Emerson

323

came remarkably close for an American: "All are needed by each one; /Nothing is fair or good alone." That one I learned as a schoolgirl. Successful hunters are not too good at killing, and successful prey must be pared and pruned.

The word I need is not "to follow after." I need another etymology: parasitism, helotism, commensalism, mutualism, dulosis, symbiosis. Local labels for the ways one solution requires another, from the bribes of fruit trees to the bacteria in my gut. Joint solutions everywhere, from ants and their domestic aphid farms to lichen, a single plant formed of two organisms that feed and water each other, breed and reproduce together.

One remarkable night, snowed solidly into a New Hampshire cottage, Dr. Ressler laid it out. "Mimicry is also an interlock. A snapping turtle's tongue depends on the shape of a fly. The beetle that borrows the look of a thorn lives off the rose's solution. Half a dozen harmless snakes ape the bands of a coral without paying to produce the poison. Jammed frequencies of passed semaphores, real, faked, intercepted, abused: everybody trafficking on the river dabbles in this pidgin." His speech was soft because the night was late, the kerosene flame revealed the blanketed world outside, and we knew we were going nowhere the next day.

"Every animal cell is itself a contract. A primitive cell may have co-opted a bacterium, enslaved it as the first mitochondrion, a genetically independent cell enclave. Believe me, we're all in this together. No cheating this economy. The books must balance. No," he said, breathing, his face obscured by the lamp, on the far side of the room where Frank and I lay touching. "The world is a single, self-buffering, interdependent organism. Or has been until this moment. Individual persistence is not the issue. Neither is species stability. If permanence were the criterion, nothing in the animate world could come close to the runaway success of rocks."

I would trade what's left of my savings to hear his monologue again, to jot down even a draft of a rough transcript of what he said. But he and his words have gone the way of probabilities, back into the loop. Death has returned him to school. I mimic him now, live off his solution.

"Why can't we speak that pidgin more fluidly than we do? Speak it the way everything else lives it? The definition of life we've lived with for too long is flawed. We presuppose the ability to tell haphazard from designed. The whole community is about to go under, pulled in by our error. Why do we want to revoke the contract, scatter it like a nuisance cobweb, simplify it with asphalt? Because we still believe, despite all the evidence, that the place was made. And what's made, by definition, can be improved. But suppose the whole, tentative, respiring, symbiotic message is no more improvable than chance. The superorganism takes its local shape—each part at the mercy of all others—because that is the configuration that chance conditions permit. Design might benefit from human ingenuity. Conditional fit cannot.

"Oh, it's worse than you think. Worse for us. Worse for you two." He looked at us as if at two crosses in a French cemetery dated a day after V-E. "Your generation, everyone from now on, faces the most serious shake-up in history. Because my generation," oblique mention of his departure from science, "has already killed life for you. I mean the old definition, the vitalist idea. We did something twenty years ago that people haven't gathered yet. It's all mechanism now. Self-creation. The game has changed. Only we haven't responded."

The night was silver and deepest blue. Outside, in the drifted conifers, owls sat dusted in branches, their eyes night-wise to the least run of rodents beneath them. Foxes scoured the surrounding hills. Tufts of grass poked above the snow like dangerous shoals, while rock outcrops were slowly digested by a two-celled limited partnership. All the while, underground, below the frost line, life waited its rechance. That night Dr. Ressler telegraphed me a part of the genetic code I just now unfold. All of this soft, conjoined precision—mutable, always slightly mistaken—was self-assembling, self-adjusting, self-nurturing information.

I thought I had the gist, on that oil-lamp evening, snowbound. I thought he was faulting science for letting the gene out of the bottle, disenchanting the natural kingdom, turning the impenetrable magnificence of the ecosystem into spent anagram. Two years later, alone, with time to think, I see he was saying the opposite. We've dismantled the biosphere out of fear. We suffer not from too much science but from terrified rejection of observation. Pattern can produce purpose, but it does so without final causes. Destination, design, is a lie stripped off twenty years ago. The only ethic left is random play, trial and error. We go on in shock, not yet disabused of success, not yet ready to save ourselves by looking.

325

Hopeless, he hoped that we might reconvene on higher ground, in an ecology of knowledge. Learning to hear the underwriting tune might at last affirm our own derivation from the theme. Adenine, thymine, a hundred thousand commensal genes, owls, foxes, the silver and blue forest of pines. His hope was simply that learning the layout of the place, the links—identifying how matter made its escape from matter and passed irretrievably through this spreading gene—might rejoin us to the superorganism at the source. Life, ordered irregularity, aperiodic crystal, signal in a field of noise, required that wonder and reverence, both coded for, beat out success if anything is to survive.

He hinted at a new discourse, a new definition. But tonight it feels like a recovery. The only, truly unequivocal success is the aperiodic crystal itself. Accustomed from long training to viewing life from the molecular level, my friend based his hope on our acquiring an awareness of the explosive potential of the genome, its implausible beauty. Anyone with eyes to see and ears to hear would know that the string is big, an ample world for expression. And anyone who once adds up the living number must act ecologically, commensally forever.

I read a throwaway bit that, like the last tumbler waiting to turn over, brings home the idea for good. Huge stretches of code called introns—in fox, owl, grasses, lichen, cabin captives—have no identifiable function. They've been carried along inside, a free rider, for a billion years. I suddenly see DNA as an ingenious parasite, a creature that has struck up symbiosis with every scaffolding it has ever invented; organisms are only the necessary evil, the way DNA has hit upon to make more DNA. To get out and see the world. Which is the most successful strain of life? A defective question, one I now relegate to the bin of exhausted fits. Life is the sole strain, perpetually becoming, a single, diversified proposition that succeeds altogether or not at all.

I check the etymology for his "pidgin." Thought to be an English derangement of the Chinese pronunciation of the English word "business." But if this business is a business at all, it must be a lending library—huge, conglomerate, multinational, underfunded, overinvested. Ecology consists of identifying, checking out, poring over, marking up, and returning all existing solutions. Passing them around. Running down another reference, another key, another published breakthrough. No competition, no success, no survival of the fittest. The word I am looking for, the language of life, is circulation.

C. *Evolution*

The envelope is as wide as the space granted by the surplus of generations, sculpted by scarcity. If anything is behind the accumulation of variations, it's reprimand. Constraint and condemning somehow rebound into bounty. Weeding out increases complexity, like gravity driving a river uphill. I can't see it; how can the shake-out sieve of death create more, when its most generous judgment is "Not quite"?

My enlightenment arrives in stages, unfolding historically, inaccurately, like the thing it researches. The best classification for gene anthologies must be laid out on the axis of time. Darwin induced the whole before he had adequate foundation. Evolutionary thought evolved only fitfully, by pangenesis. The earliest recorded text I can find already suspects the mutability of living shape. Anaximander, in translation, reads like the *Origin,* 2,400 years ahead of time. Aristotle blunders up against the notion, then walks bravely away. Linnaeus—worlds later—knew; he could have proclaimed it, incomplete, in rough outline. But he was unwilling to crawl out onto that geneological limb until humanity was ready.

Two and a half millennia after the idea's appearance, I'm still not ready. Evolution is the most explosive deflation of all time— the capstone of history's steady objectification of nature. I spend a day of quiet privacy spelling out how this unassuming model worked the most radical intellectual overhaul ever, how this near-tautology supplies the crucial cog that biology has aspired toward since its appearance. I trace every step in the synthesis, recheck, give the go-ahead to each subassembly. Still the complete machine lies one step outside credibility. I recapitulate evolution's four prerequisites in embryo:

1. Excess of issue. Surplus offspring. Seedlings rooting in the nook of an I-beam on the fiftieth floor of a two-year-old plate-glass skyscraper; maggots overrunning a scrap of meat. Viruses breeding under the electron microscope at Cold Spring Harbor, making Leo Szilard rush outside and pace the porch of his cabin to calm himself. Precisely the state this evening finds me in.

327

2. Scarcity. Common currency from day one: no amount of goods are ever enough to go around. Not all surplus makes it; none makes good in every case. Death hones away, a missed heartbeat from home.

These first two innocuous tenets are reciprocal. Yet hiding in their sum is the larger part of Darwin's bugaboo. Too much divided into too little, and something's got to change. Some die faster than others, a conclusion as inescapable as its result.

3. Variation. Differential dying creates divergence. This is my sticking point tonight. I make the catch only slowly: variation is two-tiered. First: the ten thousand wrigglers in a pound of anchovy spawn are all different. Trivially individual. Even dyed-in-wool creationists admit that poodles differ from Great Danes, let alone wolves. Man too (whatever the nausea of knowing) is not an entity, but five billion disparate creatures with different eyes, hands, and minds. I fell in love with one whose hair, height, voice, fear, and protective narcissism made him unique. I loved one man distinct from all others, or at most, two. Already halfway to difference's second tier: the difference between Franklin and that anchovy spawn. A difference of some difference—where all the tempest still comes from.

4. Inheritance. Divergence depends on a means of conserving difference. Certain individuals in a varying population solve scarcity better than others. If their advantage is handed down disproportionately, that population changes. Mendel, a great admirer of Darwin's book, inexplicably never wrote the letter that would have conferred his results to his contemporary. His work, had it been communicated, might have shown far sooner that evolution harbored more than that tautology "Survivors survive."

Even had a letter been sent, the two great innovations in nineteenth century natural science still would have faced that paradox: more comes from less. Paring away compounds. Something new derives from the not-quite, under no more enlightened guidance than annihilation. The rub starts in that antithesis, conserved difference: the ability accurately to perpetuate lapses. To preserve infidelity faithfully. It has taken Dr. Ressler's death and Todd's variation on that theme for me to understand that the word "variation" itself, like "nihilism" and "ineffable," is among the best of Dr. Ressler's perpetually sought-after one-word contradictions in terms.

The resolution of the paradox that Mendel's unsent letter would have both clarified and compounded did not come until the demonstration that genes were nucleotide sequences. A rogue protein, synthesized by a slight variation in the master base string, was inheritable. And every variation across the spectrum—fish, fowl, lichen, redwood, redhead—is born in divergent protein. Characteristics stay intact from one generation to the next, but only within a margin of error. A few capriciously altered intervals produce a new tune, a song with crisp shocks of familiar difference hiding in its four notes.

Species' diverse qualities slip down the world's gradient unequally. The specific gravity of a place settles the trait-spread into new statistical parfaits. A forbidden secret: the Bible itself is versed in the linguistics of breeding. Only, scarcity prunes more efficiently than any artificial breeder. The gap between Chihuahua and Great Dane is negotiable; the same features are visible, just remixed along a sliding scale. A theist might concede microevolution and still not throw creation itself to the dogs. But variation has a wilder trick, tweaking the quantitative so far that it kicks out something qualitatively new—wolves and sheep from the same bolt of clothing.

In sexual reproduction, rearrangement of parental haplotypes produces a genotype different from either, although cut from the same constituent stuff. If all the carriers of a characteristic fail to reproduce, that trait is lost. But otherwise, it's a closed system, however unexplorably large. Alleles mix to create unimaginable variety, but the species material remains essentially unchanged. I can rearrange my furniture in countless ways, resulting in a surprise decorating scheme for every day I knew the man, but no new furniture ever enters my place.

Speciation, on the other hand, seems to contradict Mendel's perpetuated genes. But at molecular level, I trace it to a replicating system complex enough to suffer turbulence, to err. Something new can come about through recombination or mutation. I now have enough molecular biology to find the source of genetic novelty baldly assumed by Darwin: a G grabbing a T in its negative filament instead of its proper C, a sequence of nucleotides pinched out or an intruder taken in and the whole program can change.

Terrifying, destructive anarchy, bumping blindly down dead ends and back alleys, when shaped by destruction, can shoot living things into undesignable places.

One changed nucleotide can profoundly alter the function of the protein it helps synthesize. The size of evolutionary steps, the exact scenario for speciation, is still debated. But all variants on the purposive molecule are hazards of evaluated chance. Without molecular mutation, there would be no amendment, no evolution. And yet, most bizarre to me of all, mutations are almost never beneficial. A message, carefully crafted over time, is altered at random. The text will almost certainly suffer, if it remains intelligible at all. The introduction of noise into a signal is much more likely to garble than improve. Failure is lots more probable than anything else going.

Typing too late at night, I begin to insert letters that distort my words diseasterously. Rereading, I piece some alterations back into partial sense. Only an infinitesimally few typos—the lucky comma that leaves a sentence more comprehensible—will produce clean, let alone enhanced final copy. Most swift kicks to my bum radio wreak havoc on its components. But once every few decades, I improve the signal. Mutations cause cancer, stillbirth, blindness, deafness, heart disease, mongolism—everything that can go wrong. Yet faulty copying is the only agency for change. Random tinkering, the source of all horrible mistakes, remains the "hopeful monster," the Goldschmidt variation.

We walked once in the drifted snow, the three of us, on a day written off, lost, abandoned to the world. Dr. Ressler, against the white background, speculated about the implausibility of those snow tracks, the creatures that made them. "Birds surely don't possess compositional sense, musical volition. They sing; that's all. A species' song is taught by parent to child. But every so many generations, something is lost in translation. A child muffs his riff, mislearns, wings it. If the mistake—highly unlikely—works a better attraction, this new melody will be taught to more chicks than flock average, and in time the twist becomes status quo. Insertions, deletions, transpositions: gaffs ratified or panned in performance. A species might, over considerable time, whistle its way from a G major scale into the *Goldberg* Base."

Life doesn't spring to new complexity. But small bugs, fed back into executing procreation, produce wrinkles, differences that are honed into new profiles of spread and fit. Precursors emerge

330

blindly; purpose itself erodes out of chance. At bottom, no cause: only the life molecule, copying or failing to copy. What good is a blip that doesn't yet function? Some good; even a fractional lung could keep a fraction of tidal-dried fish alive fractionally longer. Lungs are not revealed or inevitable. They are arbitrary inventions, reified in experience. They are postulated, fitfully, across immense pools of genetic potential, invariantly inherited. Or mostly invariant. Life consists of propositions about chance by chance.

In the interplay of scale between variant population, selectable individual, and occasionally stray gene, I find counterpoint enough to create a trio sonata rich beyond all design, exceeding even his hero's compositional ingenuity. All this from that hobgoblin Evolution, that drunk trapping the world into listening to its rambling shaggy dog story full of fabrication, revision, gaps, imploring every so often, "Correct me if I'm wrong."

I trace the steps, the developing embryo recapitulating its own evolutionary history. I follow the observations and inferences, mirror the young man step by step, a canon at the fifth, at a quarter century's distance. His very brain must have been electrified by the nearness of creation. I see Ressler and his love, twenty-seven years ago, listening, lying on his barracks floor in the dark, as if the danger in the notes will not notice them if they only keep still. The fifteenth variation, replication by inversion—the great, halfway watershed—completes itself as they lie in silence. A question, framed by the initial canonic voice, descends frightened down the scale ladder. A measure later, the answer, predetermined by its complement, begins an awful, mirror rise.

For the first time, unmitigated minor, as bitter as a belated gift of roses from an unfaithful lover. Sorrow creeps in, rich, expansive, and beautiful, discolors the set at the midpoint. This slow, inevitable seep is a surrender from which there is no recovery. Acute cut of chromatic, harbinger of half-steps. The meandering question, answered severely at the fifth, tripled by a bass that tries to preserve the sarabande by desperately introducing passing accidentals, combines in harmonies more unforgiving than any until late this century. The life molecule's hovering nearness threatens to sweep over the man I look for, obliterate him.

The bass falters, then fails to translate the Base into distant minors. It capitulates, lapses into the despair of part-writing freedom. The canonic lines cross, impossible for my ear to disentangle. The question begins a long—excessively, over-and-again long—

331

terminal descent into obscurity, broken only by a last, four-note, densely pitched, failed attempt to lift itself before the final fall. The answer, constrained by transcription to rise note by note, continues to do so, long after other motion stops, winding up somewhere without footing, in the far reaches of unsupported space.

The variation ends. Ressler and his love untangle their parts, the silence growing as oppressive as their finally fleshed-out understanding of just how many permutations of the four basic steps—G, A, T, C, is it?—life is condemned to examine, organize, experiment with over time. They feel the delicious, sickening thrill of evolution—lost, not just in its cold, mechanistic causelessness, but in the operation's oppressive size, its ability to go on innovating stray variations pointlessly forever.

I hear that forsaken minor tonight, canonically, at arm's length of three decades. I hear the awful, magnificently patient structure of the Darwinian revolution, more shattering than the sum of its molecular evidence. The reduction of the once animist world has thrown the human spirit into tailspin anxiety, deprived it of soul, except for the soul's distress. Convinced of the facts, I still cannot accommodate, make room in my heart for indifferent statistics. Even accepting, I am as mythless, as bitterly stripped as those who deny the evidence.

Dozing in and out of sleep to talk radio, I hear a recent poll claiming that a bare 9 percent of Americans accept evolution. Yet this debate—amazingly still raging—about the origin of wealth beyond conception is irrelevant. It doesn't matter anymore whether a fraction of the race splits off, chooses to return to a child's Eden. It doesn't matter if 91 percent of my countrymen continue to insist that species were created by father, so long as the entire planet instantly unites in acknowledging that they are, right now, being destroyed chaotically by child. Conservatively: several thousand species extinct a year. Instant, universal acknowledgment is impossible. In the hundred acres of rain forest destroyed each minute I write this, the earth loses species not yet even described in the catalog.

The arbitrarity of our origin cuts us adrift, slack as a severed marionette. In this pivotal moment of development's first dissonance, we are too stunned to see that we are driving the life crystal back into inertness, erasing the rare hypotheticals it took excruciating convolution of chance eons to propose. The situation is hopeless, huge, advanced beyond addressing. Why do I even bother to put this down? No reason. The same reason the gene in me keeps up its random postulate.

"The universe was not pregnant with life," my friend Monod writes, "nor the biosphere with man. Our number came up in the Monte Carlo game." The entire, endlessly expandable text, "the replicative structure of DNA: that registry of chance, that tone-deaf conservatory where the noise is preserved along with the music," is a fluke lottery we are losing, rubbing out by the minute. Awful, chromatic awareness fills me with a curatorial resolve. "Think of it," another friend once said. "The proper response ought not to be distress at all. We should feel dumb amazement. Incredulous, gasping gratitude that we've landed the chance at all, the outside chance to be able to comprehend, to save any fraction of it."

D. Heredity

In the last, delicious twist, the width of the restless species catalog depends on the ability of traits to persist in stillness. Evolution is the exception, stability the rule. Variation depends on a larger invariability to begin its trip from home. Procreation is not creative per se. Sex is easily accomplished by anyone with a high school equivalence certificate. I did it myself once, with help. The resulting product, except in exceptional cases, is a rearrangement of existing qualities. Innovation lies beyond even the most conscientious parent.

My mother bore three children, low for the baby boom. She arranged to interleave them by sex, feeling a good mix to be better for development. My father, bravely self-educated, lectured her endlessly about the X and Y chromosomes, how sex determination sat in the male's gamete; she had no say in the matter. She replied, "Yes, dear," and went about sleeping on her left side to make a girl and her right for a boy. The idea that the left ovary produced girls and the right boys had been passed down in her family for generations. No controls, no sample mean. The children were all the empirical evidence she needed. My father calculated the probability of her black magic: one out of eight, impressive but not conclusive. My mother offered to make it one out of sixteen anytime my father was man enough to try.

Now they're both dead. The constituent commands that assembled them—voice, intelligence, even those aggregates of obstinacy

333

and superstition—are cut loose, alleles still intact in daughters, ready for another experiment, another change-partners. What exactly is lost, destroyed, with an individual's death? Just a permutation put to rest. A combination, devastating, never to be reassembled. Its elements remain: eyes, voice, mother, father.

Meiosis, necrosis: the arcs of the ancient cycle of recirculation I'm caught in for good. Both carry on, mesmerized, churning out tireless rearrangements on the first little nitrogen, methane, lightning spark. Carry on, despite long since filling the entire surface of the earth with velvet and scum, as if some fabulous combination were just around the next chromosomal bend, waiting to be revealed. But there is no revelation. Only endless surplus versus harm.

To the population, the gene, birth and death carry no last word. Only in the chest of the next of kin does that partnership make any inroads. Slow, conservative, migratory. Once, a colt, I spoke that language. I've forgotten it all, the years I spent hungry and astonished, nights by flashlight over the illustrated encyclopedia describing mysterious, interlocked systems—water cycle, nitrogen fixation, circulation of blood, food chain. Winter weekends, whole summers out in the woods, in empty lots, in our immense, dark backyard, examining the scat of rabbits, catching bizarre electrical arthropoda in jars, convinced, sensing firsthand the terrible expanse of the place.

I remembered it this morning, to ruinous expense, so long after first elaborating the thought. It suddenly was not enough to rehash natural selection. I had to go put my hands on the gene, on evolving population, invariant heredity. I knew it would cost, that my carefully guarded nest egg would suffer. I boarded the inbound, not knowing what part of the unclassifiable, branching catalog I was after, but knowing that the biome was midtown. I found myself on the stairs to the Met, but could not bring myself to go in. Not without the one I once arranged to meet there, should we ever be separated.

Instead, I walked back through the living park and on to 53rd, the Museum of Modern Art. Time to see how Brueghel had evolved, survived, passed down to my own generation. All morning I discovered again that every observer's notebook, every act of seeing, even the harshest, most politically indicting, alienated, abstract, cynical acrylic, is a frightened, desperate, amazed recapitulation of the natural kingdom. More: an effort to mimic it. Always inexhaustibly to recombine, to classify.

I stood in front of Paul Klee's *Twittering Machine*, a created thing at once both mechanism and inexplicable bird. It had been so long since I'd looked at anything but genetics that the sleight of hand seemed crammed with associations. I thought of Emily Dickinson's secret reaction to Darwin, five years after the publication of the *Origin*. Split the Lark—and you'll find the Music. Loose the Flood—you shall find it patent. Now, do you doubt that your bird was true?

On the train back, I knew it would have to be poetry for me, as well. I scribbled my *fille de Klee* on the back of a MOMA flyer:

> star start itself
> seeds blueprint climb:
> egg alone and only gear
> for eatrock lichen or
> unlacing umbel veil.
> chance, the sole mode assay-
> able: tumult of twitter-
> ing ovation is all word
> forward can enlist to move
> embryo to ember, or drive
> cold scale from first bird.

It smacks of effusion and will embarrass me by next week. It contributes less than nothing to my understanding of Ressler's aborted bid for love, discovery, the Swedish Sweepstakes. But as poetry, it doesn't have to be good. It only has to contain a testable guess about being alive, the incomprehensible ability.

Back in my apartment I remember two things I long ago lost words for. The paradoxical breakout of life from mere preservation to runaway self-threat depends on two subtle phenomena. First, information represented in a certain way emerges as instruction. As in the gene, all observation is a command to observe. Dr. Ressler once showed me how an ordinary drinking glass is a data structure informing liquid where to go. The information in the life molecule is a similar vessel, informing itself how to describe the condition it finds itself in.

Second, small initial changes ripple into large differences. The constricted initial alphabet of four letters produces a journey many million species long. The only astonishment great enough to replace that ectomized maker: all this proliferation results from one

335

universal and apostolic genetic code. The fantastic diversity of outward form doesn't begin to anticipate the leaping, snaking, wild logic that develops in response to the far more complex internal, intracellular environment. Once DNA began to speak, not only the carrying medium but the message itself was susceptible to evolution. Even to approximate that polyphonic, perpetual baying, I'll have to go back down, square off against the living, purposive program incorporated in the enzyme.

Tonight in History—12/9/38: A coelacanth caught off Africa, a third of a billion years after it was supposed to have vanished from the earth. Not the first extinct animal to return from living fossilhood, nor the last. Far stranger things are afoot. Quaggas rebuilt from the residual ghost in their zebra cousins. Frogs cloned. Talk of reviving mastodons from single frozen cells. I sit at my desk, overwhelmed but still among those throwing their insufficient efforts against the unlistable world.

I know nothing about the place. But the nothing I've ascertained has already changed everything. I learn that I live in an evening when all ethics has been shocked by the sudden realization of accident. I must ask not how many kinds of life there can be, nor even how there can be so many kinds of life. I must learn how, out of all the capricious kinds of cosmos there might have been, ours could have lucked, against all odds, into that one arrangement capable of supporting life, let alone life that grew to pose the hypothetical in the first place. How quantum physics allowed room for a rearrangement capable of learning the outside chance hidden in quantum physics. How this tone-deaf conservatory could produce the *Goldbergs*.

I review the record of care we've given a spark we once thought was lit for our express warming. I feel sick beyond debilitation to think what will come, how much more desperate the ethic of tending is, now that we know that the whole exploding catalog rests on inanimate, chance self-ignition. The three-billion-year project of the purposeful molecule has just now succeeded in confirming its own worst fear: this outside event need not have happened, and perhaps never should have. We've all but destroyed what once seemed carefully designed for our dominion. Left with a diminished, far more miraculous place—banyans, bivalves, blue whales, all from base pairs—what hope is there that heart can evolve, beat to it, keep it beating?

XVI

12/6/85

Our Dearest O'Deigh,

Out of some terrifying collective unconscious, the phrase "Greetings from the Old Country" nags at me, although this place is one continuous novelty from Cisalpina to the Afsluitdijk. Do you remember that game show where contestants were sent into a supermarket for three minutes (our nation's chief contribution to world culture—shopping as a competitive sport)? Europe is exactly that; I've got this checklist of three-star *Schatz chambres* and a rail pass, and I can't come home until the art treasures have all been looted. Vermeers in the Rijksmuseum. Speyer Cathedral. Brueghels in Brussels. Haven't enjoyed myself so much since butterfly-collecting days.

I can haul body around faster than mind can follow—the goal all civilization has striven for since the Golden Age. I haven't words enough yet to tell you what I've seen. My teacher says (at least I *think* she says; all transactions are in Dutch, with scattered cloudy regionalisms) that words make up for lack of grammar better than grammar makes up for lack of words. The language methods here do no conjugations, declensions, paradigms. Only reading, speaking, and restoring sense to texts by supplying missing words. ("Vocabulary," beautifully enough, is *woordenschat:* word treasure. OE's word-hoard?) Only a little touring and I've discovered how beautiful Dutch is. On those city maps set up at strategic places for out-of-towners, the highlighted red arrow reads: *U bevindt zich hier.* You find yourself here.

Here's where I find myself. I now know that a bighearted person, in *het Nederlands,* is small-hearted, that the Holy Ghost and your

337

basic pigeon roosting in the carillon bear the same name, that *pijp uitkloppen,* to clean out one's pipe, is to form a *geslachtsgemeenschap,* a "sex community" (the official term is even funnier than the euphemism. But then, "intercourse" is pretty funny at etymological level). *Lenen* is both to borrow and to lend, making it hard to translate Polonius. I've had my first Dutch dream: I stopped a wimpled woman in a *begijnhof* in some forgotten Belgian town and asked, *"Is dit de weg naar de zestiende eeuw?"* Roughly: Show me the way to the Renaissance.

I've brought my *en face* French partway back from the dead, although you'd be surprised at how little Racine contributes to an exchange in your basic Wallonia pâtisserie. In the tongue of the dreaded Hun, I begin to take a special delight in imbedding clauses and dropping fat, daylight verbal runs at sentence end. I can now read museum tags anywhere in Northern Europe, although a disturbing number are already in imperial *Engels.* Toward our Frenchified Anglo-Saxon, the whole continent seems to have developed a strange love-hate. Everyone wants to speak the language of power, but secretly, not far below the surface, runs the widespread conviction that *ieder Engels is verschrikkelijk.*

Thus a little protective coloration helps. Not that I can always pass. I asked directions from a dike-obsoleted fisherman up in Enkhuizen, and following his directions to the letter, found myself halfway out in the Zuider Zee. I had to know where I'd gone wrong, so I retraced my steps, found the fellow, and told him exactly what had happened. "You followed the directions fine," he told me. "We always send you Germans into the water."

My tutor assures me that research shows that a core vocabulary of a thousand words will get one through 75 percent of ordinary conversation. Unfortunately tempera, patina, pigment, brushstroke, etc. tend not to be among the core one thousand. I have thus become adept at compound neologism. I learn nouns daily, but the arbitrarity of gender makes any decent American yearn for the syllogistic cleanliness of COBOL.

Everything I do all day depends on conversion. Exchange rates, distances. The visual road sign codes—supposedly in Universal Icon Language—are more inscrutable than I imagined. I swear to God there's one indicating that something up ahead is about to put your vehicle into a condition of religious bliss. I take no joy in driving a car, even one dangerously close to the kind Shriner clowns pile out of, in any country where mirrors on building walls assist you to take otherwise blind 90-degree turns at 90 km/h. But I am, at least, marginally better off than the Midwesterner on the *Autobahn* who kept wondering why he couldn't find this place *Ausfahrt* on the map.

All my primary sources are written in literary figures nobody has used for centuries. A greater competence than I'll ever possess would still not admit me into the *real* private clubs. Believe me, every backwater here has its secret speech. The more common the item, the more likely that the villager two kilometers down gives it a different name. That good Dr. Browne was right: jabbering is a hieroglyphical and shadowed lesson of the whole world.

The hardest code to break out here—not recorded in any grammar—is greeting kisses. Every *dorp* has its own dialect. Do I kiss this woman one, two, three, or four times? Do I start on the left cheek or the right? Do I kiss this *guy*? They don't put this stuff in the Michelin. The exchange frequently leads to jarred eyeglasses and bruised noses. There's a similar dance to find a common denominator language for conversation. Observe clothes, ported books, license plate. Try a few mumbled words. I overheard two men in the Liège (Luik, Luttich) railway station conclude, after halting negotiation, that their strongest common language was Latin. A Belgian friend's advice: if you need to address someone in Brussels and can't tell whether to use French or Vlaams, speak English and walk away healthy.

The whole EC is one, huge, macaronic verse. Who invented all these ways of saying? Does the proliferation of dialects come from innate dissatisfaction with any one set of tools? Or is it just another case of Us having to distinguish ourselves from Them? Even folk songs propagate like viruses. When one is struck up in a café, I can generally sing along, although I must substitute my cowboy stanzas for the local lyric. In any case, I'm proud of what modest Dutch I've gotten beneath the knee (under the belt). I manage a bit like that pooch I had as a child, who could sit, lie down, beg, jump, roll over, and play dead, but not necessarily to the right command. I know just enough to get me in trouble with the "strange police," who did not believe that an American could really be writing a thesis on a four-hundred-year-old Flemish nonentity. They were on the verge of quizzing me on Rubens's dates before giving me the visa.

Herri hangs around my neck. I still can't say I know the first thing about the man. I've spent weeks in million-volume libraries, half a dozen first-rate art history collections, and no end of regional *stadhuizen,* and have turned up only the tip of already familiar evidence. Bles's life span remains, despite Yankee ingenuity, framed in question marks. I've nailed down an account of Patinir, with a suggestion that Bles was the older man's nephew or cousin. Fault Flemish; *neef* means either. What to do when one language has two words that the other smears into a single concept? Modalities continue to elude me: two kinds of forgetting, living, believing, remembering. Two distinct becauses! My attempts to read primary sources are humbling lessons in how enormously my own thoughts are bound in native lexicon. Whatever I call a thing, it is never quite what I've called it. It's miraculous that my mother tongue allows me to realize even that much.

I've come across a source that confuses my man's dates with his cousin-uncle's. (I remember, two years ago, your take on those art-jargon letters *fl.* "How beautiful; it doesn't matter when the man lived—he *flourished* around 1542." Believe me: half the charm of this European supermarket raid is imagining what you would make of the Leuven town hall.) Met de Bles, or Blesse. Topknot. How's about Middle High Dutch: with the Blaze. An accident of health left a livid mark across his forehead. Or I could fake a theory: Blessé, a bleeding in of the French wound. Where's my co-conspirator when I need her?

You want to know whether I have any new angle on the paintings themselves. The most convenient conclusion would be that met de Bles was actually a pseudonym, a composite of student panelists from Patinir's workshop, an art factory at least partly documented. I've hunted down a dozen panels. In the paintings themselves (all that's left of Herri, now that his blaze has faded), nothing but the trace of competence—a jagged line, an apprentice, conventional, narrow use of color, a formulaic compositional sense. None is more than marginally memorable except the occasional pastoral arrangement with, somewhere in the background, the chance catastrophe—the painted town in the nonchalant process of being lost.

Particularly skilled in the depiction of silent crisis. His single gift is to make flame realistic but still lazily surreal enough to be congenial. Trivial, banal, quotidian cataclysm. He is no accomplished graduate of the previous generation—no Memling or Metsys, skilled in the unsurpassed stillness of reality. He holds up no perfectly burnished fidelity to the look of surprise. In verisimili-

340

tude, his eye is shaky. If the panels have any resonance, it comes from their perch over invention's chasm.

I've spent hours in front of each, acclimating, learning to read him. I have hypnotized myself in the process; his panels, undeniable Patinir derivatives, grow vastly if intangibly different. I stare at them, like Leonardo trancing out for hours on his spittle, until they become more than masterpieces—immense, jagged, Manichean battlegrounds between the real and the imagined. His expertise at depicting the imminent catastrophe waiting patiently at panel edge, tucked away in back rooms of huge art repositories, are scrolls that have waited four hundred years to tell one sleepy museumgoer that he hasn't the faintest idea of the apocalypse waiting in the front foyer.

I obsess on the idea that it is up to me, FTODD, to translate these sirens into terms my contemporaries can comprehend. I sit down to write, fired with conviction, but can get no father than "He became a master in Antwerp by 1535," before I bog down again in qualifications. Crippled by the clubfootnote. I attempt to make a case for his minor, desperate genius, and wind up trotting out that he was said to have enjoyed a friendship with Dürer, as if only this dubious acquaintance with the great Nuremberger might legitimize my fellow. What can I say about him that would be above dispute? That he may have ended his life in Ferrara, in the blessed South, some time around 1555.

The only indisputables are the fantastic, allegorical landscapes. The handful of scenes I've been able to find—after the years of authenticity debates have taken their toll—contain no stamp of flamboyance, heartbreak, or eschatological revelation, nothing to interest the armchair aesthete, no announcement for anyone except the ambivalent, diverted, ex-night-shift computer operator with two degrees from impeccable schools and two overextended credit cards. Man and work are unremarkable, irretrievable blurs— the perfect topic, in this age of reductionism, for a dissertation.

You loved the scenes, didn't you, when I first showed you them? A flat-out fascination with the threat, soberly maintaining that the only thing to do when the world begins to end is to stand aside and paint it. Uncover it. *Name* it. Your belief in the ability of words to intervene, even after intervention failed the three of us, keeps me here. The inarticulate love I have found for you, the chance that I might in some impossible future arrive on your threshold, paper in hand. . . .

341

Every morning I wait for the museum library to open, and every afternoon I ask what the point is. I swear to God no one could possibly care. The utter irrelevance of foliage technique in the face of acid rain or Afghanistan or the ozone layer, the great foregone shoot-out: paint versus proof. Remember what the professor said, just before we committed to data-terrorism? "A talking cure must be transacted in the illness's own idiom." Who speaks art anymore? At its golden apex, it was already stilted discourse, a kind of leftover court lingo. Even at the supreme Quattrocento moment, the fablespeech of pictures was doomed by the creeping success of new prose. The year Herri was born, if I commit to one of the question marks, Leonardo invented the parachute. Herri (safe to assume) was born into the same zodiacal configuration as Magellan. The year Herri turned seven, astonished Dias, emerging from a storm, found he'd been blown off course around the Cape of Good Hope. New worlds, no longer the province of the landscapist.

His fate was sealed early, apprenticed from youth, perhaps against his will, to a painter's factory, where he gained a modicum of skill in elevating ordinary countryside to travelogue. But no technique imaginable could match the travel reports then coming in. Even before Herri served out his apprenticeship, Columbus had made the most important miscalculation in history. By the time Herri flourished (your face, in front of me as I write the word), Europe was grudgingly accepting the absurd conclusion that a world existed between Here and There.

Let me be blunt: he was in the wrong line of work. That's why I sought him out, the patron saint of fallen-away technographers. He should have been on shipboard from the start. What he lacked in skill of hand he might have made up for in his demonstrated capacity for mental leaps. As fabulous first mate, he might have told Columbus, after weeks of skimming the north edge of Cuba: "This is just pitiful prologue. *Think,* man. Think *big.*" Instead, the only chance of exploration life threw his way came at night, in the security of Antwerp's back streets, under cover of dark, annexing uncharted female isthmuses.

New skills, new materials, the sluiceways of travel thrown open: the man lived on the leading edge of an age of altered maps, radical overhauls: Copernicus's *De Revolutionibus,* apocalyptic showdown in the Church, Peasants' Revolution, Mercator's *Most Exact*

Description of Flanders. When a man can't himself taste the main enterprise of the day, it wrecks him for secondhand excitement. I speak as one who picked up just enough computer competence to get his name paraded through the papers for twenty-four hours.

Still, in Herri's brief flourishing, even an archaic skill provided vicarious thrill, a whiff of the spark that charged the old atmosphere. The printed word was suddenly everywhere, proliferate, vital, and at last affordable. Even art seemed sufficient, rich beyond imagining. New perspectives filtered up from Italy. Genres opened; vistas grew ambitious. Once over the threshold, it would never again be enough just to match the effect of the previous generation. All the attention once lavished on the past was now requisitioned by the unrealized future.

But possibility is only born in a blaze. Dross must be burnt off. The doors at Wittenberg got the stigmata, and there was no turning back. Art, once healing, was enlisted in the longer war. Painting, if bolder than ever, was no longer an authority on the question it had posed since the first cave scratchings: How did I come to be trapped here on earth, at the mercy of strangers? For a long time, pigment had given the answers. Now panelists were as bewildered as anyone.

Jan-o, if it weren't for the collector's thrill—the chance to sample the mythical auras of Ghent and Delft, cityscapes whose views I have wasted my life studying at second hand—I could not keep slogging pointlessly. Every day, between the novelty of new vocabulary and the art treasure map, I am consumed with the whole debacle, how badly I abused us. I miss you intensely, in my sleep. I miss the professor. I need to talk—one more late evening with the two of you. Why have we had to keep apart this year? Tell me exactly: what was it we tried to pull off? Oh, I know the motive, the virtue we made of necessity. I've kept the clippings, the accounts of how we walked away scot-free from the corporate mauling we had coming. But I've seemed to walk away with nothing except the unmistakable sound of missed calling.

Me and my Antwerp master: no better response to looming contemporarity than to set up on a distant hill and catch the conflagration in oils. While his fellow guild members inhaled the whiff of combustion, broadening their palettes, taking on the awful, widening world, Herri staked out a modest line of sight, reworked the Wallonia horizon—the same three-star valleys I traveled yesterday—until it became a jagged, escapist kingdom, more seductive because of the lazy threat hanging perennially about it. Perhaps he was the first modern, after all.

So it is with me: guiltless, evasive sightseeing. I take the cathedral tours, sketch in galleries until the guards chase me out, rediscover the tissue of simile that passes for linguistics, learn enough Flemish figures of speech to pore over obscure, outdated books: waste, in short, whatever gifts I might otherwise have staked against the ascendancy of nonsense. Oh, I've turned up my share of objective fact. I've even indulged in small doses of induction. But data spell out so blessedly little about the man that I am free to spend my days in speculation. The principal attraction in choosing Bles in the first place. His panels were manageable; I hoped to knock out a quick study, earn the degree in two years. At the time, it struck me as courageous, to turn my back on the present—to proclaim, in those faraway mellifluous blues of a milky, indifferent sky, an anodyne for current event, a technique, if not astonishing, at least caressing, resonant enough to salve without shame.

I write you, seated at a desk by a medieval stone casement, breaking from a paragraph to stare out on an enclosing countryside that, in its essence, Herri himself once studied. The place I stay at tonight is a town like any other: a tuck-pointed, half-timbered, bacon-stripped, step-gabled Flemish village, circa 1500. It nestles over an expanse of hills like a case of cowpox. The view is succinct, following the familiar formula developed by Bles's predecessors: foreground in brown, submerged sea-green middlescape, and background of serene mineral-and-linseed blue, wandering out of the available frame and off the edge of the visible spectrum. A lily pond of slate shingles and mansards, the ideal place to produce a minor student piece about a minor genre painter specializing in minor fires.

Easy to imagine him looking out the same window, breaking the scene into constituent geometries. He still searches for the gnostic equivalence that will turn the tricks of the painter's toolbox, the daub-formulas for producing a bird, tree, or frightened stag into a vessel able to unleash, from the dark cave of mind, the animate Original. Science is still in infancy—unweaned from vital essences—but already urging the skepticism of measurement onto the senses. Paint enjoys its last few years in the lost kingdom of parable before its exile. Years when the eye for the last time, alarmed by the discovery of what actually lies outside the window, still has half a retina full of the afterimage of preexistent places.

Bles's era is the last to hope that even a journeyman drafter might assemble, from egg, oil, and slats of hardwood, a graphic equivalent of essence erupting in halftones. Painting, for the last time, is not a process of application but of stripping off, revealing underpainted layers that had been covered, steaming the glaze from between the eye and the form-doused world. Painting and science, for a brief moment before Bles's last serene panel, are after the same key: that book—tucked away in the stacks of a secondhand vendor the way a master of the next generation will tuck a nativity in a hidden village corner—that will prove to be, under its binding, the forgotten alchemist's almanac condensing, in one pass of the alphabet, the whole roll of landscape, the view from the lancet.

I trace him, embroidering the sketchy sources, in his pursuit of this index to seeing. I see him, up before six for perfunctory matins, waiting the descent of journeyman's grace. After a spartan breakfast, he sets to work in suggestive silence. There is no time like the early day for observation. He works alone, in the middle of this Brabant scene, out of reach of easy communication, so no man can say exactly what, if anything, he accomplishes.

His day's big meal comes on the stroke of eleven: fish and fowl, sauce, fruit, nuts, fresh bread to stave craving. After this heroic undertaking, he naps, to release dreams of the unity of all living things. He wakes, spends what remains of afternoon (marked out in the intervals of new mechanical clocks) in repetitive labor, waiting for the visual trick that might unlock the safebox. Lost to work until dinner, revising and undoing the morning's base. Now, if ever, with a few scrapes of the palette knife, he might turn a competent genre piece into dangerous prediction, the living syllable that pierces opaque nature.

Dinner is light, as light as breakfast—modest indulgences at day's ends, falling away from the midday feast in a curve that science will formulate three centuries later. There follows the pursuit of women by night, alluring, unattainable shapes in stone passages, shadowy countenances rendering each shiveringly desirable. He enchants these midnight nuns with a thousand verbal inventions, seductions ranging from blunt frontals to coy flanking maneuvers. None works so well as the invitation to sit for a portrait, a misrepresentation as blatant as any, since he has long sworn off studies of the face, too important a subject for his own passing competence.

Those nights when he fails to procure he is left alone, recalling that this is how he likes best to end days, in the tallow-glow of winter. Waking the next morning to the blessings of solitude, he throws himself again into the schedule of early production, midday gorging, afternoon nap. And further evenings in pursuit of that other whom he has never found, who exists only and precisely nowhere.

He follows this invariant routine for a year or three. But at the instant when habit becomes inhibiting, he upends his carefully cultivated schedule, reneges on debts, chases off his few friends, sends them away berated. He liquidates stock, leaves his rent in arrears, and packs off to another town, another time, taking nothing but his private formulae and all the panels he can carry. He chooses a direction and begins walking. When he grows hungry, he stops and sets up shop. He puts his head down to work, eat, nap, describe this new landscape, find out its fires, rousing himself from routine only when awakened by a surprise ambush of forgotten fields from another century.

He flourishes before an ornate gate unequaled in history. A few years after Gutenberg, a few before Shakespeare, unrepeatable era of giants: da Vinci, Erasmus, Michelangelo, Rabelais. All a fellow condemned to marginalia can do to avoid the sink of afternoon is turn back to the morning's unfinished panel, betray no barometer of hope except what eye can observe, hand mirror.

This, the implicit advice of his paintings, is what I search for in his biography. But a paragraph into exegesis and I gaze again out of this stone casement in the medieval attic I have sublet. On second glance, the countryside is overhauled. All vestige of Brabantine gothic dissolves, and I am in another small town, just as sleepy. The window fills with a different formula for depicting houses, churches, the tucked-away, unobserved miracle. Bles becomes, say, Thomas Hart Benton. The era of infant exploration, its flirtation with parachutes, cadaver dissections, and the sextant gives way to the International Geophysical Year, scientific discovery in full flower, the year of my birth. The moment when that centuries-long investigation, begun on Bles's doorstep, converges on a complete theory—the revelation that experiment has spent four centuries preparing for.

346

Dropped into this alien landscape of block apartments swept by overhead satellites, my journeyman is forced to abandon painting. He takes up the vocation of the times—cashes in palette for vernier gauge. He has no choice but to go on working at the same scene, his eye still after the underlying mechanism that infuses life with its surprising form. Work remains a question of catching, in one sweep, the quiet neighborhood crisis that knowledge always circumscribes. The world by mid-twentieth century has expanded unprecedentedly toward that watershed moment when it will comprise nothing except measure. Met de Bles, symbol depictor, takes up a profession still obsessed with eavesdropping on the world's interior monologue, but wildly enlarged in power of material manipulation, closing in on the symbol table itself.

You see, I start with every intention of cranking out a chapter of Bles's bio, but after a few subordinate clauses, find myself deep in Ressler's. Obsessed, reticent, demure, brilliant, intense, driven, asocial, truculent, lonely, vulnerable, abandoned: the professor, for all we got from him, remains a thesaurus of contradictions. Ressler, at my age, lived for one thing only. To unravel the complexities of personality at its source. Being alive is a one-shot affair: a window, small, blurred, but miraculously permitting a cramped, flattened, two-dimensional, distorted view of the terrain.

Before the perverse thing closed for good, the professor wanted to find the first landfall of the full map, the rule that dictates his generative unfolding. To name, translate his own breathing, his own infolded instinct for love from out of the formal language of chemistry. He is the one I want to flesh out. Why did he let us so far into his life, only to hold us at arms' length? Nature's decoder, who thought that if he could just get to the generating tape, say what "A" meant, then "AT," then "ATG," he would sniff the source, the panel's panel, and could then let the window close peacefully over him. But at bottom, laid bare, solved, the tape read only, "Obsessed, reticent, demure, brilliant, intense, driven, asocial, truculent, lonely, vulnerable, abandoned." The old thesaurus.

Being in the same room as Ressler, just sitting with him in silence, was like filling my lungs with the air of galleries. The chamois cloth of his eye sockets, those pressed seersucker suits no one has worn for twenty years emitted unfinished labwork, interrupted notebooks, glimpses under the electron microscope rendering the familiar mechanics of life alien, less survivable, more unlikely than any oil. I know more about Bles than about the man we sat with.

Think what it must have felt like, to be in your twenties, to rip out of yourself in cerebral caesarean the formulation of an idea two thousand years old. A confirmation so simple, so unexpectedly *whole* that the only available response was militant, head-bowed humility. Then think the unthinkable. At the moment of confirmation, when the connection screams into proximity, you stumble onto another discovery, one that will disperse without trace the instant you formulate it: cracking the program does not mean exemption from having to follow it.

Because Ressler too erased himself from the guild records, I am free to elaborate. Even as he rushes the unavoidable outcome, he gives in to the trivial joy of being twenty-five, more soaringly ill-considered. He can do nothing but savor, as long as possible, that temporary, timid kindness of doomed courtship. What exactly, at this watershed, does she seem to him? She manages to look beatific without being ludicrous. She commits to precious little on the surface. She limps through labwork, by turns bright, sultry, competent, demure, vivacious, dumb. Joanne Woodward's contemporary Oscar performance as a multiple personality has nothing on this woman. Her body's message alters itself at its base: in her step, arrogantly light, she conveys, over the general noise of the lab, the campus, the apocalyptic meander of 1957, that all manner of things will be well, now and in the enzyme.

For his part, he sinks to a parody of reconciled Goodwill. The continued explosion of American Vanguards, the detonation of Soviet nuclear weapons in the Arctic—the whole market of current events fails to flap him. This vestigial, infant happiness is a chemical sluicegate flushing him with unbuffered ions; a thickness in the winter air, his youth triggered by irresistible stimulus—the mechanism he had hoped to overcome by translating.

Admission discounts nothing. The moment flushes him. He feels the rush, no matter what the equation. He thinks of her all day, wants nothing more reprehensible than to spread over her surface like a roosting flock. He willingly gives her every chance to waylay him, to wreck him for what he is after. If the worst should turn out true, the contemptible clarity of his love will redeem everything. The full force of luteinized want—his body conversing with its own attraction—leaves him more laughable perhaps, but no worse off than others, who must also dodge missiles, fend off conflagrations, name the crisis of knowledge. No worse off for his petty attempts at—call it care. Under the circumstances, isn't even care born in sexual aggression sufficient and worth savoring?

Remember the night when we confronted him point-blank with the dossier you'd assembled—every mention of him ever to appear in print? Confirm me: his shoulders slumped imperceptibly, he looked off and cleared his throat, willing to answer anything, but only this once. Remember how he shrugged, a stream of sympathy, invention without cleverness? The slight catch snagging his words wrung all our ingenuity out of me, the pride of authorship I'd felt in his friendship. The valence of the fellow we'd been trying to ascertain became real. Ressler's fingers gripped a card deck, some pointless data-processing task he was about to shove into the hopper. His knuckles turned transparent; his veins and cartilage were the color of an oil-slicked puddle. A thousand cells in that hand split and replicated in the time it took us to speak again.

He'd set out to uncover the principle uniting all animate matter and discovered something simpler instead. Ear to the clicking telegraph key, to the message coming across the wire, the sequence he heard the answer to "What hath God wrought?" was "Who's asking?" Lost to science the moment he cannot put into words, into chromosome strings, why he loves this woman. Reductionism supplies no reason except her clothes, random, mismatched, pastel; her graceful gawkishness between the legs; the absolute lightness of her limbs moving against gravity in all directions at once; her globed cheeks; her wide, scared child-eyes; her visits, quick and brief as accident. No specific part but gives her an uncaring, lissome urgency, wholly beautiful because wholly ephemeral. He is condemned to loss, from that day forward, never quite able to return to the text he had been seeking, for no reason except that she has made him realize, at cell level, that the only message worth receiving will be intercepted, garbled, lost in translation.

He must have seen this before, this slipping off, recalled it from the histories, even as indifference came over him. I'm sure of it. He felt the slow unfolding, long before he showed any sign. He had all the motive in the world to keep from disappearing: the experimental method, all but resting in his hands, a trick for reading the banished original. All the magazines predicted results. Couldn't he have lasted another year?

But he knew the work would get done whatever happened to him. If he did nothing, shut down his tabulations, spoke not another word of his insights, any of countless, equally talented researchers would have his method in a year or two. His year produced a focus of scientific talent unparalleled since Herri's. An all-out marshaling of forces cutting across disciplines had already begun that grade-school recruiting process that would brush the two of us. Sputnik wasn't the catalyst, for my money. His 1957 was just the first of a stream of IGYs.

Before we said goodbye, the night we took our electronically permanent step, he reprised for me in a few, condensed measures his own bitter disappearance. Before we jimmied the packs, he thought it only fair to pass on to me details I might be able to use. "What we need," he told me, "is the code for the synthesis of the forgiveness enzyme. Self-forgiveness. Forgiveness for having wanted what we are born wanting."

Not that I can now hope to ask you for it, after everything, any more than Herri can ask me to forgive him for not being Van Eyck. He and I were born wanting the same thing, and neither of us will ever come close to it. We will never make an *Arnolfini Wedding* or a *Hunters Homeward in Snow*. Herri sees, through the stone casement, that he will be forgotten, demoted to shadowy myth, despite his sole biographer. And with his unrealized landscapes will go that compulsion to imitate, to name the crisis lingering over the indifferent town.

It has become night as I write. Soft chiaruscuro transforms the casement view into interior: has any painter ever made such a composition? The graveyard shift in an airplane hangar full of infernal calculating machines and peripherals. The machines themselves are as serene as Titians. But underneath the skin seethes a public chaos of crowds, a roll call crammed with as many encapsulations of misery as were ever wedged into any last judgment. The foreground is still blue, merging into a sea-green midrange nativity. But the background now takes its tones from the red of ambulance lights. About suffering, they were never wrong, the Old Masters. Even the minor ones. Even met de Bles, or Blesse. With the blaze. Or wound. You see I am thrown in over my head, asked to judge this contest between observation and invention. All I can concentrate on long enough to write about is those overlookable *almosts* in his aborted landscapes. I wait by windows, half-maker of the range of creation I'm supposed to describe.

Creation is at present limited to exotic holidays. Not far back, I was sitting in a *buitenlanders* language class full of earnest young

350

Germans when our teacher announced that there would be no school tomorrow. Incredibly, the most towheaded kid asked why. The teacher tactfully explained that the day commemorated her exemption from obligatory German. For *Hemelvaartsdag* I went to Brugge, an urban time capsule, where I took part in the Procession of the Holy Blood. In the town center, along a fossil gothic-walled circuit, with the great cloth hall and belfry as backdrop, comes this procession of thousands of townspeople in costume, acting out, along the length of their parade ribbon, the history of the world from the Garden to present-day politicos. Animated time flowed past me on the street, a ritual that has been going on, unchanged except for appended length, since 1150. As the procession ended, each block of crowd milled into the street, following the flow, becoming the last, contemporary, costumed participants.

Time, static stuff, is reified here. The granddaughter of collaboration can't marry the grandson of underground. I heard a German ask a price in a bordertown bric-a-brac shop. The proprietor—Common Market be damned—gave the standard reply—allusion to the million conscripted vehicles that aided the Wehrmacht in initial blitzkrieg and sped the surviving sixteen-year-olds reeling from advancing Americans: "Give me my bicycle back and I'll answer you."

Time is a place here, a tangible landscape. Last week I took a day trip to Münster. Disconcerting: still attached to the steeple of St. Lambert's, the iron cages where they displayed the bodies of the Anabaptists. The cathedral was softly disappointing. It had its great astronomical clock: Herri's contemporary universe as flywheel. But I'd expected something more articulated, nuanced. A clause and a half into a wall plaque on the south porch, I realized I was reading English. Stone from Coventry Cathedral, given to the people of Münster. Let us forgive one another as He forgives us. Caption in two languages, each translating the other.

Stupider than my towheaded classmate, I get no closer to this place's meaning than porting over. I will never fully "understand," because I can never fully "*begrijp*." The verbal myth of standing under a thing is as unrealizable as that of grasping it. I came to class last week to discover that my towheaded friend had suffered an auto accident. My distraught teacher, confusing my native tongue with the victim's, blurted out, "*Rudy ist tot.*" That much I grasped, stood under. She passed out copies of the death notice, that final declension. We students spent the morning looking up, in our wordbooks, the names of grief in translation.

It did not stand in the dictionary, but these death notices make a local *spreekwoord:* "He lies like a remembrance card." For they are always filled with love, these after-the-fact summaries. Is what I feel for you at this moment the distortion of loss, waiting until separation to say it? I think of you, want nothing more than to see you and hear your voice.

Instead, I send you this botched dissertation draft. This letter may be the closest I ever come to writing it. You alone are easy to write to, perfect audience, someone who will see, in the weak paraphrase I here throw together, that I am building my apology— explaining why I could not become a sketcher in this world. Now is not the time for drawing. What limited skill we've developed to describe the place we long ago consigned to the laboratory. It may take generations before we remember how big the world is, how much room it has for all sorts of observation.

According to the professor, one single science stands between us and our address. Only we don't see the link; we grasp it only in bits—the pay telescope that magnifies but constricts, and that snaps shut on your quarter after a lousy two minutes. Let me paraphrase the vulnerable Bede: what I put my hands on is the sense, but not the order of the words as the man painted them. For travel scenes, however perfectly composed, can never be ported from one world to another without loss. Perhaps neither beauty nor exactness nor profundity nor meaning, but something will not go over the bridge intact.

The words that might tell me who the fellow was are no longer the words of the original. A coat of metaphor between me and the life I want to write. Words are a treacherous sextant, a poor stand-in for the thing they lay out. But they're all I have—memory, letters, this language institute. Translation would be impossible, self-contradicting at the etymological core: there would *be* no translation were it not for the fact that there is *only* translation. Nothing means what its shorthand pattern says it does. Everything ever uttered requires cracking. So I keep busy, travel, learn some words. . . . "I will call the world a *school* instituted for the purpose of teaching little children how to read." Full marks for identifying.

You may find it as hopeful as I did to discover that the Dutch for "weather" and "again" are the same. Let me say at least that I love you, and all other untranslatables.

FTODD

P.S. If I were you, I would write me back quickly and affection-ately, an irrefusable letter from home. Something along the lines of "The age of Europe is past. That of America is ending. Get back fast before it's all over." In the meantime: *Waarom hangt je was niet op de Siegfried Lijn?* Roughly ported over: Why not hang your wash out on the Siegfried Line?

XVII

Halcyon Days

Ressler's write-up is accepted by the *Journal of Molecular Biology*. He will appear as second author after Ulrich. Standard practice: the glass-washer takes second billing to team leader. Ulrich edits his summary liberally. Ressler initially concluded, "It has been demonstrated that hereditary information is arranged in unidirectional, nonoverlapping nucleotide triplets, each determining a single amino acid in protein synthesis. Code redundancy may favor an in vitro method of determining codon assignments over analyses of base and polypetide sequences." Ulrich softens this to "Our results further substantiate the hypothesis of a linear arrangement, perhaps with a triplet reading frame." He strikes the crucial second sentence altogether. When the red-penned draft comes back to Ressler, he springs up and walks the paper back down the hall to the old man's office, using the distance to suppress the spontaneous fight mechanism sprung in his body.

Ulrich shifts in his chair and drops into placid register. "The write-up is first-rate. But we don't want to overstate the results." Ressler volleys halfheartedly: his conclusion makes no assertion that isn't supported. "Perhaps," Ulrich holds firm. "But what counts is not what you claim for your results, but what they claim for themselves. You don't want to dictate how to run follow-ups. That would be ..." The veteran breaks into a conspiratorial grin. "That would be leading trump."

Ressler leaves, rebuked but pleased. Ulrich's tacit advice to play things close to the chest unwittingly exonerates Stuart for not yet announcing his even more sweeping line of thought. In the premature evening of his office he follows a bibliographical trail, searching down another experiment from a pair of years ago. He dimly recalls a paper with similar elliptical conclusion that could vaporize the intractable barrier between him and the last lab step. His concentration for work is shaken by the hierarchy of ethics. Ulrich's edit can in no stretch of the term be called fraud, or even suppression. Yet aggregate reticence shades imperceptibly into misrepresentation.

He has not, under grant or tenure pressure, recreated results without resubmitting them to the experimental apparatus. No; his data are beyond reproach. He's not even on the hazier ground of corner-cutting in the name of efficiency. In school, he worked for a big-name researcher who occasionally whipped up extra runs, substantiating more careful trails but skimping on controls. The accusation's been made against Mendel himself: the smooth-versus-wrinkled ratio is too perfect. But that was something else altogether—the unconscious influence of conviction. Another, more troubling imputation against the monk asks why he studied only traits that all reside on independent chromosomes. Did he examine and fail to report inheritance patterns complicated by inexplicable linkage that would have thrown the infant theory in doubt?

Simplification, paring back the variables, far from invalidating results, is indeed required by the foundations of empirical design. The success of reductionism depends on measuring and reporting only that bit of the cloth that can be understood and tested piece-meal. Ulrich's advice partakes of the same reductionist pragmatism: let's establish the part beyond the slightest doubt, before we speculate on the whole's make and model.

Ressler releases this work—insignificant compared to the catch he now angles for—from safekeeping. But the question nags at him. The question of just what he is or isn't obliged to telegraph to the competing scientific community masks a deeper ethical issue, his secret competitive motive. Easier to tell all, free himself from the advantage of insight. He hoards the self-sabotage urge the way his fellow children of the Depression hoard tinfoil.

He lets Ulrich strike the summary and does not press his own extrapolation. Demurring is worlds away from the most defensible fraud. It doesn't begin to flirt with falsification. Even in the continuum between subjectivity and chicanery, no one would call it doctoring. But simple selective silence, cautious calculation itself, carries along, like an unsuspecting trouser cuff bearing the free-loading burr of a seedpod, some particle of self-servance. The nauseating calculus of survival flashes on him. Self-furthering strat-agems color even that perfect, informational openness, the uned-ited wonder of the most ideal human pursuit: good science.

Cyfer has a greater threat to its survival than entrepreneurism. Circumstance strips the team of its clearest-headed member. The train is set in motion on December 19, when the world weather engine is traditionally in almanac respite. The day is too warm for near-winter. The unusual front that releases the balmy air in the same breath releases a burst of tornadoes across the belt of Mis-souri, Arkansas, and Illinois. They catch the states off-guard, well past the usual time of year.

Ressler has just returned from the retail strip, where he has bought himself an early Christmas present. He has taken his last two untouched checks and a list prepared by Toveh Botkin and made a run on the record store. He returns to barracks with two LPs for every periodical still strewn about his front room. He assembles a respectable, compact music library, from Palestrina's *Missa Papae Marcelli* to Penderecki's *Threnody for the Victims of Hiroshima*.

He listens, relaxed, alert, despite just coming off of a triple shift of journal scouring, article amending, and experimental specula-tion. Finding the music precise, the notes excruciatingly discrete, he decides that the need for sleep is vastly overrated. The intensity of music keeps him from hearing that the long, sonorous, extended pedal point arising from the continuo of a bit of until-then-banal Venetian Opera is, in fact, the Civil Defense horns crying disaster. Discovering that the piercing tone is not shook out of his pho-nograph's paper speakers, he wonders if he's skipped ahead to Tuesday, 10:00 a.m., the weekly CD drill. But days can't have passed: he's still in the seventeenth century.

At the air raid's insistence, he steps outside his shack to scope out the situation. Unforgettable: the sky has gone a sickening, *Matthew Passion,* faulty-Zenith green, right out of the Crayola box. Otherworldly: everyone in Stadium Terrace, from infant to eternal student, streams in column to the stadium, toting suitcases, pulling Rapid Flyers full of belongings. No simulation would bother to be this elaborate.

Tuning in the radio strikes him as superfluous. He stares at the sky creeping toward yellow, making a break for infrared. The long-expected airburst, most likely Chicago or old Midwestern rival,

St. Louis. At 150–200 miles, a midsized device, as the papers like to call them, would kick up enough dust to discolor the atmosphere, give it this early, dramatic sunset. He goes heavy at the waist; his knees fold involuntarily. He crumbles onto his stoop, watching the refugee crowd fanning toward Memorial Stadium for an unscheduled game. Some amazing instinct has gotten it into these heads to try to save their *possessions:* scrapbooks, chairs, an antique doll, blenders, anything arms can drag or shove. He considers calling out to the lady hauling the home tanning lamp not to bother; she's getting a healthy dose of rays already.

For thirty seconds it hails, but cuts off abruptly. The violence of the wind, the backlash of pressure electrifies his skin, returns him to a child's awe at one-time forces. He watches the sky slip to a silver gray and calculates the airspeed by timing a scrap of paper tearing across the lawn. A ten-year-old boy breaks from beside his hysterical mother in the file and waves his arms like a crane, shouting: "Run from the funnel!" His clutching mother snatches him back, yelling at Ressler as if he were an abductor. So the cause is natural, not induced. It makes no difference: correction will eventually have its out. But spreading his fingers across the violet grass, he does feel something, the bulb of skin flaring after a failed immunity test: gratitude that he may have a chance to see Jeannie again.

The stream of evacuees drains to a trickle. The wind whips to such craziness that he cannot keep from laughing. In the cusp moment, he sees the vertical cloud on the horizon feeling its way, prehensile, across the harvested fields. He calculates the number of steps to the relative safety of the stadium. Even if he'd dedicated his youth to distance sprinting, the protection of colonnades wouldn't warrant that open-field gallop. It's all over except the virtuosity. He spreads himself on the ground, facedown, head to the side so he can view this performance from the edge of the pit. He sees the outlines of groundbound things tossed about where they oughtn't be going. On all sides of the cross hairs where he lies, physical law defers to easy chaos.

When it's safe to sit up, he does, slowly. Stadium Terrace is overhauled with scrub, branches, trash, furniture, pieces of wall— no longer the center of the biggest plain in the world, but a tidal zone of flotsam. Astonishingly, his tarshack and most of K block have escaped. He succumbs to childish disappointment, the one he felt years ago on seeing the picture of that domed structure that obstinately survived Ground Zero. Can't even violence accomplish something unmitigated?

He dusts off, grinning at how good his clothes feel, how wonderful the wrinkles. He takes himself back inside. He tunes in an emergency report, running only minutes behind the event itself. The twisters leave ten dead across Illinois: a misleadingly small toll, not indicating the power of the thing, the lightest flick of Coriolis effect that chose, this once, to pass over. The tornado failed to take him by only the narrowest swirl of turbulence. When the information repeats, he shuts off the radio. He picks at random from his new reference set a disk to return to. Brahms's number comes up: the Second Piano Concerto. The sound so transfixes him that he rises to place the unprecedented phone call: to Botkin, to verify her safety after the storm. The gesture moves her out of proportion to its facility. He hangs up, hands fused momentarily to the phone. No: he cannot call that other, whose safety means more than meaning.

He returns to a piercing, slow 'cello solo, music too beautiful even to listen to in this century with a clean conscience. But he listens. The homecoming of the piano, demure soloist, is punctuated by pounding on the door. Outside, it is pitch-black; near the solstice, that could mean any time after 4:00 p.m. Eva and Margaret Blake stand shivering together under a quilt feathertick in the dark. He quickly lets them in.

"Is Tooney here? Have you heard from him?" Evie asks, looking about, a timid meter reader looking for the main. "It's late," she adds, rebuking not her husband but puerile nightfall. "He never came home." Ressler settles her and gives Margaret a can of orange juice concentrate and a spoon, sufficient to delight her. He and Mrs. Blake begin the systematic round of phone calls, first to everyone on the team, all negative. Then they try the lab, every office at the Biology Building where someone might still be around to pick up phones. No one does. Only then do they resort to the finality of police, who reassure them that the twin cities have reported no fatalities. Last, the hospitals, who cannot match any injured to Tooney's description.

Eva has worked herself into a state. She's reluctant to return to K-53-A alone with the child. He insists that they stay with him. Over Eve's ennervated refusals, he makes up the bed for them, apologizing for the brutality of bachelorhood. Margaret is across the mattress and asleep before he can turn out the light. He returns to the front room and his journal pile, prepared to sit up all night, a trick that has become almost easy. He has just hit upon an article in a 1955 *Nature*—one that, for an instant, seems as catalytic as Watson and Crick's piece two years earlier—when Eva pads in, still wrapped in the quilt. "Can I sit out here with you? I'll be quiet."

"You don't have to be quiet."

"Good. *Nature* again, I see. You men are all alike." She takes the volume from him, thumbs through its thickness, and drops it back into Ressler's hands. "OK. Ask me anything."

Before he can smile, she coils up and follows the book into his lap. She collapses like a cut tree, lets out a bleat of anguish, and balls herself up against him. She is uncannily cold; he wraps her in his forearms to try to trap what little warmth is left in her. "He must be somewhere," he offers.

Evie stifles a vowel. "Keep talking." She digs into his leg, a breeding sea turtle scooping deeper into the beach.

Ressler pops the clutch for a moment before he can locate his deep sentence structures. He begins talking about Tooney and the tornadoes, the likely scenarios accounting for his absence. Paralleling in rough analogy the series turning electrical current into magnet pulse into paper motion into air wave into earbone disturbance into neural network into Brahms, his words of coded comfort drive Evie's muscles into slack acceptance. When he runs out of explication, he goes on filling up empty space. He talks about how essential Blake's sensibilities are to Cyfer, his lucid, first-rate spoiling of half-baked ideas. Tooney is the one person liked by everyone on the team. Eva acknowledges this praise with a muffled sigh. Ressler goes on, explaining how Cyfer has squared off against the coding problem, just what difficulties still lie between them and a map of the nucleotide grammar. As the details are lost on her and therefore safe, he lays out the theory of an in vitro solution just weeks away from gelling: submit the simplest imaginable message to the coding mechanism, and see what the enciphered text looks like. Crack the system by standing over the encoder's shoulder.

He stops, struck by the beauty of the thing he touches. His hands keep working, rubbing warmth into Eva in ways they would not dare with the other woman now. Eva has lost her agitation. He can stop the invented monologue. But for this perfect audience, asleep, unable to hear, he recites, "I'm in love with a colleague of your husband's. She's as married as you are. Nothing to do about it. No point." He checks each mark off, brutally succinct, but he stops short of the worst: *She is a locking template I cannot shake*.

He wakes up early to the sound of someone letting himself in. He watches fuzzily as Tooney Blake enters and sits opposite Ressler and still-sleeping Eva. "She was cold and just fell asleep here. Your daughter is in the next room." Tooney fakes a suspicious look, speaking volumes, knowing that Ressler is already hopelessly compromised. Blake does not wake his wife, but only sits, staring disconcertedly through things rather than at them. Stuart asks if everything is all right.

"Fine," Blake answers, distracted tone contradicting him. The monosyllable rouses his wife, who in sleepy euphoria attaches herself to her mate. She rises up radiant, blinking, without a hint of question to her. The night's anxiety needs no other payment: they've weathered the worst, already more than repaired. When the embrace settles, the space of reprieve gives place to the collective need for postmorteming. Something Blake needs to announce, a chance locution that threatens to change his life. He has this aura about him, difficult to miss. Blake grabs his wife by her shoulders, about to launch into *There was a ship....* "Honey," he says, "something's happened."

At the moment that the Civil Defense horns began their Gabrieli, he was across town, in the stacks. "Somebody has the whole microbiology library out on loan," he growls at Ressler, casting accusing glances about the periodical-strewn floor. "When the alarm went off, I figured I was already in as good a place as any other; no point going from one designated shelter to another. So I went down to Deck One, instinctively sought out the subterranean. I'd just gotten into a cozy study carrel when the power went out. Pitch-black, surrounded by that maze of shelves. I couldn't move without banging up against the 120s. I kept thinking, 'If this is the end, at least I'm surrounded by books.'

"After a long time, with a lot to think about, I tried to work my way to a stairwell. I found one at last, and after some trouble adjusting to the steps, I hauled myself up to the deck at ground level. *Light* coming in from the street. Cars shuttling. Life as normal, except for a few vanished trees. I groped along the aisles, doing my Theseus bit, keeping my right hand on the wall. I found the entrance and yanked the door. It wouldn't budge. Locked in. I heard the all clear go off downtown. I waited patiently in the dark, convinced that if I sat still long enough, something would happen. Sure enough, forty minutes later, the lights flooded on. When my eyes adjusted, I went to the emergency phone on Deck Five. The thing was as dead as a mayfly on day two. The lines must have come down in the storm."

Eva giggles, the low, jittery laugh of relief. "Oh *Toon*-ey! Locked in the stacks overnight! You must be a wreck."

"Strangely enough, I've never felt better in my life. They'd have to install vending machines before I'd agree to move back in on a long-term lease. But I've never spent a more important night." A comical whimper from his wife forces him to append, "Honeymoon excepted, sweet."

He lapses again into amazed gazes at various objects about the room until Ressler clears his throat. Tooney wraps his wife tighter and continues, "Realizing I was stuck awhile, I began to see the place differently. The stacks had always been a purely functional means to an end. But now, I *lived* there. A long night ahead, and the third-biggest collection in the country to pass it in. It occurred to me just what the place contained. Millions of volumes. The figure, which has always struck me as impressive, now became staggeringly real. At first, I got a chuckle going around looking up everything I've ever published. Then I began to track down every published reference *about* me.

"It slowly dawned on me that everything Ulrich, Botkin, or Woyty will leave behind is locked up in those shelves—their best insights, the record of how that trace spread or failed to catch hold. All the noise any of us has made in this world. I pulled our friend here's dissertation. I independently confirmed that he graduated *summa cum laude*." He gives Stuart a cuff. "After a while, the game of deciding which parts of each of us will live began to grow thin. It was after midnight, and I hadn't even gotten off that deck, let alone scratched a fraction of it. I had ten levels to play on, without the slightest plan of attack.

"You wouldn't believe the *substance* of that collection. A book-length study tracing a century and a half of disease among a single tribe on Mozambique. A thirteen-volume log of an 1848 botanical survey in the South Pacific. Photo cavalcades to performing hand surgery. An experimental account of chimps addicted to painting, whose work declined as soon as they began getting rewards for it. And I hadn't even gotten out of Biology yet.

"The words spread in all directions, an endless, continuous thread. I could jump in anywhere. Goethe. Glosses on the Koran. How-to dog sledding. Crackpot theories about ancient supercontinents. Accounts of Marian Anderson singing the national anthem at the Lincoln Memorial, because the DAR wouldn't let her sing it inside. Watercolors of Pemaquid Point by assorted artists. I lost twenty minutes to an article about whether or not Clara Bow had really slept with the entire UCLA offensive line."

Blake falls silent, preoccupied, sliding down the early slope of a syndrome that could drop off as suddenly as the continental shelf. Ressler tries for casual silliness. "We need to rush you to Info Detox, Tooney?"

Blake laughs, but nominally. "It's the world's damn DNA in there. Not to trivialize tornadoes, but suppose yesterday had been something more . . . extreme. How many died?"

"At last report, ten."

"Kick that figure up a few exponents. If worst-case scenario comes down to worst, there's enough information in the stacks right now to rebuild everything we have, within a narrow tolerance, from scratch."

"Provided the survivors would want to do something so ill-considered," Ressler counters.

"I'm serious," Blake insists.

"I am too."

Blake stands and begins to pace. Margaret waddles out of bed from the next room, welcomes her father back from missing personhood with a nonchalant kiss, and curls up against her mom. Eva sits at attention, not quite knowing what's going on. Nor do any of them. "How much of that information do I—any of us—actually have a handle on?" Blake pauses, the question more than hypothetical.

To get the man to go on, Ressler answers, "Almost none."

"My God, we're reaching the point where we're stockpiling more information than we can manage."

"That's what indices are for," Ressler interrupts, this time to slow his friend down.

"But we're racing to the day when even indices won't help. We're outstripping even the Index of Indices. New discovery daily, and we can't even find the damn thing by this time next week. Go spend a night in the stacks. We're committed to nothing less than a point-for-point transcript of everything there is. Only one problem: the concordance is harder to use than the book. We'll live to see the day when retrieving from the catalog becomes more difficult than extracting it from the world that catalog condenses. Book and lab research will pass one another in the drifting continents of print."

"What are you suggesting?" Ressler asks. "It seems a bit late in the day to stop accumulating."

"No! We can't afford to stop. We've got to keep on top of the stockpile. Here we are, digging in the dirt, turning up shards, millions of shards, more than anyone expected to find. But nobody knows what the shattered vase they all came from looks like. Whether it's a single vase, or even a vase at all. What we need is not more shards. We need to accumulate something else altogether. Something much wider."

Ressler doesn't follow this last leap and says as much.

"Look," Blake challenges. "Take our own field. Blown wide open lately. Which do you think will be more complex: a complete, functional description of human physiology, or a complete, functional description of the hereditary blueprint?"

Ressler considers the number, weight, and function of the purposive proteins in a working body—the countless, discriminating, if-then, shape-manipulating, process-controlling, feedback-sensitive, integrated programs composing the complete organism. As in the old Von Neumann joke, he sees at long last that the answer is obvious. "Physiology is vastly more complex."

"But the more complex is *contained* in the less complex, right? We believe in the simplicity of generating principles."

Some equivocation, some sleight of hand here. Can genetics really be said to contain all physiology in embryo? Yet Ressler concedes Blake's central point, Poe's point, in that volume buried in the 800s. Poe's cryptanalyst needed three things to turn the hopeless gold-bug noise back into readable knowledge: context, intention, and appropriate reference. A night of information science has forced Tooney to confront the full width of that triplet. "Wife," Blake says, grabbing his matched half. "Oh, Eva! I'm sorry. Something's happened to me." This all ought to be occurring elsewhere—anywhere but Ressler's living room. Eva's features are smothered in wonder. She touches her husband's head, coaxing him into relaxing the cords in his neck. "It's crazy," he repeats.

"No it's not," she says, combing him.

"Friend." Blake smiles helplessly at his wife. "I didn't plan this." Eva smiles broadly: nothing you could possibly do will upend our life. "I may," Blake says, laughing at her unconditional trust, swinging his head sideways in disbelief, "I may have to resign from the faculty."

Evie coddles him. In a very bad John Wayne, she says, "A man's gotta do...."

Ressler refuses to believe the exchange. "Quit the team? To do what? Where would you go?"

"Back to school," Eva says, almost hissing. Protecting her husband from this outsider when he is down.

It's impossible. "You can't. What about your child?"

"Who's a child?" Margaret demands.

Blake mistakes him. "My child? She's *in* school already."

"How will you *live*?"

"There's always the Civil Service," Eva volunteers.

"Tooney," Ressler says, "you've had a strange night."

Blake just laughs. "No doubt about that."

Anger fills Ressler at his friend's uncharacteristic leave from realism. "What will you study?"

Blake shrugs: the discipline hasn't been invented yet. "Look, Stuart. How can I pretend to do science, take apart the mechanism, inventory all the particulars, when I haven't even a rough feel for the sum? I haven't even dusted the spines of a fraction of the stuff they have shelved in there."

"And you never will."

"True. But I wouldn't mind a rough take on the big picture. A life of educated guesses, and I haven't even a clue what we're guessing at."

Thus the Blakes commit themselves, overnight, to hopeless generalism. They depart, Tooney shaking Ressler's hand warmly, Evie kissing him, thanking him for keeping her alive last night. After they leave, Ressler replays the man's mad argument, but can find no hook to snag him. He circles back on Blake's point: the complex can be contained in the simple. Push past the deterring convolutions—too varied to describe—and get to their underpinnings. Grammar *must* be simpler than the uncatchable wealth of particular sentences. He wants to run over to K-53-A, throw himself around the man's neck. He has never been more in need of his teammate's skills. Never more in need of his neighbor himself— his solid, dispelling humor. But Tooney is gone already. Intractable.

Over the following days, as it becomes clear that Blake really means to depart, Ressler gambles everything. He lays out for Tooney the seminal germ he has stumbled on. The beauty of the green idea sparks Blake's scientific residue. His eyes light up at the walkthrough. He grabs his young colleague's upper arms, lifts him bodily into the air. "You can do it." But the next moment he returns to his new calm, encourages the kid more soberly, and again declines to stay.

Blake doesn't even wait for term's end. He leaves in midweek, departs from Stadium Terrace, forever jumps the tenure track. He asks Ressler to take over his classes; "Mostly a matter of administering finals." They leave him with a dozen pieces of furniture. "Another long-term loan." They give him a forwarding address—Seattle, Eva's mother's. Eva kisses him courageously goodbye, on the lips, wet with hypotheticals. Tooney shakes his shoulders. "After boning up, I might come back to the lab in good faith someday."

When it comes to saying goodbye to the child, Ressler can take it no longer. He may see her again in this life, but never again like this. Process will have gotten her. The pilgrim soul will be lost in adulthood. He tries to say, "Got any poems, for the road?" but cannot get it out. Margaret tugs at his shirt cuff, spins on one heel, and disappears, giggling. He will die without raising a child.

Script

Who knows how long his envelope has been there. I haven't checked the box since Thanksgiving. I'd given up looking, achieved a degree of self-sufficiency. My only bottle-messages lately are from the power company. Checking for mail was once my day's high-water mark. But recently I've taken to clearing out the box only often enough to keep the utilities running. Suddenly this: the message I'd written off. A simple letter wouldn't have been enough. It's a longhand manuscript. I knew instantly it was from him: his runic glyphs. The packet carried the same exotic monarch as his card, pasted all over with stickers pronouncing *Per Luchtpost.* Why now, when I'd almost edited him?

I tore open the packet, knowing the weapon was loaded. I was a wreck from the first rambling paragraph. Even now, twice through the text, my organs scrape like tectonic plates. The sprawling poetics are unmistakable Todd. But someone else is in there too, someone I've never met. A dozen minutely, perfectly hand-lettered pages, both sides, and I still can't tell where he is. That landscape: the place he used to map out for me in whispers. But somewhere else too, a globe away. "Why have we had to keep apart this year?" "Not that I can hope to ask you...." Who is this? A male I once knew, stripping at a safe distance?

Plaintive Baedeker gossip, swapped cathedral stones, death notices. Frank on the ropes. Writer's block, foreign language, death of a classmate, the panels themselves after years of reproductions: tempera homesickness for the world. I make myself immune to his contents. But two paragraphs in and I hear him confessing something I never realized. He'd *been* on the ropes from the moment I met him. Easy, sociable, pelted with phone calls from friends who couldn't imagine why he gave them the slip, locked up on the night shift, satisfied with the company of a failed scientist and a failing librarian. This *luchtpost* packet confesses why he wanted Ressler's etiology, the dossier on that disease. A year's rupture; anonymity in Europe, oblique petition for help, lost in moratorium. Out of character at last: please write me back.

Something's out of joint. The cheery postcard—Flemish scene ported from Boston back to Flanders—is dated July 6, five months before this letter. He writes in the card that he's well along in Dutch. But the letter reports novice's difficulties, unlikely for someone of Todd's polyglot perversity. After a half a year, he still cannot mention Ressler's death, or give the man the dignity of past tense. Alone, unchecked, unseconded, writing me, dragging me through all his sweet, unreliable, poorly timed declarations of maybe love. God free me from this man.

Todd had a way of darting his eyes around as if the earth were the last thing he expected to see. I have forgotten that astonished tone, forgotten everything about him. He's back, wanted or not. But another sender here too, one I wouldn't know from a Dürer Adam. He is in trouble, needs me to write. As if a letter, even now, might serve as saving bedtime story.

The Question Board

Q: How often do questions appear here that you can't solve?
H.M., 8/11/81

A: More often than we'd like. According to a survey of American libraries, a third of questions to reference departments go unanswered. Ours weighs in a little under the national average, although we have no firm numbers.

J. O'D., 8/11/81

"What you need," Todd whispered into my ear, gazing over my shoulder as I typed, letting his hand loop dangerously over my ribs toward my breast, "is to copy the post office. A Dead Question Department." He lifted my hair and moistened the back of my neck. "Imagine: Question Purgatory. A smoky room full of three-by-fives, each unsolvable."

Putting One's Hands Through the Pane

Unbelievable: I can write him back at last. What I've ached to do for months, poring over atlases for clues, rehearsing the wording I'd use when given a place to reach him. Only now, I can't write the first clause. My block is worse than his: I can't even get off a salutation without seizing.

Another two readings and I still can't tell what's wrong. Indifference would feel simpler, would have no shakes. I've never written to him in my life. How can I start now, after everything? How could I begin telling him of my months reading a science I haven't any grounding in, depleting my savings, mourning the death he doesn't mention? I can't begin to concentrate on Dear Franklin until I've extricated myself from Dear Dr. Ressler. All I can do with his letter is add it to the evidence to be sifted. I can write only the same piece I've been working on for months. Why have we stayed apart all this time? Enzymes, friend.

I have only my work to answer him. The content of the coding problem compels me, twenty-five years after the facts. Discovery is a dependence that addiction only imitates. Engineered into my sequence, selected for obvious survival value, is a craving to lift the backdrop, to integrate the evidence, to mimic the tune so closely I can at last get *through* the notes. To force my hands through, touch the habitat. Assemble it. Ressler's was the desire behind all research: the pull of something simpler and stranger

367

than imagined, lying within arm's length. Curiosity must, like every built-in desire, be written somewhere in the organism it wants to discover. Ressler looked for the fundamental lexicon in primitives. Only the results of the lookup table itself can explain why he was hooked on breaking it, on getting to the name of experimental desire.

Can anything as composite as curiosity be revealed by a set of equivalences, a molecular cipher wheel? Nothing in the chemistry of nucleic acid gives the first hint of the creature enclosing it. The sequence of base pairs in the molecule, their disorderly pattern, provides the edge needed to record a message. But the sequences themselves are not yet vernacular, but a shorthand. An arbitrary string CGAGGACCGACG, without a translator's dictionary, is gibberish. The lookup table supplies that dictionary; without semantic meaning itself, it lends the first suggestion of sense to unreadable data.

The translation Ressler worked on is a one-for-one, simple substitution. My arbitrary string, pressed through the table, maps to a single protein: arginine-glycine-proline-threonine.... Transliteration to aminos alone seems to move me no nearer the evolution of heart, chest, hands, eyes—those devices against the caprice of environment. Slavish substitution appears no more helpful in finishing my triple bridge than those primitive DOD translators Ressler once tapped us into. One night, taking us on a tour through the vast MOL on-line network, he tapped into a machine translation program. He selected "French" for target language and typed in the string "I am left behind." We shouldn't have been playing with the restricted program at all, but that didn't keep Todd and me from hanging on his every keystroke. The algorithm churned away on a mighty effort of pattern matching and produced "*Je suis gauche derrière.*" He hooked up two of these software Berlitz's back to back, feeding English-to-French back into its reciprocal. "Out of sight, out of mind" returned to source language as "blind lunatic."

All I've done with codon translation is rename the elements I started with. ACG becomes threonine; I've just swapped chemical terms. And yet, the map is never quite the place, nor the place as navigable as its image. It has taken me months to see that the coding problem is just the start of the cryptography. If that were the extent of inheritance, the lookup table would produce only tautological definitions. The hundreds of base pairs in a gene, broken into triplet codons and fed through the decoder, would produce the telegram "Please refer to original dots and dashes."

All these ciphers mean nothing until I find the *difference* created in translation. The table only softens the inscrutable script, shapes the clay into executable words. Cracking the code is just the tip of the *Goldberg*. The lookup list of simple equivalences requires me to learn how to interpret, implement the text that comes out of it. For data to grow, respond, rise up and walk I must look at the secondary structures locked in the life molecule. I want a deeper definition from the string—its isomorphs of hope, ache, posted desire.

The bouillabaisse is richer than I've guessed. The punched tape running along the inner seam of the helix is much more than a repository of enzyme stencils. It packs itself with regulators, suppressors, promoters, case-statements, if-thens. Genes coding for messengers, readers, and decoders of genes. Genes to copy and build the genes' copiers and builders. Genes that may speed, slow, or reverse their own mutation. The automated factory imbeds a blueprint for its own translation machinery—a glimpse of real invention that knocks me for a loop.

How, from simple substitution, can this absurd surplus emerge? A gene and its enzyme, while code-equivalent, are worlds apart in function. The decoded string contains more than its original. My mistake has been in thinking of enzymes as simple ropes of twenty-colored beads. Even though this model provides more necklaces than the most scrupulous socialite could wear in an eternity of nights out, my metaphor misses a key point. Each color pattern corresponds to a specific necklace *twist*. And shape, in stereo-chemistry, is behavior by another name.

Protein necklaces are actually closer to wildly tangled wool fuzz. They are strings, but coiled as erratically as Norwegian hair run through a home permanent. (Wool, hair—two prime analogies.) Only, the twists that the fiber balls up into are rigid, fixed by the sequence of the aminos. I feel my first spark: the growing polypeptide—arginine, glycine, proline—folds up in a manner determined by the amino sequence coded for in the synthesizing gene. The resulting three-dimensional globule carries spatial information; a landscape of grottos, peaks, and plains gives the enzyme catalytic ability—the power to bring about reactions that otherwise might not have taken place.

Even if the strand is stretched, it will spontaneously reform to the coiled arrangement unique to its linear sequence. This complex but ordained shape turns the enzyme into a cookie cutter, machine tool, a shoehorn introducing big foot into recalcitrant slipper. Smaller molecules align with spots on the enzyme landscape where they precisely fit. Held in place, they are brought together to react with another similar squatter. Each uniquely shaped enzyme is expert at bringing about a particular reaction. The human genome codes for countless enzymes, each a chemical command, a potential engine capable of producing a specific chemical event.

DNA carries just part of the instructions for these purposive, molecular machines. The actual welding—go straight a fraction of a micron; make a hard turn, 137 degrees in plane X, north-by-northwest—depends on physics. The shape an enzyme takes, and therefore its function, results from the laws governing atoms in space. To manufacture breathing, searching, speaking, rule-defying life from out of constrained matter requires no transcendence. Every level of the hierarchy arises from the previous, without any need to change the rules or call in outside assistance. Yes, some sleight of hand: a knit sock is *just* a series of knots, a computer *just* switches, a haunting tune *just* the intervals that walk it down the scale. But what other way to grasp a thing except as the emergent interplay of parts, themselves emergent from combined performances at lower levels?

The emergence of function from codon assignments is like that child's toy: two intermeshed gears with an asymmetrically affixed pen that produces unpredictable designs. The surprise, recursive flowers the toy makes aren't hinted at in any part of the assembly— not gear, not pen, not the cranking hand. Each of these parts does only what is allowed. The flower lies latent in the aggregate rules of geometry, which know nothing about flowers. In the same way, my most inexplicable high-order ability—understanding things through metaphor, applying the light of likeness to probe the layers of the pyramid—already lies infolded, hidden in the craggy terrain, the hintless indifference of my crumpled-up polypeptides.

Solving the lookup table—itself arbitrary—is prerequisite for my locating the particle of purpose, the smallest programmed machine in that regress of programmable machines making up living tissue. In grounding Mendel's invariant inheritance squarely in molecules, Ressler hoped to position science for a theory of molecular evolution. Protein synthesis would reveal how the destructive anarchy of chance, capable only of wearing the rock away, can carve Chartres. The production of enzymes, each shaping an urge to bring about reactions that would not occur spontaneously, is the first rung up form's ladder toward free will.

The catalyzing shape of enzymes is the seam between predetermined atomic interactions and the self-ordering living library. Enzymes are the machines DNA creates and sends out into the cellular factory. They *are* the factory. The coding problem was, to Ressler's generation, nothing less than a matter of locating the fundamental message unit behind the biosphere. Just as the innermost in a set of nested Chinese dolls anticipates the shape of the outermost, the way the array of living things bends itself to the environment depends on the ability of chains of amino acids to fold into specific, reaction-promoting molds. Or a step before that: on the way nucleic acid hides the enzyme shape in a helical archive.

Addictive, naked hunger to reconstitute the real: the freshly scrubbed Ph.D.'s compulsion to locate the lookup table was, by another name, a longing to unfrock things as they are. Life that refused to push all the way down to the evidence was just a costume party. Only by demonstrating beyond doubt how unaided atoms accounted for craving, variety, the accident of being alive could Ressler see what compensation the truth of his own contingency might hold.

He and I both—desperate to disassemble the table's mechanism, to show that the cell's fundamental engines create living purpose and not the other way around. To demonstrate that blind atomic bumping can lead to anything, even sight. Long before love coiled him he felt desire, a catalyst posted from the beginning of the genetic record, bringing the parts of his substrate inexorably together. However differently his life might have unfolded, he could not have long survived the need to refuse surfaces, to come closer than flush. In the sum of their catalyzed reactions, his choir of molecular autonoma sang, *Bloody your hands. Get past it.* What would it mean to leave this place, really leave it? That is his coding problem. The message I eavesdrop on, still vibrating on the wires.

The molecular engines—still not all named by the week he died—begin to say who he was at fifty, the work he had yet to do back up the steps of the living hierarchy, here at organism level. His traits, my own, Todd's, lie tangled in the shape of proteins. But the triumph of biological reductionism, the grounding of living

371

things on molecular necessity, the establishment of chance as the mainspring of change, each successive tier rising seamlessly from the previous, still leaves me something inexplicable at the top: after curiosity, impulse, restlessness—his ability to give it all up.

My friend possessed deep in the coils of his cell an urge to unite the natural world in one internally consistent model. He hid the compulsion for years. But our showdown, forced on us, revived for a moment his attempt to put hands through the pane, a need always stronger than its decoding. Years after he thought he'd come home from the commute for good he returned to the thick of the search. His last days—and every day I knew him was one of his last—shone with all the surprise of the cybernetic enzyme. After a quarter century he was back, pitting himself against the lookup table. And this time, something more: submitting to it a uniquely landscaped command.

I Have Become a Stranger to the World

In our walking days, I talked to more perfect strangers than I ever had before or since. Todd was intent on single-handedly reviving the custom of greeting people on the street. In the city, this was tantamount to taking one's own life. But we always got away with it, and I was amazed at how many people greeted back as if old friends. We had long talks about election rigging with news vendors, exchanges over dog disobedience with retirees, leisurely debates about Western history with men in three-piece suits who must have had more important places to be. Once, we were riding the local next to a man whom Todd induced into telling us all about his combat experience in Asia. Giving us the blow-by-blow of his tour of duty, the vet asked Todd suspiciously, "What do you do?" When Franker lied, "Art history," the man let out his breath. "Good. Can't hurt me with that." Todd talked to anyone, on any excuse. Cabbies, police, Englishless immigrants, bank officials, drunks—an endless dialogue with people I'd never have spoken to alone.

I was now free to see Franklin every hour I wasn't working. He came by the library, late afternoons before he started his shift. These were my least productive hours of the day; had I not had an excellent track record, I would have been reprimanded. Sometimes, to save my job and to keep him from putting his hands down my shirt where I sat at the Reference Desk, I would send him into the shelves with questions. I remember giving him "Who was Leslie Lynch King, Jr.?" Frank came back after an hour and a half, successfully identifying him as the thirty-eighth president of the U.S. "The Public," he shook his head angrily, "is a sadist."

We met everywhere, and soon had touched one another in as many places. The MOL office was still our haunt of choice. Following the disastrous system crash that cost both men a sleepless week, the machines returned to normal. Outside of island visits by Uncle Jimmy, Annie Martens, and the janitors, we reined in our shamelessness only for Dr. Ressler.

However genuinely the professor enjoyed our round tables— freewheeling wine-and-cheese talk spiraling to absorb the spread of international terrorism, the limits to sports record-breaking, and the nuances of surviving a certain late-night cashier at the corner convenience store—he seemed as genuinely relieved when conversation ended. More often than not, he wound up, saying, "You two must excuse me. I have to supervise the workings of the North American financial network." And he would return to the gigabytes, leaving Franker and me alone to escalating experiment.

We pressed against each other, each day more blatantly, feeling the short fuse evaporate, postponing, restraining the way a bud shimmies under time lapse before falling into flower. Following an evening's wrestle, he would kiss me goodbye, dipping into my dress, saying he needed to fix my surface in his memory until he could see me again. We played deeply and dangerously. I found a meridian on his shoulders, the mere press of which made his muscles collapse and his eyes roll up. He came by but never stayed over; we were two passengers in a long-haul airport, consulting the array of world capital clocks, each still on his native time zone. My night of romance was his midday.

One night during lunch break he came to my room carrying a package he'd acquired downstairs just before my landlord's antique shop closed. I unwrapped the box to find an off-white eighty-year-old linen blouse that must have set him back a month. Along its dorsal edge ran cloth-covered hemisphere buttons the size of ladybugs, hundreds of them. The high choker owed its origins to Alexandra's tracheotomy. It rippled with multiple traceries, ruffles under ruffles that, as they could not actually be seen once the blouse was on, could only have been, like those exceptionally skilled adventures in heavy counterpoint, for the express benefit

373

of those privileged to hold the score in front of them.

"Try it on," he commanded. I hesitated, but just for pacing. I went to the bedroom, stood in my closet, the mirrored door left conspicuously open, and stripped to my underclothes. Even these I changed for the antique slips and skirts I had collected piece by piece, on account with my landlord. In a few minutes, I was clothed in a soft, lost century. But the effect was not yet done. I sat down at my vanity (another piece rescued from downstairs), pulled my hair up in a storybook pile, and made up lightly, with an eye toward the period. It took some time and extraordinary, wavering patience on both our parts.

When I stood and walked toward him, I knew we were done for. He'd watched the entire process, standing in the doorway, waiting to undo it. The clothes I had attended to so carefully shed themselves everywhere. Some stayed on, displaced and uncaring. Everything began to move slowly, underwater. I felt him, felt myself all over, both far away. Minutely mammalian, I conformed to fill every space between myself and this shape pressing against me. I could see the peach inside of his legs and sweated to match his breath condensing against the back of my neck. Strenuously, straining, but expansively, slowly, we worked, astonished to be recovering pneumatics from a manual we were born knowing. And something else to our rocking: an attempt to recall a word on the tips of our tongue. The word was *nihil*. The word was *nearly*. I felt his skin stretching, conductant, as smooth, hazel, and aromatic as the taste of food I craved for years but could never identify. My skin.

I kept waiting for my body to pitch me over those patent falls, the one I'd discovered at thirteen but which, by thirty, I still hadn't adjusted to. Instead, something unprecedented: as I realized I was invading, being invaded by, this man, that we'd surrendered to the thing we had been circling nervously for months, I was doused by first serum-surge; rather than sharpen to a cutting point, it spread, a thick, coffeed narcotic, into parts of my body I never knew existed. It vacillated, then intensified toward white, wider than I thought possible, for bottomless seconds before it faded into capillaries. I could not tell if I'd gone over or not. Stupid semantic. I was ionized.

We made love—copulated—at my apartment repeatedly over the nights that followed. I never recaptured that total diffusion, that month or later. I did catch brief bits and pieces before his body became more almond-familiar. That sustained current never reappeared, and I came in time to wonder if it had been somatic after all. The work we lavished on each other, hungry and needy, received reinforcement, often and diffuse and strange. More than enough to keep us coming back. Todd came frequently to my apartment, sometimes with more old clothes.

But it was some time before I ever set foot in his place. True, he lived in Lower Manhattan, while I lived in the neighborhood where we both worked. At last I invited myself. He was to cook for me, on a weekend we both had off. He agreed to the conditions, with whispered additional terms.

He lived in an attic—"loft" is the current euphemism—on a street straight out of "Bartleby." The corbled eccentricity of the place made him give up nicer rooms uptown, going from a relatively safe neighborhood into the heart of the urban experience. He greeted me at the street, walked me down the hall, parodying bachelor brazenness as soon as the apartment door closed. "Well. Here we are. Just throw that dress anywhere."

He took me on the lightning tour. His makeshift sitting room lay angled oddly against the back corner's fire escape. He had pitched a double bed in an old storage room and turned a large walk-in closet into a study. "Not much, but we call it home. All right: abode. Let's not niggle over terms." Museum-clutter suffused the place, somewhere between a Sotheby's halfway house and Turkish bazaar. A dumbwaiter, now dysfunctional, toted a Howdy Doody in pince-nez. Furnishings included a table made from a lobster pot, chairs made from conveyor belts, and a lilac-colored upright piano. Here and there were scattered convenience-store samplers of instant coffee, lip balm, shoe-odor pads: CARE packages dropped for a shipwreck who'd forgotten how to use them.

Art treasures—Brueghel's wheatfields and Vermeer's *Head of a Girl* prominent among them—covered every inch of his walls, and a few Tiepolo-type *trompe l'oeil*s even encroached on the ceiling. That popular seventeenth- and eighteenth-century genre, the picture gallery: one canvas crammed recursively with as many different miniature art masterpieces as could fit in the space allotted.

Not only prints: incomplete sets of Conrad and Scott, African kalimbas, a glass harmonica assembled from kit, dancing bears and Uncle Sams that swallowed dimes. Among the larger bric-a-brac was a seamstress's costume dummy from the 1920s, adjustable along all major axes. "Meet Theda Bara. I inherited her after the breakup of a college experiment in idealistic living." She had osmotically acquired a wardrobe: flapper skirt, feather boa, worn-out sneakers, a cocky hat fashioned from a post-office mailer, a brightly painted papier-mâché toucan nose, and a breastplate of buttons reading, among other things. "Liquid Courage, Not Liquid Paper." Against a wall of raw brick lay a hundred-gallon aquarium divided between soil and water. The dry land was given over to mosses, beetles, and skinks. Below lake line, turtles and eels swam oblivious of captivity. "I tried salt water once," he explained, "but it's more difficult to balance than you think."

I watched as he prepared a skillful dinner—Indonesian chicken, so he said, although it could easily have been ad lib. He chattered the while, not even stopping to answer the phone. "They'll call back. Do you think I could pass for an eighties man? The eighties man is sensitive. He wins women's hearts by saying such things as 'I feel a deep sadness welling up in me.' Do you think I'm in any position to win women's hearts?" He was nervous, profuse. I was happy, feeling how little I knew him.

We ate epically—two hours over dinner. He made me try three cabernets blindfold. We talked about his dissertation, long delinquent, and about how I had ended up in library science. When at last nothing graced the table but scraped dishes, he reached over, felt my belly, and nodded, satisfied. "All right then," he said, withdrawing his hand after only a modest amount of further exploration. "We have to talk about music now. You start." I could think of nothing but his violent reaction, on that first business dinner of ours so many months before, when the piped tape of Bach's little keyboard exercise had hurt his face so spontaneously. I wondered if it weren't music he wanted to talk about, but that taboo neither of us had raised since he first hired me to find Dr. Ressler in the historical register.

I shrugged. "I played the piano once. As you know."

Franklin smiled. "I played the accordion. I could make 'Five Hundred Miles' sound as if it had been transposed into kilometers. At eighteen, I applied to music conservatory. Chopin études on the squeeze box for my audition. Went to art school."

He looked at me, decided to get the worst out of the way. "You know, the professor came to music late in life. He says the whole enterprise caught him by surprise. Other noises, other tunes. Said he spent years committing to memory the entire repertoire. But somewhere along the way, he's pared Western music down to just

376

what he can carry." His voice fell, forced-cheery. Todd shook his head.

But this time, we didn't stop at Dr. Ressler's collapse into the microcosm of those few dozen measures. He became animated, demanding to know my favorite pieces. I gave over a couple hostages. He accused me of being hopelessly stuck on mainstream war-horses. He challenged me with a dozen composers, none of whom were more than names to me. "These are the folks who are writing music right now. Your contemporaries. But who bothers listening? We're reduced to the three-minute unison synthesizer banks while an electronic drum loop programmed to bash out every other beat mercifully drowns out the hermaphrodite wailing about how it feels good to feel bad. It's a war zone out there. Lose-lose situation. Another concert hall rendition of Finlandia for folks with the heavy jewelry on the one hand, and three anemic teenagers called 'The Styro Detritus' on the other."

In a minute, he recovered. "The trick to listening," he said, lifting me by the hand, "is to hear the pieces speaking *to one another*. To treat each one as part of an enormous anatomy still carrying the traces of everything that ever worked, seemed beautiful awhile, became too obvious, and had to be replaced. Music can only mean anything through other music. You have to be able to hear in Stockhausen that homage to the second Viennese school, in Schönberg the rearrangement of sweet Uncle Claude. And every new sleeper that Glass welds together gives new breath to that rococo clockmaker Haydn, as if only now, in 1980, can we at last hear what pleasing the Esterhazys is all about."

He was performing for me. By then we were in the bedroom, but for a wholly different seduction than we'd explored at my place. Franklin's dirty clothes were stacked into prim piles, interleaved with notebooks. He cleared away a state-of-the-art turntable, expensive but not well cared for. He went to the top shelf of his closet. There, stretching from end to end where the sweaters usually went, was a wall of records, arranged by spine color in rainbow spectrum. He dug out a disk, mumbling, "Have a seat. No. Take the bed. Lie down and close your eyes."

I did as instructed. Eyes closed, I heard everything: Todd shuffling the record jacket, the domestic argument in the flat downstairs, the sound of breaking bottles, someone being sick in the street below, Dr. Ressler putting up a disk pack on a spindle across town, the first snow of the year falling on my mother's Midwest grave. I heard the hollow of high-fidelity speakers, the muffled pop of needle touching, and the sandy scuttling of crabs across the worn record surface.

A deep harp pulse, then a double reed, followed by a muted horn choir: before I realized that the piece had started, a door opened beneath me, and I fell effortlessly into another place. An orchestral work, but deployed in a chamber, slower and more melancholy than any music I've ever heard, a sound written after the history of the human race was only a faint memory.

I didn't possess the sophistication to say when it *had* been written. I didn't even worry it. The notes took occupancy, a horizon of tones stretching in all directions; I was at the center of the sound. Someone was singing, a contralto, although it took me measures before I identified *voice* as that new, ravishing instrument that had entered. She sang in a language I didn't know but understood perfectly. The song was so agonizingly drawn-out—sustained loss unfolding in the background of a peaceful scene—that I couldn't make the pulse out. One measure became eight; eight crystallized into sixteen. I knew that sound: the last day of the year.

> Ich bin der Welt abhanden gekommen
> Mit der ich sonst viele Zeit verdorben;
> Sie hat so lange nichts von mir vernommen,
> Sie mag wohl glauben, ich sei gestorben....
>
> Ich bin gestorben dem Weltgetümmel
> Und ruh' in einem stillen Gebiet.
> Ich leb' allein in meinem Himmel,
> In meinem Lieben, in meinem Lied.

I couldn't say how long it lasted; I was stunned to learn later that it took less than ten minutes. Just as the tune seemed reconciled to ending, its texture thinned to nothing, the strings waited on the verge of resolution, that reed hung on a suspension, and the whole chord stood still in space, frozen, refusing forever to give up the moment of quick here now. Then the portal closed; I came back to this man's room, all the noises of his apartment and the street, noises I had designed my life around not hearing.

He waited a suitable moment before ruffling the silence. "Well? What was that all about?" Didn't he know already? I snapped my head up, opened my eyes, saw him again in the corner of the room, sitting amid his notebooks and clothes and rummage treasures. He hadn't moved during the piece. Had he meant to use the music to win me, heart and frozen soul, he could not have succeeded better with my assistance.

"I don't know," I answered sharply. I closed my eyes and let my head drop back to the bed. "I don't speak German."

He laughed at my hostility. "Not the text, goof. The music. What does that *tune* mean?"

I was auditioning all over again. I was to tell him what that frozen chordal unfolding contained. Against my will, I wanted to answer correctly. Wanted badly. But anything I might say would be wrong. I kept still and waited, knowing that the least sound would give me away. I could think of nothing to add to the notes. But my interviewer waited just as patiently for the thing he wanted from me. I would have hummed that infinitely patient theme out loud by way of explaining what it meant, if I thought my voice could carry it. I said nothing for as long as nothing was possible, then came out with, "It's about leaving."

Todd sat up. "I've been waiting forever for someone to hear that." Unable to leave well enough alone, he added, "The most beautiful delaying gesture ever written."

He identified the tune as one of the *Rückert Lieder* by Mahler. He would play it again for me later, under different circumstances, when it would sound completely changed. But this time, over the sea in America, in 1983, in a cluttered, unzoned apartment, between two people who couldn't, despite themselves, have the first idea of what was going on out *there,* in the real house of cartels, conspiracies, and national states, it sounded completely out of place and time: a round, bitter, beautifully inviting rearguard action against loss. But we didn't understand, yet, just how much there was to lose.

"*Ich bin der Welt abhanden gekommen,*" he said, coming over to where I waited. "I have gotten lost in the world. Although *der Welt,* feminine, seems to be in the dative: maybe 'to the world.' *Abhanden* is definitely not the tantalizing choice: abandoned. False cognates. *Faux amis,* as the Germans would say, if they were French."

I hated him at that moment. His arrogance ruined for me what sound I could still just make out. Truth was, I was not a native speaker. I had studied it once, but had gotten nowhere. Had he played any other piece, I would have heard little, maybe nothing at all. I would have flunked the audition if the piece he'd chosen hadn't been so clearly a sound track for the only thing on God's earth I have an ear for. I wanted to be outside in the cold. I wanted to be by myself, in the apartment I had left a man to get. To die away from the world's noises, to live alone in a quiet place. In that song.

Todd kept chattering amiably, as if I were another of his news vendors or street drunks. I wanted him to stop talking, but he wouldn't. He jabbered on about the composer, the exhaustion of romanticism, the absolute distrust Americans have come to feel toward European culture, toward their own past. He prompted me to join in, but I snubbed the invitation. He prodded me again, but a look from me cut the game dead. He stood, went to the window, and stared at something farther than the neighborhood. He squinted, looking for that metaphor, the outside world with its untraceable, newsprint, global urgencies closed off to us, hermetically sealed. "But I *do* love you," he said. I was the only person within earshot.

"Thank you. I mean, for. . . ." I gestured at the record player with a wrist. He turned to look at me. I saw in his face the evidence he'd been denying since the day he came by the library to ask about a disappearing man. I understood that all the people he spread himself out over—the cashiers, the subway vets, the three-piece-suiters, college friends held at phone's distance, everyone who elicited that uncalculated, soliciting, contagious charm—were grapples, last-ditch efforts to reverse the departure he was well into. He had the Ressler gene, recessive, latent, but irreversible.

He returned the record to the closet shelf. "I have become a stranger to this place," he said, not daring to look at me. I realized later that he was trying again to translate the song text, quote of the day.

XVIII

Canon at the Sixth

"Does it have any side effects?" he asked one night in my room, our habitual place for love. We lay still straddled; I crouched exhausted on top of him. Although subzero outside, we were moist from exertion. Sex, slack and slow, expansive, aesthetic, like serious wine tastings where nothing gets drunk but everything sampled, sometimes turned fierce for no reason, vocal, frantic, a muscle purge. The first such escalation scared the daylights out of us. Neither had initiated any change of pace, but all of a sudden we were both running hard, testing the edge of control. The more frightening it became, the more wildly we went at each other. Afterwards, still winded, I murmured about not knowing he was a sprinter.

"Sprinter? 'Hurdler' wouldn't half say it. You get that from a book? Private reference?" I made an embarrassed pun about open circulation. After that, even our most passive encounters—wide-eyed stroking—had a whiff of danger, as if anything could trigger fierce surprise.

Following such an outbreak, we lay motionless in my room, awkward in the impossible non sequitur, the return to nonchalance. The behavioral masterstroke, more crucial to human evolution than the opposable thumb: the ability to pretend that nothing just happened, that there is no seam. "Does it have any side effects?" he asked in the dark, after geologic pressing desperate enough to crystallize carbon. He could make himself obscure in half a dozen languages, including his mother tongue.

"Hair on my palms, you mean?"

"Can it do that?" he blinked.

381

"Can *what* do that?" Even reaching the conclusion that we didn't get each other was endlessly difficult.

He leaned toward me confidentially. "Safeguarding." I stared, unable to crack the euphemism. "Here we've been happily tilling the fields for weeks, with nary a mention of prevention. That leaves, to my knowledge, only two possible methods by which you...." His speech ground to a halt. He locked eyes and stuttered, "Uh-oh."

I laughed a monosyllable. "Idiot."

"I suppose I should have asked beforehand, huh?" He was abashed only a second. "Which is it then? I don't want you using anything that's going to give you...."

"Don't worry."

"What do you mean, don't worry? I'm worrying."

"We don't have to worry about pregnancy. Or any birth-control side effects." We dressed slowly. I stood looking outside, wishing for all the world that we could go for a walk.

After a respectable pause for a man, Todd broke into Cockney constable. "What's all this then?"

I faced him, as self-possessed as a health professional. "I had a ligation."

"You *what?*" Dead silence. "You're not even thirty."

"Pretty soon," I said, suddenly too girlish.

We lay back on the bed, fully clothed. He put tentative fingers through my hair. "Mind if I ask...?" I waited placidly, relaxed, until he put it in so many words. "What prompted you...or did you need to?"

"No. Tuckwell and I decided that, with our lives, our careers, we would never do well with babies."

"But I didn't think.... Did you expect...? Did you think you would live with him forever?"

I snorted—a sharp exhalation that expanded my lungs as it emptied them. "Evidently I must have, on our good days."

"Jesus. One of you must have been pretty certain. I mean, 'permanent' means...."

I discarded the argument that the operation could conceivably be reversed. The odds against that loophole made it irrelevant. Permanent meant permanent. "He had nothing to do with it, really." I was sorry I'd mentioned Keith at all, ashamed to have tried to palm off on him an interest in the decision. "It was all me. The idea of passing on accumulated adult knowledge to a helpless

382

infant—how to expectorate phlegm and not swallow it, how to tell the difference between 'quarter to' and 'quarter after,' how to stay off the stove, how to tell when people were trying to hurt them—was too much. I couldn't see myself selecting all those clothes and birthday presents year after year, keeping them from inserting screwdrivers in electrical outlets, nursing them through the destruction of favorite toys."

"Jan. No. You're joking." Franklin was pale, shaking. "Motherhood is tough, so you tied your tubes!"

I could have crushed him with one word. It would never be *his* pregnancy. He wasn't even responsible enough to have thought of prevention. The male model of parenthood: everything between ejaculation and tossing the football with the twelve-year-old is trivial. The matter didn't concern him in the least. The fight had begun, after all, with his wanting to *avoid* contributing to any child of mine. I had made an irreversible decision, a choice self-evident at the time, one that would have been made for me anyway in a few more years. I did not care to reproduce, and although I was still relatively young, removing that possibility meant clearing the anxiety from my remaining sexual life.

"How hard would it have been to leave the door open...? Bad metaphor. Sorry." Todd smiled queasily, about to be sick. "I mean: as negative life insurance, the pill would have been cheap at the price. Suffer the less radical premiums for a couple years, against the outside payoff if you change your mind. Or partner," he added sadly, touching me on a flank already changed to terra-cotta.

I shook my head. Having come this far, all I could do was explain the variable that had swung the calculation. I told him why it was not a question of my mind or situation changing. A few years before, I'd found on the Question Board a request for the latest scientific line on mongolism. My first response was mild irritation; any modestly educated adult ought to have been able to find a satisfactory answer within minutes. I started at the obvious place, followed the well-marked trail through reliable sources, and delivered the broadly established explanation: Down's syndrome is the result of trisomy—a third chromosome 21. Airtight, complete, exact. I couldn't imagine improving upon it.

But the day after I posted this answer, the board carried a follow-up: What causes trisomy? I felt ashamed at not answering the first question at all. I went back to the sources, beginning to appreciate the issue, how much subtlety the research in fact required. The immediate mechanism was undoubtedly genetic. But nature and nurture were not entirely distinct. That extra chromosome, research suggested, may in turn be the result of an older ovary in which chromosome 21 fails to separate in egg formation. I attached a rider to the first explanation: chromosomal non-disjunction, while not entirely understood, increased in frequency in proportion to the mother's age.

Two days later, a third question: How old is an at-risk mother? "I was exasperated," I told Todd, crawling back under the weight of his arms. "Someone was putting me through the hoops. You know: like a child, repeating 'why?' until the word evaporates?" Todd shook his head, made me continue.

The day after the third question, before I could form a definitive response, a woman materialized at the Reference Desk asking if I was J. O'D. She reached down into a stroller and lifted an infant for me to inspect. The child had the unmistakable spatulate features of deformity. She said she was twenty-three.

"I could still see, for probably the last week, a faint profile of normal boy already being drowned out by the crosstalk of that extra twenty-first chromosome. I finally knew what she was asking. Was it her fault? I asked what her doctors had told her. Her answer destroyed me: 'They're less helpful than you.' I spent the rest of the afternoon with the two of them. I showed her how to follow the citations, and we pushed them hard. At the end, we discovered two distinct etiologies. The first was sporadic, without inheritance patterns, some slow, possibly viral cause. The second, the minority of cases, was a permanent chromosomal attachment in the mother, a translocation trisomy, a fluke of a fluke that struck mothers of all ages equally.

"After some hours, I apologized: the library would have to be a lot more current and specialized, I myself would have to have a medical degree to move her any closer. But by then she was almost grateful, having learned along the way about cretinism, microcephalia, PKU, anencephaly, spina bifida. Oh, Jesus! The whole, grisly catalog."

In the middle of the list I broke down, scaring Todd witless. He sat by helplessly, uncertain whether to comfort or cower in a corner. I tried to compose myself, aggravating the shakes. My voice was still wild when I spoke again. "The girl thanked me for the one promising bit anyone had thrown her since her boy's birth.

The books said that an extra twenty-first often leaves mongols with the sweetest dispositions."

Todd did not need the rest spelled out. The endless catalog of things that can go wrong—so comforting to this woman, whose punishment began to look like commutation—had killed me. I felt a dread I previously couldn't have imagined. Because of a lucky statistical aberration, because I and everyone close to me had been born healthy, I had assumed that childbearing was a perfected process with a few tragic accidents impinging on the periphery. I now saw that the error-free lived on a tiny, blessed island of self-delusion. I could hear my own mutations accumulating; it was either hurry into a baby-making I was not ready for, or wait, Russian roulette, for my own blueprint to betray me.

Lying in the dark, I felt the revulsion return with full force. As at his apartment, listening to that Viennese song, I heard how we lived in a room of privileged music above the screaming street. I closed out the syllogism, wishing I'd stuck with the less defensible line that I'd sterilized myself because I hadn't the time or patience to bear children. "I told Tuckwell I was going in for the operation. He didn't argue. It never occurred to me to consult anyone else." Least of all one I hadn't met yet.

I watched Franklin's face as he assembled the facts. Something had been broken; but the thing was done, and even he was smart enough to see that he would only break things worse by probing. "Well," he said at length. "That answers my original question." The time for theory was over. All that was left was practice, and we fell back to working over one another's bodies again, more circumspectly this time. That night, at least, there were no side effects.

Friends of the Family

She must still be a benign, lovely woman. From the day I met her, Annie Martens struck me as impossibly well-adjusted. She worked as a remote teller for MOL's mother bank, entering the financial world's dirty linen that Todd and Ressler washed every night. She seemed perfectly happy with that deadly-dull career, preferring it to anything more ambitious. She would have gladly accepted a demotion for the good of the firm.

She was suspiciously sunny for this city. Her only claim to psychopathology involved an early marriage, which had ended in amicable divorce the year before. Uncle Jimmy reported from the day shift that the abandoning mate persisted in meeting Annie every day for lunch. The uncomplicated woman was happy to hold hands and neck in the corridor with her ex as if a newlywed.

She was infinitely patient, cohabiting comfortably with the incomprehensible, her face wearing the perpetual surprise of Mary ambushed at her prayers. She had a deep, throaty laugh, like underground water. She was intuitively musical; we often listened to her wrap herself angelically around a guitar and produce, in round pitches, old frontier songs about wandering, gambling, or brutal stabbings of love objects. Even I loved her when she played. Her face radiated. She closed her eyes when she sang, inhabiting a garden far away.

Annie had no faults except a propensity to speak incoherently. She punctuated her small talk with advertising slogans: "Betcha can't eat just one," or "Even your friends won't tell you." She was, Franker assured me, impossible to take anywhere, because she unconsciously read all wayside text out loud until the patter became intolerable. This habit explained how her husband could sue for divorce without losing his affection for the woman.

There was something else that took me months to put my finger on. She liked aphorisms, annoying if forgivable in themselves. But she could not reproduce these clichés accurately. The errors were easily missed. To recount amazement, she'd exclaim, "I flipped my wing." She'd crack a joke without apparent punchline, laugh throatily, and conclude, "That went over like a wet balloon." When Jimmy teased her, she responded, "Watch it. You're walking on thin eggshells."

Once her problem became apparent, listening to her filled me with embarrassment at the whole race. She was not a stupid woman; her problem was not imbecility in an environment requiring alertness. Rather the reverse. She was born in 1963, a year I'm old enough to remember. The date itself consigned her to another era. Todd, five years older, slipped in under the wire, old enough to know that the world is racing toward the most crucial drop since Galileo. Annie was too young to know what the good fight was and certainly would never have fought it without us.

The paintings that made Franklin's life palatable to him, that opened up a channel to a resonant past, Annie knew instinctively to be treacherous impostors. She was a matter-of-fact woman, loving what was at hand and not at all awed by what was not. Sfumato mystery, the flame of the past scumbled around her in a Washington Heights pastiche of the Cluny cloisters. *La Gioconda* munching on corn chips. *Great Expectations* abridged to fit on ninety-minute car cassette. Stains spreading into underarms to Beethoven's Fifth. Mozart's in the closet: let 'im out, let 'im out, let 'im out.

She was true to the culture she was born into, truer than Todd, who has abandoned it. She was endowed with a great capacity for care. She could cry at pop tunes and laugh at Yellow Pages ads. Her sloganeering, her mangled proverbs, her utter incomprehension of irony, her ability to recite "Buckle up for safety" as if it were a Pater Noster, marked in her genuine humanism. Along with the clear forehead and angelic chin came a propensity for what her how-to manuals called "personal engagement." The news account of a zoo giraffe that had died in copulation almost shattered her. She loved things. Anything. Rain showers. Pretty stationery. Sandwich wrappers. Her Doberman, ten pounds heavier than she was. Anything nearby and knowable Annie cared for indiscriminately with all her heart.

The need to distribute surplus care led her to sacrifice personal preference to prescribed taste. In another time or place, she might have fixed as easily on Shaw as she did on Burma-Shavian quatrain. Nothing mattered except giving compassion in the available dialect. I can't imagine what pleasure she found in staying around after hours, eavesdropping on the roundtable rotogravure. She couldn't have had the first idea of what those men were up to. When I saw her with them, wading bravely into cross-purpose conversation, I felt I was witnessing one of those confrontations beloved of science fiction: carbon-based life meets living silicon. She would clip shirt ads for Franker as a way of telling him his were hopelessly worn out, and admonish a startled Dr. Ressler about the dangers of smoking. She confided in me that the two fascinated her because they minced no bones.

She would have made herself a satellite of whoever was at hand. Todd, in one of his rare, Orphic ascents into the day shift, had accosted this stranger just as he did so many streetsweepers, cabbies, and commuting power brokers, demanding a full working account of her machine, her job, her sensibilities, and her life. That, followed by the requisite lunch, and Annie became a devoted friend. Words so freely given were to her a pact with him and all his friends. The casual contact he was so good at made Todd something real for her, not ever to be wholly understood, but cared for.

I often thought that Uncle Jimmy would have been Annie's ideal mate. They were both obliviously gentle people. They might have offered one another some protection against events. Even Todd suggested the idea to him: "Take her out to a show. See what happens."

Jimmy laughed him off. "Are you mad? I'm old enough to be the girl's father." The difference in their years was not great. But Annie was still a child and Jimmy already an old lady. He did, in fact, carry a torch for her, a crush that made him even more puppyish than usual whenever she was in the room. He flirted with her shyly, as he did with every woman who came through the suite of offices. "Have a boyfriend yet? Must be half a dozen guys who would jump at a chance to dance with the likes of you." Annie would say that she was ready anytime, say that evening. Jimmy would excuse himself, insisting that his expert supervision was required just then by the night shift. "Other men get to play with the ladies. Me, I've got to keep this ship running."

In fact, he was a nuisance, and every hour he stayed on into the shift cost Ressler and Todd two on the other end, in the early a.m. He liked to organize the stockroom and the card deck library, to create new rotation systems for the disk packs. Each scheme led to complete confusion. He would call his infirm mother. "These night-shift boys have fouled things up again; don't look for me until late."

Jimmy caught me in possession of the door password again, but this time resigned himself to my coming and going. I had free rein to let myself into the computer room as if I were on salary. A few nights after my confession to Todd, I arrived to find the entire population missing. Someone, in theory, was supposed to be laundering the day's data at all times. I sat and waited, thinking that the shift must have stepped out to an all-night sandwich dive. A minute later, all digital hell broke loose. Sys B began making the distress ah-oo-gahs of a wounded submarine. The spindles on Sys A powered up and the console spit cathode fireworks. Helpless, I ran to the screen, thinking I might at least jot down error codes. The screen erupted in animated celebration:

Our Dearest O'Deigh. Welcome to the median. The U.S. Bureau of On-Line Statistics assures us that 30 splits the country in half. As usual, you're right on the fence. Get out of that frilly blur of an apartment and acquire a mortgage. Accumulate some debt. Numbers compel you to do something middling. . . .

The display was amazing: letters grew, skidded across the screen, recombined into new words, surged in normal distribution curves, twisted into visual syntax, "fence" forming one for "you" to sit on, "frilly blur" dissolving into one, "debt" coming out gothic, "middling" in Times Roman. The letters exploded into life, accompanied by bells and whistles on the terminal speaker:

Happy B-day. We hope that 30 is your most profound variation yet. Never forget that you are living at life's critical instant. Your fellows in aging, SRESSLER & FTODD

Then the screen went blank, came back with its inscrutable system prompt politely inquiring "Command?" I looked up from the console and clenched a fist at the initiators, doubtless observing behind the two-way mirror. Todd came out, followed by a sheepish Ressler. I cold-shouldered Todd, addressed the professor. "How did you do that?" He shrugged: all Boolean. A matter of access.

I wheeled on Todd. "How did you know it was my birthday?"
"You told me."
"I only said it was coming. How did you get the date?"
He grinned, thick with significance. "We looked it up."

Operation Santa Claus

Blake's departure hits Cyfer hard. The lab is poorer without the force of his arbitrating humor, his even keel. The defection makes the remaining members suspect they've been kidding themselves; chemical inheritance will evade them. To restore morale, Ulrich turns the last Blue Sky session of 1957 into a Christmas party. He invites other department members, staff, favored graduate students: anyone who might keep the remaining team from staring at one another in stunned silence.

Christmas is an odd holiday to be observing, intent as they are on substituting a molecular model for the miraculous winter birth.

389

Nevertheless, they go through the motions, set out a wassail bowl, paper cups depicting Santa Claus in various postures of levity, a herd of wax reindeer, and a university record player on which Toveh Botkin, music committee, keeps up a stream of modal progressions insisting glad tidings of great joy.

Ressler wants to know how it has come to pass, despite his friend's exit, the flicker of the tired capacitance lights, Sputnik standing in as Nativity Star, the daily radioed word of low-level violence decimating the unwatched flocks by night, that Christmas still lodges itself so deeply under his skin. It can't be the fugitive baby on the run from the authorities, a story he saw through when not much older than the infant in question. Still, he finds himself steeped in the crusty old four-parters Botkin churns out on the turntable. Their modulations draw him toward the pitiful speakers, exhalation of synchronized air through the trachea suggesting chords that might lift the edge of the translation table for a quick look. These medieval intervals, a fossil record of his dazed arrival here in this room of reagents and gauges, this change of venue, with no quantitative test for discerning the way back. A camaraderie he wishes he could admit: he too, smothered in the stink of gingerbread and pine needles, lapsing into Lydian under forever unangeled skies, might be culpable, guilty of trying to reach beyond his grasp, of attempting to comprehend something he can't hope to name, something that might better be left to metaphor, myth, popular fiction, the beautiful counterfeit.

At the record player, he asks Botkin with his eyes for an explanation. His old friend raises her finger. At the end of the current tune, she slaps on another sprightly chorale. "Samuel Scheidt," she identifies. "From the *Köln Gesangbuch,* early seventeenth century." Ressler cocks an eyebrow at her, uncomprehending. The piece has some slight charm, aura of otherworldliness. But as full of leftover Renaissance censer scent as this tune is, it cannot minister. It has no healing power, no explanation.

Botkin notes his confusion. "Wait. Wait." She musses about in the cardboard sleeves and pulls out another disk. "O Jesulein Süss." She drops the needle down on exactly the same tune. Only everything different. The thing now arches and breathes, soars through agonizing suspensions, pours across a new, unexpected support in the bass, moves its four lines independently yet in a coordinated harmonic terrace of beauty. "Bach," she says, shrugging, the attribution self-evident.

The two works differ as a salt crystal and a spider's web. Scheidt, competent craftsman, labors on a carved doll that, however lifelike, remains wooden, while the other joiner need only apply the lightest imaginable touch to transform the clunky melody, lift the crippled thing to life. "A cradle song," Botkin glosses. "Composers cut their eyeteeth on chorales. No musical form is less sophisticated. A year of theory and you could churn them out blindfold. Bach manufactured them by the hundreds. And yet...." She points to the turntable, as if the secret behind the miraculous transformation searing Ressler lies there. On the vinyl. In the vibrating diamond.

Just as she is about to make the critical point, to identify what turns beats into *beating*, Toveh is interrupted by Dan Woytowich. He grabs them both in a friendly embrace, happier than Ressler has ever seen him, happy enough to be another person. The only happy soul in the room. Team setback can't touch him. Wife Renée, after losing two first-trimester fetuses, has finally passed the danger point and is on her way to making the couple a family. Woyty has chosen the party to announce, sure that this time the news will not turn out premature.

"Christmas music: is that the topic here? You two hear about the phantom of Urbana? Yesterday's paper. Two undergrads walking on the quad at night in the snow hear this harpsichord tinkling. Nowhere in the world it could come from. But they both hear it, and track it down, with difficulty, to one of those cast-iron grates in the sidewalk. Turns out a fellow's been living down in the steam tunnels for months. Persian rugs, stuffed chair, harpsichord, candelabra, bookshelves full of classics pinched from the library."

Ressler listens to the transformed Woyty. After a bit more banter, he excuses himself. The snippet of excruciating chorale, Toveh's interrupted explication, confirms it: some part of him has hemorrhaged. Companionship, connection to another is now as locked off as that beautiful halo of notes hanging above the winter cradle. He turns from the music, from his friend Botkin, from grinning Woytowich, turns into the decorated lab. Clots of partygoers, the forced gaiety of holiday streamers close the matter. He wanders the lab, *a priori* lost; it's not miraculous birth all these desperate preparations are for, not birth at all. Each face swinging to greet him is etched with the same scrimshaw hysteria. The thought of doing his bit for this outfit repulses him. Behind the sickening mélange of aromas—the light *Euglena* petri mildew, the smoky paraffin and dye of burning reindeer, the sweet-greasy thermoplastic mistletoe, the unguent perfumes, hair oil, deodorant, skin lotion, the beakers of astringent and rinsing acids, furtive fart vapor trails—is a smell so stand-out that not even this richness can smother it: the mammal-gland emission, out-and-out animal bafflement at being left here, spoorless, to toast in another New Year.

Then another scent, as neutral as air. Thin aromatic hydrocarbon, one part per billion in the room, catalyzes him. The smell fits; he knows it. There, shining from a corner, standing out against the sepia clumps of conversation, a still spot in the sea of relayed distress, a face as familiar to him as speech. Clear as the cold, cloudless night, a lucid journey of features framed in a shell of hair, eyes that flash recognition, that have been marking him all along, a mouth smiling broadly at his rush of relief, a young head shaking at him in wonder, in pure pleasure from across the room, announcing one, unambiguous certainty: be of good cheer.

Jeanette. *His* Jeannie. He can no longer keep away. Nor can he remember, so strong is this welcome home, why he needed to. He forces his way through the celebrants, drawn to her north. She takes a few steps to him, verifying: inevitable. In the blaring secrecy of this public place, she places the flat of her palm across his ribs. "I love you," he tells her. He expects her to spring fawnlike at the snap of a tree branch, the flush of this snare. Instead, she melts against him, catches her breath.

"Don't say it," she answers. She looks up, all forgiveness. She moves her hand minutely against him. With that gesture, she assumes all blame, confesses to a symmetrical wedge. She lowers her eyes, awaiting further sentence. Every program in his body, every enzyme, every gemule collaborates on synthesizing a single biophor: take this woman and kiss her. He does, here in the middle of danger, hard, moist, lasting. Empty symbol, leading nowhere, appeasing only the immediate edge of hunger, explodes in his brain. A hand grasps his shoulder and he steels himself to receive the blow. But it is not the enemy, the legitimate complement to this jean-home. It is Joe Lovering, pulling Ressler out of the clinch.

"OK, Buddy. Move over." Ressler, reeling, looks up where Joe points: a dismal piece of plastic mistletoe. The crowd around them smiles indulgently. Jeanette straightens his tie. He backs off, dizzy. Lovering steps into his place, looking over his shoulder confidentially as he takes his turn at grabbing Jeanette. "Sandy doesn't need to hear anything about this," he winks to Stuart.

After preliminary recon, Lovering launches his frontal campaign.

To Ressler's horror, Jeanette kisses the cretin back, with a laugh of anonymous pleasure in the license. Of course: she has to. Protective coloration, or they are both exposed. But her easy subterfuge makes him crazy. Lovering at last breaks off, pronouncing, "Hmm. In Sandy's league. Could substitute in a pinch. But doesn't quite ring the bell one hundred percent."

"Thank you very much," Koss sniffs. Lovering goes on to regale them with his astonishment at actually being more fixated on the polymorphous Sandy than when she was still a veiled novelty, so many months ago. Koss and Ressler ignore him. Unflapped, Joe snags a cup of wassail. "What *is* this stuff?" Lovering swills a mouthful, cocks his head contemplatively, and declares, "1889 Jolly Roger Green. Cheeky bouquet. Sandy's a great wine connoisseur. Me, all I know is 'Beer then whiskey, pretty risky. Whiskey then beer, never fear.'"

Koss blinks, rests a sympathetic hand on Lovering's shoulder. "Joey, it might be furlough time." Lovering downs another glass and goes on to perform combinatorial studies on the gifts from "The Twelve Days of Christmas."

Ressler mingles, his gaze scrambling back to the buoy of Jeanette's. She catches his glance with one just as helpless: *Where can we go? We need to talk.* He checks his watch; how long can the bash last? He is cornered by Ulrich and Woytowich, the euphoric father-to-be. Anxious to follow up the coup of the first paper, they are debating the next step: might the table be based on a supersymmetry of purines and pyrimidines? Never angels and shepherds for very long.

His earthbound colleagues exasperate Ressler. "Why don't we go in and have a look? Study the effect of positional havoc." He tries to take the edge out of his voice. "Induce point mutations along the length of the message. Compare the synthesized proteins. The words will fall like dominoes...."

He doesn't labor the ramifications of Ike's metaphor. The seniors smile in the thing's glare. Ressler receives, for his pedagogical pains, a clinical gaze. Woyty strokes his chin, scanning the notion for flaws. "We'd have to work out a few bugs, of course." Vogue expression, derived from the moth that crashed a complex program on one of the first sequential logic machines. Sent the coded instructions out into the electronic ether.

Ressler nods. He feels the blast of the kiln: *the* method, a complete experimental attack, all but here. He dies a slow death for

393

the chance to work it out with someone who'll grasp it, help him past the last hurdle. He bursts inside to diversify. Multiply, subdue with fruition. But he is alone—no ears to hear, no hands to understand. Except perhaps hers.

He slips out of the party, the mocked-up festive lab. He stands in the darkened hall, a hundred steps down, in a blind recess, waiting. Five minutes turns into an agonized ten. Surely she must have seen him leave. At last, she hurries out furtively, looking over her shoulder in fear, sheer erotic terror at being caught. He steps from his shadow. She stifles a shout and collapses into him, clinging.

"Listen," he orders. "*Nature,* 1955. Gale and Folkes. Test-tube protein synthesis. Incorporation. I told Tooney, before he left. He thinks it'll work. *We* place the sequence to study in glass. Out comes the offending enzyme."

"Shh," she says, convulsing rhythmically. "I love you." The sound of singing, candle scent from the far end of the hall. He holds her to him, all along his length. Her tangled hair, her face, her muscular shoulders, the small of her back, her upper legs. "Make up for lost time," she laughs, sniffling. She lets out a short, soft, pained cry midway between a howler monkey and a gothic angel's *et exultavit*. He signals her, unnecessarily in the dark: *Don't even say it.*

Deus ex Machina

Q: Who made me? Defensible evidence only please.

A molecule able to influence two others that would not react otherwise: can my miracle reside here? Does DNA, the map unfolding the whole organism, do no more than manufacture reagents, golem formulae, tinctures where soul emerges if the secret proportions are hit on? The code I am after must embody not just stuff but *substance:* process, decision, feedback. Not data alone; behavior at molecular level.

The lint-ball tangle of an enzyme—its charged terrain of twists and turns, vise-grips for welding chemical substrate—makes it a three-dimensional, supple machine. Here is the muse of fire I've been needing. Certain of these enzyme proteins become single-molecule transistors, devices that test and respond to feedback, creating a free repertoire from predictable physics. The assembled amino string of an allosteric enzyme can tangle into two different shapes. With unique twists in each shape, it thus possesses two separate sets of binding sites. The molecule may be enzymatically active in one shape and inert in the other, like a shoehorn that sometimes warps into worthlessness. A substance that binds to a site in either the active or inert shape will lock the enzyme into that configuration:

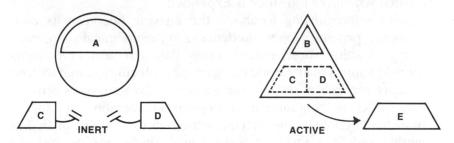

The inert shape of this enzyme has a binding site that fits substance A. The active shape has a site matching B as well as materials C and D that it transforms into product E. If A grabs the molecule first, it locks it into inert shape, eliminating those sites that accept the catalyzable materials. The enzyme is switched off, C and D can't bind, and manufacture of E stops. But if B first binds to the enzyme in active form, it locks the molecule into a shape with C and D's sites intact. The faucet is held open; the enzyme joins C and D into E so long as supplies of C and D exist.

Ressler's magic Boolean circuitry begins to emerge. The presence of A inhibits the manufacture of E; B promotes it. None of the compounds reacts with the enzyme itself; the machine remains unchanged except for switching on or off, always capable of switching back if the splint-substances detach. Even wilder: the inhibitors, promoters, and inputs, binding to independent sites, need have nothing to do with one another. A, B, C, D, and E can be *anything* at all. In theory, any chemical can be made to inhibit or promote the formation or degradation of any other. The effect can even be nonlinear; multiple binding sites on an enzyme could cause small amounts of compound to have enormous effects on the synthesis of others.

Here it is, my escape act from chemical necessity. Microcircuitry I can't begin to map: a single allosteric enzyme made up of a few hundred amino acids, weighing less than a million billionth of a gram, accepting multiple, graded inputs and producing nonlinear output, a free-floating if-then program. It smacks of religion to me.

But the conjuring act hasn't even begun. Link the logical feeds of an allosteric circuit together, and the molecule virtually lives. E, the reaction product, can be the same as A, the inhibitor. Every successful catalysis then shuts off the switch. Or E, used up by the body, might degrade into promoter B, ensuring that new E is created whenever old stock is expended.

With self-regulating feedback, the enzyme becomes its own economy, gauging supply and demand in the chemical soup, even acting to adjust these. I enter loops, linked regulatory patterns more ingenious than theistic design. One molecule's manufactured product can inhibit or promote another's. Two enzymes activate each other in conjunction or opposition. Metabolic pathways branch and conjoin, one enzyme setting off two others, or two in tandem combining to shut down a first. These *and, or,* and *not* operations create a complete propositional calculus.

Coordinated microprograms capable of changing their own environment, able to spring into production modes within an instant of encountering a trigger, create a cybernetic network powerful enough to initiate the impossibly articulated behavior of the composite cell. Q: Is the tracery of microprogramming networks too complex to have arisen through guided chance? Q: Is it complex enough to account for the autonomy that high-level enzyme by-products—Ressler, Todd, myself—all suffer from?

I've started four times today, on four separate sheets—what? Nothing. Trivial message strings going no farther than Dear Franklin. Even the adjective is problematic. After months, I have the man's address. I have a world of things to tell him. Nothing stops me. I *want* to write. But even today—Caesar crosses Rubicon, 49 B.C.—I can't. I won't. English doesn't have the modality to say what's keeping me. Writing him is fine, but words are out. A is too functional, B too forgiving. C and D are transparent excuses for E, which I will never bring myself to say to him again.

I own his mailbox, the lookup table to the one spot where he can be reached. If I could finish a fifth sheet, seal and mail it without reading... I could; I want to. The first letter of the first sentence, and I waver from one urge to the other. I am truly stochastic, indecisive. Do all inputs, computed, already drive me to one course or the other, or can they still be interfered with by some messy conglomerate circuit, *me*?

I try on Laplace's old dream—to solve the world through giant inference engine. Ressler, alert, talkative as I had never before seen him, racing through the data stacks looking for our place to cut, cracked a joke about the final triumph of the reductionist program. "NASA's eyes in the sky determine the vectors on every molecule of atmosphere. They feed all these numbers into a Cray, and the animal pounds away, megaflops, on a simulation that knows everything about adiabatic cooling, turbulence, vapor pressures, topography, solar radiation. The machine assembles and delivers a perfect prediction of tomorrow's weather. Only it takes two days to run."

The problem is irresistible. Do all my active enzymes plus the running average of the chemical soup they find themselves in, the jungle of bioeconomy (vast, uncatalogued tracts of electrochemical memory, mine and earlier), all the stimuli bombarding me from outside—the January sun's false springs out my window, the glass of water at my elbow (complete with Brooklyn reservoir heavy impurities), the feel of the keys under my fingers—do all these independent effectors sum to one unique output: write him or not? They couldn't sum to *more* than one outcome. What would it even mean to say the choice, the final cybernetic weighing were left open? Open to what? Whom?

I must be asking the question wrong. Any outcome, once reached, must have been decided *by* something. The sort of freedom I am talking about—Dear Franklin, Where are you? When can I see you? How long you have been away! Come home—must be constraint by another name. Constraint that jumps some complexity threshold. The molecules I look for need not be capable of *autonomous* behavior; the word, when pushed, probably has no meaning. But are they enough, in themselves, to escape the determinism of physical vectors? Do these microprograms, once fired up, always run the same way, water down an arroyo? Or can they self-determine, self-modify, rewrite their own program listings?

They can. Allosteric enzymes are themselves synthesized. The microtransistors are drawn up, tailored, detached, and sent into the fray by a macroprogram, the nucleotide sequence—semantic bursts of DNA thread. Worker bees, assembled by the queen in her hive, these hatchetmen, day laborers, have the critical ability to apply their logical toolboxes back on the master program. Allosteric proteins can bind to and influence DNA, inhibiting or

397

promoting the synthesis of allosteric enzymes themselves. I stare at purpose, at the molecular level. The running program—DNA synthesizing enzymes—creates and executes subroutines that double back, influence the way the master program executes, cascading into new subroutines, run-time solutions.

To the best of my metaphoric understanding, it goes like this. Codons along a stretch of DNA direct the sequencing of amino acids in a protein. This sequence constrains the lint-ball molecule to adopt one of two or more possible shapes. Held in one shape by an attached brace, its personality—the lure of its binding sites—is inert. But when that jamb is removed, the protein recoils, takes on a new surface. Part of that switched-on surface attaches to a segment of DNA, switching off that segment's instructions. The segment of code temporarily patched out could even be the one manufacturing the binding molecule itself. The substance that switches the protein's code-modifying abilities on and off theoretically could be anything, even the by-product of enzymes manufactured on that or other DNA segments. The master control and its agents combine to alter their own combined behaviors.

One allosteric enzyme, working by itself, is already a formidable machine, reactively linking unrelated substances. Thousands of them, joined into branching, judging, regulating feedback networks, can just about account for the numbing inventories, the shifting assembly lines that run the corporate cell. With metaprogramming—the ability of the central network to reset even its own switches—the last constraints of the hardwired universe are shed. The field is broken wide open. Anything can happen, and does.

But can chance alone create such structures? Oh, yes. I have become abandoned to the idea. Chance is necessity by another name, thrown over the complexity barrier. The building blocks for self-replicating molecules can emerge from a milky suspension of ammonia, methane, water, and free hydrogen treated with an electrical spark. All the other steps from polypeptide to vanished near-Nobelists can be derived.

Solution can take shape—slowly, stupidly, agonizingly inefficiently—on trial and error alone. Error takes care of itself, in the hardwired universe's unforgiving compulsion to extinguish its dead ends. The *trial*: that much emerges from quantum perturbation—random mutation that infests the duplicating life molecule with variation. Molecular rules are not fixed, but statistical. That mother lode of modern anxiety—indeterminacy—lifts the whole dance off the ground and holds out the promise of sending it anywhere there might be to go.

Who made me? My answer, all but demonstrated, ten days past New Year's, 1986, has none of the crisp, winter, nighttime traveler's comfort offered by the old Baltimore Catechism. The science I study doesn't even frame the question the same way. Each system answers only the question it asks. The magic, memorized chants of my girlhood dealt in revealed things—truths that could be got at only by leap, flash, obedience, and rejection of human comprehension. They will never be reconciled with a skepticism based on repeatable test.

Yet in both, the name is not the thing. The one scientist I really knew came within a hair shirt's breadth of being a divine. Ressler was a Franciscan minus the cassock. He of anyone I've ever met was free from use's hammerlock, the blundering functionalism that leaves us blind to the miracle of our presence here. I can't begin to describe his speech, his actions, his days—they were so empty, selfless, contemplative. For a brief moment, he achieved a synthesis between scientist's certainty in underlying particulars and the cleric's awe at the unmappable whole.

Who made him? Chance made him. But that wasn't the crucial issue. The second question in the catechism—why?—was, to Dr. Ressler, more important. In his short run at science, he had learned the trick of seeing every living creature as elaborate baggage for massive, miraculous, internal goings-on. Every itch, every craving, every store run, every spoken word arose in a switchboard of enzyme messages splaying out in an overflowing veil that made the sum of all water droplets tumbling over Niagara seem a simple, sophomore differential equation.

The knowledge left him mute, punctual, meticulous, polite, weakly good-humored, pained by human contact, a nibbler on food yet quietly omnivorous, good with words but only when pressed into them. Mostly, he took things in: listened. For some reason, a full understanding of enzymes left him still able to love me, to love Todd. Like all good Franciscans, he had this thing about affection for fellow creatures of chance's kingdom.

The answer my Catholic training years ago had me memorize, if I carry through the blasphemous substitution, turns out to be exactly the answer Dr. Ressler's work on the coding problem left him: Why did chance make him? To know, love, and serve it in this life. And be happy with it in the next. Only: Dr. Ressler knew—as now I do—that our chemicals, in the next life, will be stripped of their self-coding repertoire. There'll be no chance to be happy with chance. It won't be in the lexicon. No lexicon. Chance will resume its maiden name. I have only this afternoon, this moment, to decide whether to go on writing. Perhaps it's letter-answering time after all. I pull out blank sheet number five, take a sip of suspect water, feel the waiting keys under my fingers, study the sunny January outside. I feel unaccountably, blessedly free.

XIX

Winter Storm Waltzes

sea_change(odeigh,todd,ressler) if reawakened(ressler) or
in_love(todd,odeigh) and not(scared(Anyone)) and
journey (Anywhere).

Ressler knew we were sleeping together. Every indication suggested he approved. He toted in a sack full of squash and tomatoes. "For you." Plural you, in ambiguous English.

"They're beautiful," I thanked him. Todd seconded. "Where did you find such nice ones this time of year?"

"My cold storage. I grew them."

"In Manhattan?" we both asked, overlapping.

"I happen to live on the sunny side of the World Trade. Over several years, I've hauled three tons of soil up to my roof. My landlord puts up with it; she likes the beans. Organic gardening is the perfect supplement to a night position." These were the first of a steady harvest—jar, juice, fresh—that kept us fed all winter.

He was lighter than I'd ever seen him. One day, a blue Icelandic sweater in place of the impeccable fifties suit and tie. He talked longer, exchanged brighter banter—often off-colored, anthropological double entendres about how it was up to us young to provide the heat needed to get the race through the winter. It was Ressler's idea to do my computerized birthday card; he had pursued my birthday through the federal electronic statistics.

I hardly dared believe it: our happiness made *him* happy. A quiet, remarkable last process started up in him. He experimented successfully with a beard. Once when Annie treated us to guitar, he forced us all into descant, benevolently dictating which lines to take. "Do you know 'Smoke Gets in Your Eyes'?" he asked. Annie shook her head, embarrassed for him. "How about 'Soap Gets in Your Ears'?"

He brought in a pack of art postcards and quizzed Todd. He suckered us into outrageous debates: whether Vaughan's "I saw Eternity the other night" might be treatable these days by a few milligrams of something from Hoffman–La Roche. Whether Marx's class warfare might in the future be fought between information-rich and information-poor. He would dismiss Todd early. "Nothing left I can't run through these rough beasts myself. Take this woman to live the life she deserves." He would give me a gentlemanly cheek-brush of the lips, saying, "Your quote for tomorrow is Alain-Fournier," supplying edition and page.

quote_of_day(alain-fournier,edition(Y,page(X1)),"I still say 'our' house though it is ours no longer").

knows(jimmy,news) and curious(jimmy).
knows(annie,news) and unchanged(annie).

My new relation to Todd seemed to be public knowledge. Even Uncle Jimmy asked me confidentially, "What's this I hear about you and my junior staff cohabiting?" Todd, delighted, took up the euphemism as buzzword of the hour: "Let's go cohabit the cafeteria." "Care to cohabit a little after I get off tonight?" Jimmy's trusting grin was tinged around the edges with a droop suggesting he would have preferred Todd and me to altar the thing legitimately. Jimmy was from another time. His mother, patiently invalided at the other end of the phone, probably understood the cohabiting world better than he.

Annie too began treating us as a couple. "Look at you two, both in maroon. Cute as two peas in a pie." She told us we ought to wear more maroon; maroon was a largely misunderstood color. Annie's acknowledgment capped it: romance discloses more than it knows. Everyone saw what we were up to but us.

reawakened(ressler) if

Dr. Ressler paced the digital warehouse, slipping deeper into human ways. During machine lulls, over paper cups of wine, he volunteered topics rather than just politely annotating ours. He'd bring us colored bits of the world's specificity: "Listen to this," he said, sporting a shampoo label. "'Lather, rinse, repeat.' An infinite loop." He made us try the Dial-an-Atheist number, laughing broadly when we discovered it was disconnected. He roped us into working difficult British crosswords where puns, imbeddings, weddings, retrograde inversions, anagrams, counterpoints, and subtle substitutions combined in fluid wordplay that seemed beyond human ingenuity to invent let alone solve.

Imperceptibly he thawed. He told terrific stories of scientists. An aged teacher who'd spent seventeen years in Morgan's fruit fly room. A colleague who left his research team to surface, years later, as codeveloper of the first artificially intelligent encyclopedia. The famous Swiss botanist Nägeli, whose habit of tasting bacterial cultures was a great source of information but shortened his life. So it would go until, at the end of an evening, I would realize that we hadn't had to draw the man out once.

astonished(todd) or scared(todd).

Frank was unable to believe the turnaround. As Ressler grew daily more voluminous, Franklin clammed up, afraid to say anything that might dispel the fragile moment. "Did you see the man?" he'd ask later in bed. "Searching through his pockets for clippings to give me? Like a third-base coach giving signs!" The clipping-gifts were superfluous; Todd's notebooks had closed. He no longer needed them. The companionship they'd substituted for had sprung to life.

Frank would play the fool out of sheer terror. While the mainframes processed end-of-day transactions, he'd bait his mentor with silly challenges. "How high can you count on your fingers?" He whispered in my ear the proud target thirty-five, one hand standing for digits and the other for groups of six. Ressler paused a few polite minutes before responding with 1,024—each digit a single place in binary notation. Todd sulked. "Yeah, well...anything *higher*?"

"Always," confided Ressler. And they took to the problem together, like competing cousins at a family reunion, chucking the softball, testing each other's arms.

"It says here," Franker announced one night, "that we have genetics to thank for the killer bees heading north o' the border from down Mexico way." He spoke the word from Ressler's past,

403

sidling up surreptitiously to the conspicuously avoided issue.

Dr. Ressler nodded, not at all reluctant to take up the topic. "That's right. An attempt to tame an aggressive African strain with a docile South American one backfired. One of hundreds of plagues we've initiated by improving the ecosystem. Transplanted gypsy moths; imported rat-catching cats that destroy South Pacific islands; mongooses overrunning the West Indies: cures worse than the diseases. This one's especially damning. We haven't just replaced one pest with another. We've created a new one to call our own." He huddled us around the console, created a workspace, and whipped up a Mendelian genetics lab, a field where we could put our creations to the test. A simple simulation, but complex enough to prove his point. "There are a lot more ways to fall off the tightrope than to inch forward."

Ressler, the author of every declaration fed into the machine, was often surprised by the executing program's outcome. Todd and I, who had to have each line explained to us, were floored to see self-modifying behavior built from a few innocent assertions. I learned not only the danger of intervening in systems too complex to predict, but about declarative programming, the thin line between determined and emergent, the ability to surprise. Looking down at Dr. Ressler, newly bearded, Icelandic blue, typing keys, leading us with infinite patience through the nuances of his composition, I knew the world had lost in him not just a scientist of the first order, but something more important: a gifted teacher.

We ran the simulation many times, each time failing to steer the model toward anything but collapse. Todd threw up his hands. "The discerning intellect of Man bested by bees. I've a suggestion: we greet the little buggers at the border. Instantly upon their crossing the Rio Grande, we lavish them with Walkmen, warm-up suits, the whole nine yards. They'll shed their asocial ways in a flick of the Zippo—get ahead, secure the Mercedes, et cetera. *Adieu* national panic."

Still, the conclusion of the ecosimulation distressed Todd's Renaissance belief in the perfectability of the natural world. "You aren't suggesting we stop cross-breeding?"

"No," Ressler affirmed.

"Or that we quit with all this inheritance and population dynamics stuff?"

"No again."

"But we aren't yet ready to build a better mouse?"

"No."

This last answer was ambiguous: No, we're not ready? No, we never will be? No, that's not what I mean? But Franklin was afraid to pursue the point. I could hear him form and reject delicate questions in his head. At last he blurted out, "Bacteria engineered to protect potatoes from freezing?"

An art-history ABD specializing in obscure 450-year-old panelists, the spokesman for technological progress, versus a Ph.D. in molecular genetics, once the comer to keep one's eye on, cautioning that the possible and the desirable were not the same. Ressler fielded Todd's question without flinching. He ran his hand lightly over his head, smoothing his hair. He seemed not a minute over thirty. He was spoiling for something—not for a fight. For the mystery and heft and specificity of conversation. "If we're to do recombinant DNA, you'll need more background."

journey(north-woods) if

Todd jumped at the chance. He suggested we three drive up the following Saturday to a cabin in New Hampshire. "Belongs to a college friend who will gladly lend it for a weekend."

Inviting the professor for a camping weekend seemed just short of asking one's priest if he'd care for a round of racquetball. Had Todd run the idea by me first, I certainly would have squashed it. But Dr. Ressler broke into a boy's grin and said, "Do you know how long it's been since I've gotten out of this damn city?" Both men turned to me, and I nodded with enthusiasm.

"Should we ask anyone else?" I couldn't think, aside from our day-shift friends and the man at the sandwich shop, who Todd had in mind.

Ressler handled Todd's question with his usual grace. "Having put our hand to this three-personed plow, I suggest we stay with it. This is a congenial enough group as it stands."

That was all it took. I arranged my hours at the branch. Todd secured not only the cabin but a beaten-up Plymouth to ferry us there. I was in charge of food and Dr. Ressler of kerosene and campfire reading. They picked me up at three in the morning after their Friday stint. Todd met me at the door of the antique shop, shushing hysterically, as if this were a teen-aged prank. I guess it was.

The roads were clear, and after we jumped the city, the night was crisp and quick. We got free of the interstate, preferring seat-of-the-pants navigation up through empty New England towns. Todd drove, and we passengers were assigned the task of keeping him awake. For a stretch, Dr. Ressler had us all rolling with a dry commentary about how every road sign in existence—"Slow children," "Cross traffic does not stop"—contained unintentional slipped meaning. Todd ruddered via Boston, Saturday morning. We spent two hours in the Fine Arts, studying the conflagration he was after, and he bought a postcard of it. Then he hauled us across the Fens to the Gardner and that domestic chamber music in amber by Vermeer.

We arrived at the cabin late Saturday. I felt, by contrast, how my life in New York had become a spasm of hormone and acid jolting my system into continuous speculation on how I was going to get killed. My key to surviving, or not dying too quickly, had been to swim in stress without feeling it. Adaptation to environment. Suddenly this place: rag-quilted, smelling of sap and kindling, spices hanging from kitchen beams, squirrels marauding in the walls. A foot-pumped parish church organ stood against a wall with a Lutheran hymnal on the music rack. A five-thousand-piece picture puzzle that Franklin identified as an Aelbert Cuyp lay spread over the dining-room table. Salvation, in short. I hadn't known I needed it until I was there.

We unpacked, laughing, pitched up on the beach of the New World. We put on coats and fell into the bracing air. Snow was falling thickly. A carpet gathered around the cabin clearing and up the stony hillside. The thought passed through us: head back now, while still possible. But all we spoke out loud was, "Let's try this way."

There were so many stars that the sky seemed black gaps pasted over a silver source. The same lights as hung over the city, invisible. Todd looked up and quoted, " 'The stars get their brightness from the surrounding dark.' Dante, but who's keeping track?"

We walked in silence, in one another's footholes in the drifts. I felt, in the constriction in my chest, the intractable riddle facing the first species saddled with language: why are some things alive and others not? Snow, rock, star, lichen, rabbit scat, pine. It was the easiest, most blanketing protection in the world to imagine that everything partook of the same animation.

"Let's have it," Todd wheedled Ressler after we'd walked half a mile in chill awe. "You're the life scientist. Tell us what's happening here."

"I was never a life scientist, to my misfortune." His breath came out in white, frozen puffs against the snowy air. All our patient field work was about to come to fruition. "I was always, at best, a theorist. But before I was a theorist, I was a child. And every child knows...shh! Look. There. Just past that birch."

Ressler didn't even need to point. Against the black of the woods, a pair of eyes, reflecting dim analogy of starlight, observed us from a distance, measuring our every move, theorizing. We froze, matching it, watching for watching, not even whispering a guess as to what it was.

alive(X) if grows(X) and reproduces(X,Y) and
member(Y,class(X)) and not (equals(Y,X)) and

A long, deliberate draw of observation, and the eyes blinked off. The creature vanished, freeing us to turn and retrace our path through the drifted snow. I knew it now: the world, even in the pitch of winter, metabolizing all around us. Every ledge of it, trampled by a permutation on the first principle, each straining for a crack at the Krebs cycle, a slice of the solar grant money. "Hilbert's Infinite Hotel," Ressler described it. "Perpetually booked up, but always ready for more occupants, even an infinity of them." The place was penny-wedged, crammed, charged with doppelgängers, protean variants on the original: radial, ruddy, furred, barked, scaled, segmented, flecked, flat, lipped, stippled. Who knows how? The place was beyond counting, outside the sum of the inventory. And we, as of this weekend, were but a particular part.

As day broke, we returned to the cabin, spread ourselves in the existing beds, and slept. I had joined the night shift. I woke to soft talking in the room downstairs. Dr. Ressler was tutoring Todd, laying out the rudiments of the new, biological alchemy. It was afternoon, already dark. On the windowpane, thick flakes had been collecting for hours. I put my hand to the cold glass, leaving a negative ghost when I drew away. I hoped for the worst the elements could do, hoped harder than I've hoped since I was a girl.

I came downstairs. The men had a semblance of warm meal waiting. Flush with eating and drinking, we piled close together on the couch, in front of a fine fire. I thought: This could last forever, long evenings, passing around murder mysteries, losing weeks without glancing at the papers. A place where progress was obscene, unwanted. Todd could putter perpetually at his dissertation, I over some project in Maritime wool, Ressler fiddling with the smoky spruce logs.

Franker roused us to attack the bellows organ. He took the right pedal, Ressler the left. They each took a line in the upper staff, and I, on account of six years of piano lessons as a child, was expected to handle both tenor and bass while simultaneously pulling stops. Conquering the skittish entrances and squashing some unscored tritones, we flew along well. We pumped out *Lobe den Herren* and *Nun danket alle Gott*. After a while, we even grew bold enough to let the inner lines out and improvise on the cantus firmus, Todd laying on a counterpoint from "Mood Indigo." But human, we grew tired of hymns. Todd was the first to break off, pace back to the fire. Warming himself, with his back to Ressler, he asked, "How about it, then? Let's hear it for those man-made bacteria."

Ressler sighed with exasperated pleasure. "Ice-minus *Pseudomonas*." He returned to the couch, wrapping himself in a discarded quilt. "Not man-made. Man-manipulated. The process is neither so formidable nor so erotic as you think."

I wandered to the dining room. "Who's up for a little jigsaw?" Neither man responded. "How 'bout a big jigsaw?" Flat. "Think your friend would mind if I worked on this thing?"

"Of course not," Todd smirked. "Just so long as you take out any pieces you put in before we leave." I pottered away at Mr. Cuyp's cows, an ear posted to the conversation I avoided.

"How erotic is it?" Todd took the rocker opposite Ressler.

"The lab technician identifies, by a lot of boring scutwork, that particular restriction enzyme with the ability to clip out from the bacterial DNA the sequence that directs the synthesis of a given protein. In the case of *Pseudomonas,* the deleted protein acts as a seed for ice-crystal formation. No gene, no protein. No protein, no crystal seed. No seed, no ice at that temperature. We aren't bestowing any new characteristics on the microbe; we're depriving it of one."

"Like clipping a Scotty's tail?"

"Only this snip is inherited."

"And this sort of deletion—can it happen in nature?"

"It *is* nature. Only infinitely quicker."

"So where's the danger?"

Ressler shrugged. "Where's the danger in a mongoose?"

"But a mongoose is a separate species. Ice-minus bacteria are just a protein away."

"And you are just proteins away from either." It thrilled to hear the man, the edge of alertness in his voice, discernible only in outline until then. "Yes, the Frankenstein fear is over-blown. Transgenesis is not about creating life from scratch. It's about juggling existing genes—existing formulas for protein manufacture. Deleting, adding, moving the factory parts from one organism to the other. You're right: the whole genetic engineering revolution is only a quantitative extension of the ancient art of livestock breeding. Even interspecies gene transfer has a viral precedent. Only human snipping is a billion times faster, more facile."

"Moving around existing traits? That's all we're talking?"

Ressler smiled. "All," he said ironically. "For the time being."

Todd was high-strung. He spoke rapidly. "That just proves my point, then."

"No." Ressler shook his head painfully. "That proves *my* point. Genetic engineering is not one single thing, but an assortment of various techniques and projects, all with different risks. By far the largest is ecological imbalance. Unpredictable, irreversible environmental mayhem that used to take selective breeders a lifetime to produce can now be knocked off in a dozen weeks."

"Mayhem?" Todd sounded personally wounded. "Are we that stupid? I'd think that any science capable of reaching down into the cell with a syringe a few molecules thick, of doping out the genetic commands and figuring out just where to cut and paste, should be able to predict the effect a simple rearrangement will have once it's in place. The hard part's *doing* it. Figuring out what you've done ought to be trivial."

"One would think so. But remember our simulation, back at the office. *We* wrote the piece. We knew what every line of the code did. We knew what effect a change to a given parameter would have locally. But the only way of determining the overall outcome was to run the code." He learned forward under his quilt. "It surprised us. And *that* program was only a hundred instructions long. The human genome, in twelve-point Roman, is several thousand printed pages. The linked biosphere...."

"This strikes me as a strange argument for an arch-empiricist to be taking."

"Names will never hurt me," Dr. Ressler laughed. "I could do without the 'arch,' I suppose."

"We can learn about things by breaking them into parts?"

"That's the only way I know of to learn about things."

"But it sounds as if you're describing some impenetrable big picture. Some transcendent sum that evades final analysis."

"I wouldn't put it that way. Life is an immense turbulent system. Small changes produce large swings in outcome."

"Are you saying that even a complete understanding of the working parts can never predict how they fit together?"

"I'm saying we don't have anything close to a working understanding of any of those parts. A year and a half ago, two fellows at large state schools, using one of those miraculous syringes you mentioned, injected the gene for rat growth hormone and a promoter into a fertilized mouse cell. Their mighty mouse made the cover of *Nature*. Only: nobody knows *how* the mouse DNA took up the injected gene. It's hard to condone commercial applications of work where the basic mechanism isn't understood."

"Unfair. How can we possibly go after a breakdown of 'how' without first mapping out 'what?'"

Ressler was delighted that Todd, despite his lack of formal training, felt equal to the argument, even this deeply in. "Suppose the fault is not in what technology can tell us, but in what we are willing to hear from it?" Hope: the life cycle's lethal enemy.

I worked steadily on the jigsaw, a dozen times aching to jump into the dialogue, but knowing better than to risk involvement. Franker argued from a position of urgent altruism. He wanted to believe that by eliminating the blind, backsliding, short-interest, error-driven, groping element from the spark—the code at last rendering itself self-knowing, literate, able to grasp and correct the insensate message it has for eons posted forward to its later by-products—life might reach the verge of a new relation, cross the threshold of liberty. Dr. Ressler, for private reasons, put Franker's hope through the burner.

"Check out Chargaff's piece in *Nature*. Half-dozen years old. 'Have we the right to counteract, irreversibly, the evolutionary wisdom of millions of years...? The world is given to us on loan.

410

We come and we go. . . .' This, from the fellow who first revealed the base ratios in DNA."

"Hey lady," Todd called me. "Verify this man's citations."

It felt good to be spoken to. "First tell me where this tree branch with the two nubby end things goes."

The men came over to the table and began worrying the puzzle with me. Frank looked for spaces where particular pieces would fit, Ressler for pieces that would fit particular spaces. They were both infuriatingly good.

"Do you have an ethical problem with it?" Todd asked casually.

"That depends, I suppose, on what part of the 'it' we're concerned with. Perhaps some genetic engineer somewhere is embarking on eugenic nightmares, but that's another matter. I guess I'd say that I have no more moral qualms with ordinary gene transfer than with hybrid corn."

"Where in the world is the problem, then?"

Ressler shrugged. " 'Where in the world,' indeed. The field is only a decade old. In a little less than three years, the government has granted a dozen patents on new forms of life. Patents! There's even talk of copyrighting segments of identified genome."

"OK, then. What part of recombinatory research would you legislate against?"

"That's just the problem. Legislation is too late. Legislation is about commerce, rights, equity. Once you need to pass laws about science, you've taken a wrong turn."

"Galileo muttering 'But it *does* move,' under his breath, just after recanting?"

"Exactly. Of course, the state is right to prevent any process it thinks might harm the public interest, just as it takes action against phosphates in freshwater lakes."

"So what *bothers* you about genetic engineering?"

"It's not science. Science is not about control. It is about cultivating a perpetual condition of wonder in the face of something that forever grows one step richer and subtler than our latest theory about it. It is about reverence, not mastery. It might, from time to time, spin off an occasional miracle cure of the kind you dream about. The world we would know, the living, interlocked world, is a lot more complex than any market. The market is a poor simulation of the ecosystem; market models will never more than parody the increasingly complex web of interdependent nature. All these plates in the air, and we want to flail at them. 'Genetic engineering' is full of attempts to replace a dense, diversified, heterogenous assortment of strains with one superior one. Something about us is in love with *whittling down:* we want the one solution that will drive out all others. Take our miracle superstrains, magnificent on the surface, but unlike the messy populations of nature, deceptive, thin, susceptible. One bug. One blight.... No; the human marketplace has about as much chance of improving on the work of natural selection as a *per diem* typist has of improving Bartlett's *Familiar Quotations.*"

"But does recombination research necessarily mean selling the field into the market? We have this incredible leverage, this light source, mind. The ability to work consequences out in advance. Shed the stone-and-chisel, save ourselves...." I could make out his humanist's evolution: cell, plant, animal, speaking animal, rational animal, laboring animal, *Homo fabor,* and ultimately: life as its own designer. Something in Franker too, voting for wonder. But wonder full of immanent expectation.

Ressler was not buying, not all the way. "All we've done to date is uncover part of a pattern. We can't mistake that for meaning. Meaning can't be gotten at by pattern-matching."

"That's why work is more crucial than ever. We're so *close.*"

"The experiment you want to extend is three billion years old. It may indeed be close to something unprecedented. All the more reason why we need to step back a bit and see how it runs."

When we went to bed, Todd joined me in mine. I was up early. It had stopped snowing at last, but nearly three feet had obliterated the contour of ground. Standing out against the unbroken white, as conspicuous as the pope without clothes, conifers went about as if there was nothing more natural in the world than converting sunlight into more fondled slang thesaurus entries on the idea of green. My eyes attenuated to movements, birds, squirrels, the extension of that trapped energy in the branches. I picked up a cacophony of buzzes, whirs, and whistles—an orchestra tuning up, about to embark on big-time counterpoint. Imagining the invisible sub-snow system—the larvae, grubs, thimblefuls of soil a thousand species wide—I suddenly understood Ressler's point of the previous night: the transcendent, delivering world Franker so badly ached for: we were already *there.* Built into the middle of it, tangled so tightly in the net that we could not sense the balancing act always falling into some other, some farther configuration. The point of science was to lose ourselves in the world's desire.

Ressler came out, putting a biscuit in his mouth as if dipping litmus into solution. He greeted me happily. He gauged the snow and rubbed a palm over his temple. "The prospects of returning to the city in time to do tonight's work have apparently slipped to less than slim."

Of course they had; we hadn't left ourselves a margin to get back. We'd counted, covertly, on this emergency, and now we had it. We inspected the car, made token efforts at clearing the wheels. I got in and started the engine. Dr. Ressler wedged himself against the fender and tried to rock it down what was once the cabin path. But we were not so much stuck as buried. The back door of the cabin slammed and out ran Todd. "Brought you some traction!" Smirking like a schoolboy, he produced a salt shaker.

"Save it for the boids' tails," I shouted. Giddy, euphoric.

We rocked a while, stupidly, humanly, going a dozen feet.

"Shovel time," Todd suggested gaily.

"You're mad," Ressler said. "It's three hundred meters to the road."

"Note the metric precision," Todd told me.

"And the main road is itself under."

"Just as well. We don't have a shovel anyway."

"We'd best call Jimmy," Dr. Ressler suggested. "Not that he'll be able to do much to pick up the pieces."

"Oh God," Todd giggled, despite himself. "Jesus. East Coast Fiscal Collapse."

"Is there a problem?" Knowing what their typical evening consisted of, I couldn't conceive of their being anywhere near indispensable to anyone.

"*We* may not do anything. But those big metal boxes do. Quite a bit."

"Can't Jimmy run them?"

"Around the clock? Without cohabitors? Maybe for a day."

"At half speed," Ressler clarified.

"With the night operations procedures manual at his side."

"A book we haven't kept current for months."

"So who has a phone up here?" Todd yodeled, listening for the echo.

Ressler cocked his head in the direction of the path we'd taken Saturday night. His eyes flashed: it was not, perhaps, the shortest

413

route, but was by far the more beautiful. This being North America, it had eventually to lead to a phone. We took off happily up the drifted hill. We made slow progress, propping up one another. At the spot where that pair of eyes had looked us over in the dark, we stopped and searched but found no tracks. The snow had long since rubbed out all trace. We crested and saw, a few hundred yards off, a house that looked lived in. We threaded our way down the valley, between the bare trees, hunters returning home. Making the most of the last few minutes before human contact, Todd asked, as if nothing had intervened between their conversation and now, "So is that why you quit?"

I was walking next to Ressler, and he took my arm. "Not in so many words." And because we weren't going anywhere that night, or the night after, he suddenly had all the time in the world to tell us what had happened. And he did. In so many words.

Storm Waltz II

sea_change(ressler,koss,X) if in_love(ressler,koss) and
not(knows(X)).

Briefly humanity recalls, in a dream of distant past, that use is no use. For a week, it's again clear that the question is not ends and applications, but shape, sound, angels arriving on the raw doorstep, an ache, an instant hint, singing the new year in, in a bleak midwinter. Then back to grim progress. In a dim hall just off the Christmas party, the following afternoon in a public lecture, passing in crowded corridors, seated pointedly apart in team brainstorming, a few excruciating minutes alone in the lab: they fall deeper, more carelessly into unwished desire. Her confession of love, at the close of the old year, sweeps away his last sense that this has all been self-torture. He pays for that relief by losing all say in the outcome. He has confessed to her, too.

He feels in Jeanette a perverse urge for danger. She is crazy reckless, slipping hand between his thighs at a faculty meeting. In their stolen clinches, she strains her head around with fear at the least rattle or click, only to relax her neck desperately again, hating herself, her nerves, loving the near-escape, moaning for more, moist fear. Startled, silky, mottled, new to the place, terrified, perpetually about to bolt.

414

Away from her, he vows to break off, a resolution already hob-bled by attached fatalist clauses. Hopeless. She demands to be pressed, kneaded, her trembling animal lip down registering the punishment of pleasure they cannot forego. Creature-reversion, triggered simply by touching certain spots on her—he can't stop re-experimenting with it. The image comes involuntarily just be-fore he falls asleep, how she closes her rolling eyes, shudders, lets her focal "I" slip twenty centimeters down her spinal column. He can feel it in her muscles, in how she stands against him, indentured to the flood response of her body, teaching him how.

He too is addicted by the sense, new to him, of being victim to a thing he cannot help. *Debauched, depraved;* the words give him an erotic thrill proportionate to the *pro forma* resistance he still manages. He knows her public composure is the thinnest wallpaper patch above a seething hive in the board beneath. She wanders from the lab to the supply closet nearby, looking for something: tubing, glassware, *him.* He follows her into the distant room. She stands at the shelves, the picture of business. But turning, she grabs him like a vegetative trap, nudges closed the door, begins to mouth him as if the verb were truly transitive.

"If we get caught," he says, "we'll be dead on many levels."

"I know." She kisses him, pushing away and pulling at the same time. "Leave me alone, why don't you?" She kisses again, more circumspectly. "I must *want* to get in trouble."

He hears her struggle to keep from cooing audibly. "This is as far as I go without a note from your parents." He nearly says husband.

"Me too," she replies dreamily, drugged, aroused. "As far as I go." They catch one another's eyes. The danger is real. They sober, swing back to adulthood, agreeing they must wean from this mad-ness. "Little boy," she says, restoring her glasses, "in another life, I could take you around the block a few times."

The brave kindness, the funny, forlorn way Dr. Koss delivers it pulls him back regretfully to her face, where they lose another moment. In this bittersweet heuristic, he is not the experimenter. He is the subject of these trial runs. That car will go around the block itself if he doesn't brake.

They share lucid moments, but only under supervision. She visits him in his office, in Lovering's gaze. "I've just read Gale and Folkes," she says. Ressler looks across the office. He can't very well ask her if she'd like to talk outside, now that talk is really talk.

"And?" he asks weakly. "What did you think?"

"Incredible. 'Incorporation reactions for specific amino acids can be activated by specific recombinations of nucleotides.'"

"Spitting distance of an in vitro system that will crack the game wide open."

"You're right. You *must* be right." She smiles, her back to Lovering, a double entendre smile.

"Two Cambridge scientists..." he doubts out loud.

"...who've missed a follow-up. You've seen wrong turns before?"

He's more than just *seen* one. "A two-year-old article in one of the most prestigious journals going...."

"And no one's noticed it? No one picked up Mendel for thirty years."

"What's this over yonder?" Lovering banters. "I distinctly hear dreaming."

"Joey," Koss says, returning to the thuggish quip-trader Ressler first took her for, "call your wife, Sandy. I hear she's at home taking a delivery from the furniture man."

"She's not my wife. Sandy doesn't believe in the hypocrisy of the institution. We live in sin. And believe me, sin's gotten an undeserved bad name."

"Have you told Ulrich about this?" Koss readdresses Ressler.

"I tried to," he claims.

"How hard?" She grins.

"You know the man's bias. You told me yourself. Hung up on pushing the thing through statistically. The last time I spoke with him, he tried to interest me in doing some machine coding."

"Sounds interesting," Lovering throws out.

"Damn it, it's not." Ressler slams his hand on his desk, surprising even himself. "He thinks we can put together some kind of grind-out generator of all sequenced nucleotides, throw it up against some data structure showing every known protein, and let the thing iterate a couple hundred hours...."

"Couple *hundred?*" Jeanette almost falls in his lap. "On the ILLIAC?" CU's trimmed-down, transistor-overhauled, performance-boosted, cutting-edge version of the power-hungry rooms full of hardware, brave new programmable switch boxes, descendants of those devices originally built in the forties to assist in cracking wartime codes.

"Sounds like it would work," Lovering says.

"I'm not saying it wouldn't."

416

"What's the problem, then?"

"It's overlaborious, superfluous drudgery, that's the problem." Koss and Lovering both laugh at his adjective production line. "I can't *believe* it. Not after the success of the first paper." Ressler's first work has already caused ripples. The English and French, as well as the Californians, have requested reprints. But the more notorious the work gets, the more cautiously Ulrich pursues it.

Lovering shows his allegiance. "Come on. How hard could the programming be?"

"Oh, the algorithm is trivial. Little more than a nested loop, with cases hooked on to it. It would take a few weeks to throw together, test it, get the bugs out. But it would be a time-eating monster."

Koss blurts out, "Joey! Friend. How much programming have you done in your wee lifetime?"

"Zero. Null. Nil. Naught. Void."

"Good. I'll teach you everything I know."

"Everything?"

"Everything that can be expressed politely in FORTRAN. And Joey." She stares at him and whispers. "We'll race you there."

helps(heaven,X) if helps(X,X).

Koss and Ressler get clearance from a dubious Ulrich to try the incorporating techniques suggested by Gale and Folkes, under condition that they give Lovering a hand in formulating an algorithm for the matching program. They are to split their time between in vitro synthesis and computer tutorials. He gives them a two-month probation, not enough time for anything, yet more than Ressler expected. If they have something tangible to show by then, Ulrich will talk extension.

Ressler tries to cop assistance from Woyty, but the man is tied up reading *Baby and Child Care*. Renée, pregnancy safe from spontaneous abortion, is due in weeks. Stuart visits Toveh Botkin in her oriental-carpeted office. He surprises her, slumped back in chair, in a *Ringstrasse* Hapsburg reverie. "Where were you?" he asks softly.

"In the Café Centrale," she smiles.

"Talking to Mahler?"

She scoffs. "To Trotsky. In French. He was trying to make me pick up his check." She laughs at herself, a laugh that trails off into a tsk. "Friend, it may be time to retire."

417

"I've something that will change your mind." He shows her the article, which she devours in minutes. He tells her about the release time he and Koss have won from Ulrich.

"Let me wash beakers. Pull periodicals. Anything." Her eyes plead for one more shot at the code before giving in to it.

"We can pull our own damn periodicals. From you, we need chemistry. And the appropriate inspirational music."

"Be not afeard," she says. "The isle is full of noises."

What noises? Down the quad, over in the Music Building, Lejaren Hiller and Leonard Isaacson put the finishing touches on their composition, "ILLIAC Suite for String Quartet," spawning a new genre. They use the computer as a giant random-number generator, an engine that produces, within restrictions set by the program-mer-composers, sounds and suite airs for four-pair hands to unvary. The project reflects a dawning awareness that the life score itself is assembled from successive iterations of random mutation. It is left to the unprepared audience's ears to unalgorithm as best they can, to reverse the random process, to hear in the blips and bleeps of this new, startling conch shell the steady surf of the first sea.

```
theme(goldberg,list[g,f#,e,d,b,c,d,g,g,f#,e,a,f#,g,a,d,d,b,c,b,
g,a,b,e,c,b,a,d,g,c,d,g]).
variation(X,Y) if theme(Name,X) and equals(Y,mutation(X)).
mutation(X) if
```

"ILLIAC Suite" shares processing time with Cyfer's attempts to secure the definition of life. Compared to the tunes coming in over the transistors at that moment, it comes from a new planet. "Hon-eycomb" is the hit of the season. Even Ressler, after laborious attention now able to distinguish between Haydn's *London* and Mozart's *Prague,* dissects the disposable tune in two hearings. For the week in question, he is forced to listen to it twice an hour. The message is inescapable—the measure of the minute. It blasts from a thousand portable radios all across town. For the invention of the transistor, blame crosstown physics faculty member John Bardeen. The 1956 Nobel laureate, Bardeen has come to Urbana to continue the work that will make him the first repeat winner in the same field.

The transistor itself is a flexible current junction: small voltage differences at the base produce large differences between emitter and collector. With this simple lexicon, the transistor can serve

418

as everything from current amplifier to logic gate. In the ten years since its evolution, the device has crept into circuits ranging from ILLIAC to the portable radios giving white kids of Anywhere, America, their first taste of black sonority, racy innuendoed danger. R and B currently mutates to R and R, a dialect banned in several communities as subversive, destructive, and unpatriotic. In years, changed beyond recognition yet virtually the same, the sound will go from threat to ubiquitous backdrop: decorative prop for everything from news broadcasts to barber shops.

William Shockley, Bardeen's collaborator and corecipient of the '56 Nobel, has gone from Bell Labs to California. There he begins thinking taboo thoughts about the inherited nature of intelligence. Might it be passed along as discretely as wrinkled pods? He becomes possessed by an idea in embryo—a sperm bank for geniuses. Keep the genetic pool from pollution. The racist tinge and resultant outcry are picked up, reported, and amplified in the general transistor noise.

As for the text of "Honeycomb," it strikes Ressler as a straightforward variation on the time-honored metaphor of Love-as-Edible-Food. Nuzzle, nibble, chew, swallow your baby, your honey-pie, your sweet. Until now, he always considered the pap embarrassing, indulgent drooling. Now he no longer holds it in contempt. Soft, tuneful, pathetically appropriate. He'd like to nuzzle, suck, sing to her, even. Jeanette's form sears him with the instantly consumed melancholic cheer of radio tunes. Heartbreaking, vulnerable, in black-pleated narrow waists, peach tapering bodices, she is the core of girlishness, a fleeting goodbye to summer, sailboats on the lake, the downy, borrowed body about to be eaten and spit out by the shape-hungry world. She hovers at her last moment, soon to be expelled from visitation. He must preserve, fix her at this unarrestable peak of loveliness. He doesn't know how. All he can do is attach himself to her at the mouth.

They preserve enough presence of mind to work together on in vitro. With Botkin's assistance, they advance on a clean technique. Lab work is exciting again, not solely on account of their proximity, hours spent within touching distance, more secret because more open. Back in the barracks, doing a dish, he is struck by how much repetitive maintenance it takes just to exist. Existence is *the* cycle extraordinaire; everything tangent, constantly spinning just to stay in place. But the missing piece of the coding problem offers entrée to another process—lines, deltas. They stand

419

at the base of Jacob's Ladder. Can they be on the threshold of completing what until then had been merely repetitive climb?

For weeks Ressler has bankrolled a private research venture, exploring to what extent a toothache is imaginary. When the tooth abscesses one morning, flash burning at the stake makes him recant, tear to the dentist. In the waiting room he blunts himself into oblivion over back issues of *Life*. He reads Dulles's brinksmanship quote, which he missed the first time around. He scans the magazine's breezy treatment turning high-ranking Nazi von Braun into the Rock Hudson of Rocketry. He has a premonition: the final solution to the modern crisis will be to turn the threat of news into light entertainment.

The world is at war, perpetual war, moving at all tangent angles. All over the world, a spreading collection of brushfires extends the head-on conflagration by other means. Wars come down to the control of information. They purport to be about the attainment of battlefields, defense of property, renovation of antiquated systems of ownership, liberation of oppressed peoples, geopolitical dominance. But these are just material proxies for pursuing conflict's real end: the testing of new technologies, the stockpiling of data.

Information is ordered contrast; it can be won only by building a differential between sound and noise. The purpose of gathering information is to increase predictability. Information theory was born in the War, when Norbert Wiener was asked to build a gunsight that could tell where an enemy plane would be in the next few seconds. He's read Wiener: wars are won by making your enemies more ignorant than they can make you. A state's ability to wage war is measured only loosely in kilotonnage. A better indicator is a country's ability to wage randomness, to impose a signal-to-noise problem on the enemy, render his informational stockpile incoherent.

Since Caesar, warring states have known that the best way to protect information from enemy corruption is to disguise it as noise. A coded message already appears random, protectively colored. But since the Gauls, warring states have studied how to break the noise barrier, reverse the garble. The history of warfare is the story of cryptology. In one of the paperback cipher books he pored over when the coding problem was forming, Ressler read that the British alone during the recent outbreak sported thirty thousand information troops. The number has risen steeply since. The Cold

War marks that moment in organized violence when the number of people attached to various code books surpasses the number toting rifles.

No matter how well coded a message, how ingeniously the treasure is reduced to apparent gibberish, there is always a key that reveals the underground sense under the cloak of noise. This gives secret writing its otherworldly quality. The cryptanalyst's arcane ritual of incantations—MAGIC, as the army/navy wartime decoding efforts were named—transmutes seeming meaninglessness into firm predictions. The one who renders the message readable possesses all the import of the original.

In *Life*'s breezy treatments of Dulles and von Braun—aided by the swatch his abscess cuts across his brain—Ressler sees that even the safe haven of academia, so far from the industrial trenches, will not prevent his being conscripted. The genetic code, however selflessly and reverently, will be co-opted in the broader code war. *Life,* use's henchman, serves up as comestibles everyone from assassins to scientists ("modern mandarins, modern necromancers"). His act of pure research, done with religious indifference to consequences, delivers all organic creation, codebroken and codespoken, into warring hands.

Just as his tooth sends up another flaming wave, Ressler stumbles across a photo essay of the twenty-odd-year-old pianist, interpreter of the *Goldberg* recording that Koss gave him. Given the ends of photojournalism, Ressler is not surprised to catch the gist: the boy is young, single, romantically eccentric, a crank hypochondriac, never seen without his panoply of pills and jars of spring water. He possesses the Lovering allele of cold virus paranoia, wearing wool coats in the height of summer. He sings out loud while recording— ghostly, alternate vocalizings the technicians can't muffle. He has a carefully worked-out, outlandish theory about recordings rendering the concert obsolete. Yet the nut is a genius. He has inherited a contrapuntal brain, and the Bach decoding algorithm is congenitally embedded into his ten-bit, digital circuitry.

Suddenly the notes are in Ressler's ears, conspiring voices, sounding of lost days, lost names, affections, friends. Those variations, fragments, flint-splinters of the original: how long he has lived with them since his first, dull attempts at theory. His slow, purpose-free pursuit of the four-by-four-by-four aria, the Sixty-four Sarabande Dollar Question has become so instilled, so somatic, that he has forgotten the point of the experiment until this moment.

Jeanette! Why infect a stranger in the first place? She hadn't a clue to his nature, yet she came, brought this unprovoked birthday encyclopedia of crystallized sounds—iced trees clicking together after a storm; scrape of metal runners coasting down a hill near evening, sparking bare rock, reticent snow brushing the blades; shouts in the city; the clink of tipping scales; the slosh of ankle-dangling euphoria; summer insect swarms; plash of sun's rays lengthening over the lawn; baroque silliness; French fluff; political fervor; the chill call of last illness; the swelling sound of always, of never. Did she know already where they would arrive, long before either dared to consider the first touch? He forgives himself this once the too-brief two-manual figure in the thick of his chest, deciding that the only measure that can crack these patterns is beauty.

Ressler reads the profile three times but finds no key to the *Goldberg* code. He is called into the operating theater. As the dentist administers the composite anesthetic, preparing to yank out the offensive handiwork of bacteria, Ressler calms himself, grips the arms of the chair, and relaxes, following the contour of the seductive melody he has never really put aside since that unbirthday party long ago. He recreates tracts of the piece in his head. Preexistent knowledge of the piece, recovered in a hundred hours of close listening, allows him perfect recall. But the music, the note-for-note isomorph in his interior concert hall, is not the piece she gave him. One cannot step into the same theme twice.

His dentist saws off the tooth's crown, ferrets out the roots. His mouth is blown apart. At that moment, when pain ought to rack his body, the pain of violent mistake, murderous razor-pain, Ressler is cast adrift, at sea on sound. A Pentothal haze of realization: every sound wave ever uttered could be packed into a single generating pattern a few measures long, the world's pocket score. He barely flinches as the chunks of infected, lodged bone are ripped from his head.

    asks(ressler,koss,question(Today,X)).
    question(2/1/58,"Why can't I tell you what I hear?").
    equals(question(Day,X),question(Day+1,X)).

At home, a bloody cotton wad in his mouth, still under the protective residue of anesthetic, he calls Koss. He gets the husband. Pleasant acquaintance from faculty parties, dignified man of standing, food technologist of the first order, impediment, innocent victim, human being who has never shown Ressler anything but trust. "Hello, Herbert. Ressler here. Wife home?" No mean feat with a mouth of pebbles and blades.

"I didn't recognize your voice. Drinking?"

"Dentist."

"Ha! Not the slurred speech of choice. The wife's in the study, all bothered over this new experiment of yours. Hold on."

After gruesome pleasantry, Ressler doesn't mind being left dead on the line. He stares at where his hand has been tracing out automatic writing on the phone pad: phonenumber phonember phonembryo phenomeber.

A silence comes across the receiver, one whose breathprint he has come to hear most hours of waking and deep into sleep. Her lungs, in and out, are a muffled Morse. Those soft pulses of silence are the one message they can transmit to one another uncoded. At last she says, "Stuart!" Cheerily, a little surprised for the benefit of her husband, listening in the distant room. Yet cloaked in a subtext intelligible only to him. Quite a trick, making the word serve double purpose for two parties. Her subsequent lines are the same—masterly ambiguous hermeneutic chestnuts. It scares him to hear that actress's modulation, her flawless delivery. She lies beautifully, as confidently as Eva Blake doing crosswords in pen.

But fright is also deeply silken, burgundy, arousing. He hears her excitement across the line, cadenced so that her husband cannot. He relishes the awful irony: she lets the man think we're discussing biochemistry. And we *are*. "Jeannie," he grits out through numbed mouth. "Jeannie, I'm sorry."

"No need for that. Hold on a moment. Let me get a pad. OK. Now: were you speaking in the short or long term?"

"I'm sorry for calling. I'm sorry for falling in love with you. I've had a hundred opportunities to stop. I wanted to. I'm sorry for ruining your life."

"Oh, I'm sure it's nothing we can't salvage. What's the damage, in your estimate?"

"Jeanette," he says "Darling. Friend. We have to quit."

"We can't." Perfectly modulated. "Not while we're ahead."

"Jeanette. You're killing me. Every minute is a terror that something's happened to you." Without thinking, he blurts, "You have to leave your husband."

At the other end, excruciating, ambiguous silence.

"We have to have each other."

423

"Well?" she giggles, eighteen, baiting, ignoring the chaperon. April invitation. "What's keeping you?"

Where is Herbert? Has he stepped out? Does she no longer care? Her invitation burns like a fist of opium, warm, loose, nothing to be done. He will go over this minute, taste her, feed her, make her call out to her husband in the next room that no, she wasn't shouting. Nothing wrong. Ressler looks down at his growing list: genenumber genome genehome. "I'll die, otherwise."

"Nobody likes death," she says, hands cupped to receiver.

"Listen. I need to ask you something. When you brought me that record...."

"Record?"

No longer in control, he begins to sing, through shattered mouth, half of a twisting, two-manual arabesque. No, a third of a trio: a simple descending line that, in this instance, implies, *in abstentia,* a flowing semiquaver figure, transparent, effortless, advancing in all directions, nowhere.

"Oh, *that* record," she laughs, despite his tuneless butchering of the Base. "*De goole bug.*"

"When you bought me that record...."

"Used," she corrects.

"When you gave it to me, did you love me already?" Did you think: We'll listen to this together, in some future life, you and I, free from all distraction, from the duplicitous waltz, innocent again, free to follow the tune, to go nowhere with it? "Why do I think of you when you aren't here?" He does nothing to help her out of the bind. She must deceive her own way out, with her own sick skill with words.

"That's a tough one. We could throw that one up for brainstorming, if you like."

"I need you. God, I'm sorry I'm even saying this. Why am I saying this?"

"No doubt there's a mechanism somewhere. But we shouldn't be too hasty, hmm? Perhaps we can't blame everything on ribosomal RNA?"

"Jesus Christ."

"I beg your pardon?"

"Say that again."

"I beg your...."

"Before that."

"Aren't we being a little hasty in blaming ribosomal...?"

424

"Dr. Koss!" An electric connection. She grasps it instantly. Whatever her weakness, her acting skill, her addiction to danger, her animal need, she too is driven by love of the pattern. "Oh, Stuart," she says, hushed. "'Jesus Christ' is right!" Crescendoed in those four words almost to a yell, she lowers her voice back to business tones. "No, Herbert. Everything's all right." Giggling almost hysterically into the phone. "Isn't everything all right, Dr. Ressler?"

It is. "How could we have been so stupid? Don't answer that. The ribosome isn't our message carrier. It's not the software transcript. It's just..."

"...the reading hardware," Jeanette supplies, giving the word a delicious twist. "Our messenger boy is..."

"...someone else by the same name. The RNA we're after disappears as soon as it's read." Of course: not the stuff that persists in the cell. Theirs is another transcript, ephemeral, one that can't stick around to clog the works with old commands. No wonder vitro hasn't produced yet; they've confused identities. When he speaks again, it's to himself. "How beautiful! The thing assembles its own assembly plants. It sends out an isomorph of orders for the production run. It uses its own end product to keep the whole process running. Magnificent." Its own hardware, software, storage, executor, writer, even client. What else? The code cannot be decoded except through by-products of the code. He might have known, *he,* another of the thing's by-products. "I'll call Botkin."

"She'll flip. You can't be wrong about this," she gushes carelessly. That slight oversight of tone recalls them from the intoxicating insight. She returns to the brisk voice of science, perfect in contrivance, disguised signaling. "Stuart. You've all but done it. I'll be in the lab early tomorrow. The procedures for testing this ought to be trivial."

"Goodbye, friend," he exhales, weary.

She returns, "Good night," imperceptible overtone catching in her throat, suggesting, *Dream of me,* as if that parameter were not already an errand boy, persisting, racing through his cell.

Storm Waltz (Da Capo)

```
writes(X,Y,Z) if knows(X,Y) ,alive(X) ,alive(Y) and
helps(heaven,X) and message(Z) and (curious(X) or
reawakened(X) or scared(X)) and in_love(X,Y).
```

message(Z) if quote_of_day(Anyone,Any_source,Z) or
question(Today, Z) or variation(Any_message,Z).

in_love(X,Y) if sea_change(X,Y,Anyone).

goal: writes(odeigh,todd,Z)?

1 Solution: Z =

Dear Franklin,
    Your letter arrived just when I'd cured myself of waiting. I read
it—I've lost count how often—and it still breaks my heart. What
am I supposed to make of you? Not one mention of the fact that
has driven me for months. Do you even realize? The man is *dead*.

XX

The Wife's Message

Writing was bad enough. Posting the thing felt like killing a baby. The unreal address and Franker's dreamy prose freed me to say things I'd never have written had I for a minute believed he might read them. He'll be reading them in days.

The incurable Todd denial of time drips from his every sentence, worse than his long-distance admission of love. I loved his time-indifference once, believed in it. Now I see that he doesn't even realize his infuriating, seductive residence in the eternal present. Nothing happens to anyone; no one changes or ages or dies. Everything exists, static; *now* is a standing wave. One just moves about inside the gallery, changing vantage, tilting an eyebrow, unbothered by closing hour.

Once, making fun of my three-by-five tone, he accused me of being thirty going on thirty centuries. But he was twenty-six going on twenty-six. When I first asked his age, he improvised: "I was born in St. Paul's Maternity Hospital on June 18, 1957, and instantly fell into a deep sleep from which I have since awakened only fifteen hours a day." Funny at the time.

When he was obsessed with transferring each day's *Times,* baroquely illustrated, into his spiral books, I thought here was a fellow intent on knowing his narrow sliver instant. Just the opposite: he meant to freeze solid the world's blood bank. Full compilation of everything that has happened would at last provide a place where nothing still did. Had he possessed the sticking power, his books would have swelled, not widthwise across the shelf but downwards, mine-shaft-style. In time—for one could always be sure of more time, somewhere in an eternally spacious future—

he would have gone back to pick up the missing pieces from the vertical file: first UN disarmament conference, Reagan slips surviving marines out of Beirut, haircut ($9.50), breast of chicken again. February repeats; so does the 3rd: why not the year as well?

His letter plasters over unaccountable cracks in chronology. Days spent nosing about in collections no longer *pass*. His *Hemelvaartsdag* trip to the Middle Ages: Ascension, a good half year before he wrote. Yet he lays out the detail as if last week. He has grown so cavalier with the calendar that he postdated the letter; no other explanation for how it arrived so quickly. When he bothers mentioning Dr. Ressler at all, it's a Ressler his own age, predisappearance, present tense.

If he came to my doorstep and petitioned in person, I would not be able to help myself, although the thing he cannot abide in me remains unchangeable. But *this*—this nostalgic declaration of attachment, a connection that continues in his mind just because he chanced recently to remember that it was ongoing *once:* impossible. Not now or ever.

Return Trip

We called our distress message back to the city. Jimmy groaned. "You two know you aren't supposed to travel together." A case of closing the disk file after the bytes escaped.

We borrowed a pound of oatmeal, a packet of coffee, and an ancient grain scoop from the contemptuous local whose phone we had hiked to. Sleepless, deliciously starved, we dug out. Late the next day, the plows sliced open the access road, clearing our umbilical. But before we were freed, we heard, in meticulous detail, how Dr. Ressler left microbiology. He narrated in open monotone, feeling the pull of those way stations again in proportion to their distance. Todd got his answer to how a person might descend into moratorium and never reemerge. And I learned that the man I'd researched was not who he was at all.

Not reticent, not demure, not this neutralized retreat behind grace and syntax. The effacing fifty-year-old was a detour, not Ressler by nature, not who he was slated to become. I began to see what had done it: circumstance and a certain turn of mind had conspired to give him violent proof that the individual organism

428

was a lie. Thoughtful, precise, romantic, driven, needy: the à la carte traits were all phantom, paper bookkeeping. The self was wedged between two far more real antagonists—the genes it was designed to haul around and the running average of a population statistically indifferent, even hostile, to it.

What possible response was there, upon discovering that all responses were embarrassing, misrepresentative semaphores? Laughter was after something; even kindness had ulterior motives. Character was composed of processes intent on short-term results. The molecule, eternally rolling its repertoire against the monster-generating numbers, cared as little for a trait as for its polar opposite. Life was not the polite venture it seemed at eye level. One step up or down the hierarchy and the project grew sweeping, terrible, so indirect in means that it made *him*, the best part of his nature, seem a self-duping, shady junior partner in a fly-by-night mail-order scheme.

Even pure science—the most advanced display of living potential—was not approved by either gene or population, both indifferent to any but practical knowledge. The one was a stupid, sniffing truffle hound rooting out instant gain, the other a totalitarian juggler, insatiable for accuracy. As unsavory as that left things, the linkup between molecule and mob was still so brute-beautiful that Ressler might well have lived on curiosity alone, even manipulated, puppet curiosity, were it not for one implication in the unified theory. Life proceeded not by survival of the fittest, but by differential reproduction. It was enough simply to make more than you lost. There was no Jacob's Ladder leading higher and higher. There was only breeding, faster, hungrier, until speed, appetite, and success did you in.

Yet life in theory (more beautiful because more crystal-cold) didn't do him in; life as lived did, the twist existence laid at his door. He could not erase his traits without erasing himself—a choice he stopped just short of. But he could swear off the self-serving bouquet of characteristics in abject humility. Monasticism. The night shift.

Snow-sprung, we headed south along the fastest route. Todd drove; Ressler rode shotgun. I studied this passenger in the front seat who, for no good reason except that we'd half guessed, had just told us his life story. His eyes had become reanimated, too hopeful, too alive to possibilities to bear looking at.

429

A 443

A slight sharp in the middle brass,
teeth-freezing, three beats fast:
masked quickly, yet more conspicuous
in being virtually home, but missed.

Near-hit dissonance is a shout:
someone whom love, in the darkening yard
held at arm's length, kept *almost*.
Always the choice: there or close,
the sharp catch of near miss
or the oblivion of concert pitch.

Return Trip (continued)

We reached MOL in the middle of the night. The waiting chaos
was worse than I'd imagined. The computer room's fluorescent
composure had been shattered into a parody of flyblown *Jugend-
stil*. Tables were stacked with slopped printouts, riffled listings,
and unraveling tape bands. The rack-bound operations manual that
usually sat regal as an OED was pulled apart into signatures, spread
all over the linoleum. Disk packs, dangerously uncovered, were
scattered everywhere, piled in model babels on top of spindles.
The smooth metal chitin of the CPU had been detached, revealing
a mass of printed circuit cards. Seated on the floor in front of the
bared cage, his back to the door where we entered, a dazed Uncle
Jimmy stared listlessly at the diagnostic LEDs. "James," Ressler
greeted him, between amusement and anguish.

Jimmy turned around slowly, as if the cavalry's arrival no longer
made any difference. "Don't even ask."

From behind the aisle of drives came Annie's excited treble. "Is
it really them?" She crept out, tape spools running up each slender
arm like Cleopatra's bracelets. Her hair had fallen in a flaxen heap
around her neck. She was rumpled and white from lack of sleep.
"I've been helping tide things over."

Franker began frantically inspecting the damage. "Don't tell me
it's been just the two of you here since. . . ."

"I wish it had been," Jimmy said, hoisting himself wearily off the floor. "They've been parading in and out for the last forty-eight hours. My people. Bank people. Hardware repairmen. Outside advisers. Everyone staying just long enough to screw up another thing before heading home for the wife and kids."

"I have no wife and kids," Annie said.

"You've been a brick, woman. A lifesaver. Not that we've managed to salvage anything."

Ressler sat at the console, leaned forward to read the screen full of error messages. He managed a remarkably calming voice. "How bad is it, Jimmy?"

"I haven't been home to see my mother since.... Damn you both." Even the man's anger was ludicrously devoid of hostility.

Ressler scanned the console log and asked, "What are you running at the moment?"

"Running? You jest. See those packs over there? Those are tonight's work. Those in the corner are from last night. Monday's packs are still up on the spindles."

Todd whistled. Jimmy nodded grimly. Dr. Ressler took off his coat and glanced around the room, looking for the best angle to approach the catastrophe. Then the two of them set into motion, like the mythic ants called in to carry off the chaff. Todd sorted reports, cumulating pages. He held out a sheaf toward me, turning his head. "Take these away. I'm not privy to them."

"But I don't know the code to the listings room."

"Me neither," he said woodenly, then whispered it in my ear.

Ressler went over to the Operations Manager, still paralyzed by the CPU. "Jim, we're sorry. We owe you. Now get home to bed. We'll see you on the day shift tomorrow, *when* you get here. Go. You're no good to us in your current condition."

Jimmy nodded dumbly and gathered to go. Annie, still pretty in raggedness, bleated out heroically, "What can I do?"

Ressler had already turned his back and was busy swapping the board that had failed. "You'd better go home too."

Annie only smiled: whatever he said was right. It hit me that she too adored the man, in her fashion. "I'll pray for the three of you."

"She'll do *what*?" I whispered to Todd, after they left.

He was unrolling the console log on a cleared swatch of floor, digging back into the transcript of the last three days for clues to reversing the disaster. His lips curled at my incredulous tone. "You didn't know?"

"Know what?" I began collating, punching emergency job cards, doing what little I could to help clean up.

His answer shocked me. "She's a fighting Fundy from Spiritus Mundi." Todd spoke more to his pencil ticks on the log than to me.

"But that's impossible."

"Why? Because she likes us?"

"Because she works for a DP firm. Because she graduated from a university."

Todd snorted. "Lots of religious folks graduated from university. Abelard. Luther. Jonathan Edwards. Oral Roberts. Everybody who ever graduated from Oral Roberts...."

"Stupid. You know what I mean. Really fundamentalist?"

"Literal, noninterpretable truth of every word in the Good Book. I'm not sure if that's King James or Revised Standard."

"And she's going to *pray* for us? Heaven will expedite the data backlog you two have unleashed?"

"Don't be cynical. It's not becoming. Besides: what Bible truths are you able to refute beyond all doubt?"

"Joshua commanding the sun to stand still?"

"This was before Newtonian mechanics."

"Methuselah living to be nine hundred and sixty-nine?"

"They had more ozone layer back then." He looked up suspiciously. "How, may I ask, did you remember that number exactly? You practice closet religion?"

"Please. Don't talk to me about closets and religion. I used to stay awake nights as a girl, terrified that the Blessed Virgin was going to pop out of mine. I used to pray *not* to be granted a vision."

"A Catholic!"

"Very apostate, thank you."

"Once a Catholic.... Did you know that if you summed the letters in all the popes' names and divided by four thousand four that you get six sixty-six?" He drew red circles around telltale spots in the console timeline. Annie's faith was burlesque counterpoint, incidental to the real metaphysical question of whether there was life after the death of his firm. I continued to help fetch things and enter keyboard codes. But the idea that someone I was friendly with believed that exactly 144,000 people were going to be saved come the Rapture wrecked me. I could not help harping on the point. "Do you suppose God put all those animal fossils deep in solid rock to test our faith?"

432

Todd laughed aggressively. "See all this?" He swept his hands over the chaos of the hermetic room. "God planted the seed for all this in...." He paused to do the simple product. "In one hundred and forty-four hours."

Across the room, from inside the crippled CPU, Ressler said, "That's less time than it's going to take us to clean it up."

I stayed the night, gophering, watching as they returned the machines to the state they'd been in at derailment. By the time the day shift filtered in, they had managed, by superhuman effort and suspect shortcut, to get the Monday processing underway. That left two and a half days of backlog, with Thursday's transactions about to come in. As I left, Ressler shook his head in disbelief. He smiled his old, demure smile—but with a hint that the disguise wouldn't wash anymore—kissed me on the cheek, thanked me for the trip, and said that perhaps praying was the proper algorithm in the circumstances after all.

I went straight from the warehouse to the branch, looking as rumpled as my friend the creationist had when she left to intercede with the creator. Back at work, greeted by Mr. Scott's sardonic eyebrow at my having at last deigned to return from extended vacation, I got down to addressing my own backlog—the public sector's most urgent questions.

The Question Board

How many dimples on a golf ball? My neighbor refuses to turn his stereo down; what legal recourse do I have? Is intelligence inherited? Where did goose-stepping originate? Can we afford to stand idly by? A farmer has a fox, a chicken, and a bag of feed; how...? What is the highest form of life that can be cloned? Why 'Big Apple'? What happened to Amelia Earhart? What's the most fundamental particle in nature? Does acupuncture work? What causes inflation? Who are the eleven thousand Virgins and where can I meet one? What can I do but move from sorrow to defeat? Why sixty seconds in a minute? Why not 5,380? Who made those statues in the South Pacific? Which weighs more, a pound of feathers or a pound of lead? What is the name of the projecting blocks supporting a roof beam? "Croatoan"? How many people in this century have died for political reasons? How many were going to St. Ives? When did the Age of Enlightenment end? Who calls so

433

loud? *Or se' tu quel Virgilio?* Is it possible to service domestic debt by adjusting foreign exchange rates? Which is better, Harvard or Yale? How many secretaries of state has this country had? What child is this who laid to rest on Mary's lap is sleeping? Where is the oldest-known surface on earth? Can one still join the French Foreign Legion? What was the name of that Eisenhower aide who got in trouble over a coat? What kind of coat? What's the difference between the United States and a carton of yogurt? *Kennst du das Land? Kennst du es wohl?* What is the common name for the family Chrysomelidae? Will machines ever think? Is my tap water poison? What about radon? Acid rain? The greenhouse effect? DES? Dioxins? The ozone? What the hand dare seize the fire? Did he smile his work to see? Is it true blondes have more fun? What's your sign? Will you still love me tomorrow? What causes cancer? Who turned out the lights? What is this world? What asketh man to have? Who told you you were naked? When will it suffice? What's a heaven for?

The Coding Problem

Todd woke me the next night. I rolled over and answered the phone without coming conscious. "Hello, Reference Desk."

"Hello, Reference Desk. Frank here. Did you see? We made the papers."

"The *what*?" Swifter than smelling salts.

"You know: today in history? All the News That Fits? Well, we're on Section A, page thirteen, column four, line number..."

"What did we do?"

"Nothing less than impede the March of Progress. 'Digital Blit Ripples Through System.' Special to the *Times*. 'A rash of electronic funds transfer problems have propagated through the banking networks in the last several days, causing serious delays throughout....'"

"Good God."

"Now, now. Let's not turn theistic under pressure. That's the first signal. From there, it's just a small step to frogs, hail, bread, and fishes."

"Shut up. Do they mention you by name? Do they say MOL?"

"'Those most familiar with the increasingly integrated computerized transfer routes admit the difficulty in identifying one specific node where delays begin. "That's like trying to pull the culprit from a fifty-car expressway pile up," says systems analyst..."'

"So you're not sure it's really your outfit?"

"*Our* outfit, lady," he snickered; having come along for the vacation, I couldn't weasel out now. "*I'm* sure it's us. Ressler is sure. The president of MOL is sure. But nobody's suggesting as much to the *Times* until we've doctored all the logs."

"Don't be ridiculous. Your whole office can't be larger than twenty thousand square feet. Even the day shift only employs a couple dozen people. How much weight can you possibly swing?"

"How big is a bit?" he replied. He went on, against regulations, to list clients of the firm—credit unions and financial outfits for half a dozen *Fortune* 500 companies, including two productless conglomerates whose names perpetually pop up in defense bidding.

"By itself, all our screw-up did was mess up these folks' books for a week, delay a few checks, block the flow of transactions. Big deal: they shell out excuses, we get slapped with a fine, and everybody waits till the status byte returns to quo. Problem is, no CPU is an island. Listen: 'The minor crisis, which industry analysts hope is now over, reveals the vulnerability of increasingly interdependent fiscal networks. Particularly sensitive are same-day overdrafts, when institutions transfer massive amounts of money they do not have, under the assumption that they will receive similar transfers to cover them in the immediate future. Any interruption along the line...'"

"Paraphrase, please."

"What do you mean, paraphrase? The thing already *is* a paraphrase. Every cell has to be in place for the lung to pump properly. Small inputs run up big outputs. A single snowfall in New Hampshire..."

"...can bring the entire post–Bretton Woods banking system to a standstill?"

I meant the crack facetiously, but I heard him doing the recursive algebra in his head at the other end. "Yes," he said. "With a few well-placed shoves from basic ineptitude."

I went by the first chance I had. They were still shoveling out; the place needed only the stink of manure to be the Augean stables. They had been on continuous surgical call since I'd left. Todd was as punch-drunk as he'd sounded over the phone. Dr. Ressler looked unflustered, alert, well-rested. He'd even managed to slip back into

435

a pressed suit, thinking to intimidate the crisis into submission by proper dress. Taped to the edge of a CRT was the clipping from the *Times*. All other evidence was extinguished. That evening they processed the previous day's transactions, submitting alongside the standard decks supplementary bug inoculations. "Do you know what a 'fix' is?" Todd asked.

"I know you're in one."

"Spoiled my punchline. A fix is when you patch a tag to a program reading, 'Amendment 12: Amendment 11 hereafter invalid.'"

"What are you repealing, exactly?"

"History. We have to settle the Master File's nerves. Convince it the trauma it's just been through never happened."

"How do you do that?"

"Much the way Stalin edited the textbooks until Lamarck became viable," Ressler said.

Todd chuckled. "All the data are backed up. That's what these tape drives are for. Transcriptions of every day for the last six years. We went back to the last uncorrupt day and fed in the duplicate transaction files all over again, doctored to look as if they were just coming in. The professor's footwork, of course. It worked, except for a few tumors, which we are now in the process of postdating and zapping with microlasers."

"No four-day delay? No same-day overdraft foul-ups?"

"Never happened."

Ressler explained, "Electronic records, unlike organisms, aren't compelled to drag around the trace of everything their ancestors ever lived through. We can rewrite them, assign them any past at any moment. We, by contrast, are trapped in every stopgap success our bases have ever come up with, the running average of our every *then*."

"But how can a little flypaper dive like this cause a quake in High Finance?"

"You surprise me. I would have thought that you, of all people your age, would have picked up on the emerging, central fact of modern existence."

"Namely?"

"The smaller the thread, the tighter the weave."

"Don't get him riled up," Todd cautioned from across the room. "We still have two evenings of work to finish tonight."

But it was too late. Dr. Ressler sat me down at the console.

"What would you like to know? What wing of this incredible house of cards would you like to visit?" To hear him talk, the keyboard was, in knowledgeable hands, an index into all embraceable space—gazetteer, thesaurus, almanac, anatomy, *Britannica* annual all ready to respond to the least finger nudge. "Let's start in our own backyard," he said. Where all inquisitive children begin exploration. He stroked the keys, cross-hands, answering system prompts faster than I could read them. A string of coded digits snaked in front of us:

```
53 6F 6D 65 74 69 6D 65 73 20 66 72 6F 6D 20 68 65 72 20 65
79 65 73 20 49 20 64 69 64 20 72 65 63 65 69 76 65 20 66 61
69 72 20 73 70 65 65 63 68 6C 65 73 73 20 6D 65 73 73 61 67
65 73 00 00
```

"Here we are," he said. "A little fragment of the master text. This could stand for anything in creation. Bank account, tech blueprint, love letter, combination of all three. All we see is a systematic disorder."

Todd sighed, "A systematic disorder in the dress kindles in me a wantonness."

"This says nothing in its present form, but it clearly possesses the irregular regularity needed to mean something more than it says. So which do you think this scrap is," Dr. Ressler quizzed, inclining his head. "Data or instruction?"

I hadn't the slightest idea. But on second look, with encouraging nods from Todd, I noticed two features that made the choice obvious. "Data," I said quickly, once I'd caught on.

"Good woman." He knew I'd get it before I did. He hit another key and the gibberish turned into fair speechless messages.

"Shakespeare," said Todd, leaning over our shoulders. "What do I win? I recently saw French literature defined as English literature sans the Bard." Ressler did not pause from file manipulation to reply. Todd cleared his voice ironically, persisting. "Who said, 'The French for London is Paris'? Think he said it in French, originally."

"*Je ne sais pas,*" I said. "I'm off duty." To my amazement, I found I was following Ressler's walking tour through the system. Just by long association with these two exiles, I had picked up the rudiments of programming.

He showed us how to disassemble a program, how the machine-readable switchs can be turned—by means of another program—

back into the logical operators that had generated them. He spoke of a colored oil drop in a cylinder of water, spun slowly until it dispersed, colorless, throughout the fluid. Spinning the fluid carefully in reverse can bring the oil drop miraculously back out of nothing. "The process is not entirely reversible. We can't get from the driving bits all the way back up to the high-level source language. But we can begin to see the programmer's design."

He demonstrated some structures. While condition Y applies, do X. Do this if these conditions are met, otherwise do that. For all values in the list L, run routine R. Go here. Test that. Change the other thing. When done, return. He showed me how to build a patch: save down all current values that must remain the same. Change a byte or two so that it branches to a space in the program left blank for that purpose. Write your appended routine there, and then pop back, restoring all previously saved values.

These generic commands, he explained, were the meat and potatoes of procedural languages. Procedural languages—those that mapped out every route the machine could take—were the lingua franca of business computing. Business, Ressler showed me, as he pulled up the skeleton keys to the programs they used to process their hundred thousand clients' health, education, finance, and welfare, was nearing its finest hour. "The logical conduits on silicon have done to the ebb and flow of capital what the Dutch waterworks did to the Zuider Zee."

"Speaking of the Dutch," Todd interrupted, growing desperate, "I'd love to get caught up tonight. Wooden Shoe?"

Ressler sent him out for grocery-store wine. By the time Todd came back, we were navigating through the Federal Reserve via MOL's linkup with a battalion of bank mainframes. Under his arpeggiating fingers, portals opened, rabbit holes that we disappeared down before they closed over us. I could no longer keep track of imbedded levels, just whose system prompts we were responding to. We tunneled deep into the web, far from home.

"I had no idea," I said. "When you make the link, it's just as if you were sitting in front of the other machine in some other office?"

"With semiconductors, physical locations become arbitrary. Half our work takes place at remote sites. That's why this suite can be so small."

"These machines talk to one another? Without chaperon?"

He smiled. "Under the supervision of procedural languages."

"Can you get anywhere from anywhere else?"

"Not yet. Think of the U.S. highway system in the twenties. Lots of the local infrastructure, but the expressways still going in. Still, one can swing quite a distance along existing vines." He got us onto a system that allowed us entry to yet another nested net; in no time we were browsing machines in Washington, Oak Ridge, San Francisco. The effect was dizzying. For a man who'd stayed home for twenty years, he got out a lot.

For my benefit, he pulled up a sampler of bibliographic services, retrieval banks now creating the largest revolution in my discipline since Alexandria burned. Our branch had not yet entered the future, and I had yet to play personally with the first generation of living Reference Desks. Christmas all over again. "Go ahead," he said. "Ask it anything."

I typed: "MACHINE; INTELLIGENCE," and got back a bibliography as long as a Mannerist Madonna's neck. I highlighted one of the titles and got the full text. The strangest sensation came over me—the recovery of a lost domain, the bafflement of childhood, a displaced hope older than memory. What might we yet see, name, feel?

"In the future, you'll be able to type, 'What happens to nuclein when it's boiled in water for forty hours?' and the thing will come back, 'According to a study by Albrecht Hessel in 18....' The next step will be getting it to print articles that haven't been written yet."

I couldn't tell how serious he was. "All of this is assembled with only Ifs, Thens, Gosubs, and Elses?"

"No. These make ingenious use of tools that a person can *really* love." And he described, in tantalizing sketch, the new declarative languages. He made them sound like returns to the Ur-tongue. They relied not on rules but on simple assertions about the nature of things in the defined world. They blurred the distinction between data and instruction, set the machine free to serve as inference engine.

"Which is DNA, procedural or declarative?"

Dr. Ressler smiled soundlessly and looked at his watch. "Short answer or long?"

I felt what had been tearing at my heart the last several weeks, why it hurt progressively worse each time I saw him. He had grown ready to teach, undertake again, discover. Something in Todd's and my blundering, slow courtship had tricked him into thinking this time it could go right. I sensed in the way his eyes grabbed at every word thrown his way that he had recovered a capacity for application. But there was nothing for him to apply himself *to*. He had awakened for nothing, for a wrong number. A roof-gardener, harvest brought in for the year, receiving unsolicited seed catalogs in the depths of winter.

"It's a grim irony," he said, waving toward the screen, "that just as we are closing in on the perfect taxonomy we've always been after, we may already have spoiled the data beyond recognition. And yet, our effort to bring it on-line is beautiful. Beautiful in the way that a child's first book, all folded and crayoned over, is beautiful." He tilted his head oddly, and I realized he had in mind one particular child, whose conspicuous absence at last informed him, here at the end of the day, that he had never had a real home.

We were still at the bibliographic prompt that for the last several minutes had kept me as rapt as a toy chemistry set. Abstractedly, he typed a woman's name—last name, comma, first. After a pause just longer than anguish, the system responded, "6 Match(es)." He turned away. When he could speak again, his voice was controlled. "See what one can find? And the first integrated circuit was invented just twenty-five years ago." *The year I left the game,* he didn't add. He hit a few stop-key combinations, backing us out of binary pontoons, dropping all carriers until we returned to the dingy suite.

When I left, sad beyond provocation, I gave Todd a duplicate key to my place. "Come tonight. Anytime. Move in if you can."

He woke me up when he came in. We had a few unreal hours before I had to go to work. Ice had paisleyed over the panes with a second, opaque window. In hard February, I paid the price for my place's turn-of-the-century quaintness. Fuel ran a hundred-meter hurdle up through the Victorian insulation into the freezing night. We held one another, wanting the relieving friction but not daring to rub—like a retriever trained to carry the shot bird back in its jaws without salivating. "Do you think...?" I tried to ask, still glazed in sleep. "Is it possible... he still loves this woman?" For the first time since fullness had taken me, I thought of Tuckwell, alone in our old place, in front of that breathtaking view of skyline.

Todd answered me with such an answer. I never knew him. I never had the first idea of what men were. "Love is a pyramiding scheme," he said, and pressed my hands together until they hurt. "He never loved her more than tonight."

Frailty and Other Fixed Constants

The world churns out a tune Ressler just now learns to hear. The U.S. at last lifts Explorer I into orbit. It begins testing at Eniwetok and rejects a Polish proposal to make Central Europe nuclear-free. The Sixth Fleet doubles its presence in the Middle East; by summer's end, American troops will land there. Emergency forces will be in the Caribbean by spring. Veep Nixon's goodwill tour in Latin America will provoke open hostility. The army announces the STRAC, a 150,000-troop acronym committed to winning limited war "anywhere in the world."

One, frail fermata in that dissonant strain: Van Cliburn wins the Tschaikovsky competition, making him the most popular Texan in Georgia. Vaughan Williams dies just after the debut of his final symphony, a last holdout against Boulez and Berio. "Jailhouse Rock," "He's Got the Whole World in His Hands," and "Purple People Eater" (thinly disguised political allegory) top the pops. To the casual listener, the synthesized bass is lost in a ravishing circle of chords, lovely terror, a broken horizontal stream rushing toward greater complication. Sheer counterpoint is loosed upon the world.

The quizz-show scandal breaks. Jack Benny admits to being forty. A leading manufacturer brings out a nontoxic floor wax, to save infants that lick their way across the kitchen. According to *Time,* eleven thousand new "citizen-consumers" are born every day in the U.S., adding a city the size of Norfolk, Virginia, every thirty days. "A new wave of opportunity coming."

Science too can't help but join the footrace. The accidental clarity that Ressler and his love stumbled upon over the phone remains solid, even in the unforgiving light of following days. Botkin declares the proposed angle as right as an inevitable passacaglia. They sit in her office listening to Fauré, Franck, drawing up the apparatus needed to confirm his serendipitous insight.

In barely controlled excitement, Ressler does the week's summary for Cyfer. He begins all the way back in the uncontestable: the double helix. Not even Woytowich holds out against the model any longer. He has just become a father—an architectural marvel named Ivy. The impossible reprieve leaves him open to even the

441

most outlandish proposals about life's generating plan. Taylor's radiographs, too, transcend disagreement, proving that DNA replicates by that classic postwar cure-all, political partition. One message splits into two; two halves each restore the one message. The simplest form of molecular baby-making: divide and regenerate.

Adding a demonstration of Mendelian inheritance for mutations, Ressler presses up against the last unequivocal certainty. This double-twined ribbon pastes up, from its internal library, the army of proteins that pump, breathe, inflame, hoist the whole organism. The rest is tentative, beyond the limits of current, territorial waters.

"Our own work," Ressler casts a cold eye at Ulrich, "elaborates the decoding parameters: triplet, colinear nonoverlapping, unpunctuated bases. We know that DNA never leaves the nucleus. I submit that it sends out a courier, a single-strand RNA molecule templated on its surface, a plaster-cast of the recipe. This messenger strand carries its transcription of a base sequence—call it a gene, for old times' sake—to the ribosomes, where protein synthesis takes place." He draws a freehand philosopher's stone on the blackboard:

In Nucleus   **In Ribosome**
DNA —(transcription)→ RNA —(translation)→ Protein

"OK," says Ulrich. "Two separate processes. One directly templated, one read and assembled. Ribosomal RNA promoted to translator, not message. Valuable," the chief concedes. "But does it get us any closer to *reading* the bugger?"

Introducing a new, ephemeral, RNA messenger—itself a single-ribboned series of four bases, with uracil substituting for the thymine in DNA—doesn't change the informational nature of the problem. From a cryptographic vantage, it makes no difference whether the code word is the RNA simulation or its DNA original. They still track the old, elusive pattern. So despite the opportunity staring him in the face, Ulrich insists that codon assignment is more a symbolic problem than a chemical one. He fails to see that Ressler's clarification gives them an experimental wedge, a way of simulating nature's own mechanism, letting the cell solve the problem for them. Instead, Ulrich is preoccupied with his own pronouncement: the discovery of a way of juggling the letters to produce a pattern so satisfying that it must be correct.

442

Ulrich announces, in competition with Stuart's unsubstantiated diagram, that he, Lovering, and new conscript Woytowich may be in a position to land the Big One. "The closer we get, the better it looks. DNA splits loose along the inside seam to present the base sequence. Either edge might code for the protein, so any codon and its complement on the anti-gene would stand for the same amino. The triplet AGU thus codes for the same thing as its Chargaff anticodon UCA on the other strand. Two chains, two directions, so to the synonyms AGU and UCA, we can add UGA and ACU. Four words under the same thesaurus heading."

"Treatment by retrograde and inversion," Toveh Botkin mumbles, troubled. "Bach was fond of putting fugue subjects through both." *So was this fellow Schoenberg,* thinks Ressler, who's done his homework on the matter. But that proves nothing. He's nonplussed and can do nothing but keep still and follow the working-out.

Ulrich lists the sixty-four-codon catalog according to groups of shared degeneracy, the plan growing increasingly obvious:

Codon	Inversion	Retrograde	Retrograde inversion
ACG	UGC	GCA	CGU
AGC	UCG	CGA	GCU
ACC	UGG	CCA	GGU
AGG	UCC	GGA	CCU
AUG	UAC	GUA	CAU
AUC	UAG	CUA	GAU
AUU	UAA	UUA	AAU
ACU	UGA	UCA	AGU
AAG	UUC	GAA	CUU
AAC	UUG	CAA	GUU
GAC	CUG	CAG	GUC
GGC	CCG	CGG	GCC
AAA	UUU	—	—
GGG	CCC	—	—
AUA	UAU	—	—
ACA	UGU	—	—
AGA	UCU	—	—
GAG	CUC	—	—
CAC	GUG	—	—
CGC	GCG	—	—

"All sixty-four permutations. The set contains twelve fourfold synonyms and eight twofold synonyms." With a touch of showman's pause, Ulrich says, "Twelve plus eight equals our magic number." The pattern is stunning in its own, horrific way. The rationale for construction seems at least reasonable, and the numerology is perfect. That Ulrich has leapfrogged empirical constraints to get there seems temporarily defensible.

"But it's all wrong," Ressler whispers, glancing at Botkin for support. He's afraid to appeal to Koss, afraid to look at her in public for fear that her ephemeral face might make the day's pragmatics too much to bear. But it's Koss who comes to his aid. She objects, grounded in the best literature, to the idea that the complementary strands are being read equivalently. For all her substantiated accuracy, the facts wash up impotently against perfect pattern.

That Ulrich's subdivision of sixty-four triplets uncannily produces a hidden number equal to that of the essential amino acids carries the surprise significance of arithmetic. He is under the spell of physics, where the pursuit of fundamentals pares back a mass of data to simple, elegant expressions. It seems safe to assume that cellular mechanisms, carded back to their core, are also driven by symmetry. But it's not safe; safety and life science are incommensurate. That one can derive twenty from sixty-four with pretty, reciprocal twists may be nature's sheer perversity.

Botkin lowers herself into the line of fire. "Grammars are not usually so clean." Her cheeks contract bittersweetly: don't we always mean more than we say? Why not the we within us?

But the objection of one senior member is offset by another. Woytowich, revived by infant Ivy, wanting to be worthy of her when she is old enough to evaluate fathers, throws his hopes in with Ulrich's dash for the cymbal crash. "It's not evidence, of course; but the fit's attractive enough to do some stat analysis on those groups we think might be equivalents."

Lovering's vote is a foregone conclusion. There's only one way Ulrich can run that sort of analysis: through ILLIAC. And Lovering has proved so skilled at programming that he has replaced Stuart as Cyfer's fair-haired boy. All Ulrich's hopes are now pinned to numeric confirmation of his simple table. Ressler tries again to interest them in in vitro, but these three refuse to concede that the codon catalog is arbitrary, devoid of internal order. The debate comes down to temperament, individual hobby horses. What each feels ought to be true. The team splits down the middle—gnostics versus nominalists, formalists against functionalists. They forget the first article of scientific

444

skepticism: meaning always reveals pattern, but pattern does not necessarily imply meaning.

Ressler cannot fault Ulrich for leaping to the beautiful conclusion. Would Stuart have begun in science if he wasn't predisposed to believing that what lay behind common sense was more beautiful because more objectively indifferent, dense, feverishly specific? Ulrich sends them off with his blessing: "Both parties' results to be continuously exchanged, of course." Yet Ressler knows he will be out a fellowship come spring. He is resigned, for his own sake, to losing everything, every professional advantage, for a glimpse of the demonstrable. Only now, he has dragged Botkin and Koss into the breach with him. Against their careers, he has only a vague plan: learn the trick of the cell-free system.

They now know the tube must include synthesis-active RNA messenger chains as well as ribosomes. They'll also need an energy source, ATP, and the raw amino building blocks. Their technique is still crude: throw them together; see what you get. On evidence, he is no less culpable than Ulrich, perhaps even *more* stained by faith, hope, and love—the old triumverate keeping life perpetually on the trail of its own suspected order.

But he is not ready to tell Botkin or Koss the wildest of his suspicions: the double helix somehow codes not only for its own messenger, but also for the elusive adaptor, the ribosome assembly line, and all the enzymes needed to recognize the adaptor, affix the amino acids, promote the growing chain, and trim the finished proteins. Enzyme-trimming enzymes. Ribosome-building ribosomes. Synthesis must itself be synthesized. The machine is as self-bootstrapping, as self-*selfing* as consciousness itself. Why not? Consciousness, the thirst for exchange and research, is just the self-selfing chain writ large, considering, synthesizing itself.

Why so complex a path? Why so many intermediaries? And how can everything come from four simple bases? Ressler, even now, closing in on tendering a first, tentative model of the arrangement, is blocked by his own unspeakable desire to ambush the experiment, wreak the control by introducing the irreducible variable of personality. He hears it in the deep cell's core, lapping at the heart of comprehension. Despite the danger, he cannot help it. He must make a little room in himself for himself, for the same mistaken guide that now leads half of

445

Cyfer astray, for that terrible Pauline triplet. And of those three, most of all love.

Self Help

Each passing day has payoffs. Ressler, Koss, and Botkin daily refine the bottled-synthesis technique. He sees one perhaps uncrossable barrier in front of them. On that day when they can finally drop a stretch of active RNA into the chemical mix and have it produce its isomorphic protein, the resulting sequence will still be beyond direct chemical correlation with its source; they might still require Ulrich's ILLIAC bulldozing for any hope at analysis.

Fat chance that Lovering will be forthcoming with his do-loops for the competition's sake. Ressler learned programming as a tyro undergrad—how to octal-toggle machine code directly into Core an instruction at a time. Worse than annihilating on the nerves; not surprising that the average software cowboy ran into a breakpoint at thirty-two, sent home with smoke steaming from the circuitry. Even punching cumbersome codes into Hollerith columns seemed small improvement. While it did save wear on the neural nodes, coding remained hell and debugging impossible.

It was with the zeal of a convert that he welcomed the work of Von Neumann and others, who lumped common machine instructions together and made them available as macro commands. Assemblers—programs that take macros and generate machine-executable code—still strike him as miraculous kludges, like the first wind-catching membrane stealing upon those lizards that had been hopping about in trees. Released, the analogy spread like disease. Full-fledged compilers were upon him before he finished graduate school. Compilers, of course, are themselves written in assembly language, giving the whole tower of Boolean babel more than a facade's resemblance to the House That Jack Built. Code-writing code. Program-designing programs. Uncomfortably like the thing they built this tool to help examine. Why stop there? Why not assembler-assemblers? Application-generating applications? Jacob's Ladders off and runging, climbing themselves; tools that turn the trick of replication. Among the projects that the Lovering-Ulrich-Woytowich pattern-matching program time-shares ILLIAC with is one to write a high-level ALGOL language compiler. In ALGOL.

446

Without further refinement of their cell-free system, Ressler, Koss, and Botkin will have to stay on good terms with Joe, something that grows increasingly difficult with the man's expanding personal triumphs. Lovering, finding his vocation in programming, is on the ascendant. His well-being is consolidated by the devotion of the much-touted Sandy. Ressler has still not met the woman, but to hear Joe speak of her, she is all sweet surprise and variety personified.

The accounts Lovering sprinkles liberally over his office mate are ludicrously effusive. The woman lisps in numbers. She's built like a shit brickhouse, although Joe produces no photos to substantiate. She plays Mozart with the proper smidgen of rubato. *And* she understands Lovering's own abstruse work, without his yet conceding to bring her around the lab. "I explained the gist of the coding problem to her the other night. Granted, she didn't take in all its particulars. Who can? But in her own words—without any formal training—she came up with this beautifully intuitive formulation of framing."

"How does she feel about code degeneracy?" Ressler asks. The man's adoration of the woman grates on him. He wants to shake him violently until the blathering stops. But for reasons Ressler's reason more than comprehends, the most he can level against the self-deceiving fellow is gentle kidding.

"Go on, laugh. She anticipated the proof against overlap."

"Jesus, Joe. You'd better go nuptial. When's the date?"

"Just after yours, Dr. Ressler." Miffed, Lovering addresses his card-punch forms.

"Seriously. With a woman like this falling into your hands, you ought to cleave, be fruitful, and multiply. If they let Dr. and Mrs. Woytowich do it, surely..."

"Who says we ain't cleaving?" Lovering looks up slyly. "I told you, Sandy doesn't believe in licensing love. We've talked it over, and neither of us sees why we have to pander to the boojwah by going through with dress-ups. That's a socializing trick, all that paper signing. The only party to profit from marriage as it is currently defined in middle-class America is the State. We've drawn up our own contract."

"Joey, I can't help thinking that you've chosen the wrong moment in history to make an experiment in alternative mores. Just yesterday I read about this minister who was defrocked for using the word 'sex' when preaching the seventh commandment."

"How can they hurt us? We've just put a payment down on a house. We move this weekend. It has a room for her piano, and a garden plot, and . . ."

Botkin knocks softly and enters. Hearing the conversation she unwittingly walks into, she sits by Ressler's desk like a frightened undergraduate. Ressler says, "A house. That's nice, Joe. But how are you going to go about making babies?"

"Stuart! And you claim to be a biologist. Historically speaking, there have been some very impressive genomes born out of wedlock."

"Who you calling a bastard?" Woyty calls from the doorway. He enters, evening the gnostics and nominalists in the room. He has come hunting down Lovering with more sequences to key in. But he capitalizes on the opportunity to sentence the party to baby pictures. Seven-pound Ivy Woytowich looks to Ressler exactly the way every newborn looks: a hive of tube worms attacking a soft-boiled beet.

"Sandy's already made it plain that I'm free to sample other women, so long as all my offspring are with her."

" 'A miss for pleasure and a wife for breed,' " Botkin supplies. "As far as I have ever heard, we are the only species who seek out nonprocreative liaisons. Who get distressed when the surrogates accidentally do the job they substitute for. Do you suppose we succeed in tricking our genes into irrelevant pleasure? Or do they still get the surreptitious last laugh?"

"What is this woman *talking* about?" Lovering asks the other men. Ressler knows. Botkin looks so sadly at him that she must certainly have guessed everything there is to guess about who is fooling whom.

In the following days, the shame of that look drives Ressler to force the equilibrium of aroused danger he lives in. He will push at the precarious spot, get to know his enemy, the rightful husband. The man she sleeps with every night in abject intimacy. He cannot invite himself to their home, sit on their settee, run a semantic differential on Herbert Koss as she looks on. His trial must be isolate, valid. Life, as always, supplies its own contrivance: the Local Industries Trade Show at the Champaign Holiday Inn. This year's theme is "1983: How We Will Live a Quarter Century On." Every east-central Illinois entrepreneur in the book has banded together to reassure the consuming public that the future will continue to present no end of new things to buy. The roster of participants lists Herbert Koss as a principal. Booth 112: "Better Food in a Fuller Tomorrow." Ressler locates him on the newsprint map amidst a forest of voice-activated appliances, vibrating soap, self-regulating lawn grass, and power-driven exercise cycles.

Ressler catches the food technologist manning the booth alone. Herbert and his outfit have taken a conservative stance compared to the antigravity, space-station approach of other vendors. His predictions are modest. Hexagonal steaks for efficient storage. Vegetable appliqué that cooks on the stove top. Plastic wrap at once spoil-retardant, clingy, and edible. Herbert's brave new delivery systems attract a continuous lull. Ressler wonders if he need introduce himself; he has met the man only casually, half a minute at a time. But Herbert greets him at once, friendlily, his color deepening to rose under the convention-hall neon.

"Dr. Ressler," he blusters. "Ha! You would have to catch me in my finest hour." They shake quickly. "My wife said you were likable, but coming to say hello to a neglected huckster is beyond the call of duty." He spreads his hands over his display, deeply embarrassed. "I assume you have no genuine interest in how the future bodes for edible goods."

The man's no fool. Just an engineer making a living. His self-deprecation fills Ressler with shame for the daily transgressions of thought, word, and everything up to and all but including deed against this man, whose carriage and speech embody a quality promoting him beyond contempt: good-natured humility. Ressler has for weeks enjoyed the self-congratulatory belief that disinterested tinkering with nature was somehow more virtuous than retail. Now he stands in front of the man, quietly accepting indictment in the lines of this fortyish, kind face. His failure to pick up the conversational gambit only makes Mr. Koss more graciously awkward.

"It's generous of you to pretend to really want the spiel. This peculiar gadget seems to be garnering the most attention at this year's show." He picks up a sealed can outfitted with metal nozzle. "Believe it or not, we've injected this full of cheese that has, alas, been pasteurized until it has become virtually eternal. It is probably also flame-resistant and impervious to radiation." Herbert bites a nail, but Ressler assures him with approving silence: The humiliation is all mine.

449

"The nozzle is still a little rickety. But in twenty-five years, I hope someone can bring this prototype into production. The long-term goal is to shoot cheese out in a controlled spray." He looks up from the device: I'm sorry; it's what I *do*. Whatever work your hands can find to do, do now.

"No," Stuart objects. "Go on. Please. It looks as if it will be very ... useful." Herbert thanks him in silence. A look of complicity passes between them: Ah! But what's the use of use?

"Our main problem may not be the nozzle, however, but the plate presentation. As you see, the product at present bears an unfortunate resemblance to something you might scoop up after a Great Dane." Chuckling forlornly. In a moment, both men are laughing at a puerile species that can never stop ludicrous ingenuity, can't see what a fool it makes of itself in this world. Only invention's source, the loneliness longer than life, prevents the evidence from condemning the lot of them.

Ressler stops first. "Herbert, your wife is ... wonderful."

Koss beams, proud without pride. "I envy you both, really."

Ressler's head snaps back. "What do you mean?"

"I would have liked to be a scientist." He shrugs at the spin-offs all around him in the booth, the garden he wound up in.

Ressler dismisses him with a wipe in the air. "No difference. You've heard that Congress is deciding whether actors in white coats have to identify themselves as simulations? If they do, we'll all be undertitled." They kick around that topic: Truth in Nomenclature. Herbert contributes his nemesis—a Western senator with a touch of religious mania and a mission to legislate the labels on synthetic foods. The law would prevent manufacturers from selling juice as "Juice" unless it contains a given percentage of real fruit sap. Others would require a suitable euphemism.

"Our outlandish creation here would be forced to go forth into the world under the ignominious name of 'Artificial Pasteurized Processed Cheeselike Food—Stick Drink—Spread Mix Spray.' It simply isn't fair to the entrepreneur."

Ressler laughs. He can't help himself. He likes this man, as much as he's liked any man since Tooney left. "Our legislators would be shocked to hear that evolution's greatest successes deliberately misrepresent appearances. Nature has never abided by truth in advertising." Your wife can attest to that.

"Jeanette's convinced me that your splinter group is on the right track." Ressler smiles, wincing. "Jeannie brings the journals into

450

bed with her, and reads them out loud. We share a great deal." Herbert asks him his opinion of the possibility that cancer is gene-induced. The man may not have become a scientist, but no failure of curiosity, attention, or temperament prevented him. He is more current on this topic than Ressler, but Stuart takes a stab at the challenge. "A stretch of nucleic acid could code for a tumor-inducing enzyme, but a mutator gene is more likely, or a faulty feedback that causes other genes to run amok. All speculation, but I can at least conceive of an oncogene."

The comeback arrives from over his shoulder. "I had an Onco Gene, once."

Ressler sees her reflection in Herbert Koss's face: the painter in the convex mirror behind the subjects. The creases in Herbert's face swell like a succulent after flash flood. Even the cadence of his voice picks up conviction as he cracks back, "I remember him! Your Onco Gene and your Anti Body."

With a single-finger signal upon Ressler's back, Jeanette springs to her husband and kisses him behind the ear. The married couple exchange a few tokens of their idioglossia, the most natural thing in the world. Ressler is stunned: the husband is hopelessly in love, and the wife accepts his ministrations with a marvelous insistence on the ordinary.

"Wife, you must invite this fine fellow to have dinner with us." Herbert touches her upper arm in a way suggesting, circumspectly, that he may have found a friend.

"Fellow, you heard the man." Jeanette, perfectly modulated, relishes the idea. Ressler barely manages to mumble a transparent excuse, blanching at the look of hurt confusion coming over Herbert's face. The Know Your Enemy campaign retreats from the field in disarray, Ressler smiling but routed.

For the next several days, he avoids her. He frequents the lab at night or when she is busy teaching. When they must be there together, he makes sure it's in the company of others. She touches his upper arm as she passes—familial, furtive, questioning. But she knows the source of his silence, and neither of them cares to put it in words. She leaves him gentle and absurd gifts as apology— currants, offprints, lozenges at the first hint of a cough. She moves through the day visibly holding her breath. She sheds all trace of public sarcasm. Lovering continues to give her ample opportunity to deliver the quick cut, but the woman contritely declines the kill. One of those creatures with two-stage life cycles, having meta-

451

morphosed in front of his eyes from sylph back into cipher, she wants nothing but another chance to return to the pupa and re-emerge with all the chestnut innocence she last week lost for him.

He finds it impossible to concentrate on the empirical work. His desire to perfect the cell-free system stalls against Jeanette's opacity, more cryptic than when she was a stranger to him. Curiosity has gone, leaving in its place a fatalistic homesickness opposed to investigation of any sort. He does not love her now. And yet, a keener coveting: she is more intensely beautiful for having so far declined to confirm him. Beauty, as Botkin once read to him during their joint listening sessions, Schubert's *Winter's Journey,* is just the beginning of a terror he might not be able to endure.

He is taken by absurd urges to plead with her, to demand explanations. Of course, he cannot, even if the explanations were his to demand. He will lose her the moment his feigned self-possession admits to need. No begging. Self-preservation now depends on a deadly competition: can he escape faster than she? He slips into the lab late one afternoon, safe for the thirty seconds he needs. But immediately, tailed to this one injudicious half-minute, he is cornered by a lab-coated, dissimulating apparition.

"May I come over and play?" She walks slowly toward him, then stops, hovering near where he stands, not daring to come flush to him. She wears her lab coat, a soft, brushed olive skirt, an organdy blouse sweetly fatigued. Dark stockings hold her legs heartstop-pingly limber. She is less clinical than reckless, frightened, precariously still. She pushes back a loose forelock, then holds the nervous forearm in her other hand, to keep it from straying. She just looks, beseechingly, too uncertain to say anything. At last, she shakes her head, giving in: "You really are a beautiful boy."

Her simple, head-down, sole-scuffing benign capitulation betrays her. Passion now would be powerless against him, but soft, dependent admission of hurt calms him before he can run. She holds his gaze, opaline, opalescent. When she finally smiles, it is with relief, as if he has favored her already with his inevitable return. "Stuart. Friend. We have to talk."

He chills without missing a beat. Pith me mercifully, then. "Don't worry," he says, suppressing the trace betrayal. "We stay on the project together. In vitro is as much your province as mine. We'll just have to find a way of working in close quarters without pulling the pin."

She stares at him, slapped down, laughing through choked throat at the frailty just revealed. She looks at him, shaking her head: Boy-o, how could you think it? Don't you realize: we can't get out now, except together. "You said you loved me," she says quietly, courage enough for both. "I've been thinking of nothing else since you admitted it."

"Nothing else?" One lie and we drown in atmosphere.

She gives him a bashful overbite that would disarm the coolest Geneva negotiator. "I won't tell you what else has gone through my head since then. Not yet, anyway." She steps toward him, a supplicant. Only believe. He does not step back. He fixes on her teeth: how can even her incisors incite him? They ought to seem more like tetanus hooks than pretty advertisements. She does not stop until they touch thighs, here in the open. She does not care who sees them.

"How could you...? You're so natural with him. You're..."

Her sweet undertones flatten into a quick cat's hiss. "What were you doing tracking him down? Spying? Big buck showdown? Imagine how *I* felt, seeing you talking with him behind my back."

Her anger releases him. She might fake everything else, but not this surpassing flash of hatred. "Jeanette," he says, loving her so acutely his chest feels the phantom pain of amputation. Names he never wished to be saddled with—the photo of a luminous child who died just after the lens opened. "Jeannie. Your husband is great. Kind, bright, funny." He, in comparison: ambitious, hungry, vain. Even were he in the man's league, any trade would invalidate everything.

"Yes," she admits harshly, the tear of the barbed gaff.

He takes her at the waist, knowing even as he does it that it is the worst possible gesture. "You two love each other. I've seen it."

"He's a good man. We get along. We know one another."

"But you're not...?" He stops short of the ridiculous semantic distinction. Her nervous lock falls again, obscuring her lowered face. He reaches, brushes it back. "Something in your marriage is not working?" Temporarily reprieved by that indifference he could not rouse earlier, when he needed it.

But his detachment lasts only until her next words. Her cheeks crumple horribly. Blood rushes into her soft tissue, and she chokes for air. "We can't have children." A day later, Ressler will not remember the precise next sequence. Jeannie falls into his shirt, dry-heaving, hyperventilating sobs. Water everywhere—eyes,

453

nose, throat. Her vulnerability, her flood is at last *her,* one that he recognizes, recalls from internal phylogeny—cave life or earlier, arboreal, forest floor, or gilled, underwater. It pitches Ressler into the passion of animals. He begins to kiss her everywhere across the unrecognizable bruise her face has become. She kisses back. She bites, trying to break the skin. "Help me," she says, as if he were the only one who could. "What's *wrong* with me?"

XXI

Canon at the Seventh

They rut. No other name for the humping that takes them. He kisses her blood-filled face, scattering the hits, surrendering to dizzy inertia. She sinks her teeth into his shoulder, sick desire clamping her to him. Her frightened, little-lamb's-backsliding capitulation passes into his tissue and he can only clamp back. Sobbing, startled, she looks at him, realizing the place where they've arrived. They fall into the fabled clearing, forbidden and inevitable, the place they knew from the first caught glance they would one day inhabit. She loosens from him long enough to lead him to the back lab corner, beyond equipment shipment boxes: for form's sake, out of the public thoroughfare.

Den, hive, nest, nidus, eyrie, newlywed starter home: they build themselves a pallet on the floor. They pull each other down hungrily. He unfastens her organdy, exposing the final freshness of her breasts to the air. She stretches along the length of her flank, moans an admixture of pleasure and regret. Her exertion ripples like the paroxysms of a barometer giving up in the eye of the storm. We can't. Don't do this. Wrong, childish, wicked, degenerate. Please. Faster. Here. Home. They are to go through with it, in full cognizance, commit the self-seeking, indulgent act. It stops his breath.

He lifts the crumpled olive skirt up around her waist. Jeannie gasps once, an angry aspirant. Her stockings and panties give way. She utters sharp, soft forest noises. The sound, the pungency of her vaginal quiff undo him. He rolls into her. Her legs lift, ready to receive. The space is his only. They fit. Her small-mammal whimpers condense in violence. He clasps his hand over her mouth, but even now does not really care if every living thing just down the hall hears. He is drawn up her by capillary action, deeper than anticipated, into an encircling center. Never did he imagine a woman could have so much room. The fluid folds of that infinite passage press up against the intruder, welcome it with all the ingenuity of design. She is crying now, from the lungs, where he feels her from the other side. "Stop. I don't want," and then, throatier, garbled: "I love you," or "I love this."

Each races the other to unilateral surrender. Something more than sex: an excavation, mohole, metric and insufficient, each time farther down, nearer a remembered core. By turns, his whole body is a coition-charged conductance and something else—the effortless, mate-free budding of plants. There is no Herbert; whatever pain they cause the man is erased by his wife's abandon. Ressler's forward motion into her becomes a rocking apology: clandestine. Never again. He has her, as he needed from word go.

He owes no one anything but compassion. His lone accountability is solely to the code. This woman was long ago inscribed in his genotype. She is his working out, his text made flesh, made enzyme. He *will* join himself to her, however pointless that deposit. He cannot do otherwise. She is underneath, around him: he feels her organic list. Her voiced breath dissolves into syllables, self-defense shouts, bird's cooing. He pins her, presses a spot in her back that touches off further thrashing. Their sure lives in this moment end. Even if they escape this writhing, they can never again be safe. She heaves again. The base of Ressler's brain floods with chemical keys he will not, not ever, neither viscerally nor in mind, recapture.

Jeanette's pumping leaves her spent. Then, as suddenly, she is crazy again to pump, elude pursuers. The force of her desperation frightens him. What bloody business has she come to transact? She rolls against him, thighs first felinely soft, now shoving with a drive that would be rid of itself, of all its tensile load. Ressler cushions, absorbs, protects her from her own tranced rage, keeping this speaker-in-tongues from crashing against the sharp corners of their makeshift pew.

She is only here, nowhere else but her body, manning her cartilage factory. She spasms, an enormous sustained cramp that runs from the nape of her neck along her whole length, at last pulling the arch of her foot taut, from Romanesque to gothic. She is only here, in frenzied pleasure, knowing she will take it like this only once in life. Frenzy enough for both of them: he is lost to the dictates in the master program, locked onto her, coupled, forever sacrificed, shutting out last objections and letting the old sarabande in.

Her face, when the shock of the last muscular lift comes on it, is surprised, flushed out of the thicket in ancestral wonder. All an "O" of astonishment—her eyes, mouth, fingers circling his arms, her labia concentrated around him, drawing him over the edge into his own, rounded O. Sustained effort, every minute of recent months is here made real. Here, only here. Then, the collapse back on confusion and particulars.

They glide at the end, after violent discharge, released to familiars. His cells swim into her, spend. But for a brief ever, molecular memory of the deed persists in muscle, fades through shoulders, torso, limbs, limbic system like immense pipe-organ fundamentals banging around in the baroque dome an eternity before slipping back to nave level, sinking through flagstones into the crypt. He lies capitulate on the floor next to Mrs. Koss, sharing the last shred of companionship left them. They are free of the chief anxiety in animal delight: she can have no child. But facing a worse eventuality.

Jeanette Koss, still in the dream of remembered recklessness, stiffens, comes unstunned. She tries to sit, look at him. She succeeds painfully, staring as if he has just revealed himself. How can you do that to me? She closes her eyes again, lies down, and places a delicate, stray hand between her legs, as if that will keep the somatic impression of their animal abandon from leaking out with his semen. This long, undulating modesty, endless current of hair, hand pressed innocently and curiously to the pudenda. Residual image from the generic feminine.

She does not need to look at him to know what he sees. She smiles through closed lids, uses one finger to explore the passage he has just inhabited, withdraws it with a globe of milky, opaque fluid. She draws it to her mouth, places the drop on the tip of her tongue. Eyes still closed, she turns her lips up and pronounces, "Millions of stu-karyotes." He kisses her and she passes the taste perversely back. She hums, piano in pleasure, already wanting more. She closes her eyes, tasting, recalling.

The memory, this woman passing one unsolicited secret name to him now and for good on the exposed lab floor, will be as suddenly lost, taken from him. More than he can endure. But Jeanette only drifts her hand back under her stained olive dress, between her absorbing thighs.

Trace Mutagen

"Let's give Uncle Jimmy a raise." I picture him alert, playful in front of the console, perched on the edge of a techno-chair, ready to write his graffiti into the system at the first nod from the professor. MOL was again in the clear. Ressler and Todd had returned the Master Fille to working order. The auditors had come and gone, dragging their trails behind them. They had given the restoration a clean bill of health. The console log carried no trace of catastrophe. We passed the anniversary of the *Maine,* that explosion half-made in the American press. Ours was the opposite engineering feat: from out of real burst, erasure. The sense of delivery from disaster was still so strong that Todd's manic suggestion seemed a simple extension. "Who would know?" he asked. "The easiest thing in the world."

"What does ease have to do with anything?" Ressler replied. The two of them had developed an elliptical way of talking to each other over long nights alone. Members only. I listened but was locked out in the static.

"Tell me he doesn't deserve one," Franklin said.

"He does. Unquestionably. After what we've put him through." Ressler collected forms from the printer and collated them with amusement. "But he's not on our payroll."

"Of course not. Good data-processing procedures. Send your own checks to be cut out of house. Simple safety." Ressler's objection was so transparent that Frank didn't even counter it: one can get to any machine from any machine, if one knows the sesames. And Ressler had taught us those. Franklin talked through the steps hypothetically. "We could penny-shave him. Take every salary we handle. Round the fractional cents down, pitch the remainder into Jimmy's account. No one is out more than a partial cent, and Jimmy is. . . ." He did a calculation in the air. "Lots richer."

Ressler detached the day's log, folded it carefully for the archives. "Penny shaving means a permanent program patch."

"We could do it."

"Again, possibility is not the point. The manipulation leaves a permanent print."

"Snake the code around. Relative-address Jimmy's record so that his name isn't sitting in broad daylight. Make the siphon look like something else, an error trap."

"If someone *writes* the program, another can always *read* it. Logic is easier to trace than to scramble."

Franklin twaddled with his contrast knob. "What if we just went and injected a new figure directly into his salary field?"

"Exactly," Ressler said. "Why get ingenious, when you can accomplish the same thing by simpler means?"

"But would it work? I mean, if we cleaned up after it? Balanced all the cross-sums?"

"Never underestimate the power of bureaucracy to believe what their electronic ledgers tell them."

"So you're in, then?"

"No." Dissociating himself from the suggestion, Ressler thwacked his stack of forms in exasperation. "Good God! Pope was right on the money about knowledge. You can't teach a kid anything these days." With an affectionate shake of the head, he left us alone to our own devices.

"It *could* be done, you know," Todd murmured defensively. He riffled idly across linked data lines as he'd watched Ressler do. He punched up a prohibited, distant file, flexing his apprentice prowess. "We give him a one-time bonus. Flat fee. We enter the change in a way that could be mistaken for a Mylar typo. If the tinkering should be traced back to us—assuming the unlikelihood of anyone noticing—we can always say it was a piece of driftwood from our recent flood."

I watched him perform the surgery. He inserted a paper clip into the console print head to keep it from logging. Then, with a simple record edit, he turned the trick. Unreal. What was he changing? Just screens. Alphanumerics on the CRT. "There." He lifted his fingers from the keys long enough to warm them. "How's that for moral compromise?" He backed out to the system, signed on again locally, and returned to the familiar operations prompt. He rolled the printer platen back over the blank transcript and removed the paper clip. What could be simpler? "How's that for victimless crime?"

The Adaptor Hypothesis

"What do we do now?"

She smiles, lids still beatifically closed. "Now, you love me." Still lying indecorously on their corner of floor, she arches enough to allow him to lift her stockings, smooth the olive skirt, restore the organdy.

He places a guilty fingertip to the stain on her hem. "Do you need to rinse this?" he asks stupidly. "Before you go home?"

Her thigh moves beneath his hand. It already wants touching again. "Don't worry." She assures him with her eyes. He helps her outside to her car, escorting as if the assault has weakened her. He closes her car door, contrite, abandoning her to sneak home alone. He is ready to call Herbert, read his confession into the wiretap. Only it's not just his confession any longer.

He walks home. The premature warmth of February air blankets him. He is lost in the calendar; he cannot, for a moment, say when in the year he is or which season follows, cannot even fix the ordinary sequence of warming and cooling. Helpless in the face of a mild breeze, his skin remarks on the glorious night this night has brought in. But the breeze, the false thaw, does not displace what he and Jeanette just transacted. It must keep happening now, transposed throughout the year.

He wades in illicit, erotic revulsion: retained impression is no more than a command to repeat. The weighted average of every surviving drive compels him to another go-round with this woman. Arousing, irresistible, and like most enticing hybrids, sterile. Yet through that revulsion, this breeze insists that hope grow even in an empty place. The Base, overlaid with a contrary voice, whispers that the night feels good, nevertheless; something may yet happen; you've been surprised this far; more of the same is never just more of the same. He reaches the familiar barracks and lets himself in.

He concedes to an English muffin, then straight to music. He needs: what? To prostrate in front of plainsong from a cloister so empty that the echo relay is antiphonal? To join the high, pure head tones of boys in a Byrd Kyrie? To be knocked unconscious by a bit of dislodged opera-buffa stucco? To smile ironically at the *Eroica,* its canceled dedication? To sit quietly stewed outside the locked door of a rolling concerto cadenza just before the last, rescuing tutti? To admit the impossible poignancy of neo-romance? To make a space for grief four last songs wide? To breathe the air of a new planet? To trace the permutations in the *ILLIAC Quartet*? To lie in caged silence?

He opts for the master blueprint: music with no past or future, existing in the perpetual now, a standing Schrödinger wave. He could kiss Olga, so paralyzed has she held her plastic arabesque. Once more he lowers the needle on the scratched disk, unleashing a keyboard exercise that wanders far off the face of the earth into a canonic minor modulation as full of pathos as the first creation. Chromatic beyond recognition, the Base slips inconceivably downstream from the peaceful thematic trickle of its source Brook, the most outrageous claimant in the most unprovable paternity suit ears have ever heard.

He and Jeanette have worked upon each other's nakedness, done all they ever wanted to do. He has no inclination to go back to the lab, now or ever. He wants to resign, sign on to the obscurest work available—making pizzas, hawking Fighting Illini pennants, whatever unskilled labor the local economy will support. He is overwhelmed with the urge to trash his radio, cut the phone lines, and hole up in his bungalow alone with Olga, listening without dissection, assembling without violating the unforgiving weight of particular parts.

He wants her here, to see, speak with, listen to as she vocalizes those rhythmic, objecting stammers. She must call, *now*. But she doesn't. Those moments when she will pity him, deign to drop by, are already too rare. Each minute out of contact is awash in variables—all the accidents that perhaps have already led her forever away. Research recovers nothing; knowledge doesn't knit. He sits in the stream of sound, unable to avert a collapse of volition, not even wanting to.

Criminal scenarios edit themselves in his head. Cloak-and-dagger, skulking affairs where they press against one another for a quarter hour out of every forty-eight. Magnanimous Herbert lend-leasing her or throwing in the towel, acknowledging the omnipotent heart. Ressler appealing to Jeannie, begging for a noble, lifelong separation. His taking up surgery, returning her somehow to fertility.

Each permutation more inspired, more insipid than the last. They take him at once, gang-rape him. He sits wedged in the inseam between wall and floor, listening, thinking that he can hear distant song straining the contour of a variation beyond the variation. He's lost it; accumulated stress pushes him into the realm of imaginary acoustics. But the trace is real, waving the air molecules however faintly. Then he figures it: the pianist singing, caught on record, humming his insufficient heart out. Transcribing the notes from printed page to keypress is not enough. Some ineffable ideal is trapped in the sequence, some further Platonic aria trial beyond the literal fingers to express. Sound that can only be approximated, petitioned by this compulsory, angelic, off-key, parallel attempt at running articulation, the thirty-third *Goldberg*.

Canon at Seventh (II)

We began living together, I suppose. Not even what lawtalk would call a verbal contract. Todd had the key, and he checked in periodically. He even moved a few things over: a backpack of clothes, few but washed frequently enough to stretch forever. His precious notebooks, kept by the bed in case of emergencies that never emerged. His sketchpads, filled with closely observed nature and lacking only that last urgency to become truly remarkable. I was so pleased the day he brought them by that he felt compelled to squash any hope that he might start drawing in earnest: "Can't leave these in my apartment for the burglars to find. I'd be drummed out of grad school if anyone saw them."

"You're not *in* graduate school."

"There's still the dissertation. Any year now."

He kept his own apartment and left most of his treasures there. He gave me a copy of his key, more out of moral parity than enthusiasm. I'd been back to his cult museum at the tip of the island a handful of times since our first listening session, but it never felt right. "Should we spend more time at your place?" I asked one weekend.

"I like it better here. The curtains. The rocker. The bedspread. Your touch." It was his embroidered, endangered bastion, his last holdout in an overrun world: the amber oil lamp in the second-story corner above the antique shop, abiding in tragic coziness. There were more economical arrangements, but anything beyond this tentative fit—a nocturnal burrower braving danger to accept the handout—would be invasively unstable.

We ate evening meals together. He insisted on washing all dirty dishes. Sometimes he stocked the pantry. I took the phone off the hook when I left in the morning, to let him sleep. He came and went freely. I had no expectations. When he was around, we read out loud together, did anagrams, experimented on each other's body, assembled a list of what hurt, what was indifferent, what felt good.

We worked together on our 1040s, finishing long before they were due. On this one ballot alone did he vote his conscience and go head to head with Western Civilization. At great fiscal sacrifice, Franklin buried most of his money in tax shelters, charitable deductions, and losses until the Amount You Owe was zero. Not stinginess on his part. Just the opposite: by the time he had it all legally diverted, he had nothing left to spend. The year I saw him file, he'd accumulated write-offs that would square him for two more years.

It wasn't foresight; he never thought he'd make it to old age. "Part of me dearly wants to pay taxes. I love schools, sidewalks, museums, research funding, food relief. You simply cannot get a better return on investment. But I hate to pay for anything that can incinerate twenty million people at a pop. I know. At my infantile tax bracket, less all desirable governmental expenditures, my contribution wouldn't even cover the *decals* on one of those things. It makes no measurable difference. But withholding is all I can do."

Efficiency had Franker by the throat. He would urge bananas on me, broccoli—anything that might be in danger, in some future, of spoiling. "We've got to keep at that pilaf." He was brutal when I took slices from the fresher loaf. Yet he refused the antidote that progress held out to people with his mania: the bacteria-resistant, stabilized foodstuff, BHA added to preserve freshness. "I try not to eat anything that's newer to the food chain than I am."

He liked the dark and the cold. Saved on utilities costs, but more than that. He aspired toward that life that would not use any of the earth's resources. He deserved only what absolute efficiency could not eliminate. While he roomed with me, the compulsion got noticeably worse.

But when I pressured him to make use of the years already tied up in his obscure painter, efficiency became another matter. "I need more work. I just came across an early primary source that..."

"You already know more about him than anyone alive."

"Me? I haven't even seen all the panels."

"Go see them, then." I cringe to think of it: my suggestion. I even offered to pay, forgetting that he could write the flight off.

"Can't. Got a job."

"This thesis is your job. It's important."

He looked at me sardonically: right. Raging issue. But he did not speak the sarcasm. He seldom stooped to snideness. The words he used in his defense were so much smoke. He believed; he wanted. The project was lodged in him, staved off a worse drift. But he would never knock off a perfunctory proofwork. And putting a closely reasoned and deeply felt piece on the public auction block as a bid for self-promotion, packaging ongoing thought as a completed effort, was worse than immoral.

I frequented MOL as often as ever. I still assisted in dangling in front of Dr. Ressler the slow coax of companionship. Now that he was ready to emerge, I felt I had to make the place as ample as we'd advertised it. I couldn't have been more wrong. Yes, he loved me, loved Todd, loved, for the first time in decades, talk for pure talking. And yes he was again researching. But not what I thought, or for my reasons. What had coaxed him out again, said *go,* recalled him to the roster, was something else: the one liberating whiff.

Dr. Ressler refused to take part in my debates with the club creationist. Annie, even-tempered, devoid of suspicion, never knew these were anything but earnest exchanges of conviction.

Do you believe that the earth was made in 4004 B.C.?

Don't be silly! That was some medieval bishop. The Bible doesn't give the age. It's very old, the *beginning*. But put together in no time flat.

Do you believe that species change?

No. They were made. Look around! Two creatures that need each other to survive: wouldn't they have to be made together? One without the other would be like a ship without a carriage. They'd die if left to chance.

What of the fossil record? Small horses, huge lizards, cats with fangs?

I don't know. Perhaps the Flood—

Trilobites? Fish covered with plate bone?

I don't know.

I flush in shame. I didn't want to destroy the woman's faith, but it maddened me that I couldn't. Ressler sometimes stopped to clear up facts, and Todd liked to push the argument back on track, like a kid righting a slot car. But Annie was unshakable; she would, after a day or two of quiet thought, match any forensics I sprang on her with an equal and opposite blow for verbatim truth.

I should have known that measurement and religion will always be two split continents bumping up for the first time, without interpreters. What drove me to distraction, made me ready to jump into the breach every time however ashamed I always came away, was the woman's insistence that the spirit could address the mechanical world, but mechanics weren't allowed to mess with the spirit. She accepted the age of the earth, dog breeding, inheritance of variant characteristics, organic chemistry, even the reality of genetic tampering. But not evolution.

"Try this," she said, "it can't hurt. A simple experiment, and who knows? It might mean a lot to you in the future." She handed me a pocket Bible, which she carried at all times. "Open it randomly to a passage and read what's written there." I don't know how I managed, but I kept sober as I read the passage chance had sent me. "Does it mean something to you?" I nodded gravely, and handed the passage to Todd. He had to leave the room to keep from bursting. Exodus 22, xviv: Whosoever copulateth with a beast shall be put to death. Contemptible just remembering it.

I was guilty of believing that evidence had progressed so far that a creature like Annie, endowed with native intelligence, would have to accept it. And it broke *her* heart to fail to convert *me*. Todd and Dr. Ressler were lost causes, to be loved more strongly on earth because they wouldn't make the last cut come the signs, seals, and trumpets, unless through benevolent intercession of the Maker. But me: for some reason, Annie thought she could win me for belief.

How did I ever presume to undermine her certainty? What did I have to replace joy with? Annie was surer of her right to happiness than I ever was of mine. Even the loss of her life savings did not ruffle her. She told us of the ugly event one night, still trembling, not in anger, but at the danger she had just come through.

Three days before, while looking over the books in those stalls at the southeast corner of the Park, she noticed something on the sidewalk near her feet. Just as she realized it was a purse, another book-browsing woman also noticed it, bent down, picked it up, and handed it to her. "Did you drop this?"

Annie said no. The two women looked around, finding only one other nearby browser. The third woman also said that the purse wasn't hers. "Perhaps there's an address," Annie suggested. Still in possession, she opened it. No address. No credit cards. No ID. Only about fifteen thousand dollars in cash. The second woman yelped. They were holding the proverbial hot tuber. The three drew toward one another, herding instinct, and sat down on an empty bench. "This doesn't look good," Annie said. "Maybe we should notify the police."

"The *New York* Police?" the others objected.

They sat in a scared knot, no one knowing what to suggest. At last the third mentioned, "My brother-in-law's a lawyer." Instant relief. The second woman was parked in a lot not far from Columbus Circle, and they drove to the brother-in-law's on the Upper West Side.

The lawyer laughed at their nerves, asked facetiously if they were being tailed. "Relax. You'd be surprised at the amounts of cash some people carry on them."

"Only they usually notice if they've left it lying on the street," the second woman said acidly.

The brother-in-law rummaged in his red-spined library and found the passage he was after. "If you three can put up a cash retainer equal to a third of the amount, and if we make a public declaration of the find—a newspaper ad will do—and if no legitimate claimants show after one week, then it's all yours. Manna from heaven."

They punched the numbers up on a calculator. Adding a dash for the ads, they each needed to put up sixteen hundred dollars. They drove to their apartments, each woman running in and securing the funds. Annie and the second had to cash checks; the third, embarrassed, admitted that she kept her money under a rug. Annie's collateral cleaned her out. They left the earnest money with the brother-in-law, who notarized receipts. They exchanged names and numbers, and agreed on the restaurant where they would eat out a week from then.

"The next day, no ad. I called the first woman, and got some poor man in the Bronx. The second number gave me one of those dee-dee-deeps." She sang the no-longer-in-service triad. "I took the subway to the lawyer's office, my stomach in my throat. Cleaned out. For rent. I even tried to go back to the buildings where the two women got their money. Nobody by that name. The police say the notarized receipt is meaningless." Annie stopped, swallowed, could not go on.

466

She didn't need to, except to say that the handle on the inside car door where they had her sit was broken; her door had to be opened from the outside. "These people play for keeps." Ressler and Todd had their heads down. *Old,* their faces said. Old, treacherous, and transparent. It took a genuine naif like Annie to get so blindly stung. Yet I had never been tested against so elaborate a setup. If the con thrived, always with new wrinkles, now out of some other uptown office or in another city, marks must be in steady supply.

In the wake of the story, Annie was the first to revert to form. She said she'd planned to give the windfall to an ecumenical food drive for Africa. "Just imagine, when I finally figured things out! You could have knocked me over with a truck."

Adaptor Hypothesis (II)

Cryptography lives in the seam between sense and randomness. Its deforming rules sow noise into a signal. But by reversing the rules, the signal reforms, like Dr. Ressler's undispersed oil drop. I can't quite put my hands through this paradox: scattered nonpattern and articulated message are somehow—what can the word mean?—equivalent.

The entire Library of Congress, encoded with a single notch on a stick, like those colossi bestriding the narrow world under whose legs we book researchers peep about, keeping one foot on each of two unspannable coasts. The straddle is its own contradiction. The mark on the stick is trivial, blank, without significance. And yet, it inscribes everything in the archive. Even more counterintuitively, the mark could fall anywhere on the stick at all. An infinity of transforming schemes: take the fraction formed by the letter string, divide by its cubed root, add .344.... *Any* notch at all could fold out into the Library of Congress, including all books not yet catalogued.

Such a notch would have to subdivide quantum spaces. But not even that physical catch clears things up. The rub remains: with an infinity of available enciphering keys, a meaningful string of letters can be translated into any available gibberish. So any random string of gibberish I choose already stands for that original string, provided I can locate, out of infinity, a transform that equates them.

This unsettling two-way mapping of any sense onto any nonsense works because the key—the enciphering rule—itself contains information. Information (a science unfolding just moments before Ressler hit the scientific scene) is the degree of restriction clamped onto the set of all possible messages. Information is not meaning, but can be used to reveal it. It has, as Todd's favorite living novelist notes, replaced cigarettes as the universal medium of exchange.

Knowledge might be extracted from simple clues if given the right key: an idea as old as consciousness, existing in precursor form even in animals. Codes, ciphers, impresas, enigmas, mots, emblems, all forms of enfolded text propose not just their own hidden significance but a secret system where inscribed meaning built into the half-obscuring, half-revealing world surface is revealed.

If any gibberish string can reveal not just one but all possible patterns (given an infinity of information-bearing keys), then gnosticism—arcane manipulation until pattern emerges—can't return me to source meaning. The pattern such bit-fiddling produces would say more about its own manufacture than about the subcutaneous nature I'm after. Information between cipher, key, and source is conserved. If the key is simple, then the cipher, however mysterious, will carry much of the order of the original. But if the codetext contains little information—if it is random, full of possibilities—then information must be present in the clamped-down key. The revealing key would then be as difficult to arrive at by trial as the plaintext itself.

The veil between signal and noise never lifts as easily as it falls. Any teenager can take a car *apart,* but few would be thrilled with a complete parts inventory for their coming-of-age gift. If signal is rich and noise deafening, then the deforming garble is practically irreversible without the formula. A hard code is like a lump of peat for an engagement stone, with the instructions: Press firmly and long. From message to code is trivial; but getting back to tonic, if the clamp on possibilities lies in a complex transposing scheme, is as entropically prohibitive as the postman springing back from the pool, the dog backing away, the letters shedding their droplets and returning to dryness.

I may never come across the clause that revokes his exile. The journey back, however much it seems a birthright, a trip I ought to be able to do blind, remains as unlikely as my making it from alien Maple and Jefferson to unknown Walnut and Monroe with nothing but a world globe. Each cognate I stumble across gives a shock of recognition: *here* is the grammatical clue, something I can at last make out. The nearness is uncanny. The clues are all *eall mast, al meist, allr mestr*. But run through the decipherer, they remain *all most*. No ladders lead back up from where I've been lowered. I must lie down where all the ladders start.

Science is hard, the notch intractable. It is not secret knowledge, but nominalism. Not facts; only a means of verifying the endless, tentative list. Like Lear's look *there;* and *there*. Information theory proves that for a given purpose, an optimum code exists. But it supplies no means for finding it. The purpose of investigation seems to be to find the optimal code for purpose. Nature freely hands out isomorph variants of herself. Signals jam the air—patterns not *nature* but the shaped equivalents of her writing. Sometimes information lies entirely in particulars, and their uniting pattern lies only a light tweak away. But if the key packs a larger fraction of crucial information than the signal, reading it remains as statistically unlikely as launching at random and hitting upon life.

How is it possible, in those cases, to recover anything? I have only the old, empirical trump: set up a local peep-holed world and watch; follow the effects, trace the shadow of the key as it encodes. Eavesdrop over the codebook. Then, with the silhouette of the transforming rule traced out, its transforms become trivial. Briefly: the thing I want to hear more than sound itself is the bliss *beyond* the fiddle. But the fiddle itself remains my only conveyance.

The information of an organism is spread out over its substance, processes, organization. No one part embodies the life semantic. Nowhere in my cells does it say, "Woman, thirtyish, pretty to some, deserted, unemployed, desperate to know." The code is not the gene, nor the enzymes, nor the lookup table, although these are the core of what the code knows.

All of these assembled leave a bit of information still out: I lack a key. To make the catch, I must grab the adaptor.

What are my odds of succeeding in the time remaining? By saving chance, the school where I learn to read obeys the same laws of probability constricting the codes that life writes itself in. There is a limit on the coding mechanism, on the information it contains. Evolution sets such unlikelihoods into existence that it seems, given time, universally ingenious, eternally able to one-up. In fact, it's a patch job, short-term kludges barely breaking even, ducking down blind alleys, working only with existing parts. The map is full of places that one can't get to from here. A fin might come in time to grasp marvelously as if designed for it, and a hand turn back into a fin. An air bladder, used to solve the flotation problem, might be tucked into a structure that can sustain a crawl into naked air. But nothing is *a priori*. Other solutions *will never hit upon the particular next trick,* no matter how many eons you let spin. Life on the planet could have been entirely different: billions of years of prokaryotes, unchanged since inception, stretching on steadily until the sun dies.

The "hopeful monster"—Goldschmidt's variation—has been resurrected from the scrap heap with the suggestion that evolution need not always progress by imperceptible gradualism. But despite the haggle in step size, all jumps are essentially local, for there are infinitely more ways of jumping wrong than jumping right. Small text changes ripple into huge phenotypic differences. But the *way* the text is read and processed will never change, short of the complete annihilation and improbable respark of all life. The code key is fixed, clamped from the first fluke discovery of self-propagation. The translator, the adaptor, is information-rich, de-termined, locked in. If we stumble on the place once, in the dark, during a storm, after a quarrel that has driven us wildly from home, we may never find the way again. The accumulation of accident along the way makes the journey irreversible. Each step is sculpted, restricted, feasible, frequently brilliant, on rare occasions even optimal. But the sum of these steps is unrepeatable. It will not happen again, not in this way, perhaps not at all.

I look for a go-between. Inside the machine, deep in the cell, the molecule must take the rich hieroglyphics of the DNA string—randomly accumulated dots, crots, and mots—and, its own struc-ture housing the missing key, translate the jiggles of the varying sequence into the purposeful, programmed, cybernetic, living en-zymes. Outside, in the warehouse of time, the adaptor I look for must bridge the paradoxical equivalence of message and notch, caprice and complexity, theme and variation.

I wake to sleep and take my waking slow. What falls away is always, and is near. Why are three quarters of my analogies drawn against lyric poetry? One would have to be a lingering sap to still think, with Wordsworth, that poetry is the impassioned expression that is in the countenance of all science. I don't deny the senti-mentality charge, but perhaps I keep reverting to anthologies—the ones I have memorized over a life of erratic reading—because they too are their own evolutionary kludge, new vehicles resurrected from modified parts, an historical stratigraphy, packets announcing, "This works, or worked once; use it, or lose it in favor of something else." *I learn by going where I have to go.*

Four months from now, I'll have starved to death or will be employed again, somewhere. Either way, my education, these notes, the extended aside of this last year, will be over. Only two ways I might still get moonlight into a chamber. I can sit and wait for the calendar and capricious weather to accommodate. Or, even at this time of the night, I might find an intermediary. Get hold of the adaptor. Dress up as the visiting moon.

The Transfer Molecule

He can't explain it—maybe because from here on nothing can work out as hoped—but the morning after he makes love to Jeanette Koss on the floor of the Cyfer lab, he feels inappropriately alive. The physiological component is undeniable: yesterday's nerve-shattering release produced a sleep deeper even than clean conscience. He wakes, lies in the bunk, arches, feels the muscles in the back of his thighs, the full power of the intellectual biped.

He has had a dream: a world-renowned gynecologist, looking suspiciously like Toveh Botkin, told Jeanette Koss that her conception problem lay in sperm getting lost on their way through the egg. The doctor implanted an ultramicroscopic device, a sort of converter shaped to let the sperm enter at one end, pass easily through the cell wall, and sail through to the other end, snapped snugly over the egg nucleus.

Stretched on his back, he tenses at the obvious message he has sent himself in sleep. He knows why they haven't been able to get the cell-free system to work. He, Botkin, and Koss have assembled, in their simulated broth, messenger RNA for the instructions, ribosome material for the factory, ATP for the energy, amino acids for the contractors' materials, GTP to glue them together, two types of enzymes as cut-and-paste wage laborers, and a handful of inorganic cations as a chemical hunch, salts over the shoulder. They have left out the key, the go-between, the bridge.

Ressler, with the oceanic feeling of calm that makes investigation the most sustainable gratification available to living things, conceives of what they are missing. A molecule amorphous but vaguely

471

familiar, one of those UN simultaneous translators. At one locus, the molecule has a spot, an *anticodon* that matches a codon on the message string. Another spot on this bilinguist holds the amino acid called for in the lookup table. No: the adaptor molecules—for there must be a whole class, each with different anticodon sites and corresponding amino acids—*are* the lookup table written into matter.

The adaptor molecule is both sorter, porter, and rivet-holder. The anticodon gives it away: more nucleic acid, another RNA chain itself transcribed from—where else?—the parent DNA. Once they season their preparation with this interlocutor, they will be able to make nature break her own code, as she does constantly in the maniacal specific density of self-construction. But before he has time to work out the details, he hears the jiggle in the latch, the intrusion of human sympathy. Company, carrying something, muffled with care. Koss floats into his bedroom, crimson with cold, hazel in triumphant proximity. "Ah!" Ressler looks up, helpless to waylay elation. "The Man from Porlock." But she is so lovely, so *here,* that he can't resent the desertion of insight, its replacement by her.

"I thought," she says, looking away a little wickedly, a little shyly, "you might like a bite of breakfast." She sits at his bedside and unwraps her packages. Coffee, sweet rolls, fruit. Ressler, slack, lets her insert torn-off pieces into his mouth. He chews, eyes closed, while her hands, losing their chill, colonize the covers. Slowly, seamlessly, they are forsaken again. She undresses, this time showing him. Now they are infinitely patient, exploratory, stripped of yesterday's violence. Yesterday was public, awful, dangerous. Today is soft, secluded, trembling, expectant, admission of mutual rabbit-sin. Her throat takes over again at the end. Anyone home at this hour hears the decibels, knows what blood ritual takes place. Exultant, shouting for help, finding it.

When she transfers control from ape back to angel, that sound is the first thing she mentions. "These barracks walls are pretty thin. They could present a problem for us." Never did he expect a single word could trigger such instant, enzymatic rush. "How are the troops supposed to do their women without dispatching a communiqué?"

"Enlisted men are not permitted to have sexual relations."

"And officers do it by semaphore?"

Pretty Jeannie wrinkles her nose, kneels over his body, exploring everything in that inscribed universe. He rests a hand above her breasts, protects her even at the cost of this child-like moment. He tenses his metacarpals. "This is crazy, you realize."

Her change is astonishing. She collapses against him like a sensitive plant. She bows her head, hiding it. Muscles along her length clasp him with a desperate rocking. "Don't forsake me now, Stuart." The plea electrifies him.

The discharge is doubled by the phone selecting that instant to ring. "That'll be the HUAC," Ressler jokes weakly. He gets up, throws a blanket around him, glad for the excuse to retreat to the front room. He grabs the receiver and mumbles hello.

"Sleeping in this morning?" the other end says. The voice chills Ressler to the quick. Ulrich. His supervisor *knows*. "Not that sleep hurts. Look at Poincaré, Kekulé. Major work while unconscious."

Jeanette creeps naked out of the bedroom. She reattaches to him, curled, like a small child, a gibbon on the ground, a hermit crab displaced from its shell. Ressler strokes her hair while she strokes the inside of his legs. He cannot concentrate, makes Ulrich repeat his message.

"I *said*," the chief enunciates, amusement and annoyance waiting for each other at a four-way stop, "you'd better get down to the lab. Some gentlemen from *Life* are here to see you."

Transposon

I have made a Bush League mistake. Idiot! Pulling his words out for the thirtieth time, for the stupid pleasure of hoping they might be different this time, I see it, as self-evident as just out of the envelope. I could smother myself. The boy's affectation has been staring me in the face, begging to be understood, obvious from the day of arrival.

Had I remembered the first thing about him, I would have worked this out weeks ago. He always said the trick to picking up a foreign language was to wear it. Affect its idiom. Act. Assume a virtue if you have it not. I should have known that his method would extend even to written dates. He posted me from Europe. There, people have the good sense to arrange their calendar units in ascending order. He wanted local fluency as fast as possible. So why revert to old habits, just to write a friend back home?

12/6: Not the sixth day of twelfth month. The twelfth of the sixth. I can hardly take it in. He wrote, not in early December, but in the middle of last *June*. Not X number of weeks ago. X months. *Half a year* before I thought he'd written. The opposite season. Every word I read of his was wrong, bungled, lost over the lines. The smallest tweak of context changes every sentence. Nagging anachronism, that weird sense of collapsed time disappears. Of course he had no grief. When Todd wrote me, Dr. Ressler was still alive. One stupid transposition and I hear what the man is saying for the first time. Only, after explanation, his message is more cryptic than ever.

XXII

Alla Breve

I can't take it in. Where has he *been,* and when? After the fact, the holes in my old version are obvious. But this new timetable, for all its superiority, is still shot full of anomalies. June? Half a year from door to door! Unthinkable, even for international mail. I cross off those weeks when, lost to this project, I'd stopped checking for mail: months still unaccounted for.

Assume that Todd, in character, obliviously attached so little postage that the packet went by surface freight. Adding all possible holdups—trouble reading his nineteenth-century hand, customs opening it—accounts for a couple of months at most. Todd's refusal to descend to anything so *courante* as zip code tacks on another punitive week here in New York. I conjure up a postal strike in the Low Countries—they happen in social welfare states. Stretched to breaking, the thread still doesn't span.

Perhaps he began the letter in mid-June, but sent it later. But that's impossible. Two weeks after he started it, he was back in Illinois, dispatching news of Dr. Ressler's death. The letter makes no mention of stateside hiatus. And the imitation Flemish card wedged between? I compare postage, look up the exchange rates from the middle of last year. No doubt the card came by surface. Slow boat. Posted before the death notice.

Todd couldn't have poured out a long chapter, had his life upended, returned to the continent with everything he wrote turned inside out, and then blithely sent the thing unemended, as if nothing had happened in the forgetting world in the interim. Granted he never made sense to me. But even *he* could not have sent these bottle-messages in any order except card, lengthy letter, and obituary. Still, the gap: as if he set me up to misread chronology, invert it, hate his indifference for half a year. Now I must postdate everything, the way they adeptly postdated the console log when it most mattered. I can't set it right, can't remake myself to it.

How many times he left me kitchen-table notes, agonized trails of crotchety, contradicting explications replete with a course-of-battle map, arrows tracing out day's insomnia: "Don't worry; stepped out for a minute. Nope, upstairs; first line obsolete. Make that *was* obsolete; this rescinding is final. Two of the previous three updates are false." He *lived* in unaccounted gaps. Gone for weeks. Then waiting in the front room, smiling: *You were saying . . . ?* In the dark, before falling asleep, he would suddenly ask after leftovers we had eaten a dozen days before. He confused the order of his discoveries about Herri with that man's chronology. I'd post the anniversary of the world's first news broadcast, February 1920, and he'd go about beaming as if it had just been sent all over again.

Once, over one of my modest casserole attempts, he asked, "How do you suppose that lobster could walk away like that with his rear half hacked off?" A day later, I remembered: that seafood dive, our business lunch that turned out to be a date after all. It unsettled me: if the first date was still so immediate in him, could the gap between now and the last be any larger?

I've seen him do the same to Dr. Ressler. We and an attendant Annie sat in the control room one night on the threshold of spring. The machines on the other side of the two-way mirror blindly carried out their procedures: if balance equals debit minus credit, then goto smoothsailing, else goto errorhandle. We were deep in listening. The theme for the evening was children's songs: Schumann, Bartók, Debussy. Without even a feint toward preparation, Todd asked his mentor, "So what about that magazine?" Annie and I exchanged glances: had we missed something? But Dr. Ressler broke into a reticent grin. He shook his head and squeezed the bridge of his nose. "Come on," Todd teased. "What did you tell those gentlemen?" I finally got it. He was jumping not just the weeks between that evening and the New Hampshire woods, when Ressler told us about his one run-in with notoriety. He was leaping over the entire twenty-five years since Ressler did the interview.

"I didn't tell them anything, as you and your woman collaborator determined." Ressler winked at me, homage for the bit of detective work I'd done three quarters of a year before. His wink rushed over me, a chemical injection. I was in love with the man. The worst, most unspeakable schoolgirl's crush.

Todd was relentless, for private reasons. "You must have told them something. Who supplied them with that Miescher quote? *Should one ask anybody who is undertaking a major project in science, in the heat of the fight, what drives and pushes him so relentlessly, he will never think of an external goal; it is the passion of the hunter...*" Todd had the quote intact.

"Guilty as charged. But I was just a child." A pointed rib for Todd's benefit: your age, boy.

"I thought you did. Hacks for the glossies seldom know the literature."

"It might have been any of the other poor souls they'd cornered for the portfolio. 'Faces to Watch for in '58,' or what-have-you." Todd supplied the actual title of the piece. This irritated Dr. Ressler. "Did you need to *memorize* it?" That hushed things, and we were back to songs for children. Todd had it coming. He should have known that missing spaces, for other people, remain real. But with the quick forgiveness of one who once studied inheritance for a living, Dr. Ressler gently berated Franklin. "I thought I'd told you everything that anyone could conceivably find interesting about my case." An edge in his tone insisted that of all ways there were of learning what it meant to be alive, biography was among the least helpful.

Todd, lip out, said, "I just wanted to know how they heard about you."

"Oh, they were doing the brave new world piece they're obliged to run every two years. Somebody at Cold Spring Harbor mentioned to the journalist compiling the piece that if they were looking for bankable horses, there was a bright, young, single, obscure young man out in the Midwest who had initiated an interesting bit of work and who, word had it, was not entirely unphotogenic." He looked at Annie and me sardonically: you see how cells take it upon themselves to fall apart. He couldn't have been more wrong.

"What did this fellow ask you?"

"Almost nothing about my work. He wouldn't have been able to follow even the Music for Millions version. He wanted the usual color: twists, eccentricities. Was I a child prodigy? Did I keep my lunch bag in the dissection freezer? Did knowing the chemical nature of humanity keep me from favoring certain eye color? Did

477

I have any words of wisdom for the generation of molecular geneticists then cutting their teeth in school labs?"

"Did you?"

"I told them to read from the bottom of the meniscus."

Having bludgeoned my way through college chemistry with
limited success despite the opposable thumb, I laughed. Annie,
the picture of Sunday-school patience, blurted out, *"Life magazine?* You were *famous* once?"

Lovering snags him outside the interview, unable to wait until
he gets back to the office. "So. Big Time. The coffee tables of
America."

"Listen, Joey. I had nothing to do with this. I wouldn't even
have talked to them, except they were already here. They just
want a photo for the gallery. It could have been anybody. Could
have been you."

"Thanks."

"That's not what I meant. I mean that the press hasn't the slightest notion of what we're working on."

"Do you?"

"Touché." Happy to give Lovering the hit if it will help put the
ridiculous issue behind them.

"I heard Ulrich hasn't renewed your fellowship. Sounds like the
prophet-without-honor syndrome."

The bombshell he's been expecting these last weeks. "Ah," he
says, false-pitched. "I'm out of the running for next year?"

"So I've heard. Formal decision won't be posted for another few
days. Department's eager to squirrel away cash for the big push."
Meaning Lovering's hunt-and-peck methods on ILLIAC.

His year has been appraised and found lacking. Preferment denied, not because of the quality of his science but because Stuart
has shown himself not to be a *team player.* The vicissitudes of
funding cannot afford the solo worker. The population geneticists
have had the right gauge all along. Ulrich has every right to apply
his limited research funds to a post-doc who'll do better by Cyfer.
But the calculation embitters Ressler, and he cannot suppress a
smiling accusation. "You people are wrong, wrong, wrong."

Lovering, twitched by bad conscience, reassures him. "Oh, they
want to keep you around. You're hot stuff. Ask any coffee table."
The joke goes flatly aromatic. "But the freebie is over. You'll have
to teach or something."

478

He can't teach—not yet, perhaps not ever. To stand up in front of students and make definitive statements is unthinkable. Every definitive statement is false. Whenever he addresses a room of eager notebooks, he begins to shuffle at the lectern, cloak himself in qualifications. It's useless to explain this to Lovering, one of those surehanded lecturers who forget that skepticism is at the bottom of scientific method. Ressler adopts an obsequious tone. "I don't imagine my classroom presentation is likely to be especially stellar."

"No, I wouldn't think so."

Ressler feels an urge to smash his colleague to the wall, watch his head loll against the brick. The forbidden appeal fills him: nothing to prevent it. He is more powerful in the upper chest than Lovering, although the comparison hasn't occurred to him until this moment. Violence forever in the serum. Jacob's Ladder does not ascend; it coils forever around the same four rungs. "Joseph, I've never said 'boo' to you. What's going on here? What do you have against me?"

"What do you have against Ulrich?"

"Against...? Nothing! I just want to do my work."

"You are a very unpleasant fellow, you know. I can't think of anyone in the department who's especially taken with you."

The casual hallway conversation, at the flick of a switch, becomes puerile. He doesn't have a clue to what the switch is, let alone how to flick it off. "Listen, Joe. I don't know what to say. Is this over the interview? That's crazy. It's a puff piece. The magazine pulled my name out of a hat. They hadn't even seen my article, let alone..."

"Screw the magazine." Lovering's voice is steady. "Sandy and I don't even subscribe." His joke strews the path with shrapnel. "And screw your article, too. Sandy says you dangle too many participles, by the way."

"I don't *understand* this. I've never bad-mouthed you. I'm quiet in the office. I keep the glassware clean...."

Lovering wags his head, shedding these possibilities as beneath consideration. "If you haven't figured it out by now, I ain't gonna lay it out for you."

Ressler walks away, shaken. For days, he cannot put the weird run-in behind him. He cedes the office to Joe, abdicates out of shame and inability to look at the man. He doesn't go to Ulrich to confirm the loss of fellowship; he'll hear soon enough. He must

479

assume good faith. Difference of opinion, even divorce, must all be in good faith.

On a late-February evening he passes the closed door of Toveh Botkin's office, from which issue the dampened strains of the gallows march from that old war-horse the *Symphonie Fantastique*. He freezes in the hall—dark, drafty, and full of the smothered scent of lacquer, hair oil, methane, generations of forgotten undergraduate odors—freezes at the tentative probes of this progression. He is thrown back to the previous year, to *Summer Slumber Party,* when he did not know flat from sharp, let alone Neapolitan sixth from French overture. He is nowhere close to breaking into the inner circle of repertoire, the mysteries of tone hidden even from program-note readers and devotees. But with the help of the woman on the other side of this door, he has gone from utter illiteracy to the point where he can name this tune without ever having heard it before. He recognizes the Berlioz exclusively from the physiognomic description given in the literature.

Standing in the hall, taut with eerie last-century intervals counterpointed by clattering steam pipes, he feels the quick slip of deliverance. No matter what happens—should he be barred from the intellectual cloister, never publish fresh research again—academic year '57–'58 will in any light remain the great watershed adventure of his life: the year he intuited the rough, sole appropriate method for cracking chemical inheritance, the year he fell irreversibly in love, and, most intangible, most intense of all, the year he learned to hear. He knocks, lets himself in, walking euphorically against the harmonic wind. He lies down in his old place on the leather couch. At the movement's end, he lifts his torso and greets his old friend. "Not two flutes, you scoundrels! Two piccolos!"

Botkin needs no gloss. Her eyes brim viscous at his visit. She shakes her head, tsking. "What a student we've turned out to be."

"Dr. Botkin, do you find me unpleasant?"

"Don't flirt with an old woman. There isn't one of us who couldn't rise to make a fool of ourselves under pressure."

He thanks her obliquely but gratefully by consulting her on the adaptor notion. "We have set everything up perfectly in our tube—plaintext message, scissors, paste, paper, pen—everything except the code book itself. If we slip that in, we ought to get synthesis such as no one has seen yet."

"What, in this extended metaphor, does 'code book' stand for?"

Ressler explains: a bilingual molecule, with specific amino acid at one locus and corresponding anticodon at another. Where the messenger reads ACG, the strip on the translator reads UGC. They fit; the amino is held in position, glued to the growing polypeptide chain. He glances up from the couch when he finishes. Botkin smiles at him, but queerly. "Is there something wrong?" he asks. "Have I committed the usual bona fide blunder?"

"My friend," Botkin laments, "you have been working too hard. You have been picking over too many back issues of periodicals and not enough front." She lifts, fresh from the place of honor on her desk, a reprint of a recent article, hands it to him. He accepts the piece, a paper Crick delivered last fall to the Society for Experimental Biology, with the amalgam of trepidation and excitement of asking a pretty wallflower for a dance. Crick is coherent, gorgeous. From beginning to end, he throws open the casements and floods the place with conceptual clarity. In a few pages, the man crystallizes everything Cyfer and Ressler have struggled so fitfully to consolidate. And before it is all over, Crick hints at the same construct, even employing the term "adaptor": an RNA strain shaped to encode both reading stencil and written amino.

It chills Ressler to lie there and read the piece, the chill of recognizing Berlioz without having heard him. He does not sink, beaten. Quite the reverse. The piece breaks his heart with poignancy. It is a beautiful late-twentieth-century pilgrim's narrative—exegesis pressing outwards, refusing to stay confined to the dark backyard. It makes the work his own era struggles to produce seem unmatched by any Renaissance: a time when anything might come to be anything at all.

The shining confirmation—the correspondence between their own work and this work going on across the ocean—descends on him as relief. All sense of racing to the gate dissolves. There is still the weight of wanting to contribute somewhere along the line. But Crick's structure, so close to the one he has independently imagined, reassures him that contribution is never an endangered individual. It will be made, whatever might become of him, no matter how soon design's undertow drags him down.

Botkin mistakes the quiet that comes over him while reading. When he finishes, she consoles him. "He still seems confused between ribosomal and messenger RNA. And he has not yet picked up on Gale and Folkes."

"You think not?" He glances at the paper, frightened. Then he understands his friend is trying to motivate him to remain in the chase. How can he tell her: I *am* in, for good, forever, even if I drop out along the way? We have no choice in these things; they must be done for the greater glory of whatever there is. "Maybe not," he whispers, grinning, conceding the responsibility still wrapped inside relief. "Maybe we can add something to this." He gazes at the creases in Dr. Botkin's face, the manifestation, the final working out of a textual puzzle written nowhere in particular, everywhere in general. He hands back the beautiful draft, Crick's notes toward a score for the young person's guide to the orchestra. "Let us go after this adaptor molecule, then."

"I think we have to."

"You know what it is, of course."

"More nucleic acid?"

"Who else?" Is there any other matter so skilled at grammar that it can write one, in its own language? "Thank you for showing me that," he says. "It's breathtaking." He spills over with the wonder of it: the organism guessing inspiredly at its own conveyance, mechanisms themselves the frozen record of inspired guesses about the environment. The practical substitute of words for words seems makeshift, courageous beyond imagining. He can say nothing.

Botkin lifts a hand to her darkwood shelves, takes down a book, and slowly reads to him. The source is in German, of which Ressler has only technical reading knowledge. But Botkin's native fluency bridges this impediment. Her eyes read in one language, her lips pronounce another, without the halting searches of the simultaneous interpreter.

"'At the suggestion of Doles, the Cantor at the Leipzig Thomas-Schule, the choir surprised Mozart by performing the double-chorus motet *Singet dem Herrn ein neues Lied*. The choir had produced but a few measures when Mozart bolted upright, shocked. After a few more measures, he shouted out, "What *is* this?" His whole soul appeared to rise up into his ears. The singing ended; he cried out joyfully, "Here at last is something one might learn from."' I hope this holds up in translation."

Even in the translation of a translation. The image of Europe's prodigy, exiled in the loneliness of his abilities, unexpectedly discovering that he is not alone only augments the strange understanding welling in Ressler. "The name of that piece: 'Sing unto the Lord a new song'?"

"On the mark." He does not even ask the name of that surprise something, the someone one might at last learn from. No need to translate it into speech.

Lovering's assault seems more inexplicable after a week's simmering. But one accusation stands out of the erratic mass as possessing a germ of truth. Distance is not respectfully neutral, as he has always meant it. Socializing, like push-ups, is a necessary, unpleasant surrogate for the real thing. He has not visited Woytowich and Renée since they gazed at the evening news together last summer. Almost too late, he feels a funny, irrelevant need to exonerate himself. He finds himself on their stoop on the first of March, holding an amateurishly wrapped, postage-stamp-sized baby jumper, he hopes female.

Woyty opens the door, shouts "Stuart," clutches at his chest, burlesqueing a heart attack. "My God, man! Who died?" He rushes Ressler in, treating him just a notch below long-lost brother. Lovering is right: Ressler has let the thread of mutual sentence almost snap. "Renée honey," Daniel shouts. "You'll never guess!"

A thin voice from the distant room wafts back. "If it's the Census Bureau, tell them we're topping off at one."

"She's kidding," Daniel gushes. "She loves this motherhood racket. Come in, come in. We were just getting ready for the bassinet. Want to see?"

"I'd prefer the home movie, Dr. W." Ressler can't deliver the line without smirking. Woyty's elated regressing is infectious. He rushes Ressler upstairs. Renée fusses embarrassingly over the little jumper as if it were the coat of many colors. She retires it to the middle of a set of shelves that Dan has labeled "0 to 6," "6 to 12," and "12 to 24."

"We have to wash Ivy," Woyty sings in a high, squeaky voice, rubbing his nose into the infant's belly. "Don't we have to wash Ivy?" Ivy smiles, or perhaps it is just gas. Ivy's father undoes the enormous safety pin in her cotton diapers. "What did you do here? Did you make all this?" Daniel removes the soiled rags, showing Ressler the product, the miraculous residue left in a beaker after fractional distillation. The mocha clay—laid down in deposits—might fire in a kiln to silky porcelain.

The wrapper gets thrown into an enormous collecting sack for the cleaning service. Father daubs the holdouts from between Ivy's legs. The infant makes a confused gurgle, unsure whether to resist, screaming, or give in with pleasure. Ressler is hypnotized by the protozooic genitalia: a fatty eruption, almost tuberous, between the egg-roll thighs, a strange red rash disappearing into a discreet afterthought of a tuck, like the dimple that marks where the mold attaches.

Ivy goes into the bassinet, water warmed to half-degree precision on Renée's thermometer. She seems to enjoy returning to the drink, splashing about polywog-style with more muscular knowledge than she can muster on dry land. As he sops her clean, Daniel keeps up a constant stream of language games: "Where's your foot? Here it is! No, we haven't lost it. Where's your tummy? That's right. How did you know?"

Father and daughter have an uncanny rapport, almost spooky for the handful of weeks under the bridge. Reading Ressler's thoughts, Woyty concurs, "She's a prodigy. Renée and I are both amazed. Already twice where the books say she's supposed to be." He gazes at his wife in astonishment and pride. Renée responds in kind. Daniel goes on laving, talking, half to Stuart, half to Ivy, letting his daughter in on an awful prediction. "This is going to be the brightest baby in the world. Isn't she?" he asks, sponging the tiny creature's back.

"If Daddy has anything to do with it," Renée chuckles. "He's got the John Stuart Mill alphabet blocks strung up over her crib, and he spends an hour going through them with her every night."

"I swear she gets them already. I *feel* her catching on."

Ressler looks in the flat-focusing eyes of this baby to see if that can be possible. He remembers that other model of miraculous miniaturization, Margaret Blake. Ivy, no longer than Margaret's arm, retraces phylogeny back to some intermediary generating form. Staring at Ivy, amphibious in her bath, he begins to think that parenting may be science as well. The gradual testing, forgoing, and refinement of postulates, the constant probes of methodology and interpretation. Ivy is the subject of every lesser investigation anyone has ever run.

He loves a woman, has entered one who so awakes the possibilities buried in his cytoplasm that the urge to get her as round, as loose-draped in the belly as a medieval Virgin is now stronger than any that has ever possessed him. The compulsion to run the one experiment that can't be pared down to a manageable outcome. But every cell he will ever shoot into her will die there, in her tract, in confusion. He and Jeanette are barred forever from

484

that trial run, not just by skirtable social proscription, but by final proclamation of the law of averages.

"One, two, three, four, five," Daniel intones, peeling back the child's tiny, almond machine-shop parings. "*Seis, siete, ocho, nueve, diez.*" He frees his finger from her reflex grasp and winds up a music box. Its melodious running down sends the child into rapture. "Yes sir. This baby's either going to be a genius or one overstimulated cookie."

Ressler barely hears Woytowich to nod acknowledgment. The music-box trickle recalls him to another music box, a distant one, one he first heard in Botkin's office months ago, at the start of this *annus mirabilis,* before learning became more than he could bear. A music box, an automaton of stoic grief, faintly singing out in the fifth of five songs selected from a catalog of four hundred poems chronicling the death of a child from scarlet fever. *Kindertodenlieder.* A little light has gone out in my tent. Hail the eternal light of day.

"Yes, Ivy and I are going to teach each other a lot. Aren't we, dear? Aren't we?" A fair trade; she gets to learn where her tummy is. You get to learn what it means to cheat death. Ressler hears, in the child's music box, how the only life he will ever live beyond his own will be the life of that absurd photo and caption, trapping him in coffee tables everywhere.

Annie's alarm at Dr. Ressler's one-time borderline notoriety was so genuine, her face so amazed, during the account that his irritation at the broach of the subject bubbled away. "Yes, greatness briefly thrust upon me, and only a quick side step and swing of the red cape saved me. I was cornered by the same journalistic band that cruelly led the beach-party beauties to believe that one of them might domesticate that twenty-some-year-old genius pianist, cure him of hypochondria and his awful singing over the instrumental tracks. Even as the magazine was busy promoting that fellow, he'd already begun to trade the international concert circuit for a life where even his closest friends could reach him only by phone. *Life* never caught on that his keyboard exercises were a refusal of natural selection, a means of surviving solitude." He fell apologetically silent a minute. Speaking to Annie, as if Todd and I already understood, he said, "The three weeks when my mug inhabited the back pages of newstands filled me with a revulsion that has not diminished."

That fame was a proving ground for another notoriety then just weeks away. One evening Uncle Jimmy stayed late, lying in wait for Todd. By Franker's account, the Ops Manager hand-delivered their pay receipts for the period, reading over their shoulders as each examined his stub. Jimmy, jittery, wanted to know if their deposits checked out. He told them his pay had come through augmented by a lump sum, with no note on the stub or word from higher-ups. I imagine Todd relishing the lark, encouraging Jimmy to accept the Bank Error in Your Favor and go buy a new color TV for his mother. Of course, Jimmy, seconded by a terse-lipped Dr. Ressler, concluded that he would have to report the windfall glitch.

"Do you think it could have something to do with that whole lotta shakin' goin' down here over the last few weeks?" Todd suggested lamely.

"As you know," Dr. Ressler intervened, to keep Todd from clever admission of guilt, "all our payroll records are kept insulated from our own machines."

"That's right." Jimmy frowned, trying hard to ignore his hunch. "All our checks are cut out of house. By a rival firm."

After Jimmy's departure, Ressler gave Franklin the most severe dressing-down possible: he said nothing about the matter. They started the end-of-day processing, Ressler letting Franker stick with his story. Trust devastated Todd more than any accusation could have. Franker's whim turned real at last, on this side of the main-frame linkup.

A few days later, when a baffled Uncle Jimmy returned to what his instincts told him was the scene of the crime, he shook his head and told my friends, "Nobody knows who authorized it, but the receipt matches a valid electronic request. 'Somebody musta dunnit.' Accounting even looked at me like I was crazy for bringing it to their attention."

"James," Dr. Ressler assured him, "it sounds as if you're forced to consider this the gift of an anonymous donor."

"Pennies from Heaven," Todd suggested meekly. "The Color TVs for the Mothers of Excessively OT 'ed Middle Managers Fund."

"If the two of you have nothing more helpful to say than 'Roll with it,' I guess I'll have to. But nobody can make me like it," Jimmy said.

Or words to that effect. Unlike the Evangelist, I was not there and did not see these things. I received the revised version only through Todd, and my memory of even that is already years old. "This is the gist, but not the exact run of words as he sang them in his sleep, for even the most beautiful song cannot be translated from one language to the other without much loss of loveliness and grace." No better fit for the sad fact than Bede's famous bit— a bit no one for more than a thousand years has even been able to read in the way that a real speaker of Bede's dead language was able to. But what's a real speaker? Latin was no one's mother tongue. Why should I use quotes, if the English version of his despair at the insufficiency of translation is itself insufficient? "This is the gist" doesn't even give the run of words as Bede sang them. And yet these words *are* his gist. The same, if undeniably different. My rough guess at what Uncle Jimmy said stands in now for Uncle Jimmy. It must. There is no other.

These eight months spent trying to rig up an exact recreation have never once gotten closer than a rough gist, even of those moments that I lived firsthand. A verbatim transcript is, it goes without saying, a contradiction in terms. Yet I could not have sustained this almost-transcript this far without believing that it approximates the original, even with every original word out of order or altered. No threshold effect turns resemblance into fac-simile. Yet approximation is as close as any transcriber gets. I know now how genetics relies on ingenious but indirect measurements, reflections and not direct knowledge. Genes are mapped relatively by the frequency of their breaking and recombining. No one has witnessed a transfer-RNA molecule reading the next triplet and attaching its amino acid to the growing polypeptide. Yet the in-ference is unimpeachable, because the shadows this process casts on reflective apparatus cannot be explained so well in any other way.

Even a literal recording—another contradiction—even highest-fidelity holographic videotape of what I and my friends said and did at that precise moment would still be a rough transcript re-quiring interpretation. That pause between his sentences: anger or exasperation? The pitch, volume, and tempo of his words: do those variables, integrated across context, indicate half his impa-tience, uncertainty, wonder at what is about to happen? Everything I might say about this place involves decoding. Things say in one language and mean in another. No getting across that gap without the ultimate transitive, to translate.

Out of unshakable habit, I look up the word. English occurrence dates from the thirteenth century. Latin origin: to relocate, carry across, port over. Among the dozen definitions (including to bring to a state of spiritual or emotional ecstasy), the now familiar biochemical one: to transform the information stored in messenger RNA into a polypeptide structure by means of the genetic code. An upstart translation of the parent meaning: to move the substance of a text from one language or dialect into another. To translate Shakespeare into Bantu, or the secretary of defense into English.

I follow the idea down to its core, where, rather than reveal itself, it dissolves. I ask the Ur-question of whether translations, unlike Todd, can be both beautiful and faithful at the same time. I nudge that old impasse concerning whether to translate all "Napoleon"'s into "Bismarck"'s when porting a limbered piece across the Rhine. I live with the line about how all translations are obsolete the moment they are made, how the death of marines in Lebanon calls out for a new draft on Thucydides. What I can't decide is whether passing words from one language to another is even possible.

Pragmatically, I know it must be, for I do it all day long. Like Dr. Johnson's friend Mrs. Carter in reverse, I once could translate Epictetus as well as make a pudding. Every piece of impenetrable information I ever ported to my eternally hungry clients was born in interpretation and carried out under the guidance of rough analogy. Even now, working exclusively for myself, every genetic concept I acquire is a stand-in isomorph for an alien domain. Letters as bases. The genome as five-thousand-volume library. The ribosome as reading head, messenger RNA as strip of recording tape. Enzyme as if-then command. The presence of amino sequences inferred through the pattern of dark bands on paper. Traits located by tracking genetic markers. The ages of the earth as bands of sedimentary rock. The forms of finches radiating outwards. Sperm with heads and tails. Radiation garbling messages, introducing noise. Mendel as the Darwin of heredity. Darwin as left fielder, batting third for the Science Hall of Fame. Life as computer, steam engine, automation, animate puppet, clay shape breathed full of *spiritus dei.*

> For out of olde feldes, as men seith,
> Cometh al this newe corn fro yeer to yere;
> And out of olde bokes, in good feith,
> Cometh al this newe science that men lere.

Translation inhabits every sentence ever predicated. Nothing is what it is but by contrast, cracking, porting over. Every part of speech is already a *figure* of speech. Not long before I stopped going back, I visited Dr. Ressler, once more alone in the quiet of the control room. He was compiling a catalog, with nineteenth-century Linnaean diligence, of examples of tone-painting (I mistakenly heard "tome-painting") in Bach vocal works. We listened to scores of examples, figures as generic as joy, hastening, or humility, as literal-minded as flames, fire, sheep grazing, or the rich being sent empty away. He played a jagged, dissonant 'cello descent, buzz-saw violent. "How do they put it in the King James? 'The veil of the temple was rended'?"

"In current versions, it reads something like 'And their public religious building was damaged by plate slippage.'"

Ressler smiled. "No wonder they burned Tyndale. Of course, for Bach, it was *'Der Vorhang im Tempel zerriss in zwei Stück von oben an bis unten aus.'* Which is another story altogether."

"I thought you said you didn't know any foreign languages." Except *I do no one any harm by remaining here,* in French.

"Every scientist my age had to read a little German."

"And a little Latin?"

He shrugged. "For nomenclature."

"Greek?"

"No farther than the letter names, believe me."

"Why should I? And tone-painting?"

"Well that, yes. But is that a language?" he slid away quickly. "Is it redundant, specific, rigid, nonambiguous? Can we really hear what it means?"

"First tell me what 'The veil of the temple was rended' means."

"Good point," he said. Or words to that effect.

But just because translation is everywhere necessary, it doesn't follow that it's possible. Even the perfect translations of mathematics beg the question of what is being carried over where. The length of this two-dimensional extension expressed in *number*. The value of that number expressed as a *numeral*. If performing the same operation on both sides of an equation does not change the expression's validity, what *does* it change? Why is the last line of a proof surprising, if its truth is already hiding tautologically in the lines above?

The load is inseparable from the cart. What I say depends on what I say it with. The most resourceful conversion cannot take

489

the simple phrase "Words are very rascals" and transplant the sense, stripped of conveyance, into Oriental pictographs where adjectives are conjugated, sentences have separate logical and grammatical subjects, and verbs have no tense or mood but context, cannot perform the exchange without everything except simple-minded correspondence being lost.

Conversion's impossibility only increases when the languages have recently diverged. Mother, *maman, madre, mutter* come nowhere near meaning the same thing. I need only boot, fringe, or grid to prove that we and the Brits are indeed two people separated by the barrier of a common language. *"Ceci n'est pas une pipe"* does not mean "This is not a pipe," any more than Magritte's famous symbol is smokable. All four texts no longer mean what they separably say: they are a packet, together standing for the inability to extract thorns from dialect briars.

The decline of the world in my lifetime precipitated by Vatican II and *Webster III* is just the latest echo of the collapse of Babel. Frank's favorite painter had to do this topic twice, in porting it to another idiom. Difficulty did not begin when God caused everybody on the work crew to render "pass the hammer" in his own unintelligible idiom. It began with "hammer," a real thing in itself, separate from that solid, cold, workable weight strapped into the flat of the hand. Every assertion is already a comparison, wedding a thing to a thing, a thing to an action, a thing to a quality, temporarily joined at a given moment from a given vantage. Shifts betray without ever leaving the mother tongue. Stravinsky once called Verdi the Puccini of Music. I know exactly what he means, but could not say it any other way.

The coding problem begins with a single word, shorthand simile. Simple naming is already unstable. There is no other way to *say* a thing except by its name, yet the name never says it. Once, I knew what it felt like to be the first to use a metaphor. To invent metaphor itself. I loved someone who was sunk in winter, someone who didn't watch where he walked. Garden in his face. Nest in hair. Pearls for eyes. Wall between us. Words dispersed us like the cold points of stars. The joints splay that should pull flush. Dovetailed comparisons wear out, go threadbare. But tonight, for no reason—because of a transposition converting two very different dates—language coils, starts up again. I apply my key, my adapting bit, until something fits, shifts, carries over. The conversion closing in on me will never again be so clean as one gene, one enzyme, one metabolism. It never was that clean, even at microscopic level.

Shakespeare in Bantu, Indiana in Brooklyn, Dr. Ressler in verse, desire in biological terms: the world is only translation, nothing but. But paradoxically, inexpressibly, translation of no other place but here. All this conversion work—words into cantatas, landscapes into words—has as goal neither fidelity to the original (although valueless without fidelity) nor beauty in the target language (although without beauty, a waste). The point of every translation—the years spent in science, away from art history, wrapped in the library, trapped in this paragraph—is suddenly one and the same.

Translation, hunger for porting over, is not about bringing Shakespeare into Bantu. It is about bringing Bantu into Shakespeare. To show what else, other than homegrown sentences, a language might be able to say. The aim is not to extend the source but to widen the target, to embrace more than was possible before. After a successful decoding, after hitting upon the *right* solution—however temporary, tentative, replaceable, and local—the two extended, enhanced languages (Shakespeare changes forever too, analogies adapting to the African plains) form a triangulating sextant pointing back to the height of the ruined tower, steering limited idiom toward a place where knowledge goes without saying.

I have the likeness for the whole process in front of me. How could I have been so long in hearing it? Each alternate translation is an emblem of the generating tune. But variation grows rich in a new tongue. The tune in February. The tune as laborer. The tune in love. The tune in the Information Revolution. The tune intoned without hope or longing in the cloister of a solitary order. The tune in vitro. The tune swung round, wrenched into minor. The tune as a lost vee of geese. The tune triumphant. The tune as sudden stroke, erasing all personality. The tune as folk tune. How long you have been away from me. Come home, come home, come home. Change the signature, rhythm, harmonic underpinning, even the intervals. Where is the theme? Oh, still *in* there, in the new terms, the awful euphoria of more. It needs only a listener with the right key to find that unprecedented, surprising, radical bit that from the first, all along, it was saying.

Because he is not where I thought he is; because I had him badly figured; because I set out last June to identify Dr. Ressler at last; because Ressler died; because I thought Todd had run off to

Europe; because he in fact came *back* for his friend's death, leaving my letter sealed under some casement, waiting months for a benevolent stranger to post it; because I thought to learn genetics, hoping that way to work my way around to the man; because I loved with all the force of metaphor; because I loved those two as if they were the last similes left on earth; because I will never get the exact words and will be lucky to hint at the weakest equivocation; because I shut myself away for months for work (because I thought them both gone); because I find, tonight, in crossing over, that I was wrong on virtually every account worth being wrong on, I hear the old tune as if it were some absurdly singable new song. Sing it then. Friend, thou art translated.

XXIII

Century of Progress

Q: Why not a test ban? If satellites can read license plates from outer space, couldn't they also detect your basic multimegaton blasts going off here or there?

P.N.

A: Official line is that a test ban would not be verifiable, and thus not desirable. But many in the scientific community say tremor detection has permitted verification for at least a decade. Nuclear detonations are required by the space weapons program now under development. Measurement is never separate from motive.

J. O'D.

Q: How many humans will there be by the beginning of next century? How many other living things?

R.P.

A: Eight billion humans, by conservative estimate. There will still be many animals. But far fewer kinds....

J. O'D.

Q: My parents used to sing a song together when I was a girl, before the First World War. It was called something like "A Hundred Years from Now." It was beautiful, but I've never been able to find it since. Do an old lady a favor?

L.S.

A: One Hundred Years Hence what a change will be made
   In politics, morals, religions, and trade;

493

In statesman who wrangle or ride on the fence,
These things will be altered a hundred years hence.

Then woman, man's partner, man's equal will stand,
While beauty and harmony cover the land;
To think for oneself will be no offense,
The world will be thinking, a hundred years hence.

Oppression and war will be heard of no more,
Nor the blood of the slave leave its print on our shore;
Conventions will then be a useless expense,
For we'll all go free suffrage, One Hundred Years Hence.

J. O'D.

Change of Venue

He did not run for Europe; he came back. Ressler's death did not leave him cutting human ties, cleaning off, briskly efficient. Franklin was in the Low Countries already last spring, throwing his lot in with new words. Days after he wrote me, second week in June, he heard that Dr. Ressler was entering the last turn. He must have dropped everything and come back home.

Home to what? The death notice says nothing. "I have just heard...." Midwestern postmark; the town Ressler chose to die in. Did Franklin make it? Was he able to see the man? In my last word from Franklin, a trail a half year old, he'd just arrived stateside. No reason to believe he isn't still here. Somewhere. Today.

On the Threshold of Liberty

On March 11, the AEC concedes to angry scientists that seismic shock from last year's test in the Nevada desert registered in Alaska, 2,320 miles away, and was not limited to 250 miles, as first claimed. Ressler can't imagine how even government might think that figures will conform to decree. But he understands its temptation to dictate to measurement. Agencies sit on sheaves of results they can't ingest, a report of increasing mastery over material that grows faster than they can read it; each new breakthrough edges deeper into that place where everything is certain to happen—wider extremes of availability than the biome ever anticipated.

Foreign policy snaps precedent. Leaders are left hanging on to realpolitik, chanting the trusty, rusted formulae long obsolete. Nations haven't the first notion what to do about the eager weapons that will garble irreversibly the three-billion-year message inside the informational molecule. The lone trustee, the incompetent caretaker, is loose on the estate.

The public, even those still buying the myth of species permanence, has lately latched onto the most horrible fold in the new dogma. Life is no longer *a priori* appropriate. Creatures become sickeningly plastic, moldable, as mistakable as clay. Two-headed monsters, nightmarish collages of scales, fur, wings, and jagged things, hybrid ghouls of unbound imagination inhabit theaters nearest you. Godzillas, lagoon creatures, giant Gila monsters: nothing now prevents life from running amok in the shower of mutagenic material already unleashed. Lovering pins up a Yardley cartoon on the office bulletin board. "Radiation didn't hurt us a bit." The speaker is an amorphous blob with three eyes.

The specter is more terrifying than mass extinction. The annihilation of most of the globe seemed survivable so long as some fraction of the message remained intact. But if monstrous meaninglessness propagates with the speed and exactitude of natural transmission, everything is over. The loss of a great library to fire is a tragedy. But the surreptitious introduction of thousands of untraceable errors into reliable books, errors picked up and distributed endlessly by tireless researchers, is nightmare beyond measure.

Ressler's read Neel and Schull on the effects of Hiroshima and Nagasaki on childbirth. He'd be the first to point out the impossibility of generalizing about the effects of radiation after one generation. New lethals float around in the pool, garblings that won't reveal their consequences for several lifetimes. If a bomb can be heard 2,300 miles away, then how unacceptably far might invisible, message-melting static seep out? Government, confronted with living nightmare among its own constituency, refits the facts, making human ingenuity seem somehow survivable, benign, commensurate with being alive. The project of procreation can't be allowed to scare itself sterile on its own imagination.

If scientific fact disappears in a sea of carefully tailored editing, then the protecting officials will have induced the corruption they meant to stave off. Fear of sinister garbling is just the first, obscure public realization of molecular genetics. The greatest revolution in thought ever, the one material theory of being that isn't an after-the-fact put-up, has an even more unpalatable ramification. The sanctity of one life, the primacy of the particular, has no place in the new science. Biology has united ecology, taxonomy, paleontology, and genetics in a single grand theory of encoded nucleotides, but in doing so, it lays bare terminal grimness. Gene, organism, and tribe operate by opposing means, are driven by inimical goals. The individual is a myth of scale.

Behind the radiation-horror is another so great that it requires agencies to interdict the facts. The life script's playwright is a die; even now the script is not fixed. Smudges change it from one reading to the next. The spectacular species-fan is spelled out in a table-bumped game of Scrabble. Who can go on breathing when mutagens are everywhere in the air? A severe birth defect, annihilating a sacred existence, is to the gene just another guess, to the population, just bean-curve indifference. Ten million mutations per U.S. generation. A half-dozen deleterious genes per person.

More unlivable still: the steady generation of noise—birth defects, the eternal perjury of even healthy bodies, infection beyond death—is life's motor. The text, self-trimming, self-writing, self-reading, is also self-garbling. Necessity's chance horror is the mother of variation. Time plays with deleterious mutations strewn through the common gene pool, extracting from them, every handful of millennia, new functionality. Useful difference comes about only through decanting tons of detritus, error, waste. Weed it and reap.

Individual interests are sacrificed to the interests of the species. A billion cripplings to produce one meliorism. Radiation becomes Pentecostal, the procurement of the overspecies that will rescue the speaking animal from the general botch of things, the disastrous night it has brought on itself. Mutation as evolution's arrow: further text depends on the garble, whether from UV or Nagasaki. The garble is the code talking about itself, a decision to go forth, be fruitful, and mutate.

Even the nausea of knowing where the message hails from cannot touch him today. Even knowing that the individual is permitted by gene and tribe only so long as it serves their ends cannot, this hour, alter how he feels. Despite knowledge, he is shamefully alive, weeks away from pushing through. Discovery, once-chaotic things clicking together into a tight matrix, is so unequaled a rush that it overwhelms even the ugliness of what it reveals.

Part of this ankle-dangling euphoria is more prosaic: the absurdly pleasant spring weather that's plagued Champaign-Urbana for days. Who can feel distressed for long in the face of this breeze? The core of brutal insistence thaws with the assurance that his love—recalcitrant, unique, individual—is reciprocated. Jeanette's minutes, he now knows, are as laden with him as his are with her. To be loved reciprocally promotes them to special-interest group. He no longer cares what codes for their shared obsession, what drives them deeper when they both know it can come to no issue. No behavior is so pointless but can be ratified by a second of the motion, mutual agreement, the binding site of love.

Love, like the mutation blade, both maims and surgically saves. He knows both incisions. Today it is good; a surge of surety putting anguish to bed. He savors the slight shift in his favor. Lovely sound rings K-53-C: car honks, someone getting married. The beep persists; he smiles at the summoned party's refusing to answer. At that moment, Jeannie's head appears at the window. "Ask not for whom the car honks."

He forgets himself, the careful propriety they've learned to coat themselves in. He rushes to the opening where she and the soft breeze pour in, holds her face, kisses it in adolescent profusion. Another instant and he is shod, wrapped in windbreaker, out the door. He tears around the corner of the shack, brakes just short of flying into the woman. He stretches out an arm and messes her hair. "Do you still love me? Are you all right? Nothing's happened since I saw you last?" All this delivered at the sprinting speed of one who's just discovered how little time he can afford anything except life.

He lifts her shoulders, pinches her waist, clasps each hand in rapid succession, pulls himself away, and glances at the windows that look out on where they stand. His puppyish eagerness to touch her already gives the ache hopelessly away. She laughs and strolls with him to the waiting car, not the familiar Koss futuristic spaceship. "What's this? What happened to the fins?"

She puts thumb to lip, hesitantly bites the nail. The gesture's endangered tenderness ravishes him. "I know this sounds terribly genre-ish, but I thought it less conspicuous to rent this for the day." She looks at him: the day. The *whole* day. To be squandered together over its entire length, as if it were really theirs without constraint to be disposed of. She stares at him. "Want a lift?"

How can he help but want? He is prepared to go wherever she

497

designs to take them, today, ever. He throws himself into the camouflaged rental on the seat beside her, passenger, co-escapee, surrendered to travel. They wander out of town onto an unnumbered county road heading south, a lane unrolling as straight as the cut of a plow-scythe, the trailing arrow of a compass. The snow has melted, leaving the muted, moldy yellows of last fall's stalk residue, the blue-black of the soil, the clinical gray of a tree or windbreak hedge, the protestant white of a farmer's two-storied frame. He feels no inclination to ask where they're going. They are there already, here, in the same car with one another, released, untethered, unsponsored, on the thin crust of the earth.

Out here in rural emptiness, road calculations are irrelevant. They are vulnerable to the slightest change of mind, the possibilities presented by the infinite numbered grid of county roads leading exactly everywhere. He can't imagine how anyone taking a trip could possibly plan his destination ahead of time. One can only get from Here to There by plotting the way simultaneously from both, and hoping against odds that the tendrils will meet in the middle.

He looks at the loveliness beside him. She too needs no more forethought than the game she plays with him every time they come to an intersection. She rolls up to the node, slightly reducing speed and asking languidly, while testing the wheel imperceptibly to left or right, "What do you think? Turn here?" Sometimes she turns, sometimes not. It comes to the same thing.

Something catches their eyes in the expanse of cumulused air. She tugs at his sleeve, disbelieving the remarkable phenomenon. Above a town that before this moment barely merited the name, a plane strews an aerial milt stream of confetti from its cargo bay. Jeanette steers toward this celebration—some local cause for wonder, a marriage perhaps, or a birth. As the dispersed load approaches the ground, Ressler makes out the artificial cloud: a flurry of rose petals, storm of leaf-lets showering the town. All these miles of A-frames and straight acreage, naked fields being readied for corn, bathed in a burst of pink petal-points. He would not be able to take in this March-shower surreality except that Jeannie is there at the wheel beside him, stone-still, just looking, for all she is worth.

How long has it been since he's gotten out? Out of town, out of range, out of the lab, out of touch, out of himself? He hasn't sampled this liberating emptiness since that day, negotiated life-

498

times ago, when he Greyhounded into town through this same enchanted vacancy of may and might. The field returns, even as they pass, from black sand to the first, primitive hint of callow, new green. The challenge of this spilling emptiness cuts into him. He commits himself to feeling it, to riding aimlessly with her, to living this rented day. He stretches, feeling his feet against the floorboards, his back flexing against the car seat. He pushes out his arm, which falls experimentally across her welcoming shoulders, exercises its privilege to play with her rose neck hair. "Is this a kidnapping, by the way?"

Jeanette smiles, far away. "I sure hope not. Because you won't get any money out of my husband these days." Even mention of the man has no power over them. Herbert falls away, sinks into the road shoulder disappearing behind their wheels. When she looks over at him, lifting her eyes from the hazardless road, it is with all the dismay of care: we are abducting each other, throwing away everything in complicity.

How strange it all feels, how immediate. He has seen nothing at all except his adopted town since he hit it. And of that swaddling college village, nothing except the barracks, lab, stacks, and sycamore-shackled paths connecting this narrow net. How much finer the place he lives in, broader, more surprising than he thought. He stumbles upon it by accident for the first time. The farmers, worrying their lands' next attention, do not know their own acreage the way he knows it at this minute.

The fields call him palpably back to the moment of his arrival, the unsuspecting child he'd been. An urge comes over him to tell Jeannie of that forgotten bus ride into town, the way he has come, across the cold year, against all expectation. "When I first arrived— early summer!—Urbana seemed the perfect place for getting lost in. I sat on this endless bus, in the middle of the traveling poor, next to a man with a thyroid defect. He warned me against reading. Said he had an uncle who consumed all Zane Grey and never amounted to much."

His uncharacteristic monologue cracks her up. While Jeannie giggles, he adds, "We had been held up along the way by a flood of tortoises crossing the road. Several shells wide, with no end in sight. I could still hear them crunching under the bus wheels when we pulled into town. I saw this place and—the oddest thing. I was home, although I'd never even imagined its contour. I thought: A person could work here. Anonymous. Politely alone with nothing

499

but investigation to get through this open cipher, all the right angles." He fondles the lithe vertebra protruding from her neck. "I had no idea you'd be here. I thought it would be all code-breaking. I never predicted, until this morning, that it would be this." *This*? What, exactly? Name it. "That I would fall in love."

Jeanette arches against his hand, almost mews. She opens to him, speaks of how, at thirty, she wakes up some mornings not knowing where she is. "Sometimes I'm lost, without clue to re-covery. This isn't where I live. This isn't what I do for a living. Illinois is lunar landscape to me. Even science sometimes seems some alien routine I've learned to go through without giving myself away. I think, 'What am I doing here?' And then I think on you, and it's like coming across a favorite child's book in an antique store with my name scrawled on the flyleaf. Like being dropped into the most tangled foreign bazaar and suddenly hearing English an inch away from my ear."

Her confession scares him: does he really soften the bare rock for her, give it a breathable atmosphere? "Were you happy as a child?"

"Growing up? Oh, happy enough, from what I remember. My folks were trauma-free, more than normally immersed in their generation's long-term goal of boredom. I loved school, always did well. Forever busy improving myself. Always had some project going. Continuous science fair."

"The Home Nature Museum."

They gaze at one another in recognition. "Where were you when I was sixteen?"

"Oh." The suggestion is pain. "Wouldn't that have been a sce-nario?" It mauls him to think what the years might have been like, what chances they might have lived.

"So much wasted time. I might have been watching you learn things, learning them with you. But look! We're here. We've found each other now. That's the main thing. Even if I...." Her voice drops, inaudible. "If I've married prematurely." She stares straight ahead, oversteering. Ressler feels her neck tense and removes his hand. Suddenly she shouts so violently from the lungs it makes him jump. "Stupid. Fool! Damn it to hell." She clutches him with a free claw, turns her face on him, eyes red, puffy, pleading. "Why?"

He gives no answer. She winces and looks away. She slams the steering wheel with the flat of her palms, and it flips off the column into her hands. Weaving, the rented car reams a big chuckhole in the county road, a washout from the spring melt. She reacts spontaneously, controls the vehicle by lifting her foot off the gas and braking judiciously. At the same time, fumbling with the worthless metal ring, she hands the wheel to Ressler, fake blasé. "Here. You drive for a while."

Ressler laughs hysterically at her poise. Jeanette manages to beach the car without crashing. There's little to die against on infinite road shoulder. He finds the broken joining pin, jimmies a substitute, wedges the wheel back onto its column while Jeanette proclaims, "Damn rentals. Can't take them anywhere." Years later, when everything else, even bitterness, has dissolved into sepia, he will remember her, love her for that absurd reversion to wit in the face of near-disaster.

When they pull back onto the road, still alive, they grow as unqualified as the terrain moving through them. Their invention is subdued, the remorse lifts, the hypotheticals of where else they might have gone vanish. Jeanette accclerates, confidence creeping back, tearing along for tearing's sake, in overarching breakneck speed. The call in this confusing, rented, temporary tune is at last clear: all the two of them need do is hit the right notes at the right time, and the thing plays itself.

They know their intended destination the instant they wander into it. A pristine almost-village, a time hole lost in the previous century. They park the car, trying to make the vehicle inconspicuous. Difficult, as theirs is the only internal combustion engine in sight. The prevailing mode is horse-and-buggy: black, closed-box coaches, wood and leather, spoked wheels, draft animals in the stays. The extraordinary drivers are decked out in blue, black, and gray homespun. The women wear simple headcoverings, and the men sport foot-long beards.

Ressler can only look and look. How far have they come? No more than a few miles from that university town with its top engineering school, its transistor Nobel laureate, its state-of-the-art digital computer composers. They have fallen through time, Judge Craters, a footnote in those stranger-than-science compendia. It takes Jeannie's soft erudition in his ear to instruct him. "Are they House or Church Amish?" They have stumbled upon a self-isolated community of dissenters who have chosen to break off from the rest of the race, to hold still in the workable niche while life floods around them into new pools, speciates.

They walk by the roadside, in silence except for the creak of wheel rims and the clop of hooves. Jeannie takes to the community, ratifies its simplicity. She curtsies to a passing buggy and the driver acknowledges with a reserved nod. That one gesture gives Ressler the acute pleasure of locating the key to the chance variations of existence.

"I have lived in east-central Illinois for years," she whispers, "and I never knew such a place existed." Nor did Ressler; he barely believed in such groups when he read of them years ago in American History. "You brought me here," Jeannie insists, giving his hand a covert squeeze.

"No," he objects. "You." They pass a knot of families that gather in front of the general store. He hears accents of German. Although no one pays them any attention, he feels grossly conspicuous. He and Jeannie—glasses, wristwatches, awkwardly constraining clothes—are the grotesque, implausible by-product of a defective turn, representatives of all these people have saved themselves from.

In an unforgettably aromatic, unfinished wooden store, they buy a quilt, made by many hands over several weeks. They buy it for the haunting pattern neither of them can quite make out. It repeats yet is never twice the same, develops, yet stands in place, constantly spinning, unspun. Each time they look at it, it changes. They return reluctantly to the rental, the dead giveaway of their nonbelonging, their mark of Cain, their freedom. The anachronism vanishes in the rearview mirror, a lost place they will never find their way back to, even with detailed ordinance survey. They drive until they find a spot superlatively nowhere, even by prairie standards. There they pull the car off the road, spread the quilt, undress each other, and explore the solid sorrows of one another's bodies as if for the last time.

Jeannie is radiant, rubbed beautifully coral in the raw March air. She can stand the cold nakedness of this copse of trees only by huddling against him. Fierceness is gone. She does not use him this time to discharge her explosive, agitating thistle. No more gangster attempt to recover the androgyne. The two of them fit, couple to one other so wholly that friction is an unnecessary irritation.

Today she is downy, quilt-frightened, narcotically surprised by the unthinking pleasure she finds here. She makes love to him like a girl of sixteen. No, as if they had met at sixteen, and lost sixteen

502

more intervening years, banished from each other by some wrong turn. They roll up in the quilt, so tightly wrapped that they cannot move except to fill each other's missing spaces, conform skin to skin, vapored breathing. They lie for a long, unmeasured time, until the light gives out. The spell failing to sustain, they dress, each helping the other, keeping the other warm until clothing can take over. For the last time they return to the car, enter, hug briefly on the seat, an afterthought, then ride home north in dark, in silence.

Jeannie breaks the quiet. "Tell me that story again."

"What story?"

"How you came to Champaign."

"Why?" He tickles her under the chin. She frowns.

"I like it."

"What's there to like about it?"

"I like how I'm waiting there, in town. How you don't have the first idea of how I'm there."

"You are, aren't you?" Daring, not daring to believe. "You really are, aren't you?"

"Love," she says, with heartbreaking alto. "Whatever you think about me when you are old, I want you to remember that I never lied to you." *Never,* an overtone in her voice gives away, *about anything fundamental.* It chills him, past the rapidly falling temperature. This once, despite everything he believes, he chooses not to decode.

They creep back into town, protected from notice by the anonymous car. She drives slowly, dropping almost to zero, delaying the end of their one stolen day of unmitigated intimacy. She continues to halve their speed, but Zeno does not keep Stadium Terrace away. They sit in the front seat looking at one another, hungry again, separate, needy. They would have each other, even here, if they thought for a minute that the magically patterned quilt could hide them. A noise jars them back to the realities of K-court. A couple across the street launching into the cruelty of familiars. Someone's failure to take out the garbage, wash a dish, or pick up a sock escalates into mutual hatred. Recrimination floats out upon the spring night, elides with a cry of disgust that tears free from the back of Jeannie's throat. "*God.* Listen. I hate people. I really do. The whole wretched lot of us make me ill."

His heart is so full with her, he sees through her without thinking. Her would-be misanthropy is misguided, jejune. He is strong enough now to take on human kindness. "I know. I used to hate people too."

"And?"

He kisses her, grazing her breasts gently into agreement. "Then I met a few." He shakes her, squeezes her shoulders until she giggles. The sound salvages them. She holds on a little tighter. But in her touch, the suggestion of inevitable mitosis. Her mouth stays pursed, expressively silent. She reaches a cold hand up under his shirt, connects the moles on his back with a grazing finger. Jeanette closes to him on the narrow car seat, as if just filling the space between them a few seconds longer will fix everything. Her eyes are wide, groping for words like a drugged woman. Sexual dizziness; she is thinking herself into climax, pushing herself out over the edge again. Jeannie, his Jeannie, comes, shudders, loses herself against him, just out of holding, refusing to stunt love.

Recovering as quickly as she took off, she raises her incredulous head. "Where did that come from? Did you do that to me?" Ressler just holds her, blood testing the weak points in his veins. He curls over her, makes the first motions of leaving. Her voice originates inside his ear. "Stuart, promise me something." All play gone.

"Name it," he says, straining for humor.

"Promise first."

"I promise. What?"

"You must never die."

The Paperwork Reduction Act

So Jimmy won the salary lottery and, thick with suspicion, accepted the windfall. The next time he stayed late, it was about another fluke, linked to the first, less benign. This man, whose most extravagant profanity was "chili con carne," who could not shout except apologetically, waited furiously in the computer room when Franklin and I arrived after an afternoon of playing house. "Problems, Uncle Jim?" Frank asked.

"That's one name for it. They've dropped me from the group insurance."

"They?" The word irritated Todd, with its overtones of conspiracy.

504

"Our loyal machines. This has to be the work of independent-minded computers. No human being would do such a thing without serving notice." Good faith, touchingly misguided.

"Beginning, please," Franklin said, hanging his jacket on the corner of the CPU.

"What do you mean, 'beginning'? There is no beginning. This is the Information Revolution, son." Jimmy was shaken by being singled out to receive the random hit. "Look at this." He handed over the customer copy of a three-part micro-perforated form. The lines did not quite fit into their intended boxes—a bit of operator negligence I would never have noticed before my days of helping to load such paper. The piece was telegraphic: undernamed no longer carried on major medical group policy number XXX because of failure to pay premium during previous period.

"Failure to pay!" Todd laughed, throwing the form into the air. Jimmy scrambled to catch it. Todd's voice shifted register at the blanket stupidity. "What are they talking about? How can you fail to pay? The premium is deducted automatically from every check."

Jimmy groaned. "Supposed to be deducted." He reached into a pocket and withdrew the now heavily crumpled statement stub that had recently thrown him into moral convulsions. The one announcing: You are the lucky winner. "In all the excitement over that salary nonsense, nobody even noticed." He smoothed the ratty scrap and handed it over. Todd reexamined the figures he'd secretly produced. Jimmy didn't notice, but Frank's face changed color. He shot me a look, but in front of the victim, we could say nothing.

Cavalry-like, Dr. Ressler arrived, carrying a bag of zucchini from his rooftop garden, a plot that must have had more soil than Battery Park. "I'm glad you're still here, James," he said, dividing the crop three ways. All anxiety ceased until he finished doling out his gifts. "Now. I can tell something's up. And today," he smiled at me as if I knew the reason, "I'm prepared to solve all problems."

Jimmy laid out the crisis, and Dr. Ressler's brows narrowed over the relevant documents. He did not look at Franklin, but the refusal to mete out the punishing glance was itself crushing. He studied the forms for hidden explanation. Jimmy said he'd called around, and all the relevant executives had apologized but assured him that his not intending to skip a payment did not change the fact.

"When will they reinstate you?" Ressler asked.

"The period after the period when I first pay again. Barring further electronic bolts from the blue, I should be back on coverage within eight weeks."

"Well, that's easy, then," Todd joked. "For two months, just look both ways before you cross the street."

Jimmy managed an anemic grin. Dr. Ressler asked, "James, may I hang on to these?"

"It's hopeless. I've talked to everyone. All I can do is pay up and wait. I wouldn't waste any more breath on it."

"I'd just like to think about this before notching up another round for the corporations." More than passing inconvenience: the individual in a mismatched battle. His asking for another look before conceding inevitable defeat reminded me that the actual quote, eternally misused, was "But for the grace of God there goes *John Bradford.*" A name immortal in its oblivion, four hundred years ago swapped out for the generic *I.*

Jimmy grumbled his usual threat to enter chicken farming the next time the opportunity arose. The moment the man left, Todd began protesting. "I can't believe it. I don't know what I did. I must have tripped the preemie flag on the way out of the record." Frank was pitiful, scrambling to hide his ineptitude from his hero.

"Let me stake a hypothesis. You went in and requested a flat-fee bonus. Am I right?" Todd nodded. "You added your figure to his gross and put the total into the salary field."

Todd slapped his palm on his scalp. "Jesus. The program processed the *whole check* as a bonus."

"From which, of course, no premium is deducted."

"Christ. Who wrote that thing? What a kludge. Shouldn't it have known that the man can't get a bonus without a salary check in the same period?"

"Don't blame the code. I don't think the authors anticipated second-shift operators doing surgical intervention on their data structures."

Todd threw his hands up. "Well. Now we all know better."

Ressler took Jimmy's papers and sat at the console. Todd sat next to him at the keyboard. The two of them retraced Todd's escapade, which seemed more capricious with each keystroke. I tried to follow as they undertook flood control. I'd never noticed before how much Frank talked with his hands. He rubbed an eraser all over the screen, gesticulated at the keys, drew logic flows into

506

his sketchpad, and sculpted in the air the solution he thought they might yet go after. Ressler sat motionless, a few words doing the work.

But there was little even he could do. The letter had been sent, the coverage canceled. They could not now uncancel the cancellation. Revealing all—the corrective measure of first choice—was out of the question. Todd would lose his job, perhaps be slapped with criminal charges, and Dr. Ressler would fall under suspicion. They could undo the event electronically, but the doctoring involved too many systems: their own, the firm that handled the check, the insurance company where the policy resided. The fix might muck up something else. "Too many humans tipped off already," Todd added. "Can't jerry-rig humans, unfortunately."

"Not yet," Ressler granted.

A few weeks after moving into my place, Franklin began to seep out again. He moved his treasured stereo into my room, a breakthrough in intimacy, and he even brought the violets, blues, and greens from his massive spectrum-arranged record collection. Every few days saw a trickle of disks, gradually edging into the higher wavelengths. He himself was there as often as ever. We continued to read together, to listen, to play, to share meals.

Sex remained dangerous, a revelation about how far I might go, how far I needed to keep going once brought out. I learned no end of things about myself. Franklin could be aggressive, slow, mercurial. He could stalk like a thief looting a house. He could repeat, wistfully after we spent ourselves, the Puritans' standard caption for a needlework primer's A: "In Adam's Fall, We Sinned All." He could lie still under the covers and tell, after a too-savage unloading, "Heard the one about the hellfire preacher berating his congregation? 'Is an hour of pleasure worth an eternity of regret?' Voice from the back of the church calls out, 'How do you make it last an hour?'"

We began to get out again, as the city again warmed. We took a trip up to the Bronx Zoo. Franklin was as excited as a child, and babbled like one. "Look! Kangaroos! Do you know that the mother can slow or speed up gestation, depending on food supply?"

"The name means 'I don't know,'" I contributed. Standard trivia fare. "Aboriginal answer to white hunter's question. 'What do you call those fur-bags with the giant hind legs?' 'Haven't the faintest idea what you're talking about, hombre.'"

507

"She licks down this passage in her fur, the way to the pouch, see? So that her newborn, a wriggly blob like a shelless snail, can slog out the journey...."

"Have you actually seen this happen?" I asked suspiciously.

"Do endless wildlife shows on public television count?" Oh, he was up that day; the cages were not cages, but regional sanctuary from unstoppable habitat destruction. I couldn't help but think of the dismal visit to Central Park Tuckwell and I had made eight months before. Separate lifetimes.

He was always ready for the impulse activity, for any jaunt at any hour, so long as it did not conflict with MOL, about which he grew unusually conscientious. Obscure museums, galleries, secret spaghetti dives, performing-arts warehouses, a walking tour of the colonial remnants of the city. For the first time since leaving Indiana, I went up against the variety of New York. Yet something in the way he moved feet first through the place tipped me off that he was just visiting.

I never expected I would have him all there, every time he stayed over or we went out together. But his eternal pacing.... He had a way of obsessively measuring out a room three times a minute, even when sitting still. I thought the restlessness came from his being twenty-six, at the height of his powers, with nothing of consequence to do. I put myself entirely at his disposal as research assistant for the dissertation. "I can find anything," I swore to him. "Facts are my life." I couldn't have made a worse suggestion, even in jest. It made him pace in even tighter circles. He never dropped the boyish charm, the Midwestern politeness. He made it a point to be home more predictably, and even called on a couple occasions to tell me he would miss a standing meal. But his silence grew denser even as he pruned it.

When he was gone, I thought he might be dead, distracted, religiously converted, injured, amnesiac, overcome by indifference. Each scenario was a toxin whose cold advanced up my arms and legs. Yet I would not put on the saving tourniquet, take the necessary measures. Leaden suspicion was scarily arousing. I discovered it only slowly. My fear for him when he was away became one of those secret fetishes discovered late in life—a region on my body that when struck by that taboo person reduced me to helpless perversity I never suspected lay in me.

These were awful weeks. Every reckless afternoon proved that I had never known what I might be capable of. After making it last

508

an hour, I would draw away with a sick thrill, find myself saying, in the extremity of affected calm, "We aren't really one another's type, you know. You need someone neurotic, taller, silkier, not so verbose." On alternate days, I wanted to break laws for him, to take to terrorism rather than give up what little life with him I'd managed to win. I dwelt on the worst possible explanations for what was happening, the way someone who discovers a growth on a bone cannot help, several times an hour, feeling it to see if it has grown.

Breathless, off-balance, by turns willfully wanting to confirm the incurable worst, I would use my key privileges to his place. An attempt to track him down, to find out how he lived when away from me. When I let myself into his apartment, I always masked my humiliation in high spirits. It never seemed to bother him. He could jump out of bed as if he'd been waiting impatiently for me for hours. "So what do you know about fixing refrigerators?" Or: "You must be the French Maid. Shall we wrinkle the sheets once before ironing them?" No matter what hour I surprised him there, we did not stay around his place for long. Twenty minutes of talk or milting or cleaning up and we'd be gone, to an exhibition, for a meal, back to my place, where he would once again stay a couple of days.

I never appeared empty-handed, so that if he was not there, as he frequently wasn't, I would have some excuse for dropping in while he was out, some reward to leave him for confirming my compulsive need to prove him not at home. I'd bring by a novel, claiming I'd just finished it and it was so beautiful I had to make the impulsive crosstown delivery. I would sit at his kitchen table, too cluttered with tapes, art repros, delinquent library books, lidless half-full peanut butter jars, and dire predictions torn from the *Science Times* to be used for actual meals, and compose scraps of occasional verse by way of saying that I'd been by and we had failed to connect.

These poems, more heartfelt than skilled, were the only means I had of telling him things without cloaking the sentiment in requisite irony. In reverting to a form that most lovers swear off of at eighteen, I compounded the dangerous instability, pushing myself where something would soon have to happen.

> The first days of intimacy scare:
> exchange of histories too keen to mean

anything yet but new threat of loss.
Why thaw now? Why lay bare
all that has held in a fine hide
and stake it here against chance green?
Because we haven't any choice.
Just as two tunes catch in a chord
care moves forward, fact-gathering.
Our measured steps might improvise
a way for winter to wind down, ice
flushing crusted puddles, freeing spring.

I would copy these pathetic fallacies onto a notepad he'd made up for himself: From the Couch of Franklin Todd. Then I would shuffle them into the stack by the telephone, among the ghostly phone transcripts and the portraits made from memory of the people on the other end of the line. He never mentioned discovering them. But the older ones were no longer there when I left an addendum. He pressed them into notebooks somewhere or threw them away.

Life above the antique shop, nights when he did not show, became unbearably acute. The furnishings I had carefully selected, the old crochets, the scents that had been so evocative once, grew too much, the way slight touch is acid to a skin oversensitive with fever. Coming home from work, in days that were struggling to lengthen and stay bright until a reasonable hour, I would look up at the intimate pool of light coming from the room upstairs. I knew that the Edwardian glow was turned on by a digital timer, just as the choker collar—still capable of eliciting response from him— wrapped the neck of a woman who, that afternoon, had spent half an hour procuring the feasibility of test bans.

Unable to sleep, I would call him at the office at obscene hours of the night. Each week was a new probe to see how depraved I might, under the prose binding, really be. "Do you mind if I touch myself while you talk? Say something that might get me bothered." Franklin loved these experiments, thrilled to play along over the phone. Sometimes he urged me to wait until he got home. Others, he was as happy to tease me, take care of me remotely via analog transmission.

I had no clue where we were heading or how long I would be able to last. I only knew that every question I was asked all day long seemed a nuisance variation on the one I wanted answered. When I was away from him, I was frantic with possibility. When

I was with him, it wasn't enough. I had stumbled into a cadence, begun to believe that love had to *lead* somewhere. He was waiting for the same revelation, each of us afraid to move lest we bring about the expected QED.

One early-spring Saturday I found myself, around two in the afternoon, half a dozen blocks from his apartment. He had not shown the night before; Fridays, with their end-of-week processing, frequently became all-nighters. I had no idea where in all the East Coast he had ended up, but his place was as good a guess as any. I decided to surprise him with afternoon breakfast. I ducked into a deli and bought bagels, cream cheese, coffee, oranges, and a horrible sucrose-dripping thing that Todd, with his sweet tooth, would doubtless devour instantly. I walked up to his loft and let myself in.

He was still asleep. Evidence of disorganized entry pointed to a rough night with the machines. I stood in the foyer, wondering whether to wake him. I took a few steps toward the bedroom, then came back to the hall. However good-naturedly he awoke and greeted me, he could only be irritated, and I'd only feel more desperate to correct the impression of desperation. But coming back into the foyer, I thought: So what if I tip my hand? What doesn't he know about me already? Affection, even overdone, must be preferable to more empty space. Back to the bedroom: but before I could make it all the way there, I felt my eagerness driving him away.

I have never felt such indecision, certainly not about anything so ludicrous as whether to get a male up for breakfast. My inability to take more than a step in either direction suddenly seemed emblematic. From some reserve of self-possession, I saw how pitiful I'd become. I laughed out loud, but softly, so as not to wake him. I went to the cluttered table, composed some verses, crumpled them up, and wrote instead, "Dearest Buddy. I came by. Left you a bagel for breakfast."

But just as I was quietly letting myself out, I was again overcome by desire. This might, after all, be the last time. Effusion was the least of the two vices, everything considered. I let myself back in, scolding and cheering myself at once. I went straight into the bedroom, relieved, leaned deeply over him, and kissed him on the shaggy head. He made a soft, pleased gurgle, which was answered by another in a higher register. On the pillow next to him, there moved a second, soft, blond angelic head. An incoherent female

511

voice, lovely in unconsciousness, said, "I'm so hungry I could eat a house."

All I could think about was getting out before more groggy vocalizings brought them conscious. I made it back to the front room, went to the table, and with amazing presence of mind, crossed out "a bagel" and wrote, "Oops; two bagels," supplementing the first from the now useless bag. Out on the street, wandering at random through the press of the Village, I understood; fidelity was for stereos. Working his way through love's alphabet, the man was stuck on the A's. Annie was who he wanted.

XXIV

Canon at the Octave

He is within easy reach, unreachable. His last postmark, Dr. Ressler's forsaken Midwest grain oasis. Even there—only a thousand miles from me, on the same continent, identical landmass. Here. Now that I can't reach him, I want to. The letter I so long dragged my heels on, endlessly red-penned in my head, left lying for weeks on the bureau, and at last ambivalently sent off just before realizing my mistake has come back bearing an Indo-European grab bag of apologies saying that the addressee has vanished without forwarding address. The text of my sham indifference now sits urgent, priority mail, registered, express in my hands.

Not even the same letter, now that it's been returned. Even if I were to place it unrevised in another envelope, send it out again to his unresearchable new post node, it would not mean what it meant the afternoon I finally managed to put it together. The thing I thought to make him see then is gone. Aggregate chance has changed it—a memorandum lost in transit.

If I had his address (counterfactual) and if I could hit on the right words (hypothetical), I might send him some item from our assembled quote box—"I need to know someone"; "What is the origin of 'to make the catch'?"; "What's this I hear about you two cohabiting?"; "Oops, two bagels"—that might convey, if not the particulars of what I need to say now, at least the sense that if he were in the neighborhood (subjunctive), I'd like to see him. But even our favorite phrases, reprised over our allotted months on different occasions, repeated once more would now go enharmonic, altered, racing home even as they stay in place, changing because all other lines range freely around them.

513

I cannot say the same thing twice. The first time through, invention; the second, allusion; a third promotes it to motif, then theme, keepsake, baggage, small consolation. Brought back after years, it evokes a lost twinge never harbored in the original. Perhaps, with everything between us changed beyond recognition, one more reprise might make it invention again.

When the chance was there, who needed to say anything? Now that I can't write, predicates take shape; polyps spread across my insides, bubbling into my throat, seeking the surgery of speech. What do I want so badly to tell him, now that the channel is down? I wanted to say it—the same thing, only different—that evening at that first seafood dive. (The front end of the lobster scuttled into the tank. Todd said, "You should see how they do beef." I kept mum.) I wanted to tell him, that summer night on the swings. (I came all over him, shuddering, but disguised the event, admitting nothing.) I wanted to say something achingly similar, that freezing night under the New England stars. (Todd and Dr. Ressler talked away, trying to save life from life. I worked a jigsaw.) I wanted to say the urgent thing, that Saturday afternoon when I leaned over him as he slept. (Annie said, still asleep, "I'm so hungry I could eat a house." I slipped verbless out the door, leaving no hostages.) I always thought it was Todd, ironic, dry, who constantly pleaded that quintessential department-store excuse "No thanks; just browsing." But it wasn't. Always, from the start, it was me.

What is it that I'd give the rest of my exhausted savings to say to him, now that I can't? I want to tell him what I've learned. Todd: I have taken on science, spent the year acquiring terms, doing a blitz Berlitz in the same grammar our friend was once after. The same, only with all particulars changed. And here is the sense, if not the specifics of what I've picked up.

"There is, in the Universe, a Stair." Small, too small for me to see the steps, even with the best current optics, too small to be floor-planned except through experimental analogy. But large beyond telling, a single epic verse five thousand volumes long, three billion years old. It is smooth, spiral, aperiodic, repeating. Within the regular frame is a sequence so varying that it leaps over the complexity barrier and freely adopts any of an inexhaustible array of possible meanings.

But meaning does not reside *in* the enormous molecule, the reservoir of naked data. The Stair Dr. Ressler was intent on climbing

514

is not rolled up in the nucleus like a builder's blueprint. The plan does not map out the organism in so many words. Nowhere in DNA is there written the idea or dimensions of "tentacle," "flipper," "hand." Nowhere does it describe the shape or functioning of nerve or muscle. Tissue is not modeled to scale. Yet shape, structure, functioning, even the range of behavior: everything originates here, the repository where all significant difference is jotted down, held in place, passed along perfectly, but never twice the same.

I would tell Todd, spell it out in a five-thousand-volume letter. I would say how I have seen, close up, what Ressler wanted to crack through to. How I have felt it, sustained the chase in myself. How the urge to strip the noise from the cipher is always the desire to say what it means to be able to say anything, to read some part of what is written here, without resort to intermediaries. To get to the generating spark, to follow the score extracted from the split lark. I would tell him, at last, sparing nothing, just what in the impregnable sum of journal articles sent Ressler quietly away, appalled, stunted with wonder.

I would tell him everything I have found. I would lay my notebooks open to him. How the helix is not a description at all, but just the infolded germ of a scaffolding organism whose function is to promote and preserve the art treasure that erects it. How the four-base language is both more and less than plan. How it comprises secret writing in the fullest sense, possessing all the infinite, extendable, constricting possibilities lying hidden in the parts of speech. How there is always a go-between, a sign between signature and nature.

I would tell him of nucleic acid's nouns, its cistrons. I would show how stretches of the supercoiled chromosome are simple substitutions for polypeptide chains. Even Todd would see how breathtaking it must have been to be the first to connect metaphor to chemistry, to find the genes, those letter-crosses nesting like flocks in family trees. But I'd make the airtight case that nouns were not what Ressler was after.

I'd show him the speaking string's conjunctions, interrogatives, and prepositions—operator and promoter sites where proteins clamp, qualifying the noun, turning the cistron on or off in subordinate clauses and prepositional phrases. I would show him how Ressler lived at the moment when the ravishing, intensely cyber-

515

netic system, after millennia of theorizing, at last laid itself open. But Franklin would be the first to agree that prepositions alone would never have fed our friend.

I would tutor him in the verbs, set in animation the enzymes, programmed molecules that act, cause, do, command things to fly upwards from equilibrium. I could touch upon the adverbs and adjectives, the modifying sea inside the cell wall singing "brightly," "*langsam*," "con brio." I could deliver an overview of how the five thousand volumes produce their own lexicon of translators for reading their own messengers (transcribed by enzymes of their own synthesis) at sites of their own devising. The complete predication, the weird collaboration of disparate parts of speech into whole utterances, is now within my working vocabulary.

If Todd could sit still for this explanation, if my translation of a translation meant anything to him, he would see that none of this was what the professor was after; despite the brute beauty of the system, none of these parts of speech would have had the power to cripple the man. Then I would say what I know: that an accident of private history left Ressler, for a single, prohibited, unrecoverable moment, hearing not what the grammar says but what it *means*.

I would tell you, straight out, what I've spent the year and my savings to verify: how language makes it impossible to receive the exact message sent. I would tell that anecdote Ressler told me, the day I went to say goodbye, in bitterness over you. That account of a boyhood experiment with a friend and a tin-can telephone: how he had yelled along the muffling string, "Calling Timmy, calling Timmy." Then, dispensing with the ingenious medium and calling out directly across the twenty feet of more expedient air: "Could you hear that?" Only here, there's no jumping outside the medium to verify transmission. Only the tinny tin.

I would make metaphors for you until I became almost clear. Words are fairy tale, not a court transcript. They are those PA announcements on public trans where all you can make out is the irrelevant filler. "Ladies and gentlemen, this is your captain speaking. We're experiencing severe sdklh dhfj hryu e ahj ajd astue for alarm." Words are those slides they constantly fed you in art history, the blurred, color-poor angels of annunciation meant to stand in for the trip to Bruges. But I have no other means to tell it to you.

Ressler, when all molecular inheritance took shape in outline before him, saw it: the closest he would ever get is simile, literature in translation, the thing by another name, and never what the tag stood for. The dream that base-pair sequences might talk about themselves in high-level grammar vanished in the synthesized organism. Science remains at best a marvelous mine, not a replacement for the shattered Tower. Even at his death, despite the unstoppable advances in the state of decoding art, the human genome defies interpretation.

And yet, a man's speech should exceed his lapse, else what's a meta for? The manufacture of these working terms, names and the rules for manipulating them, the accuracy of their fit as fired in the crucible of environment, gave him a way *in* that mere possession of the thing never would have allotted. Names let him toss arrangements around, examine the implications of the message from angles that did not exist in negotiable reality. There is, in this Universe, a Stair.

If I have read the texts correctly—and who knows how wide of the mark my grasp of the blurry words is—then the grand synthesis that ten years ago today pulled all biology into a single tenet is this: a living thing is a postulate about where it finds itself. But that living thing postulates, deep in its cells, in a language that is itself also just a rough guess, a running, revisable analogy. The intermediary of language alone makes it possible to run trials, load experiment. Only by splitting the name from the thing it stands for can tinkering take place. Language, however faulty a direct describer, can get to the place, even change it, by strange ability to simulate, to suppose, to say something else than what is.

A given stretch of the epic verse, the sequence AACGCTA, may start life as a part of speech, emblem noun or imperative verb; "add this, then a bond, then another." By fault in the sentence-making system, the original utterance becomes AACGCGTA. Not much, I hear you dismiss. So what? So *everything;* you must see it. The whole parade depends on seizing mistakes. The accidental change of a single base pair can ripple through the reading process, accounting, after eons of accretion, for every implicit structure never mentioned in the string: stems, leaves, hair, hands, and—most hypothetical—brain. Evolution, the first arrangement of living things that doesn't commit the *post hoc* fallacy, lays it out: invention mothers necessity.

The feasibility of each inherited variation—theme elaborated by mutation—breeds out until there is no more single epic but four million variant variorum editions, each matched to the shelf where it finds itself. Yet the code, the language life writes itself in, is universal for every living thing, taking hold once and spinning, telling in all places at all times an eerie, inconceivably implausible story of how in the beginning there was a little water, ammonia, and methane, all trapped by trivial rules, and at the end, this woman saying over and over to herself, *I want to tell you, I want to tell.*

The scrim lifted, this is what Dr. Ressler saw. The text of a living thing, the tender, delicate, unlikely apparatus for unfolding it, does not stand for or represent or disfigure the shape of the world; it is just a set of possible, implementable maybes about what one might do about it. Nature seems to favor the what-if. Once over the complexity barrier, the simple account promotes itself to simulation. That is the magic of language: every word waits to come true. Description gives way to postulate, is refined by experiment into singing celebration. The same opaque, heavy-handed system that kept him one step away from what those emblems stand for permits this. No saying how; I've been in molecular linguistics long enough to know that language, like economics and love, is wonderful in practice, but just won't work out in theory.

The notebooks I've been keeping for you, friend, if they go on long enough, might become something new, not the thing I wanted to get at, but a live thing all the same, a living thing's living offspring. Would you approve of them? Could all this stuff still move you? To think so has become my life, what all this science writing hopes for. Every sentence ever written down is sent into the world to be winnowed or thrive according to the same accountability principle as those cistrons and their experimental apparatus. Does a given combination of words push close? Do they resonate? Or are they more noise, divorcibles, permutations to dispense with? Does the line shout out, beat around the edges of something real? Do the words make sense? Do we find ourselves arriving back at them late one surprise night, after years of traveling, thinking them dead? Is this phrase worth the ink it expends? Is it what I mean, something I need? Unshakable bits of the original Question Board. Months after quitting, I'm still working on the thing. Still pasting together. I have something almost right, something to say for no one's but your ears, if I could only reach you.

But it's stupid, to write as if he could read this. How could he know what has happened, how far I have come, how I would share him now with anyone, under any conditions, so long as I had a fraction of him to converse with? He couldn't, can't, doesn't, won't: choose your modality. Last he heard, I crossed him off, cut the tin-can string. "It has been so long since he has heard from me that he might easily conclude that I too am dead."

But I know something of him. He is here. Beached on the same island I am. I could walk to him overland if I had a map, an X to mark his spot, that Flemish, reflexive construction he once wrote me: "You Find Yourself Here." Frank, there is no other way to you but this.

The man you wanted me to name for you: his metaphors, too, were from the start just genes, as "gene" is the most successful metaphor his science has yet made to name life's notes toward a theory of experience. Dozens of words he scattered on us while alive still live. See? They keep me up at night, typing. This is what one woman might do with them. Todd, my mate, my husband, could I reach you, I would tell you how I have discovered what he was after—the secret subjunctive—and what discovery did to him. I would say how I have heard him, alone in this laboratory, his school, singing to himself. How I have made out, at last, what tune he wanted to pass on, the tune I want to sing you, the only notes worth moving mouth to mimic, and what the snippet means in our vocabulary. Franklin, just as you asked me: I have identified your friend.

Nomenclature

By spring, Ressler's trio has the kinks in cell-free synthesis ironed out. Uncanny: they can fractionate the inanimate building blocks, assemble them under controlled conditions, add a coded messenger, slip in the distilled adaptor, and—the nearest thing to golem-making to date—*manufacture* proteins, bring into being the plaintext product of the cell. It is not yet creating life. But their procedure is a close functional simulation.

They can take a chaotic soup of free aminos and arrange them, from out of a staggering number of linear permutations, into a sequence that gives them enzymatic sense. Granted, the information they introduce is not theirs, nor can they read it either before or after translation. They cannot compare the bit they submit and the batch output. The text is too complex, the print too fine.

They stand, all but there, confronting one last unskirtable hurdle. They can cause the code to be broken, eavesdrop on the process, but they can't get close enough to read the code book. For weeks, neither Koss, Botkin, nor Ressler has been able to supply any fresh suggestions. Ressler concludes that they are in need of new blood. He tries out the problem on his office mate. Since assaulting Ressler that day outside Ulrich's office, Lovering has been unreadably neutral. Enough time has passed to try reestablishing relations. This intellectual problem is Ressler's peace offering. Lovering declines the proffered branch, polite but indifferent, too busy to be bothered. To leave Lovering an honorable out, Ressler jokes, "Maybe your girlfriend would like to take a shot at the problem." When Lovering jerks his head up from his desk, eyes burning, Ressler regrets the miscalculation.

He takes a slow walk to the Woytowichs', a path he has lately reopened. They will never replace the Blakes, but they are nevertheless—what is the word?—contact. The prodigious Ivy has an undeniable fascination about her rapid development. This time Dan and Renée are between diaper changes. He and Dan trade project stumbling blocks. It gives Ressler no pleasure to hear that the ILLIAC project is just as seriously log-jammed.

"The kid's program is fine," Woyty admires. "It's terrific what he can make that machine do, after only a few months. But after every run that closes in on an occurrence of the pattern we're after, Joey changes his blessed instruction deck again. The program keeps expanding, like those radioactive tomatoes Botany is always growing. Exceptions to the latest exception-handling. The do-loops have grown do-loops on them several nests thick. Very Ptolemaic."

Ressler suggests that they might be engineering their desired result. Dan nods gravely at the possibility. Then, as if hitting on a remedy, he says, "Hey. Come take a look at this." Ressler follows Dan into the infant's bedroom. There, father arranges Ivy on the rug and sets in front of her four brightly colored blocks—rose, powder blue, eucalyptus, lemon—boldly imprinted with oversized letters. "Find the A, Ivy. Come on, little girl." Singsong, he coaches, "A is for ap-ple, aard-vark, an-gi-o-sperm."

Ivy is off and crawling. Stretching out a system of muscles she can still but pitifully coordinate, she falls on the correct block. Ressler remains guarded. "One in four." Can she repeat?

Woyty laughs confidently. He returns the child to the starting point, shuffles the blocks, and says, "Can you show me the C, Ivy? Sure you can. C is for cat and cactus. . . ."

"Cuneiform," Ressler suggests. "Codon." The baby, unperturbed, heaves herself against the correct letter in question. Ressler's eyes light, fueled from a source far away. Still in the crib, Ivy knows her alphabet. Is it real learning or just conditioning? The question, at this level, is meaningless. The scientists sit on the nursery floor. Daniel exercises his daughter's arms, strokes the ham-hock smoothness of her back, stimulating the nerve connections to solidify into a network. Ressler relates the in vitro successes and describes the block they now knock up against. They can produce plaintext proteins from ciphertext nucleic acid. But analysis cannot yet tell them within acceptable margin of error how the sequences correspond.

"So close you are almost past it," Woyty says.

"With long chains, we can label the bases in the sequence we feed the decoder. We can label the amino acids picked up in the synthesis. But it doesn't give us position. The best we can do is assign weight ratios . . . .We're no closer to actual assignments."

"It's a pickle," Daniel concedes. A missed beat reveals that Woytowich is not really following him. He's playing with the baby. The gap between them wraps Ressler in loneliness more severe than that brought on by banging on the closed codon library door. Daniel says, "I wish I could help you, Stuart." Struck by a happy inspiration, he suggests, "Let's ask Ivy."

Weeks pass, the project advancing without real headway. One day, he cannot even name the month anymore, he comes home to the barracks to find Jeanette, in lovely familiarity, waiting for him as if they were silver anniversary candidates. Their time apart cannot even masquerade as moral restraint anymore. Simple cautious terror. But here she is again, in his front room, smiling richly, once more free from the delays and wastes of time that constitute their love. He returns her kiss, goes to the record player, puts the sound track on. She follows him eagerly with her eyes. Like me. Need me. "Hungry?" he asks. "I think I have something that might have been Major Grey Chutney once."

"No thanks. I never eat when I'm in love."

"You know this from experience?"

"Do now." Jeanette makes a little space for him to sit. No sooner does he than she changes her mind. "Stuart? I've a great idea. Let's go outside."

"Outside?"

"You remember." She crooks a finger toward the window. "Trees. Sky. Living things. Perfectly safe, in small doses."

"Well. . . ." Suspicious. "It isn't the strontium 90 level I'm worried about, you understand."

"What, then?"

"It's just that, you are—how can I put this delicately?"

"Married?"

"Exactly. Walking in public, together. . . ."

"Could be that Edward G. Robinson scenario all over again." Spring has made her reckless. "Come on," she laughs. "It's tougher to hit a moving target." She will go walking, and won't hear no. Nor, after another minute, does he want to refuse.

They roll onto the lawn, turn up the block, put Stadium Terrace behind them. He is struck by the department store of smells, after the stale monoscent of the barracks. "And," he adds, thinking out loud, "there are a lot more places to sit."

She stretches herself luxuriously. Relaxing, slack on the return stroke, she slips her arm into his. Here, in residential Champaign, in front of a gauntlet of plate glass—colleagues, friends, faint acquaintances—she makes an open, unambiguous declaration. He knows what it means. She is ready now, ready to leave her husband, that blameless man, to upend her life, to break it and build it again in this arbitrary spot, to recommence, uncertain, with him, only him. Here, now, in spring. Ressler's arms are paralyzed. He cannot move them a millimeter in any direction, either to encourage her or to withdraw and spoil the happy idiocy that has come across her face. He goes numb from neck down.

The abnormal warming trend has brought on, ahead of schedule, a rush of returning life up and down the ladder. She makes first mention of the event. Her voice is low, imparting, even-keyed: *Here we are, outside, together, nothing hidden*. "Flowers," she says. "How early! But it's been so long." He studies her skin. Just below the yellow, little-girl's surface, two blue-green blood tubes in her temples pulse as deep as a spanking new bruise, as the Aegean. She catches him looking, curls up shyly. "What are your favorites?"

"Favorite whats?"

She shoves him. "Haven't you been listening? Favorite flowers."

He is every bit as adrift as when he didn't know the antecedent. "Hmm. Coleus, I suppose."

"Coleus? You suppose? Its flowers are this little."

"Sorry. I guess I meant crocus."

"Oh. Crocus is all right. First. Virginal. Paschal. Fresh schoolgirl." She pauses, putting things together. She grabs his arms, stopping him. "Wait a minute. You're an amateur, aren't you? And you call yourself a biologist!"

Ressler kicks a stone. "I've never called myself that."

Jeanette gapes, hurt by his willful ignorance toward blooms, but half excited at the thought that here, at last, is something she can be the first and only one to give him. "Wait. Look. See over there? Do you know what those are?"

He follows the line of her perfect extended finger. "Y-yes," he says, so tentatively it hurts. "I believe those are droopy, wrinkled, yellow vegetable genitalia."

"Fool. Listen to me. Those are called Narcissus. Even you can see why."

"Am I responsible for etymology as well?"

She kisses him, tongue, for the whole incorporated city to see. "Yes. You are. Now. How about these?"

"Those? Piece of cake. Those are, don't tell me. . . . Nope. I'm afraid it's strike two."

She supplies a name, which he does not even hear, so taken up is he with the soft, effusive enthusiasm in her face. Bluebells, cockle shells: could be anything. He will ask her to repeat it, explain the name here in the privacy of the world. She takes his hand with the grip of a school crossing guard. From one plant to another: who would have thought the block contained so many? Revelation creeps over him. These bee-lures, bright landing pads, reproductive export docks for photofactories temporary beyond telling, self-promoting color that next month will annihilate: each is *called* something, distinct, keen, revealing. Every item has an exotic label that, while not the thing, is the only way of latching onto it in the course of a walk through the neighborhood.

A good deal of his undergraduate days were spent committing to memory vast tracts of binomial nomenclature. But the genus and species identifiers inhabiting his past, while occasionally colorful, were functional: ratios arranging in systematic manner what would otherwise be arbitrary varietal chaos. He knows of the raging taxonomic debate between splitters and lumpers, between those who see in each individual—never corresponding to the norm, always a little bit *other*—the call for a new species, and those who

523

want to restrict the chart to broad, manageable branches. His own discipline, the tabulation of mutations at the molecular level, might solve the matter, showing gaps between species to be both discrete and continuous. But whatever the local bias, inflected, logic-bound Latin taxonomy strives to squash ambiguity, to distinguish between surfaces.

Not so Gladiola, Jack-in-the-Pulpit, Mother of Thousands, Evanescence, False Solomon's Seal, Wake-Robin. The words Jeanette whispers to him, makes him repeat, ranging speculatively across the year, are not labels at all. They are intent on a different program altogether. *Bidens frondosa,* he learns, might go by Beggar-ticks, Rayless Marigold, Sticktight, Devil's Bootjack, Pitchfork Weed. It might even be named the Nameless Wonder, for that matter, and still not strain the grain. According to this woman, a thousand different bizarrely descriptive modifiers specify the catch-all violet. The naming urge embodies the feminine miracle pouring it in his ears.

All desire comes down to naming. Yet no nomenclature will ever erase the fact: standing *for* is also obscuring. The real use of names must be something more serious than handle-efficiency. It must also be myth-making, resourceful approximation, soothing the scar between figure and ground, between the dead chemicals ATCG and the repeating uniqueness they have become. Dr. Koss, his Jeannie, moves him on, graduates him to bulbs that have not appeared yet, to stamens that never show themselves in this region. The game grows more incredible as it goes on. She says how the garden-variety pansy, one of the few lay identifiers he has taken for granted all these years, takes its name from *pensée,* French for thought. From thought to word to name to plant: the chain equating them, more fragile than the petals themselves, defies examination except through tools as fragile, of the same make. She feeds a tutoring hand inside his jacket, releasing a dam burst of labels. What, he wonders, could he call this blossomer?

"You are brilliant," he says.

Jeanette drops her jaw. "Why? Because I like gardening?"

But the germ has taken hold in him. Flowers and their ciphertexts, smearing the one-for-one trip-wire correspondence that in vitro would isolate. Can the handle relating base patterns to proteins clear this up? Or could it be that in vitro is less precise than this hopeless, associative morass: Baby's Breath, Crowfoot, Lily of the Valley, Queen Anne's Lace?

"But can we call them anything we like?" His words elicit only a confused look. "I mean," he measures, "people call flowers what their grandmothers teach them to call them. But some grandmother assigned the tag once, way back, right?"

Jeannie chuckles at his earnestness. "Several grandmothers in several places at several different times." No conspiracy.

"Why is a given common name *the* plant's name? No one in a million years is ever likely to argue with 'Black-Eyed Susan.' What makes it right?" Dark and disturbing, a flare threatening the reductionist certainty that has guided his every step since the home nature museum. The task of the skeptic is to determine, for every appearance, if the label fits the thing. Every tag must be either apt or inapt. Was Charles the Bald? Louis the Fat? Richard the Lion-Hearted? By a slow tightening of terms, exclusion of middles, improvement of instrument, each sobriquet's appropriateness becomes discernible. But the assumption is shaken to the core by the introduction of Jeanette the Misnicknamed. If the name is apt, it's not; if it's not, it is.

She tightens against him. Her waist persuades, hands help, eyes ratify, arms work their armistice. "Well, I suppose a name is right if it sticks, if it becomes *the* name."

"I'd like something more than the tyranny of the vote."

She gives him the once-over. "All right, bub. You are above average in looks, so we're gonna give you one more shot. What exactly do you have in mind?"

"These," he says, leading her by the digits. "These tiny, bulbous ones."

"Oh!" She smiles widely. "Excellent choice; the name for these is inspired. Note how puffy, spacious. And how they hang upside down. You have thirty seconds."

When he makes no reply, she patters. "Ready for this? Dutchman's Breeches." He makes a puzzled, slight tightening of the mouth, flick of fingers. Faltering, she says, "See the trousers?" There are no trousers. For one, the flowers are less than an inch across. The blossoms flare out in a three-dimensional solid, more H than Y, an oriental kite. Upside down, opening underneath. But why Dutchman? At his failure to respond, Jeannie's features deepen, ready to run from the first hint of disaster. She is more beautiful in distress than at her sunniest. He needs this woman, her scattered stimuli of joy, intensity, and fright. He will end up on her doorstep in the dark rain, waiting for her to come out and utter even so little as one not unkind word.

He drops to his knees and examines, up close, this fragile palate opening diffidently to the air. The more Ressler looks, the more iridescent the bloom becomes until it goes purple around the lip. It smells of nothing—sinister, promising, forsworn, far away, as far away as Jeannie's hair. He moves it under his eye, careful to manipulate only the stem. Glass, it would shatter at a fingerprint. Even so, nature uses him: light rearrangement of examining is enough to dust pollen across his hand.

"But what if it weren't?" he says at last. "What if it were something else? Say, the Common Speak-a-portal."

Dr. Koss, who has followed him to knee level, struggles to her feet like a newborn wildebeest. She stares at him, slowly going radiant, finding in him what she has been after. He has broken the code. Ressler too tries to struggle to his feet, but her mouth blocks his way. "Mouth" is certainly misnamed: what he kisses is something lighter, wider, more enveloping. He is set for weeks, for as long as memory holds out.

How obvious, waiting to be discovered: the tracts of rectilinear Midwest that he once loved for their reserved refusal to interfere with fact in fact consist of an indivisible density of named things. Purple-green weeds sprouting ubiquitously throughout spring. Exploding pollen packets. Seeds parachuting on currents of wind. Waxy pitchers, dull matte, convoluted packed rosettes, bright, round, fierce day's eyes, each replicating and subduing the earth, attempting to demonstrate by success the aptness of their sobriquet.

Jeanette, wetting his mouth with hers, breaks only long enough to pull him impatiently back toward the barracks. But before she can cover him in the prize she will bestow on him for his discovery, while he can still remember the wrinkle with sufficient agitation, Ressler grabs the spiral notebook that came out to Illinois with him. He has reserved it until this moment for lab notes, hypotheses, models, the verifiable jottings of procedure. The pages fill with a complete, handwritten history of the in vitro attempt. Now they seem the logical place to record the afternoon's momentous insight. Jeannie clings lightly to his back, sinking her teeth into his shoulder. She looks on, reads as she murmurs, allowing him two minutes to say what he needs. Then she will take from him everything he has shown himself to be worth. But first, he arrests in print amber the skeleton that might one day release the world from its condition of standing cipherhood: "Flowers have names."

Today in History

March 21: First day of spring, vernal equinox, pedal point of Aries, the calendar's octave. My file for the day is full of forgettable sports records, local legislation, small-time politics, standard international bickering. I can find only one thing of lasting consequence that happened on this date, one recombination that will stick, lodge itself in the permanent gene. For once, I break the self-imposed rule prohibiting birthdays: today is Bach's.

Ressler was celebrating that musical provincial's 299th the night I walked into MOL to make my goodbyes. Todd, alone in the lunchroom, was cheery. "Thanks for breakfast," he said, implying by a grin that they both had needed it. "Why didn't you wake me?"

The question, self-evident to him, knocked the words out of me. I sat down at the empty lunchtable. I had nothing left to say. I didn't even want to be there. Impulse instructed me to run, get rid of him without pointless postmortems. I would have, except for the farewell I owed Dr. Ressler, the blessing I needed from him.

"Why didn't I wake you?" I could manage nothing more than a flat, journalistic survey. Todd nodded, but betrayed the pretense by fiddling with the knobs on the microwave. I was getting softer, fainter. I felt nothing. No resentment, no desperation. Zero. A cipher. I lifted my eyebrows: I release you; now will you let me out cleanly?

"You didn't want to wake our friend?" Todd's voice tacked suddenly, came about. Its preemptive volume, front first, dropping the would-be innocence, jerked me by the neck.

"I didn't want to wake your friend," I said, this time finding the exact, disdaining disengagement I was after. He tilted toward me and rubbed an eyebrow; every natural defense lay with him. I could not lie, could neither attack nor escape. Tolerance of animal stupidity, the only religion I believe in, kept me from choking him. He had broken no rules; we had never laid down any. From the first, I could have him only without promise or propriety. But he *had* broken something, unforgivably cheated. He had not *said*. From the day he first showed at the Information Desk, all facts were to be on the table, public domain.

527

"How long?" I asked him. I might have been conducting a phone poll, a product questionnaire.

Todd closed his eyes, pressed thumb to the lids, and struggled to suppress an hysterical snicker. "How long what?"

He wanted to hear me say it, unleash my rage. "How long," I said, perfectly modulated, stewardess-clinical, "have you been packing your dick into that pretty little muff?" Hearing myself pronounce the obscenity—I still can't believe this—brought me to the first stages of arousal.

"How long have I been sleeping with Annie?" He waited brutally until I nodded at the paraphrase. He was a boy. A stupid, puerile, self-indulgent, arrested boy. His eyes looked up as if he were reading the answer there. "Since shortly after I began sleeping with you."

The moan came out of me before he finished the predicate. I covered my face in my hand, so that he would not have the pleasure of seeing the knife slice across it. Muscle convulsed under my palm, my skin burned, all over an exchange of words. Todd took a clumsy, involuntary step of compassion in my direction, but he did not dare close the gap. He could not bear to be responsible for a show of pain that compromised me. He let out a plaintive bleat, banged into a chair, and slammed the cabinet, by way of offering comfort. "You honestly didn't know?"

It helped, at least, to let my facial tics explode. "You said *nothing*. Total silence." Amyclaean, golden, consenting. Alien and unnatural in my mouth. "You *hid*. How I was supposed to know?"

He shook his head. "She's always around. Devoted. Doting." His tone was soft, pointed, regretful. "All the qualities I so patently lack."

"From that I was supposed to guess?" I went shrill, and—last symptom of losing control—didn't care. "She treated us like a *couple*. So did you, for that matter."

"I still would. So would she." *If,* he implied, *you weren't so archaic, perverse with monogamy.* "The night I first went home with her, she told me she wouldn't hurt you for all the tea in china shops. I obviously miscalculated in telling her you'd understand."

Having slighted everything else, he went after my understanding. I wanted to prove myself the most magnanimous, liberal creature on earth. At the same time, I wanted to snuff him out, arrogance and all, like a kitchen match. Hurt him beyond understanding. "You screwed with a creationist." Monotone outrage. Sex with a religious zealot: the most unforgivable miscegenation. Todd could not stifle a horrible laugh. The pained chuckle came out hideous; he knew the escaping sound would divorce us for good.

"We slept together regularly, yes."

"Slept together," I said. "Regularly." The act might have taken fifteen seconds against a wall, but the polite name promoted their every transaction to a mutual sedative between the politenesses of linen. "I don't understand." Bitter pleasantry. "How can she square this with the Six-Day God? Isn't fucking without benefit of clergy one of the bargain fares to damnation?"

Todd pinched his lip. "We've never discussed doctrine."

"What *do* you discuss?"

"Not much, frankly. You and she have always talked more than she and I."

She'd wanted to save me. God did not allow for interpretation. Thou shalt not commit. Her folk-song simplicity had fooled me into assuming she did not share creation's basic contradiction. I didn't care anything about her or her motives. The only thing I cared about, flailed at as if it alone could keep self-esteem from dissolving, was the *cause* of Franklin's infidelity. Irrelevant.

Unaccountably calm, I suddenly knew that belonging, for Todd, was another ugly name for aging. He was losing the courage to face routine, and monogamy left him in the path of exhaustion. Woman-jumping, deep in him long before I arrived, publicly proclaimed that in the end he wouldn't be around for anyone. He could never have survived, as half his life, a partner's crises, the death of her parents, her illness, aging, change. He barely survived the spring overhaul of my wardrobe. The constant terror of event unfolding in daily familiarity could only be beaten by jumping ship, getting promiscuously free.

He had ruined whatever chance the two of us ever had of looking to our joint moat. I would never forgive him that. But I needed to confirm a worse suspicion before breaking off. I spoke softly, not to repair but to cauterize. "Why, Franklin? You have to explain. Don't leave me guessing."

"Janny." A student pleading for a grade change. "I don't want to leave you at all." I retaliated now with all the secretly stockpiled silence I had stolen from him over the months. "Jan. You want me

529

to make it worse?" I waited, my fingers jiggling like voltmeter needles. "You're asking me to hit you." Yes, I thought. Say it. It will never make any sense otherwise. I will never work it out alone. "You cannot," he started. He shifted clauses. "She . . . Annie. You see, with her. . . ."

"She's still fertile," I supplied. His relief, the greatest I ever succeeded in giving him, broke all over his face. I felt, to answer it, only sick, self-confirming, disaster stoicism. Your house is on fire and your children have burnt. I knew what I needed to do, and would do it cleanly. "I'm sorry," I said. "I had no idea. You two are trying to make babies?"

"Janny." Frank was beyond trying. "Janny."

But I was right: the saving *maybe*. Every option exercised was a small murder. Open-door policy: everything had to remain possible. He couldn't write about his Flemish landscapist without first acquiring botany, geography, geology, optics, another foreign language. He could not write a life with me without a second edition being at least conceivable. He had to remain an able-semened body. My ligation robbed him of potential. His every evasion of commitment preserved the day when he might exercise his birthright, cash in and capitulate to fatherhood.

I had my explanation, and I made to leave. But stopping at the door, meaning to make a concession to closure—a last goodwill drink somewhere—I surprised myself by furiously whispering, "I told you everything early on. Why bother coming back, week after week? Why trouble to move halfway in? Why string out the thing, knowing I was useless?"

A boy, arrogantly loose on his scavenger hunt, stared at me in boyish bewilderment. "What do you mean?" He held his head, searched for the best possible word to counter my willful misrepresentation. "I *love* you."

I left him and walked alone to the control room, where I heard Dr. Ressler's birthday musical offering. I knocked and entered rapidly, before I could back out. The professor sat behind the bank of monitors, blissfully happy in the spray of dense counterpoint from his turntable. "Ah! A victim. Listen to this," he said, hungry for companionship to a degree I had never seen in him. He was now ready for anything that circumstance might throw him. And I had come to rub his readiness out.

"The D minor partita for solo violin. 'Solo' is a euphemism. Multipart polyphony from a single instrument. Last movement: the chaconne. Constantly repeated eight-bar theme...." He stopped. I had my back to him, looking through the two-way mirror into the computer room, committing the place to long-term memory. "No music lesson today?" he said gently, without patronage. Unique among males in my experience.

"Your boy says he loves me," I said, trying for lightness and missing by light-years.

Dr. Ressler lifted the needle of the phonograph and bombarded us with quiet. "That much is obvious." My long silence gave him a chance to allude to that old, shared joke. "Well, yes. It *is* obvious."

"But you see," I said, turning to him and parodying a smile, "I am no longer functional."

He looked me full in the face, searching for the missing pieces. In less time than it would have taken a professional, he had the thing figured. Against room rules, he lit a cigarette brutally, in disgust. A flare-up I didn't know could come from him. He had taken a chance on us, tenderly maneuvered us over our own flaws, poised us for a reasonable chance at happiness; all we had had to do was pay attention and try to be relatively free of cruelty.

He walked a few steps in every direction. His eyes were intent on something farther than the other side of the silvered glass. He shook his head, racing through the permutations, discarding things he might say as pointless. He stubbed out the butt and exploded. "The man is a fool." I felt a forbidden rush: Dr. Ressler needed me. I went over to him, stopped him from stepping away, and pinned myself to him. The only demonstration either of us would ever give one another. I didn't let go; instead, I pressed against him, insisting. Slowly, against his will, he pressed back. We did not caress, but held one another hypothetically, softly letting skin guess at what desire might have felt in another place, another life, halves of a botched dissection, an old whole.

We separated without explanation. He lifted my lowered chin until I had to look squarely at him. "This is not the scenario of choice for you two. You know that."

I shrugged. "It's the scenario we're in." It occurred to me: I could say: *Talk to him; shame him.* And the thing would be straightened. Ressler knew as much too, and was waiting, weight on his toes, to intercede. I didn't ask. I no longer wanted to be fixed. It was a relief to escape the waiting, the nights away—to

531

break off without it being my fault. To come away with all the benefits of the injured party.

I went home, there being no other place. Over the next several days, most of Todd's possessions politely disappeared of their own accord, vanished under bacterial rot, in stop-action film. The evacuation did leave its slight, keloid blemish. Notebooks, a record or two, a pair of socks left behind, forgotten—the crippled child in Hamelin, or props for a later, staged, happier goodbye.

The room above the antique shop once again became my private reserve. There was nothing to do on evenings off except repair the place. When I could make no more improvements to its chenille stagecraft, I began finding reasons to stay late at the branch, without compensation except the slightly more comprehensive answer.

Q: What is the largest geological feature on earth?

A: The earth's largest feature is also its youngest. The Mid-Atlantic Ridge, a ten-thousand-mile-long submarine mountain range rising to an average height of ten thousand feet and anywhere from three to six hundred miles wide, is split down its length by the breach of new rock welling up from the convection currents of the earth's molten mantle.

I lost several days to the QB. I thought I might be able to go on forever, working it into the perfect artifice, addressing every hidden need in the close-lipped questioner.

Warm days went on increasing. I began walking again, more cautiously, not so far afield as when it had been the two of us. Brooklyn is a complex biome. Two and a half million people watching the neighborhood isobars of war and truce. Streets full of Russian, Italian, German, Korean, Yiddish, Spanish, Chinese—a fair slice of the varieties of talk. But the language map is devised to keep out crossovers. I stuck to the island allotted me—branch, apartment, subway opening.

After a long afternoon at the branch rooting through *Gov Pubs,* I did not feel like going home. One evening, sitting in a convenient pizza parlor among surreal composite frescoes of Venetian and Florentine landmarks, I had time, for the first time since I'd left him, to see how I'd treated Tuckwell. While I'd been flush, I believed that the best thing we could do for old loves was be firm with them. I now saw the weak rationalization for what it was. I simply had had no stomach for messy responsibility. If it were too late to make good, maybe I could at least recant.

Keithy shouted a surprised hello through the intercom and buzzed me in. I walked up to the apartment, disoriented by how familiar the stairs still were. He'd left the door open but did not meet me. He was lying in the recliner, watching TV with the sound off, but in full three-piece uniform as if just back from the office. "Marian," he said, as if I too were just home from work. "What do you have to say for yourself?" I had *lived* here once, and all the place could say was *I remember you; wait, don't tell me.* . . . I sat next to him, ready for any sentence—hostility, abuse, sadistic wit, even affection, caresses, sex-with-the-ex, if that was the penalty he chose to extract. Any slap but casual indifference.

"You're just in time," he said, without glancing over. "Watch." He pressed a button on the remote; was it a new device, or the one we'd owned? The sound flooded on, cataclysmic *Carmina Burana*—the microphone everywhere in the orchestra at once. On the screen, a casserole apotheosis of meats, vegetables, noodles, and sauces flew through the air in an ultra-slow-motion parabola so charged and erotic that each of its subtle, glacially arcing parts seemed loaded with the symbolic curve of significance.

I watched arrested in horror as epic food rained down upon an ivory-colored antique tablecloth. Every transcendent splash was Bolshoi-choreographed. Succulent streamers of pasta twisted like living things against the sea bottom. Crosscut, pan, slow zoom: every visual stop pulled out to create a late-century masterpiece. The effect, pornographically immediate, more evocative than any Ingres or Master of Flemalle, scooped out my stomach more violently than the real event would have. Keithy killed the set just as the voice-over began to explain what the stain was selling. He leaned toward me in triumph. "No talking toilet bowls for me. When Keith Tuckwell dies, he's going to leave something behind him in the minds of millions."

"That was yours?"

"Essentially."

"Network TV? Prime time? My, Keith."

"Yes, woman. I've arrived." No trace of the old self-mockery, no suggestion of *see what you lost?* He sat back in his chair, at peace with his times. I don't know what I'd expected, what I'd

533

hoped to say to him. In thirty seconds, I remembered how hard it was to say anything at all. I asked how he'd been. "Since when?" Had he been eating well? "Well, but not prettily." Gotten out any? Been dating? "A veritable salad bar, a smorgasbord of women. Cold women who dress in red and black. Women with overbites—very frail. Women who know all there is to know about structural engineering. Black women who drift down sidewalks humming de Falla. Leggy blondes in pastel who have never known unhappiness. Women who keep great secrets. Auburn-haired beauties whose neuroses periodically flame out like...."

I let him improvise, absorbing my due. But it was no punishment. He was too happy. An intercom call a minute later, playfully rhythmic, revealed the reason. He buzzed the caller in without asking identity, and opened the door on a heart-stoppingly glamorous girl who wore, with poised authority, incredibly expensive Italian-tailored rain-forest green and a rope of pearls. Keith introduced us without a ripple. I didn't catch her name, but the way she shook my hand and said how much he'd told her of me laid out everything.

She excused herself to take a powder, something I hadn't realized women still did. "Keithy." I said. "You can't marry this woman."

He looked at me, lips cracking. "Why not?"

"She'll stay for long periods in the bathroom with the door closed. She'll be two hours dressing, just to take the trash out. You'll be miserable. This is just a rebound."

He waited an arch second. "Too late. Your invitation's already in the mail." His date returned. "We're going out," he said, his suit now giving an entirely different account of his emotional state of affairs. "No need to wait up." They left, leaving me watching television in a stranger's apartment, knowing the exact, private locking-up routine on my way out.

Nights in my apartment I sat in the rocker, watching Todd's goods disappear of their own volition. I reviewed the old photo gallery. I remembered how he arranged his notebooks near the bed, so he could reach them rapidly in the dark. How he bought milk so he could stare at the photos of Missing Children on the cartons. How, when he lost his patience with food, he could survive for days on charges of whipped cream straight out of the can. How his body sometimes lurched in an electrostatic jerk of total fear before falling off to sleep.

I was at last militantly alone. I would probably have stayed in that condition, habituating to it until I no longer noticed, had not the phone rung one night, Todd on the other end, hoarsely whispering, "I've killed the man."

XXV

Disaster

Information thrives on it, a larger part of the daily paper than anything except ads. Annuals feature it, the most prominent and dependable heading. Almanacs compile numbing numbers lists— freakish accounts aligned in fatal categories, Earth, Air, Fire, Water. The calendar is just a disaster register. March 27: strongest earthquake to hit North America, Anchorage, 1964. Worst aviation disaster in history, Canary Islands, 1977. Mount St. Helens, 1980. Next morning rounds out the elements: Kwangtung ferry capsizes, last year. Bolts from the blue, tears in the fabric. The word's etymology blames bad stars. But nothing is so mundane or ensured. All information, every signal and search, will collapse into noise, lost to sudden, shocking, disastrous commonplace.

Restricting myself to the seismic/volcanic category of *Information Please,* summing the conservative death estimates for the last hundred years, I get an average of thirty people a day dying from the locution of speech reserved for impossibility: the earth moving underneath them. Flood, drought, famine, hurricane, tornado, tidal wave, avalanche—tea visitors, daily mail. And the constructed catastrophes: hotel catwalks leaping free, tenement fires, airplanes dropping out of the sky. Motor-vehicle deaths in this country equal a large plane crashing daily. An accidental death every six minutes, accidental injury every four seconds. Only accidental birth accounts for anyone being left.

Outside accident accounts for less than 5 percent of American deaths. The rest are tiny slippages within the system, a valve shutdown, a tube burst or blocked, an instruction misread, production idle or fatally overrun. The body, too intricate to sustain, lives in what industry calls the "mean time between failures." Expected, ubiquitous friend of the family—bad stars.

The Morse name has an elegant symmetry: three triplets arranged in simple contrast that sounds panicked even in binary. No word is faster to transmit, clearer to receive than "An event again." Words—those rearguard actions—can't frame it, the infinitely unlikely disappearing into the terminally indifferent. Everywhere, this instant, unrepeatable combinations lost. Cathedrals bombed, cantatas used to wrap fish, years of space exploration going up like a Roman candle, an absurdly kind man who would choke on his phlegm rather than spit, wiped out by a fleck of loose plaque.

Disaster is modest, quiet as termites, low-key as a library dissolving in acid paper. The five-thousand-volume epic biography, life, loves—unique configuration of cells and switches—*might* be reassembled by trial and error, just as Keats's unwritten work lies hidden in the ad copy of magazines, out of order. Reconstituting Keats would be child's play in comparison.

Disaster is a junior page accidentally reshelving a one-of-a-kind manuscript by the wrong call number. Someone comes looking for the work, sure that it contains the explanatory key long overlooked. But the tome is not where the catalog assigns it. The manuscript, in any number of random places, is annihilated in improbability. How lost? Say the library is big, big beyond combing. Say it contains a few thousand books for every organism ever brought into unlikelihood. Say it contains a record of every geological tick that brought into existence, from out of bare rock and trace atmosphere, this implausibly kind man. No search will ever turn up that misshelved manuscript.

The "Disasters" sheaf in the vertical files professes to have the numbers in hand. It gives the erosion calmly, in columns of sandbagging statistics, the way good breeding compels a person to say, "Never mind; it's nothing," even when everything has now gone irretrievably wrong.

Uncle Jimmy

Franklin was worse than worthless over the phone. I'd never heard him like that. His voice was crumpled like an ancient wax cylinder recording. His sentences were incoherent beyond editing. I had to steady him, lead him with Twenty Questions. Slowly now, back up: what's happened? *I've killed him; I've killed the man*. No one was even dead. But disaster, the 65.5 per 100,000 people per year chance, had settled in. Uncle Jimmy had had a stroke. Although alive, he had been severely hit.

Franklin's hysteric claim of responsibility possessed a distant logic. Jimmy's further inquiries about his premium error had at last awakened a sleepy corporate hierarchy. He had been requested to answer a couple of *ad hoc* actuaries. Their questions had raised the possibility, in insinuating office dialect, that Jimmy might know more about the source of the computer irregularity than he let on.

Jimmy, most oversensitive of men, already nursing accumulated anxiety over his inadvertent failure to meet a premium, was so bewildered by the probe—mere formalities, all part of good investigation—that he ruptured an aneurysm that had been hiding, an inherited deficiency, secret and soft in his cerebral arteries. He apoplexed on the examination carpet, proclaiming innocence while going into coma.

Not until his evening arrival did Franklin learn it. Dr. Ressler broke the news, alone in knowing how Todd tied in. Franklin harassed the hospital where Jimmy had been rushed until the answer-givers on the other end refused to speak to him. He forced Ressler to repeat over and over that the hemorrhage was not his fault, and each time he refused to believe it. Torturing himself into organic nightmare, he called the only person in the world who might further torture him.

I calmed him as best I could, offering to come right over. He screamed in agony, "No. Not *me*. Jimmy." I said I'd be at the hospital within the hour, and that alone comforted him a little. I rang off, threw some clothes on, and was gone. Not until I entered the hospital did I collect myself enough to realize: *Jimmy*. That courtly, clumsy truism-speaker, inept and universal flirt who every afternoon called his mother to say he was on his way home, too free of complication to understand, let alone repeat, the slurs that pass for human conversation.

I felt the queasy calm of worst-case scenarios. Cool, calm, and collected: the highest rung in Tuckwell's ad world, the one that will deliver us from harm. The building's smell—alcohols, ethers, gauze—made me feel I was picking Jimmy up from the dentist's rather than heading for Intensive Care. I asked for him at the reception desk, an antiseptic module as wide as a Canadian football

538

field and as blond as Sweden. The linen nurse addressed me too gingerly. "Are you the wife?"

I smiled, despite the immediacy, to imagine Jimmy and me as life mates. I said the patient was single. The registrar nurse examined a huge, Dickensian ledger printed in dot matrix rather than quill. She flipped to Jimmy's lookup code: Steadman, James S. STEA3-J13-72-6. My correct answer apparently earned me admission, for she directed me to a waiting room. The sprawling complex consisted of an outer shell of functional, modernist passages laid out in star-shaped pods wrapped around an industrial kernel with low ceilings and forced steam heat that probably should have been trashed at the turn of the century. The two symbionts didn't quite align. Old floors ramped up to new; catwalks cut across obsolete passages. Colored stripes and system icons indexed each region of local suffering like a Byzantine underground parking lot.

Children in slippers and tunics, hair thinned to pointless patches, carried listless trucks under their arms, remembering everything about the ritual of toys except the reason. Mint-green semiconscious shapes with bloated bellies lay in half-obscured bedrooms in the care of LED banks, chins fighting for air, tubes rammed so deeply up their noses that it bruised their eyes. Some sat in pharmaceutical storms. Orderlies, acutely reassuring, wheeled people by on hydraulic flatbeds, cots that smelled of runny ulcers and fecal ooze, smells dusted over by musty astringent. Worse than Passchendaele, more hideous than Bosch: everything proceeded with supermarket calm.

In embarrassed hall-alcove clumps stood the healthy—by fault of intimacy, the go-betweens to this hideous lab. We avoided one another's eyes. An accidental exchange of glances and I found myself staring into the face of a scared woman who flashed me a conspirator's look: *Don't tell anyone you saw me here.* By the time I located the IC waiting room, I knew the dirty secret. Individuals were woundable, sickly, inconvenient, contemptible, tragic in every way except numerically, smudges on endless fanfold paper. Despite everything culture has ever insisted, hospitals were not shows. Even here, at the one moment my entire life should have trained me for—Intensive Care, 5W, North Tower, Green Wing—obscenely lacerated, lost: wanting, needing, but not knowing how to hear the makeshift, temporary metronome measuring out so obvious a rhythm, the meter of the faltering human platelet pump.

A months-old trade magazine in the waiting room declared that more Americans enter hospital every month than were alive at the Revolution. I stared awhile at the magazine's other unabsorbable facts, then matched wits against quiz TV. I sat on a wraparound petroleum-based sofa, kitty-corner to a volatile, overweight woman who had the lounge phone's receiver surgically incorporated into her double chin. She was not using the phone, just holding it, keeping the line open for a message she had long given up hope of receiving. My companion watched as I answered the one about the oldest city in the continental United States being St. Augustine and correctly gave "nano" as the prefix meaning one billionth in the metric system. The only question worth addressing at that instant was in the IC, stroked out. But I kept on answering these others, eye-calm.

The woman looked at me reverently. "You could make a lot of dough, honey." Having paid me the highest compliment, she could now let me into the intimacy of her being here. She said, "My little girl," tapping the receiver as if it were the child. She flashed me one of those in-your-own-best-interests grins. "She's down the hall, about to be cut open in several places." I apologized, not knowing what else to say. She waved me off. "I'm trying to find out who the anesthetician is. That's very important. A girlfriend's husband once died under the hands of a bad anesthetician."

Courtesy dictated my saying something about waiting to see what was left of a friend following his massive stroke. I didn't. After a pause during which she twice said "Hello" into the unresponsive phone, my partner turned again to me with the two-syllable, singsong question "Children?" She nodded reassuringly—*Easy one. If you knew St. Augustine, this one's a gift.* For some reason, I couldn't figure the question out. Did children exist? Which was the oldest? What was one billionth of one called? Up from the unfigurable field of memory came that old jump-rope rhyme: Franklin and Janny sitting in a tree, kay eye ess ess eye en gee. First comes love, then comes marriage, then comes Janny with a baby carriage.

I smiled and said I wasn't married. She made a just-as-well face, and all at once I felt Franker lean over my shoulder and whisper, "Holbein." Habit; with specialist's myopia, he would look at a tree deranged by autumn and, taking in the clash of colors, would come up for air saying, "Bonnard!" Nothing was what it was, but always a comparison to paint. When he came closest to genuinely loving

540

me, he would freeze, beg me not to move, and exclaim in a half-rapture, " 'Girl with the Pearl Earring.' " He was a lost cause, wrecked on aesthetics. Seeing Rembrandt's ox-sides in the meat case at the supermarket marked him as unfit for life.

Aesthetics could not survive the waiting room. A bit of aesthetics on his part had led, however indirectly, step by step, to a burst vessel in Jimmy's brain. I looked at the woman again; yes, infinitely more Holbein miniature than contemporary Long Island mother. I was inspecting her in the Met, with Franklin at my side. It was suddenly enough to have had a look at her real face—pinched eyes, mole, spinsterly, approving mouth—to set her in a time she matched. Empathy came on me from nowhere, and I wished her daughter every chance that medical technology, God, and a good anesthetician could give her.

Years later, when they at last let me into his room, Jimmy was sitting in bed as if nothing had happened. I wondered, What on earth is he doing here? There's nothing wrong with him. In that first moment, he seemed the same person he had ever been. Unmistakable, vintage Uncle Jimmy. Then I saw just how wrong things were. His face had collapsed on one side, as if from a bad foundation. His mouth sagged down to the left, an eighty-year-old's mouth, unable to produce anything more than a few raw vowels. His lips drooped a deep, secretive smile all over his face, the smile of a man who had seen something remarkable. His eyes bore a matte glaze, not his. Jimmy's eyes were gone.

I thought there would be others there—friends, day shift, his mother. But I was alone, except for Jimmy and the patient behind the draw curtain. My calm collapsed beneath me like a pier gently washed out to sea. My eyes grew acid. I dug my fingernails into my upper arms, trying to reverse the process that had overtaken him, reverse everything.

He must have recognized me in some sense, because as I stepped to the bed, he rippled his ruined facial muscles. He looked roughly in my direction and erupted in a horrible, unformed call like the open modulation of an underwater whale. "Hello, Jimmy." My tone was no closer to natural. He made the awful blast again. This time it seemed to possess syllables. The sound was edgeless, blurred, terrible. I had to force myself not to run from the room and deny I ever knew him. I put my hand on his gown, and my touch made the word come out of him again. "Jimmy," I said, as brightly as I could without bursting. "Try it a little softer." I put my head close

541

to him, my ear almost onto his mouth. The less air he had to push, the less muscle he needed to control, the more chance I had of making him out.

The sound came out again, softer but no more distinct. Jimmy fought to unmangle it. His whole body shook, a weight lifter at the instant when he must either jerk the bar overhead or be crushed under the plates. I thought I heard him, in shadow, pronounce "cohabit." The word he had teased me with for weeks when Todd and I moved in together. I must have projected it. I began to think he wasn't saying anything at all, just releasing animal bursts from a cortex now helpless to hold them in.

"Once more, Jimmy. Don't try so hard." But the noise was worse, vanishing. I looked at him, shook my head. "I'm sorry. I can't. I can't make it out." My own words were themselves smudged out, my voice lost in a choke, my head rocking. I could only stop myself by putting my face down onto him, where I kept it. I felt something brush my hair. His arm, its muscles contracted into a permanent claw, was trying to move, to put its weight over me in comfort. I lifted it—he could not do it alone—and put it around my neck, where it had been trying to go.

I hunted down a resident to ask about Jimmy's chances. Like most, I had so mastered necessity that when chance was at last the subject, I was lost. The physician was too professional to say what might be hoped. Hope was a function of structural impairment. But the implication was clear: Jimmy was setting out for an unknown place. Sitting in bed in the double-occupancy room, close up, flush against a place closed to every petition except disaster.

I went straight to the warehouse. Todd wanted word immediately, over the intercom, but I waited until I went up. At the top of the freight elevator, I froze, afraid to go in. Jimmy was there. The office floor was still warm where he had fallen, a delicate, blue, broken vessel stroked out across the tiles. He was there, working late, ready to scold me for unofficial use of combinations, to tease me boyishly about cohabiting with men. It was all as I had left it, every night I ever spent in this forsaken place. But the old arrangement, the Second Shift Club, had changed color, reddened upon contact with air.

I gave my faithful transcript. I told them about his face, his mouth, his eyes, his clawed hand. I told them about the sound he had made, syllables beyond guessing. I told about the doctor's hedge. Dr. Ressler listened for physiological signs, Todd for any

542

scrap that might spell forgiveness. Would it have happened without his mistake? Unanswerable, but we gave the rest of the night over to it. I couldn't think of sleep, and so sat up the remaining hours with them. In the morning I went directly to the branch, as I had before after long nights in circumstances that would never arise again.

I spent the day combing our modest collection, reading everything I could find on brain damage. I learned that a third of a million Americans suffer cerebral vascular accidents each year. I learned that the word derived from *the stroke of God's hand*. I learned that Jimmy's injury would unfold in its own way, a way research could not fix.

I found a text on the subject, reasonably up-to-date, although the pace of the field consigned all texts to the pyre every two years. The chapter on stroke recovery was a rationalist's nightmare: people who could see a sofa, walk around it, and give its name, but couldn't say how the thing was used. People who had no trouble explicating "Jack kissed Jill" but who were hopelessly gutted by "Jill was kissed by Jack." People whose right hemispheres didn't know what their lefts were doing. People in every other way intact, day after day unable to recognize their own spouses' faces.

Some accounts went beyond science fiction. I read of Phineas Gage, a Vermont railroad man who had a three-foot rod blasted through his head. He lived for twelve years, intelligence unimpaired, capable of speech, memory, and reason, but with no emotional control. I read of a woman whose one hand tried to strangle her unless fought off by her other. I read of people who could not recall anything from before their accident or who could not learn anything after. I read of a concert pianist who could play the most complex concerti from memory yet who could not point to middle C.

There was aphasia, loss of speech, alexia, loss of reading, agraphia, loss of writing, and agnosia, loss of recognition. Everything a person possessed could be taken away. I read of people who could grasp numerals but not numbers, who could define the word "pig" but couldn't recognize one, who could write complex ideas but couldn't make out what they'd written. There were patterns too bizarre to warrant names: the sixty-seven-year-old stricken into thirteen years of fastidious silence only to be awakened at age eighty by a train whistle's sixth-chord that launched him into a popular tune from the year of his wedding, a half century before.

Minds reduced to a vacant stare worked their way back into replicas of their former state. Massive paralytics rose up and walked, showing no trace other than a shuffle or droop of one eyelid. Others, only grazed by God's swipe, lived for years masking incapacities they themselves failed to suspect. I grabbed at every slight ray of optimism. Children's brains could rewire, recover from blows that would wipe out mature adults. Jimmy's gentleness might indicate a saving persistence of child's wiring. Recovery was above normal in left-handed people, and higher still in lefties who had been forced into the right-hander's world. I'd seen Jimmy type, lift, carry, write, and wave hundreds of times, but I could not for life remember with which hand.

I was so high-strung that I even found, hidden in the technical folds, rare benefits from a well-placed lesion. Violent personalities woke from apoplexy as loving as a newborn. Pasteur's massive stroke altered his work for the better. Dostoyevsky's visionary power followed from lifelong epileptic seizures. Research proved nothing except that no one could predict injury's outcome. No one knew much about the brain at all, let alone Jimmy's. The hierarchy had too many subsystems for the loss of any piece to be understood. My only question—would it still be Jimmy inside the destroyed case?—dissolved in qualified statistics. By evening I found myself guiltily hoping for the kinder, comprehensive solution.

I went back to MOL after work. Todd stood in the computer room, source of the catastrophe, scrutinizing my face as if, at panel edge, overlooked by everyone, he might find some hint of horror's miracle waiting to flame. Nothing I could report helped. My friends had news of their own, a wrinkle more pressing than Jimmy's prognosis. The hospital DP operatives—Todd's and Ressler's opposites at that immense institution—processing Jimmy's numbers, revealed that his coverage had not yet been reinstated.

"His mother called."

"How is she?"

Todd shrugged nervously; care had to be rationed, focused to a point. "She's either the emblem of strength or doesn't realize what's happened. She says the hospital needs proof of alternate ability to pay."

The man I'd seen the night before would need feeding, clothing, changing, constant surveillance, and a year of slow, expensive therapy that might come to nothing. An after-tremor could surface with the next clock tick. The hospital staff discovered the billing irregularity and served notice in under forty-eight hours: thus health science, the keepers of the human spark, in the Information Age.

Disaster (continued)

A part of Jimmy's brain had dissolved in the hemorrhage faster than a sugar cube in coffee. His was near one extreme of a spectrum of tissue failure. At the other, the best anyone gets away with is a steady evaporation beginning in late teens, racking up thousands of neurons a day, making every aspect of experience—cheerful revisionism notwithstanding—continuously harder to master and easier to miss.

Ten billion switches, by conservative estimate, are each wired to five thousand others, regulated by neurotransmitters and neuropeptides whose scores of enzyme dialects control a chaos of simultaneous translation conveying desire, fear, torture, pleasure. No sooner does the switchboard wire itself to survive the world of experience than it begins to dismantle. It flashes out in a violent short or disintegrates imperceptibly. All that varies is the tempo.

I have until now faulted words, blamed the messenger of mangled news for keeping me from my answer. I should instead be prostrate with gratitude that words can mean anything at all, given the nature of the receiver. The thing is jerry-rigged, carrying around in its own triple fossil a walkie-talkie wrapped around a shrew-screech encasing a lizard's intuition. Absurd paste-up: gothic chancel tacked onto Romanesque crypt fronted by rococo nave. The wonder lies in its comprehending anything, its ability to work its supreme invention, the shaky symbol set.

Word into synapse is even more approximate than substance into word. The brain, in the subtle dozen hours when it reaches its zenith, already wades through a dissipation that leaves it searching without success for those three syllables beginning with an "F" about which everything has been rubbed out except the certainty that they sat at the lower right corner of an even-numbered page. The word was "forfeiture." The word was "filigree." The word was "forgetting."

A hundred trillion synaptic bits, each capable of threshold effects, compressed into a kilo and a half, split into two lumps connected by 250 million cables. Twin-view parallax resolves the field into multiple dimensions. The most complex entity ever thrown together, an organ vastly more complex than the plan that assembled it, locally violates the Second Law. Every brain extends itself with a ten-thousand-item template, puts together continuous unprecedented messages for no other reason than to model in miniature everything that exists and half that doesn't. Five billion living brains, a hundred billion already dead, each sickeningly bound into a net surpassed only by the single thing they are bent on weaving.

Stockpiled deep in the magnificent kludge, buried in the cerebellum, hippocampus, corpus callosum, the device knows its own unwiring. Thought carries a little pattern of terror around inside it, the realization that it shouldn't even be around, that it will soon fall back into distributed static. "What a day," Jimmy sometimes greeted the second shift, throwing up his arms. "I should have been a chicken farmer. What else can go wrong?" He knew what else could and one day would, knew before anybody, and only his tired joke stood between him and nothing.

The map of circuits, like their mobile case, is shaped by evolution. Synapse routes that presage their own immanent shorting out must also have been selected for. What good can it possibly do to know, every paralyzing, conscious hour, that the prop holding me up to a smoky little aperture onto everything is already, even as I name the process, dissolving in a stroke or a gentle stream? Medullar terror at returning to randomness is behind every urge to pattern the world. Hardwired to fear is the breeding scream.

Desperate copulation evolved long before cerebral terror. Male dragonflies scrape a female clean of previous sperm before mating. Cheater fish slip between the throes of a thrashing couple and make their secret deposit. But the truly promiscuous, the ones who couple with everything that moves, who cannot stop propagating even to eat, who fill notebooks into the night: fear makes us father for our lives. Todd excavated me as if his organ were a fixing gauge. Learning that nothing could come of it, he left, scared off. Only wilder fear drove him temporarily back.

Natural selection edits with an eye only toward what the message says, not to what it means. It has no interest in the fittest solution, nor the most efficient. The fittest thing life could do would be to die immediately and join the overwhelming efficiency of inert space. Selection hinges on one thing alone: differential reproduction. Double faster than you die. Dissolve slower than you replicate. All organs are an attempt to leverage this edge, even this crazily immense, already unwiring circuit. I know; I can feel the pay telescope starting to flick off. By Jimmy's count, with luck, I might get six more years.

Losing the Signal

How much space might he clear away in himself for this brilliant, two-manual experiment in naming? He has no precedent, no Jeanette template, no chromosome locus synthesizing the next step. Dr. Koss is his only instructor. They test the limits of their freedom, walk openly through town, feeling the violation, not daring to believe what they do. Their walks are exercises in synchronization. Their legs cadence. They talk in overlap, complete one another's sentences, laugh at each other's jokes before they're made. A small miracle, for once in this life, not to have to explain.

She spends the night, an extended, sleepless night of semaphores. Jeanette stands peach-naked, stretches, touches her toes in morning's light, showing herself to him. "How do you like your eggs?"

He would ask: Are we wrong? Am I destroying something real and immediate in you? Are you denying your husband's sacrifice, losing the intimate, accumulated weight of your past? But her eyes are sparks, looking for affirmation of the rightness of this moment. He must not violate her joy, and says, "Ova easy."

The article appears, makes the rounds at Biology. It includes a photo of Ressler among Faces to Watch and gives a bastardized, erroneous thumbnail treatment of his mutagen investigations. It paints him as arcane, isolated—qualities that may have been requisite for serious creative effort in the past but at this hour are inimical to effective science. On pub date, log-jammed almost at solution, he wants nothing more than to be brought back into the fold, to work together with Ulrich toward some common persuasion.

The *Life* photo essay horrifies him: a sad, indelible feeling as he flips through the sickeningly permanent pages. Perpetual artifact, preserved in a thousand long-term vaults. A million copies faithfully reproduce his every imperfection. Too late to recant: his face, his thin nose, his words badly quoted and out of context, his arrogant self-assurance—Stuart Ressler, rising science star, split, flapped, and pinned out like a cat in undergraduate anatomy. Proliferated throughout the English-speaking world.

The fallout of bad-faith fame follows him into his first office visit following publication. Minor notoriety will not help patch matters between Ressler and his increasingly erratic office mate. Ressler braces on entering and shouts out something friendly. But Lovering just sits among the ruined piles of papers, his Baalbek of print, indifferent and still. Walking toward his desk, head down, hands in pocket, Ressler is shaken by Joe's voice, struggling to shake off catatonia. "Do you know the price we're all paying to improve the world?"

Ressler stops and faces Lovering. He chooses each word, multiplying the odds against the growing sentence a hundred thousand times per syllable. "I'm not sure what you mean, Joe."

"What I mean? The world. *The* world. Toot la moaned. The big picture. Come on. We're both adults. We don't have to get into semantics here." Ressler can't even respond. Scrambling through the repertoire, all inappropriate, he just bobs his head on its universal joint. "Unnatural prospect! All the way back, all the way back to fires in caves." Lovering drops into a movie monotone. "And I work for them!"

"Who do you work for, Joe?"

"Who the hell knows? Big state school. The money's been washed through so many agencies it's wetter'na Baptist. But it's the government at bottom, isn't it? All that dough."

The logic eludes Ressler. "Half the scientists in this country have worked for the government since the war."

"What do you mean, 'since'? Who told you they've stopped shooting?" Ressler backs toward his chair, out of the stumbled-upon line of fire. He can say nothing. "What does it cost to eradicate the Black Death? Ask GM. Ask Coke."

"Joe...."

"Shut up." Brutal, suppliant, drunken. "I'm talking." Ressler wants only to be out of the room, to allow the fit of latent humanity to work itself out in privacy. But Lovering won't release him. He stares at Ressler, pleading, the look of a spaniel, hindquarters smashed beneath the wheel of a car, asking why his years of service have been so rewarded. His smile changes to pity. "Education, learning, progress. You know what we're going to find out, we researchers? We're going to finally get down to that old secret code in the cell, and the string is going to come out spelling D-U-M-B space S-H-I..."

"Joe. Would you like to go out for a beer?" Ressler's intonation is so soft it startles the man silent. The invitation sounds slightly frayed coming out of his mouth. He has forgotten how to ask the question right. But Lovering remains distracted.

"What? Out? Why? Corn as high as an elephant's eye. Big, hulking, behemoth state school, out in the middle of godforsaken nowhere." He brightens, addresses Ressler as an old friend. "I've got a job offer, you know. As soon as Sandy finds someone to replace her at her office, we're outta this hole. Someplace new, fresh, different."

"Terrific, Joe. Could be exactly what you're looking for. Where are you going?"

"Ann Arbor."

Late that evening he sees Lovering again, ducking into the department's small-animal room. The lines of cages always have an edgy hysteria to them, as if the rodents know where their cage-mates disappear to. Ressler pokes his head into the room. He watches Lovering pick up a cage, shake it. Above the animal squeaks and pleas, Ressler hears Lovering doing a poor but obligatory Cagney: "You dirty rats."

"Dr. L. Which way are you headed?"

Lovering sets the cage down quickly. "Nowhere. Why?"

Ressler makes the beer offer again, but Lovering smiles and shags him off, saying he isn't ready to leave just yet. Ressler wishes him good night, and Joe replies in like manner. The next morning, Ressler notices an unnatural silence emanating from the cage room. He looks inside. The place is stripped clean. The animals are gone, cages and all. The answer stands just down the hall, where Woyty, Botkin, Koss, and Ulrich gather in a stunned lump. He walks into the circle, which opens to him with a look shared and obscene.

"You've heard?" Ulrich asks.

"Not a thing."

"Apparently, Joe Lovering drove out of here last night in a rented truck loaded with the department lab animals." The others, hearing the tale for the second time, seem unable to get past the beginning. "He drove the whole shipment back to his apartment...."

"Apartment? Didn't he say...?"

Ulrich insists. "Apartment; there is, apparently, no new purchased home. He stacked all the stolen cages neatly around his garage. Albino rats together, all the *cavia* . . ."

Ressler nods hurriedly. Get on with it.

"His landlady heard the engine running about eleven o'clock last night. The garage door was locked and wadded with rags. She had to let herself in through his apartment." Ulrich takes a breath, the same deep breath Joe's landlady took before racing to the truck to shut off the engine. "It seems Joe's decision to join the specimens was an impulse. There was a badly burned TV dinner in the oven, and a burned-out cigarette on the edge of a counter." Ulrich clears his throat, debating whether to suppress the next detail. "A Sears catalog open to the lingerie pages in the bathroom. A pocket-size spiral notebook with grocery list. At the bottom, in the same handwriting slant, an afterthought, he'd written, 'Send the checks to the Anti-Vivisectionist Society.' He was in the front seat of the truck, lying gently on the wheel. He'd left the passenger door open. Presumably because it vented more closely onto the tailpipe."

The stunned cluster of survivors turns toward Ressler, waiting. "How did you hear?" he asks Ulrich.

"Landlady called his mother. Mother called me early this morning."

"Has anybody gotten in touch with his girlfriend? Sandy? She might know something. . . ."

Ulrich snaps at his stupidity in the face of the obvious. "There is no girlfriend." Sandy is a simulation.

Ressler spends two days pacing between office and lab, fiddling with beakers, doing nothing. Ulrich distributes the official notice through the department and announces a memorial service to be held at the First Church of Christ Scientist. The service is ecumenical, so much so that it carries almost no religious overtone at all. What's left of Cyfer, their families, and the man's mother comprise the entire congregation. Each team member makes a prepared speech. Ulrich talks about Joe's sharp mind, how quickly he picked up the complexities of machine programming. Woyty, on dangerous ground, saved only by the difficulty he has controlling his voice, remembers Joey's pathological fear of catching cold, hints at the irony that another virus, in the end, got him. Botkin reads from her beloved Rilke: *Wir sind nicht einig.* We do not agree. *Sind nicht wie die Zugvögel verständigt.* Do not correspond like the migratory bird. *Blühn und verdorrn ist uns zugleich bewß.* Bloom and withering come on together.

Koss assumes the pulpit, mouths the expected homilies. She

550

turns to descend, but stops, unable to sit down without really speaking. Lovering was a scientist, she insists. A scientist going after the code. And the end of all codebreaking is to get behind the outward trappings of a thing to meaning. Joey lost the signal. Read the message wrong. The congregation makes a scuffle of collective objection, propriety offended. Ressler alone is quiet, loving her more than he has ever loved her for delivering this tract and no other. Who is the graveside speech for, after all, if not the survivors?

He is last, deferred to for the postlude, for some reason. For his act of speechmaking Ressler digs way back, into the only other text he received as inheritance from his parents aside from chromosomes and the *Britannica*. He has, in adulthood, achieved agnosticism, despite efforts by both folks to steep him in doses of received scripture. But the syntax of the Book still rattles about in him on days like this of vestigial need. So, it comes about, here in the pulpit, summarizing off to his long home a man he didn't even know except through falsified dispatches, that the only thing he can get out is Ecclesiastes.

> Whatsoever thy hand findeth to do, do it with thy might; for there is no work, nor device, nor knowledge, nor wisdom in the grave whither thou goest.

Work, for the night is coming. Inarguable, if of no practical value to Lovering now. Each human effort and each new word speeds the acquisition of the next. The maps get more exact with every effort, but the key only points out the size of the workless, wisdomless place. He might better have dispensed with speeches altogether, left the work of his colleague—the saving of a few doomed test animals by carbon monoxide, painless, reportedly lightly euphoric—as Lovering's lasting eulogy.

After the service, over the subdued hand-shaking in the narthex, Lovering's mother approaches Stuart and takes his forearm in her hands. "Thank you. What you read was beautiful."

"I'm glad you think so."

"Joseph spoke of you many times. He thought the world of you. 'The best scientist I've ever met.' He told me how much he wanted to be more like you. I'm glad you two were friends."

"Your son and I," he fits together, searching, "had a great deal in common." Vast stretches of A,T,G,C. She kisses him without apology. He wants to grab the woman, shake her until she tells: why start that cigarette? Why not extinguish it before himself? Joey had time, all the time of his decision. In less time than it takes a cell to split, Lovering turned ignition and annihilated the three-billion-year-old system. Two more minutes to hang around and finish the butt: what couldn't he bring himself to stub out?

Lovering's senseless violence will never heal, never close over in time with new tissue. Ressler will be permanently scarred by that last impertinence. A cigarette, a sorrow, a chromatic love for the things of the world unexcisable at the last minute. A garage full of animals mercifully gassed: affirmation, a yes to the same free polyphony he was sending to death. A by-product of the first, unresolvable confusion deep down at rule-level, the inner confines of language where sorrow and celebration, sender, message, and receiver collapse into the same unlikely pattern, a pattern that knows it is alien, impossibly unlikely, exiled.

How easily all decisions are reversed; everything hand might find to do is tentative at best. He, at least, is still alive, more alive for Lovering's annihilation. Stuart walks home from the service in the cold air, awake, whole, pained for feeling so. He survives the misguided man, a distant cousin, an atavistic trial run, a hypothesis that could not stand the test of experience, a failed variant. Adjacent to survivor's exhilaration, a cold capillary fluid closes on his heart. The man was erratic, dissolving in pain: a glance showed it. The best empiricist in all of his acquaintance gave no help, ignored the long distress call to friends.

Four o'clock the following afternoon brings Jeanette to him. He lets her in, unable to read the enigma of the features he prided himself on glossing the week before. After he commits to some deplorable pleasantry he sees that the message is anger: soft, silent, crying, intractable. Her rage is all for Lovering, although it is Koss she mourns for. The best he can do in extremity is extend the inadequate arm of care. He attempts to comfort her in the only dialect he is fluent in. He strokes her, but the touch feels like his own obit. No comfort in contact at this minute. If they could stop for half a measure, separate, let silence come between them, that paraphrase might teach them what Lovering meant, and more. But he cannot retreat from her for any reason now. He has only the old, obscuring burden of touching to save them.

"Jeannie," he says, lifting her resisting face. "Lovering made his own decision. We might have seen, but we didn't. Who can say

552

what difference it would have made, even if we had?" The argument his viscera have already vetoed. Jeanette says nothing. He never imagined she was capable of such anguish, acute grief for someone she never cared for. "Darling, listen. It isn't up to *us* to figure out why he killed himself. You said it yourself. Joe made a framing error. He misread the . . ."

Jeannie jerks away from him fiercely. Fully capable of defrauding her husband, Ressler, and even herself, she will not stand for defrauding science. "What the hell do *you* know about it? You, the arch-rationalist. Tagged, antiseptic passions. The double-blind study! Never known confusion in your life. Nothing a control group can't clarify. Where do you come off making sense of him?"

His mouth hangs loose on the words. Her face purple, air-starved, bruised, her features hideous, unrecognizable in the violence she would do him. He sees how deeply he hates her. Hates her as in the early days all over again, when he could not admit to need, when he was not even significant enough to her to be singled out for rejection. Even in hating, he takes his cue from her. The words for what comes next originate with her at every step, from the day this total stranger toweled his head dry.

Hatred bridges what pity was powerless to. They are both instantly in the same place. "Get out," he whispers. "Did I ask you here? Did I ask to be led through grubby little liaisons? The supply closet, for Christ's sake." Each subdued syllable leaves her slamming a fist into her temples and gasping for breath. "Go on! Tell me all about myself. Make it accurate. Then get out."

With a weird, guttural shout, she springs on him before he can hold her off. Her nails sink into his back and her teeth dig for a vein. Pinning her, he discovers: not aggression. Desperate holding on. He knows what consolation she has come for. A minute's embrace and she would lead him unsteadily off again, here, on another floor, as if their bed were anywhere the world might let them make it. She would have them do the euphemism as if it still had a point. As if the act of kind still signified, still stood somehow for kindness or could close the gap between them.

But the closest they will ever come is analogy, secret writing, codes—social, behavioral, civil, moral, criminal—constantly garbled in the thousand signal deformations passed from her hemispheres to his. She makes herself a glossary on his mouth, in his ear, asking forgiveness, tolerance, understanding, love. Or not for these weak analogies, spent conventions, but the intransigent, unmappable location she would loose herself to.

Her grief smashes against him, a convulsion scarier than any Lovering elicits. It forces his chest, cuts into it with the desire to be past things, unchanged, indifferent to how they reveal themselves here. Toward that one goal, he can assist her for half an hour. He undoes her blouse, turning it down from the curve of her shoulders as she gives, leans into the unsheathing. Then, shocked by his fingers' static charge, she jumps to her feet, pulling on the slipped clothing. She holds her hair to her head, takes a few steps in a circle. Ressler lets his breath out, saying, at the end of the exhale, "He's dead."

"That isn't," she says staccato, frantic. "That isn't it. *This* isn't it. I can't... I never meant...." Dr. Koss shakes her fevered head, comes to a decision. She runs for the door. He calls her, but she doesn't break meter. The latch closes behind her, swift and succinct. Ressler goes slack, stretched across his front room. He feels nothing, no loss, only the lumpectomy scar. From first prohibited kiss he has prepared himself for the moment when the impermissible toxin would purge itself. But he has overlooked this possibility—unexplained, unilateral panic—as too awful and obvious. He lies on the bare floor, waiting for no explanation. He stands, goes to the record player, creates his own.

There is, in the innermost core of the work, a variation that stands apart from the others, bizarre, instantly detectable, alien. He heard this outcast in the litter, picking it out from the confusion of notes the night she brought them by, even before he could speak a single chord of tonal language. Five sixths of the way through the *Goldberg* set—variation twenty-five—is the most profound resignation to existence ever written.

He has studied music for half a year, listened each evening, learned notation, sight-read scores for much of the basic repertoire. Now, after a long time away, he comes back to this little sequence coding for the moment of dispersion. It is the one text that can say how he and Jeanette, by lightest degrees, arrived at dead confusion. How could the unsuspecting initial sarabande possibly code for what has taken her? He follows in memory the way they have come. Once, he could only see it on the page. Now he can hear. The Base is intact, agonizingly fleshed out with chromatic passing tones. Above the encrypted notes a slow unraveling, shattered beyond saying, an ineffable, searing, lost line meanders into intervals where language cannot follow. Push the whole sequence down a tone, fill out the phrase with accidentals, repeat verbatim, but dropped into a key the chilling, unreachable nether pole from tonic.

The four-by-four-by-four Base, stretched out of all proportion, out of all ability of its limpid simplicity to carry, is still there, whole, note-for-note intact, only unrecognizable. His ear, schooled on recent events, detects the ancestor, the parental name now lost in daughters. The mathematical manipulation pushes on, farther than the bars would permit, grinding against dissonances more grating even than those born in his own generation. It wanders stunted through bleak modulations—G minor, F minor, E-flat minor, B-flat minor—keys incredibly distant, bearing no relation to the place where they began and must return. As testimony to the heart that made it, this too is scored as a dance. What cannot be survived, cannot be listened to, must also be danced.

Stuart lies at the close, back against the impossibly thin crust of earth. The column of air pressing his ribs is no thicker. Pinned between these sheets, he hears in this scalar mutation what called Lovering away, what tortures Jeannie: a sorrow that did not exist in its parent sarabande. No math encapsules it; no signal, no word for Not. It never was on this earth, until twisted out of insensate elements.

What are these modulations after, about, just in front of the door? Something to the tune of how mere saying, tracing, researching, conveying will never make the case for existence. Days do not carry the full conjugation table for the verb To Live. Only, at raw moments, the imperative.

He knows she is gone, as gone as his office mate, as lost as his steady, programmed shedding of cells, the tune that twenty-five comes unspeakably close to speaking. Departure. He hears in brief the only home his future can ever come back to, whatever distant relations it explores on its long, final, unimaginable spiral deep down into the innermost life of the hive, beyond grief, underneath encryption.

Disaster (conclusion)

I cannot find it in me to keep working. The cause is longer than this morning. I've been racing it from the first, and I see now that it will beat me to the finish. I've made the mistake of reading over what I've put down here since last June. A little lay chemistry, evolution in outline, amateur linguistics padded out with kiss-and-tell. The whole ream turns my stomach to look at. It was to be my way of learning a little about music, a year spent listening to the composition. Now the pattern-search is snagged on a single fact: the best potential father in the world, the transmissible gift of kind intelligence, chose to die a celibate.

"You live alone?" Todd asked him, back when we still drank contraband wine out of paper cups in the computer room. Ressler lifted that familiar lip edge that said everything and disclosed nothing. "What do you *do* with yourself?"

"I work. I read what interests me. I garden. The seed companies send me their catalogs, a little earlier every year."

Todd was unrelenting that night. "If you don't mind my asking, what do you do for women?"

"What have women ever done for me?" He pressed the advantage of humor, slipped out with an account of a recent survey of the most desirable traits in an American mate: "Women choosing men selected intelligence, kindness, and money in increasing importance. Men ranked it face, breasts, and hips."

He deliberately chose to sit and wait for complete genetic dismantling. I never saw him, until that last chance, lift his hand to assert himself. He suppressed the choice to breed along with the other vanities. The life scientist, still in his twenties, turning over flagstones in the lab, looking for buried treasure, one day, by accident, squared up against what all the secret writing graffiti'd over every millimeter of the world's surface and miles deep was saying: double faster than you unravel.

Even that much would have been bearable. Even if only a simple-minded recursion—"Copy *this*"—the pattern had authored grammars so materially satisfying, living syntaxes of such heart-stopping choreography, that it would have been enough to affirm life even in abstaining. The law compelling electrons to arrange themselves in the lowest energy configuration, the law saying that hot had to flow irreversibly downhill into cold, had become so adept at local violations, amended and invented loopholes, that the resulting biological anarchy synthesized its own sponsor. But he had stumbled upon something that ruined him for procreation.

He heard the sound—if not imbedded in the cell itself, there in the way the program runs—of an imperative variation stronger than "Copy this." A countering command: the tick of miss, of not, the leak of things going wrong. The hiss accumulating in transcription, like that party game of Telephone, slowly mauling the message so badly it no longer meant anything. Death too was just the code's last trick to promote divide and multiply. He listened to his cell incorporate disaster into its plan, synthesizing genes with no function but to make enzymes that smeared other genes, enhanced mutation, promoted runaway tumor.

Disaster says to me, softer and softer, "Quit the typewriter. Too much has gone wrong. You're not accurate enough ever to put it right." I'd say my project was in crisis, if I thought the project still existed. How can I still mourn for a man who gave me a few months of guarded, way-station amenities? Why anxiety at Jimmy's stroke, incapacitated by an acquaintance with whom I never graduated past tenderness? Throat-choking panic at the thought of a boy I kissed for four abortive months at sixteen. Anger at a devoted friend for skipping a Christmas card. Alarming dreams of parents dead for years. Annihilating ache for my old colleague Mr. Scott, who knew one joke about retiring. Everyone I've ever loved has killed me a little. Every concert I've ever attended, every tune I thrilled to and immediately forgot, every book, every reference, every patron that presented herself at my desk with every question saying, "Solve me; you have half an hour": decimating strokes, a swipe of God's hand.

I'll never solve any of it. Assembled into oppressive full score, it whispers to me, submits the unlivable knowledge that the world will be recombined, more fertile than ever after I disband. Worse, the mix will be renewed *because* I leave it. More than I can take: the stroke that erases me, the force corrupting my message engineers creation.

But the piece won't let me drop. The most chromatic catastrophe ever composed leaves me here, cashless, listening to meandering pattern stand in for plan. Accident hums the song it assembles, resigned beyond listening, intervals arcing like sparks damped in a vacuum inconceivably bigger than the code and wanting only one thing from it. The thing it makes me finish writing: how that celibate, as if only waiting for the disastrous chance, set to work living like there was no tomorrow.

XXVI

The Vertical File

Ressler alone was ready. The space of a single week showed that his slow return to engagement had been spring training for exactly this catastrophe. The bloom of the last few months, which I had nipped in the bud, sprang back fuller for my pruning. Todd was set to go to the insurance company with a signed confession and spend the next half of his life in prison if it meant getting Jimmy back on coverage. Dr. Ressler restrained him, pointing out that the grandstand clean breast would only transfer the unpayable liability from Jimmy to the fraudulent file manipulator.

Ressler organized a trip to the hospital. Todd could not bring himself to go. His need for exoneration was so paralyzing he could not take a step toward it. The sight of Jimmy in that bed, in that condition, would have destroyed any chance Franklin had of ever living with what he had done. Dr. Ressler, Annie, and I met by the registration desk. When she saw me, Todd's other mate pleaded with my eyes a moment. She came tentatively toward me and awkwardly stroked the hair of my forearm. She wanted to lay her head between my breasts like a little girl. Knocked down by the larger, unattainable forgiveness I then needed, I would have let her.

But we gave no hostages to humiliation on that trip. The hospital halls, the bald children, the tubes jammed into bruised faces—the entire ordeal of shame seemed, in the company of Ressler, whom I had not seen out of the warehouse since New Hampshire, less to be endured than understood. In the elevator, he talked to a wheelchaired victim in the extremities of MS, not about the man's disease or the work he would now never do, but about the best lines in Tennyson and which pieces of Dvořák most bore repeated listening. When we got out of the lift, Ressler turned and waved as the doors closed.

Challenge the Patient

Challenge the patient to respond
to one narcotic or another,
strap him to a quantifying screen
that feeds back digits for his number,
root out the latinate reason
from the multivolume tome,
circumvent the leak or seal it,
magnificently postpone:
he, insidious, will choose
a time that signifies at least,
chorus to a calculated close,
spread south like the vee of geese.

I led them to Jimmy's room, issuing veiled sentences meant to warn them about what they would find. But when we got to the room, Ressler greeted his old acquaintance in the same voice he had greeted him in day after day at shift change for longer than I'd known either of them. "Hello, James. Visitors. Oh! This bed can't possibly be comfortable." Jimmy, seeing us, convulsed on his good side. Whether delight or resentment, the message was lost in the spastic independence his muscles had acquired. "Franklin has to man the fort," Ressler said. "Your being away has thrown things up for grabs at work. He wants to come see you soon." Not a lie. He wants; he wants with his capacity to come see you.

Jimmy made an awful noise, not the one he had made for me. The contour was different, changed, more desperate, more out of control, less like words than the ones he had spoken to me alone. Annie shrank from the sound and left the room. Better to have stayed and cried in front of the man. Ressler leaned over Jimmy, put his ear close as I had done, if for no other reason than to ease the chest, lungs, diaphragm. "What was that?" As if he'd just been caught off guard, not paying attention. A thump in darkness, the trickle of syllables over teeth, fricatives ululating in rapids over the pebbles of a streambed. Cruel, given the smear of noise, to make him say it again. But against expectation, Dr. Ressler turned to me after the second burst and translated.

"He says, 'My father died.' "

My hands flexed automatically to grab my neck, the escape of flushed birds. We had had no clue, until then, of the condition of Jimmy's mind. Only his sagged face and vocal cords; *he* was trapped somewhere inside the hull. These first words Jimmy had gotten out since his vascular accident could not have been more grotesque. I didn't know which would be worse: a real death, a second horror laid on his, or a detached, neural wandering. Dr. Ressler leaned back down to ask a question that never occurred to me. "When did your dad die, James?" He straightened and interpreted, "Nineteen-sixty."

Annie came back, sat in one of the chairs by the bed. When shifting, I caught Jimmy in certain angles—eyes alert, face at attention—where his expression seemed almost cogent. Was he decoupled, incoherent, ruined, or just rubbed raw, shot back into involuntary memory? "Mr. Steadman," Ressler smiled, holding him affectionately by both hands, sitting down on the hospital bed that, while single, was large enough for both these men. "Jimmy. Can we get you anything?" Uncle Jimmy trumpeted again, more sedately, a breaking whitecap of pitch. But the professor was growing fluent enough to be able to understand the sentence without leaning up against him.

"He'd like us to tell him a story. He says that if we give him one he'll be good." Perhaps inept irony was still intact. Or maybe he'd become a child. I searched Ressler for his opinion. I looked into the face of a biologist who thought Jimmy's request totally understandable: anyone in the world might one day reasonably request such a thing. A story. And why not? "Either of you two any good at narrative?"

But the line between simplicity and violence in Jimmy had been whittled narrower than a capacitor gap. When Dr. Ressler tried to tell Jimmy what had been happening at the office in his absence, the invalid flared out. His mouth hung open as inappropriately as a vault left swinging on its hinges. He practically howled a word that, in its vowel at least, was clearly "no."

Ressler appealed for help, but I could give none. I had no idea what Jimmy wanted. If it was really a tale with beginning, middle, and end, I was no good to him. My skill lay in retrieving, not telling. I could lead them to the encyclopedia, give them the Greek explanation for thunder or Native American rain. I knew that *legenda* was Medieval Latin, for things to be read at gatherings. But I could not invent one. Annie grabbed a newspaper from the stand where a visitor to Jimmy's sickmate had left it. Thinking it was sound he needed, she pulled a headline off page two: "Sunni Splinter Group Shells Suspected Shi'ite Arsenal." But Jimmy's head snapped up. He gave her what must have been a sidelong glare and growled. That was no story; he was not going to be robbed of explanation by mere reportage.

It seemed he would only be kept in check by a real barrier of narrative fable. He wanted an exegesis as precise, elegant, and exact as those old origins of thunder, evil, rainbows, suffering. But those museum pieces were rusted over beyond reviving. There was a man in the room who might make a stab at why the defective blood vessel had burst, leaving a mind flooded. But that wasn't the song Jimmy asked for. He needed a more potent bedside tale. Jimmy was pinned under wreckage, a cerebrovascular accident that had failed to throw him clear of the crash. He lay propped up in bed, sense of direction destroyed, one of those compassless whales trapped up an illusory inlet. For some reason, even after damage that could never be reversed, he still wanted the sum of his experience read back to him as an adventure.

Dr. Ressler looked at Annie and me, wondering why he'd bothered to bring us along. Jimmy was growing increasingly restive, rocking on the bed, attempting to build up the momentum needed to throw his feet to the floor. Ressler caught him up gently. "Jimmy. Listen. The hospital is making threatening noises about the bill. They've asked your mother for proof of ability to meet a prolonged stay." He hushed Jimmy's long, mewled objection. "Of course that's impossible. No one has told you because no one wanted to upset you."

Jimmy lay still while Ressler related the insurance company's refusal to retroactively reinstate him. He listened passively to the legal counsel's opinion: the letter of the law lay on the side of the insurers, a business that made no provision for individual charity. Ressler did not mention Todd's plan to save Jimmy by confessing the deed. But the professor did lay out something I heard for the first time. "Don't worry about this bill for now. Your job is to come back from this as quickly as you can. I believe we can get you reinstated. But don't mention this to anyone just yet."

The admonition made me snort in pain. But neither man paid

me any notice. They were concentrating on each other. Ressler began spelling out a plan so developed that it seemed months in the making. Who knows how much Jimmy was taking in. Ressler leaned over his friend's crumpled side, speaking in low tones, as if admonishing, *behave, then, and we'll give you what you ask for*. Lie still and we'll give you that story.

The Cipher Wheel

Days go by when he can think of nothing but what he might have done for Lovering had he been paying attention. He does not see Jeanette; neither can abide what they now know about the other. In that dead period, when Lovering's chaotic half of the office still sprawls up to the dividing line, Ressler learns, from out of the diminished Blue Sky, that Daniel is suing Renée Woytowich for divorce. Impossible: Ressler was at Woyty's the other day and father and mother were on the floor playing with the kid, beyond all dignity hopelessly in love with one another and their family. All incinerated in a matter of hours. He ought to leave it, run the other direction. But he must know.

He tracks Dan down to his office, late in the evening. Ressler knocks gingerly, hears nothing beyond the door but canned laughter. He goes in, circumspect and uninvited. Woyty sits in front of the hulking, luggable TV set that hasn't been on since Ivy's arrival. Woyty's long fast from watching, causing great concern at Stainer Central, is broken with a vengeance.

"Absolutely unavailable for chatting, Stuart. Got to assign a number to *Life of Riley* here."

Stuart sits down and watches Jackie Gleason play the big, bumbling, malapropian airplane factory worker whose tag line, "What a revoltin' development this is," has become a national catchphrase. After a minute of ritual self-effacement, Dan says, "So much for the liberal humanist theory that what the world needs is more laughter. America doesn't need any more entertainment; it's entertained to the gills. I'm panning this sucker. Straight zeros. Send *Life of Riley* back to figurative speech where it belongs." He speaks as if there's something heroic in wandering out of the mode shelter in the middle of the bean curve. He fiddles with a Sputnik-sized wad of aluminum foil strung between the rabbit ears. "Reception's piss-poor here. Ghost so bad it makes *Queen for a Day* look like the Austro-Hungarian dual monarchy out for a weekend."

Ressler looks at him, neither admonishing nor accommodating. All at once, Woyty is volunteering all over the place. "You came to get the lowdown on my divorce, didn't you? Scavenger. Want to know why I'm filing? Want to know the grounds?" Ressler doesn't even nod. "Go ahead, guess." But Woytowich doesn't wait. "You got it. Infidelity."

"Good Christ!" Ressler slams the desk, shoots to his feet. "Don't be an idiot! One look at her and any divorce judge would laugh the case out of court."

"Saying she's not pretty enough? *You* wouldn't have her? Well, Stuart, I'm relieved to hear it's not you."

"I'm saying you're a fool. She worships you. She's just had a child." Ressler can't say how he knows Renée is blameless. He knows what women in affairs look like. Dan's wife is not one. "How could she possibly be running around? She doesn't have time. She hasn't been out of your sight for months."

"Oh," Woyty answers with a placid smile. "We're not talking about recent weeks. We're going back into the distant past. A year, year and a half."

"What are you talking about? Nonsense. *Before* Ivy?"

"Stuart. Leave me be. The kid's not mine."

"God. Don't tell me! Not learning fast enough. You've hit a wall in the instant-genius campaign, and the only explanation is that no child of *yours*. ..." He breaks off in disgust.

Dan gives his evidence in monotone. "Five days ago, Ivy and I were playing with the letter blocks. It occurred to me that she might not be acquiring the alphabet at all, that I might be cuing her solely on block color. I thought it might be fun to set up a control, have her pick colored disks out of a ring. She couldn't do it very well. I tried it with some large letters and she selected them perfectly. That didn't make any sense. How could she learn letters and not colors? I tried the disks again, and she was erratic. She could do blue, black, white. But it became increasingly obvious that Ivy could not differentiate red from green disks without prompting."

"Your child is color-blind." An allele that might not have come to the surface for years had Woytowich not been so keen on bestowing super-stimulated intelligence on her.

563

"I've told you. She's not my child."

Ressler summons up the textbook treatments of the matter. He recalls the central irony of sight: good vision is recessive; myopia dominant. He skims past that irrelevance and concentrates on remembering what he can about red-green color-blindness. "Renée doesn't have it?"

Daniel clucks his tongue dryly against the roof of his mouth. "I thought you were supposed to be the boy wonder. Don't you remember anything from Mendel?"

Ressler suddenly sees why the question is stupidly irrelevant. Red-green color-blindness is the classic example of a sex-linked, *X-linked* recessive. Both Ivy's X chromosomes must have the allele for her to be color-blind. If *Daniel* isn't color-blind, his daughter can't be. "And you don't have it?" Ressler asks, again irrelevantly, of the first man in downstate Illinois to have bought a color set. "What about the autosomal varieties? At least two different assortments, as I remember."

Daniel snorts. "One in several tens of thousands. Which do you think is more likely? A fluke mutation or a woman getting herself plowed?" He turns away in pain, deaf to anything further Ressler has to say on the matter. "Too bad, too. I was looking forward to showing her the egg-in-the-bottle in a year or two." Science. "The potato and iodine."

"You're not going to ask for visitation?"

Woyty just spins lazily toward him. "How many times do I have to tell you? She's not mine."

The improbability of the event, the lateness of the hour leave Stuart helpless. "So what do you do now?" Woytowich flicks a wrist toward the corner, indicating a duffel bag and toilet kit. "Oh, no. Dan. You're not moving in here?"

"Just until I find a place."

"Turning your back on them? Just like that?"

"They'll get half the checks."

The next day Ressler visits Renée. The woman assaults him with dazed protests of innocence. "Stuart. There's never been anyone but Daniel. Not now, not two years ago. God. Not even before I met him." Clearly innocent: the way she rocks the baby between denials. She confesses to one sorry, fully clothed grope with her thesis instructor, momentarily aroused for the first time since his tenure when the two of them compared the relative merits of *Volpone* and *As You Like It*.

"You've told him as much?"

"He won't listen. He has that f-ucking proof."

"He told you about that?"

"Stuart," she says, ready to debase herself. Her vowels cara-melize. "I don't *care* what inheritance says. Inheritance is *wrong*." He glances down at the bright child, tilting her head in curiosity all around the enormous room. All right, then. He's ready to accept the astronomical odds. But *his* willingness is not at issue. Ivy bab-bles, grabs Stuart's cuff, shakes it, waiting impatiently for the next letter game. The baby, however precocious, doesn't know what's hit her. But she is a fast study. She'll learn in no time.

A week later, Ressler takes his first outdoor tomato juice in months. In vitro is still jammed, and he has nothing to fall back on but the torture of relaxation. Propped in the forgotten lawn chair, he realizes that he'll soon have been in the I-states a whole year. The landscape is unchanged, but his 1958 debut stretch on the lawn is incomplete. No Tooney and Evie Blake will materialize, step out from K-53-A, glasses in hand, having waited all winter for this first lawn party of the season. No one will set up a chair at Stuart's side and kick in a conversational bracer. No decimated Woyty, now, and Jesus: no Lovering. And Koss's awful resolve to keep away, keep from seeing him, will be no weaker, no less erratic, than her original passion.

His eye scans K court, the tar-paper triplexes. He looks across the toytown street toward A through J. He imagines all the doors opening at once, pouring out their contents, Tornado Day. He animates the imagined occupants, marches them his way, stands them out on his front lawn tapping an imaginary but ample keg, trading the character flaws that are the generating spark of all beer bashes. A neighbor who studies wish fulfillment in corporate execs, a woman who conditions rabbits to do this trick with a rosary, a fellow with a theory about rag content in Spanish Renaissance manuscripts, another who claims he's in grad school but whose big trick is to sing the words to the *Gunsmoke* theme so fast you can't tell what language he's in: they are all there, behind closed doors, lined up in these row houses. Statistics and human variability guarantee it.

He has only to tap on any window and they will come out, eager to meet him. Ressler has yet to commit himself to whether dreams carry codified information or whether they're just elec-trical residue. As he nods deeper into this one, the difference

565

becomes insignificant. He snaps his head up each time it droops onto his chest. Then, from nowhere, he sees himself staring at clarity, at the rarest, most paradisiacal species.

In that moment of visitation—arriving once in a life if lucky and requiring a further lifetime to recover—it comes to him. He is afraid to move; the least muscle tic will frighten the creature off. He sets his empty glass down on the grass, taking forever to reach ground. He lifts himself slowly from the chair, feeling his knees infinitesimally unbend. He stands, turns, looks: it is still there. Everything he is after, the last bit, the complete, documented map home, squarely in front of him. His.

He stays up all night hitting it, but it will not break. He tries to knock it out of commission by reviewing the literature, but it stands up to the articles. The means are so clean, so self-evident, that the suspicion that someone must already have it sits in the crook of Ressler's gut like a silver-dollar-sized, swallowed acid drop. He is waiting for Botkin outside her office when she shows up the next morning. She's surprised enough to know not to ask anything until she opens the door. Stuart makes a beeline for the couch, where he lies back and announces, "We are so bloody stupid."

"Instantiate that pronoun. You and me? The research group? The department? The human species?"

"Whichever is largest."

"This," she says, her pitch cupping upwards with each word, "is Biology?"

He grins in a way that confirms his sweeping generalization. "We've done the thing exactly ass-backwards. We've done step two, the hard part. And we've been stuck backing up to step one, the piece of cake. Like someone building an entire internal combustion engine and then serendipitously saying, 'Hey! Why don't we put *gasoline* in here?' Stupid. Dumb. Pea-brained."

"Dull. Dim-witted. Duncical," Botkin agrees. "So tell me." She laughs, infected with the visitation of science, which she has felt once before. Laughs for this young man, for the moment of insight that will not come in this way again.

"Unbelievable. I *designed* it toward this end. I'd already realized it would have to be something like this. That was the whole point of Gale and Folkes. I'd laid it out, everything but the method itself, months ago. But I must have...." Marveling: how could it be? "I must have forgotten."

"And now you've recovered?"

And more. Romped. Routed. "You see, it was the fault of pattern. All those months of numerology we put in. I've been as guilty as Gamow, Crick, Ulrich, any of them."

"Explain yourself. Two speeds slower, please."

"We all wanted to make the codon catalog conform to some kind of internal necessity. The problem is, math does provide a few surprising, elegant, yet irrelevant ways of producing the number twenty out of the numbers sixty-four, three, and four. But you see, Nature—well, it's not even perverse, because it's not even a noun. Nature had no idea what we had planned for it."

"You're suggesting that we forget your poet's advice about forcing Homer into English—allow the result to be less than rapid, plain, direct, noble?"

Ressler nods his head impatiently. "Because no experimental evidence for internal commas exists, we assumed a self-punctuating code, got hung up on catalogs where no two successive codons create valid overlaps. The notion of a self-punctuating, error-correcting code was never far from my mind. It happens that the largest possible error-detecting, self-framing catalog is exactly twenty codons. As a result of this coincidence, I was predisposed against even *thinking* of long monomer chains like CCCCCC. Monotonous strings like poly-C carry no internal information. Not worth toying with, I thought. Couldn't be more wrong." Ressler sits up, carried forward by excitement. "The trivial chains are our entrée *into* this thing."

A slow, broad grin of understanding breaks out over Botkin's face. She glimpses it. Her pleasure confirms Ressler. She could blurt it out, fill in the missing bit herself now. But she sits back happily, waiting for him.

"We have built ourselves a working in vitro interpreter, an Enigma Machine that converts any nucleotide chain we feed it into the protein polymer it stands for. Oh Toveh!" His voice is a husky, amazed low wavelength. "Child's play. Stupid, stupid, stupid. It really is. We've built the flower, then discovered sun." He's come too far not to spell out the obvious. "Grunberg-Manago and Ochoa had polyribonucleotide synthesis *three years ago*. Accidentally, but we'll take it." He nudges the smile in her direction, stands, spins Euclidians in the narrow office. "Khorana has nucleotide-building down to a *science*. We can say anything we want to our little transcriber. So we synthesize our own RNA message, only we make

567

it the most simple-minded, open-throated, informationless whole-tone shout imaginable." In the beginning was the Word. "We make our own gene for reading, only we make it all of one base. We take this constructed, monotone string—poly-C, poly-anything—and submit it to the protein-synthesis process. I'll wager the remainder of my fellowship that the resulting protein will be a repeating polymer string of a single amino acid. We will have the first word of the code: the codon CCC codes for whatever poly-amino makes up the resulting string."

"All right," says Botkin. "We get UUU, AAA, GGG, and CCC. Four down leaves sixty to go." That takes care of transmuting lead into gold. What do you do for an encore?

Ressler's face drops before he sees that the woman's calm is affected, her euphoria about to blow out every pore. "The rest of the catalog is just sweat." It is not, in fact. He begins to see how there's always call for one more insight, one more piece of improvised ingenuity. But labeling, controlled mutagen-tailoring of the submitted message, poly-dinucleotides, combinatorics, short chains—time-consuming, meticulous, brute lexical mop-up will get them through.

"Simple," she concurs. "Dr. Johnson's dictionary." But beneath the sardonic restraint, they both know he has done the hard part. He has listed the set of imperatives for lifting the curtain. Her excitement is unconcealable, and it spills out of her in cautionary checks. "Anyone wishing to make a little conversation with the angels has to remember that *jeder Engel ist schrecklich.*" At his blank, startled look, she laughs and glosses, "Every angel is terrible. You've told Dr. Koss?"

Something, a slight rise in the woman's cheerful tone, warns Ressler that she knows the half of what she is asking. He feels the last step in an untraceable hierarchy of chemical events flush his face, conveying the source by suppressing it. Enzyme spray laces his central nervous system. He will not go on this way, pretending. He cannot bear it. And now, he need not. Heart, lungs, viscera do a Coney Island. He is diminished, augmented all at once, hung out on the first intervals of a melody that pronounce him infinitely powerful and shatteringly afraid, a pairing he needs no code wheel to read. *Promise first. You must never die.*

Now he can promise. He can go to her, say, "See what a flower I have found you." No more cause, no possible loss, no need for this denial, the refusal they have fallen into, the separation standing in for life. She must get free. The two of them must marry, must make, of the time still in front of them, the everyday miracle time already hints at. He will go to her, tell her he has sprung through to the far side. He holds the answer in his hands; hers if she wants it. He will ask her help and offer her his, daily and for good. What will it be like then, how impossible, necessary, and real, to be able to look up from anything he is thinking, working on, just look up—nothing so simple as that—and speak to her, hear her, be with her?

"I haven't told her yet," he says. "But she's next."

Theory and Composition

Sometimes we played a game, essentially Name that Tune.
Our friend would challenge us: "A sequence please, some clues,
But make it something from the repertoire I've had
some chance in this amateur's life of having heard."

The point was not mastery of the catalog, but the pleasure
in quotation: Were we familiar with those few measures,
a certain interval, a favorite leap; that abiding high G
in the 'cello, surprise rising fifths, agitation in the reeds?

He thought themes between us might make an intimacy, could
be almost like singing. We didn't get it: "How long should
the phrase be?" "How long do I need? Give it to me a tone
at a time. One after the other; I'll stop you when I'm home."

We tried him on our most obscure: Stamitz, Machaut, Cui.
Then graduated to guilty loves. At last, it grew fun to see
if Gilbert and Sullivan, slowed to a stop and in minor, might
slip him. Or "Satisfaction." "Watchman, Tell Us of the Night."

I thought: so this is melody.
Leased office, dull mechanical hum, irritating flicker of fluorescence, and a few friends, stretching their vocal cords. A little patter, a little mix of the dozen available intervals. And out of this weight on the chest, our desolation, came a sudden sweep, a quick-closing glimpse of that place beyond the incurable, where hope might still germinate.

569

We resorted to the concert war-horses. The point was to see how far they might be sliced down, pared back to their essentials, and still be recognizable. Ressler was uncanny. Even with my feeble approximations, he could get most of what I knew by heart in a few pitches. Half by reading my mind, half by the shape of the phrase, he got Brahms's Fourth, first movement, in four.

The suggestion of predictability in the masters outraged Todd. "Now how in hell, out of all possible choices—"

"That's just the point. Each note reduces the choices that are left. What pitch could possibly come after such a setup? And if you already know the next pitch, then you know the piece."

Todd persisted, confused. "Tell me: could you conceivably Name That Tune in three?"

"Not if the notes formed an ascending triad. The whole question is, within acceptable tonal syntax, how likely the sequence of intervals becomes. Where do they point? Is the next pitch already telegraphed? Some sequences are so free, so without redundancy, that they might lead anywhere. Others are more constrained. Every melody heaps up improbability until, by the cadence, it can only be the one thing it is. If your three pitches were improbable enough, they might suffice to prove the private domain of, say, Shostakovich. Or *Dragnet*."

"And two notes, then? Still possible?"

"Don't push your luck."

"One?"

"Pure potential! No edge; no message. One note could be the start of any tune at all."

It took a trained reductionist, someone who arrived at effusion relatively late in life, to see the shape of songs governed by information theory. Perhaps he did so simply to lead Frank on, force him to toughen his own indulgence toward washes of sound. Whatever the case, Ressler tested the first, tentative equation relating music to constituent melody and melody to strings of frequencies, simple sequence.

Q: I'm just your middle-distance listener. Forgive me
   asking: if it's really language, a matter of tending
      toward tonic, being driven back, how can fragments of phrase,
      motives, voices stacked into chords, moments that strain
      toward greater departure or return, how can these explain,
      begin to account for, the terrace of light, mottled rays

570

guttering back to dark, joy, loss, the scent of my own ending
in this syllable-free tune? Layman's answer please.   J. O'D.

Sound, he pronounced, always means more than it says. The
parts only start to explain the thing waiting to spring out of them.
So it is in every organized hive. Because we live on the seam
between formula and mystery, because I can recognize in the
harmonic vicissitudes the hummable tune is put through some
similar, metaphorical bend, music marks out the way all messages
go. Its contours deliver themselves, bent from the chance of experience. They live for a minute in ephemeral pattern, then collapse back to a uniform void that says nothing, carries no
knowledge, far less information. The silence they fall back into,
the nothing that they contrast with, is what notes make, for a
measure, audible.

What *else* is there in a melodic phrase? However much it
wrenches me on the promise of sound, signals from a place lost
beyond recovering, a musical line has nothing in it but notes. A
choice of twelve possible pitch-equivalents, durations scored out
by a simple-minded system of ten or so lengths based on powers
of two. What else is there in an allegro but phrase, phrase, and
development of phrase? What is there in the *Jupiter* but allegro,
andante, minuet, plus allegro? At bottom, only notes.

But notes passed through a transforming *key:* nothing is what
it is except in where, when, and how it goes about unfolding. Push
that pencil box of notes, pitch it faster, prolong it, pinch it, prod
it upwards, follow its fall, attach it to a line, stack voices on top
of it, slacken, shift it off into unlikely relation, let it breathe, grow,
summon, augment, enhance, startle everything around it, and suddenly, out of those ridiculously constrained initial building blocks,
those neutral frequencies meaningless in themselves, with only
the most elementary grammar or enzymes to shape them:

I am (at first modulation) coming home late, pressed under the
hot but changeable air, studying the warnings, the bruise-blue
striations of a storm-sky. Someone—my mother?—runs before me,
entering, crashing through the house, slamming shut windows,
spreading towels across the soaked sills. A cascade of flats, sudden
appassionato, about-face at the double bar, and I am elsewhere:
watching frigate birds dip in a graceful circle into fresh pools, an
enchanted oasis of animals studied through a slight break in the
vegetation.

571

And yet: that's still not it, exactly. It's no more an excuse to free-associate than it is equations. Besides, those associations— house, storm, birds, pool—are all too literal. Everything Ressler ever said to us was an exercise in how words might fit to music. But music into words? Don't push your luck. It will run from any description like floaters skidding across the cornea when and only when you look directly at them.

Yet it is, beyond doubt, language. It may be closer to the architectural plan for that ruined Tower than any other available approximation. I once read, when combing the literature to save Jimmy from his hemorrhage, of the way CAT scans reveal sonatas ravishing the cerebral cortex. A single tone shows up as stagnant Sargasso. Scales create regular ripples of red, yellow, blue. But tune it, trip it into a sequence, three-three-four-five-five-four-three-two, clothe it in vertical harmony, and it storms, splashes across a mass of uncontrollably firing neurons, exploding into the rose window at Chartres.

We know all the rules of air, but we will never predict the weather. Something happens on the rungs of order above the chromatic scale; something happens between the four first pitches and *Four Last Songs*. According to the scan, even the simplest compositional rules are enough to awaken primitive wonder, release the brain from the conventions of verisimilitude, free it from its constant dictionary of representation. But the scan shows something even more surprising. Composers, skilled in theory, hear music differently. CAT profiles of their listening brains show more verbal hemisphere activity, as if they don't just let the associative sensations of timbre and rhythm swell through them, but somehow eavesdrop on a point being argued on thought's original instruments. Can the effect be any less beautiful for being better articulated?

What message could anyone hear there, what terrible conversation except the same, out-of-place, inexecutable instruction carried in the Linear B script deep in the nucleus: feel *this,* grow, do more with what is scored here? Harmonize it every time you open your throat, but know you will never come close to saying, naming what it is.

Even those who can look at a score, a graph of the raw wavelengths in annotated two dimensions, who can see an ingenious inversion or stretto and feel there in the soundless study a cold stab up the spinal column, who can leap from the single cut stone to the completed dome: even they are not replying just to the notes on *that* particular page. They are hearing in the sigh of the appoggiatura the covert, coded, Latin joy at the approach of the Spanish Armada transcribed in Byrd's motet. They are remembering Lully putting the time-beating stick through his foot and dying of infection. They are repenting to Mendelssohn, unable to premier Schubert's Ninth in London because the players wouldn't take the work seriously. They are reliving late Beethoven's obsession with variation form. They are reading, where they still lie open, extant, the notebooks in which an unhearable humanity addressed the deaf man. They are scribbling addenda in those notebooks, adding unanswered questions there.

Our game was only Name That Tune. "I can name that tune in five notes, in four, three." The pieces whose names Ressler supplied had nothing to do with these snippet clues. The real works were interplays of huge motions, movements that stormed inexorably toward arrival or were forcibly restrained, parts progressing in the collision and collusion of themes, themes that constantly built toward breaking down, recombining from their phrases, lines that urged certain stabilities, expectations, setbacks, the tendencies of chords in their given instant, five or four or three of those delinquent, namable, and straying intervals sounded at once. Notes that gave nothing at all away about the ineffable message urgently taking shape so many levels above them, in the weather, in the storm.

It was a night like any other. Outside, six blocks away, people were being murdered. At a middle distance, rain was falling upstate, over the border, rain that left pines as dead as if they had been stripped for sadistic pleasure. In the wide lens, we had at last opened up our long-sought hole in the atmosphere. According to best projections, extrapolations from that week's Facts on File, the world was moving into a terminal late afternoon. Ressler guessed Brahms's Fourth in four.

We sang and quizzed and stumped each other a few times. "No, no. Listen. This part's beautiful. Damn, I've lost the thread. You have to hear it with harmony; here, hold this D." In a few months, Todd and I would split, Jimmy would be crippled for life with a ruptured aneurysm, and the professor would succumb to galloping cancer. All of that lay hiding in those melodies we had by ear. We played name-that-hosanna, but the only quote that lasted past that night was the Dostoyevsky that wound up on the board: In life, sheer hosanna is not enough, for things must be tested in the crucible of doubt.

Above us, well into the solar system, a deep-space satellite drifted; in addition to pictures of the planet we had just finished poisoning (drawings and coded information theoretically understandable to any alien creature, whatever their language), it bore a record player and recording of a *Brandenburg* concerto. Colossal misrepresentation, exaggeration, lie, really, about who we were and what we might be able to accomplish. *Homo musica.*

But that was the language we spoke for a night, a grammar of one trick: tension and release. How likely is the next note, its pitch, its catch, its duration, its tonal envelope? Where does it need to go? What detours must it be put through? Delays, silences, that brief flash showing how close beauty was to the germ of hopelessness. The poignancy of a pattern lifted beyond identity, beyond the thing it was mimicking, past metaphor, into the first mystery: the bliss beyond the fiddle, but not, for a night, beyond fiddling.

Music was no use for anything. It would not protect us from the disaster about to happen, nor even predict it. It was the one pattern not rushing to accomplish or correct current event, not condemned to be *about* anything else. It was about itself, about singing and breaking off from song. Its every phrase continuously flirted with the urge to return to constituent pitch, to give up, go back to Do. We sat quizzing, guessing, comparing recognitions, trading affections for certain expositions with no idea of the development section already in store. Ressler was as happy as a widower who, through force of habit continuing to buy two season tickets years after his wife had gone, discovered that he might give one to the child on Symphony Hall steps who until then had had to be content with echo.

I can still hear them, softly at night, trickling through the open window from the next apartment over. Those tunes still hold, locked in their sequence like the foundations of older temples beneath the nave, not only the complete morphological steps for recreating each similar April night I have ever lived—the color, the wrap, the attitude, the inclination, the range of emotional casts: how I turned from a similar window in just such a light back to a sheet of sums that had to be completed before bed—but also the difference, the closed door, the knowledge that I am no longer in any night but this.

There is only one way for day to pass into dark; today has done so along a predictable sliding scale since the Precambrian. There are only a few barometric pressures, a narrow band of allowable temperatures. But however reducible to parts—degree, pound per square inch, lumen, hour by the clock, latitude, inclination and season—however simple and limited the rules for varying these, something in the particular combination of elements is, like twelve notes and ten durations compounded into a complex cortex-storm, unique, unrepeatable, infinitely unlikely. Today in History: Bach knocks out another cantata.

I hear him listening with a code-breaker's urge, taking noise
and turning it to pattern, thinking to find with ear and voice
a surrogate, an emblem for the melody of the self-composing gene.
The absurd conclusion I cannot help but reach—that singing *means*
something—is rooted in Ressler's choice: either be a physician,
cropping the delinquent tissue, or a researcher, a musician,
mapping anatomy, the way the tissue lies. Two choices that amount
to one thing. To feel the pattern flash, summoning an account
for the gut-twist in a deceptive cadence. In either case, conspire
to produce and deliver that new song the obsolete Lord requires.

Listen and sing. That's all he wrote.
And I can name that tune in one note.

Breaking and Entering

"So you see, Jimmy, we'll need *access*."

I listened as the professor sat on the hospital bed and explained. It became clear to me what he had in mind. It even became clear to Annie, who leaned over during Dr. Ressler's explanation and whispered, "So it's time to get our feet dirty."

How he could imagine that stroked and broken Jimmy, who had wanted pitifully to tell us of his father's death twenty years ago, was in any shape to assist was beyond me. Yet Ressler spoke to him without condescension, apologizing for spelling out the obvious. His words had a confidence in the ability of signals to survive the shattered receiver. I watched Ressler reach into his jacket pocket and momentarily thought he was about to pull out a hand-held terminal and plug it into the wall jack in that hospital room.

Instead, he retrieved a lower-tech spiral notepad and flipped to a blank page. The pad was packed with illegible scrapings, although I had never once seen Ressler make a single mark into anything resembling it.

He printed methodically, in large block letters down six columns of six, the letters of the alphabet and the ten digits. "I'm sorry we have to resort to this, Jimmy. But I have to be sure we get it right." Jimmy made no sound. I thought: He might as well be talking to himself. "Let's start with the operating system lockout. You lie still. When I get to the first letter, let me know." He smiled reassuringly, betraying none of the hopelessness of this attempt, the only shot we had for getting Jimmy reinstated under the umbrella of an institution that, understandably, had no stake in private welfare. Dr. Ressler began at the top of the first column, pointing to each letter and pronouncing the corresponding name.

I stood and walked to the door. I could not stand to watch them get to the bottom of the last column, Ressler pointing and naming while Jimmy lay in confusion. Then, an agonizing twenty letters into the list, Jimmy made a noise. Not a howl or sigh. An indicative yes. Ressler's shoulders dropped in relief. He noted the letter and brought his pen back to the top.

It was a grueling process, and Jimmy had to rest twice. But after the first letter, we were home. Jimmy gave us dozens of crucial bits of information—passwords, memory locations, patch names— that until then had been the secret domain of the Operations Manager. Whatever else the flood of blood had wiped out—muscular control, speech, emotional perspective—it left Jimmy still able to remember the system words Ressler was asking him to spell. Nowhere in the dialogue was the message passed, "Betray your professional confidences, look the other way while we break the law, and we will do what we can to keep you from being killed." Ressler said only the letters of the alphabet; Jimmy made only grunts. But the transmission was there, intact, awful in its implied risk. Uncle Jimmy was the classic Picardian third: minor his whole life, promoted to major at the last chord.

XXVII

The Goldberg Variations

Its published name is wildly unassuming: "Keyboard Practice, Part IV. Composed for music lovers to refresh their spirits." One of only a handful of his thousand compositions to be published in his lifetime, in a form he never cared for, although perfected here.

Bach's first biographer tells the story, already thirdhand, of how Count Kaiserling, former Russian ambassador to Saxony, employed a young harpsichordist named Goldberg, one of Bach's star pupils. Goldberg's duties included making soft music in an adjoining room on those frequent nights when the Count had trouble sleeping. The Count commissioned Bach to compose for Goldberg something "of a soft and somewhat lively character," to assist against this periodic insomnia. A musical calmative, a treatment that now consists of two tablets and the low drone of talk radio.

Theme and variations, a form limited to "the sameness of the fundamental harmony" throughout, was just the ticket: sedative, soporific permutations jumping like counted sheep over a stile. From beginning to end, the *Goldbergs* were conceived, if not as an attempt to sing the listener to sleep, as a catalog that would at least keep the sleepless sufferer company, to hold at theme's length the nightmare of wakefulness. The best one can be is either doctor or musician. Both, if possible.

For this work, legend has it, Bach was rewarded with a goblet of one hundred gold louis, more than he was paid for scores of other works combined. The ambassador got off cheaply, taking possession of one of the supreme works in music history. Throughout the rest of his life, he referred to the piece as if it were his own composition. "Dear Goldberg, do play me one of *my* variations."

So much for the reading tale. The stuff any librarian can turn up. As for the architecture: the *Goldbergs* are twice as long as any previous variation collection. They form the most virtuosic and demanding piece for solo keyboard in any form until middle Beethoven. The set is built around a scheme of infinitely supple, proliferating relations. Each of the thirty is a complete ontogeny, unfolding until it denies that it differs at conception from all siblings by only the smallest mutation. Together they achieve a technical inventiveness and profundity unsurpassed in the rest of music, a catalog hinting at every aspect of tonal experience.

And the whole archive is hatched from an insipidly simple theme. One musicologist tried to convince a fellow scholar that the germ aria, a heavily ornamented period piece, was not even Bach's own. The eminent colleague disappeared into his study, emerging some time later (like Von Neumann affirming the obvious) shaking his head. "You're right. It's a piece of French fluff."

Bach's first act out of the block is to strip down this aria bacterium to its even simpler bass. For the longest time, until Ressler pointed it out, I couldn't hear how the wayward offspring had anything to do with parent. That's because the variations aren't descended from the aria per se. Rather, the aria itself is just another variation, built upon the all-generating, sarabande Base:

The *Goldbergs* are not even variations in the modern sense, but an imperceptibly vast chaconne, an evolutionary passacaglia built on the repetition and recycling of this Base. Music that goes nowhere, that simply is, hovering around the fixed center of diatonic time.

A line of pitches can be heard as a melodic sequence or as a series of harmonies. Bach's Base is both, at times even hybridizing horizontal and vertical. As with 90 percent of standard tonality, it is no more than an exploration of the possibilities hidden in the scale. The sequence is symmetrical to an extreme: two paired, complementary halves of sixteen notes each. Each half comprises four similar-shaped paired phrases—tension, release, tension, release—four notes long. Each pair of four-note phrases creates an eight-note harmonic section, four in all, tracing the fundamental journey from tonic to dominant to relative and back to tonic. Sixteen twos, eight fours, four eights, and two sixteens: with repeats, the trip from home and back takes sixty-four notes.

Dr. Ressler—already fighting gnostic tendencies—must have loved discovering in Bach two paired strands, four phrase-building blocks, a sixty-four-codon catalog. Bach had a habit of imbedding mystic numbers in his compositions; these ones happen to correspond to the number-game nature imbeds in its own. But this coincidence was the least of the qualities that made this music Ressler's best metaphor for the living gene.

I begin to hear, too late, how the Base's symmetry ripples through the piece, unfolding ever-higher structures, levels of pattern, fractal self-resemblances. Having made my layman's survey of the synthesis his science was after, I begin to hear in this encyclopedia of transcription, translation, and self-replication something of the catalog he carried around inside of himself for a quarter century.

Like the master molecule and its living scaffolding, the *Goldberg* schema is a self-spun hierarchy. First: the transcription of the Base into each variation, even those transposed to relative minor, is faithful, either note for note or harmony for harmony. Oh, it strays from its source, sometimes implying the sarabande while straining to leave it, sometimes filling out the step with jarring accidentals. At times it too becomes a new thing, a new theme, overhauled for all its treading water. But the basic sarabande bass, its thirty-two-note journey, completely informs each child, in turn thirty-two bar-equivalents long. The code is universal throughout creation.

The variations unfold a second level of emerging pattern. Every third variation is a canon, a strict imitation of staggered voices. "Row Row Row Your Boat" self-replication taken to terminal degree. In the first canon, the duplicating voice begins on the same pitch a measure later. In the second canon, the interval between voices is a second: the replication begins one tone higher than the original. The third canon is a canon at the third, and so on through every interval of the major scale plus one—the same scale the theme is built upon. Two canons occur in inversion: whatever happens in the first voice is mirrored upside down in the second. A rising interval is answered by equivalent fall. But in all the canons the situation is the same; the melody harmonizes not with another

579

tune but with itself, a replica of its immediate past and future.

The second voice in every canon is determined: the template first voice right-shifted, transcribed into new scalar position. Two copies twist about each other with helical precision, at ever-increasing steps, coding for their own continuation. Some of the canons are content to be canonical: the template is still audible when the replication arrives. Others push the form's limits, holding a note away from falling into a single voice or mapping out intervals so dissonant that each constrained part seems to insist on its own, discrete decisions—strict, deterministic contrapuntalism forcing freedom.

In each canon but one, strict imitation takes place over a third, persistent, unifying voice across the widening intervals. The second level of order enfolds the first: underneath each canon, the original Base matrix continues to churn. Canons at every scalar interval arch across the work like a giant backbone. But at each vertebra, the canonic lines are tied into position by the spinal cord of a theme that released them, the last to anticipate what spreading skeletons swirl around it. In the final canon—the replication at the ninth, the interval beyond the octave—the imitative voices draw up into their tag the contour of the Base itself.

That much, already a *tour de force* of both conception and execution, would have easily engaged Ressler the scientist and pattern-seeker. But the primary structure of informing theme and the secondary emergence of canons at increasing intervals does not yet account for his lifelong devotion to the piece. A third level of structure, emerging after a week of my nonstop listening, hints at the successive layers of fascination peeling from the piece, bringing the man constantly back to listen, to make his next discovery.

I have just come to hear how the variations group locally, how they arrive in threes, triplet codons together spelling out a fundamental word of human experience. The third of each set is a canon, as the second level of ordering dictates. But after the first triplet set, a regular rotation also generates the form, color, and scope of the other two members of the triplet. The first of each codon is a dance, strikingly rhythmic or in a unique musical form. These moments of clarity are followed by brilliant duets, outbursts of virtuosic display, two-manual arabesques tearing across the keys. Dance, arabesque, canon: the variations produce a triangulation of feeling, sensing, and thinking that could only have arisen from a three-chambered arrangement of body, soul, and mind in perfect coordination. Harmony consists of propositions about harmony.

The dance variations explore a variety of musical genres: a complete, compact fugue without episodes. An outrageous French overture, that most stylized of Baroque puff pieces, opening with a vertical flourish in the jungle of surrounding counterpoint and proceeding with eighteenth-century aristocratic optimism. A vigorous, syncopated alla breve. A four-voice stretto-fit of well-being over before you can say hallelujah. Two transcendent adagios, one in poignant, resigned major, the other a heart-stabbing minor where every pitch in the chromatic scale puts in an appearance, the two together an unendurable duet of deliverance wedded to dissonance, promise unwinding in pain.

Each of these formal dances is built upon clear renditions of the Base. The difficulty of satisfying the constraints of variation within the bravura of overture or the rigor of fugue is considerable. But more disconcerting than the technical accomplishment is the plan. Take the variation number and divide by three. If the remainder is 1/3, the piece is a formal genre or dance; 2/3, and it's a toccata. No remainder, and the piece is a canon built on the interval given by the quotient.

Each dance stands in utter emotional contrast to the previous canon. And each is followed by a two-manual tear that draws the ear up in a second reversal of decision upon appeal. This constant broadening of technical and emotional contrast must have taken Ressler years to train for: each variation is so arranged to throw off the spell of the previous, and before the ear has time enough to savor any crystallization of mood, a reaction at once pitches the listener into new tempi, meters, and melodic figures probing radically opposing kernels of feeling, pulling open the full complexity of the piece, the inexhaustible variety extracted from the modest four-by-four-by-four sarabande. Each variation asserts its own myth, its own melody, its lack of precedent. Yet underneath, shining through each arpeggiated outburst, the theme asserts itself as master gene.

My attending ear learns not to give over entirely to the sorrow or exuberance of the moment. The most stupendously brilliant piece in the set is also a premonition of the emotional devastation that must follow. The variations each announce the consequence each itself creates. Just after a variation harboring harmonies that will not surface again until this century comes the most rococo

581

of diversions. Grief spills over into buffoonery. Every beauty has its bitter answer. Yet each reversal doesn't *dispel* its sibling. They are all obedient, first-filial offspring of the same parent; while different phenotypes, they carry the same underwriting code. They exist side by side, superimposed in my unforgetting ear, apparent incommensurates, but one at the core.

And they are a unity in a way that becomes clear to me only as I discover an even higher order of order imbedded in the set. The aria, itself just another organism synthesized from the Base, is repeated—completely overhauled, although note for note the same—da capo at the end. So there are not thirty but thirty-two variations in the set, one for each measure in each variation, for each note in the generating Base. Any reductionist attempt to capture the work in its understandable particulars, dropping from the set down to the variation down to one measure, produces a germ that is not a *part* of anything but a microcosm of the infolded whole.

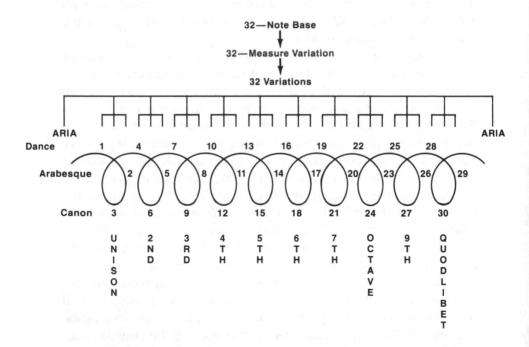

The theme is all thirty-two notes, the *Goldbergs,* all thirty-two variations. Each moment is a miniature globe, an encoding of everything above it. The *Goldbergs* are layered all the way from bottom to top and back down again, with every layer of ordering—from canonically entering canons to contrasting triplet groups, from note to measure to line to variation to entire work and back to note—contributing to, particularizing, and lost in the next rung of the hierarchy it generates.

But the severe mathematics of recursive architecture are lost in the first ornament of aria. By the time the potential of the original sequence emerges, no ear can trace any but the faintest line of that all-embracing ground plan. No; Ressler was not listening to inversions and midpoint symmetries and numerologies and the closing of the diatonic circle. He was following the death of his friends, listening to how love fled, anticipating the dissonance of Jimmy's crippling, detecting and replaying his own departure from science: hearing, in the descent of four notes from Do, the script of life's particulars, brute specifics that too often became too much, too full, too awful to bear, too unendurably, transiently beautiful.

The canons proceed beyond the octave, start all over again at the ninth, as if to suggest, "We could do this for eons." The *Goldbergs* threaten to expand the modest four-note germ of the thirty-two note Base to the scale of infinite invention, a perpetual calendar. I hear Ressler talking to his love every night for thirty-two years, using no words other than those built on the alloted four letters, and never exhausting all he had to say to her. Once a grammar passes the complexity threshold, no algorithm can list all possible well-formed sentences. The diversity of language defies physical law, or rather, endless sentence-generation displays law in a new, unprecedented predication.

Sufficiently complex, the *Goldbergs* no longer know their own sarabande. They are no longer about permutation, manipulation, pattern. They are about the bliss of the sixth, the cut of the seventh, this drooping cadence, the suspension selecting for sorrow or serenity, a snowed-in weekend, late nights of conversation, anger, abandonment, disaster, the decision to act, to rejoin for a last moment the condition of human politics, a brute insistence modulating worlds from G before coming home. The *Goldbergs* reach the threshold where each variation denies that it *is* a variation. And at that point, they no longer are.

Like proliferating species, the variants do not improve or advance. There is no question of *progress* here. Under the pressure of evolutionary restlessness, they simply spread out across the map of available biomes, unearth more of the embedded germ material, bring some as yet unrealized alternative—similar to all others, only different—into existence. The sarabande is never escaped, however much migration takes place. Its shape squarely inhabits mid-measure. It may wander freely across voices and beats, be for a few bars almost unhearable. But it is always there. The distance between any two incarnations is immense, as wide as the immigrant's awe at native idiom. It is improvisation in here tonight. We listeners can do nothing but stand back and wing it as it wings. Where will the next dance step come from, the next flying arabesque, the wilder, more cunningly contrived canon?

More than enough room in this world for him to move around in, respond to, to laugh at, to feel the quick, sure flash of recognition. He could hear in it not just the faithful transcript of lost love, his early work on the coding problem, the years of obscurity, and the premonition of a few affectionate months with us, the first hint of what today in history would call him to. The sound was also an invitation to run this experiment of independent parts—crossing, racing, colliding, mimicking, moving in contrary motion, teasing each other into brighter, freer passages, informed by what has passed and what is still to come. The variations are the working out of that instruction, buried deep in the Base string, that commands itself to translate, to strain against the limits of its own synthesis, to test the living trick of Perhaps, to love.

It is, as the young pianist on Ressler's thirty-year-old recording proclaims in the liner notes, music with no beginning and no end. Music of no particular style or period: its eighteenth-century decorum constantly upset by backward glances and embryonic predictions—by turns monkish cloister, Renaissance brass, skittish romantic soaring, and the jarring atonality of my own evening. Darwin might have found his elusive pangene, if he'd only looked in the right place: higher up, deeper down, outside the cell, in the codes the cell creates and sends out to probe and describe its inexhaustible world.

The variations take on the language of the time and place they require, obeying no formal principle except the continuance of their parent. Conflicting musical ideas tear across the page, from the page to the keys, and the keys to the ear—rising into free-fall, daring chromatics, turning triplet shorthand, leaping, crashing in exhilaration, creeping meekly across the keyboard, descending to earthy folk song, daring the dead stop of anguish. The Base on which the entire piece is built, while everywhere manifest, loses its original, independent identity. It is subsumed in the general fanfare, swallowed up in invention, changed in the accumulation of minute mutations. Its sequence becomes a sustained pedal point, a repeated, ultimately stationary strain that changes as all else changes around it.

And the immense set as a whole becomes a scalar expansion of the sarabande, each of the thirty-two notes enlarged into thirty-two variations that are themselves, apart and together, a macrocosm of a single idea. Nowhere in the patterned sequence is there the remotest suggestion of what might arise out of it. To try to locate, in the thematic germ, what Ressler spent a life listening to would be to search in those schematics—line drawings showing every subassembly of every carburetor part—for a semblance of the functioning car. The germ shares nothing with its inheriting variations except the investing metaphor at the heart of life.

Yet the only way over the threshold, down into the full sound he heard, lies along this line, parallel to the one connecting organism to circulatory system to heart to chamber to valve to pumping muscle cell to nucleus to copy of the master theme. The line sought by the systematic researcher. The thing he hoped one day to uncover on the ancient, battered disk he toted around his entire adult life, the thing every beat of the piece encoded, the thing he was living, the set inside him: the infinitely pliable four-note theme.

Ultimately, the *Goldbergs* are about the paradox of variation, preserved divergence, the transition effect inherent in terraced unfolding, the change in nature attendant upon a change in degree. How necessity might arise out of chance. How difference might arise out of more of the same. By the time the delinquent parent aria returns to close out the set, the music is about how variation might ultimately free itself from the instruction that underwrites it, sets it in motion, but nowhere anticipates what might come from experience's trial run.

The relentlessly repeating thirty-two-note Base traces out that same unintentional contradiction in terms that Dr. Ressler read to us from the operations manual on the night we sat down to commit our crime. "These two procedures are exactly similar." "Exactly similar" elicited a laugh. But shouldn't "the same" get the same? "A is the same as B." Impossible. What Ressler listened to in that tightly bound, symmetry-laced catalog of unity was how nothing was the same as anything else. Each living thing defied taxonomy. Everything was its own, unique, irreducible classification.

The *Goldbergs* were his closest metaphor to the coding problem he gave his life to studying. Exactly similar, with one exception. Bach liked to inscribe his compositions with the triplet SDG, *Soli Dei Gloria*. To God alone the glory. Even this secularly commissioned soporific possesses the religious wonder at being joyously articulate, alive to extend the pattern. But in Ressler's hierarchy of transitional rungs, the thing beyond the composer, on the other side of the threshold from articulate breath, was only dumb designless matter, arising from and led only by the shape of experience. The world's pattern was not assembled for the mind's comprehension; rather the other way around. And that made the metaphor more miraculous.

To play the piece—to buzz the length of the keyboard for an hour, to barrage, to cross over, careen dangerously—requires only a feat of digital dexterity. Just hit the right notes at the right time, and the thing virtually plays itself. To compose it, Bach insisted, required only that one work as hard as he did. To hear in the organizing software the unique, unspecifiable odds against any metaphor ever arising on this earth out of nothing, out of mere notes, requires something more. It needs the conviction, in a third favorite phrase of the provincial choirmaster, that all things must be possible, sayable, particular, real.

A Terrorist's Primer

When we returned to MOL from visiting Jimmy, Dr. Ressler set to work on the second-to-the-last experiment he would ever be involved in. He laid out the contour of his plan. "What we're looking for is a program exactly similar to this operating system." The work required over the next several days steadied Todd, gave his hands something to eradicate. We all resolved to do anything needed to keep from abandoning Jimmy to the world.

The office was in a shambles since Jimmy's stroke. The daily processing was getting out, but only just. The day shift ran on automatic, and the least irregularity would have chucked the whole operation into chaos. While Jimmy's crippling was still novel enough to play on imaginations, the staff to a person worked until the work got done, without compensation. But gradually imagination failed, folks tired of reality, and self-interest set in. Management appointed an "interim" replacement, more eager than competent. And under this blanket of confusion, Todd and Ressler, never very supervised to begin with, had free rein to implant our seed into the on-line processing.

MOL had been suspicious enough of the original irregularity to begin inquiries, inquiries quickly and discreetly canceled in light of their role in Jimmy's stroke. The insurers had dodged a million-dollar bullet; the chronology of Jimmy's skipped premium and high-profile disaster was drilled into them. All surreptitious attempts to backdate reinstatement, to sneak Jimmy in the electronic side door, were out of the question.

Frank, getting the gist of Ressler's plan, wanted to dispose of it in favor of the less subtle, more expeditious, full-frontal approach. "The easiest thing in the world: we buy a bulk tape eraser from the hobby electronics store, change the combinations, barricade ourselves in, take a few Master File packs hostage, and give them forty-eight hours to cover the man's indefinite hospital stay."

Dr. Ressler's eyes measured the extent of Frank's desperation. For a moment, he seemed about to attack. Instead, he relaxed and lit a cigarette. "Ah! The postwar solution. No, we're too close to terrorism as it stands. We can do this thing more effectively without violence or property damage." He shrugged, having said everything needed about the superiority of legitimate retaliation. And Todd acquiesced.

Combining the words supplied by Jimmy's horrifying dictation with their own batch of gradually acquired contraband knowledge, Dr. Ressler and his graduate assistant went to work on a last recombination. They raided the program listings room and before the new manager could reinstate punch-lock security, they copied all the sections of the system software they needed, stashing the copies each night in the bottom of stockroom supply boxes.

For all they had taught themselves about how the system worked, how to make it jump through hoops, they now had to figure out why it did what it did, to trace its internal logic at machine level. For four nights running, program listings littering the computer room, they dissected the routines and procedures. They raced the clock. Jimmy's mother had seen a lawyer, who had convinced the increasingly nervous hospital to restrain itself and keep the man stabilized under care while his mother looked into every conceivable financial strategy for meeting the unmeetable bill. We had no idea of how much time we had for the delicate surgery we meant to pull off.

I was there every night. I hunched over the listings alongside them, threw in my guesses as to what fit where, ran back and forth to the massive, meter-long documentation manual. They accepted my help, but when they talked, they clearly talked to each other. They were men, in the end, and had begun, in challenge, to discover just what the other might be capable of. When their eyes locked on a piece of particularly tangled code, I could sense that they threw themselves into the untangling not just for Jimmy but to earn and keep the love of the other.

In addition to helping speed things up, I wanted to leave my fingerprints in the affair, to stand implicated alongside them. Dr. Ressler allowed me that chance, giving me a list of two dozen credit unions and financial institutions, all clients of MOL. I was to check Who Owns Whom, and establish which if any had parent-child connections to the insurance company in question. He wanted to make his bullet as precise, discriminating, and manageable as possible. "Oh," he added, as I left to do the assignment. "We'll also need your entire index card collection from the last five years." I laughed.

The financial audit was trivial but surprising. A few hours of legwork in the stacks confirmed the classic postindustrial para-noiac's fantasy: four of the two dozen names on the list belonged to the same tier of the same sprawling hierarchy of ownership as our insurance company target. "I thought we might snag a couple," Dr. Ressler said mildly, when I gave him the results that evening. "Contracts and kickbacks tying together one big happy family."

"I personally think the Trilateral Commission is behind us all," Todd said, not lifting his head from the listing where he traced calling routines with colored pencils.

Dr. Ressler chuckled. "Maybe. The world certainly is more connected than anyone supposes. Perhaps in another few years, we'll all be owned by one little old lady in Kansas City." He thanked me for the work. Looking over the list of linked businesses, he grew apprehensive. "Can you get names? Addresses?"

"Child's play," I assured him. What could be simpler?

"And the quote cards? Your collection of 'Today in History'?"

"You really want those? I thought you were joking."

"Not at all. They're instrumental."

588

I brought in my massive card box the following evening, years of trivia typed up on three-by-fives. He sat down with me and in fifteen minutes taught me the criterion by which I could divide the stack into two piles, Yes and No. In the samples we sorted together, one by Swift caught his eye. Dr. Ressler instantly taped it to the front of the CPU. It inspired him throughout the most difficult parts of subsequent decoding:

> I have heard of a man who had a mind to sell his house, and therefore carried a piece of brick in his pocket, which he shewed as a pattern to encourage purchasers.

After they had deciphered the system logic, Dr. Ressler duplicated the relevant programs and data files. Then came the task of building the mutation, the exactly similar, only different system. Ressler carefully selected locations where they might place the needed patches—electronic detours and amendments. The point was to make their baby look, feel, and behave exactly the same as the template, the original operating system. But be the serpent underneath.

It seemed to take weeks. Every night I arrived expecting to hear that Jimmy had been turned out, that the hospital was suing his mother for immediate payment, or that our project to avert that scenario had been uncovered. In reality, the insertion of program patches went quickly, and the bulk of the replacement code actually got written in the few days between the founding of the Library of Congress on April 24 and the combined *Lusitania* sinking/Nazi surrender on May 7–8.

Live testing of the modifications—bringing them on-line on scores of remote terminals—was the most difficult and dangerous part. An insignificantly small alteration, whose logic is impeccable in isolation, can have unforeseen consequences that multiply out of control when dropped in the middle of a complex system. It came down either to testing a number of changes in one batch, which increased the chance of untraceable bugs, or to tracing the effects of single differences, which took far more time and showed little about the combined behavior. And each on-line test increased the odds of our being discovered.

For live testing, Annie was indispensable. As a remote terminal user herself, she could report to Dr. Ressler the effects of the modifications at a typical station. She could also enter keystrokes remotely, sequences that triggered a routine, set in motion as if by accident. This made it possible to invoke and trace changes during a normal day without irregularities back in the computer room. Annie did this in full knowledge of the risks, aware that her complicity violated the state criminal code if none of God's own minor statutes. We each loved Jimmy after our own fashion.

The operation involved some degree of what white-collar espionage calls backstopping: dummying up the record after the fact. Todd, the artist, enjoyed this part: creating on the text editor bogus console logs that looked exactly like real ones. Faking labels and directory histories for the packs they experimented on. Going into the low-level driver software and altering the dates on modified files. "Do you remember that Holmes story where the bad guys create the complete, simulated, subterranean bank vault one story *above* the real one? That's what we're up to. Hijacking an entire office."

I hadn't seen him in such spirits since Jimmy's stroke; no, before—since we began living together. As they closed in on debugging the last subtle change they meant to introduce into the machine, I saw how much the two of them enjoyed the work, enjoyed one another, the exertion. It was an elaborate game, an intellectual challenge, momentarily divorced from real-world consequences, the emergency motive. They got carried up in the charge of making it work, making it ingenious. The life-or-death matter became play, lab for lab's sake: what would happen if we put the patch here? Wouldn't it be prettier if we rebuilt the allocation table? Why not read the records directly from the cross-index?

They were both vital for a few days. Strong and inventive with effort. Alive. Franklin earned momentary respite from feeling that he'd personally crippled Jimmy. And Dr. Ressler had, here at the end, finally found an outlet, a call to put to use that superlative skill in pattern-searching and manipulation that had always been his second nature. The young post-doc would never, in a lifetime, have imagined this experiment. But after a long detour, it was his belated return to biology. To Life Science.

Canon at the Ninth

He leaves the Biology Building, walking slowly, too slowly to get anywhere, strolling into the middle of the place he's been

590

trying to reach from the start, from before childhood. The last click of in vitro reverberates in his head with the clang of a meter-thick cell door being thrown wide open. Sprung in the open air, he explores its layout, feels its foliage, wholly foreign yet still familiar. The landscape he has lucked into is wider, more surprising than he ever imagined. A difficult passage in arriving, blind alleys and doublings back that he could never retrace, reroute, so obvious is this place in retrospect.

Ressler feeds into pedestrian turbulence, the passing hour between classes. People scowl at him for failing to get out of their way, or smile tolerantly at his distraction. He cannot quite take in his breakthrough, cannot believe that his own mental construct—string-and-cardboard mock-up, manipulation of the available tools—has led him to this threshold. Research, that inefficient recombination of insufficiencies, has rewarded him with the one prize every researcher lives for but never expects: a chance to locate part of the palpable world's terrain, to summarize some fraction of the solidity that cares nothing for theory, to say something definitive about their real home, to speak some word about the grammar carried around in every oblivious mote, down *there,* inside.

His idea is simplicity itself: they must feed the in vitro decoder a stripped-down signal of their own devising that will yield a message beyond ambiguity. The peal of the carillon just now breaking out of the university bell tower rings a change in him, slows his walk further. The waves of enabled air circle him, bang up against one another, create in him a standing crest of astonishment and gratitude. He cannot accept his good fortune, the odds against it. For a moment, he has been appointed caretaker of the entire, immensely delicate experiment, trustee of the living possibility. Whatever happens from here, he will be glad to have—well, just this once—to have made a joyful noise.

The decoding can be done. He glimpses the necessary process and knows it will work. What's more, this afternoon, walking aimlessly across the quad in May air, Ressler understands that this work, the lookup table—that rung of the hierarchy linking the life principle with slavish molecular mechanics—will, the minute it is published, be turned to further work, extrapolated, taken farther afield than he can now guess. Ideas are as self-exploiting as tissue. Everyone ever pressed into service—Mendel, Avery, Crick, Cyfer—is but a primitive precursor. The problem each has worked

591

on, the postulate passing through their hands, mutates with every generation. It must, to remain viable. The concerns of those working on the codon table will soon appear as blunt and unsubtle as those old biological models of animism and spontaneous generation.

The future of his science sweeps across Ressler with physical certainty: in a very few years, the Sunday-school work of cryptography will go public, enter commercial politics. Too much need always hinges on knowledge for it ever to remain uncorrupt, objective, a source of meditative awe. After wonder always comes the scramble, the applications for patents. Perhaps, he thinks, unable to keep from grinning at the oblivious undergrads who pass him under the sycamores, it won't be patents at all. Perhaps it will be copyrights, like books and magazines: genes written, amended, and edited like any other text. Only alive. Cold goose flesh runs up his back at the word that profit requires and biology refuses to mention: *improvement*. Everything life has ever been, this magnificent accident of doubling, error, and feedback, changes forever in this minute, makes an incalculable macro-step of fatal evolution here, now, as he walks across the quad.

Yes, the message has changed before, momentously. The marshaling of the organelles, the development of the eukaryotic membrane, energy by ingestion, colonies, differentiation, the notochord, the brain, the first croak of distress, courtship, self-expression: the word has always been permanently restless, wanting only to repeat imperfectly, recast what it has been until then. Life can't be protected against a fate it's coveted from the beginning. But this break is something else again. Angelic, catastrophic, unprecedented except in the origin. Life is passing the second threshold, emending the contract. The next generation will wrap their opposable thumbs around processes he can't even begin to conceive. What can be filled in of the map will be filled in.

Worse: everything that can be done to the process will be done. The thing the adaptor molecule has for billions of years tried to articulate will, in the last click of the second hand, be channeled into massive habitat clearance, would-be property improvements, trillion-dollar toxicity, terminal annihilation. A million species lost irretrievably by the time he dies, an acceleration of slaughter that can only be ignored by an effort of will. One species a day, soon one an hour, one a minute. Not research's fault per se, but tied to the same destructive desire to grow, be *more*. And in return—he can't grasp the grotesque trade-off—a few new species that, for the first time in creation, can be signed by the artist.

The realized ability to masquerade as the creator—not achieved this week yet, but certainly next—this slim, second shot at the garden calls out for nothing less than a complete, instant maturation. Anything short of the creator's wisdom will chuck us into chaos. Ressler skims his eye across the open space of this campus: a quaint building for math, another brick Georgian for music, a curious, classical colonnade for English literature. Clearly, we lag behind ourselves, knowledge always hopelessly outstripped by available information.

At one end of the trimmed rectangle, in front of the auditorium, a boy and girl, both sweet-and-twenty, stand propping their bikes, one's thighs brushing the other's. Each pretends they are talking. Neither admits the real issue, both crazy with spring, aroused to inchoate blur by sap-distraction. These two children will be first-time lovers tonight, find a way to violate the segregated dorms. Neither realizes the historical moment they inhabit—the sad potential, the willful waste of it. They may never know the place the way he does in this minute, wider, stranger, more calamitous than he suspected, the place research from the first has been desperate to reach. They will feel rushing finality in everything they do without ever being able to name the utter change in life's program that researchers at their own school have set inexorably in motion.

He weighs the odds against the day being saved by the arrival, in the nick of time, of that judicious, adult nature that must accompany this discovery. No chance. They are on their own, lost, lost to this obscene place, a place larger than anyone can safely care for, the place his carefully isolated adaptor molecules locate and leave him to. Left to whistle in the dark the tune described in information-bearing strands that life itself will now be able to compose, perform with the chemical philharmonic he and his friends now conduct. Even now the piece must be further improvised, built up from the given ground, played on that piano roll he will pass through test-tube ribosomes. The cell-free spinet must take up the tune, singing as it goes, the way the record his love gave him sings under the reading needle.

But his experiment, a first solution to the coding problem, will put him no step closer to solving the code-breaking *urge,* a place unlocatable in either the lookup table or any aggregate survey of it. Investigation is an ache, a permanent displacement, an accidental by-product of necessity written into the program itself. He sees it briefly, the random outline thrown up for an instant in an electrical storm: he will spend what remains of his life guessing at a pattern that is itself nothing more than exactly similar. Those codons all in a row: just successive approximations about the possibilities of pattern in this world. The gene is an experiment in its own decoding. It too, like the commands it shapes, remains a beginner in its own life. An educated guess. A blundering amateur.

How can the one place where that fragile experiment thrives, how can it be protected, kept from being trampled? Investigation cannot and ought not be stopped. The command to decipher was present at the start, driving the first clunky, unshelled, self-duping, primitive amino-assembler. But if research, life, is to protect itself from itself here at the eleventh hour, the moment of its second revolution, curiosity must be amended, matured. He cannot bring that new thing to life by himself. But there is one he might ask about this idea forming in his mind, a friend who might already be halfway toward founding that new science required to save creation from the creative urge.

A nervous coed approaches him as he drifts by the library. Are you the one from the picture magazine? She thrusts out a scrap of cash-register receipt and asks him to sign his name. "Oh, no," Ressler objects. "Thank you, but this is premature. I haven't done anything yet. Ask me next year, perhaps." He grins to smooth her apology and backs away. He runs for the barracks. Sprinting, gulping air, he knows it is high time—yes, even this late in life—to tie himself forever to his companion. There is something they must find, develop together as helpmates. They will only be able to reach it in combination, each contributing a half-proposal to the corrective that pure research calls out for. It is not too late to fabricate, between them, an answer to the riot of silence awaiting life on the far side of the patent. They will put the finishing touches on the in vitro catalog. Then they will use the international reputation the work will lay at their doorstep to convince the world that it is not too late for the getting of wisdom.

This something else: he hasn't gotten it yet, he does not know its precise shape. But they can arrive at it together—the one descendant he and Jeanette can leave to this teetering place. Herbert can, of course, visit anytime he wants. Even live with them if he likes. That will not be the last concession to the law of human averages they will need to make in the decades in front of them.

594

They must perfect the only way home, the one trick of natural pattern forever unpatentable. They must learn quickly, this afternoon, to care for living existence with the tender survey of parental love. It's time for him to become a husband. A father.

He sprints the distance to Stadium Terrace, arriving on the stoop gasping for breath. He is about to stumble inside when something stops him. Through the thin wooden door, he hears a strain of music as familiar to him as breathing. She has anticipated him. She is inside, playing this disk hinting of the new science they must originate. He stands for a moment, simply listening, hearing a certain play of counterpoint for the first time. He pushes the door open, shouting her name on the air.

The record is indeed playing, Olga indeed centrifuging dutifully above it. But Jeanette is, like the decoding urge, nowhere. He thinks: *The bedroom,* enters shyly, wondering what tender, depraved rendezvous she has arranged for him. But the room is empty, the linen unmussed. He calls once, softly, pointlessly, to her attending ghost.

His answer waits in the front room, both sides of a full sheet in his laboratory notebook, left lying on top of the stack of delinquent periodicals that has become his *de facto* reference library. Every relationship he enters into on this earth comes down to a carefully printed message. Her hand, that spidery, runic script—as much as her voice, her scent, the curve of her forehead where his fits—begins carefully, perfectly across the horizontal.

> I didn't want you to hear from Ulrich tomorrow, secondhand, about what concerns you at first. I worked up the courage to tell you face to face, but as you know, courage has always been at best a periodic phenomenon with me. A few minutes of sitting, waiting for you to catch me here, and I rush into the cowardice of print. I keep thinking I can hear your step coming up to the door. I keep rushing up, shutting this thing with guilty relief. Impossible hope that you might somehow still free me from having to say all this. You always could revise even my firmest rules. Why don't you come home?
>
> Here is what has happened. Herbert, my husband, foreseeing every eventuality, knowing I might take it in mind really to fall in love with you long before I did, put in for a transfer some months back. The arrangements have at last come through. He has been assigned to—no matter where. The world is flattening out to uniformity anyway. The next choice is mine: Wife, are you coming or staying? Coming.

You will walk in now before I can finish this clause. You'll look over my shoulder, read this, laugh. You will turn and walk out, leave me, unable to understand. How could you? I told you once that I have never lied to you. It's true, Stuart. But all along, from the opening note I passed you, I've let you draw your own conclusions. The line between that and lying now seems more equivocal than it did before I turned thirty. What good is it to claim that I never misrepresented myself to you, if I never presented, either?

Oh, love. If all I had to do now was admit, make out that we two stole your baby. If I could say: my husband, all along, was the barren one. That we two, in sickness and health, in love so deep that it reached bottom, colluded to dupe you. That he told me: go find someone, someone brilliant, soft, crystal in temperament, kind. That I found the most intelligent, gorgeous seed imaginable to use. (Beautiful isn't enough: I see your tightening lids, the flush of your cheeks as you tense under me. Brilliant doesn't suffice: your leaps are like nothing I will see again.)

If only we had stung you for a little fertility. I could have lived with that on my conscience. Isn't that love, when it comes down to it? The old pollen trick? Mutually profitable trade, exploitation. I give you pleasure to match your inbred fantasy, and take, in return, a painless biopsy, a little tissue you will never miss. I could forgive myself for having tried to steal your genes.

But that isn't how it went. That wasn't how I came to you. It's exactly as I told you long ago: Herbert is fine. I'm the one with something wrong. He could leave me cleanly by anyone's rules of fairness. Give me the severance payoff, go land a twenty-five-year-old with all her parts working as advertised, and even now start a family. That's what all the tests showed. But, good radical skeptic, I didn't believe the tests. I had to run my own. All I needed to disprove them was the perfect man.

I told you I never lied to you. I wanted you, wanted to give myself to you from the moment I toweled dry your angelic hair. But from the start, want was couched in hysterical denial. I thought we might remake physiology, you and I, if we were fierce enough. All selfless and abject, but everything I ever gave you I handed over with an eye toward the impossible return on investment, your saving me. You see, I've never wanted anything in my life as I want to be a mother. Think of the deepest desire you have ever felt. Then let it last unanswered every day for ever.

He looks up from the page, up where the walls meet the ceiling. She means discovery. Science. An urge greater than what I am after: in vivo. And she will never have it.

All this makes what I did even worse. I loved you, I love you this minute. Stuart, believe none of this but that. I would retract, qualify beyond recognition, to be able to promise you again all the mutual evers we have ever given each other. That's really why I came by. Not to tell you about my going: to stare you in the face, get you to swear that you will never leave me.

The most selfless love I ever felt was self-serving. The deepest altruism I am capable of feeling is still after something, the thing I was after in you. You were going to rewrite the rules for me, or at least explain, at cell level, why I'd been singled out, left with a desire beyond solving. But you couldn't do that for me. You could do nothing for me but love me.

You have cause to trust my truths less than my lies, but believe me. Your love has become, despite my best self-interest, as necessary, as desperate, as the little window of time that we've had. I seem to have reached a pitch of knowledge with you that I will never know again. But I'll never be without it entirely, now. I see you teaching our little girls to sing rounds. I watch us selecting chemistry sets for them for birthdays, together, carefully. Oh God. It will break my heart to go on. I'll never get through this. You've let me see what it might have been like to have a real home.

I am leaving to be with a man who, during the course of my hysterical year, looked the other way. Nothing, *nothing* in it for him. He knew what I was going through—my refusing the proof of sterility. He let me sneak, granted me the dignity of pretending not to know, and when pretense became impossible, arranged to leave. And still, he booked a place for me, should I want to leave with him. I'm leaving because I'd like for once to follow something other than the calculus of personal gain. I'm not trying to be worthy of him or to offer myself to sacrifice. You see, for whatever the sloppy term means, I love Herbert. I loved him for years before I fell for you. His is the only love I can carry through without invalidating the whole shooting match.

I've made some noises about being taken on at the university twenty miles from where we're heading. It won't be much, but perhaps Herbert will agree to follow *me* for the next move. We move a lot in this country, don't we? So know I will still have our work, in some form at least, to compensate me for all I have lost in you. I will read about you in the lit, and the children Herbert and I adopt may well yet read about you in the texts. Stuart, I hope it. I know it. But you must agree that that can be all the contact we can allow.

It seems you're going to force me to get all the way through this. But I will not leave without asking what I came here to ask. Friend, love me. Marry me, in some other, hypothetical life? Barring that (and I understand perfectly if you refuse), think of me sometimes, and of the time we had. It was a time. How much will still happen to you! Tell the woman you end up loving all about me. Never let her live a day for granted. And prove to the gold bug that it is ingenious enough to crack itself. You have cause, so have we all, for joy.

He flips the page, as if everything she has written might still be canceled out by one more amendment. But she has written nothing more except "Sorry to have spoiled a beautiful notebook." The record has run out while he read. It was in the high twenties when he entered. If she'd put it on from the beginning, as fortification for her act of mercy killing, he must have just missed her. She is still in town, at the building perhaps, cleaning out her desk. He could intercept her, pretend not to have seen the note. Incite that change of mind she seems to half hope for in every paragraph. Or he could help her, just this once, to locate the sequence for love.

He stares blankly at the stacks of journals for several inaudible variations before he sees something else there. Another, out-of-place publication: a goodbye gift, a chaste kiss between yearning cousins, the pocket edition of *A Field Guide to Flowering Plants*. He searches the front pages for an inscription. She has indeed left a message there, the only possible one. In her irreproducible script she has written, "Flowers have names." But neither book nor letter—nor any communication in his possession—bears Jeanette's signature.

He flips through the book. It opens, at random, or perhaps to where she has creased the spine, to a picture of a flower—delicate, blue-purple petals piled up along a thinning stalk. He remembers having seen it before, in another, hypothetical life. The only clue to her whereabouts, her one return address. The caption gives both scientific and popular names. "*Polemonium van-bruntiae.* Jacob's Ladder."

XXVIII

The Placebo Effect

Everything she writes is borne out. Ulrich circulates a note the next day, announcing Dr. Koss's departure just before term's end. With admirable dexterity, the head of the all but annulled Cyfer manages to praise the woman's contribution to the team without once giving the reason for her leaving or mentioning her destination. For once, Ressler is left with more knowledge than information. The chief gives the note a day or two to sink in, then calls an emergency meeting. Ressler is the last to arrive. The other three are waiting for him.

"Right to it, then," Ulrich begins with more force than conviction. "Is there any point in holding this thing together?"

Ressler looks at his boss, understands. The practice of science is less about sudden shifts of insight or repetitive hours of irreproachable lab practice than it is about funding. Always a subtle parasitism on patronage. Each year's grants deadline hastens the day when the question of whether a piece of work gets done will rest exclusively with the impartial peer review.

Ulrich's poll is clear: have we still a chance to go up against the massive labs, Big Biology? Or is this curse of defection fatal? Woytowich keeps his counsel; he's ready to return to teaching, rating TV—the life of the embittered divorcer. The continuance of the project is to him a matter of immense indifference. Ressler is also tacit, ready to be dismissed. It takes Botkin's eloquent intercession on his part to recall Stuart to unfinished business. She gives the group a rundown on the state of the cell-free system, including an abstract of the conceptual breakthrough she and Ressler hashed out just days before, at the precise instant when Jeanette sat in the barracks writing her *Abschied*.

She does a better job presenting than Ressler could have. At last, when it is too late, Ulrich's eyes widen. He has been sitting on a resource beyond anything in the equipment catalogs. This generating idea, the means into the composition, puts them as close to the heart of the problem as anyone. "We have three vacant salary lines, and we can get more. I can book over eighty percent of the remaining supplies budget. We can get you both full release time, as far as the department is concerned. Just tell me what you need."

Ressler says: "I need a week to think."

He goes home and sits for days, projecting himself into the ideal scenario: he and Botkin set to work on the synthetic mapping, in charge of a small army of eager assistants. They scoop the world. They lay out the first, rudimentary lexicon of life's language. They complete the table. They lay the capstone of the first material model of inheritance. Then he imagines himself the recipient, six months from now, through the mail, in an envelope with smudged return address, of one of those black-and-white hospital shots. A small, hairless, closed-eye cross between a planarian and Khrushchev, ID tag illegible. Like the words of organic nature hidden in the lookup table, this infant's features grow more inscrutable upon closer identification. It has no one's features, neither father nor mother. Like that complete, mechanical explanation, this complete, clean account of Jeanette's departure explains nothing.

His thoughts during this brief sabbatical return to one image: that man, ready to disappear without issue, whether or not his choice of companion in this life chooses to accompany him in exile. Is even Herbert's gesture part of the "pollen-trick"?

Then, into his third week of passive disengagement, Ressler wakes to a morning blazing in beautiful light. He showers, puts on clothes stiff with laundry soap, discovers: *I am ravenous*. He walks a brisk six blocks to the pancake house, ordering the full rancher's, trucker's, bricklayer's, red-blood, high-starch, artery-clogging special, and adores every mouthful. The waitress flirts shyly with him over the check. He tells her she is lovely, then backs away, smiling affectionately, helpless in human contact.

He walks to the Biology Building, taking the longest detour that still leaves him inside the twin cities' jurisdiction. He hears, for the first time since the days of the Home Nature Museum, how different the repeated calls of a single bird are. Are these tiny perturbations in the melody random, or do they mean something? He will make a study of this. The sound of automobile tires slopping the pavement suggests a review of physics, the equations for friction. He is struck by the shape of three identical poplars: might some mathematical expression guide the branching of trees?

By the time he gets to campus, it's clear, as clear as anything will ever be in the rough translation allotted him. The self-serving, pointless duplication of giant molecules created him in its own image, set him down here with only one order: Do science. Postulate. Put together a working model. Yet the hunt for the single, substantiating thread running through all creation is just a start. It's time for science to acknowledge the heft, bruise, and hopeless muddle of the world's irreducible particulars. This field, this face, this day are not just the result of tweaking the variables, twisting the standard categories. Every alternative on the standing pattern is distinct, anomalous, a new thing requiring a separate take on what is and might yet be. And for that, theories must diverge and propagate as fast as the wonder of their subject matter.

He reaches Botkin's office, enters without knocking. He surprises her in scowling over a popular magazine with a weekly circulation greater than the population of Austria in the year of her birth. Her grin of expectation at seeing him collapses into a demure, understanding "Oh." He walks to her desk where she writes, removes the magazine. He takes her hand in his, stroking and examining it at the same time. Why should skin lose its elasticity with age? If he were to pinch hers, it would stay bunched like stiffest muslin. He holds her hand between his for a moment, and says, "I wish I'd taken more meals with you when I had the chance."

She laughs sharply. "I wish I'd gotten more into you per meal." He leans over her desk and kisses her still forehead. He glances over her desk, her dark, filled bookshelves: this room, the place of so many discoveries, bathed in the light of midday, affords him the closest thing to religious reconciliation that empiric sensibility allows.

Age does not deprive her of the responsibility of having to play the group's advocate. "But what of your work?" she says. "It can't be left undone."

"Give it a year or two," he answers, calling her bluff. The process of directed chance is inexorable. "Half a dozen people will hit on it all at once."

"It's always the numbers game with your generation. Have you ever considered taking up gambling?"

Ressler laughs; it was *her* generation that saddled them all with perpetual probability. "I wouldn't know a blackjack if one hit me over the head."

"Boychick. You can take this project anywhere, you know. Dr. Ulrich, myself: we can get you taken on anyplace you like. Cambridge. Cold Spring Harbor. The Institute. A real lab. Wherever is best equipped. Finish what you've started. Say the word. I will write letters, call in favors. You can name terms."

He shakes his head: she, of all people, knows the nature of the work he must finish. "I don't think another laboratory would be appropriate just now." He listens to what he has just said, and adds, "Or needed, really."

"You would make an astonishing teacher, given time."

Teaching: yes, that might almost be close. But teaching is the most perilously slow way man has yet devised for conveying a message. "The student world won't miss me."

"But what about *you*?" Her eyes are a peculiar, fluid mixture of maternal distress and deep, secret satisfaction that this, her star pupil, has selected to set off into the dark. *For abiding is nowhere.* "You will be all right?"

"Without the prizes, you mean?"

"Yes. Without your Prize."

He wonders how it would feel to be able to sit back, late in the afternoon, and bask in genuine contribution. "I'll be fine." Even as he speaks this, a door opens in front of him and he gets his first foretaste of just how long, how uncertain an existence in pursuit of an unverifiable idea must be. That slow, tooling nucleotide freight, that packet boat threading itself through his ribosomes, when named out loud, carries nothing more than a letter to Jeanette, to the Blakes, to Botkin, to the rest of his colleagues living and dead. Nothing more than a letter to the world, all along. But he must post it alone.

She feels him waver, and not for the last time. But it is the last time she'll be around to be of any help. "*Mönchlein, Mönchlein. Du gehst einen schweren Gang.* Can I help you in any way? Can I *do* anything?" she asks, regressing to an accent so impenetrable he has to infer her words from her face.

"Yes," he says. "Yes you can." He slides over to the dark leather Viennese couch and lies down one last time. He slips his hands behind his head, crosses his legs at the ankles. Now. How does one get started in this enigmatic trade? "You can play me something."

The Lookup Table

I brought Dr. Ressler the names and addresses he asked me to find. He took them with a last, chivalrous compliment of my reference skills and entered them grimly into the hit routine that now hovered invisibly over the MOL data bases the way Bles's fire quietly waits to run loose through imaginary Flanders. "I've made you an accessory," he said, half to me, half to the console where he typed.

"No, *I* did." From the day I had signed on. I had also taken the initiative to retrieve a different set of addresses from the archives, and when Dr. Ressler reached a pause in his work, I produced my scrap of hurriedly copied chart:

BASE 1	BASE 2				BASE 3
	U	**C**	**A**	**G**	
	Phenylalanine	Serine	Tyrosine	Cysteine	U
U	Phenylalanine	Serine	Tyrosine	Cysteine	C
	Leucine	Serine	(Terminator)	(Terminator)	A
	Leucine	Serine	(Terminator)	Tryptophan	G
	Leucine	Proline	Histidine	Arginine	U
C	Leucine	Proline	Histidine	Arginine	C
	Leucine	Proline	Glutamine	Arginine	A
	Leucine	Proline	Glutamine	Arginine	G
	Isoleucine	Threonine	Asparagine	Serine	U
A	Isoleucine	Threonine	Asparagine	Serine	C
	Isoleucine	Threonine	Lysine	Arginine	A
	Methionine (init)	Threonine	Lysine	Arginine	G
	Valine	Alanine	Aspartic acid	Glycine	U
G	Valine	Alanine	Aspartic acid	Glycine	C
	Valine	Alanine	Glutamic acid	Glycine	A
	Valine	Alanine	Glutamic acid	Glycine	G

The genetic code for mRNA as determined in vitro, considered universal across all living creation. "That's the ticket," he said, his eyes on the paper, studying it for some revealing nuance that he and everyone else had so far overlooked. Without meaning to, I'd reduced him to embarrassment. He continued at that vanishing decibel. "Doesn't look like much, does it?" I told him I'd spent half an hour in the library learning how to read the thing before figuring out that it was a simple substitution in three variables. Two years would pass before I had even a rough, reflected image of what the table described.

"No question. It's an interesting time to be alive," Ressler said, tapping the sheet of paper as his documentary proof. "We have attained ancient wishes, the plan to dig all the way down, to the *bottom,* like little children in the backyard shooting for China. In twenty years, we've put together a comprehensive, physical explanation of life. Only, at every way station on the way down, the destination slips one landing deeper. Heredity is not only chromosomes. Then, not only genes, not only nucleotides. My generation found it was not only chemistry, not only physics. Seems life might not be *only* anything." He traced three rays with his fingers, verifying that UCG coded for serine. "No question. An intellectual achievement: those of us understandably prejudiced toward seeing life from chicken level, realizing that chickens are just the egg's way of perpetuating the egg."

Todd joined us in the control room, dusting his hands in a parody of manual labor well done. He came from the computer room, where he had been erasing the packs containing the old versions of the programs and data files. We had crossed the backout point. The only existing copies of the disks containing the complete financial histories of tens of thousands of people now carried the changes that Dr. Ressler and Todd had engineered into them.

Todd and I had spoken little in the handful of days since my return. The catalyst that brought me back was too pressing, Jimmy's hospitalization too real for us to waste time on private reconciliation. He offered no apologies, tried out no resolutions. We were both there to assist Dr. Ressler in getting Jimmy back under coverage. There was nothing to explain, to remedy. One night, seeing Jimmy for the first time since the stroke, returning to the offices to try to lose himself in an intransigent bit of machine code, Todd had weakened. "Would it be impossible for me to come home with you? One Day Only?"

I felt myself waver at his exhausted attempt at humor. "I don't think that would be a good idea."

"You do know that the lovely Ms. Martens and I are—"

"It's no business of mine." I did not want any news on the matter. Were what? Married? Divorced? History? It no longer concerned me. Annie too had tried to mumble something about intentions and ignorances and getting past misunderstandings. After the second blanket forgiveness I gave her, she stopped trying to approach me about anything but technical matters. In fact, none of us had much occasion to talk about anything except the specifics of our data terrorism. For the first time since I started visiting, actions ran ahead of words.

But that evening, as Dr. Ressler inserted the executive address list into place and Todd joined us in the control room, dusting his hands after putting the original, unedited disk packs to sleep, we were at last forced to sit down with each other as we used to, thrown back on the old, limited compensation of talk. Todd took my scribbled sheet of hieroglyphs from Dr. Ressler. As he looked it over, trying to catch up with the conversation, the professor slipped in his last bit of pedagogy for his only graduating class. "The spookiest thing about the code is its contingency. Some order in it, the symmetries of significance. But matter very well might have missed hitting upon even this configuration, no matter how large the reservoir of time it had to move around in. It might never have arrived at even this bootstrap translation had initial conditions been even a hundredth of a percent different. Or even exactly the same," he said, with a wicked glance at me, setting in motion the chain of idea-links that would eventually make me lose a year to the study of variation.

"But we got the sucker now," Todd said, facetious emphasis on the plural pronoun; nothing could be further from his field of expertise than this cryptic chart.

"Yes, we have it now," Ressler said, interpreting the phrase a little differently. "Perhaps other codes arose at the same moment, but this is the one that won out. It will never happen again; too much inertia now. Places we can't get to from here. Unlike what they teach in schools, the master builder can only proceed by patching onto existing patches."

"Having recently authored some pretty ugly kludges myself, I am glad to hear that."

Ressler extended the idea. "Efficiency and accuracy are not the same thing. Like it or not, life can only revise itself like a library saving or pitching books strictly on the basis of how frequently they've been checked out." He spoke obliquely to me, tailoring his metaphors to an end I could not then see. "We like to think of nature as unerring. In reality, everything it does is an approximate mistake. Its every calculation is short-term, a quick fix. 'Kludge' is right, Franklin." Under the shadow of what we were about to launch, the rules of decorum were changing.

"Take our species: the apex of engineering. We've all but completed our systematic destruction of the whole, buffered web. The evidence is there, for anyone paying attention. Even if we stopped this evening.... And yet, something in the joy of building—something in my inherited, egoistic firmware—still insists that we also possess the first, flawed, rough prototype that might, in time, take nature beyond the knee-jerk, blind short-term. You see, we can *project,* unlike any other postulate in nature, unlike nature itself. Model. Foresee. Think. But we have no one to help us make our projections wise."

He stubbed out a butt and checked his watch. "There is talk in the genetics community about the Human Genome Project. Sequencing, base by base, the entire five-thousand-volume DNA string. But whose string? Yours? This fine woman's here? What of the volumes for gray whales, horned toads, diatoms, four million species in all, lost by the thousands while we talk about them? Even the complete library, unattainable, will never begin to hint at the books, the stories the string might have produced."

Todd, my Todd, stood up, realizing what was at stake all around him. Life was suddenly too real to get out of alive. "Christ. What do we ask for, then?" Frantic, he asked the man he loved blindly, the woman he cared for a little, the general night—anyone who might answer. The question tore him like a marathoner's cramp, his rib trying to free itself from imprisonment in its side. I never loved him more than at that moment.

"What do you mean?" Ressler asked, elsewhere, years away.

"I mean: we have this office sewn up; the records are in our power. A Defense Department contractor, a major financial institution, a dozen municipal outfits. Five years of transactions. Half a billion dollars would vanish into a giant Mylar null if we say so. We could take a day of data, scramble it beyond all recognition. 'What's a day, *one* day, worth to you?' What do we ask for? A new Clean Air Act? Save the Whatever-it-is Seal?" Ressler chose his moment to say nothing. Todd looked at me, his voice wobbling into the shimmies. He assumed, all at once, the entire, terminal, toxic clot the race had laid over the place. The anguished understanding that he might, possessing these files, cut a deal, force a rescue on one bit of the botched job, was like alcohol in an incision. Todd was in real pain, drowning in causes. "An industry-free zone in the Antarctic? Ban the personal AK-47 from over-the-counter sale? Free food for the starving? Russians out of Afghanistan?"

"U.S. out of North America?" I suggested. It helped briefly to undo the urgency, to thin the tangible sickness calling on all sides for instant cure.

Ressler took my handmade chart back from Todd and gave it one more glance before answering. "Yes, the only question worth asking, now that we've all turned activist." This is the sense if not the sound of his words as he sang them: we have it now, have extracted knowledge from information, and it's not enough. We need to ask ourselves what we want to be when we grow up. We need that thing, that arithmetic of ecology that should have preceded knowledge, too easy, too obvious to bear repeating, too embarrassing and indicting to mention by name. The lookup code for care. "I suggest, seeing as how everything is already at stake, that we ask for the one essential in the triumvirate that life is too large and crucial to care about."

Todd looked at him without comprehension. "Meaning?"

The baggage of the gene, the curse of populations. "Keep to the original plan. Ask for Jimmy."

We sat in silence, reluctant to take the machine on-line, to bring up the doctored version of programs whose results, both digital and analog, we had no way of forecasting. Todd retrieved a sketchbook and began doing portraits, lightning contour studies as controlled as anything I'd ever seen him do. Dr. Ressler surprised us both by asking to keep two. We dragged our heels, postponing the launch for a few seconds, and we all three knew it. I half-jokingly suggested that we wait a few more days, until the anniversary of Morse's first public telegraphic message on the line between Washington and Baltimore. The notion tickled Dr. Ressler, but by that point he could only laugh gamely and say, "I dearly wish we could."

Delay was no longer just a question of losing time, of being outraced by the hospital collection bureaucracy. We had systematically destroyed all chance of returning to the old program. The files were gone. We could allow the vested interests

607

no other program to fall back upon, or our changes would be quickly suppressed before they could produce their desired effect. We could run the new version or nothing at all. And running nothing at all, as Todd pointed out, would be the equivalent of performing a lobotomy on a chunk of the city's working interests large enough to create a seizure throughout the rest of the interdependent network.

"That first remote message," Dr. Ressler asked, stubbing out another butt and starting anew. "Was it really 'What hath God wrought?'"

"That's how the books report it."

Todd snorted. "Probably backstopped. Jimmied up after the fact." His inadvertent verb stopped the conversation. He fiddled with a CRT contrast button. "Sorry. The fellow must be on my mind."

We rehearsed for the last time how we would put our claim once our variant system software was in operation. Dr. Ressler said, "We haven't talked about it yet, but we ought to try to minimize prosecution, once the project has had its run."

"Ha!" Franklin discounted. "Information Age criminals never get prosecuted. They get hired on as consultants to the DOD."

Dr. Ressler smiled; that was the precedent. "All the same, I'll link your immunity to the other conditions. Should push come to blow, you two and Annie haven't the first idea of how this bug slipped into the works. As far as you are concerned, you don't know your ASCII from your ALGOL."

"What about you?" I said, indignant at the suggestion that we scatter and leave him alone, answerable to everything.

He smiled and exhaled. "They can't do anything to me," he answered. "I'm already spoken for."

Willfully or just ordinarily oblivious, we went on to other matters. "Well, as long as I still know you for another day yet," Franklin cackled, "can I ask you one thing?"

"Name it." His voice acknowledged that he still owed us an explanation. He knew what this last petition to the Question Board would be: the same question that had started us here, before love, before knowledge, before disaster.

Todd began gingerly enough, accelerating only slowly into a semblance of courage. "I understand . . . I can see how one might not be able to trap certain feelings off in a side panel. I mean, I can see how, if the attraction, if the need were large enough. . . ."

608

He shot me an involuntary glance. "That a person might choose to go on caring, as if . . ."

"As if it still counted?" Dr. Ressler assisted.

Something broke in Todd, and his urgent attachment to the man, his innate need to prove that neither of their disappearances was inevitable, flooded the room. "I can understand the torch-bearing. Celibacy. Self-denial. But son of a *mother*. . . . It seems to me that the worst thing, the worst hurt anyone could possibly have inflicted on you, shouldn't have been enough to. . . ." He trailed off, afraid at the end to ask.

But he had as much as asked already. Dr. Ressler had only to coax him to put it into words. "Enough to do what?"

"To make you give up science." Todd's eyes swam with confusion. Shouldn't you have thrown yourself into it with redoubled effort? How could you desert the one place that might have given you some comfort?

It was Dr. Ressler's turn to be surprised. This was not the phrasing, not the question, he expected. "Oh," he said, alerted into softness. "But I never quit science."

Franklin and I exchanged astonishments. Todd dismissed him bitterly. "I mean something more than keeping up with the journals."

"So do I." The professor returned a self-conscious grin. "Look. Analysis depends on breaking down complex hierarchies into understandable parts. That's indispensable to good science, and I did it for years. Even got a paper out of it, as you junior sleuths insist on reminding me. But analysis is just part of the method. When you catch a glimpse of your smallest, discrete components, and even these don't explain the pattern you are after, sometimes the situation calls out for another motion, a *synthetic* cycle.

"Remember John Von Neumann?" he asked. " 'Yes, it is obvious'? The sharpest systematic intellect of the century. Games theory, contributions to quantum mechanics, father of digital computer software." He gestured through the two-way mirror into the computer room, suggesting that something of those old language generations still floated around in the newest machines. "Codeveloper of the hydrogen bomb and advocate of the preemptive strike. Once told *Life*, 'If you say why not bomb them tomorrow, I say why not today? If you say today at five o'clock, I say why not one o'clock?' Claimed to have invented a whole mathematical discipline while riding in a taxi cab. Wrote a pivotal book, published posthumously by my old I-state research university, called *Theory of Self-Reproducing Automata*, in which he proves that machines can be made complex enough to copy themselves.

"Von Neumann, the cleverest product evolution has yet offered, thought that the language of the functioning brain was not the language of logic and mathematics. The only way we would ever be able to see the way the switches all assembled the messages they sent among themselves would be to create an analog to the language of the central nervous system." He fell silent, perhaps wondering whether sheer cleverness is ever enough. "The firmware language of the brain. That's what I have spent the last twenty-five years pursuing."

The revelation stunned us. Todd rubbed his temples. "I don't get it. No institution? No grant? No laboratory? What are you doing here?"

Ressler laughed. "It's not a particularly popular or accredited line of research these days." He held up a finger, holding the floor. He went to his attaché case, brought it back to the table, and unzipped it. It poured forth, like a flushed warren, long, stiff, manila-colored, heavily penciled-over scores. Musical scores. "This one is a woodwind octet," he announced self-consciously. "Look here. I stole this bit from Berg. But he stole a similar bit from Bach, so I'm safe from lawsuit."

Todd flipped through the penciled staves, looking for some explanatory key. I collected myself first. "You're a composer," I said, a thrill coursing at the forbidden word.

"Yes, I guess I am." He sounded as startled by the revelation as we were. "I even went back to school awhile, although the pieces have remained hopelessly amateur."

"And?" I asked. I could not help myself, took his hand between mine. Nothing he could say or do would ever surprise me again. "Research results? Anything to write the journals about?" Could there really be another language, cleaner than math, closer to our insides than words?

He answered me figure for figure. "Precious few conclusions, so far. Soft, slow passages more effective when contrasted with loud, fast ones. Nothing much more definitive. But bear in mind, the field is still in its infancy."

Todd, recovering his wits at last, plied him with enthusiastic questions. What had he written, and how much? Lieder, chamber works, symphonic? Problems of instrumentation and registration, color, timbre. The trade-off of genre. Tonal? Serial? Aleatoric? I tried to follow this tech shoptalk but found myself hearing something else, absolutely silent: a monk, late twentieth century, working in total isolation, locked in a cell for longer than I could imagine, a lifetime, just composing, trying to emulate, recreate, variegate, state, consecrate the sound he had once heard while standing on his front porch on a spring morning, about to enter, thinking his love waited for him inside. I thought of all the experimental, heuristic, and botched compositions that kept him company over long years, and how, whatever the orchestration, form, choice of language, all pieces amounted to love songs, not just to a lost woman, but to a world whose pattern he could not help wanting to save.

What he had done, how he had chosen to spend his energies, really was science. A way of looking, reverencing. And the purpose of all science, like living, which amounts to the same thing, was not the accumulation of gnostic power, fixing of formulas for the names of God, stockpiling brutal efficiency, accomplishing the sadistic myth of progress. The purpose of science was to revive and cultivate a perpetual state of wonder. For nothing deserved wonder so much as our capacity to feel it.

I did not know the letter names yet, but I gathered that this biologist had discovered that A, T, G, and C spelled out endless variations on the old Socratic imperative in the cells. To say that the variants came from the same command was not to say they came to the same thing. Each still had to be identified in its particular texture. For that, one could only remain alert, stay flexible, keep deep down, work. All human effort now hung on the verge of revealing something unexpected, from the simplest of beginnings. The system ran undeniably toward randomness, but along the way, a steady stream of new nuances accumulated, each complete in its complexity, each incorporating the issuing theme. Dear Goldberg, play me one of *my* variations.

And at that moment, losing the thread of the conversation, I blurted out that colossal contemporary irrelevance: "Have you had any pieces performed?"

Dr. Ressler looked as nervously delighted as a little boy about to do his talent show number. "Opus One debuts tomorrow," he declared. "The sole work by which I hope to be remembered."

611

He punched up the system time on the screen, and we were struck by the work still left to do before the arrival of the day shift. "Oh Jesus," Todd let out.

The geneticist-turned-musical-recombiner threw his portfolio back together. "Sorry. My fault. That's what happens when you begin to solve the globe's problems. Before you know it, it's a quarter to six in the morning."

We fell to the cleanup tasks. I shredded the printouts of our last-minute test runs. Todd dummied up a console log, leaving no clues about the nature of the program that would soon be executing. And Dr. Ressler performed his *coup de grâce*. He selected, at random, a string of zeroes and ones deep in the system firmware. Using it as a cryptographic key, he ran the sequence against the program code of the impostor routines, storing down the scrambled product. Then he manually single-stepped into the loading procedure a pointer back to that random sequence, so that the scrambled programs would be deciphered into intelligible code when and only when they fed into the machine at run-time. When the corporate programmers went into the packs the next day to list the files and see where the unexpected behavior came from, they would find only gibberish. The trick was not uncrackable, but would slow the reversing process down.

The self-enciphering spread across acres of digital storage. "All right," he said, when the task came up complete. He took a deep breath and lifted a significant eyebrow. "Time to collect the songbooks." Our bit of genetic engineering was done. For better or worse, Franklin brought down the last remnant of old firmware. We held our breaths like rocket scientists as he attempted to boot the complete, new system. The status indications flashed one by one across the console without producing any unexpected warnings. Up came what seemed to be the old, original cold-start screen.

Ressler, ensuring that his name would be the only one traceable to this new boot, used two fingers to type it in. The screen prompted "password:" and echoed its demure x's as he entered his. It waited an ungodly whole minute, long enough for us to realize that a crash now would leave us with Jimmy on the street, his mother without a mortgage, and the three of us plus Annie in prison. Then, having put the fear of God in us, the system at last decided to flash:

System Date and Time: 05/15/84   06:35.45
User sressler logged in.
Last user logout was 00/00/00 at 00:00.00

Command?

Uncanny. We had created a new species, registering its own day one. No previous user. Ressler had even added the humorous touch of patching in a new version number for our new animal. But when he answered the command prompt with the standard request to bring up the start of the day's on-line processing tasks, up came what cosmetically resembled in every respect the old operating system. And yet it was only a simulation.

We breathed again. At least it ran. If the wrinkles we had introduced behaved in context the way they tested out in isolation, we were in business. Ressler grinned, as if Opus One had never caused him the least stress. "Looks good on this end." He produced, from behind the CPU where he had stashed it who knows how long before, a bottle of our old favorite drugstore vintage and the requisite paper cups. "To our friend's physical therapy," he proposed. And we clinked wax rims.

"To musicians and physicians," Todd added, and we sipped again.

Two sips to the wind, it was my turn. "To the language of the central nervous system."

At the Cadence

What would I add to the list of things we did that night? How would I interpret the account, two years and a handful of evenings after the fact? We thought to engage in a very old-fashioned gesture, or one so modern as to still be, like music, in its infancy. We acted according to a new complex mathematics, one dependent on the tiniest initial tweaks. The attempt was an absurd mismatch of scale—the notion that the entire community was accountable to the infinitesimal principle of a single life.

I would say: at the same moment that we tried to bring our premise into being, we were also testing its validity, objectively, if not without passion. We worked on the same problem that had occupied Dr. Ressler from earliest adulthood. Now that he had half-unraveled it, he concluded that the bulk of the text down at ATCG level was still in the infinitive: to look, to want, to stand amazed. We simply read those verbs out loud, extending the synonym list. To try. To investigate.

On the day I heard about Dr. Ressler's death, I posted a quote, one of my last, about the God of the scientists making men in his own image and setting them here with the single command to go and figure out how everything worked. Tonight, I would sneak fugitively into the library and add a complementary quote by the same author: "Trouble throughout the modern age has as a rule started with the natural sciences...." Or better: "Everything has become perishable except perhaps the human heart."

I learned that night, as we put our last touches on the on-line replacement, that science, the chief, most miraculous project of the modern world, the source of all the trouble, was itself a self-reproducing automaton. Empirical wonder did not stop short of those forbidden infinitives, to protect, to hope, to assist. They too were embedded deep in the coding problem. In order to say "Copy me," the string had first to say "Read me." Naturally such a command would result in time in the need to do science. What else could it become?

Doing science was simply a question of getting up the courage of curiosity. But the courage that made Dr. Ressler automatically interfere on Jimmy's behalf would have paralyzed Todd and me had we recognized its source. I can't pretend I had no idea. He hinted at it—his personal immunity, his already being spoken for. It's there, obvious, in his toss-off about being remembered by posterity. But that evening, while we finished our entry for the science fair, these were just words I couldn't afford to make sense of.

Tonight, the project that enlisted me is all but ready for print. I have finished my book lookup; the self-assigned homework is done. I have retrieved from the stacks the gist, at least, of what his science thought to retrieve from the world. I can now hear, in the set of variations, the shattering process he spent a life listening to. Like the best of reductionists, I can pull it apart into base molecules that, through a circus tumbling act governed by physical law, learn how to fill every conceivable niche of sound. All this, and it hasn't even come down to the wire; by the time-honored creative method of not eating, I have enough reserves left to start the job search or finance a full-scale retreat to the blood relations in Elkhart.

In my time away, I have managed a layman's guide to nucleotides, a miniature map of the man who so badly wanted in. I've come to the verge of declaring that the code codes only for the desire to break it. I've managed to name everything except the one thing, that evening, that Dr. Ressler *knew*. The Ur-text, the certain certainty that by itself motivated him, the in vivo foster parent of empiricism.

I'd seen the glow for months, but had chalked up his gradual return to solid things, to Todd's and my company. I should have known, by how quickly Dr. Ressler threw himself into Jimmy's cause, that he followed a fuller preparation, long in motion. He felt the mass packed in his abdomen. The composer knew, weeks before any physician, that the oncogene had been triggered. Information was going back under, was about to disappear again into silence. His long apprenticeship to science was soon to be rewarded with a Name Chair in oblivion. The pattern behind the pattern, the mutation shaped into something significant, the mystery, the only muse, the built-in desire for discovery, was coming home. He knew. There was a fire loose in the landscape, in the library.

XXIX

The Threshold Effect

In that museum in Rotterdam where my friend's broken-off research tour of the known world took him, a room away from Brueghel's great *Tower* (already crumbling in mid-construction around the base) hangs its twentieth-century counterpart, the contemporary reply to the scattering of languages: Magritte's *Threshold of Liberty*. The painting opens on a sealed room whose walls divide into panels. Each panel is itself a painted window, hinting at what lies on the other side, beyond the pane: sky, trees, fire, lace, more windows, or just a further wooden panel, the wall the painted imitation hangs upon.

In the center of the bare room stands a cannon, a paint cannon, but about to discharge itself all the same. The painting is an enigma, an absolute cipher. It is *about* enigma, the screen of knowing only through language, the threshold effect, the accumulation of small variations that transform a change of degree into a change of nature. Life stands on the threshold of some new twist it will never be able to name but must live through all the same. I will get no closer to liberty than thin explanation, this diminishing metaphor of panels porting images into the closed room. But it interests me to imagine Todd standing in front of that cannon just about to fire, shatter the painted chamber, flood the place with moonlight that until that moment had been only postulate. I stand next to him in the narrow gallery, looking, waiting.

My sabbatical is up. The last text I read says that the doubling time for genetic knowledge has dropped to less than a year. Twice the field it was the day I started studying. And I've nothing to put

616

down by way of synopsis except this belated discovery that I don't much care to die apart from him.

A Child's Guide to Surgery

The mutations we set into the system began to take effect the next morning. MOL data enterers, sitting down at their terminals, coffee cups in hand, saw on their screens the message: "Would you mind if your major medical coverage were instantly dropped? (Enter Y or N to continue)." An "N" looped them back to the identical question. A "Y" cleared the tube and put up a string of phosphors reading, "Then please make some noise about your colleague James Steadman," before freeing the terminal and dropping the users into their ordinary dialogues.

Midmorning, when the firm's remote clients began requesting digital transmissions, the modems behaved flawlessly, the reports came over the wires, and the remote printers executed the ledgers without hitch, until the bottom line. Just where the balance should have been, the slavish dot-matrix printer pasted a boldface, near-letter-quality Q:

Q: Your company is financially linked to an insurance organization that does not honor the spirit of its contractual commitments. What can you do to keep it honest?

A: Drop a line to the CEO below.

Underneath, the dumb printer knocked out the appropriate address. Two lines beneath, like the denouement sports score doled out only after the public service announcement airs, appeared the accurate but upstaged bottom line.

Surprise blits began to infiltrate banking facilities in distant parts of the city. Tellers presenting transaction receipts to customers found that the innocuous little slips, universally distributed for the express purpose of being instantly thrown away, carried the announcement that today in history a certain stroke patient in a hospital in a neighborhood across town was about to be turned out onto the street. The slips were still thrown away, but not before a few of the bottle-messages reached civilization.

By afternoon back at the MOL offices, the day shift's crisis man-

617

agement, printing out the first batch of the day's mass statements, noticed, after several hundred had been printed, something wrong. Each otherwise faultless statement contained, in the bottom strip of the universal financial form usually reserved for such stuff as "We wish each one of you a warm and personal New Year," the emergency signal: "A stroke victim is about to be cut loose." Just below came a random selection from the "Yes" pile Dr. Ressler and I had made from my stack of quotes of the day:

In a few years we have learned virtually to ignore things that would have petrified the world. . . .

Hark, the dominant's persistence till it must be answered to!

> For who would lose,
> Though full of pain, this intellectual
> being. . . .

I am sure that the power of vested interests is vastly exaggerated compared with the gradual encroachment of ideas.

> Care is heavy, therefore keep you,
> You are care, and care must keep you.

Le vent qui éteint une lumière allume un brasier. For a rough translation, please call . . .

Verses-turned-viruses under the pressure of environment. Each message contained a contact where curiosity could be directed. Some quotes were canonical, others more transient. We'd clipped from *Bartlett's,* the daily newspaper, private stock, selecting on how well they made anonymous tragedy real. Others we picked for the roll of the words. Still others had nothing to do with Jimmy. We just liked them, favorite bits of recognition.

The first, astonished operator to notice this issue of literature all over the credit union forms may have tried to abort and restart the statement run. If so, he got exactly the same result, with whatever parameters he called up the print job. A glance at the tampered file, any attempt to list its logic, showed it scrambled beyond recognition. The daytime operations staff faced a few unacceptable choices. They could go over the thousand statements by hand with a black magic marker. This would take prohibitively long and would raise more curiosity than the snippets themselves; worse, it would not look *professional*. They could fail to send the batch out at all, which would result in stiff penalties for failing to meet the DP contract. Or they could send the infected financial stubs out as is and hope, as with the personal New Year's greetings, that no one paid any attention.

This they elected to do, notifying the targeted insurance executives whose numbers appeared, assuring them firm to firm that this sabotage was not the work of MOL but of some runaway individual from within. When Dr. Ressler and Todd showed up for work that evening, they were taken into police custody.

I sat home alone that night, expecting the phone to ring. I had no idea what was happening to them, although I suspected they had been rounded up. Every ten minutes I had to check myself from going over to the offices, now doubtless crawling with software experts trying to crack Dr. Ressler's Chinese box. I scoured the city news, waded through the schoolchildren slayings and neo-Nazi resurgences, but there was no mention of anomalous mass-mail hijacking. I could not see the statements going out or eavesdrop over the relay circuits. I had no way of finding out whether we'd succeeded in grazing the banking industry with our tetanus prick.

When my doorbell went off, I almost tore a ligament. I opened without even checking. It was the last visitor I expected: Annie. "You shouldn't be here," I shouted. But I wasn't about to let her leave, now that she was. Annie was pale with excitement. Acting publicly and illegally, taking legitimation from the cause itself, was so new to her that she shook to talk about it. She was discovering the thermodynamics of pressure politics and wanted, that very evening, to expand into it like nature filling its abhorred vacuum.

I gave her the apartment tour. She was as surprised at my assemblage of escapist Victoriana as her lover Todd had once been erotically charged by it. She kept snatching looks between me and all the embroidery, as if I were having her on. We sat in the living room pouring drinks, the radio news on low in the background, polling the air for waves from the pebble we'd chucked into it. Annie was transformed on activism: could we succeed in saving Jimmy? If insurance companies ran at a profit, wasn't that essentially exploitative? Weren't the central money centers the same ones who were fanning the fires in Central America and Africa? I told her I didn't know.

I didn't mind her talking. It filled the space. At one point she stopped and, complete non sequitur, announced, "You know. I've been thinking a lot about all the talks you and I used to have. You might be right about at least one thing. Species don't hold static. They don't keep still." The first awful concession: she wasn't admitting anything else. But she let me know, made me take responsibility for ruining her faith for good.

When she made to leave, I walked her to the door. There—having written down everything else from that year, I can hardly suppress this—we fell into a fumbling, confused moment, and all at once found ourselves kissing. I don't know who *I* was putting my mouth to. But Annie was definitely kissing *me,* attaching to me by her hands with the same excitement of discovery she'd had on arriving. We struggled and broke off. She looked at me, imploring, needing, hoping I might now ask her back in. I stood still and let her leave as if nothing had been transacted.

On day two of the information blitz, the mechanical messages were shuffled and sent out again a little differently. Dr. Ressler had inserted a clever routine that made sure, even though the idea-genes were distributed randomly, that no target received the same message twice. The enhanced statements went out to a new batch of recipients. Our doctored programs also began dispatching little-known facts: premium-to-payment ratios for major medical plans in the U.S.; number of days in a hospital bed required to wipe out average life savings.

I went to work but could concentrate on nothing. Ignorance of what was happening to Todd and Ressler together with my anxiety over Jimmy incapacitated me. I remember going to pieces over a trio of submissions left in the question submission box: Q: How old is the minicam? Q: How many rats are living under Brooklyn? Q: Should we go to Mars? That afternoon I was picked up for questioning.

Annie was interrogated separately, as well as a first-shift data entry clerk, completely innocent. Both were released in hours. I do not know what the others said. Aware that Dr. Ressler must certainly have been somewhere nearby, denying that anyone else had any involvement in the matter, I laid out exactly what I'd done and why. I said I had no idea at all how to stop the runaway software. That much was true.

For safety's sake, only Dr. Ressler knew. He had written the patches so that they would all unwrite themselves like the magician's self-vanishing knot the instant a certain word was typed at the command prompt on the system console. The word existed nowhere but in his memory. I don't know what Ressler told the authorities, but I know that he stopped short of dealing for Jimmy's reinstatement, a proffered swap that would have converted us all into felons.

I'm not sure which terrified the vested interests more: the suggestion that masses of sensitive data might be threatened—a notion that none of our messages even hinted at—or the acute embarrassment produced throughout the financial sector by this amateur theatrical showering of Milton and Robert Browning on the upper stories of the gleaming, inviolable World Trade buildings. In any case, no one had any use for me as soon as it became clear I could not help them stop the flow of messages. They sent me home over my own protests of guilt.

The press, a day late, caught wind of the event, and I was videotaped in conjunction with the story, walking down Vernon Boulevard. I felt strangely exhilarated, dosed with questions I had no intention of answering. That rush accounts for my looking so unlike myself in the pictures on file. Beautiful. At home the next morning, I watched myself on the breakfast sampler of area news. An hour after the spot aired, I got a call from Keith, enormously amused by the escapade. "I did my part, doll. Called the front desk of the villainous outfit for a full explanation the minute I saw your pretty mug interfering with our agency's morning spots." Suddenly scared, not at what would happen to me but at what would never happen again, I begged Keithy to stay in touch. "Never fear. Every Christmas, a card. Like clockwork."

I don't know how many bewildered New Yorkers phoned in for a gloss on Beaumarchais or a verification on our claims figures. Perhaps a mildly curious couple dozen. Public rallying on the stroke victim's behalf amounted statistically to nil. Naturally. Ours was an equivocal case at best. Had the press not picked it up, it would have been less than insignificant, less than those people with the sandwich boards crammed with schizophrenically tiny writing who parade their imagined grievances in front of City Hall every day for twenty years. The city is full of suffering causes beyond affordability.

The press, for its part, barely mentioned Jimmy except as a side-thread to the paisley, surreal cloth. What they found locally sensational was that this mailing campaign had been a *computer* crime, then still a novelty. Reporters circled with weird fascination around the violated machine, its ephemeral files, the proximity of Dr. Ressler's virus to a network of sensitive information. When the hacks asked our targeted insurer for a comment, a self-assured executive, who'd had a full day to look over the paper trail on the matter and who thought that discretion was the better part of value, shrugged in front of the camera and said, "The man is covered. There was a clerical foul-up between ourselves and the hospital that we cleared up some time back. I don't understand any of it."

Neither did seven eighths of the sane world, let alone half of the breakfast television audience. We were a brief, bizarre human-interest trailer, one of those thirty-second spots that mitigate the impact of the day's real news. Our act of criminal conscience was newsworthy only until the mass of continuous diversion that passes for current event rendered it archaic trivia-game stuff. We would join the marginal list of those instantly forgotten local celebs that well-informed people, if they recall at all, suspect themselves of inventing. On day three, when the whole eccentricity was already dead, a city news reader closed the books on the story by reciting a canonical quote meant to parody our statement telegrams: "Across the wires, the electric message came/'He is no better, he is much the same.'"

At the same moment that the company spokesman denied any payment problem, Dr. Ressler surrendered the unscrambling word. They released him and Todd, a transaction that never would have happened had the two of them not been the only ones able to return the system to listable, patch-free status quo. Both were instantly fired, ironically losing, along with all other benefits, the coverage they had won back for Jimmy.

They might have fared a lot worse had it been easier to formulate a charge against them. They could not be prosecuted for vandalism. Only cosmetics had been touched, and returned unscratched. An employee in a position to do so had simply taken it on himself to redesign the corporate product. They could not be hit for electronic blackmail, as no one had ever leveled any threat. They might have been sentenced—and I with them—for malicious moralizing, capricious use of quotes. But wisely deciding that the best thing was to let the story die out as soon as possible, and perhaps afraid of vestigial viruses still in the system, neither MOL nor any node of the offended financial network spreading along the Eastern Sea-board leveled any case.

I worked quietly, wondering if I too would be fired. My col-leagues, however, came to my unqualified support. Everyone I worked with was sufficiently acquainted with my character to know beyond doubt that I was not capable of being personally involved in such a passion play. I had simply let love temporarily turn my head, had fallen in with the wrong boyfriend. A healthy regimen of reference work would erase any blot still attached to me. Mr. Scott teased me about my public record for a few days, then dropped the matter.

Some weeks after the event, I came home to discover that my apartment had been visited. On the table, wrapped in abandoned sketching paper, was a bottle of our going wine, a book, and a note reading, "To paraphrase the saint: 'Nobody likes to burn.'"

I could understand the wine—a late toast to our having brought the cause off. The note, too, was self-explanatory: I was to let him back in if I wanted. But the book. It was a tiny collection of two dozen color plates, details from Brueghel's sprawling universe of children's games. Each enlargement showed one of the games from the painted catalog and an *en face* text description. A nostalgic invitation to recover our earlier, museum-going days. But his choice of subject was so brutally insensitive that I felt my face go hot and all I could think of was how I had stupidly failed to get back the copy of my apartment key I had given him.

I thought I would let any residual notoriety extinguish itself, then, after a month or two, try to contact Dr. Ressler. I'm not sure what I had in mind, what sort of friendship I imagined we two might still have, after all that had happened and failed to happen. He beat me to it. He called me at home, late one night, waking me from sleep. He, at least, was still on night-shift hours. He was halfway through his long, decorous apology for waking me before I realized who it was. "You!" I shouted stupidly, happily, into the receiver. It seemed physically impossible. De-spite his ability to write self-vanishing code that would send *Paradise Lost* out over modems, Dr. Ressler had always been acutely uncomfortable with telephones. I'd never seen him use one voluntarily and never dreamed he would ever call me. "You! Are you all right?"

He told me, in a few abstracting words, the details of his grilling and release. "The end of a promising career in the burgeoning field of information."

"I've missed you so much." I was still asleep, saying things that would make me cringe the next morning and for a long time after. Not anymore. Now I wish I'd said worse.

"You've missed your friend Todd," he said. The words lay in that crevasse between assertion and educated guess. He did not wait for me to deny. "Have you been by to see James?"

The silence on my end worsened by the second. The truth was, I had thought three times an hour for weeks about paying him a visit, but I could no longer stand seeing him that way. Dr. Ressler, mercifully as always, let me off. "He's getting some light motor skill back. It'll never be much, but he could not have been blessed with a better temperament to face the next thirty years. The slightest advance, and he's triumphant. They've transferred him to a good muscle therapy clinic." He gave me the address, which I wrote down eagerly but already hypocritically.

"Can we see one another sometime?" I asked. Shier than a teenager. "Meet somewhere? I'm almost out of squash."

He let out a little puff of air. "I wish I could stick around long enough to keep you in tomatoes." I didn't dare say anything. "Jan, that's why I'm calling. I wanted to tell you that I'm on my way back to the I-states tomorrow. I've signed on to a new research project, back with the . . . I can't really say the alma mater, can I?" I could hear his lip pulling up ironically. Far away, the faint cross-talk of a bad connection.

"You *what*?" The news was so extraordinary that all I could do was laugh with joy. "You what? Incredible!" Was science that forgiving? Yes, and why not? No field could expand so fast that return would be impossible, even after so long away. If the man was sharp enough, his learning curve steep, he might even have the relative advantage of the late starter. "I can't believe it. What will you be working on?"

Just as I asked the question, I finally woke. As he spelled it out, I anticipated him by a thin syllable. I was one of those contestants who knew all the answers, but only the instant that the cards are flipped over. "Jan, it's a cancer study."

I hung on the edge of making it out—a phrase in foreign but ghostly cognates, the language I myself would still be speaking if the populations hadn't drifted. The phrase book of runaway cells. I gripped the silence on the line, palpating it as if pressing the secret hard spot. The first thing I could think to say was, "Does Franklin know?"

"He's known for a while."

"Listen. I can dress in a minute. When do you leave? I can call a cab."

"I'd rather you didn't. And I've never been much for writing letters, either, I'm afraid."

"I love you," I said, without help, wide-awake.

This time his words lay in a further crevasse, between assertion and command. "You love your friend."

Then, nothing between that phone call and Todd's curt note. But no: Franker's postcard and his long letter were first, written first, anyway. I did receive one other communication in that blank time, that year I spent doing nothing, working, trying to rehabilitate my own light motor skills. A handwritten card from Jimmy, delivered care of the library where he remembered I worked. Half printed, half cursive, the letters look like a first, helpless effort in penmanship written with the opposite hand. As best as I can transcribe it, it says:

> Dear Jan, I thank you and all of you. I mostly expect that there are many things still ahead. And hard. But yesterday was it possible for one whole book page to get through. As you see, I can drive this pen too, though clutch pops some. My words! I'm getting so that anyone can mostly make me out.

I wrote him back but failed to say anything. I never wrote Ressler. I never wrote Todd until after he'd left the address. I never said anything I wanted to say to anyone. I've misinterpreted the whole set from the start. That table of data in the nucleotides isn't about reading at all. It's about saying, out loud, everything there is, while it's still sayable. The whole, impossibly complex goldberg invention of speech, wasted on someone who from the first listened only to that string of molecules governing cowardice. Obvious, out in the open: every measure, every vertical instant infused with that absurd little theme insisting "Live, live," and me objecting, "But what if it should be *real*? What if it all means something? What if someone should hold me to my words?"

I should have heard it, the night that amateur composer ordered me to. I listened to him disappear into dark fieldwork, this time as subject, on the other side of the instruments. He asked for nothing from me but a little music, a keyboard exercise from the next room over to ease him across his last insomnia. I knew the tune by ear, for years. I might have said something, might have made some noise.

The Perpetual Calendar

June 6: 1520. Henry VIII hosts a Renaissance extravaganza for arch-rival François I in an attempt to secure an alliance. The feast fails to bring about any lasting political effect....

1918. For the next nineteen days, the marine brigade of the American Second Division meet the Germans in the forested area of Belleau Wood, in the Aisne region of France. Expending more than half their men to gain...

1944. Operation Overlord, involving the close coordination of 4,000 ships, 10,000 planes, 180,000...

2004. The planet Venus will make its next transit across the sun....

Political effects will be negligible. It feels as if I have done nothing but fiddle masochistically with the card set, waiting for the resulting pain to convince me that things have happened. A desperate, deluded attempt at triangulation: the old Laplacian engine applied to today in history. If one samples enough points, writes out all the differential equations governing the days' independent paths, the resulting vector might be somehow solvable, the long consequence lying patiently in the repetition might be revealed. The coward's hope that if I go over the three-by-five events again, I might catch the bit I missed, the bit that renders inevitable exactly what it was (and always had been) that was supposed to happen today, just what part that I was meant to play in it. I can add nothing to the June 6 dossier but a classified ad:

1986. Position Wanted. MLS. Years in the public service. Some programming experience. Hands-on knowledge of genetics. Good with data.

There are no more events to go over, no more data to manipulate. The data stream will only widen, deepen, strengthen in current; I can get no closer to where I need to be than these particulars. I lived a year, I lost a year, I spent a third in the archives. It's time to go back, to dust off the résumé.

When I started on this tour, I was afraid that the place he inhabited might be bigger than I could safely live in. I have confirmed that hunch by direct measurement. It is immense beyond surviving, larger than the space between brilliance and brittle stars. Older than the oldest soft tissue in the fossil record. As densely populated as a drop of water. More complex than anything I *can* imagine, as complex as self-reproducing automata. As long as the entire text of history's card file. As terrifying as the threshold of liberty. I have put it down here as a notch on a stick, afraid to name it any more closely than code.

I have lost them all, lost those few days when, as inimitable Annie said, we got our feet dirty, lost them by saying nothing at the critical moment. But I have at least this. This field notebook. My after-the-fact year of mapping. But the map is still not the place. I am ready to follow him there, all the way into the locus itself, without benefit of intermediary, to live in it for a moment, everywhere and nowhere, the space between pine and everglade, between adjoining nucleotides, disappearing with the rain forest, glazed with acid rain, vanishing like habitat, like the magician's knot, but carrying on, varying, learning by trick to subsist on poison, on heavy toxins if I can, living on just a little longer, shouting with all the invented parts of speech for a little assistance.

But how to get there: how can I find it? All at once it is clear, clear as the first, aperiodic crystal. The double helix is a fractal curve. Ecology's every part—regardless of the magnification, however large the assembled spin-off or small the enzymatic trigger—carries in it some terraced, infinitely dense ecosystem, an inherited hint of the whole. He said only what the texts say: the code is universal. Here, this city, me, the forest of infection on my hands, the sea of silver cells scraped from the inside of my mouth. Every word I have I knock out of its component letters. Every predication, every sculpted metaphor, sprung from the block. Let's save what life cannot. Play me, he asked, all he ever asked: play me one of *my* variations. What could it hurt to carry that tune a little longer? Perhaps I might be up to it after all.

XXX

Today in History

6/23: Midsummer Eve. Everything and nothing happened: one day, one gene, one enzyme, one reaction, one island in the perpetual calendar. I feel, with reasonable professional confidence, that I could extract if not the sum of the day's doctored console log at least a rough transcript. After a long while, one hits on the illuminating idea of building the room around the moonlight.

Today caught up with me a week ago. Last Monday. I had closed the notebooks and started in on the job search. My main problem in putting myself on the block was how to account for my year off without seeming to host some secret pathology that might flare up again at any moment. I tried to pass it off on the résumé as a school year, but my inability to claim any accredited course of study seemed conspicuous, to say the least.

But that did not stop me exploiting my old employers for my own purposes. On Monday, early, I went downtown to 40th Street and began researching the registers. I was looking for a certain kind of outfit—conservation, public awareness. Places that worked to preserve those stakes now dissolving. It seemed the career change of choice, whether or not there was still time left for it. By midafternoon, I had a dozen addresses. It was slow going, culling them by hand. The next time I job-search, the whole world will be on-line.

I broke for packed lunch and in the afternoon decided that I would need an interview suit to restore some of the credibility my résumé now lacked. I needed cash, and stopped at an automated teller that would take my bank card. I punched in my four-digit sequence and watched the screen flash "Incorrect code.

Please try again." Before I could reason with the machine, it cleared its screen and posted a new message: "Hello old friend. Here's an easy one." And out of that simple, vibrating speaker, designed to make no more than a few inarticulate flutes and beeps, came music. More than easy: I knew the piece before it even started. I knew the melody at once, both melodies as they entered, all three, four. A gathering of old friends, as easy to me, as familiar and close as my own name.

The Quodlibet

The Bach family, gathered at home, would begin with chorales and proceed to feats of extemporary combinatorics. One would start in with a popular tune, eighteenth-century radio music. Another would add, transposed, augmented, or diminuted to nestle down in perfect counterpoint, an older folk melody. A third would insert something racy, suggestive, even obscene, and a fourth might lay on top of all these a hymn. The words would fly in all directions, as would the piled-up melodic lines. But the whole would hang together, spontaneous, radiant, invented. *Discovered* harmony.

This is how he ends the set. No canon at the tenth, as the variation's position demands, although the snippets of trivial folk tune enter imitatively, in double counterpoint. No last flash of virtuosic brilliance. Just home: solid, radiant, warm, improvisation night with the family. Two of the folk strains—as recognizable as snatches of bus-stop melody heard this morning—have been identified from out of the thicket:

Ich bin so lang nicht bei dir gewest. Ruck her, Ruck her, Ruck her
I've been away from you for so long. Come here, come here, come here!

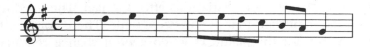

Kraut und Rüben haben mich vertrieben. ...
Cabbage and beets drove me away....

629

This song's second part also enters the contrapuntal fray:

Hätt mein Mutter Fleisch gekocht, so wär ich länger blieben.
Had my mother cooked meat, I would have hung around longer.

High-spirited, but as steady as creation gets. The musicologist Mellers quotes the best explanation of the effect in words. Thomas Browne again, the Doctor's religion:

> Even that vulgar and Tavern Music, which makes one man merry, another mad, strikes me into a deep fit of devotion, and a profound contemplation of the first Composer; there is something in it of Divinity more than the ear discovers. It is an hieroglyphical and shadowed lesson of the whole world. . . .

But there is another joke coded in the text, wrapped inside the tavern music. I've been away from you for so long. Cabbage and beets did it. Had my mother cooked up meat. . . . The complainer is the sarabande Base, back at last, in unmistakable outline underneath the flurry of simultaneous quotes. I've been a great distance, a long time gone. Sometimes unrecognizable. But it's not my fault; had my mother served up more than thin fare, all this circumlocution would never have been necessary. Bach's apology for not being a better cook. Molecular evolution excusing itself: had I been a little more skilled, I might have spared the world all this terminal variety.

Now no matter: the theme is back for good, in the left hand of the quodlibet, incarnate in the material of this last, apologetic child whose parent in no way could have foreseen it. The quodlibet changes all the previous variations after the fact. The irreducible is now less important than the irrecoverable. There comes a time in the search for the plaintext when even a chance rendezvous with the still encrypted cipher seems a glimpse, a real step in the hard passage on. The sense of all tune is to continue singing, in as many simultaneous melodies as possible. Come here, come here.

630

I'm home. In the innermost hive, inside the cell's thread, I never left. Was always there.

Quote of the Day

I stood on the sidewalk, gathering a crowd, alerted bystanders in a jaded city closing an amazed ring on the pavement around me. He had said, once, that it's infinitely curious that people are not infinitely more curious than they are. Here it was, his private lesson in inquisitiveness, remarkable enough to draw an audience, even in midtown.

Monophonic speaker playing its own harmonies: he had explained to me a long time ago how that might be done, how Bach himself had done it in the solo partitas. Just hit the right notes at the right time. With a little programming, everything is possible. But I couldn't in all of creation take in what was happening. Even while this bank-teller automaton spewed its music out into the city soot, I couldn't see how he, a year dead, could be lodged inside this circuit, playing to me. I clutched at the keypad of the machine, as if I could reply to him there. I felt the tunes running out and was powerless to keep them from reaching the last measure. They cadenced together, joke, chorale, folk song, Base. In the return of silence, the screen displayed: "Machine adaptation by SR." It cleared and wrote one more quote to compound the quodlibet: "He is a man. Take him for all in all." Another thirty seconds later, it changed again to read, "Please enter your transaction."

I yanked my card out in a daze. All the glands in my face opened and ran, without so much as polite consultation. I could still hear that music; it had never stopped. Something of divinity in it, beyond the ear. I stepped away from the machine, reaching a pitch of synthesis I will never recover. I took in the entire block in a single, vertical moment. The ring of bystanders in front of me blinked, grinning that ridiculous grin city people use in those few seconds when the danger of surviving lifts. A heavy man, medium height, thick glasses, indeterminate race, spoke for everyone. "What on earth was that?"

I was in the middle of such a convulsed colloid of sob and laugh that I could only get out the words by shouting. "I couldn't begin to tell you."

631

A Walking Tour of the Known World

I had to tell someone right away. But there was only one man I could possibly tell: the one I was supposed to take for all in all. Where was he in this world? How could I get there? Like an arctic tern on moving day, I swung uptown, toward that other information booth, the place where he had once told me, "Meet me here if we ever get separated."

I cut through the Park. My walk took forever; it didn't last long enough. The Park was just a simulation, a mere children's zoo of the full system. But I had been away from the real thing for so long that even this thin intermediary stood in nicely. It had been a long time since I had felt any sort of real link to chitin and chlorophyll. I had thought that words, the distraction of language, enforced a separation, banished me to the nowhere of descriptions. Crossing the Park, I realized that no living piece of tissue could keep its head up above the Second Law without the power of speech. In shape, function, unfolding: they were all shouting, speaking, feasting on words like lichen on rocks. Everything was a grammar, and we might come back in if we wanted.

I reached the Met at last, made my contribution, and practically ran to the wheatfield. He wasn't there. Of course not. But I had to go through the motion, for the time-lapse singing telegram Dr. Ressler had sent me was still an inch from my ear and I had to tell Todd while I could still hum. The painting, at least, was still around. I stood in front of it for a long time, thinking of the day we two had come to see it. It seemed a different object now, a completely changed composition. I had never seen it before. I looked at the harvesters, the gatherers, those just stopping for a meal, the man sprawled asleep under the tree, the two birds lifting up over the inlet of grain, the distant figures deep in the background, children at games again. Somewhere in my head, scattered by later atheism, a poem the nuns had once forced me to memorize tried to break the surface, an equation relating wheat and sleepers and time and reapers.

I wandered through the galleries, knowing I could not expect to find him there, having to content myself with the go-between of paint. I played with the idea, the inverse of the one that had struck me while cutting across the Park: everything ever painted—

tree-catalogued landscapes, still lives with fish, flesh, and fowl served up with a sprig of sliced lemon, interiors, abstractions, all backwater genres—was an attempt to classify, backdrive the alluvial branching, locate the common term of natural history. Even the endless crucifixions seemed more about anatomy—the suffering capacity of the body, the way the thumbs curved in toward the palm when the tendons were severed—than they were about metaphysics.

After a while I stopped noticing the paintings altogether, so much more diverse was the international, drifting crowd trying to decipher them. This sampling of people, muddying the halls from Egyptian to Expressionist, had been specially selected for extremes of characteristic. The varieties of human face began to seem almost comical. This random assortment of particulars had nothing at all in common. Each one had a privacy that defied and redefined all the others. My texts had it right: we differ more from one another than man does from ape.

I left in late afternoon, not knowing where to go, with the bank machine's message still in me, pressing to be ported. I stopped at another automated teller, but got nothing except the usual cash. I turned home, walking the whole way, miles, taking my life in my hands through the dangerous bouquet of neighborhoods, across that beautiful bridge, finding that slower, less accurate steps prolonged the afternoon message sprung on me.

But it was fading, unarrestable, going back to that place where wonder hides out from habituation. By the time I reached the Heights, late, after dark, it was just a sentence. Hello friend; here's an easy one. Still a block away from the antique shop, I saw the light on in the second story. Living, just existing, presses probability to the threshold of unlikeliness. I looked up at a window shadow, a violation of physical law, a miracle of coincidence that could be neither reverse-engineered nor repeated. I almost apoplexed letting myself in; the shape could mark only one person, the person I was out hopelessly tracking down. The only other one with a key. He was sitting in his favorite stuffed chair, head back on the antimacassar, under a soft, shaded, fifty-watt pool of light, reading my notebooks. "You!" I shouted from the door. "How did *you* get here?"

As if he had no other way of answering except with a musical riddle, he began whistling "Take the A-Train."

I dropped everything and threw myself violently on him,

grabbed hold, as if grip could arrest and fix this. It startled him, seeing me bare, begging to be spared. "What'd I do?" he laughed, protecting himself from the attack of my hands. "Tell me what I did."

We dispensed with talking for a record three minutes. Then, all I could find to repeat was, "This is impossible. I can't believe this."

The Question Board

"What's impossible?"

I told him. I skipped everything of importance—the year of enforced waste, the year of science. My quitting my job. The genetics texts. My anxiety over not hearing from him, then hearing, then not. I skipped everything, and started in with the bank machine playing the last *Goldberg*. "The quodlibet. He was *in* there, Franklin; I swear to you. Do you know what he told me?" I waited, put my hand to his chin, the same line of bone, and made him shake his head. "He told me you were a man. That I was to take you for all in all."

"He said that?" Franklin reacted in a show of disappointment. "Damn it. I had expressly asked for 'One man loved the pilgrim soul in you.'"

I reeled from the implication. "He's *alive*?"

Todd buckled his shoulders at my stupidity, my untreatable addiction to hope. "Janny, don't you see? I primed the pump myself, last week. He told me, when I went to see him in Illinois at the end, that he'd left a little virus on-line for you. He gave me the number that would bring it to life. Said I might use it if I ever needed to soften you up."

I took my hands from him, moved to a spot on the floor. No coincidence. Todd had cosigned on the telegram. "You never needed," I said, half to myself. "Never needed to soften."

"I've been punching into the damn tellers every afternoon, to see if you'd tripped it yet. Paranoid that someone was gonna pick me up for breaking and entering, recognize me as a monkeyer from way back. Don't you ever withdraw, woman? You above cash? Much relief this afternoon when you finally got around to it."

Matter-of-fact affectation, tough humor against the odds, as if the separation might as easily have been two days or twenty years. I dismissed the sixty-four thousand closest questions and asked,

"How long have you been back?" As if the tourist's itinerary would tell me anything.

He looked at his watch. "Ten months or so. Jersey City, actually. A shade cheaper."

"Ten months! Franklin. Oh God. Jesus. Why on earth did you wait?" Even as I asked it, I knew the question was out of line. Wait for what? To come see a person who had told him that visiting hours were over?

"I could not drop by earlier," he said, parodying Euclid, "because I didn't want to show up here empty-handed." He reached into a rucksack that had been lying innocuously by the side of the chair. He had arrived packed. He extracted a sheaf from his overnight bag and handed it to me. A stack of beautifully typed watermark bond. "I figured that you wouldn't even say 'boo' to me unless and until I wrapped up the dissertation."

My hand caught, afraid to turn over the cover sheet. "Todd. Don't start this again." I felt myself laughing, stricken, beginning to believe.

"Done. Portrait of the Artist. I'm out from under it."

I turned the cover page and began to read. I knew what it was with the first paragraph, the first sentence's description of a young post-doc's Greyhound bus arrival at a laboratory deep in the interior. He too had served his sentences. The story of one life; the math of the central nervous system. I could not read on. I began straightening the sheaf of papers, throat, hands, eyes, all in wild counterpoint.

"Who'da thought it?" Todd said, filling the silence. "Years of art history, and I wind up in biography after all."

You should talk, friend: all I ever wanted to be was a researcher, and here I am, plunged into information science. To keep myself from complete regression, I asked, "What have you been living on all this while?"

Todd shot back, speaking through the corner of his mouth, "Patrimony. The old man's life policy. What's it to ya, doll?"

I began to cry, quietly. He came and sat beside me on the floor. He began to tell me about his last visit to the professor. "The man pretended to be furious at me for leaving Europe just to come see him like that, a skeleton. We managed to sneak in a car tour, out to the woods, before he got too weak. I plied him for buried biographical details. I asked what it felt like, slowly dissolving into bad instructions. I asked him for his odds on humanity. I asked

635

him if he was happy with the way he'd spent his time. He told me: 'It seems my answers to all the important questions are doomed to remain qualified.'

"No bursts of false hope, no journal entries celebrating *I kept my meals down today. Let's hope tomorrow is still better.* Nothing left behind, no bequest to first filial but the ongoing experiment. Janny, his hair had turned white. *White.* As white as a fresh sheet of paper. I asked him if the cancer study he'd hooked up with had reached any conclusions. '*I have, in any case. It hurts.*'"

So did the punchline. So did having to laugh. The muscles around my rib cage contracted all together, against the blueprint, more like a swimmer's cramp than laughter. Todd made another feeble, black crack, for my sake: something about the absurdity of a language that made oncology and ontology differ by a single mutation. A little while later, I thought I might try breathing again.

"He told me a story: 1982. The year before you meet him. He's passed fifty, gratefully out from under the immediate jurisdiction of endocrinology. Through decades of training, he now thinks of Dr. Koss only three times a day. He's living in a world where clipped, rewritten supercoiled strands of nucleotides can be sent from anywhere to anywhere. Where everybody's got his own ILLIAC. Three golf balls on the moon.

"He's working steadily on the night shift, the month before I get myself hired. On a whim, he turns the radio on, fiddles with the dial, and freezes it on an old friend. It's the Canadian kid, beyond a doubt. The inimitable playing style, that muffled humming in the background tracks trying for a Platonic, thirty-third variation just beyond the printed score. Playing the piece that woman gave him. Ressler is amazed to find how vividly the structure of the past is still encoded in him. Stadium Terrace, Cyfer. That reverse-telescope dilation, where distant is closer than near. He discovers he still loves Jeannie as intensely as the day he first stumbled upon the evidence.

"But in an instant's listening, he's shocked to hear that it's not the same piece, not the same performance. It's a radical rethinking from beginning to end, worlds slower, more variegated, richer in execution. A lot of the variations enter attacca, without pause, the last notes of one spilling into the first notes of the next, anxious to hear how they might sound all at once, on top of one another.

"He can't believe his good luck at getting a new recording. But the party dissipates at the end, after the return of the ossified aria, when the announcer reports that the pianist has suffered a massive cerebral hemorrhage just after releasing this take two. He leaves the radio on all night, and the next, as if letting it air out. When the piece plays again two days later, he knows why. He sits and listens the piece through in its entirety, weeping like a child for the death of someone he didn't even know."

I saw then why Todd came back to pass all this on to me. I raised my head, knowing I looked hideous, thinking that if he could see me this way and not run away, it might begin to signify some chance. When he saw my face like that, Todd laughed, reached out a finger, and smeared a little saline pool around in the bogs under my eyes.

"He sent you back to me," I said.

"My suggestion. He supplied the dowry. A trunk packed with handwritten full scores. He thought we might like to try to decipher them together." Todd reached his hands around my waist from behind, closed them around mine, then moved both sets in a pantomime of that old pump-organ enterprise we had once indulged in, up in the woods. This time the keyboard was only four-hands.

I freed myself from his arms. The thought of Dr. Ressler's compositions pinned me against the stakes of being alive. The readiness that the singing bank machine had released in me vanished. Everything I had learned in my year off, every stunted enzyme for courage that I had managed in isolation to nurse alive, was about to seize up and go dysfunctional again, knowing all that now rode on it. I tried to steady myself; if I could tell Todd everything I'd done, from the beginning, I might begin to retrieve myself. "I've been toying with a little biography too, I'm afraid."

"So I see," he said, picking up the notebook I had caught him reading. "Pretty strong stuff here, Missy. Sex, love, espionage, the works. You're sitting on a gold mine, you know."

"Don't be absurd."

"No. I'm serious. I have this great idea."

All of a piece, I knew what it was. "Out of the question. Don't even think of it."

"Come on. A few edits, a little cut-and-paste...."

He made me laugh. I couldn't help myself. "I believe 'splicing' is the bioengineer's term of choice."

He made a great show of collating, a little courtship-dance of paper-shuffling to win me again, for good. "Come on. Let's do it. Let's make a baby."

I shook my head. "No," I said, dead sober. "It wouldn't be enough. A man like you will always want the real thing someday. Or at least the chance. It would never last."

"My dear Ms. Reference." He edged over to me, taking me up against him. "Why do you think the Good Lord invented sperm bank donations?" He placed his hands over my face, exploring the burning landscape there. "And let me ask you another thing." One for the perpetual Question Board. His eyes were full beyond measure. His whole throat shook like a beginner's in wonder at the words he was about to discover. "Who said anything about lasting?"

ARIA

Da Capo e Fine

What could be simpler? In rough translation: Once more with feeling.